THE HEIR'S DUOLOGY

J. HOUSER

Painted Wings Publishing

Note from the Author

The Heir's Duology omnibus consists of *The Heir of Exile* and *Soren's Legacy*, plus a bonus story, *To Love a Monster*. This duology can be read as a standalone story, but I do feel it packs more of a punch when read after the *Seeder Wars* trilogy (*Seeder Shadow Wars, Trouble in the Green Lands,* and *Unitas: Trio*).

If you're reading this as a standalone duology, I recommend reading *To Love a Monster* after *The Heir of Exile* to avoid spoilers.

If you're reading this as a series continuation, I recommend reading *To Love a Monster* before both books.

*Annotations are designated by a small coordinating symbol such as (a) which can then be matched up to commentary in the back of the book.

**Extra books, merch, and more can also be found on my site!

Table of Contents

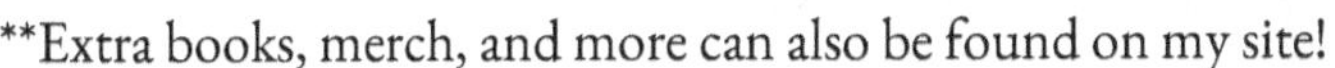

Content and Trigger Warnings

While this series is not particularly dark or graphic, some topics and scenes may be hard for some readers or inappropriate for younger audiences. While it's impossible to list every possible concern, I've included a list of some of the most common or serious concerns.

<u>Swearing:</u> Minor
<u>Romantic heat level:</u> Includes fade-to-black scenes and discussions of sex
<u>Violence:</u> Discusses war and assassination and depicts violence, but is not graphic/gratuitous
<u>Possible triggers:</u> Manipulation, mental health struggles, grief/loss, thwarted/brief mentions of sexual assault, discrimination, racism, ableism, abuse of a minor, and mentions of suicidal ideation

I love a good adventure and romance, but I also bring up meaningful topics in a fantasy setting that can spark conversation and help readers feel less alone in their struggles.

I aim to tactfully include sensitive topics, and have had positive feedback from beta readers and editors about the way they're approached here. My intention is never to glorify or justify harmful behavior, even if a fictional character doesn't get it quite right. If you find yourself struggling with any of these issues in real life, please know you're not alone, not past hope, and not beyond help from professionals, friends, and family.

~J. Houser

Pronunciation Guide

People

Acacia: uh-KAY-shuh

Beata: bay-AH-tuh

Boman/Bomen: BOW-man

Camry: CAM-ree

Eleana: el-ee-AH-nuh

    (**Leah:** LEE-uh)

Elanna: ee-LAWN-nuh

Elonta: ee-LAWN-tuh

Elonto: ee-LAWN-toe

Grayas: GRAY-us

Guillen: GUY-en

Kaylah: KAY-luh

Lycha: LIE-kuh

Murialsdotter:

    MYUR-ee-ulz-daughter

Piot: PEA-oat

Scanlon: SCAN-lun

Tain: TAYn

Tobias: toe-BYE-us

    (**Toby:** TOE-bee)

Places & Things

Boloru: bowl-OR-oo

Guenjalis: gwen-YAWL-iss

Sanath: SAN-uth

Selen: SELL-en

*To hear an audio clip by the author, go to JHouserWrites.com/swpronunciation

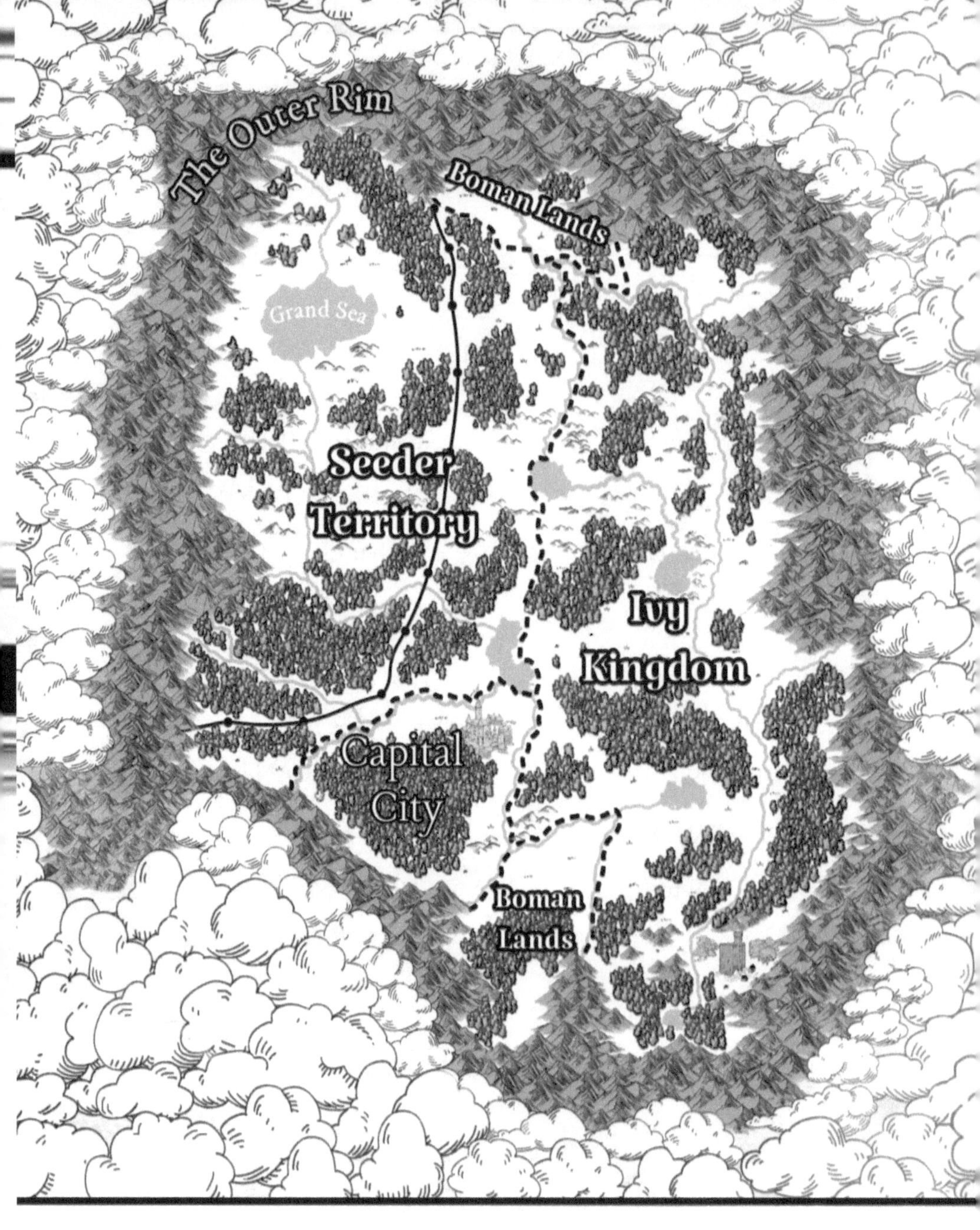

The Green Lands

THE HEIR OF EXILE

BOOK 1

Prologue

Beata lay in bed, restless as the sun peeked through the windows. She smirked. It was still so majestic—life in the palace. The stained glass was intricate, the ivy-lined ceiling magical. Pondering the dreams and plans that had been set in motion, she drew a deep breath.

"Mmm, you're awake," Soren said in a groggy voice, wrapping his arm around her.

"You are *astonishingly* perceptive." She rolled over for a kiss.

He grinned. "How are you doing?"

She wrinkled her nose. "I've been better."

"I know what always makes *me* feel better." He nuzzled her neck.

She laughed. "Yeah, well, I don't think that cures maternal sickness. Pretty sure that's what caused it."

"Damn right it is." He moved over, straddling her.

She sighed, gazing into his stunning green eyes. "I don't really feel like it right now."

He pursed his lips. "What was it you said when I asked you to marry me? 'I'll do what you want, be what you want.' You gave me an oath."

They stared at each other for a moment before she replied. "Yes. That's what I said. And I'll stick to that. I didn't say no. But that doesn't mean I can't be open with you and give you a chance to pretend like you're considering my feelings now and then."

He rocked his head back and forth. "Mmm, maybe that's true." He leaned forward, giving her another kiss. "We should talk, anyway."

"What about?"

He rested his hands on her stomach. "You ... and the baby. And what we'll do if they take on the palace again."

Beata raised her eyebrows. "You've tripled security. You've dismissed or killed half of the servants and guards to weed out the disloyal ones. You're still worried?"

He shrugged. "You know me. I like to have plans."

"I intend to stay here. By your side. You don't have to worry about my loyalty."

"I don't want you here if it happens. Your aides have been instructed on where to take you if we're under attack."

She scowled. "I'm not running away like a coward."

"I'm the king, dammit."

"And I'm the queen."

His eyes narrowed. "You're a queen because I made you one. You don't control the Vines."

She resented that reminder, staring into his cold eyes. His position of authority was just as precarious as hers. "I'm a queen because *we* made me one. It might have been your idea, but we *both*," she lowered her voice, "did things we can't speak about to get here. Don't talk down to me."

He nodded in thought. "I won't budge on this one. Not when it comes to my child."

"*Our* child."

His jaw clenched, and a signature spark rose in his eyes. "You'll leave as I order you to."

She'd never been afraid of his temper. "This kingdom needs a united front."

He raised his voice. "Did I stutter?"

She closed her eyes, breathing deeply. Hopefully it would never come to that. Soren's plans were well thought out. "I'll follow your orders."

His smile returned. "That's what I wanted to hear."

Her lips formed a hint of a grin. "I love you."

"I love you too. I always knew I was picking a strong girl. You just have to remember our deal." He leaned forward again, nibbling her ear. "Now, should I stay in bed, or should I find out if one of the new maids wants to see what it's like to please her king?"

Beata wasn't even fazed by that threat. She knew the man she'd married. He'd never devoutly promised to be faithful. But when possible, she always preferred to keep him happy and closer to her. "Stay with me."

Chapter 1

Leah loved to shop, though not in the same way her peers did. Not with a gaggle of gossipy girls, browsing through the pretty things and emptying their parents' bank accounts.

Leah loved it for the thrill.

Pulling down her hoodie sleeves, Leah glanced around to make sure the coast was clear, then picked her target. She placed her hands on the edge of the store shelf, where they could clearly be seen by someone passing by or a hidden security camera. Not as easily spotted were the vines she extended from her wrists. Green vines peeked out, as thick as her pinky, lined with several small leaves. She reached them forward, grasping the small trinkets she was aiming for on the shelf below, and reeled them in, smoothly tucking them into her sleeves. With her vines fully retracted, she moved her hands to her pants pockets and let the items slide down her sleeves.

She grinned and walked to the next aisle. The rush always lasted from the moment she picked her first target, to the moment she unloaded it all in her bedroom. Every time. Without fail. She didn't even really care for half of the items she'd take.

Spotting her next targets—bottles of nail polish—she followed her usual routine. One of the bottles tipped over, and she focused on flexing harder, picking it back up. Her deformities had some perks, but a good grip wasn't always one of them.(a) She tucked away the first pair of polishes and sized up the other colors, deciding if she wanted to add any others to her collection.

A sudden pain in Leah's ear took her by surprise. She clenched her teeth in anger. "Put them all back!" the woman hissed while pinching Leah's earlobe.

Leah stood stiff, scowling. "I don't know what you're talking about."

"Don't be a brat. I saw you do it. Empty your pockets. Now."

Leah rolled her eyes. "Fine. If you promise not to tell Mom." She glared at her Aunt Cheryl.

Aunt Cheryl glared back. "I don't keep secrets from your mother. Would you rather face her, or the cops?"

Leah sneered. "Would you rather me walk out with a few items, or have the cops find out about our family of freaks?"

Cheryl pinched and twisted her ear harder.

"Ouch!" Leah reached into her pockets. "Fine." She dumped her pilfered treasures onto the shelf, and her aunt released her ear, giving her a shove in the direction of the store exit.

They marched out of the store without purchasing anything, not saying a word until they got in the car.

"Buckle your seat belt!" Aunt Cheryl was always uptight. She hated Leah, and she hated the world. Sometimes it seemed she even hated her own sister, Leah's mom.

Leah buckled her seat belt. "None of the stuff I had was even that expensive. The store writes off that kind of stuff without a second thought."

"You're a disgrace," Cheryl muttered without taking her eyes off of the road. "Just like your father."

Leah looked down at her lap. It was a complex insult. Cheryl had made it clear she'd never been fond of Leah's dad. She seemed to blame him for things her own mom didn't. Why that was, Leah never knew.

But Leah smirked a little at being compared to him. They so rarely talked about him. All she knew was her dad had been a good man. A man who had loved her and her mom, worked hard, and been ambitious. And died far too young, in a tragic accident at work before Leah was born. And that she'd inherited his stunning green eyes. That was all her mom would ever tell her.

Fighting a frown, and the ache of never having met him, she kept her smile. She'd imagined a million times what it would have been like to grow up with a dad. She'd always painted a picture of what their relationship would have been like. He would have been the kind of dad to step away from demanding work to play with her, to talk with her. He would have been there to stand up for her when she'd needed it, and to provide more stability in her childhood.

"Did my dad know about our deformity?" Leah asked, running a thumb across her wrist.

Cheryl pursed her lips. "Never mind him. We just moved to a new city. Why is that?"

Leah gazed out the window as they passed unfamiliar buildings. "Because you and Mom like to see new places?"

Cheryl threw her a dirty look. "Or perhaps it's because you don't know what it means to stay out of trouble! Do you want to move again already? Then get caught shoplifting again. Sneak a boy into your room again. Get kicked out of school again. Have someone other than me spot you using those things. Might as well stop unpacking if you're going to do this."

Leah shook her head. "You and Mom use them, too. Don't pretend you don't, when you think I'm not looking and you're multitasking."

Cheryl huffed, braking at a stop sign. "We might extend them in private. That's a completely different story, Eleana!"(b)

Leah rolled her eyes again, and stared out the car window for the rest of the ride. *Stupid family secrets. Stupid rules.*

As they pulled up to their house, Leah sighed. Her mom was already home. Both she and Cheryl worked full-time, on different schedules, so Leah was always supervised when she was home. They treated her like she was a baby, or a psychopath or something. Sixteen was plenty old enough to be left alone. She could admit to herself that she hadn't exactly done anything to *earn* their trust, but maybe if they backed off a little, she wouldn't act the way she did. At least not as often.

Navigating her way through a maze of boxes and furniture, Leah took a sharp left after the living room, heading down the main hallway, straight to her room. She sat on her bed, staring at the bright orange comforter. As much as she pretended it didn't bother her, she hated moving again too.(c)

A soft knock on the door announced what she'd known was coming—the lecture following Cheryl's tattling. "It's unlocked."

Her mom opened the door, disappointment painting her face. While Leah had her dad's eyes, she shared her mom's short thin nose and jet-black hair.

"Hi, princess," her mom said.

Leah bit her lip, her head cocking to one side. "Hi."

Her mom entered the room, closing the door behind her and sitting on the edge of the bed. "Why'd you do it?"

Leah tucked her knees up, hugging them. "You wouldn't have to ask that question if Aunt Cheryl knew how to keep her mouth shut."

Her mom scolded her with her eyes. "Aunt Cheryl is keeping you out of trouble. And this isn't about her. This is about *your* behavior."

"She hates me."

Her mom frowned. "She doesn't hate you, sweetheart. And ... we owe her a lot. You need to be nice to her."

Leah gritted her teeth. "Whatever." Whenever her mom was physically and emotionally present, she was there for Leah. Despite all the trouble she'd gotten into, her mom usually believed her. Except when it came to Aunt Cheryl. Then again, Aunt Cheryl never threw her most venomous insults in front of Leah's mom, never laid a hand on her in her mom's presence.

"So, why did you do it? You have an allowance. You could have bought those things."

Leah shrugged, avoiding eye contact.

"And using your vines in public?"

Leah bit the insides of her cheeks.

"Sweetheart, we're just trying to keep you safe."

Leah's eyebrows bunched. "Is that it? You think a mob's going to come after us because we're a little different? Because it seems to me it's less about safety, and more about being ashamed of yourself, and your own daughter."

A disheartened look crossed her mom's face. "Eleana, I'm not ashamed of you. It's ... complicated. Some things should be kept private."

Yeah... Private. Suck it up.

"Can you please just try to behave and make some friends here? I'm so tired of moving."

Leah stared at her mom, then went back to looking at the bedding. *Make friends? When we'll probably just move in a few months anyway?* She traced the flower pattern on the comforter with a finger. She'd screwed up a lot. But not *all* of the moves were her fault. Sometimes, they'd pick up and leave without any explanation at all.

"Princess? Sweetheart?"

Leah met her mom's gaze.

"I love you—you know that. And you're bright. You could have *so* many friends, if you'd try a little more."

Leah shook her head. "Friends that I can't allow to know the real me, right? I'm pretty sure I could join a circus. That would make some good money, and then I'd have plenty of friends that are freaks just like me."

Her mom sighed, rubbing her temple. "You're not a freak. I love that you have something special about you. I know you don't understand my opinion on this, but I'm *absolutely* not ashamed of your vines, or you." She rested a hand on Leah's. "And what's different about you, physically—that doesn't define you. If you want people to know the real you, let them see how smart you are, how sweet you can be … when you want to be."

Leah gnawed on her bottom lip. "I'll try to do better."

Her mom gave her a half-smile. "That's all I'm asking. Now…" She tapped Leah's knee. "Since Aunt Cheryl returned empty-handed, and we don't have any groceries, how about we order something in? Celebrate a fresh start? Anything you want."

The first day of school was never fun. Especially when it was Leah's first day at a new school that had already been in session for three weeks. When 'Eleana Edwards' came up on each roll call, she had to inform her teachers she preferred to go by Leah. And she tried her best to stay positive, but it didn't come easy.

At lunch, she found a half-empty table in the cafeteria and sat down by herself, digging into her small basket of fries. She hadn't even eaten two bites before a pair of girls approached. They claimed seats across from her without even asking if she'd wanted them to.

"Hi. You're new, right? I'm Jackie, and this is Tina."

Leah finished her bite, looking the two of them over. They both donned bright smiles—a brunette and a blonde. She didn't need a pair of Mary Sues to pick her up as a charity case. Without a word, she stood, grabbed her tray, and walked away.

Finding a door to the outdoor courtyard, she took her tray outside. It was a beautiful day, and she loved the outdoors anyway. Near the far corner, Leah spotted an empty table and sat down to finish her meal in solitude. While she picked at her food, her mom's plea sounded in her ears: she should be trying to make friends. But she wasn't a pathetic loner, and she *wasn't* desperate.

Though, she did enjoy eavesdropping on a table of guys sitting behind her. They were a bit raucous, but it was entertaining.

"You guys still coming over tonight?" one asked.

"Yeah, you can count on me."

"Of course we can. His crush is gone." A different voice snickered.

"You're an idiot. I barely knew her."

"Take it from a bowman(d) that's lived here his entire life: don't waste your time with the green-eyed girls. You never know when they're gonna get sick and have to leave for the rest of the school year."

Leah furrowed her brow. *What's wrong with girls that have green eyes? And are they seriously making fun of sick girls? Is that supposed to be a jab at eating disorders or something?* She adjusted her position to see the guys out of the corner of her eye. None of the trio were particularly distinctive—all brunets, average height and appearance.

"Yeah, well, I'm a bowman too. But if I was actually interested, that wouldn't stop me. I could see them when I go back home." He took a drink from a soda can. "I'm just saying, I barely knew her. It's not like we had a thing."

"Sure you did. You're a momma's boy," one teased with a smug grin.

"Momma's boy?" He raised an eyebrow.

"Yeah. She's a green-eye, right? You've got a soft spot for them."

Both of the other guys instantly looked perturbed.

"That's not cool, man."

The guy the teasing had been aimed at spoke again. "Screw you, Tanner."

Tanner rolled his eyes. "Come on, Marcus. Learn to take a joke."

"You thought she was cute, too." Marcus scowled. "Don't be a dick."

Tanner shrugged. "I can appreciate a pretty face without wanting to date her. I'm old school."

Marcus sat straighter, narrowing his eyes. "How old school? Why are you even here? Socializing with the likes of us?"

Tanner frowned. "I did *not* mean that. You know I'm not like that. My parents never would have let me come here if we thought that way."

Should Leah be minding her own business? Yes. But these guys were ... weird. Intriguing. She left her tray, turning and sliding into the empty seat at their table. They all looked surprised at her uninvited appearance.

She rested her chin on a fist. "What's wrong with girls that have green eyes? I happen to think they're beautiful." She batted her lashes to show off her favorite feature, making a point.

All three guys immediately donned smirks. The one whose name she hadn't heard yet—the shorter of the three—did a poor job of stifling a laugh.

She squinted at him. "What's your name?"

"Jake."

"Well, Jake," she stole a fry from his tray, "did you know only two percent of the population has green eyes? I'd say that's pretty unique." She bit into the room-temperature fry.

His smile grew. "Fun fact. A statistic I'm sure is true for *some* parts of the world."[e]

She shook her head. "Worldwide."

He still wore a contented grin. "Okay."

"So?" She lifted her eyebrows.

"I'm Marcus," the one sitting opposite her said. His hair had a bit of a curl to it. "And who are you?"

She faced him. "Leah."

"Don't worry about these two idiots. They didn't mean anything by it."

Jake and Tanner shrugged.

"Right..." Now it was awkward, with them clamming up. She wasn't going to move back to her table, and she wasn't going to head back inside for the rest of lunch. She twisted to grab her lunch tray and continued eating with them. "So ... I just moved here. What's there to do in this city?"

Jake took a bite of his hamburger. "Mmm, that's a question for me." He pointed a thumb to himself. "These two are both new here this year."

"Really?"

"Yeah. I'm foreign exchange this year," Tanner said. His hair was a lighter brown than the others.

She detected no accent. "Where from?"

Jake grinned. "Yeah, Tanner. Where from?"

Tanner rolled his eyes. "Canada."

Leah smirked. "*Very* exotic."

He scowled.

"What about you, Marcus?"

He stabbed at his side salad with a fork. "Oh, I'm spending a year with my grandparents."

"And what brings you here?" Jake asked.

Leah wore a grin of her own. "My mom didn't approve of my friends or extracurricular activities in our last place."

Tanner smiled. "Sounds like fun."

Jake raised an eyebrow. "Sounds like trouble."

She looked at Marcus, curious whether he had an assessment as the bell rang.

He took another swig of his soda. "Sounds like it's time to head to class."

Chapter 2

Leah stood at student pickup, waiting for Aunt Cheryl to come get her at the end of the day.

"Hey. It's Leah, right?"

The voice belonged to none other than her new acquaintance. "Yeah. Marcus, right?"

He nodded, tugging on the straps of his backpack. He wore a dark grey crewneck t-shirt. "I hope you weren't offended by what the guys were saying earlier. It's more of an inside joke than anything. They don't actually look down on people with green eyes."

"Good to know."

He smiled. "Yeah. Kind of a stupid thing to judge someone by."

She chuckled. "Yeah. That would be."

They stood awkwardly for a little while, teenage giggles and chatter, and cars driving by, filling the silence between them.

"So ... no car?" he asked.

"Nope. My aunt picks me up. You?"

He shook his head. "Grandparents."

"What did you guys mean when you were talking? You and Jake said something about being bowmen?"

Marcus smirked. "Oh, you heard that? Eavesdrop much?"

She shrugged. "The conversation was interesting enough, and you weren't exactly whispering. So, what does it mean?"

He scanned her face. "What do you think it means?"

She scoffed. "I'm the one that's asking, right? I don't know. Are you talking, like, bows and arrows?"

He looked down, scuffing the sole of his shoe on the cement. "Yeah. You're right. Jake and I, uh, both like to shoot bows."

"Doesn't that make you archers? Is bowmen even the right term?"

Marcus swatted a hand in the air dismissively. "It's a nerd hobby, anyway."

"No, I think that actually sounds really cool." She tilted her head slightly, looking into his brown eyes. She'd never met anyone who knew how to shoot a bow. "Would you mind if I came sometime to check it out?"

His cheeks reddened. "Yeah, we could totally do that."

She smiled. "That sounds like way more fun than hitting a movie theater in a new town. What's your number?"

They exchanged numbers right before Aunt Cheryl arrived in her red sedan.

"Cool. Text me." She smiled again, tucking her phone in her pocket, and hopped in the car.

"How was your first day?" Cheryl asked. Her voice was neutral despite the perma-scowl wrinkles on her face.

Leah rolled her eyes. "Like you care."

Leah sat at the small desk in her room, snacking on sour-cream-and-onion potato chips, sorting through her homework.

"Hey, sweetheart. I'm home." Her mom appeared in the doorway.

"Hi. How was work?"

Her mom opened her eyes wide. "Adult jobs ... *full* of thrills."

Leah chuckled. Her mom had worked a number of jobs over the years. She didn't complain about any of them all that much, nor was she enamored with any of them. Her current job in this new city was as a receptionist at a car rental.

"How was your first day of school?"

Leah closed her textbook. "It was school."

"I see you're doing homework?"

Leah twisted in her chair. "I'm not a *complete* failure, you know."

Her mom frowned, tilting her head forward. "I never said you were."

Leah returned her focus to her American History papers.

"Make any new friends today?"

She mentally ran through her day. "Yeah. I think so."

"Someone I'd approve of?"

Leah laughed. "Yeah. Pretty sure he's a Boy Scout."

"I'm glad to hear it. Want to come help me make dinner?"

Leah clamped the bag of chips closed. "Sure."

They stood in the kitchen, Leah's mom stirring a pot on the stove, Leah picking through a bag of spinach for salad.

"So, you said your new friend is a boy? Are we talking boyfriend potential? Or boy that's a friend?"

Leah sniggered. "I'm definitely thinking the latter. What about you? Any dashing suitors at your work?"

"Oh, you know me. I am not looking to date. I don't need anyone in my life other than you."

Leah frowned, leaning back against the counter. "But is that healthy? I mean it when I say I wouldn't hold it against you. You deserve to be happy."

She wished her mom would go to therapy, would talk about her problems. Would even allow Leah to go to therapy. But they'd put that idea to bed years ago. Her mom had resolutely declared that therapists were useless. They just turned your own questions back on you and meddled in people's business when they ought not to.

Her mom faced her with a forced smile. "No one in this world could compare to your father. I'm really not interested in dating right now."

Leah bit her lip. "Why won't you ever talk about my dad?"

Her mom dodged eye contact, looking at the tile floor. "I talk about him."

"You've never even told me his name or shown me a picture of him. Do you know how weird that is? Sometimes I feel like he was a one-night stand and you're just ashamed you don't actually know who he is. And if that's the truth, I'm old enough for you to say so."

Her mom scowled. "Don't you dare think that of me, of us. We were legally married. We dated for *years* before we got engaged. And I've told you—we lost a lot of things in that house fire when you were a baby. I'm sorry I don't have more for you."

"Okay," Leah whispered.

Her mom lightly rested a hand on Leah's arm. "Princess, I know you want more. And someday, we'll talk more about it, alright?" She closed her eyes. "Just ... not right now."

Leah sighed, trying to move on from the topic of perpetual vagueness. It hurt, after all these years, that her mom still hadn't gotten over his death. That it was too painful to talk about him.

After dinner, Marcus texted to see if Leah had Friday evening free to go shooting, and they set a time. It brought a smile to her face, giving her a fun new experience to look forward to.

The next day at school, Leah considered where she'd sit at lunch. She could try to make more friends, but that required effort. And caring. She took her lunch straight out to the courtyard, and sat at the table she had the day before, by herself.

The trio from the day before sat at their table again. Marcus glanced at her a couple of times. "Do you want to sit with us, Leah?"

She waved her hand while finishing a bite. "No, I'm good."

He shrugged. "Okay."

She thought it over again, then picked up her tray and joined them. "So ... will you be there Friday, Jake?"

He was visibly confused. "Friday?"

Marcus cleared his throat. "Oh, um ... yeah. We're going to go do archery. Leah and I talked about how you and I like to shoot, after she overheard us talking yesterday about being *bowmen*."

Jake smirked. "Sad to say, I'm otherwise engaged. Love a good bow and arrow." He slapped Marcus hard on the back. "And my skills could *never* compare to this guy's. He's a regular Robin Hood, this one."

Marcus shook his head, looking Leah straight in the eyes. "That's a major exaggeration."

Tanner laughed. "No, it's not. He's *seriously* impressive!"

Marcus threw him a dark look. "Shut up."

Leah grinned at their teasing. Now she *really* wondered how talented he was at the sport.

By the time Friday rolled around, Leah was definitely looking forward to her first time at an archery range. It was a nice break from homework and unpacking. Marcus swung by to pick her up, briefly meeting her mom and sharing the range's address before being allowed to take Leah.

Marcus looked all sorts of nervous on the drive out to the archery range. "This'll be my first time coming here. You know, since I'm new in town."

She nodded. "Cool. How many years have you done archery? I don't think I've known anyone that shoots."

"Oh, really? Yeah. I guess it's not that popular. Pretty cool little niche though, right?"

She smiled. "I guess we'll see."

An electronic bell dinged as they walked in the front door of the archery shop, and an employee quickly greeted them. Leah surveyed the area while he guided them to the counter. In the main lobby area, well over a dozen round racks were crowded with bows and clothes, most of the clothes camouflage or neon orange. Hanging high on the walls were different styles of decoys, targets, and a few mounted taxidermy animals—not exactly Leah's cup of tea. Looking past the products for purchase, she caught a glimpse of the shooting range. At the end of a long room lit by overhead fluorescent lights, bales of hay had been stacked to the ceiling. A number of targets were secured to the bales.₍f₎

"Yeah, we're wanting to rent some bows to shoot," Marcus said.

"Right this way." The employee directed them to a sign behind the counter, and quoted prices. "Do you have a preference?"

Marcus's hands were shoved in his pockets, his arms rigid. "I left mine at home. I'm not sure what the best rental equivalent would be."

"What's your weight?" the man asked.

"Um ... one-fifty?"

The man smirked. "Right... You say your bow's at home?"

Marcus cleared his throat. "Yeah. You know, it's *her* first time. Maybe you could recommend a good option for a first-time shooter?"

The man kept grinning, facing Leah. "Alright, now, it's up to you. We have a lot of nice compounds, but I'm of the camp that believes a beginner should start with a recurve." He pointed to a row of more basic-looking equipment—these bows were made of wood. "Simpler to start off with."

She shrugged. "Then we'll go with that."

The man turned back to Marcus. "Would you like to go the same route?"

"Yeah. Sure. Why not?"

They pulled the string back on a couple of bows each, landing on something that gave a comfortable resistance. The employee went over the rules of the range and set them up with all sorts of other rental accessories. He tried to explain some of the basics, but Marcus thanked him and said they could handle it from there. "It's really not that hard," he told Leah.

She let him go first. His first shot went wild, finding its place in a hay bale absolutely nowhere near the target. "Just takes a little getting used to. You know, using one that's not mine." The second shot had him clenching his teeth and grasping his arm where the string had hit it.

"Hold your arm straight, kid," a white-haired man shooting nearby called out. "And wear your armguard. Gonna hurt like the dickens if you do it that way, especially being double-jointed."

Marcus rolled his eyes, taking a little more time to aim and shoot a couple more arrows. Neither hit their mark, but he had a nice red spot where the string had gotten him again.

Leah fought a smirk. He was clearly a fish out of water. But he figured out where the aforementioned armguard belonged, strapping on the piece of leather he'd tossed on a folding chair behind him, onto the developing welt.

"Choose an anchor point and stick with it," the older man called out.

Marcus shook his head, his nostrils flaring. Leah frowned. It was kind of fun to watch him suffer, since he'd obviously lied. But he was a nice guy; maybe he deserved a break.

She slipped on her armguard. "How about I take a turn?"

"Yeah." He set his bow down. "Maybe I'm just nervous with everyone watching me."

Leah picked up one of the other accessories they'd been given—a leather finger guard. Her arrows had neon-green and orange plastic fletching instead of feathers. Picking one up, she rested it in position on the bow, clicking it onto the string with the plastic nock at the end. She placed her pointer finger on the string, above the arrow nock. She then rested her middle and ring fingers underneath, as the employee had briefly demonstrated, the leather guard separating her fingers from the string. Closing one eye, she carefully pulled the string back; there was a springy resistance. Once it was pulled all the way back, she did her best to line up the arrow with her target.

As she released her grip, the string snapped forward, and her arrow launched across the room. From yards away, she thought she could hear the rip of paper as it punched through. She'd hit the target. Kind of. The arrow jutted from the bottom right corner of the paper her target was printed on, not actually having hit any of the rings.

She tried again and didn't do much better, until she asked for a few pointers from the elderly gentleman so eager to help. She asked Marcus if he wanted to go again, but he declined. By the end, her arrows were still scattered, but they were forming tighter groupings with more practice. She insisted Marcus try again with one more round before they took off. He reluctantly obliged, redeeming himself with a couple of decent shots.

They approached the counter to return their equipment and pay. Marcus had tossed his target in the trash after retrieving it; Leah held hers to take home, marking her first experience with archery.

She reached for her wallet.

Marcus held up a hand. "No, I've got it."

"You sure?"

"Yeah, I'm good."

The employee grinned as he took the bows over the counter. "We've got affordable lessons, if you two are interested."

Marcus pressed his lips together. "Thanks. How much was it for tonight?"

Leah smiled. "Hey, I'm going to use the restroom before we head out." She turned the corner and stopped to eavesdrop once the employee started talking again.

"Word to the wise? If you're going to lie to impress a girl, do a bit more research if you're going to pick something like archery. Or take her to something a little less complex, like bowling."

Marcus huffed. "Yeah. Thanks."

"Oh, yeah. And in case you two want to come back: your weight? You were pulling thirty-five pounds back there; your girl was pulling thirty."

Leah stifled a laugh and headed to the bathroom, folding her target and slipping it into her back pocket.

Returning to the lobby, she found Marcus browsing the different displays of equipment. She leaned in close. "Looking to add to your collection?"

He jumped and spun, smirking. "Yeah. Definitely."

She bit her lip and laughed. "Let's head out."

They got back to the truck and buckled up.

"So ... not an archer?" She raised an eyebrow.

His face was red. "Picked up on that, did ya?"

She laughed again, and he joined in this time.

He rubbed his forehead. "I'm sorry. That was stupid. Hands down my worst date. I mean, not that you, obviously, you know, just... I promise I don't usually lie."

She pursed her lips. "Is that what this was? A date?"

His eyes shot up to meet hers. "No. I mean. No. I don't know why I said that. Obviously just a hangout."

She shrugged. "We can call it a date if you want to."

He rolled his eyes. "I know how to get a proper date, thank you very much. I don't need you calling it one out of pity."

She rubbed the knee of her jeans, feeling awful about this train wreck of an evening. "Date or not, how about ending it with frozen yogurt? My treat."

He smiled at the olive branch. "Sure."

They sat down to eat their frozen yogurt in a shop bustling with families and couples.

"So ... why did you lie?"

He held his bowl against the welt on his arm. "It's ... complicated."

"What does that actually mean, then? Bowman?"

"It's a nickname, really." He stabbed at his dessert. "Just another inside joke."

She picked out a spoonful of fruit boba, allowing the juicy spheres to pop in her mouth. "But you're not going to tell me? Lots of inside jokes. Is it a perverted guy thing, and that's why you're not telling me?"

He shook his head. "No. Not at all. Just don't worry about it. It's stupid. Seriously."

Hmm. "Okay. So, let's talk green eyes. The guys said your mom has green eyes?"

He rocked his head side to side. "More or less."

"And you have brown eyes, so that must mean your dad has brown eyes."

"No. Actually, my dad has blue eyes."

She hesitated, having learned a thing or two about genetics and eye color. "Green and blue eyes are recessive traits. Sorry to tell you, but..."

He wore a soft smile. "It doesn't matter. I'm adopted."

"Oh. Okay. It was about to get awkward if you didn't know that." She chuckled. Her tone got more serious. "Either way, sorry to hear that."

He furrowed his brow, swallowing another spoonful. "Why would you apologize?"

"Well ... I just know that can be a sensitive topic for some people."

Marcus shook his head, scooping another bite of his frozen yogurt. "My parents love me. I'm really okay with it."

"That's enough for you? Do you have any memories or information about your birth parents?"

He drew a deep breath, looking down at his treat.

"Sorry, I really shouldn't ask."

He wrinkled his nose. "It's fine. Is it enough?" He met her eyes. "Most days. I don't remember my birth parents, and I have no desire to ever meet them."

She nodded pensively. "I guess I'm curious because I never got to meet my dad. He died before I was born. It's always just been my mom and aunt and me."

He gave her a sympathetic frown. "Sorry, that sucks."

"Yeah. Luck of the draw, right?"

Marcus sat up straighter. "Well, anyway ... what about you and your hobbies? You were ... vague."

She'd been right about him being a Boy Scout if he'd been that embarrassed about a little white lie over archery. "I don't think it's your style."

He gave her a dimpled smirk. "Alright, we both get to keep some secrets. Fair enough." He pointed his spoon at her. "But ... fun fact: I'm actually decent at throwing knives."

"Intriguing. And we didn't do that tonight, instead of that shameful display at the archery range, because...?"

He chuckled. "Because I was already committed to *that* lie."

"Here's a free tip." She raised her eyebrows high. "You suck at lying, almost as much as you suck at archery. And that's saying something. Stick to the truth, Squeaky Clean."

He widened his eyes. "I can promise you that."

Their playful banter was interrupted by a call on Leah's cell. Her mom.

She sighed, picking it up. "Hi. Yes. Sorry. We'll be back soon. Chill. Love you too."

She rolled her eyes after hanging up. "Sorry, my mom is a tad overprotective." It wasn't like she hadn't already texted her mom to check in at the archery range, per her mom's usual paranoid requirements...

"No worries. Let's head out."

Marcus drove Leah back to her house. "Sorry again," he said while putting the truck into park.

"Don't be. It was still a lot of fun."

"Cool. Well, since this is *not* a date, I'm going to stay here and *not* walk you up to the door."

She smiled. "Have a good night. See you at school."

Chapter 3

Leah's mom furrowed her brow upon her return from the frozen yogurt shop. "You know the rules, Eleana."

Leah threw her hands into the air, sitting across from her in the living room. "I know. I'm sorry. You're the one that tracks my phone, anyway. Why I even have to check in with you is beyond me."

Her mom rubbed her temples. "I shouldn't *have* to track your phone. I should be able to count on you letting me know when your plans have changed!"

"We went out for frozen yogurt afterward. It's not a big deal."

"Maybe not to you. But I have my rules to keep you safe!"

Leah raised an eyebrow. "To keep me safe? Is that it? Or is it because you don't trust me? Although, even *if* you trusted me, I have a feeling you'd still monitor every last detail of my life. It's not about safety. It's control you want."

Her mom shook her head. "You may not like my rules, but you're afforded plenty of freedom. Maybe *too much* freedom."

She glared at her mom. "I already said I was sorry. It was an innocent mistake. Can we be done now?"

Her mom slumped back in her chair. "Yes. Go."

Leah beat the guys to the lunch table on Monday. They were already in the thick of a conversation as they joined her.

"Come on, man," Tanner said. "It would be really cool to attend. Just think about it."

"No." Marcus furrowed his brow. "And it's *super* awkward that you would even ask."

Leah nibbled on a french fry, curious about the topic of the day. "So ... what's this exciting event?"

Marcus opened a can of soda. "My older brother's getting married."

Leah looked at Tanner, surprised. "You're inviting yourself to a *wedding*? Isn't that weird? And why? Weddings are boring." She dipped another fry in ketchup.

Tanner leaned forward. "Hear me out. The bride's side is going to have hardly anyone there, anyway. I could totally blend in. And there's going to be some pretty big names attending! I'm just saying, it would be cool."

She took a swig of water. "Big names? Like actors and musicians, or boring politicians?"

Marcus shot a dirty look at Tanner. "It doesn't matter. You're not invited."

Tanner appealed to Jake. "C'mon. You have to agree with me on this."

Jake shook his head before shoveling a huge bite of pizza into his mouth. "Not my thing. Sorry."

Tanner huffed and dug into his lunch as well.

"Why isn't the bride going to have many people attending?" Leah asked.

Marcus looked down at his tray as he answered. "It's a long way for them to travel."

She picked up a fork for her side salad. "Then shouldn't the wedding come to them?"

"It's ... complicated. My mom has a thing with her health. She can't really travel, either."

Leah gave him a sympathetic frown. "Sorry, that sucks. Kinda rock and a hard place, huh?"

"Somehow, I think they'll all survive," Tanner drawled.

They moved on to another topic as they plowed through their meals. With a few minutes left, Jake perked up. "Hey, I almost forgot. How did archery go this weekend?"

Marcus and Leah exchanged a small grin.

"It was great!" Leah exaggerated. "I was *really* impressed. You guys were right."

Tanner and Jake looked at her in full disbelief. Marcus's grin grew to a smirk as he focused on his tray.

Tanner clicked his tongue, stacking the garbage on his tray. "Why do I have a hard time believing that?"

Leah put a hand to her heart. "I'm not even kidding. Really talented. And frankly, the best date I've ever been on."

Marcus's eyes shot up, narrowing.

She bit her lip, reaching across the table and stroking the back of his hand. "Best kisser, too." In the split second it took his face to turn beet red, she winked and grabbed her tray, standing up. "But maybe I've said too much. I'll see you guys later." She sauntered away, suppressing a laugh.

At the end of the school day, Leah waited for Aunt Cheryl to pick her up again.

"Why did you do that?" Marcus asked as he approached.

"Do what?" she asked with a grin.

"Lie. About everything." He gave her a disapproving look.

She laughed. "Because sometimes it's fun to stretch the truth."

He rolled his eyes.

"Come on, Squeaky Clean."

He glared. "Don't call me that."

She gently nudged his arm. "I didn't mean anything by it. I was just having fun."

"Whatever." He pulled out his phone, scrolling through messages.

She frowned. "Are you really mad at me? I didn't lie about having fun on Friday. I meant that."

He met her gaze. "Fine. Whatever." He returned his focus to his phone.

She gave him a warm smile. "You're kinda cute when you're flustered. We'll talk tomorrow? I'll let the guys know I was joking."

He sighed as his grandma pulled up in a white minivan. He shoved his phone into his pocket. "Yeah. See you tomorrow."

Leah smoothed things over with Jake and Tanner the next day so things were less awkward by the time lunch ended. At the end of the day, she sorted through her locker, packing her backpack.

"Hey, so this is your hallway, huh?" Marcus said, stopping to chat.

"Yep. Guess you found me."

"I was just passing by, but I wanted to say thanks for—"

While she was paying attention to Marcus, one of her books on the top shelf tipped over. Without even thinking about it, she extended a vine to balance it before it tumbled from her locker.

"What the freak, Leah!" he whispered, eyeing her wrist.

She panicked, having slipped and been caught. Another screwup. Another move across the country. Her heart raced. "I don't know what you think you saw, but you're wrong." She scowled. "And I'm not a freak!"

His eyes narrowed. "I never said you were." He glanced around, continuing in a whisper. "But you can't just pull out your vines in public like that. Not around humans!"

She read his face while rubbing her wrist. *He... This doesn't make any sense. He actually knows about the deformities? And...* If there was one thing Leah hated more than moving and making new friends, it was feeling stupid, being out of the loop. "You're right. I should be more careful."

He cocked his head. "Ya think? Don't screw it up for us."

She shook her head, still trying to understand his reaction. "Yeah. Sorry."

He narrowed his eyes again. "Why have you been pretending this whole time?"

"What do you mean?"

His tone reflected growing annoyance. "Like you're not one of us. I know we all have to blend in, but come on. Pretending you don't know what a bowman is? And why weren't you at orientation over the summer?"

"I, uh ... was sick. And ... visiting family." She studied his expression, still *absolutely, positively* clueless about what Marcus was talking about.

"Yeah, but lying the whole time? I thought you were kidding about enjoying it, but I guess I was wrong."

He seemed to know more about her than she did about herself; this was an opportunity she might not get again. "I promise, no more lies. I was just seeing how long I could go before you found out. Like you lying about archery." She smirked to lean into the lie. "Don't be mad because I'm more convincing than you."

His expression softened, and he chuckled. "Touché." His face lit up. "This is really cool. I'm guessing it's okay if I tell the guys? Then we don't have to be so secretive."

"Um... Jake and Tanner?"

"Yeah, of course." He continued to whisper. "We had a seeder girl in the group at the beginning of the year, but it sucked that she had to go home so soon once her bloom started."

Leah slowly nodded as though she knew what any of that jargon meant. "Yeah. Sure. Or maybe let's wait to talk about it at lunch tomorrow, okay?"

The whole ride home, and that evening, Leah was distant, lost in thought. She wasn't alone. It wasn't just some weird genetic defect that only ran in her family. She'd scoured the internet and had never found anything to explain the freaky secret she shared with her mom and aunt. The only thing she'd been able to pin down was that the leaves resembled ivy plants, but no medical diagnosis was listed online, and her mom had insisted they didn't need one.

But Marcus had clearly seen the growths, and even called them 'vines' like her mom did. As if they were even ... *normal.* With her mom as touchy on that topic as she was about Leah's dad, Leah wasn't about to broach the subject with her again. The fact that she had a group of peers like her in that weird way... She needed to get as much information as possible.

The particularly unsettling fact that weighed Leah down ... was the way Marcus had talked about humans. As if *he and she* weren't. She shuddered at the thought. Not only was she making friends with weird and quirky guys ... but maybe with *crazy* guys. But ... how crazy could they be, if they were just like her?

The next day at lunch, Tanner beat everyone else to the table and started normal chitchat with Leah. Not much later, Marcus and Jake joined. No one said anything about the hallway incident from the day before, but Marcus flashed Leah a couple of knowing smiles. Halfway through lunch, he must have tired of waiting for her to bring it up.

"So ... Leah ... any news with you?" He challenged her with his eyes, sipping from a water bottle. "Anything to share with the group?"

Jake and Tanner looked at her in anticipation. Her face warmed. She genuinely didn't know what to say. "Oh. I thought *you* wanted to be the one to tell them."

Marcus grinned, keeping his voice low. "She's ivy."

Jake lifted his eyebrows. "You're kidding me."

Tanner beamed. "Nice! Add one to the scoreboard for Team Ivy."

"Not a bowman?" Jake asked.

Marcus shook his head.

Note to self: Marcus and Jake are bowmen, whatever that is. Obviously not archers... I'm ... ivy, like the leaves on my vines...

Marcus continued, "I caught her using vines yesterday. *In school...*"

Jake gave her a chastising look. "Not cool, Leah. You're lucky it was one of us that caught you."

"Yeah. Sorry. I'll do better."

"Give her a break. It's like second nature to use them sometimes," Tanner defended. He glanced at her. "I mean, still … don't get caught. I barely even use mine at my host family's house."

Jake cocked his head. "Why did you hide it from us this whole time?"

She grinned. "To see how long I could get away with it."

He busted out laughing. "Seriously the best prank I've seen in the Garden Club. The sheer terror on poor Marcus's face at having to put on an archer act—that was *priceless*."

Marcus rolled his eyes.

"No kidding," added Tanner. "Leah *totally* could have been in covert ops back in our parents' day. She's convincing."

Marcus uncomfortably side-eyed Tanner. "Is that supposed to be a compliment? What kind of person wishes the war was still happening?"

Tanner threw a hand up. "Of course, I don't mean that. But come on, even the *queen* was a master of covert ops!"

Marcus narrowed his eyes in obvious disgust. "This. This is exactly the kind of reason I'd *never* invite you to the wedding. She's not exactly proud of that! But you act like it's something to hero worship." He stood up, grabbed his tray, and walked away.

Leah sat still, not sure what to do. Nothing made any more sense now than it had when the conversation started. Ivy? Bowman? Queen and covert ops? She wanted to go after Marcus, but had absolutely no idea what to even say. Instead, she picked at her fingernails, waiting to hear what the other two would say.

Jake sighed. "Tanner, you really need to stop it." He also took his tray and left.

Leah pursed her lips. "Well, that was fun."

Tanner huffed. "Word of warning? Those two are a bit touchy. I'm not racist. I'm just saying, some bowmen think we're all out to get them or something. But honestly, just because they're both Ivy Kingdom, I mean, it's not the same. Right?"[g]

She studied his face, swallowing hard. *All these words. Racism?*

Luckily, Tanner didn't expect an answer. "Jake's family are expats and barely even go to visit. And with Marcus's family being mixed... I get that they've had persecution, but..." He shook his head. "Anyway." He smiled. "I'm doing all the talking. I'm excited to learn more about you."

She was speechless, her mouth dry. "Um... What do you want to know?"

He shrugged. "I don't know. What part of the kingdom are you from?"

She took a sip of water. "South."

He peeled back the film cover of his mixed fruit cup. "How far from the palace?"

"Oh ... um ... I don't know, really. Pretty far south."

"Cool. I'm north central."

After a few more questions she had to give vague lies to, the bell rang.

"Hey, we're doing a Garden Club hangout tonight at Marcus's place. You down?"

"Garden Club?"

He chuckled and pointed at her. "You're good. I still can't believe you had us all fooled."

She stood to join him. "What can I say? I've got skills."

He grinned. "I'd love to learn more about all those mysterious skills and extracurricular activities of yours. It's nice having a girl from back home at this school."

She blushed at his obvious flirting. She may not have understood the hodgepodge of information they'd spat out, but she gathered Tanner might be the only one of the group really like her, with the vine growths. "Yeah, I should be able to make it."

Chapter 4

Marcus greeted Leah with a smile. "Hey, glad you could join us! Come on in."

She warily walked into his house, unsure what to expect from this 'Garden Club.' When they'd texted about it, he'd said she didn't need to bring anything. She wasn't really interested in growing plants, though she figured, like most things with these guys, it probably stood for something else.

"You don't have to worry about being yourself here," he said. "My grandparents are both human, but they were host parents for my mom during her seeder youth. They understand all the green-folk stuff."

"Cool." She nodded. *Wish I did...*

He led her to the family room, where the other guys were already hanging out. They sat on a long leather sectional in front of a large entertainment center. Tanner had his feet on the wooden coffee table.

"You up for games, Leah?" Tanner asked.

She shoved her hands in her pockets, shrugging. "Sure? What kind?"

"Xbox."

"Yeah, I'm down. As long as you don't try and drag me into a D&D group, I'm down."

Tanner and Marcus laughed, glancing at Jake. Jake rolled his eyes.

"That's Jake's thing," Marcus said. "He got a human group together; he's trying to convince us to join."

"You might find it fun, if you'd give it half a chance," Jake defended.

"Anyway..." Marcus said. "Help yourself to the snacks, and just chill." He gestured at a folding table set up to the side, loaded with chips, cookies, a veggie tray, and various drinks.

Leah sat down, and Tanner handed her a controller, but not with his hands ... with his own set of *vines*. He caught her eye, smirking.

"Using vines during the game is *cheating*," Jake warned with a pointed glance at Tanner. "Sometimes we have to remind Tanner."

The entire evening was a pretty standard hangout. Games, chatting about school, and only minor mentions of the inside secrets she was trying to learn about. A bit disappointed, Leah decided to try her luck, focusing on something Marcus had once said.

"Since I was late moving here, did I miss anything in orientation?"

"Not really," Jake said. "It's just a recap of all the prep courses you take before coming over as an exchange."

That isn't helpful in the slightest. "I guess I just want to make sure I don't forget anything important."

Tanner counted on his fingers. "Let's see... Don't get into trouble, don't break human laws, don't get discovered."

She smiled. "Like using vines at school?"

He winked.

"Honestly, you really had me fooled," Marcus said. "You seamlessly use electronics and everything."

"Yeah. Electronics are nice to have, right?" she replied as casually as she could manage. *What kind of place do these guys come from that doesn't have electronics?* She'd started to wonder about the possibility of aliens, but that required spaceships and stuff... She wanted nothing more than to have it all laid out for her, and was tempted to confess she was out of the loop, but she couldn't do that. It didn't feel right. She privately scoffed at the irony. She didn't want to feel like an outsider ... to a group of outsiders.

"I haven't been here that long, but I can already see why your brother's marrying a human and moving to the human world," Tanner kidded before crunching into a chip.

Marcus chuckled. "Yep, that's *exactly* why he's marrying her and leaving the Green Lands. It's all so he can use the internet and game on a daily basis."

Green Lands? That ... sparked something. Something she'd almost forgotten from her childhood.

After returning home, Leah retreated to her room and tried to think of everything she could remember about the Green Lands. It was such a silly thing, really. Her mom used to tell her about a beautiful and strong princess, bedtime stories about majestic mountains and magical people. She'd called the paradise just that—the Green Lands. *It can't be a coincidence.*

Leah toyed with the idea of bringing it up to her mom that night, but couldn't get herself to do so, not right after hanging out with the guys. If there was one thing Leah needed, it was the freedom her mother gave her, despite the phone tracking and frequent checkups every time Leah wasn't at school or in her mom or Aunt Cheryl's custody. The level of freedom Leah currently enjoyed had been bought over the years, despite all of her mistakes, by the healthy amount of guilt her mom carried about them having to move so much, and because she refused to talk about Leah's dad. Associating the Garden Club with something her mom had kept from her all these years didn't seem like the best way to keep her freedom to hang out with the guys.

The next morning, Leah was deep in thought, running a brush through her hair.

When home, Aunt Cheryl usually kept to her room in the opposite corner of the house, and might not have even picked up much about Leah's friends or her comings and goings. Even so, Leah wouldn't risk braving the waters with her, either.

"You almost ready?" Aunt Cheryl asked while tossing her purse strap over her shoulder.

"Yeah, I just have to pack my bag."

"Hurry up." Aunt Cheryl left the bathroom doorway.

Leah tucked her hairbrush in its drawer.

"Leah... What is this?" Aunt Cheryl's voice was low, sharp, threatening. She reappeared at the bathroom doorway, holding up one of Leah's notebooks. Her face was fierce, a look Leah had seen before. That was the look she'd given Leah once in elementary school—right before they started to pack up and move.

Swallowing, Leah tried to hide her panic. She hadn't realized Aunt Cheryl had left to go shove her school things in her backpack, and that Leah had left a notebook wide open on her desk. All over the top of the page were doodles of 'The Green Lands.'

"That means nothing. You shouldn't be going in my room." She stood rigid, terrified.

"Eleana! What's this about?"

She started to sweat. "It's nothing. Seriously. Let's go." She tried to snatch the notebook back, but Aunt Cheryl held it out of reach in the hallway. "We're going to be late." Leah stepped forward to leave the bathroom, but Cheryl shifted to block her.

"I'm not going to ask again."

Maybe I should have just asked the guys.

She glared at Aunt Cheryl. "You're crazy. It doesn't mean anything."

Cheryl grabbed a fistful of Leah's hair, practically shoving the notebook in her face. "Is that where you heard this phrase? School?"

Leah winced at the pain as her breathing picked up. Maybe she could lie and pretend she'd meant to somehow write 'Greenland' the country, but that was a pretty weak claim. "No! No. It's nothing. I just... I remembered bedtime stories Mom told me when I was a kid."

Cheryl's eyes narrowed. "And why would you remember that all of a sudden?"

"It's a writing assignment for English. Memories from our childhood!"

Cheryl released her grip with a skeptical stare. "Forget about *stupid* fairy tales and places that *don't* exist. Write about learning to ride a bike like a normal kid."

"Okay. Fine. Can we go now?"

After another moment of staring her down, Aunt Cheryl tore out the page with Leah's doodles and part of her math homework, crumpling the page and pocketing it. She picked Leah's backpack up, cramming the notebook in without any care that she'd bent back several pages, and shoved the backpack at Leah.

After Leah flung it over her shoulder, they made their way to the car. Leah kept glancing at Cheryl's pocket. What would Cheryl do with that paper? Show it to Leah's mom as proof they ought to move again?

On the ride, Leah kept her eyes on the window, rubbing her sore scalp as they drove to school in silence.

They pulled into the drop-off line. "You're not lying?" Cheryl asked.

"Why would I lie about an English assignment?" Leah asked as though she were confused. It was a sad excuse, especially given the doodles hadn't even been in her English notebook, but it was the best she could think up at the moment.

Cheryl pursed her lips. "Forget those stupid stories, and don't even bring it up with your mother."

So she's not going to tell Mom? "Fine. Done."

"You okay?" Marcus asked at lunch as Leah mindlessly stabbed at her Caesar salad.

"Yeah. Of course." She forced a smile.

She looked the guys over as they chatted. They were her only hope to figure out what she really was. After the bell rang and they dispersed for classes, she chased after Tanner.

"Hey. Question for you," she said.

"Yeah. What's up?"

"I was wondering if you wanted to hang out sometime." She bit her lip. "You know, just the two of us."

He grinned. "Yeah. Sounds like fun. Have anything in mind?"

She shrugged. "Just talk ... and chill. I'd say we could hang at my place, but my mom and aunt are always home."

"Yeah. We can work something out."

They were set to meet up that Friday, but then it happened again—sticky fingers. Well ... more like sticky vines. At least this time it was her mom who caught her and not Aunt Cheryl. She was now grounded, stuck in her stupid house for anything except school.

Leah sorted through her bedside table drawer, where she always stashed the pilfered things she'd successfully stolen under the radar and had actually decided to keep. Her mom and Aunt Cheryl of course didn't know about this collection, and her mom didn't search her room that often. Even then, the plastic basket full of lifted goods was usually hidden by a few books she laid on top of it.

Small glass bottles clinked against each other as she raked her hand through her collection. For a girl who didn't paint her nails often, she sure owned a lot of nail polish. 'Owned' in a very loose sense of the word, since she'd never purchased a single one of them. She sat on her bed, starting on her toenails. *This sucks. All of it.*

All of Leah's lifelong—and new—questions ran through her mind. She shouldn't have risked stealing this time. Cheryl and her mom were getting more vigilant every time they would allow her to go shopping with them. And instead of hanging out at Tanner's, she was a prisoner at home.

Once her nails dried, now sporting a coat of azure blue with a holo glitter topcoat, Leah got ready for the night. Peeking into her mom's partially opened door, she spotted her mom writing in a journal. She wrote in there a lot. This time she seemed deeply lost in thought, wiping away a tear.

"I'm heading to bed," Leah said.

Her mom stopped writing, setting down her journal and gently covering it with a pillow. "Okay, princess."

Leah frowned. "I'm sorry."

Her mom sighed. "Are you sorry you did it? Or are you sorry you got caught?"

Leah looked down at her feet, wiggling her sparkly toes. "Both?"

"What's bothering you, sweetheart?"

"Nothing."

Her mom cocked her head. "You sure? It's not like there's an exact science to it, but I've noticed you tend to have more troubles when you're stressed."

What could Leah say that she hadn't said before? They'd already hashed and rehashed it all.

"I'm fine. Really."

Chapter 5

After two weeks, Leah's sentence had been served. She'd missed out on a couple of Garden Club hangouts, and she was itching to get out of the house. More than anything, she was looking forward to one-on-one time with Tanner. Alone, she could get to asking more questions. He'd been giving her flirtatious glances the last two weeks at lunch, too. She wasn't mad about it. He was cute enough, even if he was a bit arrogant.

He picked her up, and they went back to his place. She didn't want to go anywhere public, so they could be more open with their conversations.

He welcomed her in. "So ... this is my place for the rest of the school year."

"Nice house." She scanned the front room. It was tidy, bright, and looked like it could have come from a magazine. "You get along with your host family?"

"Yeah, they're cool."

She hadn't noticed any other cars parked outside. "Will I be meeting them?"

"Oh, um... It's just going to be us. My host parents took their kids out to a movie."

She raised an eyebrow. "Really? Are they okay with me being here?"

He grinned. "You didn't want to hang out at your place because of your mom and aunt, so ... I thought..." He cleared his throat. "Well, anyway, yes. They know I have a friend over."

She smirked—did they know the *gender* of that friend?

He led her down to the basement family room. "Want anything to eat or drink?"

"Some water, maybe?"

He filled them each a glass of water, and they sat down on a plaid sofa.

"So, what did you want to talk about?" he asked.

She mindlessly stabbed a decorative pillow with her finger. "Just ... stuff, you know. Green Lands and all that."

"What about it?"

"I don't know. What do you miss from there?"

He furrowed his brow. "Hmm. Haven't really been gone that long to miss a ton. I mean, obviously the lack of ambient energy, right?"

"Yeah. Of course."

He frowned. "Are you homesick?"

"Maybe a little."

He set his glass down, lounging more comfortably on the couch. "What I've been wondering, though, is that you said you live with your mom and aunt?"

"Yeah. Since I can remember—just my mom and Aunt Cheryl and I."

"So ... are you just here for the one year?" He ran a hand through his light-brown hair. "They're sacrificing a whole school year so you could come study in the human world? Or what? I thought that was weird instead of just connecting with a host family."

"Oh, that? We move a lot. They like a good adventure." She shrugged it off, taking another sip of water. "I didn't think it was too weird."

"No. I mean, that's cool. I had to *beg* my parents to let me come."

She set down her glass of water too, shifting to face him more directly. "I have a weird question for you."

"Okay?"

"What all do you use your vines for?"

He glanced at his wrists, poking his vines out a bit before retracting them. "Same as anybody else. Just, you know, multitasking ... catching you when you fall, wrestling... Why?" He rubbed his chin, a playful look on his face. "Do you have any fun extracurricular activities you use yours for?"

"Hmm... Well, I *did* get grounded recently..."

He perked up. "I wondered about that..."

"I ... well..." Her face grew warm. "It's a bad habit." She fidgeted with her hands. "My mom thinks I'm a klepto, but really it's just a teensy bit of ... shoplifting ... now and then."

He pressed his lips together, nodding. "Interesting hobby."

She wrinkled her nose. "I guess maybe not the best use of them, huh?"

He grinned. "I don't think I'd have the guts for it. But I'm not gonna lie, that's kinda hot."

She raised her eyebrows. "Hot, huh?"

He reached over, stroking her arm. "When I found out you were also ivy, well, I mean, you're cute. I *really* want to kiss you."

She bit her lip. It was not at all the reason she'd come over, but she wasn't a stranger to a good make-out session. "I'm not opposed."

He scooched over, giving her a couple of soft and sweet tester kisses. There was some decent chemistry there. It became apparent rather quickly that he was also experienced.

He drew closer, sliding his hands to her waist. Her hands landed on the nape of his neck, pulling him in. In his enthusiasm, Tanner leaned into her, slowly bending her back.

She preferred to have more control in the situation. Putting a hand to his chest, she pushed him back against the couch, lips still locked.

Pulling away, she gave him a grin and caught her breath as she straddled him. He smirked and drew her in, his hands on her lower back.

Hot and heavy was on the menu.

Until he moved a little too far outside of Leah's comfort zone for a first make-out session.

He started to move his hands up the back of her shirt.

Without skipping a beat, she arched her back. "No." She leaned in again for the part she was thoroughly enjoying.

Tanner didn't get the hint. Before she knew it, vines extended up her shirt, undoing the clasp on her bra with quick and expert precision. She leaned back, pinning his head against the wall with her hand on his throat.

"Did I stutter?" She glared at him, clenching her jaw, her chest rising and falling with each breath.

He smirked, unfazed. "C'mon. I'm not saying we have to go all the way. But ... you know, if we're going to make out..." He glanced down at her chest, and then back up. "Might as well spice it up with some vines. We were talking about extracurricular use, right?" He gazed into her eyes while moving one of his vines again, slipping one of her bra straps off of her shoulder.

Beyond pissed, she extended one of her own vines. Grasping it between both hands, she pressed it against his throat. "You think that's funny? You want to play with vines? I said no! What part of that is so hard to understand!"

The harder she pressed and the angrier she became, the quicker his expression faded from cocky to panicked, to furious.

Tanner shoved her off his lap, onto the floor. Caught by surprise, it took Leah a moment to recover.

"You psycho!" he belted.

He clutched his throat. As he removed his hand to look at it, she understood his anger. Blood was smeared on both his throat and hand.

Her eyes grew wide, darting between his neck and the wrist her vine had already retracted into.

"Get out!"

Her heart thumped wildly in her chest. *I cut him?* Her stomach lurched at the sight of the bright red blood. She certainly hadn't planned on going so far as to slit his throat! "I'm sorry. I ... didn't know... I didn't mean to..."

He slapped his hand back up to his neck. "Did I stutter, Leah? Get the hell out, you psycho!"

She scrambled to her feet, barely able to take her eyes off the blood. "I'm sorry, really, you have to believe me."

He seethed with anger, pointing to the staircase. "Out. Now!"

Her breath shuddered as she ran up the stairs and left out the front door. Not knowing where she was going, Leah marched down the street. She rubbed her wrist, pacing once she stopped at the end of the street. Shaken, confused, and without a ride, she called the only person she thought she could trust.

"Hey, what's up?"

She started to cry. "I need your help."

"Umm ... yeah. Are you okay?"

She whimpered. "I hurt Tanner. I didn't mean to. I need a ride. Can you come?"

"Is he okay?"

"I think so. I just—" She sniffled.

"Where are you?"

"I'm down the road from his house." She glanced at the crossroad signs. "Fourth and Elm."

"Okay. Stay put. I'll be right there."

In the ten minutes it took for Marcus to borrow his grandparents' minivan and arrive, Leah rehooked her bra and gathered herself emotionally. He pulled up behind her, and she hopped in.

He looked her over. "You're sure Tanner's alright?"

She rubbed her wrist again. "I honestly don't know. I think so. He was standing and everything." Her hands were even shaking. "He kicked me out."

"Okay ... well, we'll assume he's fine, then. Are *you* okay?"

She twisted her lips. "I don't know. I... Can we just ... talk for a bit?"

"Sure. Do you want to go back to your place?"

That was a resounding no. "Maybe just a frozen yogurt parking lot or something? Then I can text my mom where I am, and she won't suspect anything."

He raised an eyebrow. "Suspect anything?"

"Just ... please?" She wilted. "I want to get away from here, and I'll explain everything."

Marcus nodded. "Alright." He turned the key in the ignition, and they drove away without another word.

Leah bit her nails, staring out the window as they drove in silence. Once Marcus parked, she texted her mom the change in plans and location so it would match up to her phone's tracker.

"What happened?"

She faced him, her nerves still tightly wound. "I cut him. On accident. With my vines."

Marcus raised his eyebrows in surprise. "What the heck were you doing?"

She pressed her lips together.

"Or ... maybe I shouldn't ask that."

She rolled her eyes. "It's not a big deal. We were making out."

He cleared his throat. "Yeah, maybe I don't want all the details. I didn't realize you guys were..."

"Oh, give me a break. We're not. It wasn't even a date. It was just kissing. Don't judge me."

He put his hands up in the air. "Go on."

"He, well ... anyway..." She shook her head. "It wasn't anything I couldn't handle."

He furrowed his brow. "Tanner did something while you were kissing that you had to *handle*?"

She chuckled. "It sounds dirty when you say it *that* way. I wasn't *handling* anything. Just forget that part, alright? He pissed me off."

"But ... are you okay?" Marcus asked cautiously.

She scowled. "I can take care of myself. I didn't call you for help with that. Let's move on to the part where I *literally* cut his neck with my vines. I *promise* I didn't mean to. You have to believe me. I didn't even know I could."

He nodded, his face skeptical. "I'm just a bowman ... but how do you *accidentally* cut someone? And not realize it's possible?"

She gnawed on her lower lip, taking a deep breath. "Because I grew up thinking I was a human with a freaky genetic defect. I have *no idea* what half of the crap is you guys are talking about. I don't know what a seeder or bowman is. I don't know where the Green Lands are. I don't know any of it."

He studied her face in silence. "So, you want me to believe you were lying about lying?" He cocked his head. "Leah, you're a bit hard to keep track of."

Her shoulders dropped. "I'm not lying this time. Can you please just explain what I am and what the hell is going on?"

"I... Well ... I still don't get it. How do you not know? And why wouldn't you have just asked us?"

"My mom and aunt have always lied to me. I thought my vines were just weird growths that ran in our family. But when you caught me... I guess, I felt stupid not being in the loop when you guys acted as if *not* being human is something normal."

He gave her a scrutinizing glance. "You've lived your whole life in the human world, not understanding what it is to be an ivy?"

"That about sums it up."

He ran his hand through his hair. "I gotta be honest. That's weird. Most ivies who have permanently moved are here because, well ... they're racist or elitist. And sore losers when they lost the war. But ... they hide their true nature from the human world, not their kids."

"My mom isn't racist!"

He paused. "You've never heard her say 'seeders' or 'bowman' or anything like that? Or referencing green eyes? It doesn't have to be about skin color to be racist."

She spoke firmly, more than annoyed at his accusations. "No. Never."

"Bowman wasn't even a label that was used until after the war ended. She never makes fun of people for their differences or disabilities?"

"No! She's the one always telling me our physical differences don't define us."

He put his hands up. "Okay. I believe you. Maybe, I don't know... Maybe she got so fed up with all the chaos that she's trying to leave all aspects of our realm behind." He shrugged. "Even then, most ivies who move away end up coming back. The energy of the realm is something we all crave."

Leah leaned her head back, exhausted with all the lies. Both hers and her mom's. "Right now, I just want to know the truth."

He glanced at his phone. "There's a lot to explain. How much time do you have?"

Chapter 6

Marcus drew a deep breath. "Where to start? The Green Lands—it's our homeland. It's another realm located on this planet."

"Where?" Leah asked.

He chuckled, running his hand across the steering wheel. "Honestly, no one really knows. It could be an island; it could be a hidden valley somewhere. It's surrounded by an outer rim of incredibly tall mountains that no one has ever been able to get past. Even by flying. Pretty sure there's an energy barrier there, as well. It keeps it safe."

"Then how do you go there?"

"Only way in or out is rifting." He clarified when her expression twisted in confusion. "Like energy doorways. It's so beautiful, too."

"What else?" This was her chance. No more lies. She needed to know it all.

"There are two races. Seeders and Ivies. You're obviously Ivy. Within each race, you'll find bowmen like Jake and I. It just means we're born into Seeder or Ivy families, but we're pretty much your standard-grade human—no vines, no powers." He gave her a warm smile. "That's B-o-m-a-n, singular. No W. No arrows. It stands for 'Botanical Human.'"

She nodded, happy to finally put that piece of the puzzle in its place.

"My mom's a Seeder. That's why I'm adopted, because Seeders, Ivies, and humans can't have kids together. Anyway, back in the old war days, Seeders had to hide their daughters in the human world until high school, when their powers came in. It's complicated, but my mom understands what it's like to not know what you are your whole life."

Leah licked her lips, taking it all in. "Interesting. It would be cool to talk to her sometime. Are your parents planning on visiting while you're here?"

"Well ... my dad might. But ... Seeders are complicated. They're the more powerful race, but they have lots of limitations. My mom *literally* can't leave the Green Lands. It has to do with their strong connection to the energy of the realm. That's why the wedding's taking place over there." He shifted in his seat. "Well, the main wedding. They're doing a human ceremony over here, too, for the bride's family. It's pretty exclusive which humans know we even exist."

Leah soaked it all up like a sponge. "Tell me about Seeders."

He thoroughly described them—their culture and abilities. They were a floral race that lived more simply, in wooden cottages and homes, had kids in batches— *twenty-four* at a time—and could fly, able to transform and wield energy differently than Ivies. They even had more abilities and strength than the Ivies. Just like Ivies, Seeders could conceal themselves in the human world if they wanted, walking amongst humans with no way to really be detected.

"And Ivies. Like you ... well, there's the vines. Like an extra appendage. As you ... unfortunately ... discovered, you can flex the leaves to be rigid, sharp."

She still couldn't believe that. "I wish I'd known."

Marcus's voice was kind. "It's okay. You'll sort it out. He's lucky you didn't poison him. He didn't seem dizzy or anything, right?"

"Poison?!" She read his face. "Um ... should we check on him?"

He waved a hand dismissively. "No. It's not lethal to Ivies. And I think you have to be pretty intentional on that one. But yeah, you can administer chemical compounds through those leaves. Like numbing, or even plant fertilizer."

She looked down, rubbing her wrists. As if she hadn't been a freak before...

Marcus explained basic Ivy culture, how it was ruled by a queen and king.

"And Bomen, where do you fit into it all?"

"Here, there, and everywhere." He chuckled. "Lots moved here after the war, like Jake's family. But back home, Bomen live in our kingdom, in the Seeder nation, and some in their own colonies. Lots of variety."

"You guys talk about this war a lot."

His mouth hung open. "There's a lot of baggage there. Over two hundred years at war. It finally ended, actually, around the time you and I were born. You know, people still have prejudices and differences of opinion, but it's nothing like what our parents grew up with."

She leaned her head back, mulling it all over. "Thanks. For being understanding, and honest with me. It means a lot. Gives me a heck of a lot to think about." She bit the insides of her cheeks. "I really want to go check out this place now. You said there are portals. How does that work?"

"Seeders and Ivies have different abilities for rifting. But honestly, people pretty much exclusively use the cave networks now. They're monitored, and you have to have a passport." He frowned. "I'm not so sure you can visit without your mom's permission, and without going through the legal process."

She picked at her fingernails. That wasn't going to happen. Not if her mom had spent Leah's entire life concealing that part of her.

"Well, anyway..." She blew out a puff of air. "I don't know what I'm going to do about Tanner. He was livid. And I don't blame him."

Marcus shrugged. "You're going to have to be honest with him, like you were with me."

Every ounce of her pride revolted against that idea. "I hate looking like an idiot."

"You don't." Marcus pointed at her. "But just telling him you didn't mean to, without him understanding where you're coming from, is like a human scratching someone's eyes out and saying they didn't realize their fingernails were capable of doing that."

She choked back a laugh at the comparison. "I get it."

He nodded. "Should I take you home?"

"Yeah. Let's do that."

Minutes later, Marcus pulled up to Leah's house and parked the van. "You going to be alright?"

"Yeah. Just lots to process."

He toyed with his keys, which still dangled from the ignition. "Tanner can be a real jerk sometimes. You're sure you're alright about him, too?"

She smiled. "You're really sweet. I'm good."

Was she good? Kind of. She'd dealt with worse than what Tanner had just done. She'd learned to numb the side of her that acknowledged what had just happened.

What would she do about it anyway? Tell her mom? This wasn't Leah's first make-out session gone bad. She had a type. Her mom would be there for her, just like she'd been before. The problem was ... her mom's version of 'taking care of things' usually involved moving far away and starting all over again.

And then there was Aunt Cheryl. Under the thick layer of denial Leah laid down in her heart, Cheryl's biting words nipped at her. Leah was a slut. It was her fault. It wasn't like Tanner had pinned her down. It wasn't like Leah hadn't jumped at the opportunity to make out in the first place.

"Do you want a hug?" Marcus asked.

She grinned, taking in his kind face, his curly hair. "I'm not really a hugger. But maybe I could use one tonight."

They both got out of the van, and she met him on his side. He pulled her in for a perfect tight squeeze. "Are you going to talk to your mom, now that you know?"

She swallowed hard. Tanner? The secrets of the Green Lands? They'd moved for less. "I don't know if that's a great idea. We'll see."

He pulled back from the hug. "See you Monday?"

"Yeah, of course." She cocked her head. "Thanks for being a great friend, Marcus."

"You're not such a bad friend yourself." He rocked his head back and forth, shoving his hands in his pockets. "When you're honest."

She blushed. "No more lies. I promise."

"I appreciate that."

Leah ambled to her front door and unlocked it, all the while lost in thought. Marcus drove off only after she stepped inside.

"You returned with a different friend than the one you left with?" her mom questioned once she entered.

Leah huffed, weakly gesturing at the front door. "You've met both of them. Just friends. Calm down. We were at Tanner's house, then went out for ice cream, and Marcus volunteered to take me home."

"Alright. I'm going to head to bed, princess." Her mom smiled and strode back to her room.

Leah also smiled as she went to her own bedroom, mulling everything over. 'Princess' was such a juvenile pet name. Sometimes it annoyed her. But in a lot of ways, her mom's nickname for her was also sweet and indicative of their relationship.

Despite all the moves, and drama with Aunt Cheryl, and their arguments ... her mom was a good mom. Leah never doubted her love.

But why the lies?

Monday at lunchtime, Marcus searched out Leah in the cafeteria. After he found her, they stood in line together, selecting their food and getting caught up.

"How was the rest of your weekend?" he asked.

"I guess as good as it could be?" She grabbed a carton of milk from the refrigerator.

"I half expected you to call or text again." He made eye contact. "You can reach out, if you need to talk."

"Thanks. I'm good." She glanced at the cafeteria doors. "Though ... um ... I think I'm going to eat lunch on my own today."

He bunched his eyebrows. "Why?"

Really? "Tanner? I don't know that I'm ready to go through that yet."

Marcus shook his head. "Then let *him* sit somewhere else. If he ... well... I don't know what all happened. But I'm just saying, what you did was an accident. I hardly doubt whatever he did to piss you off was." He picked out a banana from a bowl of fruit, placing it on his tray. "Jake and I would prefer you be there. Or if you want, I wouldn't mind leaving those two and coming to sit with you somewhere."

She appreciated Marcus's willingness to back her up. "I'll come sit with you guys. We'll see how it goes."

Jake was at their table by the time Marcus and Leah arrived. She trained her eyes on the door to the courtyard to see if Tanner would show his face. A few minutes later, he peeked through the door, tray in hand. The moment their eyes locked, he turned and went back inside. She thought about it. *Why put it off?* She excused herself and went after him, leaving her tray behind.

"Tanner!" She caught him before he found a new place to sit in the cafeteria.

"I'm not really in the mood to talk," he said.

"Please. It's important." She blocked his way, sparing a glance at his neck. He had three regular-size bandages on it.

He wouldn't make eye contact.

"I promise I didn't mean to do that. I can explain. But," she looked around, "somewhere more private."

He rolled his eyes. "Fine."

They walked into an empty hallway and sat on the linoleum floor.

"You went too far," he said, setting his tray on the floor next to him.

She glared. "We both did. Don't pretend you weren't in the wrong."

He met her gaze, his head tilted to the side. "Yeah, but seriously? Cutting me?! You just had to say 'no' another time, or get off of my lap. It's not like I was ... *forcing* myself on you."

She scowled. "I shouldn't have to say 'no' two, or three, or four times for you to get the message!"

He swallowed and looked down. "No. You're right. It won't happen again."

"I seriously hope not. And it definitely won't happen with me. That was a onetime thing. I never meant anything by it."

He shrugged. "I didn't either." He looked up, raising his eyebrows. "But seriously. What you did went too far, too. That was—"

"An accident." She wrung her hands. "I've been lying to you guys because I felt stupid for not knowing. I was raised human. I didn't know I was capable of that."

He squinted, studying her face. "How's that possible? We all learn to use them super young. Like ... learning to walk."

Ugh. This conversation all over again. "My mom lied to me. Yeah, the vines were just kind of part of me. But other than basic reaching and grabbing ... I didn't know. I didn't know *any* of it until I had Marcus explain it to me after I left your place."

Tanner fidgeted with his hands, seemingly nervous. "Marcus knows what happened?"

"Not everything. He knows we got in a fight. And I hurt you on accident, and was freaking out." She took a deep breath. "I needed a ride and answers." She didn't want to rock the boat more than necessary, and she *could* have a temper. She'd been expelled before after standing up to an ex-boyfriend who had used her. Granted, she hadn't known she harnessed Ivy energy that could make her stronger than these human guys, but she probably wouldn't have cared at the time, when she'd kneed him in the groin so hard he'd fallen to the floor, and hadn't gotten up before she'd stalked off. Just one more thing that had forced one of their many moves for a fresh start.

Maybe this time, she'd just let it go. Pretending Aunt Cheryl didn't exist usually served Leah better than standing up to her. Why should it be any different with this situation? And frankly, Tanner may have taken things too far, but he might have more information Leah craved to know about who she was.

"Can we just ... be friends?" she asked. "Move past this?"

He averted his gaze. "Is it going to be awkward with the other guys, and all of us hanging out?"

"Only if we make it awkward."

He slowly nodded, picking up his tray. "Let's see how it goes."

They walked back out to the courtyard together. Jake and Marcus were having a discussion. Marcus's eyes followed Tanner and Leah to the table.

"What's with the bandages?" Jake chimed in without wasting a second.

"Shaving. Had to get a new razor," Tanner said, lowering his head to look at his food.

Marcus glanced at Leah before turning his focus on his own tray.

Leah forced a smile. "Jake, how was your weekend?"

Chapter 7

Leah had answers. But not enough. After the reality of the Green Lands and green folk settled in, the fact that her mom had kept something so essential from her screamed out. She considered trying to force her mom's hand, confronting her with the truth, but she didn't want to face Aunt Cheryl's fury. And doing so, revealing that she'd found the truth, might mean another move. Away from her friends, away from those who gave her such important information.

One night as she was preparing for bed and saying good night to her mom, Leah spotted her doing something she'd seen her do many times over the years—writing in a journal. A journal Leah sometimes wondered about—who wouldn't want to know what was said of them? But now, she wondered if there was something hidden in there, compelling enough to break the tenuous trust they had between them.

And how to read it without her mom finding out...

With either her mom or Cheryl almost always home, Leah didn't have much luck in trying to snoop. She bided her time, trying in a few snippets of minutes alone to search for where her mom even stashed it. After a few close calls of getting caught in her mom's room, Leah at least knew a few places it *wasn't*.

Eventually, the day came. Right after Cheryl left for work, Leah got a call.

"Hey, princess. I'm so sorry, but I'm going to be late getting home today. They really need me here, and I'm going to be a couple of hours late."

"No problem. I'm just doing homework."

"Okay. There's leftovers in the fridge, and I expect you to stay home. No boys. No trouble. I'll know if you left."

"I'll be good," Leah drawled. *I have absolutely no plans to leave home tonight.*

With two hours to herself, she entered her mom's room, and continued the search. Eventually, she looked in the closet. Her mom had a pair of medium-sized safes, and Leah worried she might be out of luck. Making sure no stone was left unturned, she carefully shifted things around on the shelves, taking care to return them to their original places so her snooping would remain unnoticed. As she moved one of the safes, two journals tipped over, having been tucked behind it.

Jackpot!

She took them both down, carrying them to her mom's bed to peruse. Flipping through the pages, Leah glanced at the dates at the top of the pages, also noting that one of the books was only half-full. The full one started with a date that preceded her own birth date. She decided to start there.

"I don't know what to do. Other than wait, and worry, and write. I should have stayed. We should have slowed down, been more patient. Or maybe I'm wrong, and we should have been more aggressive..."

"No one's come. I sent out Amy to get news three days ago, and she hasn't returned. We might have to move to a new location. If things are bad... If she was caught... I can't sleep..."

"I sent Ada over to find out the state of the kingdom. It can't be good if we haven't received word. He was supposed to send for me when it was safe again. I can only imagine the worst..."

"I can't bring myself to even write it. Then it makes it real. But the truth is ... he's gone. He'll never get to meet his own child, his heir. This baby will never have a father. And it's all Kaylah's fault. That traitor will do nothing but undo all the hard work we put into our proud kingdom. She's always been jealous, weak, and making friends with the wrong sorts. I told him we should have killed her right away. Damn it, he should have listened! But now she sits on his throne, destroying everything his family worked for. What we worked for. That bitch killed the love of my life, and I have nothing left..."

In a daze, ravenously reading each new entry, Leah paused a moment, running her finger over a portion of that last entry. The page was wrinkled, the ink smudged. *A tear.* She read on.

"I felt the baby for the first time today. How is it the best things can bring the most pain? I'll do anything to keep it safe. But it reminds me so much of him. Sometimes I tell myself that if our people turned things around, ousted Kaylah from the throne, I could take my place again. Maybe, just maybe, the day Soren's heir takes his place, I could have some sort of closure. But I know that's false hope. And even if we got our kingdom back, I don't know how I could ever rule without him by my side..."

"It's a girl. I think he would have loved that it's a girl. She has his eyes..."

"Eleana…" Her mom's voice startled her.

Leah glanced up from the pages. Expecting anger on her mom's face, she was instead greeted with a look of profound sorrow.

"Sweetheart, you shouldn't be reading that."

Leah glared. How many years had she felt like an outcast, had been clueless as to why they'd moved around so much? "You shouldn't have been lying to me my entire life!"

Her mom lingered in the doorway, shaking her head. "It was to keep you safe."

"You said my dad died in a tragic accident at work! You don't think I deserved to know the truth?!"

Her mom's eyes narrowed as she raised her voice. "He died far too young. That was tragic. That was devastating!"

"You left him to die!"

"Don't you dare, Eleana." Her voice shook. "I loved him and would have died by his side. I was loyal to him and always will be. He *ordered* me to leave. If I hadn't, I would have faced execution right next to him, and you never would have been born to even have this conversation!"

A tear rolled down Leah's cheek. "You could have done *something…*"

Her mom spoke softer, defeated. "Me and what army? It ended as quickly as it began. Your father was ambitious, but his dreams were too big."

"And now, what? We're just going to live as outcasts for the rest of our lives? You think he would want that?"

Her mom marched to the closet, pulling down one of the safes. She set it on the bed and opened it. "You want your birthright? You want to be a real princess?" She gestured at the open safe. "Here you go. You can have my old tiara. That's all we have left."

Leah studied the sparkling accessory; it was simple, but stunning. Golden ivy leaves intertwined with precious gemstones. It was beautiful, but that wasn't the point. She looked up, scowling. "I don't care about any of that. If what he was doing was best for your people, you shouldn't have given up so easily!"

"The moment I go back to that realm, my life is forfeit. I'm never going back. And neither are you."

Leah held up her wrists. "We don't belong here!"

Her mom erupted into tears. "Eleana! This is not up for debate. Sometimes you have to know when to give up hope. No, we don't belong here. But we don't belong there, either. You and I—we don't belong *anywhere!*"

Leah looked down at the journal, with so many pages still left unread. A tear of her own landed on the page, and she snapped it shut. Without another word, she got up and stormed out of the room and into her own. Slamming her door, Leah launched herself onto her bed, sobbing.

Her dad hadn't died. He'd been murdered.

After a good half hour, there was a soft knock on Leah's bedroom door. Her mom slowly opened it when she didn't respond.

"Can we talk?"

"I guess so." Leah sniffled, grabbing a tissue from her bedside table and sitting up.

"Princess, I'm sorry I didn't tell you earlier."

Leah glowered. "Don't call me that anymore."

Her mom joined her on the bed. She reached over, tucking Leah's hair behind her ears. "You'll always be one to me."

Leah rolled her eyes. "Were you ever going to tell me?"

She pursed her lips. "Of course. And maybe I should have earlier, but I wasn't really sure when. I needed to know you could keep it secret. At this point, I was waiting until your eighteenth birthday."

Leah considered her friends... None of them were old enough to have been involved in the war that had ended her dad's life, but their parents would have been around then. Truthfully, she didn't even want to know where they stood with it all. She couldn't lose her new friends, not her only other ties to the homeland she'd never known.

"Do you and Aunt Cheryl have any friends like us at all? With the vines?" She wanted to ask several more questions, but realized she needed to continue to seem ignorant about other things Marcus had told her.

Her mom frowned and shook her head. "Doesn't mean we haven't run across some. But ... it's dangerous. They might be like us—having left after we lost the war. But they might not share that opinion. And if they went back and reported us... Eleana, now that you know, you need to help Cheryl and me keep us safe. I'll go over some basic things, and if you see or hear them, you need to let us know right away."

Leah hid a frown. "We'd have to move, right?"

Her mom nodded. "Where we're from, people can blend in like humans, but there are a few different traits to look for..." She described Seeder appearances like

Marcus had, down to the glowing green eyes. She brought up some of the same terms: green folk, Green Lands.

"I remember you telling me stories about the Green Lands when I was younger."

Her mom quietly rubbed the fabric of her dress pants. "I shouldn't have. I was still foolishly clinging to hope."

"But we can talk more openly about it all now, right?" Leah asked, yearning in her voice.

"It's still really hard to talk about." Her mom's tone and demeanor echoed that of a woman who had never fully healed. "How about I tell you more about your father?"

Leah beamed. "I want to hear it all."

They snuggled up next to each other, and Leah leaned her head against her mom's shoulder.

"He was so handsome. Dark brown hair, those stunning green eyes. A smile that lit up my day. We met fairly young, at a party. I was fourteen, he was fifteen."

"Was it a fancy ball, or something like that?"

"Not a ball, but a medium-sized gathering of some youth near the palace. I was lucky he picked me." She chuckled softly. "He was actually being kind of a jerk, trying to show off for the girls. He liked that I didn't put up with his crap. Gosh, after that, we saw each other as much as we could."

Leah thought back to the journal. "Why couldn't you have at least told me his name growing up?" Soren—it sounded kingly.

There was a long pause before her mom responded. "I couldn't risk anyone finding out." She whispered, "And I couldn't … bring myself to dishonor him or his memory by giving you a fake name."

That made sense. "When did you know it was love?"

"Hmm… I don't know, sweetheart. He was passionate and goal-oriented. He had my heart pretty early. I didn't get to see him much for three years, though."

Leah smiled, imagining their cute love story. "Why didn't you get to see him?"

"He was doing assignments for his uncle here in the human world. They were really close, and worked together on their attempts to end a ridiculously long war. His sister killed him, too—their uncle. That's where things really started to fall apart."

That was like a punch in the gut. "His sister? The one you wrote about, Kaylah? His own sister killed him?"

"Yeah, his younger sister," her mom whispered. "They never got along."

"That's horrible."

Her mom drew a deep breath, poking the comforter. "Yep. And last we checked, she's still in charge."

"Why wouldn't the people have gotten rid of her by now?"

Leah's mom scanned her, then opened her mouth, hesitating. "I won't lie to you. Your father wasn't perfect. Not everyone agreed with his views or his tactics. But it was war. Things were messy. You can never make *everyone* happy."(h)

Leah nodded pensively. "I'm sure it's complicated." Her mom hadn't written much about the specifics of the war in her journal, at least not in the portions Leah had just read. It wasn't like her mom had been writing a history lesson all those years ago.

But Leah couldn't resist thinking of what little information Marcus had given her about the war, and the guys hadn't talked a ton about it, but they'd said things in passing back when she was clueless about everything. She couldn't remember enough to know what to make of the situation. And she didn't want to question her parents, but it sounded like the Green Lands realm was relatively peaceful now... "What's the realm like now?"

Her mom bobbed her head. "Well, a war that spanned over two hundred years is now over... So, there's that..."

"That sounds like a good thing..." Was her Aunt Kaylah really so bad if she'd ended such a long war?

"I wouldn't go that far," her mom said. "Seeders—the enemy, the only other race in the Green Lands—are massively overpowered, especially now. Their territory is now twice the size it was when your father and I ruled, and they can now freely walk about our lands whenever they want."

That made Leah uneasy. Would tensions rise again? "Do you think they'd attack again?"

Blowing out a long breath of air, her mom considered. "It's hard to say. Honestly? Probably not. People have become complacent, despite the fact that half of Ivies lost their jobs when the war ended, and Kaylah threw them into financial disaster. They're lazy."

Leah didn't know what to make of it all. She'd never found American History that interesting, and she couldn't make much of a judgment call about a realm she'd never stepped foot in. Her confusion must have been apparent, because her mom spoke again.

"Seeders drove our people from our lands centuries ago. Look at it this way: the human world is much, much larger than the tiny realm we come from, our little corner of this planet. In how many human nations do the indigenous people coexist with their colonizers? They're not in open war, but that doesn't mean there's not resentment, that wrongs were righted."

Leah nodded again. Her parents had obviously fought to the best of their ability, and this Kaylah had only brought peace by giving in to the Seeders. Just as her heart ached for the father she'd never met, it ached for the homeland she'd lost.

She wanted to brush away the heavy topic for now to allow herself time to ponder it. "What was it like, being a queen?" She smiled. It was still so mind-blowing. Just as much as finding out about her identity as an Ivy, imagining her parents as actual, real rulers of a nation was so crazy.

"I'm sure in peacetime, it would be a heck of a lot more enjoyable. It was stressful. But we were also newlyweds," she gently poked Leah in the arm, "and discovered *you* were on the way, so that made it all worth it."

Leah's smile grew. "Did his being a prince have anything to do with your interest in him?" She batted her eyelashes.

Her mom grinned wider. "I'd be a liar if I said no. But it definitely wasn't just that. We were meant for each other. He loved me. He loved you, too." She leaned over, giving Leah a kiss on the head.

Leah's mom entertained her with a few more stories about their courtship. Before her mom left the room for the night, she addressed one more thing.

"I know you and Aunt Cheryl don't get along, but please try to work things out." She looked down at her hands. "She's not really your aunt. She's one of my aides who helped me escape." She frowned. "We owe her our lives. She's the one who's gone back to check on the state of things. She was there to help me through your birth. Human doctors would be clueless when it comes to Ivy births." She met Leah's gaze. "Eleana, she owes us nothing. Be grateful."

Leah nodded, whispering, "Okay." Before her mom left, Leah thought to ask, "If you knew then, what you know now, that this would happen, would you have done things differently?"

"Absolutely," she replied wistfully.

After settling in for the night, Leah lay restless in bed. She loved being able to form a mental picture of her dad. And being royalty ... still a shocker. But the betrayal, her mom's heartache—they didn't deserve that. Leah might not be able to take back her dad's kingdom, or secure her mom's position to do things differently, to be successful in a kingdom they could be proud of. But she had to be able to do *something*. Her mom was held back by fear—she was broken.

But Leah—she was angry. The more she thought about it, she wasn't content to give up the world she should have had a place in, while the traitorous woman who had taken her dad's life sat on his throne.

Chapter 8

Leah got ready for school the next day. As usual, Cheryl met her at the bathroom as she finished, trying to speed her along.

"Cheryl?"

"What?"

Leah frowned. "I talked with my mom last night, and—"

"She said as much."

"I didn't realize what all you've done for us."

Cheryl's reply dripped with sarcasm. "Is that a hint of actual gratitude?"

Leah clenched her fist in an attempt not to roll her eyes. "Yes. I wanted to say thank you."

Cheryl scoffed. "Well, I didn't do it all for *your* spoiled ass."

Always such warmth and love. "Right. Do you miss the Green Lands?"

"Of course I do."

"Could you teach me how to get there?"

Cheryl scowled, shaking her head. "You're out of your mind. You think we've spent all this time in the human world for you to just pop in and be discovered?"

Leah sighed, putting in a pair of stud earrings. "It sounded like my mom wasn't very far along when you left. Would they even know to look for me?"

"That's not the point. I'm not risking our lives for a spoiled brat like you."

Leah stood taller, squaring her shoulders. If Cheryl had been one of her mom's servants, that meant she'd been loyal to her dad as well, the king. "You don't think my dad deserves justice?"

"He got what he deserved." The words rolled off her tongue venomous and cold.

Leah's heart ached, the tears from the night before threatening a reprise. "Why would you say that?"

Cheryl's eyes narrowed. "He was young and foolish. He took risks and failed. And now we're stuck *here*, away from the family and realm I grew up in. This is all *his* fault!"

Leah couldn't look her in the face; she instead slipped past Cheryl to pick up her backpack. "I'm ready. Let's go." Cheryl would be no help in getting to the Green Lands. But she wasn't the last person on the list who might be able to help.

<hr>

Weighed down, still forming her decision, Leah skipped grabbing any food, and went straight to the Garden Club's usual lunch table. She was the first one there, and to her luck, the next to arrive was Tanner.

"Hey, I've got a favor to ask of you," she started in without a proper greeting.

"What's up?" Fortunately, things were mostly back to normal between the two. Not that she didn't often think about how much of a jerk he'd been, but they did a good job of pretending nothing had happened, for the sake of avoiding awkwardness in the group.

"Could we meet up sometime? I have more Ivy questions. Not so sure Bomen could help me."

He shrugged. "Sure."

She gave him a casual smile. "You're awesome, thanks."

Marcus and Jake joined the table with their usual greetings.

"Not eating today, Leah?" Marcus asked, picking up his plastic fork.

"Mmm ... not hungry."

He arched an eyebrow. "You okay?"

She pursed her lips, thinking about it. Could she mention any of the new information she'd learned? No. Who knew what their parents thought... Like her mom had said—wars were messy. Whether or not they'd agreed with her dad's reign, drawing attention wouldn't be good. Though, she internally smirked—she could have been a real princess. What would these guys think of that tidbit?

"Yeah," she finally responded.

"Well, that was a long pause for a 'yeah,'" Jake poked fun.

She chuckled. "Yeah, I'm okay. I didn't say I was *fantastic*."

<hr>

Tanner and Leah met up at a nearby park after school, per her request. As with every outing in her life that wasn't at home or school, Leah texted her mom the plan and location.

"What did you want to talk about?" Tanner asked as they walked side by side on an asphalt path.

"A little of this and that. Our powers and culture," she said.

"Sure. Shoot."

"Who are the current king and queen?"

"That would be Queen Kaylah Elonta and her husband, Eric. He's a human."

Leah nodded. *So, she's still there.*

"Does she have any siblings?"

"Yeah. She has two younger brothers—"

Would they be like her dad?

"—and she had an older brother, but he died in the war. Lots of drama with that one."

Trying to hide a frown, Leah nodded again. "Why do you like the queen?"

He shrugged. "From the stories I've heard, she's pretty badass."

Leah clenched her teeth. *As if murdering is something to praise.*

"And I mean, she's a queen. It might be a small kingdom, but royalty is still pretty cool."

She relaxed and internally smirked at that. If he knew who Leah really was, practically a princess, with them having made out—he'd eat that up.

"Gotcha. And this part is kind of awkward for me to be asking you, but I don't have anyone else I can ask."

Tanner side-eyed her. "Okayyy?"

"Just, self-defense... How can I hurt people?"

He laughed. "Sorry, but the way you worded that. 'How can I hurt people.'"

She rolled her eyes.

"I mean, you understand the sharp leaf thing now."

"Yeah, I practiced a little with that last night. I think I understand how it works now, with the flexing. But I'll need to practice more."

He held up a finger. "I'm not a test dummy."

She huffed, tucking her hands into her pockets. "Wasn't asking you to be."

"Other than making them sharp, the other main thing is poison. But I couldn't teach you about that—that's a girl thing. And you'd need a proper teacher."

Ugh. This is stupid. And getting me nowhere. "Am I capable of killing a person with my vines?"

His face scrunched uncomfortably. "When did this escalate from self-defense to killing someone? You kinda scare me sometimes."

She tried to laugh it off. "Come on. I just want to make sure I don't hurt someone on accident again."

He rubbed his neck. "Yeah ... probably good to be careful..." He cleared his throat. "I can show you vine manipulation techniques sometime. Maybe before the next Garden Club at my house? No, uh ... extracurricular activities this time."

She smiled, grateful they hadn't burned their bridge. "I'd really appreciate that."

"Yeah. No prob. You can't enlist in the army nearly as young as you used to be able to, but my dad served back in the day. Granted, the way they teach history, it sounds like *everyone* was enlisted." Tanner bent down, plucking a dandelion and popping off its head.(i) "Anyway, he showed me some moves."

Questions kept coming to her mind, kept pushing her, prodding her, like the barely there breeze blowing at their backs. "Which side did he serve on?"

Tanner grimaced. "That's not really a polite question to ask, you know? Kind of touchy for people."

She bit her lip. "Sorry. I'm not really familiar with everything, remember? But I'm guessing by your reaction that he fought for the king that lost?"

Tanner looked down, shrugging a single shoulder. "Yeah. Not something you really talk about with others, though. I definitely wouldn't bring it up in Garden Club."

She nudged him with her elbow. "Your secret's safe with me." She couldn't decide if she was grateful to hear of someone who had supported her dad, or bitter that he was one of the troops who had surrendered, who had abandoned her dad and allowed him to die.

Nearly reaching the end of the path, Leah sat down on the grass, and Tanner followed after her. "What about getting to the Green Lands?" she asked. "How do we do that?"

"We have a cave network."

She already knew that wasn't an option—no passport. "Marcus said something once about Seeders and Ivies having different abilities with that, about opening a portal of some kind?"

"Yeah, that—rifting. Technically, we rift in the caves. But we can rift through trees, too." He blew out a puff of air. "At least we *used* to be able to," he drawled.

"What changed?"

He pointed at Leah. "That's one thing I definitely *don't* agree with the queen on. We used to be able to practically come and go whenever we wanted." He gestured at the park around them. "Any tree. Anywhere. No passports. No security checks. But not long after she got into power, she banned it."

Leah bunched her eyebrows. "That sucks."

"Right! And it's not fair. That's something unique to us, as Ivies. Seeders can still rift in their unique way. She didn't stop *them*. Granted, I doubt many do, but it's not like they can't." He glanced around as if to check that no one was nearby. "Some people would call her a weed-lover, not that I'd personally put it that way..."

"What does that mean?"

He cringed, leaning over to retie a loose shoelace. "You know, pretend you never heard that. It's... If the other guys heard me say that, they'd pummel me. Not exaggerating. My point is, the queen's best friend is a Seeder, right? She used Seeders to help her win the war—they got to keep their rifting practices. Her husband is a human—they weren't even capable of going through rifts until she let them in. But who's looking out for *our* rights?"

Leah shook her head, her gut heavy, her ears warming. This was the kind of confirmation she needed. This queen was no saint—she was oppressing her own people. She needed to go.

Leah was trying to be rational, not just be ruled by her emotions, but the evidence was stacking up. Her dad deserved justice. And his people deserved better. "Sounds like you're not too fond of humans? Or just humans being over there?"

Tanner waved a hand. "Humans are fine. I don't have any problems with them in their own world, but they used to not be able to enter the Green Lands. Do you know how vulnerable that makes us now that they can? What if we became public? If people came to experiment on us? To destroy our lands like they have their own paradises in the name of tourism or growth? It's not right. It should only be Ivies and Seeders over there."

Leah considered Tanner's words, running her hand along the grass. "You make a fair point."

"Yeah. Like I said—not her finest policy."

"So, there's no way to rift over there at all? Other than the monitored caves?"

"I've heard some people in certain jobs might get special permits. But no, not really. The only time we're allowed to tree-rift is in emergencies."

Hmm... "What if I needed to leave? What if I had an emergency? Would you teach me?"

His mouth opened, but nothing came out for a moment. "I, uh ... don't feel comfortable with that. What I've been taught is only theoretical, and you have to have specific location names to know where to go ... there's a lot of rules and stuff."

She made eye contact. "Come on. Please?" She could really use this.

He averted his gaze, plucking up a few strands of grass. "I'm not trying to be a jerk. But ... I'm going to have to say no. It's illegal. If you want to be taught, you should ask your mom."

Leah clenched her teeth, frustrated. She had three options—threaten him, and she wasn't there yet; give more information about herself, and perhaps he'd cave, but she couldn't be sure it was worth the risk; or try to convince him in other ways ... the kind of ways he'd definitely enjoyed before, but they'd agreed to not go there, and it wasn't guaranteed to work. That third option made her particularly sick to her stomach.

With a mix of hope and guilt, Leah recalled previous conversations in the club between Marcus and Tanner. There was still one more option. Her last option. And truthfully, her best option.

The queen would be attending Marcus's brother's wedding.

And Marcus had no plus-one.

Chapter 9

Leah wasted no time enacting her plan the next day. After lunch, she quickly and quietly asked Tanner if the queen or her brothers had any kids. It dawned on her the queen might be attending Marcus's brother's wedding because they were somehow related. Even if Marcus didn't know it, Queen Kaylah was Leah's aunt. A horrible waste of space, but technically her aunt. And Leah needed to make sure she wasn't trying to date a cousin; just the thought of it made her gag. Luckily, Tanner confirmed the queen and her younger brothers didn't have any kids yet.

Leah grabbed Marcus's attention as they waited for their rides at the end of the day. "Hey. I was wondering if you wanted to go on a date this weekend. Teach me knife-throwing?"

He raised his eyebrows, clearly surprised. "A date? Or hangout?"

She grinned. "I said the one I meant."

"Um..." He averted his eyes. "Well..."

Okay... So this might not be as easy as I thought. Did I misread his signals? I thought he had a bit of a thing for me. He's the one that called our first hangout a date...

"Will ... it make things awkward?" he asked. "With you and Tanner?"

"Oh, that? No." She shook her head. "Definitely not. We've discussed where we're at. Just friends. It was a onetime thing. Didn't mean anything."

"Okay..." Marcus hesitated.

Unless he's judging me for it... Great! "Do you think it's weird? I didn't think you guys were that close," she added.

He scoffed. "You know where we stand with that. We'd never be friends back home. The only reason we tolerate each other is because it's nice to have people from back home who understand green-folk stuff."

"So, that's a yes?" she asked with some pep in her voice.

"I just..."

For. The. Love. Seriously? Take the bait. It isn't that hard.

She shifted her weight to the other foot. "I didn't expect you to have to make a pros and cons list... It's just a date..."

He loosed a breath. "I just thought we were doing the friend thing."

She tilted her head, looking him in the eyes. "You're a great friend. You're kind, and considerate, and funny." She tapped his shoe with her own. "You're also cute and sweet. I'm just saying ... we could give it a chance." She hadn't planned for his resistance, hadn't rehearsed the compliments. They flowed naturally; they were genuine.

He gave her a soft smile. "Yeah. Of course. I don't know why I'm making a big deal of it. Friday?"

"Cool. I still can't drive, so are you able to borrow a car from your grandparents? I'll pay for dinner?"

"Yeah. That works. And I'll sort out the knife-throwing."

Cheryl pulled up. Leah grabbed one of Marcus's hands, giving it a gentle squeeze and making eye contact again. "I look forward to it."

Leah smirked, thinking of the archery fiasco as she waited for Marcus to pick her up. He had no reason to lie about his knife-throwing skills. Her smirk faded as she thought back to the notebook she'd started, hidden in her room—her plans. *How do you assassinate a queen?*

She had five months until the spring break wedding. That should be plenty of time for her to win Marcus over, get an invite to the wedding, and figure out how she'd actually be able to kill someone. She wasn't crazy, or some superwarrior. She was a regular teenager. Kind of.[j]

The notebook included a pros and cons list. The reality of what she was planning was ... terrifying. Successful or not—killing *anyone*, especially a queen, wasn't an action to take lightly. She didn't want to go into this based on rash emotions, but the dad she'd yearned to know all her life had been taken from her. By someone who, based on more than one account, didn't deserve to be there and was making things worse. And it wasn't only justice for her dad. Leah would be helping out all of the Green Lands, and her mom, herself, and even—not that she cared much— Cheryl. In the end, if all went as planned, Leah would have until the last minute to decide. Plan, prepare, and if she couldn't make it happen for one reason or another, she'd return home, and everyone would be none the wiser.

A knock on the front door pulled Leah from her thoughts. *Worry about that later. For now, have fun and get things started.*

She opened the door. "Hey."

"Hey. You ready to head out?" Marcus asked with a warm smile.

"Sure thing," she replied, tucking her hands into her back jeans pockets.

They hopped into his truck, heading to a new Greek restaurant Leah had picked out.

"You're looking sharp," she said. She could swear he was wearing the same cologne he had at their archery night fiasco, too.

"You don't say." He cleared his throat. "Is that a reference to knife-throwing?"

She laughed. "No. I didn't spend all afternoon coming up with that one."

He threw a quick glance her way as they approached a stop sign. "You look nice, too."

"Phew! I'm glad I don't look *mean.*"

He chuckled.

They enjoyed good conversation over their dinner, just like they had in the last several weeks of their friendship.

Leah figured she might as well start with some hints. "I didn't realize the hummus would have so much garlic. That could be an end-of-the-night killer."

He blushed, not responding or making eye contact.

Trying to date Marcus was going to be a new adventure. Not wholly shy, he was still reserved in some ways. And like she'd called him before ... squeaky clean.

They ended up going back to his house for the knife-throwing; he had set up a couple of targets in the backyard.

"I'll show you first, and we'll go from there?" he suggested.

"Sounds great."

Marcus pulled out a set of specialty knives, standing several yards back from a wooden target. Grasping his first knife, he raised his arm. He launched the knife with controlled force, and it soared through the air, finding its mark in the target with a firm *thwack.* She smiled at his confidence as he threw five more, each finding its place on the target.

He retrieved the knives and approached Leah, a smile creeping across his face to match hers.

"Maybe a *smidge* more impressive than your archery skills." She winked.

He teemed with pride. "I've had a lot of practice. My dad taught me." He handed her the knives. "There's lots of different styles of throwing knives. Some of my favorites are back home, but these are nice."

She looked them over and felt their heft.

"Do you want me to give you tips, or just take a shot at it first?" he asked.

"I'll give it a go first."

Leah tried her best, knowing she wouldn't master it right away, just like archery. Only one of the knives barely stuck into the wood. Most of them smacked against the target before falling amidst the rest with a *clang*. She gathered them up and returned to his side. "I'd say I'm a natural."

He laughed again, clutching his hands to his chest. "I'm in awe."

She grinned. "Alright, I'm your humble student. Teach me your ways."

"It's all about force and form," he said. "You gotta throw it like you mean it, but do it in a controlled way. So, throw a little harder. If needed, you can also adjust how far back you are."

She nodded, taking it in.

"And when you go to throw it, don't flick it with your wrist. Let it *glide* from your hand," he coached.

Figuring she could layer the hints and have some fun, she asked, "You don't want to do that cliché guy thing where you stand behind me? Putting a hand on my waist and another on my hand to show me proper technique?"

He stared at her, a shy smile peeking through. His throat bobbed. "Probably not the smartest idea to stand that close to a girl when she's learning to fling sharp objects."

Leah giggled. "You may have a point." She glanced down at the knives in her hand. "And a sharp point, at that."

He chuckled as she took her place in front of the target again.

She tried a couple more rounds, getting a little better with more advice from Marcus. He took another turn as she watched. She couldn't help herself—she couldn't stop smiling, admiring. His biceps flexed with each toss. He was assertive, confident, and in his element. She liked this side of him.

Leah's smile faded as she swallowed hard, her guilt threatening to ruin her casual fun moment. She was using him. This wasn't just a date. It was part of a plan. And not just for an invite to the wedding. Her notebook had a page listing *all* the ways she might be able to kill the queen. She had five months to learn how to use her vines, and to learn any other feasible options for success. Who knew ... maybe throwing knives might be an option? She wasn't going to dismiss any possibilities.

Marcus gathered the knives and smiled at her, walking back to the throwing point. She gave him a half-smile back.

Could she really kill someone? This was crazy. *Who does that?*

But she wasn't just a regular human. And this queen wasn't just some useless politician. She had denied Leah and her mom the life they could have had. *Should* have had. This woman had stolen her dad. He deserved justice.

Leah watched Marcus, frowning. He'd never done anything to deserve being used. And she genuinely loved spending time with him. She fixated on his curly hair, his physique, his...

This is bad. I just have to focus on my goal...

But ... there's nothing wrong with actually enjoying being with him, too. I can keep them separate.

At the end of the evening, Marcus dropped Leah off back home. With this having been a proper date this time, he walked her to the front door.

These are always so excruciating...

He shoved his hands in his pockets. "I had a lot of fun."

"Me too." She hummed playfully. "Even more fun than archery."

He let out a breathy chuckle. "You and I remember that event differently. You had fun; I was being tortured."

She grinned. "You brought that one on yourself."

"I won't argue on that account."

She drew a deep breath. *Time to seal the deal.* "How do you feel about kisses on first dates?"

He pressed his lips together. "I'm going to have to say no this time."

Her heart sank. *What's that supposed to mean? 'This time.'*

"I thought ... things went well."

His mouth opened, but nothing came out. He closed it and cleared his throat. "I have a date with someone else tomorrow. I just don't feel like it would be right."

"Oh..." *That sucks.* She scanned his face. "Can't blame her. You're a great guy."

He bit his lip, slowly nodding.

"Oh... You did the asking." *Was this a pity date?*

He frowned. "I'm sorry. This is awkward. I should have said something. I literally asked her, like, an hour before you asked me."

Every ounce of Leah's pride screamed to cut the line. Sure, there was chemistry there. But she was *not* the type to chase a guy. If they didn't like her for who she was, they weren't worth pining over.

But there was more weight to this potential relationship than others she'd been in before. She couldn't just ask to be invited to the wedding. Tanner's interactions had made it incredibly clear that Marcus wouldn't take someone who seemed interested in the queen, in being a social climber. Leah needed this.

"I'm guessing asking you if you want to go on a second date would be awkward, then?" she asked. "Since you don't know how tomorrow will go?"

He rubbed the back of his neck. "Let's talk Monday?"

"Sure." But she couldn't lose him. *What if he enjoys tomorrow more?* She internally gagged. *I don't fight over guys. I'm not insecure like that.* "Then maybe this is weird, but I want to put it out there, anyway... the Sadie Hawkins dance is in two weeks. I think we'd have fun." She paused for a moment. When he didn't jump at the opportunity, she added, "But no pressure. I just wanted to put it out there."

He pulled his keys back out, fidgeting with them. "We'll talk?"

"Yeah. I'll see you Monday. How about a hug?"

He smiled. "I'm down with that." He pulled her in for a squeeze. She happily took what she could get. And he was a great hugger.

The weekend was absolute torture. This was all so foreign to Leah. Guys were simple. Dating was simple. Sometimes, she just wanted to kiss without strings attached. When she wanted something a little more substantial, she could flush out her type and get into a relationship easily enough. If they weren't sure about wanting to date her, they were out. If they didn't want what she had to offer, they weren't worth the investment or energy.

But this was far from simple. She agonized the entire weekend. Not texting Marcus. Wanting desperately to know what the other girl was like. If they were having fun.

She pouted as she watched a movie with her mom, picturing Marcus teaching his date to throw knives, too. What if he kissed her, having decided he liked her better?

Leah moped, imagining him inviting the other girl to his brother's wedding. She had to be a human. Would he do that? Could he? Based on what Marcus had told Leah, revealing the Green Lands and green-folk secrets to humans was a very serious step, not taken lightly. But he had months to grow close to the mystery girl. And it wasn't like humans weren't allowed into the Green Lands at all... Just like green-folk teens came to the human world as inconspicuous foreign exchange students, a few humans in on the secret were allowed to spend an exchange year in the Green Lands, too...

Leah frowned as she stuffed a spoonful of peanut-butter-cup ice cream into her face, straight from the carton. He *clearly* already liked the mystery girl better, because he'd actually asked her. Maybe Leah could break them up in time for him to still give her a chance and invite her.

Oh my gosh, I am not that girl. I'm not desperate. I'm not pathetic.

But it wasn't just about wanting to date him. It was about the end goal. Maybe she could get lucky, and he'd take her as his plus-one just as a friend? Whether or not he had a girlfriend? She couldn't count on him deciding to do that on his own. And she'd only ever have one shot at asking him. If he didn't take the suggestion, that trust would be severed. That was only a last resort. Leah's anxiety rose as she envisioned her limited options.

Calm the heck down!

Leah happily joined her mom on a shopping trip to get her mind off of things. With a stern warning from her mom, Leah went to another part of the store in search of a couple of items on their list. But ... she was itching for another nice distraction. Strolling near the makeup wipes, she figured she might treat herself with something small ... like a lifted lipstick or two. She picked out colors and made sure the coast was clear. Starting to extend her vines, she hesitated. She quickly retracted them with a sigh. If she got caught, got grounded—it would jeopardize the big plan. And Squeaky Clean probably wasn't the type to understand her hobby.

Leah let out a long puff of air, returning to meet her mom.

Her mom raised her eyebrows in accusation. "That took a little longer than I expected for two things."

Leah scowled, placing the list items into the cart and turning her pockets inside out. "I was just looking around." She cupped her hands over her boobs. "Nothing stashed here, either."

A man in his seventies was shuffling by them. He gave them an uncomfortable glance, cleared his throat, and moved along.

Her mom lightly swatted at her arms. "Stop that!" she hissed.

Leah put up her hands in innocence. "Better than a strip search in the middle of the store. Just trying to make it clear I'm being good."

Her mom closed her eyes, pinching the bridge of her nose. After a second, she actually started to chuckle.

Leah furrowed her brow in confusion.

Her mom opened her eyes, reaching over and smoothing Leah's hair. "Just ... in another time, in another life, I'm imagining the shock on the face of your father's entire family. His heir, groping herself in front of strangers in the cracker aisle in the, well, *here*, wearing a t-shirt and jeans."

Leah frowned. "Sorry." She'd never be who her mom wanted her to be.

Her mom matched Leah's frown. "I didn't mean it like that, sweetheart." She gently put her hand under Leah's chin. "Prim and proper, or just as you are, I love you. And they would have, too." She lowered her hand, her expression full of longing for a future they'd never have. "I could have spent your youth teaching you the proper fork to use, or putting you in classical dance lessons, or any number of things. But that's not who we are, anymore. You're free to be you." She grinned. "Though, we should maybe keep the self-groping in public to a minimum."

Leah busted out laughing.

"The next time an old man walks by," her mom added, "he might have a heart attack, and we're trying to keep it low-key."

"I'll try my best."

Her mom gave her a soft smile. "That's all I'm asking. Now, what else is on our shopping list?"

They turned back to the cart, and Leah hooked her arm through her mom's. "I think we need more ice cream." She paused a moment. "And I wouldn't hate it if you taught me about different kinds of forks."

Her mom hummed wistfully. "I could do that."

Chapter 10

Monday finally came. *Longest weekend ever.*

Leah was a bundle of nerves as she approached their lunch table. Marcus gave her a tiny smile. It had been nice sharing bonding time with her mom, but Leah could only stay distracted for so long.

The rest of the meal, Leah and Marcus didn't look at each other. A few minutes before the bell would ring, Leah piled up the garbage on her tray and stood. "I'm going to get some fresh air before lunch is over."

Jake glanced around. "We're eating outdoors. This isn't fresh enough for you?"

She playfully chucked a plastic spoon at him. "You know what I mean. Stretch my legs. See you guys later."

"Okay if I join you?" Marcus asked.

Her stomach did a leap. "Yeah." She'd hoped he would pick up on that. She'd dreaded the idea of waiting until after school, with the possibility of being interrupted by their rides arriving earlier than wanted, or even worse—having the conversation over the phone.

They took care of their trash and trays, strolling out onto the school lawn.

"How was your weekend?" he asked.

"Like any other weekend." *Except for the torture.* She gave him a smile. "Except for a pretty cool Friday night."

He returned her smile, and they walked in silence for a while. "I guess I should say something."

The tension was killing her.

"I, uh... Well ... she's a nice girl, and ... she asked me on a second date."

Leah glanced at him out of the corner of her eye, trying to play it cool.

"And I said yes."

Her heart sank. He'd never wanted to date her, after all.

"But…" He rocked his head back and forth. "I swear I'm not, like, *that guy*… I just… I want to try a second date with you, too." He winced. "Is that weird?"

She shrugged. "We could give it a try." Normally, she'd have given it a hard pass. He wasn't a trophy to win, and she wasn't a player in a game. But she needed this. As much as she appreciated her mom's efforts to allow Leah a normal life, Leah couldn't let that nagging feeling go—that she didn't belong here, that the queen needed to answer for her crimes. If anything, growing closer to her mom made Leah want to do this even more.

"And she knows," he said. "Not like I'm being a creepy jerk, keeping this from either of you." Marcus stopped, facing Leah. "But … if you still want… I'd love to go to the dance with you. No matter how things go, I know I'd have a lot of fun with my friend." He gave a hopeful smile. "But I understand if you don't want to, or don't want to commit to it, now that you know, well, you know…"

Leah drew a contemplative breath. This was a good sign. Whether or not the other girl had asked him to the dance as well, Marcus was still keeping Leah close. "Let's plan on it. I didn't want to go with anyone else."

His face was bright and happy. "Sounds like fun. And thanks for being cool with all of this."

She swallowed and nodded. "Yeah, of course."

But cool with it, she was not. It was a full week of doubting herself.

Friday night, Marcus picked Leah up, putting her out of her misery. They grabbed a bite to eat at a local pizzeria and enjoyed a game of bowling. She couldn't resist admiring his figure again in the dark jeans he wore, and he'd caught her glancing once. She was pretty sure he'd checked her out once or twice, as well. She'd picked out an outfit accentuating her best features, after all.

The end-of-the-night door scene was just as awkward as the last, with the exception of Leah wondering whether there would be a kiss. He gave Leah another of his signature hugs and thanked her for another fun night.

She pursed her lips. "I'd tell you to have a good weekend, but I kind of hope it's not *that* good."

He gave her a shy look acknowledging the awkwardness of the situation. "We're still on for the dance, right?" he asked.

"I'll be there."

Monday came around. Marcus had gone on his second date with the other girl, too. Leah was going out of her mind, imagining him being so indecisive as to ask for a third date with each girl.

Instead, he said nothing.

Leah returned home from school, frustrated. After Cheryl left for work and her mom came home, Leah decided to try rehashing another strategy to make it to the Green Lands.

"I got to thinking about something you said." Leah dipped her toes in the water, carefully. "That Cheryl goes back to check on the state of the Green Lands now and then?"

"Yes," her mom said, unpacking groceries in the kitchen.

"How does she do it?" Leah folded up an empty plastic bag. "Like ... how's it even possible? You never explained that to me." She knew good and well it was somehow done through trees, but her mom had avoided anything on that topic.

"You don't need to know that."

"But no one over there knows what I look like, right? I wasn't even born by the time you left." She folded another empty bag.

Her mom shook her head, opening the produce drawer and placing a fresh pack of celery inside. "Not worth it." Her tone carried a firm finality.

"You expect me to *never* even see the place?" Leah's frustration grew.

"It's not safe for us."

Leah huffed. "You can't stop me forever. What if I go off to college and spot someone like us? Maybe *they'll* teach me how to get back."

Her mom frowned, closing the fridge door. "Sweetheart, please." She sighed. "Maybe we can revisit this conversation when you're eighteen."

Leah rolled her eyes, shifting gears. She thought of the current Ivy policy of emergency tree rifting. "What if someone comes for us, and I need to get away? Isn't it important to have options?"

Her mom rested her hands on her hips. "And you think the Green Lands is the answer? Even if you found a way to get over there ... where would you go? I'm sorry it was taken from you, but that's not your world. It may never be."

Leah's well of hope was drying up. She remembered with perfect clarity the night she'd discovered the truth about her dad—her mom had said they didn't belong *anywhere*. That ached more deeply than her mom understood. It hurt. Once, when she was twelve, tired of being a freak and having to hide it, she'd taken scissors and a knife to her vines. Despite tugging a bunch out, hacking it off, then doing it a few more times until she literally passed out—they grew back the next day. The realm of the Green Lands was part of her, whether or not she wanted it to be.

In one last attempt at getting anywhere, Leah continued her focus on safety. "Fine. No Green Lands. What about our abilities? If I need to keep myself safe, is there anything else I'm capable of doing?" She knew about the ability to sharpen her leaves ... from experience now, and the ability to poison. Tanner was going to teach her some techniques with her vines, but Leah was willing to take anything she could get.

Her mom remained silent, sizing her up. "We're always home to keep you safe. And that's why we have you notify us of your plans and give you mace, for when you're out with friends." She pressed her lips into a thin line. "But I suppose it's time I teach you a little more, for your own safety." She held up a finger. "But this is only in an absolute emergency, because once someone sees your vines... Just, be careful."

Leah nodded. "I will be."

The next day at lunch, Tanner was picking on Jake. "I doubt you even realize what you're missing after living over here so long."

Marcus was glaring at Tanner, obviously growing tired of the conversation.

Leah was too. "How about you shut up and get over yourself, Tanner," she scolded. "You're the one who chose to come here. You could have stayed home. There's nothing wrong with Jake living here." She huffed. "And some people don't get a choice, do they?" She stood and stomped off.

Marcus followed after her. "Hey, wait up."

She jutted her thumb over her shoulder, gesturing to the courtyard they'd left behind. "Remind me why we hang out with him."

Marcus twisted his lips. "You okay?"

She slowed her pace to walk with Marcus. "Yeah. Of course. Why wouldn't I be?" She crossed her arms.

"I just wasn't sure if that was you telling Tanner off 'cause he was a jerk to Jake, or because of ... you know, your mom keeping you out of the loop."

She shrugged. "Can't it be both?"

"Yeah. It can be." A moment of silence punctuated their footsteps on the green lawn. Marcus swung his arms with nervous energy. "Sorry for not getting back to you yesterday about where we stand."

She braced herself for bad news—as much as she could, what with only mildly caring in the moment.

"I, uh, told her I wasn't interested in a third date."

A small smile grew on Leah's lips as the news gave her a ray of hope. "Thanks for letting me know." She stopped to look at him. "Where does that leave us?"

"That leaves us at the dance this Friday, right?"

Sadie Hawkins was casual dress, but Leah made sure to get a little more dolled up than usual. She wore her favorite pair of jeans and a black top—sleeveless, with a rhinestone swirl near her waist. Wearing her hair up in a ponytail, she finished her ensemble with a deep red shade of kissproof lipstick.

Marcus picked her up, complimenting her outfit. Leah's mom mortified her by taking pictures despite it not being a formal dance.

"Sorry you're always the one having to drive," Leah said as they got into his grandpa's truck.

Putting the truck into gear, he looked over his shoulder and backed out of the driveway. "I really don't mind. I spent a ton of time this summer learning so I could have some freedom and blend in."

"What's school like over there? Do you guys have dances?"

"We study some of the same stuff. Obviously some things like history are different."

More often than not, lately, her mind kept wandering to this mystery realm, to the Green Lands. What would the history books say about her parents? She wasn't stupid; she knew they would speak ill of them. With the woman who'd ousted them still in control, she could choose the propaganda fed to her people.(k)

"As for dances," Marcus continued, "we've got them, but nothing like they do here. And the music is all performed live."

Leah nodded in approval. "That sounds cool."

Being an informal event, hardly any attention was paid to decorations in the school gym, but the obligatory disco ball and light show were included.

Not long after they arrived, Marcus introduced Leah to a group of his other friends. She hadn't made more at this school since her arrival. They danced with the group, and she loved how carefree Marcus was during the fast songs.

The first slow dance came on, and he offered his hand. She slid her arms around his neck, pushing him to dance closer, with both his hands on her waist. She loved this, how conversation flowed between them. Their playful banter, their shared secret of being green folk. Her heart pounded as she glanced at his lips.

After a couple more fast songs, and with the stifling heat of the school gym becoming unbearable, they headed out to the open courtyard, to their usual lunch table.

"This DJ's not too bad," she said.

"Yeah. Good songs for dancing."

They sat side by side on the small table, breathing in the cool air, and planting their feet on one of the seats.

"What do you want out of this?" he asked.

She turned her head and smiled. "I thought I was pretty clear about wanting to date you."

"But are we talking about a relationship, or friends with benefits?"

She frowned, looking down at her shoes. "You're judging me. Because of Tanner."

He sighed. "No. Though, I'm still a little worried it'll make things weird in the club. But I just want to make sure we're on the same page. We're not the most obvious couple, you know?"

She met his gaze. "I don't care what Tanner thinks. And I didn't think you did, either. If he has a problem with it, then ... well, that's *his* problem. As for obvious couples, does that matter?" She furrowed her brow. "I like spending time with you. I'm attracted to you. Isn't that why people date?"

"Yeah. And I like spending time with you, too." He gave her a shy smile. "And I'm attracted to you, too. You look really great tonight. I don't remember if I told you that already."

She grinned; he had. Though she doubted she still looked *that* great with a bead of sweat running down the back of her neck. "Then let's give it a go."

"Okay. You and me. Exclusive?"

"Yes."

"Then I'm in."

She smirked wider. "Does that mean you'll finally kiss me?"

He chuckled. "I think I can manage that." He shifted a little, getting a better angle. Leaning in, he offered up a sweet, simple kiss. He pulled back, getting lost in her eyes.

She studied his face. There was a spark there, with room to grow. But after the way he'd made her wait, she wasn't going to let him get away with a tiny kiss like that. She leaned closer, moving a hand behind his neck, and caressing his lips with her own. He returned the kiss with mirrored enthusiasm, but stopped short of a heated make-out session.

When they pulled apart, he bit his lip. "You're not shy, are you?"

She laughed. "Not when it comes to something I want."

He drew a deep breath, rubbing his knee. "How's this going to work with the club? Should we say something at lunch?"

She leaned against his shoulder, breathing in a hint of cologne. "Mmm... I think that would be awkward. Let 'em figure it out on their own."

He extended a hand, offering it palm up. "Like when they see us holding hands?"

She slid her palm onto his, intertwining their fingers. "Exactly."

He gave her hand a squeeze, kissing her on the cheek. Another couple came out to the courtyard, interrupting their solitude.

"Are you cooled off enough?" Marcus asked. "Wanna get back to the dance?"

She took her hand back, hopping off the table. "Let's do it."

At the end of the night, Marcus dropped Leah off at her house. She'd finally get a proper end-of-the-night drop-off with him.

"Thanks again, for saying 'yes' to the dance. And for giving us a chance."

He grinned. "I'm already glad I did. On both counts." He held her waist and didn't hesitate to give her a goodnight kiss.

Leah went inside with a smirk on her face. The front room was dark, and a sudden noise made her jump.

"Does that mean he's a boyfriend?" Cheryl asked.

Leah blew out a breath of relief, a hand over her heart. "Scare me half to death, will you?" She huffed. "Yes. We're dating," she muttered.

"You know the rules."

Leah threw her hands in the air. "I planned to tell her just now. We only made it official tonight." The rules were stupid. Friends, boyfriends, friends with benefits— the moment her mom or Cheryl saw more than a hug from a guy, they wanted to know *every* detail of his life. She had to admit that they at least gave her *some* level of freedom with all of their concerns—it could be worse. She shook her head at the hypocrisy, though. When she'd asked her mom about how her dad had proposed, her mom wouldn't give a play-by-play of the event. They'd dated for four years, and her mom described him as 'aggressive' and 'passionate,' and 'affectionate' but also 'not really romantic.' It was pretty clear they hadn't exactly been innocent and inexperienced.

Leah peeked inside her mom's room. "Home from the dance. Dating Marcus. Interrogate now, or in the morning?"

Her mom sighed, sitting on her bed. "Let's talk in the morning. How was the dance?"

Leah leaned in the doorway. "It was good."

Her mom gave her a single contented nod. "Okay, then... Have a good night, princess. Um ... sweetheart."

"You too."

Leah wiped off her makeup and brushed her teeth. After tossing her clothes in the dirty hamper, she climbed into bed in a fresh pair of cozy pjs. She mused on the kissing from earlier that night. Marcus didn't seem that experienced, but not completely new to the practice. Their first kiss had been basic, though the door drop-off was evidence of them finding their groove.

Chemistry wasn't going to be a problem. Keeping her lies straight might be.

She'd already formulated a backstory for Marcus, one that omitted any hints of being a Boman or knowledge of the Green Lands. She just had to remember it, and make sure he kept up the guise anytime he might be around her mom or Cheryl.

Leah's phone chimed, and she opened the message.

<Thanks for a great night. Let me know if you want to get together this weekend.>

<I'd love to. Free tomorrow?>

<Free all day. Just some homework to do.>

<Ditto. I'll bring mine over?>

<I look forward to it ;)>

<Sweet dreams.>

Leah set her phone down but didn't smile. Like a moth to a flame, Marcus was falling for her plan. How could she ever truly enjoy this relationship when she planned to use him? She was the flame on a destructive path, and he was going to get burned in the process.

Maybe not. She rationalized that she could still enjoy it. Using him to get to the queen was merely an option on the table. She wasn't so delusional that she couldn't see the plan would be nigh impossible to pull off. Not knowing the venue, or the timeline of the wedding events, or how many guards... With so little actually known, her desire was a long shot, at best. For now, she pacified herself with the thought of enjoying her time with Marcus, while it lasted.

Chapter 11

The next day at Marcus's place, the new couple hit their homework first. They got plenty distracted, chatting and making jokes as they worked. After finally completing it all, they went to the backyard for more knife-throwing. After a few rounds each, they cuddled on a rocking bench in the backyard.

He held her tight. "Gotta admit, I like having a girlfriend." He quickly added, "Not that I haven't had one before, just, you know, having one here."

She enjoyed the warmth radiating from his arms. "I'm a fan."

"I think it's kinda funny. I come all the way to the human world for school, and end up dating a girl from back home."

She drew a deep breath. "Actually, we need to talk about that."

He faced her, raising his eyebrows. "Uh-oh... We need to talk? Not my first relationship, but maybe my shortest..."

She rolled her eyes, then stole a peck on the lips. "I'm what you call green folk, but I'm not exactly from 'back home,' am I?"

He frowned. "Yeah, sorry. Didn't mean anything by it."

"It's fine. I just want to make sure we keep my mom thinking I don't know about green-folk stuff. I may have fudged a few details about your family."

He squinted. "You still don't think you could come clean with her about knowing?"

She shook her head. "No. Trust me. It wouldn't go well."

He shrugged. "Okay. We'll make it work." He traced a zigzag pattern on her knee. "I already have a cover story, you know. I guess we didn't know each other that well before you discovered my secret, but each of us has to memorize a story to keep details of our realm hidden from humans."

She nodded, feeling stupid for not thinking of that. "Yeah..." She winced. "I kinda already told my mom one I made up last night. Your cover story doesn't happen to include your parents being a nurse and a doctor, does it?"

He scrunched his nose. "Not so much. But we'll make it work. My mom can heal, and my dad likes to fix things ... so it's close enough to remember." He poked her leg. "Why'd you pick doctor and nurse?"

She gave him a warm smile, grabbing his hand and interlacing their fingers. "You've met my mom as my *friend*. But not as a boyfriend. You just lost twenty points."

"Dang it. How many points are there?"

She gave him a toothy grin. "Twenty."

He looked at the sky, forming a fist with his free hand and shaking it dramatically. "Noooooo!"

She giggled, happy to be there, happy things were going her way. If they could pull this off, there would be no moving, and things could proceed as planned. And in a way, Marcus had passed his first test—he was willing to bend the truth to what she needed. This might be *exactly* the loyalty she needed to get her to the Green Lands.

Marcus smiled, once again focusing on Leah. "In case I need more than respectable jobs for my parents to earn points, maybe I should teach you how you increase your luck in our kingdom."

She raised her eyebrows, fully curious, though hesitant, given the hint of mischief on his face and in his voice. "Luck is good. Do tell."

He cocked his head. "It's two parts." He paused.

"Okay?"

"So, the first part is this." He leaned closer, slowly pressing his lips to her neck.

She couldn't hold back a bright smile.

"And the second part..." He pressed his lips to her neck again, blowing a huge raspberry.

Leah jerked her head away, bursting into a fit of laughter and smacking his hands off of her. Marcus joined in with a hearty chuckle.

"You are *such* a dork!" She couldn't stop laughing as she rubbed away the tickle from her neck.

Marcus put on a serious face, placing a hand over his heart. "Leah, that's an *integral* part of our culture—-who we are. Now we'll both have good luck for a week. I'm hurt you're not taking this more seriously." He feigned devastation. "This is special."

"BS. I don't believe that lying face for a second!"

He smirked, shrugging. "I guess we'll just have to see how the next week goes."

She playfully narrowed her eyes.

His face softened, as did his voice. "I'm really glad we started off as friends."

Guilt washed over her. She didn't deserve to enjoy any of this. Not when she had ulterior motives. A battle ensued on her face, her heart tugging her muscles into a frown while her mind forced as genuine of a smile as possible to remain.

He squinted ever so slightly, reading her face.

She quickly wrinkled her nose, rubbing it. "Sorry, fighting a sneeze."

His smile bounced back. "Bless you."

She couldn't handle another lie that day. The truth was easier right now. "I really like you."

"Ditto. Do you want to stay for dinner and maybe watch a movie?" he asked.

She gave him another kiss. "I'm having way more fun here than I would be back home."

"I'm having more fun than if you were back home, too." He moved in for another longer, more involved kiss.

The Garden Club was set to meet at Tanner's house the next week. As promised, he met with Leah earlier than the official start time. She'd been nervous about spending time alone with him again, but the human family that hosted him as a foreign exchange student was upstairs this time.

Seemingly having learned his lesson, Tanner carefully showed her some basic fighting and protection forms he'd learned from his dad, from his days in the Ivy army. She appreciated being that much closer to having viable options for her plans. Combined with the basic poison and protection techniques her mom had reluctantly taught her, Leah had even more tools at her disposal now.

"Thanks again," she said, taking a glass of water from Tanner. "Before the other guys arrive ... I figured it might be good to give you a heads-up. Marcus and I are dating."

Tanner lifted his eyebrows, nodding. "Okay."

"Is that weird?" She wiped the condensation from her glass, the ice cubes tinkling against each other.

He took a sip from his own glass, his eyes widening. "Are you asking me to rate your relationship?"

She glared. "I think you know what I mean."

He tentatively held up a hand. "You do you. We agreed that was a onetime thing, right?"

"Yeah. Thanks for being cool about it."

Not much later, Marcus and Jake arrived. Leah had told Marcus ahead of time that she wouldn't need a ride. The group decided to watch a movie. Leah sidled up next to Marcus, and he offered his hand. She loved that; it had been a while since she'd had a real boyfriend, and he was so sweet.

She caught Tanner's knowing glance a couple of times. Halfway through the movie, Jake got up to use the bathroom. Leah spotted a spark of realization in his eye on his return.

The group knew, no drama—she wouldn't have it any other way.

A month passed, and things were good. All the balls Leah was juggling were in the right places. She and Marcus were great as a couple. She was staying out of trouble, and her grades were even better than normal.

"Happy birthday," Marcus said as he handed Leah a wrapped gift. They stood in the driveway after eating at her house.

"Oooh, thank you." She started to unwrap the heavy rectangular present.

"It's, uh ... maybe kind of a stupid gift." He blushed. "I wasn't sure."

She beamed. "I love it!" She leaned in for a kiss, holding her brand-new set of throwing knives.

"Good." He grinned. "I figured it was very 'us.'"

He wasn't wrong. It was definitely still one of their favorite activities together. Her technique was slowly improving.

"Is it me, or did your mom almost seem to even like me back there?" he asked with eyebrows raised.

She chuckled. "I told you she doesn't like anyone I've dated. But you've definitely won some points with her. You're keeping me out of trouble, and I get all my homework done on time."

He inched closer. "I do enjoy a good study date."

She grabbed his shirt, pulling him in the rest of the way. "Me too. Especially at *your* place, where we have more privacy."

He laughed.

"I'll see you tomorrow?" she asked.

"First, I wanted to ask you…" He pressed his lips together. "Well, I'm assuming, since we're dating… But I wanted to be sure we're on the same page… Would you want to go with me to—"

Finally! The wedding. Just needed some more time.

"—winter formal?"

Internally she groaned, but quickly recovered with a smile. "I'd love to."

"Awesome." He gave her a brief smooch. "I better head home."

"Okay. Thanks again for my present."

Things were going great. Until they weren't. Just a week later, after an argument with Cheryl, Leah slipped. Since she'd been caught, her nail polish collection didn't grow.

"I won't budge this time, Eleana," her mom said, taking her anger out on the vegetables she was chopping for dinner.

"Please! I'll do *anything*."

Her mom shook her head. "A month. No dance. No friends. I'm tired of your excuses and this behavior! You would think that when you realized who you were, who your father was, you would've come to your senses."

Leah frowned. She'd been doing *so* well with Marcus unknowingly keeping her in check.

"Your father would be so disappointed. His daughter, his heir—a common thief and a liar."

Leah's eyes stung with tears. It was true. She didn't even know why she'd done it.

"Thanks for chatting with me," Leah said as Marcus strolled with her on the soccer field during lunch the next day.

"Of course, what's up?"

She took her hand back, sliding it into her pocket. "I can't go to the dance."

"Why not?"

She couldn't look at him. "I'm grounded. She won't budge."

"Seriously? How long? What happened?"

She huffed. "A month."

"Ouch. Why?"

"Doesn't really matter." She rolled her eyes. "It was stupid."

When she finally looked at him, he studied her face.

"Just ... homework..."

He furrowed his brow. "Why would it be a whole month for not doing a homework assignment?"

"Just... It doesn't matter."

He let out a frustrated sigh. "It matters if you're lying to me, Leah. I don't believe you. What's the real reason?"

She wilted, her heart dropping. "Why is it a big deal?"

"It's a big deal if you're lying to me. You promised you wouldn't lie to me again."

She shook her head. "You don't want to know."

"Try me." Marcus crossed his arms.

She bit the insides of her cheeks. There was no way she could get out of this one. And there was no way he would understand. "She caught me stealing," she mumbled under her breath.

"What?"

"My mom caught me stealing."

His eyes grew wider, reading her face. "What did you steal?"

"Why does it matter? It was just small stuff, from a store. It was stupid." She looked down at her feet. "I've been doing so good."

"That means you've done this before?"

Great job, Leah. Keep digging. She met his gaze, her shame complete. "Yes. But I promise, I'm done. And no more lies."

He shook his head, his jaw agape. "This is crazy, Leah. How can I even believe you?"

"I'm sorry! I'll do better. And I'm sorry about the dance. I really am."

He scowled. "You think I care that much about the dance? I came here for *one year* of human-world exchange. And yes, I wanted to spend that time with my girlfriend. But I'm pretty sure her lying to me and being a criminal is a little more important!"

"I don't know what you want me to say! I've made mistakes. I'm going to do better. You've been a good influence on me."

His tone and expression were unforgiving. "Why do you even do it?"

She kicked at a rock on the grass. "I don't know. It's just a bad habit."

He glared. "Biting your nails is a bad habit. Shoplifting? Not so much."

Her eyes welled with tears. "I started 'cause... I don't know. It was something I could do with my vines, when all I knew about them was that they made me a freak. And then, all the moves..."

"That sounds like an excuse."

"What do you want from me, Marcus? I'm being honest right now."

He ran his hands through his hair. "We should take a break."

"You mean break up?" Her heart threatened to do just that. "Please, give me another chance. I swear."

"I didn't say break up... Just ... take some time apart..."

Her shoulders were limp, her hopes deflated. "You're my best friend."

"Then maybe you should take some time to figure out your priorities." He read her face. "We'll see where we're at when I get back from Christmas Break."

She looked down, sniffling. "Fine."

Leah had thought it was rough waiting two weeks for Marcus to choose to date her in the first place. Waiting an entire month for him to decide if he could stand to be around her was going to be unbearable. She'd meant every word. She wasn't going to steal again. Or lie. At least she *wanted* to mean it.

Not sure of Marcus's plans, Leah couldn't show her face at their usual lunch table for the two weeks left before Christmas Break. A couple of days into those two weeks, Tanner came looking for her. He found her sitting alone; she still hadn't made more friends. She'd always been the type to commit more fully to smaller groups of friends. More people meant more investment, and more people to lose.

"There you are. The table's a little boring with just me and Jake," Tanner said, sitting on the linoleum beside her in the hallway.

She didn't look at him as she took another bite of her pizza. He'd confirmed Marcus was keeping his distance as well. She sulked. Marcus was probably off with his human friends. Maybe even rekindling things with that *other* girl. It was just a waiting game for him to call things off altogether, realizing he could do much better.

"You coming to the club hangout this week?" Tanner asked.

"I'm grounded for a month." Leah set the slice of pizza down, wiping her hands on her jeans.

"Oof. That sucks. You and Marcus were going to go to the dance, right?"

Yes. Please rub salt in the wound. "We wouldn't be going together right now, anyway."

"Gotcha... His absence makes more sense. Thought you two up and ditched us for good."

She held back tears. "Well, we'll see how we feel about things after Christmas. I might leave you guys as just the original group." *And be forced to start all over. You'd think I'd be used to it by now.*

He sat there, not saying a thing.

She needed to talk more, and Tanner already knew this secret. "He knows about my shoplifting. Guess he wasn't a fan."

Tanner smirked. "He's vanilla. What did you expect?"

She scowled. "Shut up." They'd only dated a little over a month, but Marcus was the best boyfriend she'd ever had. He'd respected her, and never pushed her to go farther than she was ready to. He was funny and sweet.

"Sorry." Tanner frowned. "I didn't realize you guys were that close..."

They weren't supposed to be. Marcus was supposed to *think* they were. He was supposed to fall for Leah. Invite her to the wedding. Give her the opportunity to make things right for her family. She was supposed to have fun with Marcus while accomplishing her goals, not fall for him.

Leah respected Marcus's request to not contact him while they took a break. It killed her when they caught each other's eyes while waiting for their rides after school. The only time she couldn't help herself, she texted him another brief apology, on the night of the dance. He didn't respond.

It was the worst Christmas she could remember. Perhaps second worst; it had been horrible having to pack up and drive cross-country one year. But this one was a close second—being stuck with Cheryl, who hated her, and her mom, who'd imprisoned her and put a wedge between her and Marcus.

Leah had more than enough time to herself to think about things, especially during the two weeks of Christmas Break. She wanted to be with Marcus. She couldn't imagine being at that school without him. That meant she needed to change. Another misstep, and her mom might decide it was time to move on again. Leah wouldn't be stealing again. It wasn't worth it.

She opened her bedside table drawer, full of her pilfered goods. She stared at the bright collection of nail polish and accessories, supplemented by a random trinket here and there. The deed had already been done. But more than a useless New Year's resolution, she needed a fresh start.

Leah threw away every last stolen thing in that drawer, and emptied it completely. Instead, she placed a single object inside—her set of throwing knives. She closed the drawer, slowly exhaling. Then her eye caught on the notebook she'd been taking notes in—an assassination plan. She'd tucked it between her mattress and the bedside table.

What kind of lunatic even thinks this way? She chucked the notebook in the trash, staring at it with a frown. She couldn't do both. She couldn't be happy and honest with Marcus, while using him to fight for the memory of a dead man. Justice wouldn't bring her dad back.

But ... she hadn't actually done anything wrong with the notebook. Perhaps it was just a cathartic release, writing those things in there. It was a way of expressing her grief. She wouldn't actually carry out those plans. What kind of sane person could? Maybe she wasn't completely off her rocker. Perhaps she was just rushing into it all.

She pulled the notebook out of the trash, clutching it in her arms. Even if Marcus invited her to the wedding, it wasn't like she *had* to do anything to the queen. Maybe she'd just enjoy the chance to see what her home realm was like, and feel out the situation. The queen was still young. If Leah's dad hadn't gotten proper justice after seventeen years, she could wait another year, until she was at least eighteen.

Leah put the notebook in the drawer, accompanying the throwing knives. She took her trash to the outside can and drew a deep breath, moving on.

Chapter 12

With both hope and fear, Leah awaited a text from Marcus at the end of Christmas Break. The day before school started back up, it finally arrived.

<Just got back into town. Up for a walk?>

<Name the time.>

Marcus came over, and Leah greeted him at the door. No hug. No kiss. Just shy half-smiles and hands shoved in pockets. They shared awkward glances as they started out on the sidewalk in front of her house.

"I really missed you," she said.

He nodded ever so slightly. "I missed you too."

Her hope cautiously grew. "Before you say anything else, I have something I want to show you."

"Okay."

She reached into her pocket. "Hold out your hand."

He obliged, and she placed a bottle of bright red nail polish and a receipt in his hand. He raised his eyebrows. "Not really my color."

She gave him another half-smile. "I bought that yesterday. It's the first nail polish I've ever bought with my own money. I threw everything else out."

He nodded and handed it back.

"I'm really sorry," she said, sliding the bottle and receipt back into her pocket. "For being an idiot, for being a horrible person. And for lying to you."

The sharp, chilly air accentuated his long exhale in a cloud of vapor. "I had a lot of time to think. And ... the question that keeps coming back to me is: how am I supposed to know you're not hiding things from me again?"

She took a minute to consider his question. It was valid. "I don't know. All I can do is make a promise. And follow through." She still couldn't be forthcoming about her family secrets. Doing so would endanger lives—they weren't hers to tell.

He bit his lip. "Then let's just take things slow. Give it another go."

She wore a genuine smile. "Really? Thank you! That means the world to me." She gazed into his eyes. "So does your friendship. And ... boyfriendship."

He chuckled. "Boyfriendship?"

Oh, how she'd missed his goofy chuckle, his sweet eyes, his soft heart.

They strolled a bit further. "Not that I'm doing myself any favors by asking, but can I ask why? What do you see in me?" She'd given that question a lot of thought during their break. Especially with their relationship having been capped at mild making out and cuddling, combined with her screwups, she was genuinely both elated and surprised he hadn't broken it off completely.

"Well, it's no surprise I find you attractive. And then there's the kissing." He winked. "But being back home gave me a lot of time to hang out with family and appreciate what you and I had. What we have. My parents are best friends. I think it's important to be with someone you can laugh with, that you never run out of things to talk about with when you're together," he shrugged, "that you can work through hard times together with."

Her heart melted in agreement. She wanted nothing more than to kiss him, but reminded herself he'd said they'd take it slow.

"Honesty is really important in my family," he said. "Don't betray my trust again."

She nodded, her heart in turmoil. She didn't want to betray him. And she wanted to meet his family, who he obviously loved. She desperately wished her parents could have had a chance, that their family could have had that kind of chance, to grow together. "I won't."

He offered his hand, and she willingly took it.

"I want to hear all about Christmas Break in the Green Lands," she said. "And about your family."

"Mmm. Christmas in the Green Lands. Well ... it doesn't snow there, so no snowmen. As for religion and observance, it's all across the board. There's a larger variety represented in Seeder culture because of the way they used to raise their kids. Ivies know what Christmas is, but there aren't a lot who observe human holidays."

She loved hearing more about this place she yearned to see for herself. "Your dad's an Ivy Boman, and your mom's a Seeder, right?" She thought back to the injustices Tanner had talked about against their people, that the new queen loved Seeders more than her own kind. "Is it hard for your parents to be together?"

He nodded. "They've been through the wringer. They got married around the end of the war."

She studied his face as they walked. He loved his parents. She imagined him being like his dad—kind and wise. His mom ... well, even if she was a member of the race that was part of the problem, it wasn't like *every* Seeder had to be bad. She'd obviously shown good taste by marrying an Ivy, and by settling in the Ivy Kingdom, even with the problems brought on by the new queen. "They *chose* to live in the kingdom, right? It's not like they're there against their will or anything..."

He looked both ways as they stopped at a crosswalk. "No, they like living there. They're both closer to his family than hers. And when they got married, it wouldn't have been safe for him to live in the Seeder nation anyway, with him being a Boman."

That was sickening to hear. *What do Seeders have against Bomen?* If Jake and Marcus were decent representatives of their kind, Seeders should be ashamed of themselves. More evidence that Queen Kaylah didn't deserve Leah's dad's throne.(m)

While Marcus had given Leah the basic rundown on Seeders and their powers and culture, discussion with her mom had helped clear that picture up a bit more. Marcus had initially told Leah that Seeders were the more powerful of the green-folk races, and Leah's mom had confirmed that when discussing how the war had ended, how Queen Kaylah had won by turning on her own people, using the force of the Seeder army against Leah's dad. It stung a little that Marcus hadn't truly addressed the monsters that Seeders were, that he spoke of them in such a neutral way. But then again, she couldn't expect him to hate his own mother. Leah had to remind herself that just like humans, and their religions and political parties—it was impossible to judge them all the same. In every group, both good and bad could be found. If anything, it sounded like Marcus's mom was a pioneer of sorts—a visionary—for leaving her kind to marry Marcus's dad.

Leah squeezed Marcus's hand tighter. "Your mom sounds smart."

"She is. Is it weird if I say you remind me of her a bit?"

Leah batted her eyelashes, recalling their first meeting when Tanner had teased him about his mom. "The green eyes?"

He chuckled. "Not quite. Did I ever tell you her eyes are actually brown? They're only green when she shows them with her Seeder energy. I just meant you remind me of her because you can be tough, but sweet. And you go after what you want."

She grinned. "Not always."

He lifted an eyebrow. "No?"

"No. Like right now, I really want to kiss you. But I'm not going after it. Because you want to go slow." She met his gaze, not expecting ... but hoping...

He hesitated. "Give it some time," he said softly.

She could be okay with that.

It didn't take long for the couple to get back to their regular routine. Another month passed, and Valentine's Day was right around the corner. Marcus and Leah sat in his family room, cuddling after watching a movie.

"Is this your favorite kind of movie?" she asked. "Sci-fi?" She shifted, lying down on the couch and resting her head in his lap.

He took a strand of her hair and tickled her nose with it. "I don't know. Don't have them back home. Seems cool enough."

She smiled, swatting his hand away. "It's funny to realize the truth is sometimes stranger than the fiction in movies and books. I mean ... Green Lands? Secret societies and botanical beings?"

He grinned. "If you could do anything at all, no constraints, what would it be?"

It didn't take long to find her answer, though the way her grief slammed into her took her by surprise. She fought tears, frowning. "Honestly? Meet my dad."

Marcus's carefree expression did a one-eighty; he frowned with compassion. "I'm sorry." He rubbed her arm. "I wish there was something I could do for you."

She studied his face. Nothing would bring back her dad. But if she could get a glimpse of his kingdom ... with or without killing his traitorous sister...

Leah sat up, locking eyes with Marcus. "Thank you. That means a lot to me. *You* mean a lot to me." She leaned in, gently caressing his lips a couple of times. Her heart beat faster, her mind running a mile a minute.

Marcus's grandma had just left to go pick up her husband from across town; he was having problems with their truck. Marcus and Leah were alone.

She leaned back, studying his face again. Maybe she wanted to thank him for being such a sweet boyfriend. Or push him along to invite her back home—to the Green Lands, to the wedding. Or maybe she wanted something to help console her empty heart. Or something that just felt good. Maybe ... she wanted them all.

Leah pressed her lips against his, baiting the hook with a hint of tongue. Marcus didn't take long to get the picture, deepening the kiss into one more passionate than any other they'd shared before. She shifted onto his lap, straddling him. He slid his hands to her hips, and she moved hers down, grabbing the bottom of his t-shirt, and slowly pulled it up. Parting lips for a moment, she got it up over his head, tossing it to the side and smiling.

He was breathing as hard as she was. "You're, uh…" He swallowed and struggled for words.

She smirked. "I'm what?" He didn't tell her to stop, so she continued. She nibbled his ear, and trailed kisses down his neck and chest.

His chest rose and fell. "I, uh…"

"Yes?" She straightened, locking eyes once more. Then reached down, unbuttoning and unzipping his pants.

He took a sharp breath. "I think we should stop."

She stopped, resting her hands on his bare sides. "You don't want to?" She furrowed her brow.

His eyes exuded passion. "Oh, I want to."

She cocked her head. "Is it, like, an Ivy/Boman thing? Are things different?"

He bit his lip. "Well … yeah, there's kinda stuff … but that's not why." He closed his eyes. "Can we have this conversation with you not on my lap?"

She gave him a soft smile, knowing full well the agony he was enduring in the moment. "Yeah." She moved over as he buttoned and zipped his pants back up, then grabbed his shirt and tugged it back on.

"Maybe we just need to talk about this," he said. "I was raised to … you know … wait until I'm older, more committed."

Leah pursed her lips, nodding. She'd hoped for more, but couldn't be too surprised by his confession.

"Not that I'm judging you for being different in that way," he added.

She nodded again. "Yeah. Whatever you want."

He looked down with a pensive expression. "Whatever *I* want? What about what *you* want?"

She sweetly ran a finger down his forearm. "I thought I was making that pretty clear."

He smiled and shook his head. "I mean us. I'm only here for a few more months. Do you know what you want?"

She picked at her nails, taking her time to answer. She didn't anymore. Her goals and desires all contradicted each other.

"I'd be willing to come visit you over the summer, and during school breaks," he offered.

She met his eyes, smiling. "Let's plan on that."

"Okay. Should I take you home when my grandma gets back?"

"Yeah, I guess so."

They played a board game until she returned, mostly in silence, then borrowed the van.

As they neared her house, Leah couldn't help but ask, "Does that mean you're a virgin?"

"Would it matter to you if I was?"

She shrugged. "Not necessarily. Would it bother you if I wasn't?"

He put the van in park, facing her with a smile. "Not necessarily."

She gave his hand a squeeze. "Good night, Marcus."

"Good night."

Chapter 13

Luckily, things weren't too awkward after their heated encounter. Leah and Marcus picked up where they'd left off—a great friendship, homework dates, Garden Club, lunch at school, and sometimes going out for something more fun together. More excited and nervous than she'd been before about a dance, Leah looked forward to junior prom. Unlike senior prom, held closer to the end of the school year, their school put on junior prom before spring break.

She went dress shopping with her mom and almost settled on a beautiful burgundy one, but decided last-minute on a forest-green ball gown—it felt more fitting for her journey that year. Her mom loaned her some real diamond earrings, and Leah put extra effort into curling her hair. With perfectly smokey eyes and her favorite brand of kissproof lipstick on, she glanced in the mirror, making sure she was all set.

Her mom stood at the bathroom doorway, a hand on her heart. "You really do look like a princess. Just missing your tiara."

That was a gutting reminder. They *actually* owned a real tiara. How many girls could say that? And how many moms said their daughters looked like a princess, while knowing they actually could have been one?

"I'm sorry I'm not what you and dad wanted."

"We wanted you!"

"I just mean, you know... I don't do a lot to make you proud. And I'll never be a real princess like you wanted me to be."

Her mom pursed her lips as her eyes welled up. "We're doing the best we can, right? I will *always* love you." She wrapped her arms around Leah, giving her a tight hug.

The doorbell rang, breaking them apart. Leah wiped away a tear of her own and drew a deep breath.

"You've got your purse?" her mom asked.

"Oh, yeah." Leah strode to her room, grabbing a little clutch with a thin metal chain, and throwing it over her shoulder.

"Just a second." Her mom stopped her before she answered the door. "Not that I'm giving my approval, or that a human could get you pregnant, but you have protection, right? Just in case?"

Leah tried to hide a grin. If only her mom knew. Marcus had clarified that an Ivy Boman could still knock her up. Seeder Bomen were sterile. Powers or not, Ivies didn't have nearly as many biological restrictions as Seeders did. And Marcus had already turned her down, and wasn't likely to be ready for that anytime soon. "We're good."

Marcus beamed when she answered the door. They exchanged a corsage and boutonniere. Her mom took pictures, and they went on their way.

"You look *stunning*," Marcus said as they got on the road.

She bit her lip, looking him over in his tux. "You clean up pretty nice yourself."

After an extraordinary Italian dinner, they arrived at the hotel where junior prom was being held. They walked in, arms linked. Without hesitation, after leaving her purse at the check-in, Leah pulled Marcus onto the dance floor to get the night started. After some time, Tanner and Jake found them, accompanied by their dates. They claimed a table together and enjoyed punch and chatting. The two other girls left for the bathroom; Leah opted to stay with the guys.

"I don't need to go with them and gossip about you guys, when I could stay here and gossip about *them* with all of you."

Marcus smiled, giving her hand a squeeze. "But it's not a horrible idea. I think I'm going to follow their lead." He stood up, pursing his lips. "I mean the men's room, not women's. And this nose doesn't need powdering." He winked at Leah.

She watched him walk away, admiring how he looked in his tux.

"Does that mean we gossip about Marcus, too?" Jake kidded.

Leah shifted her gaze to Jake, stretching her arms out on the table toward him. "You and Emily are cute together. You guys have gone out a couple of times, right?"

He grinned, tugging on the sleeves of his suit jacket. "Yeah. She joined my D&D group. She's pretty cool."

"That's awesome." Leah faced Tanner. A knot in her stomach told her she shouldn't give much commentary on Tanner's date. Not after their past. "Brittany's in my history class."

Tanner nodded. "Cool. She's nice."

Leah picked at her nails.

"So how long is it for you and Marcus, now?" Jake asked.

Leah focused on her hands. It depended on whether you counted their month apart. She decided to include it. "Four months."

"You guys are good together," Jake said.

"I'm going to get Brittany and me a refill," Tanner said, standing up.

Jake was still clueless about what had transpired between them, and about the fact that Leah had lied about her knowing she was green folk, that she'd been raised as a human. Jake genuinely wasn't the kind of guy to pry or judge, and she hadn't wanted to confess to yet another person that she'd grown up in the dark about her own identity, and that she'd lied to the group.

After Tanner walked away, Leah returned her attention to Jake. "Thanks. I really like Marcus. Does Emily have girlfriend potential?"

He gave her a goofy grin. "I was gonna bring it up tonight."

She cracked her knuckles, her mind struggling with a thousand questions she'd wanted to ask in a thousand different ways over the months.

"Why did your parents decide to move away from the Green Lands?" she asked. Supposedly, all green folk could sense the energy that flowed in the realm—it was a part of them. Bomen didn't feel it as strongly as Ivies or Seeders with powers, but they could still perceive the lack of it.

Jake cocked his head, a look of confusion covering his face. "Well ... my mom was pregnant with me already before the war ended."[n]

That meant nothing to Leah. They sat in an awkward stare-down. She pulled from a tidbit Marcus had once told her: Bomanism was rare. Unless a Boman was born to a Boman parent, the chance of an Ivy randomly being born as such was exceptionally uncommon.

"Sorry if that's an awkward question. I honestly haven't met a lot of Bomen back home, you know." She hoped it came across authentic.

Jake shrugged it off. "Yeah. Just, it was dangerous for us in our kingdom, you know? Things were unstable when Queen Kaylah took over. People took advantage of Bomen. My parents got out the first chance they were given."

That had to have been so hard, to give up their home. She could only imagine her mom, also pregnant, fleeing at the same time.

"I'm glad they made that choice, so I could meet you."

He gave her a sweet smile, accented by a single dimple.

She dared to push a little further. So many questions loomed, but she'd never wanted to give away her family secrets, or jeopardize their safety. And she didn't want it getting back to Marcus, ruining her chances.

"How much do you know about Marcus's friends and family back home?" she blurted.

Jake scrunched his eyebrows. "I don't know. Probably less than Tanner." He shrugged again. "You know—he's private about his family."

Exactly. "Do you know why the queen is going to be at his brother's wedding?"

Jake's eyes narrowed. "You really don't know?"

There was that feeling again... Stupidity, being out of the loop.

"Why don't you just ask him yourself?"

She glanced down at the table. "I don't want to scare him off."

"Why would that scare him off? You're not dating him to get in the limelight, right?"

She looked at Jake, biting the insides of her cheeks. "No. Of course not. That's exactly what I'm afraid he might think, though."

"Well—"

Marcus was approaching, returning from the bathroom. "Never mind. You're right. I'll ask him myself. Pretend I never said anything."

Marcus sauntered up behind her, massaging her shoulders. He leaned down. "Want to dance some more? Or do you want to sit for a little longer?"

She moaned. "I'll stay in this spot for the next hour if it means you'll keep massaging."

Marcus laughed, and Tanner returned to the table with a couple of punch cups.

"You know what? Let's dance." She kicked her heels off under the table. "But I'm done with these shoes for the night."

Marcus stepped to the side, holding out his hands to help her up. "Sounds good. I promise not to step on your feet."

She raised a skeptical eyebrow, grinning.

"Okay. I promise to *try* not to step on your feet."

She chuckled. "Deal." They left the table, hand in hand, as the other girls returned.

He held her close as a slow song came on. She knew what the answer would be, but figured she'd still ask. "Did we have any plans for after the dance?"

"We?"

"I just ... you know..." It *was* prom.

He hummed knowingly. "Wanted to see if I had a room key in my pocket?"

She bit her lip. "Just checking."

"I'm not planning on it. Not that I wouldn't mind some kissing." A shy grin formed on his face as his hands pulled her in even closer.

"You're cute when you blush," she said.

His gaze was piercing. "You're cute when you anything."

She smirked, standing tall and giving him a peck on the lips. "I'm really glad you were my first friend at this school."

"And I'm really glad I gave us a chance."

She nodded, her smile fading. "And thank you, for a second chance."

His cheerful expression dropped. "That's past us, right?"

"Yes."

He smiled reassuringly. "I noticed you're wearing black nail polish tonight. Very dark and mysterious for prom."

She was surprised he'd noticed that mundane of an accent to her ensemble, though given the topic, it wasn't like she'd explicitly shown him a black nail polish with accompanying receipt. "My mom and I got a mani-pedi together."

He nodded.

"I've been good. I promise."

He kissed her forehead. "I'm glad to hear it."

She leaned her head against his chest. He was still checking on her honesty. She didn't need him questioning her motives for wanting to go to the Green Lands, to the wedding.

As the dance floor cleared and the evening grew late, the Garden Club and their dates arranged to meet up for milkshakes.

On the drive over, Leah stared out the truck window, lost in thought.

"What's wrong?" Marcus asked, putting the truck in park.

She pulled out her phone to text her mom their location. "What do you mean? Nothing's wrong."

"You were practically chewing your fresh manicure off the whole way over here. Did I say something? Or?" He raised his shoulders.

She looked over at him, frowning. "Nothing you did."

He furrowed his brow. "Then what is it?" He took her hand, shifting to face her.

Off-the-wall assassination plot aside, it was eating away at her that he hadn't even asked her if she would be his date for the wedding. She'd assumed Green Lands weddings were similar to human ones, that he could take a plus-one to his own brother's wedding.

She sighed. "It's more of what you *didn't* do."

He pursed his lips, rocking his head back and forth. "I thought we agreed to wait. I didn't think—"

"I don't mean sex."

He searched her face. "Okay. What didn't I do?"

She paused. "I don't want you to judge me. I don't want you to think I'm like Tanner."

His eyes narrowed in obvious confusion.

"Why haven't you invited me to your brother's wedding?"

He perked up, sitting straighter. "We seriously haven't talked about that? Of course, I want you to come."

She instantly donned a smile. "Really?"

He gripped her hand tighter. "Yeah. It's, uh, the second Saturday after spring break, and—"

"Wait," she said. "I thought it was *during* spring break. Are you talking about the one here?"

Marcus cocked his head. "Yeah. You're talking about the one in the Green Lands?"

She rubbed the back of his hand. "Yeah. The one your mom can attend, the one all of your side of the family will be at."

He pressed his lips together.

She frowned again. "I keep wondering if you'd be ashamed because, if they know my mom is weird about Green Lands stuff, or about, you know ... the ... stealing thing."

He shook his head, his voice soft and kind. "No, that's not it at all. I haven't told them about any of that."

Her heart felt lighter. "Then why?"

"Because you can't go. You don't have a passport. And..." He stroked her palm with his thumb. "You say you go after what you want, but you're too afraid to even bring it up with your mom, to try getting a passport."

She freed her hands, running them across the fabric of her skirt. "I have." She had no choice other than to lie. It was only a partial lie. "I tried bringing up the Green Lands after I met you guys. I remembered her telling me stories as a little kid. It … didn't go well."

Marcus's face was painted with confusion. "So, she's known I'm a Boman the whole time? Does she not approve?"

"No. That's not it. And she doesn't know about any of the club. And it needs to stay that way." The pain of Cheryl grabbing a fistful of Leah's hair was enough of a sore spot to be believable. "My mom was livid when I even mentioned it. She wants to put that world behind her."

Realizing she could lace the half-truths with another truth he could latch on to, she added, "She finally told me how my dad really died. It was in the war you guys have talked about. It was really hard on her." She regretted saying it out loud, now fighting tears. She hoped, like Tanner had said, that it was too much of a taboo to talk about sides, so she wouldn't have to lie more.

Marcus took her hands again and rubbed them. "I'm sorry. A lot of people died in that. Both of my parents barely made it out." He frowned, his eyes sad. "That still leaves us without a passport."

"I know. And if it were just about visiting the Green Lands, I could wait until my eighteenth birthday to apply alone." She shrugged. "I just didn't want to wait that long to meet your family."

A look of adoration crossed his face. "I would love nothing more than to show you off at the wedding."

She swallowed hard. "I wouldn't need a passport if I could tree rift."

"That's illegal." He squinted. "Did Tanner tell you about that?"

"I know. That's what he said." She read his face. "I got to thinking about how my mom and I have flown before, and she's forgotten her ID. She lets the TSA agent know she's forgotten it, and they interview her, then let her get on the flight. I thought maybe we could show up and say I realized the night before that I'd lost my passport, or something like that." She averted her gaze. "But I know how you feel about lying."

He scratched his arm. "Maybe we could try that? It's not fair you've been denied your homeland your entire life."

Her heart filled with hope. "Really? You'd do that for me?"

He smiled warmly, confidently. "My dad has some pull. He'll be on this side to greet my grandparents and me."

She matched his smile. "You don't know how much this means to me. I know we have to peg down a story, and logistics, and I have a billion questions. But I..." She shook her head, then planted a kiss on him.

He grinned after stealing one more. "Of course. But don't thank me yet, we still don't know if they'll make the exception."

She nodded. "I understand. If they don't, I could get a ride home, right?"

"Yeah. But I hope it works out." He caressed her face, pulling her in for a decent kiss.

Chapter 14

Marcus and Leah strolled into the ice cream shop; their group was already sitting and chatting. Jake's arm around his date gave Leah even more cause to smile. They must've had the talk about becoming an official couple.

Jake glanced at his watch. "Supposed to make out *after* ice cream, so you don't make your friends wait." He smiled.

Leah rolled her eyes. She and Marcus showed very little PDA in the club, not wanting to make things awkward. "We were talking." Which was true, for the most part.

Tanner looked directly at Leah, and laughed. "*You?* I'm *sure* that's true."

All the joy from Marcus's wedding invitation drained from her face. Tanner's meaning might be misconstrued by someone who hadn't been there, but his arrogant tone and smug grin told Leah all she needed to know. Leah wasn't the kind of girl to *possibly* be capable of sitting in a vehicle and just having a conversation, was she? Not by his estimation. Not when she'd so willingly made out with him the first time they were alone, when she'd sat on his lap, when *he'd* taken things too far.

She hugged herself, her mood soured by his pointed mocking. The double standard. If she'd done the same to him, he'd proudly own up to their make-out session. Instead, she was the slut? She glanced down the restroom hallway. "I'm going to the bathroom."

Marcus placed a hand on her back, stopping her. "Do you have a problem, Tanner? Do you have something you want to say?" He'd apparently picked up on Tanner's meaning as well.

Tanner looked between the two of them, holding up his hands. "Just having fun."

Marcus glared. "Have fun with someone else."

Leah shifted so Marcus's hand was no longer on her back. "Calm down," she snipped, trying to avoid a public conflict.

Jake was already raising his eyebrows at the tension.

Marcus clenched his jaw. "Do you want to go somewhere else?"

"No," she whispered. "Just take a chill pill. I'll be right back." She left for the bathroom, calming her breathing, attempting to focus on the good news of the evening, the almost-perfect dance.

By the time she returned, now fully recomposed, Marcus had joined the others, sitting down. Everyone was chatting except for Marcus. He was slumped in his seat, scrolling on his cell. She gave him a reassuring smile and a squeeze on the shoulder before sliding in next to him. He put away his phone. "Ordered your shake for you. Hope you don't mind."

"Mmm, depends on what you got me," she said playfully.

"Peanut butter cup. Right?"

She grinned. "You know me." She placed a hand on her chest. "Heart and soul."

He perked up. The group soon enjoyed their treats, critiquing the décor and music from the dance. Tanner avoided direct discussion with both Leah and Marcus.

After polishing off their shakes, Leah and Marcus said their goodbyes to the group and walked out to his truck. "Hold up," she said, before either of them got in. They watched and waved as the others took off. "Come on. Back seat."

He stood in place. "I don't know that I feel like kissing a whole lot right now."

She scolded him with her eyes. "We can't just talk?"

"We can talk in the front seat." He tilted his head to the side.

She took his hand. "I just want to talk. You and me. No barriers."

He opened the extended-cab door, allowing her to get in before going to his own side. "Okay."

"Why did you say anything to Tanner?"

He scowled. "We both know what he was alluding to."

It wasn't like she hadn't suffered from her number being written in a bathroom stall before, after hooking up with the wrong guy. "Maybe. But all you did was make it worse."

"How's that?"

"I told Tanner you didn't know anything, so it wouldn't make things awkward in the club. And honestly, you really *don't* know anything about what happened that night."

Marcus looked down, scratching his arm. "Does he still like you? Has he hit on you since we've been together?"

"No! And even if he did like me, I don't care." She stared at him. "Hey."

He met her gaze.

"For all of my faults, I'm not a cheater. I would never do that to you."

"I know. I believe you. Doesn't mean he wouldn't try something."

She furrowed her brow. "You're getting mad about a *hypothetical*?"

"No. I just—" He ran his hands through his hair. "I don't know. You're right that I don't know what happened that night. I would feel a lot better if I just knew."

She fidgeted with her hands. "That's not really any of your business. That was before we started dating."

He pursed his lips. "I know that. But I know something happened. And I can't just forget that. Every time I see you two sitting next to each other..." He paused. "I would just feel better knowing *what* he did."

She shook her head. "What is with this possessive side?"

"It's not possessive!" Marcus snapped. He rubbed his face. "It's not. It's just ... couples take care of each other. I know you say you don't need my help. But I *want* to help. What's so wrong with that?"

"It happened before we were together! What gives you the right to know about every guy I've kissed, or done anything else with, before you?" She shifted in her seat. "Unless it matters more to you than you're letting on," she whispered. "You said it didn't matter that much."

He frowned. "You have a past. I get it. But we eat lunch with him—every day. We hang out with him—every week. It's different. And you keep saying it all happened before us, but what he did tonight," he pointed to the building, "was not before us. That was aimed *right* at you and *right* in front of me."

"I'll take care of it. And I really don't think he'll be a problem anymore." Leah had given it some thought back in the bathroom. Tanner had originally only shown an interest in her after finding out she was an Ivy. "I think he's just annoyed he can't be as free about who he is with human girls."

Marcus rolled his eyes. "Won't be a problem anymore? For you? Or for anyone?"

She glared. "He learned pretty quickly how I felt about things once I *cut his throat*. Remember that part? And what are you, the morality police?"

"What's that supposed to mean?"

She pinched the bridge of her nose. "It means I want to go back to how happy I was with you before we went inside. Please don't do this."

"Don't do what? Care about you?" He huffed. "You're okay with me helping you come to the wedding, but I can't help when he pulls a dick move like that? *You* get to choose when I'm allowed to help?"

"Yes. That would be respecting my wishes."

"Fine. If I see you getting mugged, I'll wait until I have your consent to help out."

Her ears were warming in her anger. "Who's being the dick now?"

He opened the truck door, getting in the front seat and turning the key. She buckled up, stewing in the back seat as he drove to her house. Once he parked at her house, neither of them moved.

"Is this how we're ending our prom night?" she asked, still upset, though aching at the wasted evening.

"It seems like this conversation should have ended before it began."

She got out, also moving into the front seat. "I get that you want to know everything. I do. But not everyone's so open about their pasts and struggles, Marcus. Sometimes, people want to sort through it alone. Or just ... do their best to forget about it."

Frowning, he nodded. "I just don't know how to step back from it. I can't not care."

Leah gave him a half-smile. "That's because you're the most caring person I know. We just have to figure out where to draw the line." She fought off memories of experiences she'd give anything to have never endured. "It honestly doesn't bug me that much, what Tanner did. At least not anymore." She picked at her nails, sick to her stomach, dead inside. "I've had guys do worse. And you can't fix that, either."

Marcus read her face. "I'm sorry. For anything that's happened to you."

She shook her head, a tiny smile forming. "What are you apologizing for? You didn't do it. You couldn't have stopped it."

He silently bobbed his head. "I know. And you shouldn't feel like you have to tell me."

"It's probably not as bad as you're imagining with Tanner." She grinned. "You and I have been closer to getting in trouble than he and I were."

Marcus gave her a shy smile.

"Yeah. Look at that. Squeaky clean."

He rolled his eyes, his smile growing.

"I promise. It was just kissing. He got handsy. I said 'no.' I had to repeat myself. Like I said, I've had worse."

Marcus's smile faded, and he gave her a look of resigned acknowledgement. "Okay."

"And what are you going to do now that you know more? Go pummel Tanner?"

He cocked his head. "I'm guessing you're against that."

She poked his hand. "A little bit. We already worked it out. I think tonight was a fluke. We were just off tonight."

He blew out a puff of air. "I'll try to be chill."

"Thank you." She rested a hand on his knee. "I was really excited to start planning for the wedding. Let's not allow Tanner to spoil things for us."

He slid his hand to hers, interlacing their fingers. "Deal."

"How about you walk me to the door and give me one of those signature hugs of yours?"

He smiled. "Am I turning you into a hugger, after all?"

She laughed. "Not on your life. I only like hugs from *you*."

They got out of the truck, and he pulled her into a perfectly tight squeeze. He really did know how to do the job.

"Marcus?"

He pulled back. "Yeah?"

"I'm really glad I met you. I mean it. With how often I've moved over the years, I ... don't always make the best friends right away. I don't always connect with people." She played with a button on his shirt. "I've never actually had a boyfriend this long."

His smile could melt an iceberg. "It's not about the quantity. It's about the quality. The right kind makes things work." He gave her one more short squeeze and a kiss on the forehead. "We'll talk tomorrow?"

She nodded. "Wouldn't have it any other way."

Leah ambled inside the house, letting out a long exhale from the ups and downs of the evening.

"No making out at the door?" Cheryl said. "Must've already shacked up with your boyfriend in a parking lot somewhere?"

Leah scowled. She was used to them spying on her. She was used to Cheryl's insults. But tonight, of all nights? "No. Not that it's any of your business."

Cheryl scoffed. "Isn't that the only way you manage to keep them around?"

Leah gritted her teeth. "What the hell do you know? You're just a bitter old maid too afraid to move on with her life."

Cheryl glared. "You are the most ungrateful—"

"*Go to hell.*" Leah's voice was low and threatening, carrying with it a thousand unspoken curses she'd wanted to mutter over the years. "We don't need you anymore." Before Cheryl could lash out again, Leah turned, striding down the hall to her mom's room.

"I'm home," she announced with all the perk she could muster. Cheryl's bedroom door across the house slammed shut.

"Were you good?" Her mom glanced up from her journal.

Leah pursed her lips. "I think most human moms would first ask how the dance went."

Her mom smiled gently. "How was the dance?"

Leah rocked her head back and forth. "I'd give it four out of five stars."

Her mom nodded. "And were you good?"

Leah rolled her eyes, cracking a smile. "Yes. Like I told you, Marcus is a Boy Scout." After providing a few more details about the dance, she headed to the bathroom to shower.

All cleaned up and in fresh pjs, Leah glanced at her phone, opening a text from Marcus.

<Sorry again for being an idiot. Hope you sleep well. CU tomorrow?>

She wore a soft smile. <Not an idiot. Just caught up wanting to be Prince Charming. ;)>

<Maybe I am. Does that make you my Princess?>

She chuckled. <More than you know :P On for tomorrow. Sweet dreams.>

Setting her phone down on the bedside table, Leah glanced at the bottom drawer. Opening it up, she grabbed her set of throwing knives for the next day. The only other thing in there stared at her until she picked it up. *Seriously, what kind of person plots an assassination?*

She flipped through the pages she'd written on. Her heart ached at her list of reasons for why the queen deserved to die.

But it won't bring him back. Move on.

Leah frowned, tearing out the pages, crumpling them up, and tossing them in the garbage.

She was going to the Green Lands to visit her homeland. To attend the wedding. If and when the time came for her to meet the murderous queen again, she'd have more than vague plans about how to kill her. She'd find a way to make her hurt. But that wasn't what this trip was about.

After crawling into bed, and turning off her lamp with a click, Leah fell asleep with a smile on her face.

<h1 style="text-align:center">Chapter 15</h1>

As planned, they hung out at Marcus's grandparents' place the next day. "You're sure we're good?" Marcus asked as they pulled into the driveway.

"Would I still want to come over today if we weren't?" Leah asked.

"Okay." He smiled. "Let's have a good day."

They made their way to the backyard, throwing a few rounds of knives, then sharpening them. Hungry for lunch, they went inside to make sandwiches.

"Wheat?" he asked, undoing a twist tie.

"Yes, please." Leah reached into the fridge, grabbing mayonnaise and mustard. She went back for the rest of the fillings, having trouble finding the lunch meat. "You guys usually have ham, right?"

Marcus came up behind her, placing his hands on the fridge. "Yes, there on the left." He leaned in, caressing her neck with his lips.

She turned. "Did you hide it so you could corner me?"

"You know me. Plotting and planning." He winked.

"Yes. You're the *most* mischievous person I know."

He beamed. "I'm such a scoundrel. What can I say? I can't help myself. I think you're pretty *cool*."

She lifted her eyebrows. "Is that because I'm standing in front of an open fridge?"

He busted out laughing. "Yes." He snuck a kiss, grabbing the lunch meat and backing away.

"You are so punny." She grinned.

"I do what I can." He laid out the pieces of bread, spreading on the mayo. "Enjoy the lunch meat, you'll learn to appreciate it after a week in the Green Lands."

"Right. Vegetarians." She opened the lunch meat and layered it on the bread. "Thank you, again. I'm really excited."

"I'm excited too. You'll love it there. And I think my family will really like you."

"You *think* they will?"

He threw a teasing glare. "I know they will."

"I'm sure I'll like them too. But I'm going to have a million questions to get ready."

He grabbed a bag of chips, picking up his plate. "Let's get to it."

They sat down in the family room, eating and chatting. "Who all will I be meeting?" she asked.

"*Lots* of people. It won't be your usual scene."

"Yeah. Kind of nervous. Sounds like a pretty big shindig if the queen is going to be there." She dared to probe more, now that she had the invitation. "I understand it's a pretty small kingdom compared to some human ones, but ... does she attend a lot of weddings?"

He shrugged. "It's not like I track her schedule." He took a bite, looking down at his plate. "My parents have connections. I don't really like to talk about that kind of stuff."

He always did that—he was happy to talk about his parents, but only vaguely. "Okay. It's not like I'm going there to meet *her*. I'm there to be with you. You know that, right?"

He met her gaze. "I know."

"Good. But ... I've never been around royalty. So, you're going to need to coach me so I don't screw up. I don't know anything about what to wear, or customs, or geography. Any of it." She fought a grin, thinking about taking her mom up on formal dining etiquette lessons. "I guess I shouldn't say I don't know *any* formal customs. A particularly smartass Boman once taught me about a custom for good luck." She threw a chip at him.

He wore a toothy grin. "You didn't have any bad luck that week, did you? Maybe that's going to be the ticket to getting you back home."

She refused to let him win, refused to smile or laugh.

He raised his eyebrows. "Or do you need one now?" He slowly leaned over, lips puckered, aiming to give her neck another raspberry.

She held her ground, raising her hands as if she knew karate. "No."

Marcus grinned again, leaning back. He picked up the chip she'd thrown, chucking it back onto her plate. "Here. You lost this."

She grabbed it and crunched down on it defiantly. "So. Back on topic. Is it taking place at the palace?"

He shook his head, kicking his feet up onto the coffee table. "No. But it'll be at a pretty big manor."

They talked for a couple of hours, discussing how the week would go. Marcus's grandparents would drive, as they were also attending. She'd meet his dad at the rifting cave. The cave they'd arrive at in the Ivy Kingdom wasn't far from his home. He'd planned on taking the whole of spring break for a visit. They had two days before the wedding, then more family time after that.

"If you need to go home early, we can arrange that, too," he said. "Um ... even if we can fudge the truth to get you over, how are you going to hide this from your mom?"

She swallowed hard. "Don't worry about that one. I'll figure it out." It was better he didn't realize the lies she'd be piling up.

He frowned, hesitant. "Okay. I just ... don't want you getting in too much trouble."

She scooched closer, leaning against his shoulder. "I'll be fine. This will be worth it."

He kissed her on the head. "I'm excited. I bet my mom will *love* getting you all sorted with a beautiful dress and everything."

"Right. Can't exactly carry much through a rift, right?" She drew a deep breath. "Will there be many Seeders there?"

He rested a hand on her leg. "I guess you haven't met one yet, huh? There should be a decent amount at the wedding."

She frowned. The enemy of her dad. The ones Pretender Queen Kaylah had sided with to steal the kingdom. But ... Marcus was close to his mom. She had to be a decent Seeder, and it only made sense her family would be invited. "Why did your parents settle in the Ivy Kingdom? You said it wasn't safe for your dad as a Boman in the Seeder nation?"

He gently traced a finger up and down her leg, between her knee and midthigh. "Well, Bomen Lands didn't exist when they got married, and they're almost exclusively home to Bomen, anyway. Not that my mom wouldn't be allowed to live there, but it wouldn't be as comfortable. And she's not as close to her Seeder family as others might be. They're a lot closer to my dad's Ivy family."

Leah smiled, her anticipation building to meet them both. "Tanner once said pretty much everyone was in the old war. And you said your parents fought?"

"Yep. That was another reason they stayed in the kingdom. War's ugly... They wanted to help the kingdom with all the aftermath."

"Yeah. War's ugly," she whispered.

Marcus's grandpa, Brad, poked his head in the family room. "We're getting dinner going. Will you be staying, Leah?"

"If that's not a problem?"

"Never is."

She leaned forward. "I wouldn't mind helping. I cook with my mom all the time."

"We might take you up on that sometime. We're all set for now, though, thanks."

Marcus took the opportunity to wrap his arms around Leah as his grandpa left.

"Is this the house your mom was raised in?" Leah said.

"No. My grandparents, well ... there's been some family drama. It's kind of complicated. But my grandma moved shortly after my mom rooted in the Green Lands."

Leah gave a breathy chuckle. "Complicated families—I get that."

⁂

The next Monday rolled around, and Leah walked through the high school hallways with a spring in her step. She was going to visit the Green Lands. She was going to experience the energy, her culture, all of it. And with the person who made her the happiest.

That joy faded as she spotted Tanner at his locker. Her frustration bubbled up, and she decided to have a word with him. She marched up, kicking his door shut. It was perhaps a *little* dramatic.

He raised his eyebrows. "Wow. Moody much?"

She glared. "Why were you such a jerk after the dance?"

He sported an insincere frown. "Did I ruin the mood for you and Marcus? Did *he* end up with bandages?"

"You're not funny. Why are you even bringing that up?" She squinted. "It's not like you want to date me."

He shrugged. "Maybe I just realized you and I would have had more fun together on prom night." He smirked. "A girl like you, you've probably screwed a dozen guys." He glanced around briefly, lowering his voice. "But none of them your own kind."

She slammed him against his locker. "What I do with my life is *none* of your business. Sorry there's not another Ivy for you to enjoy screwing. But you and I will *never* have anything again!"

He rolled his eyes. "I don't need you or the stupid club. You're not very exciting now that you're dating Mr. Boring, anyway."

"Screw you, Tanner." She clenched her teeth. His smug look was too much to resist. She balled her fist but stopped short, instead shoving him against his locker again. "Bring it up again and we'll find out if a kick to the 'nads hurts you as much as it does a human."

He picked up his backpack. "You *are* psycho. Go take care of your boyfriend's 'nads and leave me alone." He stalked away before she could do the damage she desperately wanted to do.

Unsurprisingly, Tanner was a no-show for lunch. Leah was still in a sour mood. She wished she hadn't confronted him after all. Leah, Marcus, and Jake sat around their usual courtyard table, recapping their weekends.

"I'm happy for you and Emily." Leah forced a smile. "Too bad she doesn't have the same lunch hour as us."

"Yeah." Jake shrugged. "Especially if Tanner's going to be a no-show."

Leah and Marcus exchanged a look.

"So..." Jake said. "What was all the tension about the other day? Or am I going to be the only one in the dark?"

Marcus focused on building his hamburger.

Leah bit her lip. "Just a disagreement. He, um ... might not be spending time with us anymore."

Marcus looked up with questioning eyes.

She averted her gaze, taking a sip of water. "He told me this morning that he wants to focus on human interactions for the remainder of his exchange year."

Marcus remained silent, slipping a hand under the table to squeeze her knee. She rested a hand on his. In the end, they were all going to be better off without Tanner.

Jake took a bite of his burger, shrugging again. "I won't cry any tears if he wants to hang out elsewhere."

Leah was finally calming down. Her past wasn't perfect. She'd made bad decisions, one of them being having done anything with Tanner. But her mistakes didn't define her.

She was doing her best to pay attention in English class, until she was called to the office. *Great. This is never good.*

"Ms. Edwards. Take a seat." The vice principal pointed to a black pleather chair in her dark and stuffy office.

"Yes, ma'am." Leah's stomach was in knots. She'd had her fair share of office visits over the years.

The VP crossed her arms. "I've had a report of you being involved in a physical altercation earlier today."

Leah fidgeted with her hands. "I, um … just had a disagreement with someone."

The VP raised her eyebrows. "A disagreement that involved you shoving him against a locker?"

"Is that what he told you?"

"'He' being Tanner Holgrum?"

Leah looked her in the eyes. "Yes." This was low.

"I spoke to him, too."

'Too'? So someone else reported it?

"But I'd like to hear things from your side."

Leah bit the insides of her cheeks. "He was being a jerk. We argued. I lost my temper."

"You have nothing else you'd like to add?"

Leah rubbed her wrists. How many times did girls like her get dismissed, especially after waiting to report something? How many times had her mom jumped straight to moving because she was trying to protect Leah? They owned their own furniture dolly, for heaven's sake. "Nope."

The vice principal sighed. "Your transcript shows a lot of moves, and a few problems along the way. Is there anything else you'd like to talk about?"

"Nope."

"I'm trying to help you."

Leah matched her gaze. "I don't need help. I'd like to get back to class, unless there's something else."

"This is your first offense here. If there's nothing else you'd like to add, you can return to class. You'll have in-school-suspension for the rest of the week."

Leah's jaw dropped at the prospect of being cooped up in detention during lunchtime. "ISS? I didn't even hurt him!"

"It's violence against another student. Unless you have something else to add, you're dismissed, and I don't want to see you in my office again."

Leah clenched her jaw. "Yes, ma'am."

Marching back to class, Leah fumed. People needed to keep their noses out of her business. She should have made it worth her while and actually punched or kicked Tanner like he deserved. Just before she reached the classroom, her phone vibrated.

The text was from her mom. <I'll be picking you up today. Be at pickup right away.>

Oh crap.

Leah promptly made her way to student pickup after classes.

Marcus found her, wrapping an arm around her. "Hey, beautiful. How are you doing?"

She blew out a long breath. "I've been better."

He frowned. "Do you want to talk about what happened with Tanner?"

She scrunched her eyebrows. Had Marcus somehow been involved with her visit to the office? "What do you know about it?"

"Nothing... You mentioned you talked to him."

She closed her eyes, shaking her head. "Right. I, um..." Her mom pulled up in her blue hatchback. "I'll talk to you later?"

He gave her hand a squeeze. "Sure." He bent over, looking in the car. "That's your mom and her car. Not your aunt today, huh?"

Leah gave him a quick kiss, her heart dropping. She hadn't genuinely worried about her mom forcing them to move for a while. But was she overreacting about the ISS? She'd already had three shoplifting strikes in this city...

Leah decided to give Marcus a quick hug as well. "I..." She ran a hand through his handsomely curly locks. *I need to calm down.* "I'll talk to you later."

Chapter 16

Leah got into her mom's car with a gulp. After a moment of silence, she decided to be the first to speak. "Why are *you* picking me up today?"

Her mom's jaw clenched as they drove down the street. "I would like to wait until we're home to have this conversation."

Leah's breathing picked up. "Are we moving?"

Her mom didn't respond.

She endured the rest of the ride in painful silence. Once they got home, walking to the front door felt like walking down death row. Surely this wasn't all about the ISS... But maybe it was the last straw after the shoplifting...

Leah panicked—the notebook pages in her trash can. Had she taken out her trash? Had her mom? Had she discovered her plans and now knew that Leah had exposed herself to green folk? A thousand fears ran through her mind.

"Sit down!" her mom ordered once the front door closed. She tossed her keys onto the coffee table and crossed her arms. "Eleana." She shook her head, balling her fists.

Leah kept her mouth closed.

"Why do you think I'm upset?"

Leah shrugged.

"I had to leave work early today. Because of you. I got two phone calls. *Two!*"

Leah furrowed her brow. "Two?"

Her mom plopped down in an armchair, burying her face in her hands. "Let's talk about the school office call first."

Leah bit her lip. "He deserved worse."

"In-school-suspension? You hurt another student. Why?"

"He was a jerk."

Her mom cocked her head. "Everyone who disagrees with you could be classified as a jerk, right?"

Leah scowled. "He..." Her mom knew she'd had trouble with guys before, though just the tip of the iceberg. Leah struggled to get the words out of her mouth. "Even *you* would have approved of more than me shoving him."

Her mom softened, frowning. "What did he do?"

"I don't really want to talk about it. I'm fine. I'm just saying ... he deserved it."

"Did you tell the vice principal?"

"That's none of her business."

Her mom sighed. "Life would be easier if you would allow people to help you."

Leah locked eyes with her. Wasn't it her mom who had said therapists were useless, that she needed to learn to take care of herself? Wasn't she the one who had kept secrets from Leah her whole life because she was afraid? "You're not the most talkative, either."

Her mom looked down. "Is Marcus causing any troubles?"

"No! You've met him. He's a good guy."

"You two have been dating for a while. And you spend a lot more time over there than you do over here. Maybe it's time I met his grandparents."

"No. Why?"

"Is there a problem with me meeting them?"

Yes. They know I'm an Ivy and don't realize it's a secret... "Of course not. I just don't need you making it weird. I'm perfectly safe over there. And Marcus is a good influence—you know that." She sat up straighter. "What have my grades been like? And ... I haven't had *any* problems at the store since he threatened to break up with me over it before Christmas."

Her mom nodded. "Even then, I wish you two would spend more time over here."

"We can, if that's what it takes." Leah wrung her hands. "But his grandparents are retired, they're always home. We never go in his room. We know the rules."

"Fine. For now." Her mom sat back, crossing her legs. "Moving on. The other phone call I got today."

This one was the mystery. Leah couldn't even begin to guess.

"Take a look around."

Leah glanced around the room. There was nothing too spectacular in their living room. The decorations were simple from her mom having grown tired of packing and unpacking things over the years. Though Leah *did* notice a couple of items missing. Most notable were Cheryl's coat and purse, absent from their place on the coatrack. Leah had assumed, or perhaps just hoped, that Cheryl was under the weather, forcing her mom to come pick her up. But she wasn't there... "Okay?"

"Cheryl took a job over two hundred miles away."

Leah's heart froze. "You just said... Marcus... I don't want to move yet!"

Her mom's face became stern. "We're not. She made it *very* clear she no longer wishes to live under the same roof as *you*."

Leah crossed her arms. "Good."

"That's not something to be proud of, Eleana!"

"Why not? She was always mean to me! You can only turn a blind eye so much." A scowl covered Leah's face. "She hurt me, and you never did anything about it."

Her mom glared. "Don't pretend you're an innocent little angel."

Crestfallen, Leah fought tears. "I'm not. I never claimed to be. And I get that she was your servant, and you felt like you owed her something, but she wore out her welcome a long time ago."

Her mom threw her hands in the air. "Our lives are full of compromise. You know that. We don't belong here. She was my last connection to our home."

A tear fell from Leah's eye. "*I'm* your last connection, right?" Her voice trembled. "You and me, we don't need anyone else."

Her mom frowned. "Of course. I didn't mean that, princess. It's just..." She shook her head. "You don't understand how much we really needed the money she brought in."

Leah sniffled. "Well, I... I can give up my allowance. I can get a job."

"No. It's not that simple. I'll agree to the allowance. And I'm going to see if I can get more hours from work. But we've managed things like this for *years*. How am I supposed to work so much *and* watch out for you?"

"I'm old enough to watch out for myself. I'm safe with Marcus. I'm safe at home and school."

"And you've been listening to make sure no one from the Green Lands is in your school?"

Tanner wouldn't do anything in retribution, would he? He knew she was keeping secrets from her mom. "Yes. I've been listening. We're fine."

"We'll see how things go for now." Her mom stood, holding out her hand, palm up. "Two weeks of grounding."

"Why?" Leah whined. "Because you have to work more? I—"

"Because both of your problems could have been handled better."

Leah was done with the conversation; she never won this part of the fight, anyway. She pulled her phone from her pocket. "Can I at least tell Marcus?"

"You'll see him at school."

Leah wilted, handing it over.

Her mom tapped away at the screen, as she had on more than one occasion before. She wouldn't dare leave Leah without a phone for safety's sake, but she *could* activate a parental setting that suppressed most of the functionality of the phone, only allowing approved numbers to be called or texted—those of herself, Cheryl, and 911. "And since Cheryl and her car are now gone, you'll be taking the bus for now." She handed Leah's phone back to her.

Leah shuffled to her room, a mix of emotions. Maybe she shouldn't have pushed Tanner. No, she should have *punched* him and made it worthwhile. She prayed her mom could get more hours so they wouldn't have to move to find a better paying job. She considered the irony of how she could steal things to help with expenses, but she'd only be punished more for it.

Leah was less than thrilled to wake up even earlier to take the school bus for the first time in her life. It was noisy, dirty chaos.

She'd never been allowed social media accounts like her peers. Leah now finally understood the reasoning behind that decision—it wouldn't do well to have pictures of King Soren's exiled heir floating around the internet. But even then, Leah was used to texting Marcus, or looking up videos on social media without actually having an account. She kept rubbing her pocket, longing to turn her phone on and wipe away the world around her. Instead, it was like a brick against her hip, only good for emergencies and tracking.

The bus got to the school with barely enough time for her to stop by her locker, allowing no time to chase Marcus down. She tried dropping by his locker when she could between a couple of classes, but missed him. She reported to ISS as ordered, feeling the prisoner vibe through and through.

It was only between her last two classes that Marcus tracked her down at her locker. "Hey, what's up?"

She let out a sigh of relief, pulling him into a huge hug. "Gosh, am I glad to see you. I tried to find you earlier."

He pulled back, squinting. "Something happen to your phone? Missed you at lunch."

She pursed her lips. "ISS this week."

He raised his eyebrows. "Do tell."

She threw on a forced, cheesy smile. "I may or may not have gotten physical with Tanner."

He frowned. "Did you tell them what happened? Not that I even know what happened, but I'm sure he more than deserved it."

She grabbed his hand. "He did. But don't worry about it. He didn't show at lunch again, right?"

Marcus shook his head. "But they still suspended you?"

She twisted her lips.

He sighed, tucking a strand of hair behind her ear. "Next time he does something, I'm taking care of it. You can be as mad as you want."

She swung their joined hands. "We'll see."

He bent down, giving her a kiss. "For the record, if you had let me handle it, it wouldn't have happened on school property." He placed his hands on her arms, rubbing them reassuringly. "That explains lunch, but why haven't you been answering my texts?"

She swallowed hard. "Grounded for two weeks, no phone. Well, no phone service. It's locked."

"Seriously? Because of ISS?"

"Yeah, that's part of it."

He slowly pulled his hands back, tucking them in his pockets. "What's the other part?"

She shook her head, deflated. "It would be really nice to not have my boyfriend jump to conclusions."

"I'm trying not to."

"It's not what you're thinking. It was just a family argument. I promise. You can even ask my mom."

He took a moment before answering. "Okay. I believe you."

"Thank you."

He grabbed her hands again. "Not gonna lie. Sucks that I'll only get to see you in the hallway and at pickup."

She groaned, leaning forward and burying her head in his chest. "Yesterday was a bad day," she mumbled.

"Come again?"

She pulled back, taking a deep breath. "My aunt moved out, too. I have to take the bus now."

Marcus smiled. "My grandparents wouldn't mind giving you a ride. Would your mom allow that?"

Leah shrugged. "We could ask."

"She's got work, right? So, she won't even know who drops you off..."

The tardy bell rang, and Leah grinned. "You're supposed to be rubbing off on me, not the other way around."

He smirked. "I'd say..." He pressed his lips together, clearing his throat.

"What?"

"Never mind." He looked her over. "Better get to class." He snuck one last quick kiss. "See you at pickup."

Marcus was right; his grandma, Samantha, happily gave Leah a ride home. And Leah happily rested her hand on Marcus's thigh as they sat next to each other in the van. "Thanks again, Samantha," she said.

"No problem, sweetie."

They pulled up to Leah's place, and Marcus walked her to the door. "Hopefully you can talk your mom into being okay with this arrangement."

She played with the hem of his t-shirt. "She's depriving me of my study partner. So, if she wants me to keep my grades up, she should concede that I deserve to shorten my ride so I have more study time."

"I like your logic. And when you're off of house arrest, I vote we have a big date." He slid his hands to her waist. "Dinner, movie, all of it."

She frowned.

"Or not?"

"It's complicated. Maybe we'll just hang out at your place."

He felt her forehead. "Are you okay?"

"Yes..."

He put his hand on her waist again, pulling her closer. "You'd rather be supervised at my place than spend time at the theater alone?"

She gave him a half-smile. "It's..." She wrapped her arms around his waist as well. "Free is good. I won't have an allowance for a while."

"I don't mind paying."

She bit the insides of her cheeks. "Giving me rides is more than enough. I don't need you always paying for me. I don't want your charity."

He scoffed. "Since when is any of that charity? Because I want to spend time with my girlfriend? If anything, you're doing me a favor."

She rolled her eyes. "We'll see."

He leaned down, kissing her and sliding his hands lower, into the back pockets of her jeans. He then studied her face. "Is this okay?"

"Your kissing? That's more than okay."

He squinted. "Not what I'm asking about."

She grinned. "You know where I stand on that kind of thing when it comes to you."

"Just because you wanted it once, doesn't mean I can just assume."

She gazed into his warm brown eyes. *This one. He's a keeper.* "I usually like to handle things myself. But it's safe to say I'm alright with you handling me this way."

It was his turn to roll his eyes, though he grinned while doing so.

"Pretty bold, though." She wiggled her eyebrows. "With your grandma in the van."

He stole a glance over his shoulder. "She can't see from this angle. And if she's parked, she's reading a book."

"Thanks for asking. Did you take some sort of gentleman's class back home?"

He laughed. "Yep. Private class. My brother and I. My dad was the teacher."

"I really look forward to meeting him."

Marcus wore a hesitant frown. "Is this going to jeopardize our chances of you coming to the wedding?"

Having analyzed the situation, Leah figured her punishment was probably more about her mom being stressed, than angry. Hopefully this wouldn't have any further repercussions.

"We'll make it work."

Chapter 17

After Leah's week of in-school-suspension, she was over the moon to spend lunch with Marcus and Jake again. Luckily, her mom consented to allow her to also get rides from Marcus. After a couple of days of lunch with Jake, Leah and Marcus agreed to leave early, allowing for some private planning and talking time.

"How are things going at home?" Marcus asked as they strolled across the school lawn.

Not fantastic. Her mom hadn't been able to pick up extra hours yet. "Not bad. And we talked about going to the wedding."

"Really?" His face lit up.

"Yeah." She smiled. "I told her it's in Detroit, and that we'll be supervised the whole time. She's still thinking about it." Her stomach twisted, revolting at the lie. She'd tried the Detroit story. The answer had been a resounding 'no.' She wasn't surprised. But Leah wouldn't take no for an answer. And even if it ended up being the final answer, she might fudge the truth anyway.

"I'll take it." His happy expression faded. "One problem, though. You'll have to be able to make your own rift."

"I thought you said they do it for you at the cave."

He winced. "Yeah, well, I wasn't thinking about the fact that you're not a Boman. We can pretend you forgot your passport, and have you present your vines, but we're not going to have a good reason why you can't make your own rift. All regular Ivies and Seeders are expected to."

She frowned. "I... I could pretend I'm a Boman?"

He shook his head. "My grandparents will be there and know you're not."

Why is this so complicated? "How hard is it to learn? You don't think you or Jake could coach me through the theory of it?"

He shrugged. "We don't know what it's like."

She couldn't really expect more of them, since they'd been born without powers. Leah swallowed hard. "Then I'll talk to Tanner."

Marcus scowled. "No."

"What other option do I have?"

"*Any* option that's not him."

"Which is none."

"Just ... let me think about it. We've still got two and a half weeks."

Leah's anxiety was building. It was just a wedding. She was just going to meet Marcus's family. But it was so much more than that. She wanted to see her homeland. She wanted to size up the woman who had destroyed her family.

The next day, Leah approached Tanner's locker between classes.

"Tanner."

He looked past his locker door. "Stay away from me. I wasn't the one who got you in trouble."

She rolled her eyes. "I know. Not that you obviously said the truth, either."

"Leave me alone, psycho."

"I need help."

He laughed. "I don't care what it is. The friendship shop closed up a while ago."

"Please." She whispered, "I need to learn to rift."

"So, you are crazy, then? Even if I liked you, I told you—it's illegal."

"A cave rift."

"And yet I still don't care." He shut his locker.

"Please! I'm begging you."

His attitude exuded arrogance. "Begging, huh?"

She rested her hands on her hips, glaring. "Yes. What do you want, a blow job?"

He grinned. "Is that a genuine offer? I don't think Marcus would be okay with that."

"No." She clenched her teeth. "You owe me for not talking about what you've done."

"Not like there were witnesses."

She balled her fists. *This was a bad idea from the start.* "Why are you such a dick?"

He leaned against his locker, crossing his arms. "Why do you want to go so much right now? Doesn't your mommy still have you on a tight leash?"

She huffed. "If you must know, I'm going to the wedding. And my mom gave me permission."

He savored a deep breath with an air of triumph. "Leah... You might have Marcus fooled that you're a reformed citizen, but not me. If your mom gave you permission, why doesn't she teach you herself?"

Leah wanted nothing more than to wipe that smug look off his face. "You don't know me as well as you think you do." Thoughts of her parents came to her mind. She could have, *should have*, rightfully been a princess. Real royalty. Over him. "And someday, you might regret that."

His eyes grew wide. "Maybe you need a therapist. But seriously. Heard of a restraining order? Touch me or threaten me again, and maybe we'll look into that."

Out of nowhere, Marcus appeared, placing a hand on both Tanner and Leah's shoulders. He smiled disingenuously at Tanner. "Tanner, buddy. Next time you mess with Leah, I'm going to break your face." He released his grip as Tanner rolled his shoulder, throwing daggers with his eyes at Marcus.

Clearly enunciating, Marcus added, "I think we both know this could get *much* worse for you."

That vague threat stole all the color from Tanner's face.

Marcus faced Leah. "You, me, let's go to class." He grabbed her hand, yanking her away.

"Why the hell did you talk to him?" Marcus scolded.

"I really want to go." She scowled at the ground.

"You will! But you couldn't give me just a couple of days to get it sorted? Maybe put a little faith in me?"

She met his gaze. "Fine. It was stupid. He said 'no' anyway."

He stopped walking, holding her hands. "I found you a teacher."

"What?" She read his face. "Who? Where?"

He grinned, looking around to make sure no one could hear him. "A sophomore Ivy at another school."

Her eyes lit up. "That's great!" She gave him a huge hug. "You're amazing!"

"Well ... don't thank me yet."

She backed up. "Why?"

He scrunched his face. "She lives two hours away, and is only willing to meet us halfway. I don't know that your mom is going to be cool with us driving that far out with the way she keeps tabs on you."

Leah gnawed her lip, thinking. A light bulb flickered on. "I'm off of house arrest on Saturday. I have a plan."

Leah, Marcus, and Jake sat down at their usual spot for lunch. The couple exchanged a glance, and Marcus cleared his throat. "So ... Jake. What are you doing Saturday afternoon?"

Jake shrugged. "Emily and I are probably doing something. Not sure what yet."

"How would you feel about a double date?" Leah asked. "Except ... not actually doubling?"

He raised his eyebrows, taking a swig of soda. "I'm not following."

"You know how my mom is crazy about tracking my phone and everything?"

"You've mentioned it."

Leah nervously stirred her applesauce. "We kinda need my mom to think we're out for dinner and a movie while we're doing something else for three hours. We were hoping you'd take my phone?"

Jake bunched his eyebrows. "Three hours? What are you guys even—" He held up a hand. "Never mind. I don't think I want to finish that question."

Leah smirked. "Oh, you better believe it. I mean, three hours is *impressive* stamina. But Marcus is pretty amazing." She seductively bit a knuckle in challenge to Marcus's disapproving glare.

Jake closed his eyes, turning every shade of red. "Leah, I never want to hear those words from you again."

Leah busted out laughing. "Fine. Whatever."

Marcus rolled his eyes. "You know me, Jake. Would I ask you to do something like this if it weren't important?"

Jake sighed. "Just take the phone with me to dinner and a movie?"

"Yes," Leah replied. "We'll meet you at the restaurant for the handoff. Then you'll text my mom as me when you're leaving there and arriving at the theater. I'll have it typed up; you just have to hit send. We'll meet you there after the movie."

Jake hesitated, looking between the two. "Fine. But what if she calls?"

"That's why it's at a movie theater and not just leaving a phone at Marcus's place. She won't call."

Marcus texted Jake from the restaurant parking lot once he and Leah arrived. Not knowing all the details, Jake wanted to leave Emily out of it, so he intentionally left his wallet in the car, giving himself an excuse to leave her momentarily.

Leah handed Jake the phone out of the truck window. "Thanks a million!"

He looked down at it, making sure it didn't require a passcode. "Sure."

She couldn't help herself. "Don't worry. We have plenty of water, snacks, and protection."

"Seriously?" He glanced past Leah to Marcus. "Got a muzzle for your girlfriend?"

Leah smirked. "Hmm ... I packed the whip and handcuffs, but a muzzle?"

Marcus started to roll her window up from his side, and Jake turned, walking away.

She yelled out the window before it closed shut, "Thanks again!" She faced Marcus, still smiling.

He shook his head. "Why are you doing that to him? Are you really that horny?"

She giggled. "Come on! You can't tell me that's not a satisfying reaction. And you—I've already told you how cute you are when you're frustrated or blushing." She winked.

"You'll be the death of me," he said in that same exasperated tone he always used when she teased, the one that had a hint of a smile to it, like he secretly enjoyed it. "Let's get on the road."

She grabbed his free hand after he shifted into drive, ready for their first mini road trip.

Marcus and Leah made good time arriving at their rendezvous point, which was just shy of an hour's drive. They parked at a diner and went inside, texting the Ivy girl they'd arranged to meet. Leah was a ball of nerves, more anxious with each minute that ticked by. She was excited to meet another Ivy, but terrified of having to let someone in on her secret. Or at least the tip of the iceberg that Marcus knew about.

A tall girl with short blonde hair approached their booth. "It's Marcus, right?" She squinted.

"Yes. Kara?"

The girl nodded, sliding in. She didn't even acknowledge Leah, instead intently focused on Marcus. "You're *the* Marcus, right? I didn't realize that's who I was meeting today!"

Leah glanced between the two. Kara was positively giddy, mouth agape, fangirling over her boyfriend.

Marcus looked uncomfortable. "Just Marcus."

Kara closed her mouth. "But I'm right, right? You're Sir Guillen's son?"

'Sir'? What's that supposed to mean? Is that like 'Mr.' in the Green Lands? Or is that some kind of proper title?

Marcus cleared his throat, sitting straight. "Yes. But I'd rather not discuss my family, if that's okay."

Kara swallowed. "Yes. Of course. Sorry, I'm being rude."

The waitress dropped by. "Would you like to add to your order?"

"We already ate on the way here, but I've got the bill. Did you want to eat anything?" Marcus offered.

Kara pointed at the lemonades they'd started sipping. "I ate too, but I'll take one of those."

Marcus smiled at the waitress. "We won't be here long, so if you could bring the check with it, that would be great."

Once she left, Kara perked up, placing her hands on the table. "So ... what's up?"

Marcus slid his arm around Leah. "This is my girlfriend, Leah." The girls exchanged 'hellos' before Marcus continued quietly in the noisy room. "She's like you. And we need help on something I can't do, because, well ... if you know who I am, then you understand."

"Right. Yeah." Kara furrowed her brow. "But what can I possibly help with?"

The waitress brought a lemonade and their check.

Leah shredded her straw wrapper, tying it into knots over and over. This was all so awkward.

"It's a little unconventional," Marcus said. "So, we'd need you to be discreet, and keep this between us."

Leah leaned forward. "My parents have some weird rules, is all. It's not a huge deal, it's just embarrassing, you know?"

Marcus gently rubbed Leah's back. "Can you teach her how to rift?"

Kara raised an eyebrow, taking a sip of her drink. "You don't know how to rift?"

Leah bit her lip. "Like I said, kinda stupid and embarrassing. I know how to use, you know," she held up her wrists, "for other stuff, but they didn't let me learn rifting."

"But why?" Kara appeared thoroughly confused. As Marcus had taught Leah, any other Ivy would have learned a decade ago, at the latest. And wouldn't likely be in the human world without having created their own rift to get there in the first place.

"Just trying to keep things simple. It's not like we're asking for help with the *illegal* kind," Marcus stressed. "And we have a tight deadline. We've got today and next Saturday."

Kara nodded knowingly. "The big wedding?"

Marcus confirmed with a nod of his own.

Kara shrugged. "I've never taught someone before, but I'll do my best. We better get going."

They took a final sip of their drinks as Marcus left a few crisp bills on the table. Having scouted the location with online maps beforehand, they left on foot for a nearby walking trail.

"How are you liking your foreign exchange year?" Leah asked.

Kara smiled. "It's fun. I'm really glad I got to come. What about you guys? And did you meet here, or back home?"

"Loving it here." Marcus squeezed Leah's hand. "And we met here."

"Neat. What region are you from, Leah?" Kara asked.

"South. Not far from the palace." Marcus had already drawn her a map showing her roughly where major landmarks were, so she wouldn't be in the dark.

"Cool. I'm way north," Kara said.

"How about your Garden Club? What's it like at your school?" Marcus asked.

Kara swung her arms. "It's really nice. Two guys, another girl. I'm the only Ivy. The other girl's a Seeder Boman, and the guys are standard Seeders."

Leah cringed. "How does it feel to be outnumbered?"

Kara chuckled. "I don't know? It would be cool to have another Ivy, I suppose, so it's fun to make a new friend." She gave Leah an encouraging smile. "What about your school?"

"Just a couple others," Marcus said. "Another Ivy Boman, though he's a permanent resident on this side. And another Ivy."

Kara's eyebrows scrunched as they cut off of the path, out into the woods. "She wouldn't teach you?"

Leah rolled her eyes. "He. And he's a jerk."

Kara reached for one of her dangly earrings, straightening it. "It happens. I'm glad to help."

Chapter 18

Arriving at an area with fallen trees and large boulders, the group stopped for the training session.

"Since I'm not much use with this part, I'm going to patrol and keep an eye out for any humans who might stumble off the path and see something they shouldn't," Marcus said. He gave Leah an encouraging squeeze on the shoulders before heading off.

Kara and Leah sat down on fallen logs. "So, you said you know other Ivy stuff, just not rifting?" Kara asked.

"Yeah." Leah carefully extended a vine, glancing around. It was so foreign to show it off without being scolded or fearing being caught. "I've got down maneuvering them." She grasped a pebble, picking it up and chucking it to the side. "And flexing the leaves to be sharp." She did as she'd practiced, flexing and swinging her vine with enough force to have a couple of leaves stick into the log next to her. "And then, you know, the chemical stuff."

Kara nodded. "Okay. Just not rifting?"

Leah shrank with embarrassment. "Yeah."

"Right. No problem." Kara moved, sitting next to Leah. "I'm right-handed, so I always use that vine. And the rifting channel is the central one."

Leah froze, her heart beating faster. It was like meeting the Garden Club all over again. Terminology she'd never heard, trying to pretend she wasn't completely in the dark. "Right. That makes sense. The central channel for rifting?"

"Yeah. Between the numbing and growth channels."

Leah stared blankly at the ground.

"Um... Well, maybe we should talk more about that..." Kara addressed the elephant in the room. "What chemicals have you been trained on?"

Leah frowned, meeting Kara's gaze. "Please don't judge me. Or say anything. I ... guess you could say I'm homeschooled on Ivy stuff. And I didn't have a very thorough teacher."

Kara chuckled. "It can be our secret. Does Marcus not know about that part, either?"

Leah shrugged. "We don't really talk about the abilities like that."

"I've never dated a Boman, but I can see how that might be tough."

Leah furrowed her brow. "Why would it be tough? You wouldn't date a Boman?"

"Oh, no. I'd date one. I've never actually had a boyfriend. But, you know, just the differences between you."

"Do people care that much about Bomen not having vines and green-folk energy?"

Kara grinned. "I guess it depends on who you hang out with. And if we're talking about PG topics or not."

Leah remembered her and Marcus's close call in the intimacy department. Marcus had admitted there was a difference, but had never elaborated. "What's different?"

Kara blinked, a look of embarrassment crossing her face. "That's probably a conversation to have with Marcus. And we should focus on rifting, right?"

Leah straightened her posture. "Right."

"What do you know about the chemical arts?" Kara asked.

"A poison? Haven't really practiced, though."

"Basic self-defense poison?"

"I guess so?"

Kara rubbed her hands together. "Alright. Imagine a multilane highway between your mind and the vine you're trying to activate. There are different lanes, or channels, we'd normally be trained on. Things like numbing, coagulation, various levels of poisons, fertilizers, and so on. Of course, some are really advanced, and everyone has different skill sets, so don't feel bad if you don't know them all."

Leah appreciated her kind reassurance.

"The one we really care about right now is the central channel. In a way, it's hidden under what you know for the self-defense poison. That kind of poison is a crude combination of the others. So, if you reach underneath, there's a central channel that's easy to find for rifting. That's the one that goes both ways, working in tandem with your target to open the space."

Leah closed her eyes, imagining all of these channels. She thought she maybe, perhaps, could sense it. "What do I do with it?"

Kara pointed to a small mushroom. "Extend a vine. See if you can detect the connection between that channel and the mushroom."

Leah followed her direction, feeling a hint of warmth, or clarity. It was amazing to awaken this part of her. "I think I get it."

Kara smiled. "Great. From here, it's pretty tricky. My understanding is tree rifts are a lot more intuitive because you can pull that energy from the tree. Cave rifts are a different thing altogether."

Leah choked down her anger. *The stupid murderous queen took the more natural route from her people. Sure, that makes sense.* "Right. A rock isn't living ... so how does that work if we can't connect?"

"It takes a lot more concentration, but it's not supposed to be as draining as it used to be, since all modern caves in the network are jade-enhanced."

No idea what that means, but okay... Leah drew a deep breath. "Just tell me what I need to do."

Kara coached Leah on connecting to a few more small plants. They moved to the downed trees, which were no longer alive, but still had wisps of that living energy. Touching a rock did nothing for Leah; it was literally like trying to communicate with a brick wall. She tried time and time again. Frustrated and feeling a real energy drain for the first time in her life, Leah took a short break.

"You know Marcus's family?" Leah took a swig from a water bottle she'd brought.

"No, I've never met any of them."

"But they're a pretty big deal, right?" Leah tried her luck.

Kara gave her the same almost-incredulous look Jake had given her before. "Do you really not know who his parents are?"

Leah swallowed hard. "Of course I do. Sir Guillen, right? I guess I was just curious if you knew if they *acted* like a big deal, you know—stuck up."

Kara fiddled with her earring again. "Not from what I've heard. But you never really know with public figures, right?"

Right... Public figures. Important enough to have a queen attend their son's wedding. Leah kept the other thousands of questions to herself, having already given away too much about her lack of training and Green Lands knowledge.

They got back to practicing with boulders, Leah trying to push her energy down her extended vine. Marcus checked in on them. "How goes it?"

"I think she's promising." Kara smiled.

Leah threw a discouraged frown at Marcus.

"Anything I can do to help?" he asked.

"Actually, do you keep your personal jade on you?" Kara asked. "Maybe we can somehow use it to enhance her training, like the caves do?"

"Couldn't hurt to try." He sat on a large stump, pulling off a shoe and working off an anklet with a square green stone strung in the middle. "Just be careful. Make sure I get that back." He handed it to Kara while looking at Leah. "I checked with Jake. Everything's fine, but we should probably leave in the next fifteen to twenty minutes."

Leah's heart dropped into her gut. She was nowhere close to accomplishing anything worthwhile. "Okay."

Marcus left to go patrol the perimeter again.

"What are we supposed to do with that?" Leah asked.

Kara studied the stone. "Honestly, I don't know. I just figured it wouldn't hurt? Let's put it around your wrist and keep trying."

They tried for another fifteen minutes without any notable progress. Marcus returned, marking the end of their training session. He came up behind Leah, massaging her shoulders. "So, what do we think?"

Leah sighed. "Kara's been doing great. I just don't even know what it's supposed to feel like."

He wrapped his arms around her from behind, resting his chin on her shoulder.

Kara frowned. "Sorry. I tried my best."

"Could you meet up again for another hour next week?" Marcus asked. "I can pay you, pay for your gas money, all that."

Kara waved a dismissive hand in the air. "I don't need your money. But I can make some time next week, no problem."

Leah felt a smidge of hope. "Thank you so much, seriously."

The group walked back to their parked vehicles, finalizing plans for the next week. Kara encouraged Leah to practice what they'd been covering before their next meeting. Marcus and Leah hopped in his truck, getting on the road without delay.

"You seem pretty frustrated," he said.

"Yeah, well, I am." Her head was swimming, and she genuinely didn't know if it was from frustration or Ivy energy drain.

"Was it helpful at all?"

She leaned her head back. "Maybe. It's humbling, that's for sure."

"You could try to look at it as an exciting new step? Pretty cool to learn to master your powers, taste your potential."

She appreciated his sweet attempts to reassure her. And it wasn't like she had much room to complain about learning to use her powers, when he hadn't been born with any. She still felt defeated. "What's our backup plan? Are there any other options to open a rift if I can't get it?"

"The only thing I can think of … is the employed gatekeepers would understand if your energy was too low. But that's a stretch, considering how little it takes for someone who's rifted for half their life."

"How would my energy be used up?"

"If you used up several strands of vines and expended a lot of chemicals."

She laughed. "So, our backup plan is to make me look like a serial killer that ties people up and poisons them?"

He chuckled. "Yeah, I guess so." He reached out his hand, and she took it. "Things will work out."

She looked down at her wrist; his anklet was still there. "I'll do my best." She smiled at the stone. "Is this like wearing your boyfriend's letterman jacket?"

He stole a peek. "Not quite. I'll want that back as soon as we return."

"No one's mentioned this. What's special about it?"

"It's used more in Seeder culture, and by Bomen in both nations. Regular Ivies rarely use jade, other than in the boosted caves."

"What do you use it for?"

"Even with help, I can't get through a rift without it."

"Oh." She gently stroked the stone, noting the swirl carved into it on one side. "Then I'll definitely make sure you get it back. When are other ways it's used in the kingdom?"

"Community coordinators use jade, and if you're in the palace."

She glanced at him. "Have you personally been in the palace?"

His mouth hung open for a moment. "Yes."

"You really don't like talking about your family and their connections? Not even with me? Kara called your dad 'Sir Guillen,' what was that about?"

He sighed, checking his blind spot and switching lanes. "I'd just like you to meet them first."

"That's kind of … odd, though. That you're keeping that from me."

He frowned. "I'm not keeping it from you. I just… You don't like accepting help; I don't like talking about them."

Fair enough. Not like I'm sharing important details about my own family. "Would you at least explain why the queen will be at the wedding? That's pretty intimidating, to be honest. You said your dad had connections to help us get through the caves. Kara acted like your family's famous. I don't want to look like an idiot."

He hesitated. "Whether people like them or not, my parents played a big part in the war. My mom does a little of this and that now, but my dad still does a lot of work in policy and Bomen rights. He reports directly to the queen."

Leah's eyes grew wide. "Does he like his job?"

"Yeah. He likes helping people. He's done a lot of good for Bomen. Both of my parents have."

"Does that mean they're politicians?"

He huffed. "Tip of the iceberg of why I don't like talking about this kind of stuff. It's not like they're corrupt human politicians, you know. They're good people. And even though the war ended almost two decades ago, there's still a lot of mixed opinions. Just like how some people don't agree with my parents being in a mixed-race relationship, or my Seeder mom being allowed to adopt Ivy Bomen." He shook his head. "It's complicated. I just want you to get to know them for who they are without any preconceived notions. Is that so bad?"

Marcus had explained Seeders and their limitations, that it wasn't possible, even back then, for Marcus's Seeder mom to flee the Green Lands with his Ivy Boman dad. Seeder women, after their powers came in during their teenage years, 'rooted' in the realm, and couldn't survive in the human world long-term after that. Now, Leah was even more excited to meet this 'Sir Guillen' who'd chosen not to flee the Green Lands like Jake's parents had. It wasn't just for his love of his wife; he'd been brave enough to stay behind in the chaos brought by Queen Kaylah's reign, to fight for his people's rights.

Leah squeezed Marcus's hand. "They raised you. You love each other. And if they're making things better for Bomen, then I'm a fan." She paused, wanting to reassure him she wasn't trying to be a social climber. "But not a creepy superfan." She winked at him when he glanced over with an appreciative smile.

Chapter 19

Marcus and Leah arrived at the movie theater just in time as the movie was ending, getting out of the truck to stretch their legs. Leah handed Marcus back his jade anklet, and he slipped it on as a bracelet.

Jake and Emily emerged from the theater. "Hey, what are the odds of seeing you two?" Emily said. "What movie are you guys coming to see?"

Leah did her part to distract Emily as Jake slipped Leah's phone to Marcus. "We haven't decided yet. It looked like there's a couple of good ones."

Emily adjusted her glasses, smiling. "We should double sometime!"

"Yeah," Marcus said. "We were going to see if you guys wanted to do dinner and a movie together next Saturday."

"I'll have to check with my mom first. But pencil us in, you two." Leah smiled as Jake pointedly narrowed his eyes.

"I'm free," Emily said.

Jake glanced between Marcus and Leah. "We'll talk."

Jake and Emily drove off, and Marcus turned to Leah with a smile. "It worked."

She pulled him into a hug. "Our plan to get training worked. The training, not so much. All the other steps, I guess we'll see."

He stepped back, holding her at arm's length. "One step at a time. How about you text your mom and let her know we're capping off our date night with some ice cream?"

After driving to a nearby ice cream shop, Marcus parked in the far corner.

Leah smirked. "Are we actually getting ice cream?"

He grinned. "We can get some to go, can't we? It's been two weeks since we've had time to just chill together. Is that so bad?"

"I won't argue with that."

They ordered shakes to go and reconvened in the back seat of the truck. "I missed you," she said, leaning against him.

He set his shake down in a cup holder, wrapping his arms around her, caressing her neck with his lips. "I missed you too."

She giggled. "Not wasting any time."

"How do you feel about hickies?" he asked.

She faced him, surprised. "Really?"

"Yeah." He bit his lip.

She studied his face. "I'm actually not a fan."

Marcus blushed. "That's fine."

"Why do you want one?"

"Just kind of thought it was sexy. You know, if we each had one."

She wrinkled her nose. "I don't love the whole 'marking your territory' or bragging kind of stigma that comes along with it."

He furrowed his brow. "No. I didn't mean it like that. It wouldn't be visible. I wouldn't want you in trouble with your mom or anything."

She set her shake down, wearing a mile-wide grin. "Not visible? Where were you going to ask to put it?"

He tapped on his knee, looking down. "I don't know. I, um … just…"

She lifted his chin. "Sometimes, you are so shy."

He let out a breathy chuckle. "I thought, like, under your shirt, but you know, you'd still have your bra on."

She beamed. "I *am* corrupting you, aren't I?"

He rolled his eyes. "No. I'm just happy with you."

She took his hand. "How about this? When you decide you're ready for *everything*, we'll revisit those hickies."

He nodded with a shy smile. "Okay."

She swallowed, ready to add to his awkwardness. "What's different about a Boman in the sex department?"

His knee nervously bounced. "I'm not a green-folk sex-ed teacher … but I guess you deserve to know."

She'd already learned a little of this and that, but not too many specifics. "Yeah … I mean … I don't think there's anything different about me from a normal girl, 'cause…" Their eyes met.

"Because you've been with a human guy, and he didn't freak out?"

She looked down, her face warming. "Yes."

"Then you know what it's like to be with a Boman. In those essentials, we're the same. Though ... um, even if the person you were with didn't say anything..." He dodged eye contact this time. "Well, they say Ivy girls are better than human girls. But that could just be talk."(o)

She bit her lip, nodding slowly. She'd never had complaints from the guys she'd slept with, but she didn't want to dwell on them right now, and she was perfectly happy with Marcus assuming it had only been one. It wasn't like the count reached the dozen Tanner had flippantly accused her of.

Truthfully, though, there had been far more regret and pain with each of them, than happy memories. Each of them had started with hope, or at least a desire to numb some part of herself. Each had soured in some way—earning her a reputation, trauma, a bucket of distrust, a stalker, or the inability to look her mom in the eyes for a month. There was an irony somewhere there, that her relationship with Marcus had only started to help her reach a goal, that she never would have pursued him if she hadn't come up with a harebrained idea to assassinate a queen in another realm.

But Leah *really* didn't want to focus on past experiences right now. Not now. Not ever. "But you admitted there's something different between regular Ivies and Bomen in that regard."

He scratched the back of his neck. "Ivy guys are different. Let's just say ... normal green-folk guys..." Even his ears were turning red as he cleared his throat. "Well, guys talk. Either stuff is really great, or if they're trying to do things so a human girl doesn't recognize ... it's just not very enjoyable ... to hide what you really are. And Ivy to Ivy, like Seeder to Seeder, there's even a difference, because your body recognizes the compatibility."(p)

She wanted to know more, but it was obvious he wasn't comfortable. "I guess I don't need *all* the details. I'm not dating any of the other kinds, right?"

An embarrassed but relieved smile crossed his face. "Right."

She twisted her lips. "Is it weird at all for you? The differences? 'Cause girls really don't care about that part of it. They care about who it's with and how it's done. And I think you're perfect the way you are."

He gently tucked her hair behind her ears. "I think it's normal to compare yourself, but I'd like to think I'm confident in myself in that way. And I appreciate your vote of confidence."

She moved over, sitting on his lap. He wrapped his arms around her.

"In what ways *aren't* you confident in yourself?" she asked.

"Hmm. The usual stuff. Or maybe there's no such thing. But fear that I won't be successful. Fear that I won't be judged on my own merits. What about you? Where would you say you lack confidence?"

She looked into the distance, out of the truck window, turning inward. "That I'll make stupid decisions. That I'll disappoint people." She frowned. "I'd say I do a good job at proving both of those are legitimate shortcomings."

He squeezed her tighter. "We're all works in progress."

She gazed into his soft brown eyes. "Yeah, we are." She leaned forward, caressing his lips with her own. He slid a hand up to the nape of her neck, reciprocating. His lips met hers time and time again, in perfect synchrony. Eventually, Leah's phone pulled them apart.

Leah calmed her breathing before answering. "Hi, Mom. Yes, we're just finishing up at the ice cream shop."

Marcus grabbed his shake and noisily slurped up the partially melted portion of it.

She winked in appreciation of the background noise. "Sure, we can do that. Okay. Love you."

Leah hung up the phone. "Mind if we swing by the grocery store on the way home?"

He squeezed her knee with his hand. "Fine with me. Do you know if there's train tracks between here and there?"

"I don't know."

He grinned. "Then maybe she won't know, either. How long does it take to get stuck behind a train?"

Leah giggled. "I guess a few minutes." She leaned in, kissing some more.

Leah returned home with eggs and a gallon of milk. She took them straight to the kitchen to put them away before stopping by her mom's room. "I'm back." She leaned in the doorway.

"Thank you for swinging by the store. You were good?"

Leah rolled her eyes. "You should assume I'm being good for as long as I date Marcus. He's a good guy. I feel like a broken record."

Her mom sat on her bed, patting a space next to her. Leah joined her, sitting cross-legged and leaning back against the headboard.

"You really like this one, huh?"

Leah grinned. "Yeah. How did you know it was love with my dad?"

Her mom's eyes grew wide. "Love? Marcus?"

Leah's cheeks warmed. "I'm not saying that. I'm asking about *you* guys."

Her mom hummed softly. "It's so rarely in one instance that it happens, or that you know. At least that's what I think. When is it flattery or infatuation? And when is it the real deal?"

Leah smiled; she loved hearing about her dad. About her parents together. "Was he your first?"

"Yes, he was."

"Were you his?"

"Mmm, no."

"Did that bother you guys?"

"Are we talking about me and your father? Or you and Marcus?"

"I can't just ask questions?"

Her mom gently poked her arm. "Just because a guy doesn't sleep with you, doesn't mean he's perfect."

"I wasn't bringing up Marcus. We talked about Marcus. I changed the topic to my dad." Leah rolled her eyes again. "And it's a bit hypocritical of you, you know. It's not like you waited until you were married."

Her mom sighed. "Not hypocritical. Wanting you to learn from my mistakes."

Leah turned to face her mom, brow furrowed. "He was a mistake?"

"No! I didn't mean it that way. Your father wasn't a mistake. Becoming sexually active so young just complicates things."

Leah raised her eyebrows. "You never specified *how young* you were when you started."

Her mom cleared her throat. "That doesn't really matter for either of us at this point."

Leah looked down in thought. "Was I an accident?"

"Why would you think that, sweetheart?"

Leah shrugged. "I don't know. Just a question. If you knew he was going to die, would you have held off on getting pregnant?"

Her mom shook her head. "Never question that. You weren't an accident. And you're that piece of him I have left. I would never give you up." She smoothed the bedding. "It wasn't the best timing; I'll give you that. We were just starting our reign, and our family, in a chaotic war. We didn't realize it would end so soon."

Leah scooted closer to her mom. "What's it like in the palace?" She thought of what Marcus had said about the palace using the jade stone, whereas most Ivies didn't use it for anything. She wanted to ask more about it but couldn't think of any questions that wouldn't give away she knew too much.

"Mmm, the palace. So beautiful. I loved the stained glass windows. A lot of fond memories in that place from our dating." Her voice faded off in a melancholy whisper. "Until it all ended."

Leah felt a pang of guilt. "I'm sorry about Cheryl leaving. Did you guys reminisce about the Green Lands much?"

"Not really. Not for a long time." She nudged Leah. "I like talking to *you* about it now."

Leah smiled. It truly did sound so foreign, so majestic there. The realm was eternally spring.

"Oh yeah, and my favorite room." Her mom perked up. "It's called the Queen's Room. So unique, vines everywhere. Very peaceful."

"Is there a King's Room too?"

"Mmm, no."

"What happens in the Queen's Room?"

Her mom smirked. "What did prior generations do? Or what did your father and I do?"

Leah arched an eyebrow. "For the love... I appreciate that we can have mature conversations, but I think we're stepping over the parent-child line here."

Her mom chuckled. "We were newlyweds. Don't judge us!"

Done with all the sex talk for the day, Leah was ready to move on, focusing on something that had genuinely bothered her earlier. "You taught me that poison stuff, with my vines. Is there anything else I can do?" Kara had described *several* channels. Why would her mom be keeping them a secret? What else was she hiding?

"Not that I'm aware of. Of course, I wasn't a nurse or soldier. It was just standard training. And I'm sure I'm a bit rusty."

It sounded like an honest reply; Leah would ask Kara more the next weekend. "How's it going, trying to get more hours at work?"

Her mom averted her gaze. "I'll figure it out."

"I mean it when I say I could get a job to help."

"No. It's my responsibility to take care of you."

Leah looked her mom in the eyes. "I'm old enough. I'll be eighteen next year. You know I'm practically an adult, right? And that someday you'll have to let me go?"

Her mom frowned again, looking down into her lap. "I'll take care of things."

Leah studied her, frowning as well. What would her mom be, if left alone? She'd had her husband, homeland, and all the rest of her family and friends taken from her. She didn't deserve it. Leah also feared her mom might never really be able to let her go.

Chapter 20

Marcus went to Leah's house the next day, because her mom had asked for Marcus to come over more often. Since Leah's house was so much smaller than that of his grandparents, they did a lot more whispering and cuddling than having open discussions and kissing. Marcus let her know he'd confirmed with Jake that they'd repeat the phone exchange the next weekend. Jake wasn't excited to be involved in keeping secrets, but he begrudgingly agreed to help his friends one more time.

"I'll need to spend as much time as possible practicing trying to rift," she said as they snuggled in her living room.

"Does that mean I won't be seeing as much of you this week?" Marcus asked.

"I still have homework to do. And I'm pretty sure your place is a better option for concealing activity." She smiled. "But if you want to go hang out with other friends, I get it. I'm sure it would be boring to watch me try to figure it out."

He squeezed her hand. "We'll see. I don't know if you've noticed, but I like spending time with you."

Her cheeks warmed. "Okay. How are we feeling about everything else?"

He rocked his head back and forth. "We'll see about the rifting. The biggest thing other than that is making sure your mom lets you go. I think we can count on my dad understanding." He scrunched his face. "At least I hope so. I *really* hope this works out. I'm getting pretty excited."

"Me too. But I'm going to be relying on you to help make it look like I'm not a complete noob over there." He'd explained the wedding would be taking place in Capital City in the Green Lands—neutral territory crawling with Seeders, Ivies, and Bomen from both nations.

He leaned closer, nuzzling her neck. "I've got your back."

She giggled.

Leah loved learning her new abilities. Being able to sense the life in simple vegetation around her was nothing short of astounding. The evening before their second meetup with Kara, Leah and Marcus had an after-school picnic at a little park. With the area empty, Leah did some practicing. She almost wondered if she was at a level where she could attempt a tree rift, able to sense a balance in living things. Touching her vine to a rock still felt useless.

"Want to borrow this, m'lady?" Marcus handed her his jade anklet.

She smiled, taking it from him. "M'lady?"

He made a silly face.

She was about to put it around her wrist, then decided to try something different. "If the caves are jade-enhanced, maybe having it in contact with the rock is more helpful than in contact with my skin." She wrapped the anklet around the rock she'd been practicing on, then extended a short tendril, trying to push her energy down the lower central channel in her mind. She physically and mentally poked at the rock. The rock blocked her energy, stubborn and immovable.

She sighed. *This is a waste of time. If I knew the locations for tree rifting and how to get around...*

Marcus knelt behind her, holding her in his arms. "We've still got a week. Don't stress so much."

Leah closed her eyes, allowing her muscles to relax. She savored the warmth of his embrace, and envisioned the warmth of the energy of the Green Lands as Marcus had described it. Not just a temperature warmth, but a richness that flowed in the realm, the source that fueled all green-folk powers. Extending her tendril again, she touched the rock, exerting pressure and focusing on the path her energy was taking. The energy hit the rock, but didn't immediately bounce back. Like a spark of flint over a campfire, a trace of energy jumped past.

Her eyes shot open. "Something happened!"

"Really?" he whispered excitedly.

"Yeah, let me try that again." She sat straighter, this time doing it with her eyes open. There was no visible spark or glow, but something passed from her. It was just an inkling, into the unknown void. It had no direction or destination, but there was *something*. She grinned, her heart beating a mile a minute. "I don't know if it's enough, but something's definitely different."

"That's awesome." He squeezed her tight, his arms still around her. "You're amazing."

She leaned back in his arms. "I think you were right. That some of it was in my head." She blew out a puff of air. "Now the question is, will you be able to hold me like this so I'm calm enough to do it at the cave?"

He gently kissed her cheek. "I wish. But every second before and after that, I'm there for you."

She tried a few more times. Pushing out the stress of lies. The worry of her mom's job. The pain of her family problems. And it seemed to work. Further attempts didn't yield anything bigger, though she wasn't disappointed—she'd hardly expected a giant rift to open with beginner techniques using the enhanced equivalent of a caveman's power saw that she'd created by simply strapping the jade to the rock.

Taking a break from her exertion, she lay on the picnic blanket with Marcus, pointing out shapes in the clouds as they drifted by.

"I'm really proud of you," he said.

"Thanks." She smiled. "I think we should be optimistic ... but also realistic. This is going to take a lot of things to line up to get me over like we're planning."

He sucked in a long breath and let it out slowly. "Like your mom's approval?"

"Actually... I wanted to surprise you, but I guess I don't know why I was waiting..."

He rolled over to face her. "She said 'yes'?!"

Leah grinned wide. "Yes. She agreed I've been doing good, that I've earned it." She rolled onto her side and gave him a peck on the lips, moving a hand up and playing with one of his curls. "And she's seen how good you are. And how good you are for me."

He smiled, then it faded. "Kind of makes me feel worse, knowing we're lying to her."

She frowned. "She lied to me my whole life, and is keeping me from there, though, right?"

He pursed his lips. "You're right. You told her it's in Detroit?"

"Yeah. Don't worry. I've got everything worked out. My phone will have an 'unfortunate accident' so she can't track me. And I have an old friend who's going to fake some emails to keep in touch."

He furrowed his brow. "Is it enough? What's going to happen if you get caught in this lie?"

"A decent grounding. But it's worth the risk."

Concern was painted on his face. "But you said before that you moved here because she didn't approve of, well ... stuff in your past. You don't think she'd lose it and make you move again, do you?"

"No. I've lived all my life with her. I can gauge her reactions. Just trust me, okay?"

He interlaced their fingers. "Okay."

Leah forced a smile as her stomach knotted tighter. That was all a lie. Her mom, of course, had said no. But that didn't mean Leah hadn't come up with a plan. A plan that *had* to work. "Everything will fall into place."

He gazed at her lovingly. "It will." After a moment, he sat up. "Do you want to go back to your place?"

"No. Let's go to yours." *Have to keep them apart to prevent the stories from unraveling. One more week.*

The next afternoon was a repeat of the previous Saturday. Jake gave a stern reminder at the initial phone handoff that he wasn't doing any more favors like this, and Leah decided to keep her teasing to herself. The drive to the rendezvous was nice, and Kara was right on time. Leah explained her practice and progress to Kara as they walked to a well-concealed training area.

"That's brilliant," Kara said. "I hoped the jade might help, but it makes more sense to put it on the element you're using. If jade was capable of magnifying our powers, I'm sure every Ivy out there would be wearing it."

Leah nodded thoughtfully, a question coming to her mind that she tucked away for later.

They reached their training spot, and Marcus surrendered his jade for them to practice. "I'm going to go make sure no one wanders down this path. Probably for the best you practice without me." He winked.

It took Leah a while to clear her mind properly and get back to the place she had been the day before. "How do I even know this is the right thing? How will we know when I'm good enough and doing it right to open a cave rift?"

Kara winced. "Honestly, I'm not sure. This is kinda hypothetical." She furrowed her brow. "Let me try what you're describing and compare it to how a rift feels."

Kara extended a tendril, pressing it against the rock with the jade strapped to it. She stared off into the distance; it didn't look like she was even doing anything. After a moment, she nodded, facing Leah with a smile. "I see what you mean. That's kind of cool. I think you're on the right track."

Leah's heart lit with hope. "You think I could make it?"

Kara shrugged shyly. "I want to say yes. But you won't really know until you go to try it in the right place."

Leah glanced around, making sure Marcus wasn't approaching to check in. "I don't want you to take this the wrong way, but I was wondering about tree rifting. It doesn't seem like such a big thing to me."

Kara's eyes grew wide. "That's illegal."

"I know. Don't get me wrong. I guess I was thinking ... like a trial run. I didn't think it was such a big deal." She was getting increasingly annoyed by everyone's shock at such a simple request. It wasn't like she was asking for help robbing a bank.

Kara shook her head. "It's legal if it's on your own private property. But most people still don't do it. And you'd have to know the name for your departure and arrival points. I'm assuming you know your arrival point, but..." She gestured at the trees around them. "I couldn't tell you how to do it from a random place like this. They say it's intuitive, but I had to have the program coordinator help me with the names of places around my exchange-host home and school, for an emergency exit. I don't know how to do that myself."

Leah sighed. *Why can't this be easier?* She didn't know departure *or* arrival names. You couldn't rift without these names, the GPS code words associated with each rifting location in the human world and Green Lands. "Thanks for explaining. Please don't mention that to Marcus or anyone else. It was just hypothetical, you know?"

Kara read Leah's face. "Yeah. No prob."

Leah decided to push her luck a smidge more. "You know the jade thing, how it amplifies energy in some ways?"

Kara nodded.

"I've heard there's some in the palace. Do you know what it does?"

Kara looked surprised. "That's kinda cool. Didn't know that. Did Marcus tell you that?"

Crap. Worse than Marcus finding out, would be a royal fangirl gossiping about a politician's son's know-nothing girlfriend blabbing about something the public didn't know. Leah didn't need a spotlight turned on her. She shook her head. "No. Don't remember where I heard that. Maybe it's just a rumor."

Kara nodded like she bought it. "I could see it being true, though. Maybe it amplifies the energy at the palace in some way."

Leah's eyes rested on the jade. *Energy meaning power.* If the palace was somehow enhanced, was that part of why her dad had died? Along with his throne, his sister had decided it was something worth killing for?

At the end of the training session, they returned the jade to Marcus, and Kara offered to stay in touch in case they needed more help or to hang out another time.

Marcus stressed how proud he was of Leah as he started the truck. Leah's mind was focused elsewhere. Web of lies? It felt more like a *tornado* of lies—a messy whirlwind that would someday spit her out without an ounce of mercy. She stared out the window on the ride back home, listing them all. Lies to her mom, to Marcus, to Jake, and maybe even to herself, just to name a few.

"Leah?"

She blinked, looking at Marcus. "Yeah?"

He raised his eyebrows. "You okay?"

"Yeah, just kind of out of it."

"I asked if you wanted to meet up with Jake and Emily for ice cream after we get back. A thank you to Jake. A celebration for you." He smiled.

She squeezed his hand. "Yeah, let's do that."

"Are you worried?" he asked.

"About what?"

"Creating a rift? Going over?"

She adjusted her seat. "Maybe that's what's bothering me. What are we going to do if they realize we're lying at the cave? What kind of trouble can we get in?"

"Don't stress so much. My dad will either cave, or he won't." He laughed. "Pun not intended. Anyway, I doubt he'd know we're lying." He huffed. "Gosh, I sound like a horrible person. He's not naïve, you know. He's just trusting, and likes to give people the benefit of the doubt. And coming from me..."

She frowned. "I'm sorry I'm making you lie to your dad."

He glanced over. "Are you twisting my arm? If it ever came out, I think he'd understand in the long run why we're doing this. He definitely believes in sticking up for people who've been wronged."

Leah nodded with a half-smile. His dad was standing up for Bomen rights during Leah's aunt's corrupt regime. Of course, he'd understand that her mom keeping her from her home realm was wrong.

"As for the cave employees," Marcus continued, "I think at most, they'd be confused as to why you couldn't properly open a rift alone. They wouldn't jump to any conclusions about you being some sort of outlaw or something." He chuckled. "Are you good at fake crying?"

"Um... I could practice?"

"Couldn't hurt to say you hit your head or give them some tears about being so stressed out your powers weren't working right. You know, like getting out of a speeding ticket. Just as a backup plan." He squeezed her hand. "And ... if worse comes to worse, and you get denied, we'll survive. It would really suck, but you could apply for your passport on your eighteenth birthday. You don't need your mom's signature or approval at that point."

True. It wasn't ideal, though. "What's needed for a Green Lands passport?"

"The standard stuff. Parent names, place and date of birth to prove green-folk heritage. Maybe a background check?"

Leah's heart dropped. Her eighteenth birthday didn't matter. She'd *never* own a passport. The corrupt regime would never allow that. She'd only be putting a neon sign over their heads announcing where she and her mom could be found. She literally had to rely on their plan for the wedding, or—someday, somehow—figure out tree rifting if she wanted to experience the Green Lands for herself.

Her mind wandered, remembering something Tanner had once said. Her mom hadn't talked much about other family beyond Leah's dad. But Tanner had mentioned other siblings to the queen. "The queen has two younger brothers, right?"

Marcus furrowed his brow. "Where'd you hear that? Was Kara gossiping?"

Why does he get so worked up about it? Just because his dad's a politician and deals with the royal family, now I can't ask about anyone remotely related to the queen?

"No. Actually, Tanner mentioned it a while ago. Forever ago. I don't know why it even popped into my mind. I guess I was just wondering about all the people I'm going to meet at the wedding and if they'd be there, too." She gave him a warm smile. "But I promise, I'm not a weirdo like Tanner. I won't kiss the royal family's feet or anything."

Marcus made a comical disgusted face. "I usually avoid kissing *anyone's* feet. Rather unsanitary."

She chuckled.

"Umm, yes. She does have two younger brothers."

"Will they be there?"

He shrugged. "It's not my wedding. I haven't tracked the guest list or RSVPs. I'd imagine they were both invited, but I'd only give it a fifty-fifty chance either would show."

"Why is that?"

"Well..." He rocked his head back and forth before changing lanes. "I guess I don't know how much of our history you've gleaned, but things got real ugly with the royal family. Between the queen and her older brother, their parents. The two younger kids got mixed up in all of it. They were pretty young. They're not exactly living in the limelight these days."

"Do they like the queen?"

Marcus laughed again. "I get that you and your mom are pretty close, but you know most adults don't go around confessing their struggles and feelings to teenagers, right? I've met them, but I wouldn't know how close they really are."

Leah nodded. Maybe she'd been looking at this all wrong. Maybe she wasn't just yearning for justice for her dad. Maybe, like her mom, she was yearning for that connection to family. She hoped she would get to meet her uncles at the wedding. Marcus, her uncles, her homeland—that could be enough.

Since they were on the topic, Leah figured she could safely push a smidge more. She didn't remember her mom bringing them up. "The queen's parents, are they still alive?"

"No. They were assassinated in the war."

She struggled to hide a frown. Queen Kaylah had taken her dad *and* her grandparents from her. "Guess that's some serious family drama, huh?"

"You could say that again."

Several miles down the road, Leah still couldn't shake the fact from her head—her aunt had also murdered her own parents. "This Kaylah, she didn't agree with her parents' policies, did she?"

"What? Oh, no. Definitely not."(q)

Chapter 21

Leah and Marcus arrived at the movie theater on time, discreetly getting Leah's phone back from Jake, and heading over to their favorite ice cream joint. It was nice spending normal time with normal people. Though, Leah almost let some green-folk talk slip. She'd gotten so used to being free around the Garden Club that she forgot Emily was a human not in the know. Even as expats like Jake, green folk didn't easily give up their identities and secrets to humans.

After dessert, Leah and Marcus lingered at her doorstep for a few minutes, enjoying each other's company. Leah smirked internally; grateful creepy Cheryl wasn't around to watch them from the window. Leah's mom at least respected their doorstep drop-offs more tastefully, and both Leah and Marcus appreciated those last few minutes together.

Marcus pulled back from their kissing, catching his breath. "One week. Can you believe it?" He tucked her hair behind her ears. "I'm going to have to remember to not steal the focus from the bride and groom by showing you off too much."

She grinned. "I can't even believe this is all real. Less than a year ago, I didn't know that place even existed." She gazed into his eyes. "Or that I could find someone so amazing in every way possible."

After another short smooch, Leah went inside the dark house, turning on lights as she went. She popped into the bathroom to clean up for bed. She paused, listening carefully and furrowing her brow when she heard what sounded like sobbing ... coming from her mom's room.

Concerned, she knocked on her mom's door, then turned the knob. Her mom sat on her bed, now quiet, sopping up her tears with tissues.

"What's wrong?" She'd never seen her like this before.

"Nothing. Don't worry about it." Her mom looked down, blowing her nose.

"This is not nothing." Leah approached the bed, sitting by her mom.

Her mom moved a pillow to make space for her. She had puffy eyes, and wet hair as if she'd just showered, and was already in her silk pajamas for the night.

"Is this about work? Do we have to move again?"

Her mom sniffled. "No. I got that all taken care of."

Leah tilted her head. "That's good, right? You'll just be working later?"

Her mom averted her gaze, shaking her head. "No. I, uh... I asked for a raise. We'll be okay."

Hmm... "Really? Enough to make up for losing Cheryl's income?" That seemed like it would be a significant increase for only having worked there for a few months...

Her mom took her hand. "You let me worry about finances, okay? It's *my* job to take care of us."

Leah nodded. "I love you."

Her mom pulled her in tight, laying her head on Leah's. "I love you too, princess."

Still confused, Leah asked, "If work and money are okay, then why are you crying?"

Her mom finally responded after a long pause. "You know me. I just get too sentimental sometimes."

"My dad?"

"Yeah. Him. Other family. All of it. But I'll be okay. Sorry you had to see me this way."

Their relationship was complex. Sometimes, her mom was her best friend, other times her warden. Sometimes she was ready to go to bat for her daughter, other times she was in denial, or too depressed to handle more. "I'm a good listener, I think."

Her mom kissed her head. "I know, sweetheart."

When her mom didn't start sharing anything, Leah carefully crafted a related inquiry. "I'd love to hear more about your family, and dad's. Would you tell me about them?"

Her mom gave her a gentle smile before obliging. "I had three sisters. I guess I should say *have*... Last I heard, they're all still alive and married with kids."

More family Leah would never know. Aunts, uncles, cousins.

"Sometimes I imagine what it would be like for you to have grown up around cousins." Her voice grew cold, from nostalgic to hurt. "Last time Cheryl checked, my parents were still alive, but not in great health."

Leah frowned, wishing she could check in on them or somehow inquire. "Do you still keep in touch with Cheryl? Even if she doesn't want to live with us, would she be willing to go check things out for you?"

"Let's not count on Cheryl for anything."

Leah's guilt grew. If she'd been better behaved, better tempered... She hadn't thought about how Cheryl was the main go-between for news from the Green Lands. Being an aide to an exiled queen had to make it far less risky to show her face than the actual queen.

"What about my dad's family? His parents? Any other siblings other than the one that ... killed him?"

"His parents died in the war, too. He had two younger brothers."

"What were they like?"

Her mom took a deep breath. "Truthfully, I didn't know his brothers well. Around the time we got engaged, the boys were being taken care of full-time by staff. And his parents... They were interesting people. I don't know that they wholeheartedly approved of me, but they were pleasant."

"Why didn't they approve of you?"

"This and that. I'm sure it didn't help that I was just a lowly peasant. Not exactly lowly, my family had some status. But you know, not close to the royal line."

Leah poked a pillow. "Oh. Then maybe they weren't so great. 'Cause I think you're a fabulous mom."

Her mom wiped her nose again. "Don't think badly of them. They were pleasant to me. I hold no ill will against them." She let out a breathy chuckle. "And they had good taste. Your dad was their favorite, after all."

Leah smiled. "Maybe it's a good thing I'm an only child. I don't have to worry about my parents picking favorites." She loosed a breath. Every moment of warmth and wonder that she enjoyed while learning more about her dad and family was tainted by the bitter taste of the betrayal they'd all suffered. "I still can't believe she killed her brother, uncle, *and* her parents."

After a moment of silence, her mom spoke up. "I'm pretty tired, sweetheart. How about we head to bed early?"

"Okay." Leah gave her a big squeeze.

***

Sunday passed.

Practice rifting.

Keep the lies straight.

Monday passed.

Focus on school. Practice rifting.

Keep the lies straight.

Tuesday passed.

Focus on school. Garden Club. Practice rifting.

Keep the lies straight.

Wednesday passed.

Double-check every aspect of the plan. Focus on school. Practice rifting.

Keep the lies straight.

Thursday passed.

Doubt every aspect of the plan. Double-check every aspect of the plan.

Focus on school. Practice rifting.

Keep the lies straight.

Friday passed.

Try not to freak out. Doubt every aspect of the plan. Double-check every aspect of the plan. Focus on school. Practice rifting.

Keep the lies straight.

And Saturday morning arrived.

Leah woke early. She needed to get things right. She picked out her cutest clothes that wouldn't make her look too conspicuous. Listening intently for the sound of the shower, she began to pen her letter.

I'm sorry to do this to you. I love you. Please, PLEASE don't worry. I'll be safe. This isn't Marcus's fault—I lied to him and his grandparents. They bought the ticket for me already, and it was nonrefundable. I just really wanted to go to the wedding. I know it's wrong to leave like this, but I'm not a little kid. I hope you can forgive me. I'll be back by the end of spring break, and I'm willing to face the consequences, even being grounded until the end of the school year. It means that much to me. I hope you can understand that someday. You know I've been doing so good for MONTHS. Please allow me this one thing. I love you. ~Eleana

She folded the letter, letting out a long exhale. She couldn't have her mom risk her life by frantically coming to the Green Lands in search of her. It would be better this way, thinking she'd gone to Detroit. And hopefully the way she'd written the letter—framing her reasons, justifications, and hinting at a lesser punishment than she feared—would help on her return.

As she stared at the folded paper, a darkness overshadowed Leah's mind. This was the right thing to do, right?

She resolutely set her pen to a new piece of paper and forged a second letter, tucking it away in case it would be needed later.

The bathroom door closed, and Leah jumped up—this part was crucial. Picking up a large glass of water she'd already prepared, she quietly crept into her mom's room as the shower started. Finding her mom's cell on the bedside table, Leah plunged the phone in, taking it back to her own room to soak.

Leah pocketed the few items on her checklist and put the letter to her mom under her pillow for now. She perched on the edge of her bed, her knee bouncing up and down.

Marcus texted. <Still on?>

<Are you sexy?>

<LOL. I'm guessing that's a yes.>

< :D >

Leah took her mom's phone from the glass of water; it should be damaged by now. She clicked the button. *Crap.* It was an older phone. It should have worked already. Her heart beat faster as she plunged it back in, and the shower turned off.

She shot off a text. <Stall a half hour?>

Panicking, she shoved her cell in her pocket, leaving her mom's to soak. Stepping into the hallway, Leah was met by her mom in a robe with a towel on her head.

"Good morning, princess. Why are you up so early?"

Leah shrugged. "Just woke up and couldn't fall asleep again. Craving bacon. Wanna make breakfast together?"

Her mom's smile was warm. "Yeah, I'll be right in."

"Cool, I'll get it started." Leah turned down the hall, her heart thumping in her chest. She hurriedly threw a pan on the stove, then yanked bacon and eggs from the fridge. Her phone chimed.

<Sure. See you then.>

She let out a sigh of relief. Leah ripped the bacon package open, slapping strips haphazardly into the pan. As they began to sizzle, she pulled bread out and ran back to her bedroom to check on the phone.

You've got to be kidding me. DIE!

She plunged it back in, a little water splashing on her dresser. Her mom's bedroom door shut.

"Eleana, have you seen my phone?"

UGH!

Leah left her room, heading to the kitchen. "No. Where did you see it last?"

Her mom reached into a cupboard, grabbing breakfast plates. "On my bedside table."

Leah dropped slices of bread into the toaster. "Did it fall under your bed? Or between the bed and table?"

Her mom sighed. "Maybe." She finished setting the table, then went back to her room.

The toast popped up; Leah feverishly buttered the slices, considering alternate options with the phone. She flipped the mouthwatering bacon and dodged a wild pop of grease from the pan.

Her mom returned, scrunching her eyebrows. "Still couldn't find it." She pulled a container of strawberries from the fridge. "Could you call it for me?"

Leah's eyes grew wide. "Sure. Take care of the eggs? I've got to go to the bathroom first."

Her mom kissed her on the forehead. "Yes. And thanks for the breakfast idea. We should do this more often."

Leah summoned her most authentic forced smile. "I agree." Pacing herself to not run, she casually and quietly stepped into her room, retrieving the phone.

Still working.

She huffed, crossing the hall to the bathroom. Hoping the sizzling of breakfast in the works could mask the sound, Leah held the cell under the bathroom faucet and turned it on high and hot, directly into the charging port.

Please. Please. Please. Please. For. The. Love. Please!

She turned the phone off and on a few times, flushing the toilet after a while. She got on her knees, still holding the phone under the running water, trying to figure out what to do. Leaning her forehead against the bathroom cabinet, she considered using a bobby pin in the charging port. If her mom's phone worked, she could track Leah's phone. She could call Marcus or his grandparents. Marcus's dad or the officials at the cave could try to call her to ensure Leah had permission to travel. This *needed* to work.

Leah stood and clicked the phone on.

It didn't light up.

She clicked a couple more times. *Nothing.* She turned off the water and dried the cell with a towel. Leaning back against the bathroom counter, Leah closed her eyes and let out a long, slow breath.

I will spend the rest of my life rescuing puppies and kittens and hugging trees. Thank you.

She double- and triple-checked that it was out for the count. Luckily, it showed no water damage behind the screen—it just wouldn't start up.

Leah left the bathroom, strolling into the kitchen. She held up the phone, shaking it playfully. "Forgetful in your old age? You took it to the bathroom."

Her mom was visibly perplexed. "I really don't remember taking it in there." She took the phone back and set it down on the kitchen table. "Grab some juice from the fridge? I think that's all we're missing."

Leah did as asked, then sat down at the table, trying not to stare at the phone. Her mom soon joined her, and they dug into their breakfast.

"You're all dressed and everything. Very cute, might I add," her mom said, scooping eggs onto her toast.

Leah smiled. "No shoplifting. No cheating, stealing, plundering, murdering, or anything else. *And* I got dressed early on a Saturday morning." She puckered her lips, nodding. "I see Ivy League colleges knocking down our door without me even applying."

Her mom chuckled. "My little princess—all reformed." She tilted her head. "All joking aside, I *am* proud of what I've seen in you lately."

Leah choked down the lump in her throat. "Thanks. I've been really trying."

Her mom frowned. "And I know you're not too happy with me for not letting you go to that wedding."

Leah pushed around the strawberries on her plate. "I'll survive. I know you're worried about me." She glanced up, raising an eyebrow. "Even if I think it's overkill."

She pointed her fork at Leah. "I'm a mom. Even normal human moms worry, you know." She picked up a strawberry. "But I was thinking about having a girls' day so you weren't just bumming around the house. Kick off spring break with something fun. Go out to lunch? Some shopping therapy?"

Leah winced. "Marcus and his grandparents are taking a later flight. He's coming over any minute to pick me up. We're just going to hang out for a little while."

"Hmm ... when is his flight? We could do dinner instead?"

Leah's phone chimed.

<Be there in ten.>

"Yeah, dinner sounds great," she said while texting her reply. <See you in ten. Text when you're here. Mom = bad mood, best to stay out there.>

"Seriously? This piece of junk won't even turn on?"

Leah looked up. The dead phone refused to resurrect, despite multiple attempts by its owner. "Did it run out of battery?"

"No. I charge it every night." Her mom kept jamming the buttons. "I've had it for a while, anyway. I swear they make phones sturdier, but at the same time make them so you feel like you have to replace them every six months."

"Good thing you got the raise, right?"

"Yeah…"

Leah rushed to finish her breakfast and went to brush her teeth, opting to not have bacon breath for today's momentous occasion. Wanting to put on her best face, she included a coat of her favorite kissproof lipstick and stared at herself in the mirror. As she gazed into her own bright green eyes, her heart sank. She wasn't a great person. Not like Marcus. She wasn't even a good person. She was a liar, through and through.

Leah bit her lip, pushing past that truth. It wasn't the *only* truth. She was a caring person. She loved her mom, and even though this would hurt her, it was right. Leah deserved to see her homeland, to see the place her dad had ruled. He had shared her bright eyes. He would have wanted her to see what she could have been the heir of, before she became the heir of exile. The heir of nothing—nothing but pain.

She shook her head. She also cared for Marcus. He was just as elated as she was to have her attend the wedding and meet his family.

Leah's phone chimed.

<Here.>

She looked in the mirror one more time. *You can do this.*

Leah popped into her bedroom, pulling the letter to her mom out so it was visible on her bed. She turned off her phone, leaving it in a dresser drawer. The scene was set. Her mom had no reason to go in there for a while.

She left her room, finding her mom back in her own room. "I'm headed out." She gave her mom a hug. "Love you."

Her mom squeezed her tight. "Love you too, princess."

As Leah passed the doorway, her mom called out to her.

Leah turned back, itching to leave. "Yes?"

"You have your phone, right?"

"I'm a teenager. A teenager that knows her mom tracks her phone. I think that's a solid yes."

Her mom smiled. "I'm going out to get a new phone while you're gone. I'm trusting that you're following the rules and you're only going to Marcus's place? I'll text you once I have my new one set up."

Leah cocked her head. "I haven't been murdered while going to the movies or lunch with him yet, but yes, we'll stay at his place. His grandparents will be there. We'll be good."

"I'm trusting you this time," she emphasized again. "I love you."

Leah's heart dropped. Things would never be the same between them after this. "I love you too. Bye."

Chapter 22

Leah left through the front door, making a dash to Marcus's van. She hopped in and gave him a quick smooch. "Let's go." She buckled up.

"Everything okay? Your mom's still cool about this?"

"Yeah, of course. I told her the flight was delayed. She's fine."

"Should I," he shrugged, "go thank her for letting you come?"

She furrowed her brow. "No. I told you—she's in a mood. Let's go before she changes her mind."

Marcus laughed. "Fair enough." He put the van in reverse. "You okay? Anxious or excited?"

She stopped biting her nails. "Both."

"Ditto." He backed out of the driveway, heading to his house.

"Just remember to follow my lead," he said. "And I'll try to whisper hints along the way for customs, and stuff we may not have gone over. In a lot of ways, it's really not all that foreign over there."

She bounced her knee. "Great. Will do. As for following the other person's lead..." She cleared her throat. "I've had a lot of time to consider possible problems. And it's not something to brag about, but we both know I'm a better liar ... so, let me take the lead on that kind of stuff, okay? I'll squeeze your hand twice or something if I need your backup."

"Maybe that's for the best." He threw her a quick glance. "It's okay what we're doing, right?"

She faced him. "I thought we agreed on this. That we both want it."

"Of course we do." He grinned. "We both want other things, too. But we're waiting on that."

Smiling, she grabbed his free hand. "We have the rest of our lives for that, right? Your brother's wedding only happens once."

He squeezed her hand. "You're right."

"Happens on occasion."

After a few minutes, they pulled into Marcus's driveway. He turned the van off. "Crap! We're going to need to swing by your place on the way there."

Her eyes grew wide. *No. No. No. No. No. We need to flee. Not return.* "Why?"

"You didn't bring a bag. You think your mom is going to believe you flew to another state for a week without so much as a carry-on?"

Her heart froze as she thought up an answer on the fly. "She didn't see me leave. She won't notice. And I'll email her from your phone at the cave to let her know I forgot it but it's too late and I'll just buy new stuff there."

His face twisted with hesitance. "Are you sure?"

His grandparents came out the front door, locking it behind them.

"Yeah. Let's not delay this any more than we have to. I think my heart might give out from anticipation if we wait any longer."

He chuckled. "Okay. If you think she'll buy it."

"It's better this way. Going back now would only raise suspicions with your grandparents."

"Ooh, you make a good point!" They unbuckled and crawled into the back seat.

Marcus's grandparents got in the van.

"Thanks so much for letting me ride with you guys," Leah said. "My mom wanted to take me but had to go into work."

"No problem at all," Samantha said.

Marcus scooched closer to Leah, slinging his arm around her. She rested her hand on his thigh, and he reciprocated with a wink.

"Of course, we offered to just swing by your place on the way," Brad said. "Would have been easier."

Marcus and Leah shared a glance, and he grinned. "What can I say?" Marcus asked. "Part of Marcus's foreign exchange year in the human world means getting to drive as much as possible."

Samantha and Brad reached over the center console, holding hands. "Plus, sweetheart, I believe we were young once," Samantha said. "Teenagers need a few minutes to *properly* greet the person they're dating without their fuddy-duddy old grandparents peeping in on them."

Leah laughed. "You're the coolest grandparents I know. You're not so bad."

"High praise. We'll take it," Samantha said as they got on the freeway. "But what about your own grandparents? Won't they be jealous if they find out you gave us that title?"

Leah hid her hurt. The grandparents who had been assassinated by their own daughter, Queen Kaylah? Or the ones in poor health who she'd yet to meet? "Fair enough. Coolest grandparents I'm *not* related to."

"Shouldn't have pointed it out to her," Brad said playfully. "I don't think they make a coffee mug for 'coolest grandparent I'm not related to.'"

Marcus leaned over, whispering in her ear, "You're going to fit right in."

They drove far from the city limits into a more forested area. Leah's heart skipped a beat when she saw the Green Lands cave building. A bit uncharacteristic-looking, it was disguised as a nature preserve, complete with a legitimate human-friendly set of displays. It was overpriced and in poor shape—the online reviews were atrocious. Good enough to keep away any smart human, but still available for the poor saps willing to fork over the money and contribute to the poor reviews after their visit.

The building was nestled into the side of a tall hill, providing covered parking for green-folk patrons, and disguising the cave within.

Marcus handed Leah his phone once they parked. "She needs to text her mom that we got here safe. If you guys want to head in, we'll be right behind you."

Samantha grinned. She'd caught them kissing and cuddling enough in her house to make plenty of assumptions. "Lock up and don't keep us waiting too long."

Marcus smiled as they left. "Decided to email about your forgotten luggage?"

"Yep." Leah turned the screen so he couldn't see it. <I love you. Look on my bed.> She sent it off. There was no going back. Her mom couldn't call Marcus or his grandparents—all of their phones would be left behind in the car. And their house would be empty. But she couldn't just leave her mom hanging, in case it took her forever to look in Leah's room. The moment she got a new phone synced, that message would come through and she would *freak*.

Leah turned off Marcus's phone, leaving it in the seatback pocket. "Is there anything else I should know?"

He rubbed his chin in thought. "Um ... I feel like you've got the basics down. You've done great so far." He cringed. "Well, I guess one thing: my parents don't know I'm dating anyone. I, uh ... didn't tell them about you over Christmas Break."

Nodding, she pressed her lips tight. "I get it. You weren't sure you wanted to date me anymore."

He kissed her on the forehead. "I was just mad. And I figured it was better to say nothing rather than something I'd regret." He gave her a half-smile. "But being away from you, and not being able to talk about you... I'm pretty sure all that did was make me want to see you more."

A soft smile grew on her face. "Then I'll take it."

He furrowed his brow. "One last thing—my dad. I suppose I should correct what Kara said. You can call him 'Sir.' Or 'Guillen.' But don't call him 'Sir Guillen.' He hates titles."

"Okay, I'll remember that." Skipping the copious kissing Samantha probably assumed they were doing, they headed in, hand in hand.

They left the parking garage down an elevator to the ground floor. Striding past the dumpy little displays of dusty, poorly labeled taxidermy animals and bugs, Marcus guided Leah down a winding hallway, past the bathrooms, and into a door marked 'Employees Only.' They crossed the back room and passed through another door marked 'Restricted Access.'

And then they were there.

Leah took in the crazy view. A well-lit, simply decorated lobby was occupied by a couple dozen people. The main focus at the end of the room: a cave opening twice as tall as Leah. On the left stood a pair of guards, reviewing passports and guiding guests through an abbreviated customs. No one packed baggage due to the inability to carry much when rifting, but there were still items restricted from the realm for the safety of its inhabitants—fauna and flora one might be able to tuck into a pocket. To the right of the cave, small groups of people trickled in, greeted by loved ones there to pick them up.

Near the door where Leah and Marcus had entered, his grandparents stood chatting with a tall man Leah recognized from pictures hanging on Marcus's grandparents' walls. Leah's heart raced. There really was no going back. Well ... technically, the worry was mostly about *having* to go back. Either way, she and Marcus were at a pivotal point they'd been working toward for a month, and for Leah, really, it was five months of preparation. In some ways, her whole life.

Marcus ushered Leah forward with a supportive hand on her back.

"Hey, buddy!" His dad smiled, a brunet in his lower forties.

Marcus gave him a hug and stepped back, eyebrows lifted. "Buddy?"

His dad cleared his throat, lowering his voice. "Right. Not cool or manly." He faced Leah. "And this is the infamous girlfriend I heard about five whole minutes ago."

Leah smiled and extended a hand. "Leah. Nice to meet you, sir." She noted his pale blue eyes and a large scar on his temple. She had expected a politician to be bald or round, and less approachable, but he really hadn't changed much since the photos she'd seen had been taken.

He wore a charming smile. "Sir or Guillen. Just not Sir Guillen, please."

Leah grinned, and Marcus took her hand.

Guillen rubbed his hands together. "Hope you're ready for a lot of nonstop family chaos. We all ready to go?"

Marcus squeezed Leah's hand as she focused on hiding her panic. "Could we talk for just a second, Dad?" He glanced at his grandparents. "We shouldn't be long."

Samantha and Brad seemed confused, but obliged. "We'll be on the other side, waiting."

As they walked toward the cave entrance, Marcus took the lead. "Well, um... We kind of have a small problem."

Leah's grip tightened on his hand.

"What's that?" Guillen asked.

"Leah couldn't find her passport this morning."

Leah frowned, as did Guillen.

Marcus shifted his weight from one foot to another. "We were hoping you might be able to help with an exception."

Guillen sighed.

"I'm really sorry, sir. I hate to put you in this position. I thought I knew where it was, but then I went to grab it, and..." She laid on another frown. "I understand if you're not able to help."

"We were just really looking forward to Mom and everyone getting to meet her," Marcus added.

Guillen rubbed the back of his neck, wincing. "I'm sorry, Leah." He shook his head. "The wedding isn't for another couple of days. Would you be able to take some time to look for it and meet us before then?"

Marcus gripped Leah's hand even tighter.

"I'd say yes, but we just moved," she said. "And my mom is kind of horrible at organizing. It could be buried under dozens of unmarked boxes."

Guillen pursed his lips. "My in-laws said you're Ivy?"

She raised her free hand, extending a short vine tendril. "Yes, sir." She was definitely starting to sweat.

Guillen gave them both a disapproving look. "I don't appreciate being ambushed like this." He focused his gaze solely on Marcus. "You know I wouldn't normally make an exception of this kind."

Marcus cocked his head. "Everyone knows the security checks are mostly for human control in and out, anyway."

Guillen huffed, tucking his hands into his brown trousers. "We shouldn't expect to be above the law, Marcus."

Leah's stomach was in tight knots. *This isn't going to work.*

Marcus looked down. "It means a lot to me, to have her come."

Leah gnawed on her lower lip, wondering if she should just concede, not sure how else they could appeal to him. This part of it all was reliant on Marcus's guess that his dad would cave. She was an idiot for sending that last message to her mom. If she'd never done that, if their cave strategy didn't work out, she might have had a chance to take a cab home and hide the letter, and the truth, before she was discovered. But she'd burned up that lifeline.

Guillen focused on Leah, then glanced at their tight hand-holding. "I'd feel better if your parents had come here so I could meet them. Taking a minor through a rift with this kind of exception makes me extra uncomfortable."

"I only have a mom." Leah laid it on thick, fishing for any sympathy she could garner. How many times had she *not* gotten in trouble for shoplifting, after all, because she could tell a half-decent lie? "And she had to go into work today."

"Humans can fly anywhere in the United States at our age without parental approval," Marcus said.

Guillen pointed at Marcus, his face still disapproving. "Going between realms and between human states are very different things." He turned again to Leah. "How about we call your mother?"

Bingo. "She's not allowed to answer her phone at work, so it's turned off." She hoped and prayed he wouldn't still call and leave a voicemail that pointed to the Green Lands. Marcus had explained that a lot of green folk were cautious about leaving any sort of electronic or paper trail pointing to their true identities. "But she wrote me up a permission letter." Leah pulled out her second folded letter, forged that morning.

Guillen read the note. "She knows where you'll be? If she needs to come over and reach you?"

"Yes. Of course."

Guillen bobbed his head in reluctance. "One time only."

Marcus instantly beamed, releasing Leah's hand and giving his dad another hug. "Thank you. Thank you. Thank you!"

Leah relaxed her muscles, relieved at having cleared a giant hurdle. "Thank you so much, sir. We've been talking about coming to this wedding for weeks."

Marcus wrapped his arms around her, kissing her on the cheek.

Guillen smiled. "Let's not make your grandparents wait any longer."

The relief of his permission was quickly replaced by crushing anxiety about the most unpredictable part—her rifting skills were unproven. The trio walked over to the departure line, waiting for their turn. Leah played through her mind the many facts Marcus had relayed to her. She thought of the jade he and his dad had on their person at all times. His grandparents had gone through the rift with a different kind of jade, specifically made for humans.

Their short line progressed slowly as groups of people came through the incoming side at intervals. Departure and arrival coordinators staggered groups to avoid any type of backup or crowding in the rifting spaces.

Her heart beating harder and stomach tight, Leah paced her breathing as they approached the guard for their turn.

"Sir Guillen." The man nodded without asking for a passport.

Guillen nodded back politely, gesturing at Marcus. "My son."

Marcus pulled out his passport, a small green booklet. A decorative symbol had been embossed in gold on the front—A flower blossom, surrounded by the outline of an ivy leaf, resting on the background of a handprint. He presented it to the guard. The man did a quick look-over, handing it back. "You have your token?"

"Yes, sir." Marcus tucked the passport in his pocket, wrapping his arm around Leah again.

"Last in our party," Guillen said. "Name's Leah. Ivy. No passport. I'll be vouching for her under a diplomatic visa for the week."

'Diplomatic visa.' That sounds so formal, so official, so big.

The guard nodded, pulling a notebook from his podium. He clicked a pen, ready to take down details. "Last name?"

Leah swallowed. She and Marcus had created a bit of a cover for her, including what region she came from, picking an obscure rural one. But Marcus didn't suspect her mom of being in hiding—Leah couldn't lie in front of him about their names. She trusted her mom had changed her name as part of their cover in exile. "Edwards."

The man jotted it down. He asked for her parents' names, kingdom address, and duration of travel. Leah had already casually asked Marcus about common names in the Ivy Kingdom, and had picked a fake one for her dad that would fit in. Guillen provided his home address as where she could be found in the Green Lands for the duration of the visa. The man tore off a copy and handed it to Guillen. "She'll want that for the return." The man then looked at Leah. "Ivy? Vines, please."

She showed her vines, and he allowed them to pass.

"Thank you for your assistance," Guillen said as they moved into the cave entrance.

The final phase—the one that relied *solely* on Leah.

A few yards into the artificially lit cave, the small group met up with a couple chatting in front of them. They waited while a group of incoming rifters came through on the other side, separated by a rope divider. The couple recognized Guillen and greeted him, starting up a conversation about recent mundane policy changes.

Marcus held Leah from behind, whispering in her ear. "You'll do great. Just breathe."

Leah focused on the floor, and the warmth of his embrace, as she tried to calm her rapidly building nerves. She readied herself to observe the couple in front of them, hoping they were also Ivy so she could witness it for herself. It was so odd to not know—they could be anything.

Almost as much as Leah wanted to see an Ivy make a rift, she was curious to see a Seeder rift, and how rifts were made for Bomen and humans. Only Seeders could make cave rifts that others could go through.

The departure coordinator—the first person Leah *knew* to be a Seeder— informed the awaiting group that they were set to go. The first two people approached. Leah watched with bated breath.

The coordinator stepped forward, swiping their hand in the air, and a shimmering rift opened.

Two Bomen or humans, incapable of making their own rifts. Great... I don't get to watch anyone make an Ivy rift. Her chest rose and fell with anxiety.

"Should we go first, Dad?" Marcus asked.

"No. Leah's under my supervision now. I've got to make sure she gets through."

Leah appreciated Marcus's attempt to lessen her audience. Which they now had—a couple more people were now behind their group.

Marcus squeezed Leah tight one last time before releasing her.

As important as her ability to make this rift work was her ability to make it look like she'd been doing it for years. Her heart thumped in her chest as she gnawed on her lip. She stepped forward, spotting a line of jade embedded in the floor.

Focusing her mind, Leah thought of the words, the coordinates Marcus had given her. *Selen to Boloru.* She held her breath and extended a vine, exerting pressure, and trying to connect to the stone. *You've gotta do this on the first try.*

Feeling something there, she swiped her vine along the jade in the floor—not too fast, not too slow—the energy pulling with her. Somewhat hesitantly, but there. She dragged the energy from left to right, as if unzipping a seam between the worlds. As she finished her stroke, a surge of energy ran down the channel from her mind. A barely visible rift shimmered before her. Only *imagining* the look on Marcus's face, she retracted her vine and did her best to casually walk through.

Chapter 23

Every inch of Leah's skin was caressed with a warm hug as she strolled through the rift. Her view changed from the back of a cave, to a flash of warm light, to the natural daylight of a new room on the other side. She hadn't expected to be emotional, but she instantly fought tears. This was the biggest moment of her life. She drew a deep breath and tried to compose and orient herself.

"Please move on, ma'am," the receiving employee said.

"Oh. Yeah. Sorry." She rushed along.

This cave looked different, artificially carved out instead of naturally formed. Large skylights allowed daylight to fill the area. Leah was met by Samantha and Brad, and their warm smiles. She joined them, peering back into the cave. She beamed. Matching her gaze and smile was Marcus, approaching right before Guillen. Leah wanted to cry. She wanted to run up and kiss Marcus, and thank him, and gush over the experience. But she bottled it up. This was normal. She'd done this before, obviously.

He still gave her a quick hug, whispering in her ear, "You're amazing."

"Sorry about the wait," Guillen said to his in-laws. He turned to Leah, holding her folded temporary visa. "Don't lose this."

She nodded and happily tucked it into her pocket.

It would be a half-hour walk from the cave to Marcus's house. Electricity didn't work the same way in the Green Lands—something about the rich energy and its magnetic properties disrupted human technology like cars.

Marcus and Leah lingered at the back of the group, holding hands and whispering as Guillen got caught up with Samantha and Brad.

"Your first time. How was it?" Marcus asked.

"Terrifying!" Only now was her heart calming, her skin cooling.

He chuckled. "But you did it. I'm seriously proud of you." He kissed her on the cheek again.

She grinned, feeling the unique energy of the realm soaking into her body as Marcus had previously described. There was an instant sense of home to this place, something she'd never experienced in the human world. She understood why her mom and Cheryl longed for this place.

The charm of brick streets and stone buildings with lush plant growth added to the brightness of the day. A hummingbird buzzed nearby, drinking nectar from a creeping vine with orange and yellow flowers. It truly was a paradise here, a whole other world. Much of the flora and fauna mirrored what could be found in the human world, though some were uniquely present in this realm.

The air was warm, just right. The Green Lands existed in a perpetual state of spring.

Without warning, the truth collided with Leah's joy. She'd run away. She was hurting her mom. There would be consequences. She was jeopardizing her own safety.

Forget that. Enjoy it for what it is. Live in the moment. You're going to be fine.

"I know we're going to have tons of your family around, but we will be able to have some time alone, right?" she asked.

Marcus smirked. "Oh yeah. We'll make time."

She bit her lip. "Good."

He pulled her in tight, sliding a hand in the back pocket of her jeans as they walked along, whispering about the agenda of the week.

"Come on, now," Guillen called back to the straggling couple ten minutes into their walk. "If Marcus is going to surprise us with a girlfriend, I've got to get to know her."

Marcus slid his hand up to her waist, and they picked up the pace to join the adults.

Guillen asked how they'd met, for details about Leah and her family, her interests, hobbies. Leah shared partial truths she and Marcus had worked out.

As they approached the two-story home, Guillen gave a warning. "Take a deep breath now. Lots of chaos between now and the wedding, and you might not find the time to catch your breath along the way."

Leah smiled. Everything was so foreign. She still had so much to learn. And she wasn't the biggest fan of crowds, but there was something endearing about a large family after growing up with only her mom and an abusive fake aunt.

"I'll add to that," Marcus said. "Lots of huggers. You've been warned."

Leah laughed. "I'll try to survive."

They walked into the beautifully crafted home, which was constructed from a combination of raw wood and stone. Warm spices filled the air, as well as the chatter of a few people. From the entryway, they moved past a stairwell and a kitchen, into a large living room where a few people were talking. The home, like everything else Leah had seen so far, was a lot more primitive than what she was used to in the human world, but not quite as caveman as she'd feared.

A charming brunette in her late thirties smiled and hopped up at the sight of the new arrivals. Guillen reached her with a hug and a kiss. She hugged Samantha and Brad, then Marcus. She looked at Leah, who was hanging back, fidgeting with her hands. "Looks like you picked up a spare along the way," she said playfully.

"Mom, this is Leah," Marcus said. "My girlfriend."

Leah stepped forward, extending a hand. "Nice to meet you, ma'am."

The woman grimaced. "I might be in denial, but I refuse to believe I'm old enough to be a ma'am, yet. Please call me Rachel." She shook Leah's hand.

"Okay." She examined Rachel, taking in her brown hair and eyes, but knowing her hair could glow yellow and her eyes green, with her Seeder powers. And under the skin on her arms, sharp green blades hid, a dormant weapon any Seeder with powers possessed.

The adults sat back down while Leah's focus turned to the younger adults.

"And the bride and groom," Marcus introduced them. His older brother, Tobias, had straight hair a darker brown than Marcus's, and a much wider nose. Camry—his bride—had chestnut hair that extended just past her shoulders, subtle freckles, and wore a light purple-pink lipstick. Leah shook their hands before she and Marcus sat down near the couple on a long couch.

"Well, now the wedding's *ruined*," Tobias drawled.

Camry raised her eyebrows. "Why's that?"

"The count's off. No one could have imagined Marcus being capable of bringing a date," Tobias razzed.

Marcus glared.

"None of that," Rachel warned.

"Be nice to him." Camry lightly punched her fiancé in the shoulder.

Marcus sat straighter, his arm still around Leah. "You wanna get started already?"

Tobias flashed a crooked grin. "Five rounds."

"You're on." Marcus stood.

Tobias got up. "Are you ready for Leah to see you cry?"

Marcus shook his head. "She knows how good I am." He squeezed Leah's shoulders. "I'll be right back."

"Boys!" Guillen raised his voice. "I think we need to talk about the big problem here."

The brothers exchanged a glance.

"I'm not even invited?" Guillen said, his hands in the air.

Tobias laughed. "You and Marcus can be a team, old man. You'll both need the help."

The boys left the room, turning down a hallway. "I do not," Marcus protested.

Guillen got up, releasing Rachel's hand. "But I might." He followed after them, his voice trailing off. "Old man?"

The room fell silent, just the three girls and Rachel's parents left behind. "I have no idea what just happened," Leah said, wide-eyed.

"A house ruled by boys." Rachel chuckled. "Welcome to my world."

Camry faced Leah. "You must not have brothers."

Leah shrugged. "Only child."

"I have brothers. No matter how old they get, they stay the same."

"What are they even doing?"

Camry nodded at the large glass windows in the living room providing a view of the enormous backyard. "You'll see."

"Do you guys want any tea?" Rachel offered her parents. "Leah?" They all accepted.

The steam curled up from Leah's cup as it cooled down enough to drink. She took in the room—the simple construction and décor. Natural. No human electronics. Unadulterated, basic, peaceful.

"Well, we certainly didn't get much of an introduction before they stormed off like that," Rachel said. "Tell us about yourself, Leah."

Leah glanced out the window at the boys. They lined up on the lawn near the window, all barefoot by now. They crouched in runner's stances and took off, racing down the yard. "Um ... what do you want to know?"

"Anything and everything."

Leah introduced herself. Most of it was true. There were obvious omissions. Some things were outright lies—either to protect her and her mom's identities, or bending the truth as she'd agreed upon with Marcus to avoid any judgment on their characters as 'the wrong type' of Ivies that had left when the war was ending.

"You're not just there for a foreign exchange year?" Rachel asked.

"No. My mom and I move a lot. She likes variety. A little here, a little there," Leah said.

Rachel sipped her tea. "Well, that's nice. If you're able to travel and you like it, then why not?"

Leah gave her a polite smile. Marcus had explained that his Seeder mom couldn't leave the Green Lands anymore. She could still travel anywhere *within* the Green Lands, and was even capable of flying, but she was confined to the realm as a matured, fully-rooted female Seeder.

Leah glanced out the window again; the guys were on the fourth lap of their game. Once they ran to the end of the yard, they stopped and threw knives at a target, having to land them well, then ran a lap of the yard, retrieved the knives, and aimed at the targets again.

"Marcus said you guys have been able to do a lot of traveling around the realm, right?" Leah asked.

Rachel's face was kind and gracious. "Comes with the territory of our work, but yeah."

"That's really cool." Leah looked at the other people around the room. "I've been excited to get to meet Marcus's family. He talks about you guys often. I hope it's not too much trouble, me just showing up like this."

"Not at all," Rachel insisted. "Did you have arrangements for somewhere to stay, or will you be staying here?"

Leah pursed her lips. "We were planning on me staying here, if that's alright."

"Sounds good to me. Same rules as at my parents' place—no young couples in bedrooms."

Leah nodded. "Yes, ma'am."

Rachel lifted her eyebrows.

Leah smiled. "Yes, Rachel."

"Speaking of," Samantha said, "where would you like us to stay?"

"Mmm." Rachel's cup clinked as she set it down. "We just finished the upgrades on the guest house. Let me show you." The three got up. Before leaving down the hall, Rachel turned to Leah. "Whenever you're hungry, feel free to raid the kitchen. I've got all sorts of platters in the cooler and on the counter. I know the time change on rifting days can be a bit odd, so we'll probably just graze here and there today."

"Okay. Thank you."

Leah wrung her hands as the group left, staring out the window. The boys approached the house at a sprint, until Tobias tripped Marcus and they started to wrestle. She grimaced. "Are they going to be okay?"

Camry chuckled. "Yes. And if they break an arm, it's mighty handy having a Seeder for a mom."

Leah had forgotten that part of Rachel's powers—healing. She had a million questions to ask the woman, but couldn't really go there, needing to pretend Rachel *wasn't* the first Seeder she'd really ever interacted with. "Right. Yeah. This is kind of weird for me. First time meeting a boyfriend's parents so formally."

Camry waved a hand dismissively. "Don't be nervous on account of their positions or connections. They're really down to earth. I think you'll fit right in."

"Thanks." Leah realized she might be able to relate to Camry more than perhaps anyone else here. Camry was human. "How did it feel for you, when you found out about the Green Lands and everything? You met in the human world when Tobias was an exchange student, right?"

"Yeah. It was a bit of a shock. I kind of didn't really believe him until he brought me here. You know, Bomen can't exactly show the extra stuff like the vines to prove they have green-folk heritage." She sighed, playing with her engagement ring. "They really welcomed me. My personal token was made with Rachel's blood. It's a pretty special sacrifice, you know? She couldn't come meet me. I couldn't come here to meet her. But she knew how much Toby loved me, so they went through the process of having it made up."

Leah smiled, recalling a conversation she'd had with Tanner ages ago. Allowing humans in posed a risk to green folk. But if it was the right humans, like Camry, maybe it wasn't so bad. "She sounds pretty awesome for a Seeder."

Camry cocked her head. "I don't know about awesome for a *Seeder*, but awesome for a mother-in-law."

"Have you met many Seeders?"

Camry shrugged. "Some of her family, employees at royal functions and at caves, really."

So, not many... She also remembered something about Marcus's parents choosing to live in the Ivy Kingdom because the Seeder nation wasn't safe for Bomen. Exceptions like Rachel obviously existed, but any group of people that were hostile toward people like Marcus, and his dad and brother, weren't the type she could ever associate with. She hid a frown. Her dad had understood that. He'd tried to stop the war with the Seeders. *Without* giving in to their demands like his murderous sister.

That's not why you came here. Enjoy the moment.

The brothers came bursting into the room from the hallway they'd originally left down. Tobias stood in front of Camry, arms wide open. "My love! A hug for the victor?"

She giggled at his mud-smeared shirt and face. "Not a chance. Go clean up."

A set of hands rested on Leah's shoulders, and she looked up at a less muddy but very sweaty Marcus. "Victor?" he scoffed. "You tripped me!"

Tobias feigned innocence. "I don't know what you're talking about. I'd love for an impartial judge to decide." He gestured to the girls. "And I don't think they're going to help."

"Toby cheated," Camry coolly declared.

Tobias's jaw dropped as he gasped. "My heart!"

She snickered. "Go get cleaned up, and we'll see what we can do about fixing that heart of yours."

Rachel returned, sitting back in her original chair. "Who won?"

Guillen came in, breathing hard and clutching his side. "I'm pretty sure I did." He plopped down next to his wife.

"Sure, Dad. Whatever you want to believe," Marcus said. He squeezed Leah's shoulders. "I'm going to hop in the other shower if you're alright out here."

She looked back up. "Yes, please."

Marcus took the stairs near the entrance. Guillen slumped in his chair, facing his wife. "I think he might have had a point, calling me an old man."

Rachel grinned. "Yeah. I think I saw another white hair the other day."

He put a hand over his heart. "Et tu?"

Rachel playfully poked his shoulder. "Maybe you should shower too."

Guillen pulled himself up with some grunts and groans, leaving the three girls alone.

"So, Leah," Rachel said. "Let's talk clothes and shopping."

Chapter 24

Leah raised her eyebrows. "Are you trying to tell me I can't wear these clothes for the whole week, wedding included? I've always worn human t-shirts and jeans to important events."

Rachel picked up on her sarcasm, chuckling. "It might be frowned on."

"Leah can use some of my visiting clothes for regular days," Camry said. "You guys still have them, right?"

"Of course," Rachel said, then turned her focus back to Leah. "And as for your dress, we could carve out some time tonight, or there are a couple of openings tomorrow."

Leah's schedule was pretty much a blank slate. "Um ... whatever works for you guys. It's not like I have a set schedule."

Rachel bobbed her head. "Let's say tomorrow morning?"

"Deal. I didn't bring any Ivy money on this trip, so we'll need to exchange my human money before we go shopping." Leah had brought the rest of her savings, hoping it was enough.

"Don't stress about it. My treat."

"Thank you, but I'd like to take care of it myself," Leah said.

Rachel took a deep breath, smiling. "We'll see tomorrow."

"Do you want to take a look and see if my stuff will fit you?" Camry offered.

"Sure."

"In the same room, Rachel?" Camry asked.

"Yes. And we'll have Leah stay in that room."

Leah followed Camry down the hallway, past a bathroom and patio door. At the end, they took a right and opened a door to the small guest bedroom.

"I've stayed here *many* nights on visits," Camry mused, opening a small chest. She knelt down, pulling out some clothes. "They're all green-folk style, but I think they're comfy and cute."

The simpler cuts with intricate designs mirrored the styles Leah had seen worn by most of the people they'd passed that day. Everything was made of natural fibers. "I really appreciate it. I think those should work fine. You're sure you don't need them?"

Camry flashed her a guilty look. "I might have enjoyed too many shopping trips on previous visits. I already have a stash at the inn my parents and I are staying at." She took the clothes and put them back in the chest. "Obviously, we can pick you up some underthings of your own tomorrow morning, too." She stood back up. "That's the nice thing about prices here. In a society where you can't take much with you when you travel, they make it affordable to rent or purchase the necessities." She shook her head. "Of course, you already know that." Blushing, she added, "You're from here. I keep forgetting that."

"No worries." Leah took in the room. It was simply but tastefully decorated. A blue tatted curtain draped across the window. A small vanity with an ornate oval mirror was pushed up against one wall. Aside from the closet and chest, the only other thing in the room was the bed. On the vanity sat a large ceramic bowl; Leah decided to empty her pockets of the things she'd stuffed in there earlier that morning.

She pulled out her human currency, placing it at the bottom of the dish. In the same pocket was the lipstick she'd brought.

Camry laughed, pulling out a tube of her own. "I do the same thing. Gotta bring the trusty stuff with you."

Leah smiled. She reached into her other pocket, taking out the temporary visa and her forged letter from her mom. Falling out of her pocket and onto the ground was a single condom packet. Her eyes grew wide. She snatched it up and shoved it under the pillow, then placed the papers on the top of the bowl. She faced Camry, mortified.

Camry grinned, eyebrows raised. "So, you and Marcus are pretty serious."

Leah sat on the bed, biting her lip. "No. Well, I mean… We haven't … yet. Please don't tell anyone about that."

Camry shrugged. "I'm not here to judge or lecture or tattle. Marcus is a good kid, a smart kid. I don't know you that well, but you seem smart too." She crossed her arms. "If you were Seeders, you'd likely already be considered adults."

Leah almost made a snide remark about that having to be the reason they had so many kids—because they started so young—until she remembered they actually *didn't* have children super young and had no choice as to how many they had, if they chose to have them at all. Twenty-four kids or none—Seeders were a weird bunch. *You really need to shut up, and not comment or ask questions that will give away that you're a noob!*

"Right. Well..." Leah fidgeted with her hands. "I hope it's not weird that I'm crashing your wedding."

Camry waved her hand dismissively. "No. Definitely not. Things are just different here. I've accepted that. It's ... not exactly what I've grown up with in the human world, you know? The family structure, a kingdom, all of it. Heck, I had to buy the dress here." She frowned. "And only my parents are able to come to the ceremony."

Leah mirrored her frown. "None of your siblings, other family?"

Camry wrinkled her nose. "You know the laws. None of the rest of them are in on the secret." Her smile recovered. "But then again, how many girls get to have two weddings? When we return, we'll have a full one there, too. And they're both equal in my eyes."

Leah nodded. She wanted to ask if they were being forced to live in the human world after the wedding, or if they just didn't prefer being here with the current state of affairs. But again, she realized she might give away some naïveté.

"Actually, no pressure..." Camry perched on the wooden chest. "How would you feel about being my maid of honor? I have local bridesmaids, but I never picked a maid of honor for this wedding, and Marcus is the best man."

Leah swallowed hard. "You're sure? I've never done it before. What would I have to do?"

Camry leaned back against the wall. "Really not a big deal. Hold a bouquet. Walk up the aisle with Marcus. It's a bit of a human-Ivy combo theme on how we're doing things. It's not like you have to give a speech or anything crazy."

Leah considered the request.

"Hey, Cam." Marcus poked his head in.

Leah got up, greeting him at the door with a hug. She then surveyed him; it was so odd seeing him in more traditional Ivy garb. His hair was extra curly, still wet from the shower.

Camry stood. "Is Toby out of the shower too?"

"Yeah."

She glanced at Leah. "No pressure. Just let me know?"

"You know what? Why not. I'd be honored."

Marcus wrapped his arms around Leah's midriff, squeezing her tight and kissing her cheek. "What's that?"

"I guess I'm going to be the maid of honor."

"Thanks, Cam," he said with a soft smile in his voice.

"No. Thank you," she said.

Marcus pulled Leah backward into the hallway so Camry could exit in search of Tobias. Once Camry was out of sight, Marcus left a trail of kisses down Leah's neck, making her giggle. She turned around with a smile as he held her hips.

"I have been informed that I could work on my manners and not abandon you like I did earlier. Sorry." He pouted. "And that I should give you a tour of the grounds as a proper gentleman."

She couldn't resist digging her fingers into his curly locks. "I really didn't mind. And I don't always want you to be a proper gentleman with me."

He smirked. "Either way, let me show you around."

Marcus gave Leah a tour of the house. It was an odd configuration, but she liked the unique layout. As strange as anything else she'd seen were the bathrooms and kitchen. They were primitive by her usual standards, but familiar enough that they wouldn't be too hard to get used to. Instead of normal faucets, they used water pumps. Replacing light bulbs, they used skylights for daytime and candles for the nights. The occasional clear-quartz and jade lightkeeper hung on the wall, but only Rachel could use those; only Seeders could channel the energy that made those devices work.

In the kitchen, they used an old-fashioned coal stove for cooking, and without electricity, had to access underground cellars for cool storage.

Marcus's bedroom was upstairs; Leah only got a brief sneak peek from the doorway. It was pretty tidy for a teenage guy's room, compared to what she'd seen before. A nature painting hung on the wall, as well as pictures of family.

Heading out into the backyard, he showed her the guesthouse, a swimming pond, a large garden, and a water pump. He stopped at a flower bed and pointed out a patch of fire-orange flowers. "This is one of the plants that aren't found anywhere else but the Green Lands. They're named Guenjalis, and they're actually related to Seeders."

Arching an eyebrow, Leah studied the flower. "*Related* to Seeders? Is that your mom's great uncle or something?"

He laughed. "I told you before—they're a floral race. In exchange for their support in the war, the queen helped them with research, and they discovered there's some kind of symbiotic relationship between Seeders and this flower."

Nodding, Leah tried to smile and act intrigued. She didn't want any more history lessons. No more mentions of the queen and what she'd done—betraying her own people by giving in to Seeder demands and slaying Leah's father.

Marcus led her to one last thing on the grounds—a large tree house.

"Let's take a look," he said, climbing up the ladder first.

Leah followed, daring to be free enough to use her vines along with her hands to pull herself up. They looked out over the property, and Leah felt more at peace. It was vibrant and well-cared for.

Marcus sat down, and Leah cuddled up on his lap.

"Mmm, some *us* time." She smiled. "You didn't use up all your energy playing earlier, did you?"

"I'll *always* save some energy for time with you." He gazed into her eyes. "How are you liking it so far?"

Her heart was full. For him. For this place. "I love it. Your family's awesome. The energy here is awesome. You have no idea how much this means to me."

He gave her a contented smile. "You have no idea how much *you* mean to me." He stole a quick peck on the lips. "Sounds like you're getting along well with Cam."

She nodded. "I really like her. I wish we had a girl like her in the club." She leaned into him. "Do you and your brother get along?"

"Yeah. We get along fine. We tease. We fight. Normal sibling stuff. He was older than I was when we were adopted, so I think he might remember some stuff, and he can get kinda sensitive. But it's the typical older kid thinking the younger one gets whatever they want, and the younger one getting stricter rules because of mistakes made by the older one. You know how it goes."

"Actually, I don't," she said wistfully.

"Right. Sorry... Do you wish you had siblings? That your mom had remarried?"

"Maybe? I guess I don't know about siblings. It's always kinda been us against the world, and I love that part of us. Even when I screwed up, we were a team. But she deserves to be happy; she just can't get over my dad." The hurt dug deeper with every mention of him. "But he was a great man that died too young. I guess I can't blame her."

Marcus held her tight. "I'm sorry."

"Thanks." She hesitated, considering how beautiful and peaceful everything had been thus far in the Ivy Kingdom. They weren't exactly walking through the slums that likely covered the map under a tyrant's rule. "Are your parents ... well-off?"

"We're ... comfortable," he answered, as though he *hadn't* been comfortable with the question.

She stroked the creases in the sleeve of his shirt. "That probably came off all wrong. I guess I just mean that I'm not sure what's considered a normal home or neighborhood here. Obviously, your parents have important positions, so it makes sense they would be." She smiled. "Your mom is taking me dress shopping tomorrow. She told me she wanted to pay for it. It didn't seem like she's going to take 'no' for an answer."

He kissed her on the cheek. "Let her buy it."

Leah shifted to better look at him. "I can handle it."

He grinned. "You won't win this one. You don't know how stubborn she is."

Leah shrugged, ready to take on the challenge. "I guess we'll see."

He chuckled. "Yeah. *You'll* see."

She stuck out her tongue.

"Oh, really?" He stole a kiss. And then another, and another.

Leah happily, gladly, giddily enjoyed some alone time with him after a phenomenal adventure, only possible thanks to him.

After what could have been a mere minute, or a healthy hour, Leah pulled back, getting lost in his warm brown eyes. Her heart was swelling. Nothing in her life compared to this experience. Nothing. She shifted, straddling him.

He smiled, keeping eye contact.

"I..." she started. Somewhere in her heart, she had to let it out. But fear choked her back.

Leah glanced down, rubbing the linen fabric of Marcus's shirt. "I, um..." She'd never said those three words to anyone but her mom.

After another moment of hesitation, Marcus spoke up. "You know, the last time we were in this position, *I* was the one incapable of forming complete sentences."

He wore another handsome grin, and she blushed.

"Hey, Marcus! Stop making out!" Tobias called from below.

Leah slapped a hand to her mouth, stifling a laugh.

Marcus nudged her off of his lap. He leaned over, looking out the entryway. "We're capable of holding conversations, you know."

"Don't lie. We all know teenagers only go up to tree houses to make out," Tobias said.

Camry's voice came next. "Be nice. Don't pretend we didn't do the exact same thing."

"You're proving my point."

"What do you want?" Marcus scowled.

"We're heading out for the rest of the day," Tobias said.

"Okay. Cool. Thanks for letting us know," Marcus said. "Anything else?"

"I thought ... you know ... I'd remind you that a dozen or more people will be in and out of the house over the next couple of days. And they'll all know you're out here swapping spit with your girlfriend if you're up there all the time hiding away."

Leah couldn't stand it any longer. She stood up and leaned against the railing, grinning without an ounce of shame. "You're right. And I'd give it four out of five stars for a make-out spot. It could use some pillows to be more comfortable."

Tobias glanced from her to Marcus. His face barely cracked a smile as he pointed to Leah. "I like this one. She's honest."

Marcus rolled his eyes. "Glad you approve. See you tomorrow."

Camry smirked knowingly and grabbed Tobias's arm, nudging him along. "Later, Leah."

Marcus and Leah popped back into their hiding place with a chuckle and a couple more stolen kisses.

"I suppose he's right. I *did* say I was going to show you off, and I can't do much of that from up here."

She rubbed his hand. "True. Before we head out, can we go over more of the details for this week? We spent so much time preparing to get here, but I'm starting to get more nervous about what it's all going to look like."

They discussed the rest of that day's agenda. Mostly visiting—family and family friends dropping by in preparation. Marcus might see if some of his friends in the area were free and he could introduce them. The next day, Leah would shop with Rachel, and then it was more family. They would want to be available for any last-minute tasks they might be asked to do as maid of honor and best man.

And then it was the wedding day. A close family breakfast in the morning, but a large luncheon in the early afternoon. The official ceremony would begin at dusk, followed by a reception. The rest of the week would be a lot more casual and laid back.

"I'm still nervous about being around royalty. When will we be around them?"

Marcus puckered his lips. "Royalty is a broad spectrum. But if you're talking about the queen and king … they'll be at the luncheon, and obviously the wedding. She's officiating it."

Leah sat straighter, surprised. "Officiating it? Not just a guest?"

He grabbed a twig and poked at the tree house floor. "Yep. And then the queen- and king-in-waiting will be at both of those events, too."

She furrowed her brow. "What are a queen- and king-in-waiting? Like, their kids?" It was obvious by now that Marcus wasn't a prince in hiding or anything like that, just a politician's son. She'd initially made sure to rule out the possibility that Marcus could be some unknown cousin, wanting to avoid a creepy romantic connection with her big plan. But Tanner had confirmed Leah didn't have cousins on her dad's side. And her mom didn't come from royal lineage.

Marcus shook his head. "No. Next in line. They're actually set to officially take over in just over a month." Marcus cleared his throat. "The queen-in-waiting is the current queen's cousin."

Leah's mind ran a mile a minute at the news. "Why? Are the current ones getting kicked out?"

He laughed. "No. Why would you think that?"

"You know the replacements? Are they good people?"

He gave her knee a squeeze. "They're the best kind. I'll introduce you."

That at least gave Leah some comfort. But less than a month left with Queen Kaylah being in her position… "What are the current ones doing after they're replaced?"

"Dunno. I suppose they're going to take a nice long vacation."

Leah's very core ached, her patchwork reality of a life unraveling. The queen had murdered Leah's dad for the power, just to turn around and give it all away seventeen years later? Queen Kaylah wasn't even that old! And she was stepping down to go on a 'nice long vacation'? *Nothing like murder and betrayal to reap the benefits of a cozy early retirement.* "I'm nervous I'll do or say the wrong thing. Will there be a ton of guards? I don't want to get in trouble."

He intertwined their fingers. "Don't stress it. I mean, don't lunge at them, but they're pretty approachable. And yeah, there'll be guards to make sure everyone's safe. Just pretend it's a normal wedding."

She nodded, trying to conceal her concerns. Could she really be in the presence of that woman? Be within mere feet of her during the ceremony? Or was the universe trying to tell her something about her original plan?

Chapter 25

Marcus and Leah went back inside the house, greeted by visitors from all parts of the Green Lands. Many more would gather in Capital City territory on the day of the wedding, which would be a short cave trip away from where Marcus lived.

For the rest of the evening, they socialized with visitors, and Marcus took Leah around the neighborhood, introducing her to friends. She tried her best to enjoy it, but old pangs of hurt and rage began to fester. How could she be near that woman—the queen? Leah was finally witnessing the smallest inkling of the life she and her mom could have enjoyed—full of family, friends, the warmth of the Green Lands.

She went to bed with a heavy heart, trying to override her frustration. She was there for the experience, for the wedding, for Marcus. But this might be the only chance she may ever have to be here. What mattered most?

The next morning, Leah had an early wake-up call. It would be just her and Rachel walking to a dress shop. They shared pleasant conversation. Leah got to hear all sorts of stories about Marcus growing up. She tried to hide the pain, hearing happy stories of a whole family. The queen had taken that from her.

With the first shop in view, Rachel finished another story, this time about what it was like sending both of her boys off to the human world for their foreign exchange years. "You know, you look kind of familiar, Leah."

Leah stiffened. "Really? I don't have any family in the area. I've never actually been this far south..." No one in this realm should recognize her. She hadn't even been born when her mom fled. She *did* look a lot like her parents, but that was actually fairly uncommon for green folk. Seeder families looked nothing alike, something about their genetic makeup. Most Ivy children bore a faint resemblance to their parents, but it also depended on which ancient clan they descended from. In very rare instances, Ivies known as 'whispers' were born, the trait seemingly random. They had exceptional gifts, and their offspring tended to share a closer resemblance.

Marcus and Leah had discussed all of that a while ago when talking about Ivy powers. Leah had wondered if one or both of her parents had the special gift, but there was no way of knowing, and no way to safely bring it up with her mom.(r)

Rachel shrugged. "I'm sure I've just seen your doppelganger somewhere."

At the first shop, they picked up the basic necessities Leah needed for the rest of the week. Leah fought off her old demons, the itch to take a memento from the shelves. Perhaps her mom had been right about that point, that Leah's shoplifting habit was partially connected to her stress level.

The second destination was a dress shop, filled with a wide variety of styles and colors. A third of the store was solely dedicated to rentals. Rachel made casual references about how impractical it was to go by foot and pack much when traveling in the Green Lands. No beasts of burden resided here, no electronics worked. And the few steam engine trains they utilized were always overcrowded. And rifting constraints didn't allow more than what you could easily have on your person—carrying more volume that wasn't an actual part of you was either draining, or impossible.

"That works fine for me. I can afford a rental," Leah said.

Rachel steered her toward the new dresses. "No. Let's get you something of your own. Like I said, my treat."

Leah frowned, staring at the dresses. They didn't even matter.

"It's not hard to see how much you two like each other." Rachel smiled softly. "I'd imagine we might see you back here for a visit later? We wouldn't mind storing the dress for a future visit."

Leah hugged herself. "I'd still rather buy it myself."

"It's not charity, you know." Rachel drew a pensive breath. "My husband and I adopted two boys, and I love them to death. But once Camry came along, I realized how fun it could be to have a daughter. We just met—I get it. I'm not your mom. But let me treat you, okay? It would be a favor to me."

The more Rachel talked, the less Leah wanted to allow her to buy the dress. Leah didn't deserve it. Not with the dark thoughts running through her mind. A heaviness had set in when Rachel mentioned keeping the dress for Leah. That was the problem—Leah would never be back. She'd never get a special visa like this again. She could never qualify for a passport. She didn't know when or if she could ever learn to tree rift to come back. This might be Leah's first, last, and *only* visit to the Green Lands.

Rachel stood there, waiting for an answer.

Arguing over who bought the stupid dress was the least of Leah's concerns. "Okay."

Rachel's smile brightened. "Great! Since you're the maid of honor, we'll want to pay attention to the color scheme. Something in light green or lavender."

Leah scanned the dresses in a daze. A dress didn't matter. Or maybe she should take care to pick out a nice one, with this being her only shot here. She leaned toward a cute simple one with thin straps until she looked past it at a rack mounted on the shop wall. Long sleeves.

There hung a floor-length, lacy lavender dress with long sleeves. "Is that too fancy?" she asked, pointing at it.

"Nope. Anything in here would work."

Leah took the dress into a changing room. It hugged her just right, with a beautiful scoop neck. She tugged at the sleeves. It was crazy, absolutely crazy. *What are you thinking?* She looked at herself in the mirror. Her dad's eyes looked back at her, framed by her mom's nose and hair. *Who are you? What's your past? Nothing worthwhile. She stole that from you. What's your future? Nothing worthwhile. She stole that from you.*

Her eyes filled with tears. Her mom was home, hiding in exile. Terrified, panicked, livid. Alone. Leah was selfish for leaving. *But not as selfish as the queen.* What could Leah's legacy ever be? What would the man with matching eyes tell her if he were there today? He had died for what he believed in. Could Leah do the same?

Leah sniffled and wiped away her tears. She wasn't committing to anything. It was just a dress. A dress with sleeves.

The kind she might be able to use to help conceal a weapon.

Leah exited the dressing room with dry eyes, the dress draped over her arm. "Let's get this one."

Each holding a bag of purchases, they hit the road to walk back home. "You okay?" Rachel asked.

"Yeah. I guess I'm just nervous about meeting the queen for the first time." She felt like a broken record, but it was the easiest and vaguest truth to tell.

Rachel slung her arm around Leah. "Don't be. She doesn't bite."

No. But she murders to get what she wants.

"Yeah. I think I'm also just tired. Must not have slept well last night."

"I know that feeling all too well. And weddings are crazy. Especially with *our* family. But no one would judge you if you snuck a nap sometime today."

Leah smiled. "Thanks. Maybe I will."

Leah took Rachel's advice to lie down. She didn't need sleep as much as she needed clarity of mind. Her mom's comments cycled through her mind. *'Sometimes you have to know when to give up hope.' 'You and I—we don't belong anywhere!'*

Why had Leah even come? She was hurting her mom for what? A guy? A vacation? Her mom didn't deserve this. *What is your life really worth? Where do you really fit in? You're here talking about buying dresses and BSing your way through a week of fun instead of trying to get justice and honoring your dad's memory.* Maybe Cheryl was right about Leah: she was a disgrace. She'd never amount to anything.

The more she thought of her mom, the more Leah's heart hurt. What had Leah really ever done to make her mom proud? Her mom wasn't stupid, either. Could Leah spend the rest of her life keeping this visit a secret? Did her mom *already* know she was in the Green Lands, instead of in Detroit? Even if she didn't know that part of it, her mom *absolutely* knew Leah had run away. For a week. With her boyfriend. *My life as I know it is over.*

Leah knew, without a shred of doubt, that the moment she came home, they were moving. The boxes were probably already half-packed. No more Garden Club, or green-folk lessons. No vine training. No Marcus.

She fought tears unsuccessfully, each drop imbued with pain as it soaked into the cream pillowcase. When she returned home, she was going to lose Marcus. Trying to take out the queen—and in the process ruining his brother's wedding— she was going to lose Marcus. Either way, she was going to lose him.

I love him.

We're only teenagers. It's not love. And even if it was, how could it last? That's stupid. You've had a good go at it, but just like every other relationship, it has an expiration date.

The only constant had been her mom's love. Other than that, and more important than any other relationship in Leah's life, was the memory of her dad and his lost potential. His people would never see his dreams come to fruition. His wife would never have her husband back. Leah would never know her dad's love. Or even her grandparents' love. Or aunts, uncles, cousins. Yes, she liked Marcus's family. But compared to her own, what did she really owe them?

The queen deserves to die. It's not a question of if I'm crazy *enough to do it. It's a question of whether or not I'm* brave *enough to do it.*

Leah took a shaky breath and wiped away her tears. It wasn't a question of whether she could live with such a serious decision. Perhaps the question she should have been asking the whole time was whether she could live with herself if she *didn't* take action. Maybe her life had been preserved in the first place for this event. And how could she really deny it when it had fallen right into her lap?

A soft tap sounded on Leah's bedroom door. It slowly opened. "Leah?" Marcus whispered.

The decision isn't final until I'm there. Leah quickly and subtly wiped up any remaining tears, then sat up. "Hey." She forced a smile.

"You okay?" he asked, peeking his head in.

"Why wouldn't I be?" She got up, reaching for him in the hallway and soaking in a long warm hug.

"Just worried since you've been in there so long," he said.

She smiled a little more genuinely. "Maybe just overwhelmed. You know how much I *love* hanging out with tons of people. The girl that has a flock of friends at school."

He chuckled. "Fair enough. Want to come see something fun?"

Enjoy him while you have him. You're going to lose him either way. She grabbed his hand. "Lead the way."

Marcus led her down the lane from their property to a little stone cottage a mile away.

"And what is this?"

He gestured at the cottage with wide arms. "A wedding gift."

"That's ... quite a gift."

"Let's take a look." Marcus led her around to the back, pulling a key from its hiding place under a large rock. They stepped inside the quaint one-bedroom setup, which was fully furnished.

"This whole place is really a wedding gift?" she asked.

"Yep. That way when they come to visit, they always have a place they can call home."

A place to call home. A place in each world to call home. And I don't belong anywhere.

"That's really cool," she said.

"Want to see our gift to them?"

"Who is 'our'?"

"From you and me. Hope you're okay with it. My dad and I went to the market while you were out with my mom." He pulled her to the front entrance. "This painting." He rocked his head back and forth. "Do you like it? Maybe I should have waited."

She wore a melancholy smile, taking in the colorful brushstrokes of an abstract painting. It was framed in a striking striped wooden frame that was delicately hand-carved. "It's beautiful."

"Wanna sit down for a while?" he asked.

"Sure."

He claimed one end of a couch, and Leah lay on her side, her head in his lap.

"What's wrong?" he asked.

"Nothing's wrong."

He sweetly moved her hair from the side of her face. "I would definitely disagree."

Marcus was kind, and loving, and smart. What was Leah? A liar. A thief. A subpar person. She was going to lose him anyway, and she'd never deserved him in the first place.

"Just ... I guess a little jealous of your family." She rolled over, looking up at him. "You have both parents, and lots of grandparents, and aunts, uncles, cousins. Everything. I have my mom."

He frowned. "I'm sorry." He played with her hair, smiling. "They'd happily adopt you. The more the merrier."

She flashed a half-hearted smile. "I'd love a family like this. They're all really nice."

"You have a good relationship with your mom, though, right?"

She nodded, gazing into his eyes. "What's the hardest thing you've ever had to do?"

He pursed his lips. "I can admit I've had an easier life than some. But I guess it's just ... trying to figure out who I am. Or at least who I want to be." He shrugged. "But maybe that could be said of every teenager. What about you?"

She pondered her own question. The last several months had been some of the hardest of her life, and also the greatest. Her choices had never mattered as much as they did right now. "I agree with the way you worded it. Who I am. Who I'll be. It's tough. And we don't all have the same journey."

Was there any chance he could ever understand hers? What if she just told him her secret? If anyone could understand, Marcus would, right?

It wasn't that simple. It was *far* from simple. His parents worked for the woman who had murdered Leah's dad. Having met the lot of them, Leah had tried to ignore one important truth. It wasn't like anyone had gushed about the queen like Tanner had, but it certainly didn't seem like they were plotting something against her either.

Leah was alone. No one in either world could fathom how this felt. She trusted Marcus with everything, except maybe this truth. With her and her mom's lives in the balance... He might overreact and turn them in, for all she knew.

After some silence, Marcus attempted to coax Leah from her somber mood. "If you could pick, which realm would you live in, now that you've been here? You'll be able to choose once you're eighteen, and your mom would have to accept it if you came here and only visited there sometimes." He winked. "Like I'll visit you until you turn eighteen."

I'll never have that choice. "I like it here." She looked away, considering his pronouncement. If she assassinated the queen at his brother's wedding, they were done. She probably wouldn't even survive the attempt. Either way, they were done—he wouldn't be visiting. If she cowered from the task, she'd go home, and her mom would move them and deny contact—he wouldn't be visiting. But if she warned him ahead of time that she would be moving ... he'd still come see her in the human world, and they'd find a way to make it work, right? "What about you? Do you want to live in the human world, or here?"

"Guess that depends a lot on who I'm with at the time." He grinned. "Tobias moving there for Cam makes more sense with her being human. I think I'd have a harder time moving away from family. But I'd be willing to, under the right circumstances."

She had a glimmer of hope. Maybe she'd been thinking about this all wrong. He'd be willing to come see her, to be with her. But after tasting the energy of the Green Lands, could she so easily give it up? And in reality, how long would he stay with her? He hated her lies. More would come out eventually. It was inevitable. And what would happen the next time she screwed up? What if her shoplifting habit picked back up when she got stressed? She'd already been sorely tempted just earlier that day.

I'm going to lose him one way or another.

"Do you think your parents are proud of you?" she asked.

"I hope so. I think so..."

Her mom wasn't. Her dad wouldn't be. And she'd done nothing to earn their pride. But maybe she could. She could make a difference, make a statement, have a purpose more grand and noble than a regular teenage human could even fathom. After all, she wasn't regular, and she wasn't human.

Leah and Marcus didn't linger long at the cottage. After heading back to his house, it was more of the same—meeting new people, visiting and helping with the wedding preparations. Leah did her best to appear as though her mind weren't running a marathon. As though she wasn't contemplating the unthinkable the next day.

They gathered for a small quiet dinner with Marcus's family, bride and groom included. Leah glanced around the large wooden dining table. Tobias and Camry were glowing. Rachel and Guillen complemented each other so well. Samantha and Brad had a natural chemistry. Leah wanted that with Marcus. And in a lot of ways, they had that. But she was going to lose him anyway. And it was all one woman's fault that Leah would never sit at a table like this with her own parents. She caught Marcus's eye with a sweet smile. *I wish.*

Leah pondered the agenda for the next day. The queen would be there at both the luncheon and the ceremony, officiating the latter. If she could muster the courage, Leah could try getting to the queen at either event. The luncheon would be less public, so perhaps there would be less security detail. But at the wedding, she'd be literally tasked with walking right up to the woman. Surely, she wouldn't have a dozen guards standing right beside her then.

Camry announced they couldn't stay for long after dinner. They were going to spend the rest of the evening with her parents on final preparations.

"Oh, I almost forgot." Guillen frowned. "I got word that Catrina might not be able to make it to the luncheon, but she *definitely* will still make it to the wedding."

Rachel frowned as well. "How come?"

Guillen shrugged. "She's plenty busy. She sent her apologies."

Camry nodded. "It's okay. Thanks for letting us know."

Marcus leaned over, whispering in Leah's ear. "Catrina's the queen-in-waiting."

"Oh. Cool." Leah gulped. That made the decision easier. Assuming both women had security detail, with one less queen in attendance at the luncheon, she stood a much better chance.

After a short discussion with the bride about her duties the next day, and a few hours hanging out and playing card games with Marcus's family, they called it an early night. Leah went to her guest room. Despite the warmth of Green Lands energy, it felt cold. Despite the busy, welcoming family, it felt lonely.

Leah lay in bed, imagining the next day a thousand different ways. She wasn't sure she could actually do it—take a life. But she made her list, and it felt less wrong than she'd imagined it should. It wasn't just about her family. The entire Green Lands could benefit.

She rolled around in bed, restless, unsure. There was only one thing Leah was certain of: she couldn't trust herself.

Chapter 26

Unable to sleep, and uncertain where the next day would take her, Leah got out of bed. It was wrong to go see Marcus, given she might hurt his family the next day. But maybe spending time with him would help calm her, help clear her mind.

Leaving behind the beeswax candle and striker she'd been provided, she relied on the moonlight streaming in through windows around the house. She tiptoed out of the guest room, walking down the hallway as stealthily as possible. Climbing the stairs, she quietly made her way to Marcus's room. Only one of the steps scolded her with a muted creak. She stood at his door for at least two or three minutes, contemplating this decision. What was she going to accomplish?

Taking a deep breath, she gently knocked on the door. She waited a minute, realizing she might have to knock louder if he'd fallen asleep. But she couldn't risk waking others. As she went to turn the knob, it opened from the other side.

The room was pitch black. "Yeah?" Marcus said, barely above a whisper.

She lunged forward, holding him tight. She hadn't anticipated the amount of flesh she'd be touching. He wasn't wearing a shirt. She slid a hand down until she reached a waistband. Even if he slept commando, he probably wouldn't have opened the door that way.

He let out a breathy chuckle, resting his chin on her shoulder. "Can't sleep either?"

She soaked in the warmth of his embrace as his hands rubbed her back. "No. Can I come in?"

"Um... Well... You know my parents' rules. They'd kill me if they found out."

She frowned. "I just want to talk, and cuddle."

Silence. What else could she say? 'I'm trying to decide if I should ruin your brother's wedding?'

"Sure. Just for a little while." Marcus pulled Leah in. The door clicked softly behind them. He led her by the hand to his bed, where he lay down.

She joined him, cuddling up next to him. After a minute, she shifted positions, instead facing away. He followed her, spooning her with his arms around her.

"What's up?" he asked.

She sighed. "I guess it's just nerves about tomorrow. First time being a maid of honor. First time meeting a queen. A lot could go wrong."

"Mmm, feel you there. My first time being a best man. My mind's playing everything I need to remember on a loop. And imagining myself doing something embarrassing like tripping and face-planting." He chuckled, then squeezed her tighter. "As for the queen, you *really* don't need to worry about her. It's not like this is some official royal function all about *her*. This is Tobias and Cam's wedding."

Leah calmed the smallest degree with his reassurances. Just the feeling of Marcus's chest rising and falling behind her gave her the tiniest spark of hope in the sea she found herself drowning in. He was good for her. She wished she could say the reverse.

His voice softened. "Maybe it's good to just rip off the bandage tomorrow. Introduce yourself to her; then you can finally let go of these nerves." He kissed her bare shoulder. "And she's going to love you."

Leah internally scoffed. *Not likely.*

His lips placed another kiss on her shoulder. "Just like I do."

Her entire chest ached as she fought back tears, unsuccessfully. That was not what she'd come to hear.

"I mean, I don't know if it's love. I guess ... just ... I really care about you, Leah. You're special to me." He kissed her shoulder a third time.

Tears streamed down her face onto his sheets. She couldn't breathe. Couldn't speak. She wanted to reciprocate. She loved him too. But she couldn't say that. She might do the unthinkable the next day. She was going to lose him either way. "I care about you, too."

They both lay still and silent for another moment. Maybe he deserved to hear it. As a goodbye? Maybe it wasn't a goodbye. She might chicken out.

As much as she needed something to shut up the nightmare in her mind, she needed to show him she really *did* care.

Leah rolled over, feeling his face and finding his lips. She caressed his lips more sweetly and softly, more intentionally than she ever had before. It was slow, intimate, deep. It was 'goodbye.' It was 'I love you.' It was 'thank you.' It was everything she felt for him, all rolled up into one.

He reciprocated perfectly, gently, passionately.

Her heart pounding, she came up for air. His lips grazed her neck, his thumbs slipping under the waistband of her pajama bottoms.

"I, um…" he whispered as he caught his breath. "I'm ready. I want to. Do you?"

Leah pressed her lips together, her heart breaking completely. She wanted it. He wanted it. *Why now?* "No."

"Oh. Um… Okay," he whispered in obvious confusion. "I, uh … have protection. Or … we could do something else."

She stared into the darkness that obscured his face. "No." Her mind was spinning, her heart faltering. Maybe she owed it to him(s), knowing what she might do to his family. Maybe she owed it to him as a goodbye. Maybe she owed it to herself, to enjoy one last special thing with him before putting herself in danger.

She couldn't. She knew Marcus. It would only hurt him more. "I should go."

"You're sure?" The hurt in his voice only made things worse. "We can just go back to cuddling if you want."

"No. We both need our sleep. This was a mistake. I'm sorry." She rolled over and quietly left his room, closing his door with a soft click. Back downstairs after climbing into her own bed undetected, she wetted her pillow with fresh tears, hating the unfairness of every aspect of her life.

You're going to lose him either way.

How do you pretend to be happy and normal on the most important, and possibly last, day of your life?

Despite taking forever to fall asleep, Leah got up fairly early and helped Rachel make breakfast. Rachel flipped sunflower oatcakes on a griddle over the coal stove while Leah stirred a bowl of granola.

"I appreciate the help," Rachel said. "I usually don't mind cooking; it helps me focus on my to-do list. But today's going to be a bit crazy." She folded her arms with a spatula in her hand. "I'm so old."

Leah smiled. "You guys don't seem that old to me. And I'm happy to help." *It's keeping me busy, distracted, calm.*

Footsteps descending the stairs to the right announced Marcus's approach. Leah clung to her facade. He joined them with a hand on her back.

"Hey, handsome," Rachel said.

"Hey." He flashed Leah a hesitant, shy smile.

Leah bit her lip and looked down, her resolve breaking. "I, uh… I should go shower." She spotted a frown in the brief moment she dared to glance at Marcus as she left.

She hurried in the solar-heated shower and got ready, everything in place but her fancy new dress. Marcus avoided eye contact as much as she did during breakfast. Their awkward silence wasn't noticed amongst the excited chatter of other family members. Leah trained her eyes on a large painted family portrait on the wall. Rachel's old friend and mentor—another Seeder—had painted it for their family.(t) What if Queen Kaylah hadn't murdered Leah's dad? There could have been just such a painting hanging in the palace of her own family that Leah would now kill to see.

"Is it okay if Leah and I go for a walk?" Marcus asked his parents as they finished up.

Rachel glanced at a pendulum clock ticking in the corner. "We leave for Capital City in an hour."

"Just along the canal."

"It's up to you. An hour. That means both dressed and heading out the door."

He looked at Leah, pleading with his eyes.

"Yeah. I'm sure we can be back in plenty of time," Leah said with a forced smile.

They left out the back door. Leah frowned as they walked past the tree house. *How did things change so fast?* Exiting through a side gate, they turned down a dirt path alongside a canal. They walked side by side for a couple of minutes without a word.

"Are we going to talk?" he asked.

She focused on her feet. "You're the one that wanted to go for a walk."

Stopping, he took her hand. "You won't even look at me?"

She looked up briefly to meet his gaze. "I'm just tired."

He huffed. "You're a better liar than that." He drew a deep breath. "Did I freak you out by saying I love you?"

Biting the insides of her cheeks, she shook her head.

The hurt in his voice cut deep. "What did I do wrong?"

She studied his face. "Why would you think you did anything wrong? You're perfect."

His mouth hung open as he grappled for words. "You… Have you just been teasing all these months? You were the one who said when I was ready … that you would be, too." He threw his head back, running a hand through his hair. "I realize how much of a dick I sound like when I say that out loud." He sighed. "I'm not trying to guilt you into it. I just... I'm confused about what changed."

"You didn't do anything wrong. I'm not mad. It wasn't you. I'm just..." All she could manage was another shrug.

He narrowed his eyes. "Are you seriously pulling an 'it's not you, it's me'?"

She gave him a half-smile. "I guess I am. It's the truth."

He scrunched his eyebrows. "Are you breaking up with me? On today of all days?"

"No!" *But maybe I should.* She fought back tears. "I don't want to lose you."

"Why would you lose me?" He studied her face. "What don't I know?"

He wouldn't understand. He couldn't.

Better to give a less shocking truth. "I just worry. Thinking of back home. If this didn't go off perfectly, and my mom makes us move when I get back."

He squeezed her hand. "So, we'll have to work harder to see each other. I'm up for the challenge. Because I *do* love you, Leah."

Her lip quivered as she broke into tears. He pulled her close.

"I don't know what's going on with you, but I'm here for you, okay?" he whispered. "I know the lies to our parents are bugging you. And you're sad about family stuff. And nervous about today. And I shouldn't have put any extra pressure on you last night when you just wanted to talk. I get it. I'm not in a rush."

He released her, holding her at arm's length. "What can I do?"

She gnawed on her lip as he wiped away her tears. She was thinking about this all wrong. She needed to live for today. "How about another hug?"

He obliged, not letting go until she first started to. He studied her face again. "Are we okay? Are you okay?"

She nodded. "You're right. Just too much going on, I guess."

"That's what's nice about being a team." He kissed her hand. "Sometimes, when one person is down, the other can help lift them up."

"Yeah. We should get back."

He wrapped a reassuring arm around her as they returned to his house to get dressed.

Marcus looked sharp in his medium-brown slacks and vest over a cream button-up shirt. Leah felt that much better after their walk and chat. This wasn't about her, or them, or anyone else. This was a wedding day. She liked Tobias and Camry.

"You look amazing." Leah wore a genuine smile at seeing Marcus dressed up in this more traditional Green Lands formal attire.

"You're stealing my lines now?" He winked.

The family headed to the cave they'd first rifted into. Confused, she whispered to ask Marcus how that would work for his mom—she couldn't rift anymore. He clarified that it was only interworld rifting mature Seeder women couldn't do. They could still rift within the Green Lands because of the energy on both departure and arrival.

Still plenty nervous, but with a successful trip under her belt, and more energy coursing through her veins here, Leah opened her own rift to make it through.

Capital City was a bit of a misnomer. It was the name of the city, but also the colloquial term for a wide chunk of territory, what was left of neutral territory after the war ended. Leah wondered if it would be better or worse for her, if she did go through with her suicide mission. But she looked down at her hand, held firmly by someone she genuinely cared for. Genuinely loved. Someone she actually invested in and had allowed into her life. Who'd helped guide her to her true identity.

Leah had thought Marcus's family property and the surrounding homes were breathtaking—but the manor for the wedding was beyond words. It was massive. She couldn't believe it wasn't a palace.

After touring the picturesque grounds for a while—complete with a dozen flower gardens, and likely twice as many chiseled statues—and getting instructions on her part in the ceremony, Leah and Marcus went back to meeting and greeting people as they trickled in. The luncheon was only supposed to be family and close friends. Leah's opinion soured a bit at the thought of them also inviting the queen and king, no doubt as a show of status. *They worship her.*

As an 'intimate' gathering involving a Seeder family, there were over three dozen attendees. Leah nervously eyed the people she assumed to be Seeders. They looked just like Ivies, just like humans. But beneath their skin, they were lethal. Sharp blades could extend on their forearms, between their wrists and elbows. Some of them could shoot darts—wooden stakes—from their fingertips. The women were able to easily harness two to three times as much energy as Leah could.

The hairs on the back of her neck stood at attention, her pores clamming up at the thought of being so surrounded by her parents' enemies.

The moment Queen Kaylah and King Eric entered the room, everyone stood. She was gorgeous, thin, elegant. He stood next to her with broad shoulders, his handsome face accentuated by a sharp jawline. The queen and king gave off quite the air of authority as they politely nodded to the room, then sat at the end of a huge banquet table.

Leah was sick to her stomach. Just the sight of this woman bombarded her with so many emotions. Between Marcus and Samantha, Leah sat down when everyone else did. *Stupid, murderous bitch needs to have people worship her at a wedding. It all has to be about her?*

"You okay, Leah? You're looking pale," Samantha remarked.

Leah choked down her hatred, focusing on her food. "Yeah, fine. Thank you." She forced a smile.

Marcus placed a hand on her knee, rubbing sweetly. "See, not bad so far, right?"

"Yeah. It's great." *Why is it so much easier to lie about shoplifting than to get through a simple lunch?* She took a bite of food, looking up when a cackle of laughter traveled down the table. *She even has a stupid laugh.* The queen had jet-black hair, intricately braided, with a tiara to finish it off. It was simpler than the tiara Leah had back home. Wearing bright red lipstick, the queen kissed her husband, then carefully wiped away a smudge of transferred lipstick with her thumb.

Leah's heart became hollow. Had she *ever* seen her mom that happy?

Queen Kaylah had murdered Leah's dad for this throne. A throne she shared with a human. The throne she was stepping down from like it hadn't come at a precious cost.

Leah's mom's words played through her mind. They didn't belong here. They didn't belong in the human world. They didn't belong *anywhere*. Leah would never meet the man who'd given her the bright green eyes she loved. Her mom wouldn't date again. They'd never be whole again. Leah wasn't supposed to even be here, alive.

Leah stared more than she ought to, her reality crashing down around her. The room was caving in, and no one else could see it, could feel it.

A servant approached the queen and whispered something. The queen's gregarious expression vacated the scene immediately. The exchange was short, but telling. The servant shrank in size as the queen's face turned stern. She jabbed a finger at one of the doorways, her jaw set, her nostrils flaring, as she made some type of demand. The servant timidly bowed and left the room.

Something in Leah snapped.

"I'm going to use the restroom." She set her napkin down on the table, heading through the dining hall exit into the hallway. Leah hugged herself in the bathroom, trying to control her breathing as her face heated. *Can I seriously do this?*

Planning an assassination and actually carrying it out were vastly different things. *Could* she really do this?

There had to be more to the story, right? Yes, Leah's mom had lied to conceal the Green Lands and the horrible truth of her husband's demise, but she hadn't lied about anything else. *Everything* Leah had ever heard from the Garden Club and Kara backed up the fact that this queen *wasn't* a good one. But maybe, perhaps, there was a tiny sliver of something redeemable? Something Leah had missed? Maybe the queen had changed? Then again, look how she treated her servants...

Leah ticked off a list with each of the queen's offenses.

She'd murdered Leah's dad and grandparents, and others.

She'd destroyed her people's way of life, leaving many jobless, devastating their economy, and outlawing some of their natural abilities.

She'd taken the coward's way out of the war by giving in to Seeder demands and forfeiting Ivy lands.

She'd created an unhealthy atmosphere for Bomen, at least in other parts of the kingdom, or for those not employed by her for her own agenda.

She treated her servants like crap.

How many offenses did the queen need before taking her out became the right thing to do? Like Leah's mom had once said—people had become complacent in accepting her rule.

Leah splashed her face with water and toweled off. She tucked a stray hair behind her ear, gazing in the bathroom mirror. Those green eyes. "This is for you, Dad."

Leah returned to the dining hall with a carefully crafted smile. Marcus grinned, likely proud she was so well composed. The room buzzed with excited chatter and the scraping of silverware against plates. Everyone here was happy; maybe the queen wasn't so bad? Hadn't ruined things as much as Leah's mom had let on? But Leah's time in the Green Lands was hardly representative of the whole of it. These people were royalty, politicians, the enemy of her father. They were well-to-do. They were there for a wedding. Of course *they* were happy. The room pressed in on Leah, suffocating her.

Once Leah sat down, she leaned over, daring to broach the topic as she hadn't dared before. "We talked about the queen having two younger brothers, but I was wondering about the older one. She killed him, right?"

Marcus furrowed his brow, whispering in return. "Yeah. Not really the best conversation with her or this group, though."

"Why did she do it?"

He looked annoyed at the impertinent topic. "He was bad news. I can tell you all about it later."

"That's what they teach in schools?"

He took a sip of white grape juice. "Of course."

A numbness took hold of her, her heart teetering at the edge of a precipice. "You believe it?"

"We really shouldn't talk about this right now, okay?"

She stared at him. "It's a yes or no question."

He tilted his head in warning. "Yes. I believe it. Where is this even coming from?"

And with that confirmation, Leah had her answer—what she'd known all along. Her dad's memory was being tainted by his murderer. And Marcus believed it.

She'd screw up eventually. He'd break up with her eventually. And his belief in this fake queen's propaganda meant he didn't truly love the real Leah. How could he? *I was going to lose him no matter what.*

She shook her head dismissively, chomping down on a grape.

Later during the meal, she glanced down the table at the woman responsible for all the pain in Leah's life. All the pain in her family.

The queen had to die.

Chapter 27

Before the lunch plates were cleared, Leah needed to make use of those dress sleeves. She needed to use her old skills to stash a knife.

"Who are all those people down there?" she asked Marcus to distract him. He began naming everyone at the far end of the table. Shoplifting when no one else was in the same aisle was one thing. Tucking a knife up her sleeve amidst dozens of people, guards included, was a whole nother feat. Luckily, there was plenty of conversation—and eyes focused on their tablemates and not on the table—as plates emptied.

Leah placed her napkin on the knife, then rested her hand at the end closest to her. Not that different from a store shelf, really. She slowly, carefully extended her vine just enough to touch her mark under the napkin as her eyes darted around the room.

Servants began to clear the plates at the end of the table; she panicked. Swiftly grasping the blade, she reeled it in faster than she'd meant to. One of the serrated teeth caught on the end of her lace sleeve. She tried to tug it free.

With every second that passed, a servant grew closer to clear Leah's plate. She focused on freeing the knife, making it quick, and pretending to pay attention to Marcus's ramblings about who was who.

The queen stood up.

Leah set her free hand on the napkin to hide the wiggles and apply pressure. She yanked her vine free. "Is the queen leaving?"

She looked to her left; the servant was almost there. She extended her vine under the napkin again, carefully angling the knife to scrape against her skin and not the dress.

"No. She'll be around for a bit. It's probably the best time to meet her now, before the hordes show up for the actual ceremony." He smiled.

Leah successfully tucked the knife up her long sleeve, retracted her vine, and moved that hand onto her lap. The servant reached for her plate. Leah put the napkin on it, and he whisked it away.

One heart attack down. One left to go.

"How about I introduce you to her?" Marcus offered. "Not too many people swarming around her right now."

Leah glanced around the room. People were just barely starting to get up. Many sat in place. Some approached the bride and groom.

Now or never. The actual ceremony will have more guards, will be more public.

"I'm afraid I'll be nervous, and her guards will tackle me or something." She tried to sound genuinely anxious in a lighthearted way.

Marcus chuckled. "I mean, don't lunge at her or anything. Otherwise, you're fine." He reached for her hand. "Let me introduce you."

Leah moved her other hand to cover the one hidden under the table so he wouldn't feel the knife. "I want to go alone."

He raised his eyebrows playfully. "Really? You look terrified. I know her. It's not a big deal."

She swallowed hard, answering too curtly for a good show. "I want to do it alone!"

He raised his hands. "Fine. Whatever. Just ... go say hi."

She filled her lungs to capacity, gazing into his eyes. "I need you to know it wasn't your fault."

His face grew pink as his eyes darted around. "You're bringing *that* up right now?"

He didn't know what she meant. He soon would.

"Never mind. Just in a weird mood."

He kissed her on the cheek. "I can confirm that." He chuckled again. "It's all family here. Just breathe. If you want to go meet her on your own, go for it. Then I'll tell you something fun, okay?"

She nodded. "Thanks."

Leah stood, concealing the knife under her sleeve. She crossed her arms to further hide it as she approached the front of the room where the queen stood. Each footstep closer required twice the effort to mask Leah's rage, her terror.

The king—a handsome tall blond—stood a few feet away, busy speaking with someone else. No one really talked about the king much. Leah hadn't asked. But it just now dawned on her that the humans had probably played as significant a role in helping the queen in the war as the Seeders had. What resources had *he* brought to the table? That was why kings and queens from different kingdoms and lands paired up, wasn't it? To combine resources, to conquer.

The room wasn't filled with wedding guests prattling on. It was filled with ghosts, with screams only Leah could hear. The human world—the majority of the Earth—was *massively* larger than the little tucked-away Green Lands realm. Her dad's troops had really never stood a chance, not when the queen had paired up with Leah's father's enemy *and* the humans.

Red clouded Leah's vision. She sweat, her breathing shallow.

The queen chatted with a couple of people. Leah stood close, waiting for her chance. She assessed the room and spotted only two guards nearby. They weren't that close. If Leah could get within striking distance, this whole thing could be over before anyone even knew it began.

It felt like a decade waiting for her turn to talk to the queen. Leah was tempted to look over her shoulder, but she knew she'd catch Marcus's attention. She couldn't look at him again. They were over. Everything was over.

Queen Kaylah acknowledged Leah with a warm smile, no doubt an expert at charming everyone she was around. She'd duped Marcus's family. The two other women walked away, and the queen invited her to approach.

Leah shuffled forward, her feet each weighing a ton. She clutched the arm with the knife to her chest, ever so slowly moving it down in front of her. Almost forgetting, she dipped into a half curtsy.

Queen Kaylah gave Leah a wider smile, tilting her head to look past her. "Marcus's date, right?" She narrowed her eyes playfully. "I thought I heard girlfriend."

Leah couldn't find her voice. She didn't need one.

Cupping her left hand under the other wrist, she allowed the blade to slide down. Past the serrated edges, Leah let her vines push it out enough to grasp.

In a swift and decisive motion, she raised the knife and aimed for the queen's throat.

The blade barely meeting skin, the queen grabbed Leah's hand, quickly wrapping her vine around Leah's arm.

"Your Majesty!" someone yelled.

In the split second it took the queen to recognize the attack, Leah launched her vine from her other wrist toward the evil woman's throat, the queen's eyes boring into Leah with fury.

The queen caught the vine with her free hand, wrapping her second vine around Leah's other arm.

The whole thing happened within the blink of an eye, and now Leah's arms were numb. Panic, defeat, and rage warred within her as her heart pounded, useless emotions that wouldn't change her fate now. She was done.

"Everyone stay where you are!" someone boomed.

"Leah!" Marcus yelled.

The queen's jaw was clenched, her nostrils flared. Two guards—Ivies—came up to Leah, securing her with vines as the queen released her own.

"*Marcus?*" Rachel called for answers.

"I... I don't know!" he replied.

"Take her," the queen seethed.

"*I hate you,*" Leah said. "I HATE YOU!"

The guards yanked Leah to the side, pulling her toward the back exit. Her last view of the room showed a multitude of shocked faces.

Worst of all was the soul-wrenching look of shock and betrayal on Marcus's face. "Leah?"

Leah's jaw clamped shut. A river of tears cascaded down her face as the guards pushed her out of the room.

The guards weren't gentle, even though she wasn't resisting. They swiftly shoved her down the hallway. Leah was a jumbled mess of adrenaline, still unsure of what she'd just done. Still unsure of whether or not she regretted it. Opening a door at the end of the hall, the guards moved her inside the small sitting room, securing her to a chair with more vines.

Leah said nothing. They said nothing. One stayed in the room while the other exited, shutting the door behind him.

Leah's eyes fell to the marble floor as she tried to process what she'd done. She'd just tried to kill someone. But her life was a messy web of lies and failure, anyway. She was calmer than she'd expected to be.

Until she thought of Marcus. She began to cry again, and hated that she wasn't able to do more than wipe her moist cheeks on her shoulders. Marcus was good. Even if he bought the lies about Leah's dad, he couldn't help it any more than she could have helped her mom hiding the truth from her most of her life.

Her mom. This had been far too rash. Leah had promised in her runaway letter that she would come home. That was never going to happen. You didn't try to off a murder-happy queen, or any queen for that matter, and get let go.

This whole predicament could have been prevented. Choose Marcus and deny her true self, or not allow herself to fall for him in the first place. She never could have had it both ways. *Why did I waste so much time caring about Marcus? If I had focused, I could have done it.*

The door opened, and Leah looked up. The queen stood before her, entering and grabbing a chair to sit across the room. The door clicked behind her as she sat down, crossing her legs, straightening her dress, and staring at Leah.

Queen Kaylah took a composed breath as the remaining guard watched on. "Leah, right? Or is that name a cover?"

Leah glared into the woman's dark brown eyes. "It's Leah. Eleana, actually." She instantly frowned. "Please don't hurt Marcus. He had nothing to do with this. I promise. He didn't know anything!" She was downright desperate, unsure how corrupt the queen was. She'd killed her own brother, so why not her employee's innocent son?

Queen Kaylah raised her eyebrows. "I believe you. Marcus is a good kid. But maybe a little too trusting. I would never hurt my favorite cousin's son."

Leah's eyes grew wide. "Wait. What?"

The queen smirked. "I have a hard time believing you didn't know Guillen is my cousin."

Leah read her face. She had to be lying. Marcus had never mentioned he was actually *related* to royalty. *But ... back in the dining hall, he just said something about it all being family in there.* She'd thought he'd meant it as a generalization, with the obvious exception of the queen and king.

The queen examined the injuries on her hand. As she'd caught Leah's flexed vine, she'd sustained some cuts. The serrated knife had done enough damage to draw blood on her neck, though not much.

"But I want to talk about you, Eleana. Who sent you? Why do you want to kill me?"

"No one sent me. You *deserve* to die."

The queen rocked her head back and forth, far too casually for the mood. "Some people think that. Comes with the territory." She pointed to Leah. "But why do *you* think so?"

Leah looked her dead in the eyes. "Because you murdered my dad."

Queen Kaylah bowed her head, frowning. "I'm sorry if that's true. Whether by my hand or my orders, many lives were lost in the old war." She looked again at Leah. "I assure you, I took no pleasure in any of them."

"Oh, I think you took pleasure in this one." A sapphire necklace around the queen's neck gleamed in the daylight pouring in through several windows. "Seems to have done you a lot of good."

"No."

"No pleasure? Not even when you killed your own brother?"

The queen's head twisted slightly as she sat straighter. "What do you mean by that?"

Leah twisted her head to match, trying to figure out her game. "Kill more than one of them? Did you lose track?"

The queen's eyes narrowed. "No. I only killed one. What is your father's name?"

She proudly spoke it. "King Soren."

Queen Kaylah went pale. "And your mother?"

Leah shook her head in confusion at these stupid questions. "Who else? His wife, the queen." She didn't even know her mom's real name, since she'd adopted an alias in her self-exile, and hadn't yet shared it.

The queen remained silent, studying Leah's face. "You look like her," she whispered. "Where is your mother?"

Leah swallowed hard, looking down. This was bad. This was exactly why her mom never wanted them to return to the Green Lands. And in her stupidity and anger, Leah was leading them right to her mom. She could only pray her mom's careful, watchful eye could help her elude them. If not, Leah would never be able to forgive herself. "I'll never tell you."

The queen's voice rose. "*Eleana! Where is your mother?!*"

Leah met her gaze in loathing, her eyes clouded with a coat of tears. "I'd rather die."

Without another word, the murderous queen got up from her chair, leaving the room without even trying to deny her part in the assassination of Leah's dad.

Chapter 28

Kaylah got less than ten steps out of the room before leaning against the wall and sliding down. She stared at the floor, trying to find her breath. She couldn't breathe, couldn't formulate a coherent thought.

Soren?

Her breath became rapid as she grew numb to the world around her.

"Henry, go call for him," one of the servants said.

"May I please heal you, Your Majesty?" someone asked.

Kaylah remained on the floor, dazed, focusing on a pattern in the marble that resembled a little tree with its leaves stripped from the branches.

Soren?

"Kaylah, sweetheart." Eric crouched down, visibly concerned. "Are you okay?"

She didn't answer, her mind playing back a memory from so many years ago.

He said she was pregnant.

Eric rubbed her arm. "I'm here for you. You'll be alright."

Kaylah blinked, fully registering her husband's voice. "Soren had a daughter."

Eric's eyes searched hers. "You're sure?"

She nodded slowly. He knew better than to ask that question. Soren wasn't a name she uttered casually. Not after the horrible things he'd done to so many people, to her.

Eric's throat bobbed. "Will you please let the healer clean you up?"

Kaylah held out her hand, and the Seeder healer stepped forward. The hand and neck injuries took barely any time at all, then she began cleaning up the blood.

"What do we do?" Eric asked.

Kaylah took calming breaths. In and out. She needed to collect herself. She was a dignified head of state, not a fragile teenage girl. She'd had years to grow even thicker skin. But this had completely blindsided her. She looked at a guard. "Three guards for the girl. She says she acted alone, but keep things under lockdown." She stood, Eric aiding her. "We need to talk to Marcus."

Guards led Kaylah and Eric to a larger sitting room where the bride and groom and their closest family members were being watched over. Tobias and Camry huddled in a corner with her parents. Rachel and Guillen stood on either side of Marcus. Sitting, he stared at the floor, his head bowed, still in shock. The moment Kaylah walked through the door, he frowned, tears forming. "I promise. I don't know what that was about. I'd never be part of that."

"I know." Kaylah matched his frown, hurting for the kind-hearted boy. He'd spent so much time in the palace growing up. She didn't doubt for a second his innocence in all of this.

He went back to staring at the floor. "I don't know why she did that."

Kaylah knelt before him, gently placing her hands on his knees. "Look at me, Marcus."

A tear rolled down his cheek.

"I don't blame you. She told me you weren't involved."

He shook his head. "Why did she do it?"

Kaylah bolstered her courage. He wasn't ready to hear it yet. "Tell me about Leah's home and family."

He furrowed his brow. "She just lives with her mom. Her dad died in the war before she was born. Her aunt moved out earlier this year, but I don't know where she went."

Kaylah nodded. "I need her mother's address."

He looked back down. "Why?"

"Marcus!" Rachel chastised. "This is serious."

He remained silent.

Kaylah needed that answer, and there was no time to waste. "I'm asking as your family. I'm ordering as your queen."

He met her eyes in shame. "720 West Ash."

"Thank you." Kaylah nodded at the guards, and one left. She stood, surveying the group. Eric lovingly rubbed her back. All eyes other than Marcus's were on her, waiting for an answer. "She's the daughter of Soren and Beata."

Rachel gasped, clutching a hand over her mouth. Guillen's eyes grew wide. Marcus looked up, losing all color in his face.

"No," Rachel said.

"You're *absolutely* certain?" Guillen asked, reaching out to hold Rachel's hand.

Kaylah nodded. "His eyes, the rest looks like her mother. If we'd known she existed, we would have been idiots not to see it. And the age is right."

"I thought she looked..." Rachel wore a familiar crestfallen expression. "I had nightmares last night."

That was a gutting confession to hear, though no surprise to most in the room.

"He told me she was..." Rachel whispered. "I thought he was lying."

"Me too," Kaylah offered.

"Soren? That's that guy, right?" Camry asked Tobias.

He glared at Marcus. "Yes." His voice was hard. "That's the one."

Guillen ran his free hand through his hair. "This is my fault."

Kaylah furrowed her brow in confusion.

"I..." He glanced at Marcus. "She showed up at the cave without a passport. She said she'd lost it in a move. I issued a temporary diplomatic visa. Any security checks would have led to me. I'm so sorry."

Kaylah shook her head. "No. No one here is to blame. Her mother put it in her head that I murdered 'King' Soren."

Marcus got up from his chair, stomping to the door. A guard stood in his way, and Kaylah nodded to allow him to leave.

Rachel let out a heavy sigh, glancing between her two devastated sons. "What now?"

Kaylah frowned, addressing the bride and groom. "I'm sorry, but we're going to have to cancel today. We're in neutral territory, and I can't be sure it's safe with all the people coming. And it's ... a sticky family situation and political nightmare." Her frown deepened as the bride's eyes filled with tears, and she nodded in understanding. "I'm so sorry. This wasn't the best time for this to emerge." She turned to a guard. "Send notification to the cave network to intercept guests where possible. Ensure they're discreet."

"Yes, Your Majesty."

Rachel squeezed Guillen's hand. "I'm going to check on Marcus."

"I can stay here," Guillen said.

"I'm going to talk to the girl again," Kaylah said.

"I'll come with you," Eric offered.

She pursed her lips. "I'd like some time alone."

Eric wrinkled his nose. "You're sure that's for the best?"

She nodded. "They know where to find you. Stay with the family, please."

He returned the nod, sitting down on a settee.

Kaylah turned to head out.

"Are you okay?" Guillen asked.

She looked back with a forced smile. "Of course I am. I always am."

He gave a sympathetic frown.

She grinned, shaking her head. Guillen may have only been a cousin, but he was more of a big brother than Soren had ever been. Both Guillen and Eric always had her back. "Don't you two gang up on me now."

Chapter 29

The utter silence made it feel like decades passed in the room where Leah was held captive. All she could do was look around at the expensive decorations and the guard. The tingling in her arms announced the queen's numbing poison was wearing off. *How could I completely forget she has vines and that there are these different chemical channels I haven't learned?* She huffed. Even Tanner in his idiocy had described the queen as 'badass.' Leah was beyond stupid—and that stupidity had earned her this fate.

The door opened, and the queen came back in—she didn't have a scratch on her. *Of course she'd have a Seeder healer on hand to take care of her every need.* The lack of blood soured any satisfaction Leah had felt. But she hadn't been able to see herself trying to live a 'normal' life anymore, and she certainly wouldn't be able to now. Her life was anything but normal.

The queen sat down with the poise of a ruler this time. "I think we should talk about your parents, and find out what your mother taught you all of those years in hiding."

Leah scowled. "You admitted you murdered my dad already. That's enough for me."

"Executed. Not murdered. That's an important distinction."

Leah rolled her eyes. "The victor always gets to label things and tell the story the way they want."

Kaylah continued. "You called your parents the queen and king. They never had that legal title. They were frauds."

Leah glowered, her face heating. "I trust my mom more than I ever could the bitch that stole their place. I've seen her tiara, and I've heard enough from outside sources to know the truth."

"Why do you think they had the right to the throne?" Kaylah asked coolly.

"Because he was the oldest. Obviously."

Kaylah cocked her head. "We're matriarchal. Did your mother teach you about the Mother Vines?"

Leah clamped her mouth shut. She'd never heard that term. "It doesn't matter."

"Leah, *none* of my brothers are eligible for the throne. It's not just tradition. It's a dictate of the way our powers work. That's why the next heir is Marcus's aunt."

Leah read her face. *The queen-in-waiting is even more closely related to Marcus?* "Tradition or not. Powers or not. You shouldn't be ruling if you're nothing but a tyrant."

Kaylah scoffed. "What could your mother say about me being a tyrant? She ran away before my coronation."

"*She* never mentioned that. I have it on multiple accounts. You strip your people of their rights and give extra to the horrible Seeders. All you did to stop the war was pacify the enemy."

Kaylah almost seemed amused. "What rights have I stripped?"

"Tree rifting."

"It's been limited, yes. It's forbidden in the human world. Each tree rift requires a tree sacrifice. That's not our world to ravage. It's severely restricted in our own realm. Between previous generations of selfishness in the royal line, and irresponsible rifting in our own lands, we *decimated* our entire kingdom. It was necessary to get it under control. And tree rifting became a waste once we got our cave networks up!"

Leah rolled her eyes again. All lies, excuses, and justifications. If any of that was true, her mom or the guys in the club would have mentioned it.

"What else did you say?" Kaylah asked. "Oh yeah, horrible Seeders. How many Seeders have you met? Was Marcus's mom horrible?"

"There are exceptions," Leah grumbled. "She chose to move here because she married Guillen. I know they did it because it wasn't safe for him as a Boman over there. I can't believe you're related to Bomen and tolerate Seeders that would harm them." She mumbled about how family obviously didn't matter to Kaylah anyway.

Kaylah buried her face in her hands. "How is it possible you have *everything* wrong? Yes, once the war ended, it wasn't safe for Ivy Bomen in Seeder lands. Part of that is because it took a lot of hard work to get to where we are right now, having peaceful relations. But the bigger part is because *we* literally poisoned those lands! Did your sources talk about how the Ivy Kingdom tried to wipe out the Seeder nation for almost two centuries? Guillen, Marcus, Tobias—they would have died over there because the land wasn't survivable for them."

Leah gritted her teeth with annoyance. Kaylah had an argument for each point of proof Leah had. Why were they even having this conversation? "I have no reason to believe anything you say. You stole my dad and made my mom and me live on the run. *And* you killed your own uncle and parents. Who knows how many more innocent people?"

Kaylah's eyes narrowed. She wasn't amused by *this* accusation. "Is that what your mother told you? That I killed my own parents?"

Leah tilted her head. "So, this one you'll deny?"

Kaylah was stone-cold sober. "I will absolutely deny that. Categorically. Your parents killed them. They both had a hand in it."

Leah shook her head. *Proof of her lies.* "My dad was their favorite child."

Kaylah gave her a wry smile. "You're right. He was. We'll look past the fact that parents shouldn't have favorites, or at least not let their children know it." Kaylah stood, clasping her hands in front of her. "Soren was the oldest and the favorite. But he didn't have a right to the throne, and he killed his own parents for more power. That's as simple as it gets. I'm sorry if that's hard for you to hear, but you'll need to accept it sooner or later."

"Shut up!" Leah belted. "Why are you even telling me all this? My dad was a *good* man! My mom is a *great* mom!"

"Does a *good* man rape, Leah?" Kaylah threw daggers with her eyes. "He was younger than you when he started ordering servants to his chambers, and I know damn well it wasn't always consensual!"

"He would never!"

"Does a *good* man torture his sister in a dungeon for days, Leah? I happen to be that sister!" Kaylah's face grew more fierce with each offense she spat. "Does a *good* man kill his own parents to get gain? Does a *good* man take countless lives without a single regret?"

"SHUT UP!" Leah screamed. "I don't believe a single thing you have to say!" She'd heard enough. Her mom was a good mom. A great mom. They both loved her. This woman had no reason to tell the truth.

Kaylah stood tall. "I'm not going to mince words with you, Leah. You're old enough to think for yourself. Ask yourself why we're having this conversation, and why you haven't already been carted away to a dungeon. I'm well within my rights to order your execution posthaste for an attempt on my life. But why are we talking?"

"I don't know. I don't know how it works inside a killer's head."

Kaylah quietly scoffed. "Says the girl who tried to kill her own aunt before getting the facts straight. I'm throwing you a lifeline. Don't waste it." The murderous queen shook her head, leaving the room again without further comment.

Leah's thoughts turned back to her mom, hoping more than anything she was still safe.

Chapter 30

Kaylah returned to the sitting room. Tobias and Camry had moved to another room with her parents to talk. Kaylah sat next to Eric, leaning against him as he threw an arm around her.

"How are you?" Eric asked.

She closed her eyes. "She's in complete denial. She thinks her parents are saints."

"What are you thinking?" Guillen asked softly.

She looked down at her hands. "I'm not sure how objective I can be about this. We'll see how things work out when her mother's brought in, and when Catrina gets here."

Rachel returned to the room, taking a seat next to Guillen. All eyes focused on her.

"Well ... his broken hand, I could heal. His broken heart is a completely different issue." Rachel winced. "There might be a couple more broken things in that guestroom I can't fix, either."

Kaylah imagined there might be a dented wall in whatever room he'd found to let out some steam, but that was the least of their concerns right now.

"He really fell for her, didn't he?" Eric asked.

Rachel nodded, biting her lip. "He thought he loved her. Completely blindsided." She took Guillen's hand. "He admitted to knowing she didn't have a passport."

Guillen shot up. "You're kidding me!"

Rachel spoke in a calming voice. "He understands now how serious that was, what his lies have caused."

Guillen scowled. "But does he *really* understand? The *only* reason people respect our family is because we don't abuse our privileges. I *explicitly* told him I didn't appreciate what they were asking me to do. He went too far!"

Rachel stood next to him, holding his arm. "I remember a handsome young man willing to do *anything* to rescue a girl he loved."

A smile crept onto Kaylah's face at that response. Guillen had been Kaylah's first recruit in the revolution, and one of her elite spies selected to help rescue her best friend, Rachel. In a lot of ways, these two had saved each other.

Guillen glanced down, shaking his head. "That was different. I never got anyone hurt. I wasn't being manipulated."

Rachel gently lifted his chin to meet her gaze. "He thought he was helping a girl in need. Don't fault him for having a big heart like his dad."

Guillen's shoulders dropped. "Should I go talk to him? Is he okay?"

Rachel pursed her lips. "Give him some time." She faced Kaylah. "But I'd like to talk to Leah, with your permission."

Kaylah raised her eyebrows, unsure how that would go. Rachel had more reason to hate Soren than anyone in the Green Lands—and now Leah had hurt her son. "What's your plan?"

"She hurt my family. I don't really have a plan. But I deserve to have a word with her."

Kaylah hesitated. "She doesn't understand who her parents really were."

Rachel's tone dripped with anger. "Then I'll help clear that up."

Kaylah slowly nodded. "Be my guest."

Leah had known the dangers of trying to take out the queen. Somehow, she hadn't envisioned the part that could involve years in prison, or nonstop silence while tied to a chair. The queen's lies replayed in Leah's mind. What was her point? Why would she say such things? What did she hope to accomplish? Leah would *never* join her ranks. If anything, that would only disgrace her dad's name more in the public eye.

The door opened again, and Leah expected a third round with the queen. Prepared for more indoctrination, Leah went numb—Marcus's mom now stood in front of her.

"I never meant to hurt Marcus." Her throat was sore from screaming at Queen Kaylah.

Rachel's eyes shifted from brown to a terrifyingly unnatural neon green—a Seeder trait tied to their energy, powers, and sometimes emotions. "Let's not start with lies."

"That's not a lie. I'm sorry I ruined the wedding. And that I hurt Marcus. I ... love him."

"You came into my home. You broke my son's heart. You destroyed my other son and future daughter-in-law's big day. You lied to my husband and jeopardized his respectability. You can't tell me you didn't intend or predict those consequences!"

Leah sniffled. No one would believe her. They wouldn't understand that she really did love him. Love them. They wouldn't understand how hard the decision had been. How much she'd fought with herself over it. "I'm sorry for all of that, but what she did to my family is something I couldn't live with."

Rachel shook her head. "What Kaylah did to *your* family? Let me clear something up for you. It was the other way around. Kaylah is one of the most selfless people I know. And I know her better than anyone else."

Leah shrugged. "Even horrible people can be nice to their friends."

"Your parents earned themselves multiple death sentences. It's not just about me thinking Kaylah is a good person. It's also about me knowing your parents *weren't*!"

Leah scowled. "Did you even know my parents?"

"Your mom, Beata? No. But her crimes are well documented. Your dad, *better than most*." Rachel swallowed, looking away. "You're sad your dad died. I get it. But you didn't know him. He was a monster."

"Stop it!" Leah yelled. Each lie aimed at her parents was like a punch to the gut. "Stop talking about them like that!"

Rachel looked her squarely in the eye. "You deserve to know the truth. Your dad destroyed my family. My human parents, the ones you've spent countless hours with at their house? He and his uncle put them through *hell*." She paused. "And the things he did to my people..."

Leah pursed her lips. "War's messy." *Good or bad, winner or loser, no one comes out unscathed.*

"Yes." Rachel cocked her head. "But Soren *enjoyed* it! That's what separates us. Ugly things happen in war. But he was sadistic."

Leah rolled her eyes. "The woman I was raised by is a great mom and law-abiding citizen. I don't believe anything you say."

Rachel paced the room. "You don't believe me because you don't *want* to believe. But I don't give a shit about what you believe, Leah! Facts don't change based on someone's belief!"

"Then maybe you got your facts wrong!"

Rachel stared into Leah's eyes again. "You say you care about Marcus? How would you feel if he was a slave?"

That was a horrible thought. *What is she talking about?*

"That's what he would be, if your parents had it their way."

Leah frowned. "No! Kaylah made things worse." She shook her head, distinctly remembering that Jake's parents had fled when the war was over. His mom had been pregnant with him, scared for him.

Rachel pulled up her dress sleeve, pointing to a faded tattoo—an Ivy leaf outline surrounding the number five. "Kaylah stopped this. This is the kind of mark my sons would have been forced to take. Bomen were considered worthless, disabled disgraces, better used as slaves. By fourteen, they were taken from their families, not considered worth educating, forced to do manual labor, and had their rights stripped from them. They weren't even *allowed* to have children; it was outlawed. That's how it was for decades. Your parents wanted to continue that—actually, to make it worse."

Leah's heart ached at the description. *Why am I letting her get to me? It's not even true.* "My mom isn't like that. And you're not even an Ivy Boman—why would that tattoo be proof?"

Rachel's demeanor softened a degree, her eyes fading to brown again. "You really don't know much about our world and family, do you?" She stood with her mouth open. "I volunteered to take this mark in the war to go undercover with Guillen. We fought with Kaylah against your parents."

Leah felt hollow, Rachel's words piercing her. Leah clearly wasn't a good judge of character. She never would have pegged Marcus's family as being so involved in her dad's demise, in her parents' downfall. She stared at the ground, searching her thoughts. *What if … if I'm not a good judge of character when it comes to my mom? Or a man I've never met? Maybe only the parts about him are true, and my mom never understood? Maybe they're all true. Maybe none of them are.*

Rachel reached for the door, glancing back. "I liked you, Leah. And so did Marcus. But I've had to kill for my family. I won't let anyone hurt them. Your dad did his best to destroy my life and that of my family. Don't take on that legacy."

Chapter 31

Leah sat in silence for much longer, stewing over the things Rachel had said that cut deep. The things she and Kaylah had said about her parents, about her dad, were unfathomable. Leah ached, particularly at the thought of Marcus living as a slave. It couldn't be true. But if it was... Her stomach churned.

The door opened again, and Leah's heart shattered. It was the last person she wanted to talk to at the moment.

Marcus slid in, shutting the door behind him. "Can we talk alone?" he asked the guard.

The guard, who'd been standing silent the whole time, shook his head. "Sorry."

Marcus glanced at Leah. "Does she have to be tied up that way?"

The guard nodded.

"I'm sorry," Leah whispered. "Why didn't you tell me you're related to the queens?"

Marcus frowned, shrugging. "Why should it matter? Would that have made a difference? Do you only murder people who *aren't* related to the person you're dating?"

She met his challenge with a faint scowl. "Tell me, Marcus, if you knew who my parents were, would you have given me a chance?"

It didn't take him long to consider her question. "No."

It was like a knife in her heart. Why hadn't she just kept up the lies? Or told him she'd loved him? "Then doesn't that make you a hypocrite? If family relationships don't matter?"

He threw his hands in the air. "That's different! I'm told you won't accept the truth about your parents. What all did my mom tell you about her relationship with your dad?"

"That she knew him well. That your parents fought against him."

Marcus huffed. "Your dad dated my mom at our age. For *three* years."

Leah's eyes narrowed. "I know that's a lie. He started dating my mom when he was fifteen!"

"I don't deny that. But he *also* dated my mom. The difference was my mom didn't know he was cheating on her. She didn't know what he was, that he was manipulating her." He looked Leah dead in the eyes. "Until he kidnapped her. And tortured her. And..." He looked down, wringing his hands. "There's stuff she won't talk about to her own sons, but you hear things." He shook his head. "The irony of me worrying about what Tanner did to you. What other guys did to you. When your own dad did all of it and worse to other women. He hurt women. He didn't respect life. If that's the man you're worshipping, you're no better than him."

Her lip quivered. If she could believe anyone, it would be Marcus. He could be misled, manipulated—she knew that. But he was good at heart. He loved his family. Why would he lie about that? "I don't know what to believe," she whispered.

Marcus's eyes filled with tears. "Tell me, Leah, have you ever witnessed your mom having a panic attack? Or been woken in the middle of the night by her screaming? Because I have. And that was all because of *your* dad."

A tiny squeak of regret rose in Leah's throat. She couldn't bear to see him cry.

"I guess the apple doesn't fall far from the tree," he said. "Manipulating me. Using me."

She frowned. "It's not what you think."

He shoved his hands in his pockets. "Then explain it to me. *Convince* me you had no idea who I was, and that you didn't use me for revenge."

Leah swallowed the lump in her throat. "It wasn't all a lie. I..." She searched her thoughts and memories. "I really did like you. I really didn't know who I was when we met."

He raised his eyebrows in disbelief. "Then when did you find out?"

"You were the person that taught me about green folk and the Green Lands. That was all true. I was so lost. But then ... it wasn't much later that I found my mom's journals and learned they were a king and queen, that he was murdered by his sister."

"*Fake* king and queen. *Executed.* Not murdered," he clarified. "So, the entirety of our relationship was a lie geared to me bringing you here."

Her chest tightened. "It... I... Sometimes, yes. But most of the time it was just me being me! I talked myself out of this a dozen times!"

He scowled. "Should have done it a dozen and one."

Tears welled up in her eyes. "I love you."

"Don't you *dare* say that to me."

"But I—"

"Don't, Leah!"

"I'll say it because it's true!"

He glanced at the guard before returning his attention to her. "So true that you wouldn't sleep with me? Teased me for months, and then when I finally thought we were on the same page, you realized you couldn't go through with it? Why bother? You were already getting what you wanted."

"No. I didn't do it *because* I love you. I... I knew I couldn't trust myself. I didn't want to hurt you more."

"Then you failed miserably. How many times did you lie to me, Leah? How many times am I supposed to believe you and be disappointed?"

"You lied to me too! You should have told me about your family!"

"*I never lied!*" His face reddened. "You want to know why I didn't tell you more? Why I'm so private about my family life? You're living proof of why! I'm related to royalty. Everyone in the Green Lands knows my parents' names. They're in the damn history books, Leah!" He jabbed a finger at his chest. "Why the hell would I choose to keep that close to me?"(u)

He stared into her eyes, tears forming again. "I'm proud of them. I love them. But I didn't want to be *defined* by any of them. Hate me or love me, I wanted to be judged for *me*. Not them. I wanted someone to love me for *me*!" A tear rolled down his cheek. "I thought I found that in you." He wiped away his tears. "I was going to tell you my relationship to Kaylah when I offered to introduce you. I was going to tell you *everything* this week, but you ruined that."

She looked at the floor. "I'm sorry. I'm sorry I screwed up everything."

He paced the room. "Sorry doesn't fix things. My brother won't even speak to me right now. I ruined his wedding. Do you know what kind of drama this could cause? What kind of old battle scars... What kind of outrage this is going to stir up? How much trouble my dad might get in, because you convinced me to lie to him!"

"I lied to my mom, too." She met his gaze. "She never would have agreed to me going *anywhere* overnight. She didn't say I could go to Detroit. I ran away from home! She's sitting at home, worried out of her mind."

Marcus averted his gaze.

No! "What did you do? Please don't tell me you..."

He wouldn't look at her. "I didn't have a choice. What did you expect me to do?"

She sobbed. "She's a good mom! She loves me! She liked you! She was nice to you! She didn't know my plans!"

"She's a war criminal," he muttered through clenched teeth.

Tears streamed down Leah's face. "She's a good person! What are they going to do to us?"

Marcus opened the door. "I don't know." His voice shook. "And I don't care."

The door clicked closed, leaving Leah to her heartache and the silent guard in the corner of the room.

Chapter 32

Guillen frowned, talking to his wife with Kaylah and Eric. "He won't say much. He's still pretty hurt about it all."

"Do you think he helped get through to her?" Rachel asked.

Guillen shrugged. "I don't know. But from what you two have said, she's pretty brainwashed."

Kaylah sighed. "I'm not so sure. I saw the doubt and confusion on her face. We're going to have to see if we can bring back her mother and go from there."

Eric held Kaylah's hand. "I think we've done enough to assess the threat here. It's time for all of the luncheon guests to go home. You guys should be with your family."

Rachel frowned. "You guys are family too." She took a deep breath. "But you're right. Tobias and Camry need us right now. Her parents have to be pretty rattled, too. And I expect Marcus will still want to be alone, but his room back home will be more comfortable."

Kaylah forced a smile. "We'll send an update when we have one."

Rachel and Guillen stood. "Send word if you need anything from us," Guillen said.

"Will do," Eric said.

Kaylah dismissed the guards as Rachel and Guillen left the room.

"Hmm... I like it when the guards go away." Eric grinned.

Kaylah flashed him a genuine smile and gave him a sweet kiss on the lips.

He gazed into her eyes. "I'm sorry this is stirring up a lot of rough memories. What can I do to help?"

That was always a hard question to answer. She tried to push down flashbacks from almost two decades prior. Rachel and Guillen had almost lost their lives to save hers. Many others loyal to her had made the ultimate sacrifice. The entire Seeder nation had honored their alliance with her to end a war more than two centuries old. And risking his life for the cause, putting his life on hold for her, had been a loving high school sweetheart, a human.

She looked down at their hands, giving his a squeeze. The day she'd been able to figure out how humans could make it through a rift, and the day she first saw the love of her life in her homeland, right before her coronation—those were days that gave meaning and hope when the weight of the realm felt too heavy to bear.

And right now, Kaylah's heart was heavy. *That poor girl.* The idea of Soren being a father was a nonstarter. Leah was better off without him, no matter how confused she was. Kaylah was physically ill, imagining the sick pleasure Soren would've had about this. She'd sent him to the grave all those years ago, but he was still able to reach out and hurt people, long after he was gone.

"Babe?"

"Yeah, um…" She hadn't had episodes like this in years. "What?"

He asked again, "What can I do to help?"

"Today? Just be here for me."

He raised his eyebrows, giving her a gentle smile. "Am I being reduced to a pretty face today?"

She chuckled softly. "You're more than a pretty face. You're my rock."

He pulled her in tight and kissed her head. "I feel like I cuddle better than a rock would."

Kaylah stood outside the door, ready for a whole new round of lies and bad memories. This time she wouldn't be rattled. Straightening her posture, she opened the door.

She stared into the face of a woman she hadn't seen in almost two decades. Black hair, cut shorter than Kaylah had seen it before. She wasn't that same young girl, following Soren wherever he wanted.

Beata wasted no time. "Where is my daughter?!"

Kaylah kept her composure. "I know you've been hiding in the human world for a long time, but you're out of touch. We haven't used teenage assassins for as long as you've been gone."

"Where is she?!" Beata seethed.

Kaylah tilted her head. "And to send her so untrained."

Beata glared. "I didn't send her. I kept her safe from *you*. And if you hurt a hair on her head, I will rip out your heart myself. *Where the hell is my daughter?!*"

Kaylah remained calm, reading Beata's face. They both claimed Leah had acted alone. With Kaylah in the human world so much during the years Beata and Soren had dated, she hadn't known Beata that well. What she did know of her, from their limited interactions, hadn't impressed Kaylah.

Beata was an enigma. Seemingly kind at times, but capable of cruelty. Strong in her own right, but often willing to submit to Soren's demands or whims.(v)

Soren had loved mind games, and Kaylah knew how to play them, too. She chose the higher road. "Leah's fine. Only one of us in this room is a murderer." She rocked her head back and forth. "Then again, she's fine ... for now. We haven't decided what will become of her. Attempted assassination of the queen—you know what kind of sentence that carries."

Beata didn't skip a beat. "I'll take her place."

Kaylah raised her eyebrows. "It's hard to die twice. Your crimes have already earned you a death sentence."

"Leave her alone. She's innocent."

Kaylah sat down. "See, that's what we're trying to figure out. It seems someone has filled her mind with all sorts of bullshit fanfare about the outstanding character of her parents."

Beata scowled. "You're too close to this. You always hated Soren. You were always jealous of him."

Kaylah scoffed. "Jealous? Of what?"

"Your parents loved him more than you," Beata stated matter-of-factly.

Kaylah leaned forward in her chair. "I didn't need their love. I wonder how much they loved him when the two of you murdered them."

Beata sat straight, defiance in the set of her jaw. "I'll never admit to that. And any crimes you put on me were under his orders. I didn't have a choice."

Kaylah pointed a threatening finger. "Don't mess with me. We have plenty of witness accounts of the types of things you knowingly allowed to happen. Entering the Queen's Room is just one of *many* crimes listed under your name. I don't need to prove them all."

Beata swallowed. "Soren named me queen when we married. I had a right to be there."

"*You had NO right!* You were never a legitimate queen, and you damn well know it!"

"You weren't up for the task. And you would have killed your own parents, anyway, if we hadn't beat you to it. Don't pretend you're morally superior!"

"You're probably right. But we'll never know. I would have done it to save lives and bring peace, if negotiations had failed. You did it because you were greedy."

"He did it because he had big dreams! He did it because he loved me!"

Kaylah narrowed her eyes. "But *did* he really love you? You and I both know how it works. The moment he caught me, he could have killed me and the next five heirs down the line. That's how he would have made you a *legitimate* queen with power over the Vines. But he didn't do that, did he? He kept me in the dungeons," Kaylah's eyes betrayed her, misting at the memory, "torturing me, and servants in front of me, while you lived in the lap of luxury higher up in the palace. Don't pretend you weren't aware of the kinds of things he was doing."

"He did love me. And I loved him! I'll never forgive you for taking him away from me!"

Kaylah took a breath to recompose herself. "I'll never ask for your forgiveness. I did what needed to be done. And I'm prepared to do it again."

Beata whimpered. "Spare Eleana. She didn't know what she was doing."

Kaylah sat back in her chair, a million questions running through her mind. "How did you even get by all these years?"

Beata sneered. "By working harder and living more simply than someone like you could ever understand."

"Marcus told me you had a 'sister' living with you? I know that's not true."

Beata's expression changed to a look of confusion and surprise. "Marcus?"

Kaylah smiled. "You really didn't know Leah's plans, did you?"

"Her name is Eleana. And no. I told you I didn't. What does he have to do with this?"

"Tell me about your aides. We were told four went missing with you. We only captured one."

"You'd be surprised how loyalty wanes when the hidden funds of the assassin networks dry up," Beata muttered bitterly.

Kaylah nodded with a small grin. "We knew we missed some of those accounts. The human world is a lot bigger than here, isn't it?"

Beata sighed. "Just let us go, and you'll never see us again. We haven't bothered anyone."

"Out of the question. You'll be sentenced for your crimes."

"It was a long time ago! All I've done since I left was try to be a good mother!" Beata frowned. "I'm only guilty of anything because of Soren. He already paid the price. Why can't that be enough?"

"Don't pretend you were under his thumb. You, my parents, and my uncle were the only people who had any sort of say with him. You followed him around like a lovesick puppy. You're not innocent!"

"He loved me, dammit! And I loved him! And he would have loved our daughter! War is ugly. Making my daughter an orphan, or worse, won't fix it."

Kaylah stood, clasping her hands and putting them to her forehead. "You're right. War is ugly. But that excuse can only go so far." She eyed Beata. What should she say to her? She could destroy her. Soren had never planned to make her a proper queen, not the way she seemed to think. She could also tell Beata about his last moments. About how he'd screamed for her. About how he'd been tortured for information. She could do *a lot* to hurt Beata before she ordered her death. And she *wanted* to hurt Beata.

But pity grew within Kaylah. Soren had only ever used people as tools. Beata's parents hadn't won any awards for citizenship. Was Beata just a product of her upbringing? Her surroundings? At what point did a victim become responsible for their actions?

Kaylah rolled her shoulders, choosing compassion. "If Soren was even capable of love, I believe he might have loved you. I saw the way you two were. And in his last days, he never gave you up."

Beata cried.

Kaylah searched her face again. *This isn't about getting a confession. I have evidence enough. Her fate is sealed. This is about Leah.*

Kaylah sat back down with a sigh. "He told us you were pregnant. We didn't believe him."

Beata frowned, nodding. "He ordered me to leave so she would be safe."

"Was she planned?"

Beata gnawed on her lip. "What couple doesn't talk about having kids?"

"In the middle of a war? When your resources are stretched thin?"

"He wasn't ready," she softly confessed. "But he didn't get mad when he found out."

"Does Leah know?"

"No. She doesn't need to know that. He was happy to have an heir on the way!"

Kaylah nodded, processing everything she'd gleaned from the conversation. As it often did, her need to balance justice and mercy weighed on her. "There's nothing you can say or do for your case. You know our laws, Beata."

"But—"

Kaylah held up a hand. "However ... Leah still has a chance. If she has *any* shot at living a decent life, she needs to know the truth. If you love her, tell her the truth. Think of *her* for once."

Beata stared into Kaylah's eyes for a full minute before responding. "I'll answer her questions. But I will *not* admit to my daughter that I had any part in taking away her grandparents."

"I've already told her as much. And she'll hear about it as she learns history. It's a matter of public record."

Beata clenched her teeth. "She *won't* hear it from me."

"Suit yourself. Just remember when I bring her to see you that *you're* the one determining what the rest of her life will be like."

Chapter 33

Leah was much more comfortable at the change of guard. They allowed her to use the restroom and hydrate. She splashed her face with cool water to wash away dried tears. The mirror reflected a stranger. Could it be true—what they were all saying? What would that mean for her? Lies stacked on top of lies. Who was she?

A pair of guards escorted her back to the room she was being held in. This time, they secured her wrists with a wide band, something that prevented the use of vines. But they didn't strap her to the chair. What was going to happen next? The guards wouldn't say anything. But she knew one thing—she dreaded each time that door opened.

And soon enough, it did... Kaylah again.

"What now?"

Kaylah slid her chair closer and sat down. "How are you doing? Do you need anything?"

"To go home?"

Kaylah frowned. "Sorry, kiddo. No can do."

Leah pressed her lips together. "Why should I believe any of you? How am I supposed to know what to believe?"

Kaylah blew out a puff of air. "It's complicated, right? I can vouch for the honesty of myself, and Rachel and Marcus. But I understand that might not hold much weight for you." Kaylah leaned forward, resting her elbows on her knees. "I want to talk to you as your aunt, okay? Not the queen. Not the enemy."

Leah shrugged, studying the bands on her wrists. "The only aunt I've ever known wasn't even my aunt. And she was horrible. Then I learned I had a different aunt, but she killed my dad before I was born. I doubt it'll do you any favors."

"I'm sorry you didn't get to grow up with family. I truly am. No one deserves that. But I know your mother loves you very much."

Leah's eyes shot up. "You have her, don't you?"

Kaylah nodded. "We've talked."

Leah hated herself, and wanted to cry, but she had cried all of the tears she could. All she wanted now was to turn back time.

"I'm going to allow you to see her before we discuss consequences for either of you," Kaylah said.

"Okay."

"Before I take you to see her, do you have any questions for me?"

Leah ran through all of the information thrown her way in the last few hours. "Is it true they used to treat Bomen like slaves? That Marcus would have been taken from his family?"

"Yes."

Leah was instantly sick to her stomach. "But my dad didn't start that, right?"

"No. That became law long before him. But he had no agenda to stop it. He was unkind to Guillen because of his differences. He had ... plans to further exploit Bomen in the long run."

Leah nodded. "Marcus said my dad hurt his mom and other girls."

"Yes."

Leah felt dirty by association, if it was true. "I never knew him. I can admit that. And if he was as bad as you all say he was, then ... it sounds like my mom isn't guilty of anything. I'm sure he forced her to do anything she had to do. She shouldn't be punished. She's a great mom."

Kaylah took a deep breath, then slowly let it out. "She loves you. And I don't doubt she did her best with you. But that doesn't make her innocent. We have witnesses. We have confessions. And I know her well enough to understand the dynamic they shared. She wasn't forced to be with him. She wasn't *forced* to do anything."

Leah was numb, trying to sort through all the allegations. "Like help kill my grandparents?"

Kaylah bit her lip, giving a single nod.

Leah searched her face. Her mom's reactions would help her make sense of it all. "I want to see her."

Leah followed Queen Kaylah into another room, her wrists still bound. It killed her to see her mom strapped to a chair.

Her mom tilted her head, frowning. "Sweetheart. You shouldn't have come. Are you okay?"

Leah nodded. "I'm sorry. I really am." She glanced at Kaylah. "Does she have to be tied to the chair like that?" She realized she was now in Marcus's position, asking that question. She hated seeing her mom tied down—so captive, so undignified. And she almost wanted to hug her, but she also couldn't imagine doing it right now.

"Sorry. She'll stay as is for right now," Kaylah responded. "Let's take a seat."

Two chairs had been set up opposite Beata. Leah moved hers a little to be more in between the two, but off to the side.

"I was told my dad dated someone else at the same time you two dated," she started.

Beata sighed. "It wasn't like that. Don't let them put a wedge between us. He wasn't cheating on me. I knew all about the mission he had to do."

Leah read her face. "*Every* detail about it?"

Beata raised her eyebrows in chastisement. "We weren't even engaged at that point. I doubt he told me *everything*."

"But you knew he was dating another woman. A Seeder. And that he kidnapped her and tortured her?"

Beata took a moment before responding. "War's ugly, Eleana. I don't expect you to understand. I told you not everyone agreed with his tactics."

Leah's gut twisted. "That woman is Marcus's mom."

Beata's eyes grew wide, looking to Kaylah for confirmation. Kaylah gave a tiny nod.

"Marcus is a Seeder?" Beata asked, unable to hide her disgust.

Leah had never seen that expression on her mom before. "No. He's an Ivy Boman."

Beata glanced away, her face still unhappy, as though that wasn't much better.

Leah's mouth hung open. "You're the one that always told me our physical differences didn't matter!"

Beata shook her head, looking at her daughter. "I meant that about *you*, sweetheart! What was I supposed to say to my daughter? My daughter deprived of a normal life and hating her own vines? Hiding and dating humans who would *never* be worthy of her!"

Leah swallowed a lump in her throat, remembering a previous discussion. "You never dated again because you didn't think humans were good enough, either. It wasn't just about missing my dad."

Beata looked away again, not answering.

Dismayed, Leah kept her voice soft. "I love Marcus. And I've ruined things with him because of you and the pictures you painted in my mind."

"You don't understand everything yet, Eleana. Don't let them turn you against me. You and I, we're the same."

Leah shifted in her seat. "You really think my dad would have loved me?"

"Of course!"

"What about my grandparents? Would they have loved me? The ones you killed?"

Beata threw a quick glance at Kaylah. "They would have loved you more than you know. I'm sorry you won't get to meet them."

"Sorry because you killed them?" Leah intently looked into her mom's eyes.

Beata was an expert at dodging eye contact. "I told you your father was ambitious."

Leah's eyes narrowed. "Answer the question. Did you kill my grandparents?"

Beata met her gaze. "There's a lot of tragedy in your family. Your father didn't like taking no for an answer. That's all I'll say on that."

That was as good as a confession in Leah's eyes, but she still didn't fully know what to make of her grandparents or their deaths. "But Kaylah didn't kill them?"

Beata shook her head.

But ... she told me Kaylah killed them. Didn't she? Leah searched her memories. The truth of the matter tore into her very soul. *No. She didn't.* Marcus had mentioned they were assassinated, but hadn't named the assassin. Leah had only *assumed* it was Kaylah, and when she'd mentioned her shock about that news to her mom...

The memory was now strikingly clear. Her mom hadn't responded. Hadn't confirmed or denied the claim. She'd allowed Leah to believe what she'd wanted to believe, that Kaylah had been to blame. Her mom's silence, her every denial right now, screamed her guilt.

Leah gathered her composure, pressing further. "My dad didn't like taking no for an answer. How many women did he not take that answer from?" Leah balled her fists. Maybe her mom didn't know as much about this. Maybe this one wasn't true.

"He didn't do that as much once we were engaged," Beata defended.

"You knew he raped women, and you stayed with him?!" Leah shouted in disbelief.

"No one understood him like I did! It wasn't that simple. And it wasn't always like that. There were plenty of sluts happy to spend time with a prince or king. Sweetheart, you didn't grow up with a life of privilege. It's complicated."

Kaylah spoke up. "Don't you dare blame it on privilege! He understood the meaning of 'no' as well as I did! He hid his escapades from our parents. And when he got caught by our uncle, he had his ass handed to him. Your weakness in accepting his behavior doesn't excuse his actions."

Leah closed her eyes, trying to process her thoughts. Her mom was strong and brave. How could she also be this other woman? She opened her eyes, focusing on her mom's face. "Did he ever hurt *you*?"

Beata only shrugged slightly. "He could be rough; I told you he wasn't perfect. But it wasn't like that. I could take care of myself. I wasn't some weak, battered wife."

"Which makes it worse." Leah's eyes burned with anger. "You let Cheryl hurt me. If you knew he hurt other women, and he hurt you, why the *hell* do you think I would have ever been safe with him as my dad?!"

Beata shook her head fervently. "I never would have let him lay a finger on you!"

Leah frowned again, wishing she could take back the last day, wishing she could have made the right choice. "I love Marcus. I never would have made either of you proud. And if my dad loved me at all, it would have been because he was proud that one of his sperm performed its most basic function." She found her tears again. "We were never in hiding to keep *me* safe. We hid for *you*."

Beata spoke softly. "I've made mistakes, Eleana. We both have. But I love you."

"It's not possible to love both him and me. Which is it?"

"I wouldn't have had to choose. I love you both!"

"Then you choose him."

Beata sobbed. "No. No! You don't understand what I've had to do for you. Especially after Cheryl left. I've broken... I..." Her eyes glazed over. "I chose you. I always have. I always will."(w)

While Leah found comfort in her mom's profession of love, her heart filled with terror at her confession of having needed to do something for them. "What did you do?" She imagined more bodies, blackmail, any number of things.

Beata shook her head, defeated. "It doesn't matter anymore, does it?" She looked up at Kaylah with a scowl. "Nothing associated with our lands or people that you can add to your list."

Kaylah shifted in her seat. "I think we've heard enough. Is there anything else you need to know, Leah?"

Leah stood, her heart heavy. She hugged herself, grappling with all the chaos of the day. "No. That's enough."

Kaylah walked to the door; Leah followed her.

"I love you, Eleana!"

Leah stopped in place. Despite everything, she couldn't turn her back on her mom. "I love you too." She faced Kaylah. "What's going to happen to us?"

Kaylah glanced between the two. "It hasn't been decided yet."

Leah had nothing left. No parents. No family. No friends. No Marcus. No trust. No self. Her heart and hope were gone. "If you kill her, you should kill me too."

"No!" Beata screamed.

Kaylah furrowed her brow. "Why would you say that?"

Leah exhaled. "Because I never would have been born if you'd caught my mom when you did my dad. Why should it be any different now?"

Kaylah spun. "Is that what you told her?! No wonder she tried to kill me!"

Beata returned her anger. "You would have put me right next to Soren. Don't deny it!"

Kaylah balled her fists. "I would like to think I'd have given you the benefit of the doubt, to confirm whether you were pregnant first!"

"So, what? I'd give birth. You'd take her straight away and make her an orphan then? That's better, right?"

Kaylah narrowed her eyes. "Did you get knocked up hoping for a pardon?"

"No!"

Leah trembled, the last ounce of her identity crumbling before her. "Can I please go?" she begged.

"Yes," Kaylah said curtly, escorting her out of the room.

Halfway down the hall, a guard walked up to Kaylah. "Lady Catrina has arrived. She's in the sitting room."

"Thank you."

Kaylah returned a tear-filled and silent Leah to her room. "You'll be the first to know what we decide."

Chapter 34

Kaylah entered the sitting room, a raging headache engulfing her. She rubbed her temples and plopped down next to Eric. Lady Catrina—her cousin, Guillen's younger sister, the queen-in-waiting—and her husband sat opposite them.

"Sounds like quite a day," Catrina said. She had always been a more proper lady than Kaylah. Soft-spoken, dainty, logical, kind.

Kaylah cleared her throat. "Eric and Stephan, can you please give us some time alone?"

The men nodded and headed out. Kaylah didn't usually shoo them away. She and Eric were a team, even if he was 'only' a human, married to an Ivy queen, as some would say. And Catrina and Stephan often sat in with them when discussing policy, in preparation for handing over the crown. But legally, it was Kaylah's call on what Beata and Leah's fates would be.

"A nightmare." Kaylah blew out a long breath.

"I can't believe all of this. Imagine Soren as a father..."

"Like I said—nightmare."

Catrina tilted her head. "What's she like?"

Kaylah frowned. "She has his eyes. Other than that, I still really don't know. She tried to kill me today, but I just saw her devastated by the truth of who her parents are. The dust has to settle."

Catrina matched Kaylah's frown. "I heard Marcus took it pretty hard."

Kaylah nodded. "That poor boy. He's so sensitive."

Catrina picked up a goblet of water from a side table. "So, what are you thinking at this point?"

"You know the limits of the law."

Catrina's jaw dropped. "You could do that to her? The girl?"

Kaylah rolled her eyes. "No. Not the daughter. I'm just saying, it's within my rights. Soon enough, you'll be having to make this kind of call."

Catrina pressed her lips together. "I know it's been a hard reign for you. But Stephan and I are hoping we have significantly fewer threats and attempts on our lives."

"And we're lucky we didn't have to get your mother out of the way."

Catrina looked down, rubbing her thumb along the goblet stem.

"Sorry, that was insensitive. You know, well…" Kaylah's aunt, Catrina's mother, would have been next in line before Catrina. That woman had been stubborn. She'd loathed nearly everything about the changes Kaylah had worked so hard for. Right up to the day she died.

Catrina nodded. "I know full well your meaning. I think it's possible to love and forgive someone at the same time you hate their actions."

Kaylah sighed. "Right. So—the girl. She didn't understand what she was doing. Of course I won't execute her. But…" Her heart reached out to Leah. *That last outburst.* "I worry about how things will go for her… She said she wanted to die if her mom dies. They were pretty close."

Catrina bit her lip. "That's not great. Do you think she'd be serious about it?"

"I have no way of knowing. And … I don't feel right about changing her mother's sentence."

"Let's go over that one." Catrina took a sip of water, then set down the goblet. "You mean execution?"

Kaylah nodded. "Her crimes are proven. The trial held in her absence still holds."

"She entered the Queen's Room," Catrina said. "That's a death sentence. But really? When was the last time someone was actually put to death for that? And you yourself wrote that out of law, even if it's still forbidden by tradition."

Kaylah scowled. "She did it while it was still in law."

Catrina gave a slight nod. "And she helped assassinate your parents. Which you were also prepared to do."

Kaylah's jaw dropped. "You're defending her?! That was both illegal *and* for the wrong reason. Don't put me on her level!"

Catrina raised her eyebrows. "I'm laying out the facts. I'm not trying to justify her crimes. We're just talking." She crossed her legs. "We still don't fully know how culpable she was for that crime. Unless you know more than I do."

Kaylah's annoyance flared. According to all accounts, the only people who had made it out of the room her parents had died in were Soren and Beata. No one could confirm who had done the actual killing. "I don't."

"Okay. Then that leaves us all the other crimes Soren committed. Which we're only aware of her being a part of in the sense that she's condemned as an accomplice."

Kaylah crossed her arms. "So, we should let her walk away? Full pardon? Slap on the hand?"

Catrina's voice wavered from its gentle nature. "Will you calm down? Maybe you're too close to the situation to make an objective decision."

Kaylah glared. "Too close? Was I too close when she was upstairs screwing Soren while I dripped blood on the floor down in the dungeons?"

Catrina swallowed. "I know this is bringing up a lot of horrible memories, okay? I'm not unsympathetic to that. You know I love you. And I know they were wrong. But thinking about that girl, and more importantly our kingdom and treaties—that's more important." She gestured with a hand in the air. "I'd say life in prison."

Kaylah pinched the bridge of her nose, frustrated at herself for letting her emotions get carried away. It had been years since she'd even heard Soren's name, then to have this all crashing back into her life again... What was best for the kingdom? And peace with the Seeders? This had happened in neutral territory. Would Seeders demand Beata's life? Or even that of the girl? Would they need that satisfaction to appease old anger easily stirred up? What about the Bomen?

What about her own people? There was peace, and so much had changed in the last eighteen years of her reign. But that didn't mean there weren't still die-hard Soren dissidents out there, or those who agreed with at least some of his vision. Would the appearance of the girl and her mom cause an uprising? If Leah and Beata lived, would it give their cause hope? Would Kaylah's people see her as weak if she didn't execute them? Or ruthless and vengeful if she did?

These were not simple policy decisions or mundane social displays. These were deep wounds reopened.

Kaylah needed fresh air. She walked to a window in the sitting room. The early sunset sang the very definition of beauty and peace. She gripped the windowsill, waiting for inspiration to strike her. She wasn't always the best with words, or considering others' feelings, but she wanted to be. Sometimes she relied too much on logic or on anger. But she was blessed in her station—she didn't have to call the shots alone.

She strode to the door, addressing a guard in the hallway. "Call for our husbands, please."

"Yes, Your Majesty."

The men shortly rejoined their wives.

Kaylah took Eric's hand. "Beata's crimes remain as we once knew them. Nothing has changed. There's no statute of limitations on them." She and Catrina shared a glance. "Catrina thinks life in prison would be best for Beata, for the sake of her daughter. I agree. I'm still not sure what's best for the kingdom, however. I'd like your input."

"I agree with Catrina," Stephan answered.

Eric nodded, looking down in thought. "I feel like ending our reign with an execution that could be seen as a personal dredging up of old family issues isn't the way we want to go."

Kaylah's heart fought it. "Fine. And what about the girl? What are we supposed to do with her? She has a lot to learn about her own people. She has a lot of healing to do."

"You're thinking of keeping her in the kingdom, right?" Stephan asked.

"Of course!" Kaylah replied. "Her days with the humans are over. We're not just shipping her off. I just ... don't know where is best. A good family willing to take her in? I wouldn't dare put her with anyone in Beata's family."

Eric squeezed Kaylah's hand. "But she should be with family. I know we never planned on kids, but it's not like we didn't help raise your brothers."

Kaylah's little brothers had only been eight and ten at the time of their parents' assassination, and their older brother's coup. Once Kaylah had regained control of the palace, she'd also had to fill the role of mother for brothers she had hardly known growing up. And with all the trauma of their childhood, and the stress of being in the public eye, neither had really turned out to be the ideal citizen, or member of the royal family. Kyas was nothing short of a social recluse now, and Rian had a known drinking problem.

But this wasn't about them. This was about Leah, and what was best for her. Kaylah's eyes welled with tears. "I want to say yes. But ... I—I don't know if I'm strong enough to look into those eyes every day. And I don't think she could stand living with someone who took away her parents. I'm sorry. I know it's selfish."

Catrina frowned, rubbing her barely showing belly. "Not selfish. We all have different things we struggle with." She glanced at her husband. "Maybe we could take her in?"

Kaylah shook her head. "A two-year-old, one on the way, *and* a troubled teen? All while you're moving into the palace and taking over?"

"We're up to the challenge," Stephan answered confidently. "Like Eric said—she should be with family."

Catrina clasped her hands together. "Let's not look at her like a burden. She can be seen as someone to bridge the gap of our reigns. From war to peace. Hope in the new generation? I know I haven't met her yet, but ... do you think that's possible?"

"Hope in a new generation?" Kaylah repeated. "That's hard to say. We can't parade her around like propaganda. But it seems like everyone loved her ... until she showed her true colors."

Catrina's voice and smile were ever calm. "We'll treat her like she's worth believing in, and she might just rise to the occasion. Plus, once we move into the palace, I think it's a sign we're willing to move on from our family's past."

Kaylah smiled weakly. "And Soren's followers might be pacified, seeing her in there."

Eric looked around the room. "Then we're all agreed?"

The nods were unanimous.

Chapter 35

She had been in her new home a week. Leah lay in bed, still struggling to grasp the reality of her situation. The family was welcoming and kind, but this wasn't home. It might never be. Granted, in two weeks it would quite literally not be her home, or theirs. They were moving to the palace.

She rolled over, hugging a pillow. What was that going to feel like? She'd be in the place her parents had always wanted her to be, but without any title, not that she deserved one.

Staring at a stack of books on an ornate vanity, Leah sighed. They didn't force Ivy history down her throat, but they'd assigned her a tutor and made it abundantly clear that she was free to ask any questions. She'd perused, though it was hard to do so.

The first couple of days following her assassination attempt had been the worst of her life. Before her mom was moved to an official Ivy prison, Leah had been given one more chance to talk with her, this time all alone. Despite the multiple witnesses against her mom, and even her mom's own confessions, Leah had worried the confessions had been coerced out of her.

In full shame, an absolute wreck, her mom had sworn over and over that she'd tried to do right by Leah. She'd admitted she hadn't been forced to say anything that day. She'd begged for Leah's forgiveness. Leah didn't know if she could give that.

Thoroughly devastated, Leah had cried so hard that night that she threw up. After telling Kaylah she'd be willing to die with her mom, and being in such bad shape, they'd put her on suicide watch, regularly checking on her.

Sometimes, she found it in her to leave her room to dine with the family, or to sit in the sunny library to read from these books, but most of the time she still stayed in her room, trying to make sense of it all.

A knock sounded on her door. "It's open," she answered, despondent.

A servant peeked inside. "You have a visitor, miss."

Leah rolled her eyes. "It's not 'miss.' It's Leah."

The servant nodded once. "My apologies, Leah. It's Marcus."

She shot up out of bed. "Really? I'll be right out." She grabbed clothes from her closet, quickly changing out of the pajamas she'd been sulking in all day. She looked in the mirror, regretting doing so due to the disheveled mop of hair disgracing her head. She bounded to the front sitting room, her heart lit with hope and aching all at the same time. "You came."

He stood, hands buried in his pockets. "Not by choice. I'm on my way back to school. What do you want?"

She frowned. "Just to talk."

He shrugged, not meeting her eyes. "Then talk."

"I'm sorry. Very, very sorry."

His expression was blank, his voice soft. "You've said that already."

Her heart sank. "I love y—"

"Don't! We're not together anymore. You can't seriously think I could forgive you after what you did."

She'd cried more tears in the last week than in her whole life put together. "I didn't understand."

"You understood enough." He shook his head. "And you're going to move into the palace. Sounds like you got what you wanted in the end, anyway."

"I never wanted that! I don't care about servants or titles, or any of that! I cared about my family." She looked down in shame. "I just didn't understand who they were."

"If you want my forgiveness, I... I'm not ready for that. I don't know if I ever will be."

"You're my best friend," she whispered. "You're my only friend. I guess ... not even that, anymore."

"You don't stay with someone because you pity them. You stay with them because you have mutual respect. And that ship has sailed."

Leah met his gaze. "Who even am I? Tell me that. My dad was a monster. My mom's in prison for life! Who am I, Marcus?"

He glared. "I'm not your crutch. Figure out your own damn life."

"Please. I'm begging you." She frowned in desperation, wiping away fresh tears.

"I get that you didn't win the parental jackpot. I really do. I didn't either, Leah! Why do you think I was put up for adoption? The day my birth parents realized I was *defective*, they wrote me off, tossed me away like scraps in a compost pile. Same happened to my brother. We don't get to *choose* our parents. Learn to deal. Make a name for yourself that *you* will be proud of."

She fidgeted with her hands. "It's not the same. Your birth parents aren't infamous. And you have amazing adoptive parents."

He narrowed his eyes, his hands gesturing at the large room around them. "I'm sorry. Is my aunt's generosity not good enough for you? You have family willing to give you a chance. And you're right, my birth parents are some nameless nobodies out there. That just means you have more eyes on you. Maybe it will help keep you in line. Maybe you'll snap under the pressure. Maybe you'll tell the doubters to suck it, and move on with your life."

"Marcus," Catrina scolded at the door, her toddler breaking away from her side, hugging Marcus's leg. "She's trying. Go easy on her."

Marcus picked up the toddler with a huff, then faced Leah. "You have choices to make, but that doesn't invalidate that I get to make my own choices." He gave the toddler a hug and set him down. Marcus stalked toward his aunt, about to pass her. He stopped with a sigh, giving her a hug, too. "Good luck with your coronation preparations."

Catrina gave him a gentle smile. "Thank you. Good luck with school. Love you."

"Love you too." He left the room with Catrina standing at the doorway.

Leah sat, biting her nails and sniffling. "I don't know why I even tried."

Catrina frowned. "Do you want to talk?"

Leah shook her head.

Catrina picked up her little boy, holding him on her hip. "Just give him more time."

Chapter 36

Leah strolled down the lane, lost in thought, a guard trailing a few paces behind her. She still had so much to learn. About her homeland, culture, family. About herself. Eventually, she'd had to come to terms with the truth. And as much as she hated her mom's actions, she understood some of them.

Beata had never had a good influence like Marcus in her life. Her parents had been in charge of the old Bomen communities, not that they used any nice names for their quasi slaves back then. Leah still didn't know how much she could forgive her mom for her twisted prejudices and perspectives, despite the home she'd grown up in. Was *any* level of leniency just giving her an undeserved free pass?

Leah still held a special place for her mom in her heart, and suspected she always would. On a recent visit to the prison, she'd come to understand her more, and had been grateful for her mom's frankness. Beata swore up and down that Soren hadn't always been so brutal, so horrible, even if Kaylah disagreed on that point. Beata had believed he was a good man when they'd first met, but over time, he had started doing more things she found hard to stomach. She hadn't protested his actions as much as she ought to have. She'd been too taken with him. He'd talked her into too many things she hadn't been comfortable with. And once she'd lost him for good, her grief broke her, and she could now admit she'd remembered things with rose-colored glasses.

Leah stumbled on a rock in the path, almost twisting her ankle, but catching herself. She should pay more attention, but her mind still played back her previous conversation with her mom.

Her mom still wouldn't confess what she'd done in the human world to earn them money, not fully. She had opened up some about that, though, too. Losing Cheryl and her income had pushed her over the edge in desperation to watch out for Leah. The same day Leah had found her mom sobbing in her room, she'd done something that earned them a healthy sum. She still wouldn't give specifics, but it had something to do with a promise she'd made to Leah's dad years ago.

It was hard to hear her mom confess that she realized she hadn't been putting her daughter first, that she'd been clinging to Soren's memory for far too long, to an old promise. But that day, she really had chosen Leah. In her heart, she'd let him go in a way she'd never imagined. Even confessions like that were heartbreaking for Leah. It had been too little, too late.

Since Cheryl had abandoned them, and Beata knew her current address, Beata had given it to Kaylah in hopes it would help her and Leah. Cheryl was brought in, and just like Beata had blamed Soren for her actions, Cheryl swore she'd never wanted any part of it, but had been forced to help Beata as her aide back at the palace. Leah didn't buy a word of it, still fully believing she'd just been a bitter old maid hating the life of exile in the human world, and taking it out on Leah. Where Beata had let Leah down, Kaylah didn't. She heard her out. She believed her.

Cheryl was sentenced to thirty years in prison for child abuse, and aiding and abetting a war criminal. Leah never wanted to see that woman again, and was promised she wouldn't have to.

Leah took a pensive breath as the breeze rustled leaves high above her head. A chipmunk scurried up a nearby fence post, and Leah plucked up a long velvet grassweed, swishing it in the air. She still obsessed over her mom, unable to reconcile her behavior of the past and present.

Ironically, the fact that her mom *hadn't* blatantly lied more was somehow frustrating to her. Her mom hadn't taught her more of the chemical arts—the other things she could do with her vines—because she hadn't actually known them. Like cave rifting, Kaylah had been the revolutionary to lead her people away from war, to a better understanding of their own powers, and to a more sustainable way of life.

Most of the real lies and misunderstandings were taking shape for Leah over time. It took her a while to wrap her head around why Jake's parents would have fled at the beginning of Kaylah's reign, because Bomen hadn't even been physically capable of travel to the human world until Kaylah and Rachel had discovered that option. Queen Catrina had helped clear that one up for Leah. Like Jake's parents, many Bomen, especially ones like his mom—illegally pregnant with him—had fled once Kaylah made it possible to, fearing she would be deposed. Kaylah's parents and then brother were all assassinated or ousted in less than a year's time. It was understandable that the most vulnerable population took the chance they were given to flee in a time of uncertainty.

Leah shook her head. *Everything* had been twisted. She'd chosen to hear and believe what she'd wanted to. Now, she was having to carefully reframe her every decision that had led up to the failed assassination, and every decision after that. She'd written a long letter of apology to Camry and Tobias. *What a horrible and public way to ruin their special day.* With Leah having lost her mind, her hope, and even her faith in Marcus's family, the couple's wedding had felt like the smallest consideration, as collateral damage.

Turning the corner at the end of the street, nearing her next destination for the day, Leah sighed. Queen Catrina and King Stephan were nice. And despite being so busy, they made an effort to ensure Leah was as comfortable as possible. Leah felt guilty for tainting Catrina's special day, her coronation. Leah was the black eye the Green Lands hadn't seen coming.

Leah chuckled to herself. She'd once asked Marcus if Catrina was taking over because Kaylah was being kicked out. It was far from the truth. Kaylah and Eric had served their best, but it had been a rough reign—trying to redesign a kingdom that had spent centuries oppressing Seeders and their own citizens. And unable to have children together, with Eric being a human, they could produce no heir of their own. Once Catrina's awful mother had died, and Catrina was married and having kids, she was in a good place to rule. Catrina had always been a proper lady, immensely helpful, yet barely even part of the old war. Her name and reputation held no negatives in the public eye.

The guard still walking behind Leah broke the silence of their travel. "Her Majesty wanted me to remind you of this evening's state ball, miss, and to allow extra time for one more dress fitting."

"I know, thank you. I doubt this will take long," Leah replied. She'd given up on fighting Catrina's staff calling her 'miss,' and she was growing even more fond of the pretty dresses.

Out of nowhere, Leah's mind went back to her journal entry from the day before. As horrible as it was that Leah's dad had slept around, Leah had been holding out hope that maybe it meant she had a half-sibling out there somewhere. *What kind of person wishes that on a kid, anyway? Especially if the mother is one of the women he forced himself on...*

But Soren had been careful to ensure he didn't have illegitimate children floating around. Leah was still alone as his only living offspring. Living, because records indicated she wouldn't have been all alone. When prevention hadn't worked, he'd had things taken care of. He hadn't just taken Seeder lives, or servants' and soldiers' lives, he'd taken some of his own children's lives. That was the shadow Leah lived under. That was the shadow she was fighting every day to break away from.

Rachel poured tea for herself and Leah before sitting back down, tucking her legs underneath her. "How are the lessons going?"

Leah smiled, sipping her tea. Rachel was actually the hardest person to look in the eyes, after how much Leah and her parents had hurt her family, but she was more understanding and forgiving than Leah could have hoped for. "Thanks again. You make the best tea. Even better than at the palace."

"High praise. Do I need to share my secret blend with Catrina's cooks?"

"Yes please. As for lessons, um ... I mean ... having to be tutored during the summer sucks. But I get it." She set her teacup down. "But if we're talking powers, I think I've got down numbing real well." The history lessons were kind of a given.

Rachel smiled. "Nice. I understand that one can be tricky."

Leah rocked her head back and forth. "I'm just doing local numbing, really. There's still lots more to learn."

"Hey, Mom, what's with the extra guard out—" Marcus stopped once he walked into the room. His eyes swept over Leah. "Oh." He turned and headed past the kitchen, upstairs.

Leah sighed. "I thought he was ready."

Rachel returned a sympathetic frown, shrugging.

Not a minute later, footsteps came back down the stairs, and Marcus peeked around the corner. "Go for a walk?"

"Yes." She looked at Rachel. "Thank you again for the tea, and everything."

"Anytime."

After a few paces in silence along the canal, Leah decided to get the conversation started. "I know I sound like a broken record, but I'm sorry for everything I've done. And I say that without any expectations."

He nodded, looking straight forward.

She swallowed. "How was the rest of school? How's Jake?"

"It was good. Well ... it was alright. Jake's good." He met her gaze out of the corner of his eye. "I could see Jake being up to a visit next time he's in-realm."

She furrowed her brow. "Do you mean visit me? Or you?"

"Either. Both. He's pretty forgiving. And doesn't really delve deep into Green Lands politics."

Leah smiled fondly, wishing she'd spent less time planning and plotting, more time getting to know Jake better. "Is he still with Emily?"

Marcus smiled as well. "Yeah, he is."

"Did, uh... Well, I know word doesn't always travel fast between the realms, but did Tanner give you any problems?"

Marcus smirked, rubbing his hand. "Not after I broke his nose."

Her jaw dropped. "You didn't!"

"Oh, I did. He had it coming."

She wrung her hands. She couldn't assume it had anything to do with her. Tanner was a jerk, plain and simple. "I'm sure he deserved it."

"You know him well enough." Marcus paused. "Have you gone to see your mom in prison?"

"A couple of times. At what point do you stop loving someone because of their mistakes? Or I guess ... at what point do you keep loving them, despite them?" She meant it as much about herself as her mom.

"You're not her. And you're not him. You made your own mistakes."

"Yeah. And I learned from them."

Silence hung in the air. *Next topic... Um...* "I hear Wedding Two-Point-Oh went off without a hitch. No crazy murderers on the guest list."

Marcus frowned. "It was really nice. They still kept their human-world wedding date, so they were already legally married over there. That one was nice too." He rocked his head back and forth. "I think Cam would be up to seeing you next time they visit."

She smiled. "And Tobias?"

"Yeah ... we're still working on things. He knows how to hold a grudge."

She nodded. "I don't blame him. I'm surprised the rest of your family has been so nice to me."

He raised his eyebrows. "They're your family too."

She blushed. "I know. Did that make things weird, when you realized that? It took me a little while to process it, with how we ... well..."

He stole a glance but didn't stop walking. "We're kinda related. Heavy on the kinda, light on the related. It's not like we're cousins. Our dads were. And I'm adopted, anyway." He looked back at Leah. "Is it weird for you?"

Her heart still clung to hope. "Not really."

Marcus reached into his pocket. "This is what I went up to my room for." He handed Leah a bottle of red nail polish.

She scrunched her eyebrows, accepting it. "Nail polish? This is why you asked me to visit?"

He rubbed the back of his neck. "Yeah, um. Well, no. I think they threw away the receipt, but when they were clearing out your old place, they asked if I had any input on what you'd want that could be taken back."

She looked at the almost-full bottle. "You can bring back anything that will fit in your pockets through a rift, and you brought me this? They gave me my childhood photos weeks ago."

He opened and closed his mouth a couple of times. "Yeah, well. I don't know." He pointed to the polish. "If I remember right, that was the first one you bought with your own money. I thought it was a nice reminder for your new life."

She smiled, her heart warming. "Thanks. I've been doing loads better. You'd be proud of me." She tucked the bottle in her pocket.

He nodded. "I've heard. And, um ... I also brought your throwing knives back home. I just didn't bring them for the walk. I figured you could take them when you leave to go back to the palace." He glanced over his shoulder at the guard walking several paces behind them. "Assuming they'll let you have them?"

Leah rolled her eyes. "I'm assured she's around for *my* protection, not to protect the world from me. I'm still allowed to eat with a full set of cutlery at the dinner table, thank you very much."

A look of embarrassment flashed across his face. "Sorry, I didn't mean—"

"No, Marcus." She stopped abruptly, facing him. "You don't need to apologize. For anything. Ever." She hadn't expected her eyes to mist, but her heart couldn't handle skirting around the topic. "I was in the wrong. I know that. Completely. And I don't expect you to take me back. I don't deserve that. I know that too." A tear rolled down her cheek. "But I hope you can give me another chance at being your friend. I miss you."

He wiped her tear away. "I'm pretty sure I'll do something over the course of my life that requires an apology." He smiled. "At least one." He studied her face. "I can do friends." His smile grew to a grin. "I think my parents would prefer we started there."

Her heart leapt. *Started?*

Marcus's cheeks took on a shade of pink. "It was an … *interesting* discussion with my parents about why my girlfriend came prepared with a condom stashed under her pillow."

Leah's eyes grew wide, her face burning. "Oh gosh. I'm sorry! I really didn't think things through. I didn't exactly do an inventory when they returned my clothes and lipstick." He was still smiling, but she felt horrible about adding to the stress he had to have gone through after she was taken into custody. "You didn't get in too much trouble, did you?"

He chuckled, looking up at the sky. "Let me see if I can remember what they said. Something to the effect of 'You are not to, under any circumstances, ever even *consider* sleeping under the same roof as any girl that you are dating, or considering dating, or even think is pretty, unless you're fifty years old or married to her.'"

Leah did a poor job of stifling a laugh. "I'm really sorry."

He got more serious, gazing into her eyes. "You don't have to keep apologizing. I've … forgiven you. Don't say you're sorry anymore."

A huge weight lifted from her shoulders as she lunged forward, hugging him. She was about to pull back, realizing things were still touchy, until he reciprocated with one of his tight squeezes. It felt like home.

Leah leaned back, searching Marcus's face. She was acutely aware of his hands lingering on her waist. "I don't have to apologize, *ever*? Because I'm pretty sure I'll do something over the course of my life that requires an apology." She smiled. "At least one."

"Then try to make it something only needing a small apology. For my sake?"

"Deal."

He slid his hands down, grasping hers.

She looked at their hands, her heart racing. "What does this mean to you?"

"It means I missed you, too. And I care about you. And I want to get to know the new, real you. And give you a chance to know the full me, family notoriety and all. We'll go slow."

"Yes."

He grinned, squeezing her hands, then turned, dropping one of them and continuing on their stroll. After another minute of Leah's heart overflowing, Marcus cleared his throat. "Will I see you at the ball?"

"Yeah. Save me a dance."

"I'll save you two." He pressed his lips together. "You know that if we had kids, they'd be like me, right? All Bomen."

Her jaw dropped. "Kids? We have a year left of high school!"

He chuckled. "I didn't mean to give you a heart attack. That's years in the future. I'm just saying... I want to make sure you understand that about our people. That you know what you're signing up for ... if things lead down that path someday. A lot of people around here still care about that, still consider Bomanism a curse."

She stopped him, gazing into his warm brown eyes. "I understand how it works. And I might still be figuring out who I am, but I know who *you* are. And the world could use *a lot* more people like you."

Epilogue

The ballroom glittered as candlelight bounced off chandelier crystals, and reflected off the gilded wainscoting. Glassware clinked, girls giggled, and adults everywhere mumbled in greeting.

Leah sat at her table, alone, sipping grape juice and trying her best to mind her posture. Marcus and his parents had been busy conversing when she'd entered, and she hadn't wanted to bother them. After slinking to her designated table, she people-watched as the room continued to fill, as the violins played upbeat tunes, as the gaze of literally every person in the room rested on her at some point.

It was lonely in the corner. In part because she didn't really know many people yet, other than the servants who occasionally swung by her table to check on her. In part because her personal guards were doing a more-than-sufficient job of gatekeeping her company that night. They wouldn't take any risks at Leah's first ball. Everyone here at the palace was theoretically pro–Queen Catrina. That meant they should respect her wishes to welcome Leah and help their kingdom move on. That also meant they might despise Leah for being the daughter of Soren, one of the most hated men in the history of the Green Lands. Leah hadn't done herself any favors either, by attempting to assassinate their much-beloved Queen Kaylah.

The whispers and glances were hard to ignore. Leah knew what it felt like to be slut-shamed. She knew what it was like to be the topic of perverts in the locker room. None of that compared to this experience.

Closing her eyes and taking a deep breath, Leah forced herself to repeat Catrina's pep talk. She'd only ever be able to clear her name, to claim her future, by showing she was above the gossip, above the hate. It probably would have been easier if it was just her peers throwing looks of disdain her way, but the adult eyes on her made things that much worse.

"How are you doing, miss?" one of the guards asked, leaning close.

Leah forced a smile. "Doing well."

"Good... Would you like to dance?"

Arching an eyebrow, she turned to face him better. He had to be more than twice her age. "What?"

He nodded to his right. "Jaxon Withers, son of Governor Withers."

She almost giggled when she realized the guard had meant a boy her age wanted to dance, not that the guard had intended to ask her himself. She eyed the governor's son. He stood tall, holding his hands in front of him. His straight black hair hung below his ears, and his suit was as sharp as any of the other men's in the room. He looked at her with a smile and a small nod from a few feet away. The fact his request was even being passed along to her meant he was on an approved list of some sort, that the queen's security team felt this boy could be trusted. Leah didn't know whether to be annoyed with him or grateful he was attempting to rescue her from her island of solitude.

"He can ask me himself," she told the guard.

The guard waved Jaxon over. He glided over to Leah's table, bowing. She remained seated.

"My name is Jaxon."

She gave him a nod. "I'm Leah, but I guess you already knew that."

His smile grew.

Leah took a sip of her water. "How can I help you, Jaxon?"

He looked confused, glancing at the guards. "Oh, I thought they told you. I want to dance."

She wore a grin. "They did tell me. But I wanted to hear it from you."

"Oh." He rested his hands on the back of the chair across the table from her. "Well, I'd love to dance."

Studying his face, she figured she might as well have a little fun. "Then I'd say you came to the right place. I hope you enjoy your evening."

He narrowed his eyes. "So ... that's a no?"

"I can't say yes or no to a question I haven't been asked." She folded her napkin. "All I know from you is that you hope to dance tonight."

His mouth hung open. "Yeah. I came over to invite you to dance with me."

She opened her eyes wide in mock surprised shock. "Aha. I didn't realize you were asking *me* to dance."

He smiled again. "Yes. That's why I'm here."

Straightening her unused utensils, she matched his smile. "Why do you want to dance with me?" She was trying to be playful, though she genuinely was curious. She hadn't expected many approved suitors would even try socializing with her that night.

Losing his cool, Jaxon squinted with a frustrated expression. "Why do I want to dance with you? It's a ball. That's what people do. If you don't want to, you can just say so."

She sighed. Her sense of humor was lost on this boy. She knew she shouldn't toy with him, and that Catrina would likely already disapprove of their conversation—it hadn't been 'gracious.' Sparing a glance in Marcus's direction, Leah yearned for him to be the one asking her, but he was busy talking to a row of dolled-up girls.

"Yes. I'd love to dance." She rose and took Jaxon's outstretched arm, and he led her onto the dance floor.

Luckily, he eased her into the dance with simple steps. She'd taken lessons at Catrina's urging, but hadn't practiced as much as she ought to have in preparation.

"So, how are you enjoying the Green Lands?" Jaxon asked.

Leah puffed up her cheeks. "Um... Good? Yeah, it's good." How was she supposed to have a conversation with anyone? 'Yeah, pretty good. Minus that whole bummer thing about finding out my parents are murderers, and I almost joined their ranks. How about you?'

"You like it at the palace?"

"Uh... It's," she glanced at the room around them, "shiny."

"Shiny?"

Another awkward question. What had he hoped she'd say? 'I'm glad to have lost both parents and am now being forced to live in the lap of luxury, at the same palace my dad's death sentence was decreed from?'

"It's beautiful." She forced a gracious smile.

"I understand you'll be touring the kingdom soon?"

"Yep."

He nodded. "How do you feel about that?"

Was he a therapist in disguise? "Why did you want to dance with me?"

His mouth was agape. "Do I need a reason?"

A diplomat, she was not. "*Need* one? Nah. But you *have* one. There's always a motivation behind what we do, right?"

"I just ... wanted to dance with you."

"Hmm…" Catrina would not approve of the words about to come out of Leah's mouth, but it wasn't Leah's fault she hadn't developed a filter overnight. "Well, I'd say you either asked me to dance because you think I'm pretty, and you like the way this dress looks."

His eyes wandered over her deep plum dress for the shortest of moments before he blushed.

"Or you're doing this as an aspiring politician, like your father."

Jaxon studied her face skeptically. "It's just a dance."

"Or…" Leah bobbed her head. "You're one of those sick fan club people that fall in love with serial killers and write to them in prison."

He was not amused. "Excuse me?"

"Just call it like I see it. Which is it?"

He glared, but didn't miss a step in the dance. "You have no culture or manners. If I was less of a gentleman, I'd walk off of this dance floor right now."

Should she be ashamed of herself? Yes. Was she? Not really. She laughed loudly, playfully nudging his shoulder. She wore a giant toothy smile as if he'd told a great joke. "But it's all about appearances, right?"

He wasn't smiling. Instead, he ignored her for the rest of the dance. Leah was okay with that, for the most part. Her guilt grew a little with each step. She didn't even know this guy, but if there was something Leah was good at, it was burning bridges. And it was hard to imagine *anyone* not having an ulterior motive, given her story, given her precarious place in society.

Without conversation to occupy her, Leah watched the people who were watching her right back. A pair of soft brown eyes caught her attention. Marcus was watching. And then a girl rested a hand on his bicep. *Ugh.*

As the music slowed, Leah allowed her guilt to prompt her to speak again. "Sorry, Jaxon."

He didn't respond. As the dance came to an end, he released her, bowing.

"I really am sorry. That was rude of me."

He scanned her face. "Thank you for the dance."

"Did someone ask you to dance with me?"

He squinted. "No. I thought you could use a friend, and a kind introduction. But perhaps, Miss Eleana, you ought to get more help before you come out in proper society again." He gave her another bow and then turned on his heel, gliding off the dance floor.

Yep. She was an uncultured swine, alright. One that happily skulked off to her familiar corner.

Couples were already dancing away to the next song by the time she returned to her table and accepted a pastry from a passing servant carrying a tray. Marcus danced with a girl wearing a pink dress. Leah was green folk, alright. Very green. Jealously green.

She picked at her pastry, eating tiny crumbs, constantly stealing a glance at Marcus and his partner. The girl was striking. Her long blond hair cascaded straight down her back to where Marcus's hand held her. Her smile was perfect, her footwork graceful. And that dress—it was like a custom-fit beaded wonder with strips of fabric flowing away from her as she spun.

Leah guzzled some water. *This is going to be a long night...*

At the end of the dance, Marcus bowed to his partner, and she curtsied. Leah looked away. She was the epitome of an obsessed ex-girlfriend right now. What she didn't need was gossip about how she'd gawked at the queen's nephew all night, how she was probably plotting the assassination of every girl who stood in her way as she pined for him.

Instead, she stared at her nails, trying to not pick at or bite them. It was a messy habit.

"Free for this dance?" Marcus asked.

She looked up. He'd already reached her table, not needing to be approved to approach.

Leah glanced around the room. Couples took to the floor, but more eyes than usual were on them right now. The entire kingdom knew what had happened, the entire realm.

"Are you sure?" she asked, her pulse quickening.

"Of course." He extended a hand.

So many eyes rested on them both. And now that she had really learned more about Ivy society and Marcus's place in it, this felt risky. It wasn't surprising he'd been upset to find out his girlfriend had shoplifting and lying problems. He was the most eligible bachelor their age. His family had a reputation of being saints. People had expectations of him.

"I... It probably won't be great for your reputation," she said.

"You let me worry about that." He extended his other hand as well. "You promised me a dance. And right now, the only reputation you're giving me is that of a guy being royally shot down by the prettiest girl in the room."

She bolstered her courage. "Yeah, sure." She took his hands, and he led her to the floor. He rested a hand on her waist, leading her in the dance. Leah furrowed her brow at the song being played by the orchestra. "Is that human music?"

He gave her a charming smile. "I asked them to play our song."

"We have a song?"

"I don't know. I remembered us dancing to this once."

It was undeniably sweet. "Thanks. It kind of makes it feel a little more like I'm home…" That was a depressing confession. She *was* literally home, in her new home, in the palace.

"Are you enjoying it at all?" he asked.

She gripped his hand tighter. "I'm enjoying this right now."

"Jaxon's a better dancer than me."

She smiled at his fishing. "I figured you were too busy with your fan club to notice."

"Hmm…" He spun her. "Is that a hint of jealousy I detect?"

"Yes."

He wore a triumphant grin. "It would be hard not to notice you tonight."

"Hmm. That might be true. Jaxon probably thought so, since he claimed the first dance."

Marcus's eyes narrowed a bit. "He's kind of a nitwit."

She batted her eyelashes. "Is that a hint of jealousy I detect?"

He pulled her closer. "Yes."

"Good."

They took a few more steps in silence. She couldn't resist stealing a peek at the others in the room. Rachel smiled when their eyes met.

"That really is a … stunning … dress," he breathed.

She blushed, focusing on him. "Thanks. I had to fight Her Majesty and the seamstress to let me wear it the way I wanted."

He didn't say anything. He didn't need to. Queen Catrina was genuinely very kind, but could be a bit strict. She'd insisted Leah should try harder on showing a good face to work on her respectability. It wasn't like anyone in the Green Lands knew the kind of reputation Leah had left behind, but a young lady trying to prove herself ought not to show so much cleavage.

Leah had wanted a breathtaking sweetheart gown, or to not go to the ball at all. They'd compromised. Leah attended, and had a shawl. A shawl she took off and draped over her chair the first moment she could.

Leah lifted a hand, wiggling her fingers. "You didn't compliment my nail polish."

Marcus spared a glance at the red polish, the one he'd just returned to her, then smirked. "It's your color. You'll have to forgive me for not noticing it. That dress doesn't accentuate your nails."

She stood taller, puffing out her chest. "Tell me, Marcus ... what *does* it accentuate?"

He shook his head. "You're going to make this hard on me, aren't you?"

She feigned confusion. "What?"

"Dancing with other guys. Wearing a dress like that. You're going to make it hard on me."

She looked him dead in the eyes. "I heard what you said the first time. I just wanted to make sure. You said I was making something on you ... hard?"

His face bloomed red. "Leah!" He stole glances around them, not that anyone would have been close enough to hear her say it. He would never *not* be cute when he blushed. "You can't just say stuff like that in public."

It was a playful moment, like those they'd shared before. And his response was more shock than censure, but it threw her into a melancholy mood.

They continued to sway. She swallowed. "If we're going to do this... Friends, or more than friends... Even if we didn't, and we just saw each other at royal functions and awkward family gatherings, because there's really no escaping those anymore... I need you to know I'll never be the girl they want me to be."

He searched her face.

"I'll practice the dance steps. I'll do the curtsying. I'll attend the right royal functions. But I'll still be me. I'm going to spout off gosh-awful puns, and fight with the seamstress about what I wear, and make *wildly* inappropriate jokes while dancing in the middle of a ballroom filled with people watching and waiting for me to fail. That's what you're in for."

He nodded, pensive. Disappointment painted his face.

But then an almost sinister grin overtook his lips. "Do you promise?"

She matched his grin, her heart melting completely.

"I know you don't love being the center of attention," he said. "I'm used to this. You'll get used to it too."

Doubtful.

"But ... if they're all going to stare and spread rumors, what do you think about giving them something to sink their teeth into?"

"Um... What are you thinking?"

He wore a cat-that-ate-the-canary smirk. "Hold on."

"What?"

His hands gripped her tighter, and yanked her into a wild spin. She let out a short scream, then giggled as they spun around and around. She quickly became dizzy, and almost lost her grip, but shot out vines behind his back to secure herself.

When he slowed, the song was coming to an end. She was still laughing, but almost out of breath. He was laughing, too. They helped steady each other, and she leaned her forehead against his chest. "Yeah, people might talk about that..."

He chuckled a little more.

After taking a second to recompose herself, she stood straight. "Well, that was a dance."

He bowed graciously, and she curtsied. "Still saving me another one?" he asked.

She almost grabbed his hand, but held herself back. "Yeah. Of course. I can't wait to see what we'll do next."

They lingered a moment.

"Well..." He fidgeted with his hands. "If you want, I could introduce you to a few people..."

She glanced past him at the group he'd spent time with earlier. She recognized a few faces he'd introduced her to weeks ago, but several were new to her. A cute blonde stared right at her—and then her pupils flashed an unnatural green, Seeder green. "No. I think I'm good in my corner right now." Leah forced a smile. "Baby steps."

"Okay. We'll chat?"

She nodded, and started walking away. The Seeder girl's eyes were no longer neon, but they followed her back to her table.

The next hour or so, Leah sat at her designated spot. She took more than one bathroom break, and chatted with guards and servants. She festered over the situation, and over the Seeder girl. Had she been jealous that Marcus made a scene with Leah? It was public knowledge they'd dated. It was obvious to everyone now there was still something there. But it might not have anything to do with Marcus at all. It might have just been Leah's parentage.

A couple of guys even inquired about dancing. Leah declined. She wasn't in the mood anymore. And she couldn't handle much more of being a wallflower, either.

Needing a break from the noise and crowds, she sauntered to one of the open balconies, escorted by her security detail. They kindly gave her some space and waited just inside.

Leah looked out over the expanse of the kingdom before her. The moonlight lit giant mountains in every direction, and landed on the sea of treetops surrounding the palace. It was positively ethereal, but it only helped a little.

"I shouldn't be worried, should I?"

Leah glanced over her shoulder. "No, Your Majest— I mean, Highness."

Kaylah smiled. "The titles are confusing sometimes, aren't they?"

Leah blew out a puff of air as Kaylah joined her at the edge of the balcony. "Yeah."

"Of course, *you* don't have to use one with me."

Leah nodded. It was still weird. How could it not be? To just call her 'Kaylah' to her face? Or ... 'Aunt Kaylah'?

"You're not enjoying the dance," Kaylah said.

"I know. I should try to at least look happier."

Kaylah adjusted a bangle around her wrist. "I don't know about that. I think people understand the position you're in."

Leah didn't really care for a heart-to-heart right now. She just wanted peace and quiet. She continued to take in the scenery.

"Well... I just wanted to make sure you were okay out here."

Leah gripped the balcony railing. "I'm not out here to fling myself off the edge."

Kaylah said nothing. They'd also put Leah on suicide watch those first few days because Kaylah's ruling hadn't been an official one. Kaylah had met with the Seeder and Bomen councils to address the issue of Leah's assassination attempt, and her very existence, during that time. It had taken a while for Kaylah to report that her decisions had been upheld.

"If you ever need a break from the palace, the invitation's always open to visit Eric and me at our place."

Leah nodded. She'd been there once already for tea. The grounds were expansive, and it was beyond serene. It was actually a tempting offer.

"Fewer servants," Kaylah continued. "And don't get me wrong, I love Catrina to death, but toddlers and babies, and dignitaries... Gross!"

Leah couldn't resist a tiny smile at that. "I'll give that to you. You're probably more fun, too." Perhaps that wasn't very generous of Leah to say. Queen Catrina was a sweetheart, but the rules upon rules… It was quite the contrast to what Leah had grown up with.

Kaylah splayed a hand on her chest. "I'm the fun one? I'm the fun one!" She balled a fist in triumph. "Yes! I didn't know if I'd ever be an aunt, but if I turned out to be, I for sure wanted to be the fun kind!"

Leah's smile grew. Kaylah admittedly had a decent sense of humor. And Eric was a fantastic listener. "Don't get too big of a head about it. Your tiara won't fit."

"That's why you get different sizes." Kaylah nudged her.

Leah chuckled.

"But I'm sorry you're not having more fun. Other than that rather unique dance you shared with Marcus."

Her stomach flipped at the mention of him. "Yeah. I'm sure I'll hear more about how wrong that was later tonight."

Turning to face the palace, Kaylah drew a deep breath. "You know, we Elonta women might be blessed to rule, but we kinda suck at fitting in sometimes."

"What?" Leah raised a skeptical eyebrow. Strictly speaking, she *wasn't* an Elonta, and had absolutely no place in the line of heirs to the throne, but that wasn't what Kaylah had been getting at. "I'm sure it's rough having millions of green folk adore you for fixing their problems. And from what I hear, Catrina's never even sneezed when she ought not to."

Kaylah grinned. "Okay. Way to call me out. Yeah, Catrina doesn't count. Maybe I just meant *this* Elonta struggled to fit in."

That was still hard to believe.

"We won't even mention the whole Seeder drama… Or Bomen. Or the family legacy I had to fight tooth and nail to disassociate myself from. Just me as a person… I'm not everyone's cup of tea." She straightened her gorgeous off-the-shoulder red dress. "I started my reign when I was just older than you. I wasn't properly prepared. I flubbed things left and right. I said stupid things that got people I love hurt. I didn't always have the best filter."(x) She pursed her lips, then softly chuckled. "My friend, Saff, once described me as 'flippant and callous.' She wasn't wrong. And frankly, the list goes on. I dressed wrong. I wasn't a coy, proper lady. I was the monster who unilaterally decided to allow humans into the realm, and then, Lights of the Afterworld forbid, I married one." She pointed at Leah. "Mind you, his existence wasn't even public for almost two years until I announced it and refused to pick a sperm donor just to birth gremlins of my own."

Kaylah sighed. "Anyway, I didn't mean to make this about me. I'm just saying, people might not be ready for you yet. Yes, you'll have to accept some give and take. But they'll get there. And so will you." She cautiously wrapped an arm around Leah's shoulder, giving her a gentle squeeze. "Okay?"

Leah nodded. "Yeah." Kaylah could get a tad preachy, and as Leah had learned at the wedding luncheon, she could be fierce, but mostly, she was pretty down to earth. That was only one of a million things Leah had gotten wrong, had made assumptions on, and had felt like an idiot about later, once she'd learned the truth. She'd seen Kaylah's rough interaction with one of the servants at the luncheon as a sign she was a tyrant. That hadn't been the case at all. There had been royal wedding crashers outside of the manor causing problems, and she'd been curt, frustrated that her guards needed to barge into the family luncheon when they ought to have been able to handle the situation on their own.

Kaylah broke her reverie. "Are you too polite to tell me you want to be left alone right now?"

Leah smiled, averting her gaze.

"Alright. I can take a hint. Just know I'm here for you. Love you, kiddo."

Leah opened her mouth, but nothing came out for a moment. "Thanks." It was still too soon to go there with Kaylah, despite how much she tried.

Kaylah gave her a sad smile. "Good night."

Once the click of Kaylah's heels became muffled in the distance, it was just Leah, her thoughts, and the faint breeze. Tomorrow would be better. Things were better when she was busy with tutors, her counselor, and knife-throwing, and honing her skills, fine-tuning her powers.

Tomorrow would be better.

A warm hand caressed her back, and she sharply inhaled.

"Sorry," Marcus said.

She blew out a shaky breath. "I don't expect people to sneak up on me so much when I have a security detail watching my back."

He smiled gently. "You okay?"

She rubbed her forehead. "Did Kaylah send you?"

"No... Should she have?"

"No. Just don't need everyone checking up on me every two seconds."

He pursed his lips. "Sorry. Just hadn't seen you in a while. Though, I should learn my lesson." He cleared his throat, tugging on his vest. "I dated this *superhot* girl once, and she tried to teach me that girls don't always want to be saved. I wasn't the best student."

She grinned. "Maybe she was too stubborn to admit she sometimes *does* need saving."

"Yeah?"

Her smile grew. "Yep. You just have to be able to read her mind to know when and how."

He busted out laughing.

An owl hooted from a nearby treetop, and Marcus scooted closer.

"Are you only here with me, trying to work things out with me, because you feel bad?" She gazed into his eyes. "Or because this is one of those 'for the greater good' things where we show we can put aside our differences and make up for our parents' mistakes?"

He didn't answer right away, instead lifting a hand to her waist, then sliding it to her hip. "No. Not at all." He spoke softly. "Part of me..." He stared at his hand as he stroked her hip bone with a thumb. "Part of me wants to pick up where we left things ... that night ... in my room." He met her gaze, exuding passion. "The night I told you how I felt, before things went wrong."

She took his other hand, placing it on her other hip. "I'd be okay with that."

He panted an exhale. His look of wanting washed away as he removed his hands from her body entirely. "But part of me, the part that's been used before, even before I met you, *needs* to go slow this time." There was hurt in his expression. "Please don't rush me."

She nodded, gutted at that confession. He'd never told her that before, not that it likely would have made much difference when she'd been blinded by idiocy to use him in the first place. "I can be patient." Perhaps that wasn't the whole truth. She could *try* to be patient. They both still had healing to do. Unfortunately, she felt like her healing would best be done with the one she loved by her side, and his needed to be done with some distance.

"But I will say..." She wanted to lighten the mood. "Try not to take too long. There's only one of me, and frankly, every single day, the guards have to fight off *dozens* of sexy suitors trying to pound down the palace doors to get a chance to date me. So, I'm just saying, hot commodity right here."

He smirked knowingly. "They would be, if they knew you the way I do."

She blushed. "So, we're friends. Ish. Friend adjacent. Friends that have a look in their eye and a tenderness to their touch that friends ought not to have."

He pressed his lips together. "Sorry."

"It's okay. I want that. But I'm afraid we're going to be five years down the road and I'm still waiting for you to call me your girlfriend, just to find out you thought we were back together after a month."

"Trust me, when I'm ready to be exclusive again, you'll know. The whole realm will."

She smiled, a calmness settling in her heart. "Okay."

Marcus furrowed his brow, looking off into the distance. "Can I ask you something?"

"Of course you can."

He lightly ran his hand over the railing. "What do you like about me?"

"Really?" It felt like a ridiculous question, given she'd told him during their time together. But then again, it wasn't a ridiculous question at all... They were starting from square one again. He didn't know how much of anything she'd said during their time together was genuine. It was going to take a long time for her heart not to ache in situations like this. The old Leah would have moved on, would have protected herself by washing her hands of him. The new Leah knew she'd be an idiot to let him go.

Marcus didn't respond, didn't look at her.

"I love a ton of things about you. You're studious, and love your family, and you like to help people. You're ... forgiving."

He gave her a cautious understanding glance at that mention.

"And I love your sense of humor, and," she lifted a hand to his bicep, its beauty wasted in the suit he was wearing, "you're strong, and talented, and have handsome eyes."

He smiled.

She slid her hand up to his shoulder, then the side of his neck, and ran her hand through his naturally curly hair. "And I love this, the curls."

His smile grew, and he stared at her. Her lips yearned to be kissed. Her heart nearly beat out of her chest in protest at the absence of his arms around her.

But he still didn't snatch her up, didn't draw her close. Didn't kiss hope back into her.

As the moment floated away, she stopped playing with his hair, and lowered her hand. "Anything I've ever said about why I like you has always been true."

"Thank you," he said softly. "Did I tell you what made me change my mind about you? About us?"

"No. You didn't."

"It hurt to hear you say you, well, that you loved me. For the first time, only *after* what you did."

Her heart was a pincushion. "I'm sorry."

He rubbed his chin. "It sucked. And I came to understand that you couldn't help yourself, given what your mom had said. You didn't know the big picture. And in part, I was to blame."

"No you weren't."

He side-eyed her skeptically. "How much history did I teach you?"

She frowned. "You were my boyfriend, not my history teacher." She poked his arm. "Plus, you taught me lots of valuable things, like how green folk earn good luck."

He instantly donned a toothy grin.

"Though I will say, the servants and guards all get *super* creeped out when I ask them to blow raspberries on my neck. I could use some good luck! Your aunt has forbidden me from chasing them around the palace asking them to do it, and I can't figure out why!"

Marcus's laughter was music to her ears. After a moment, he sighed, growing serious again. "Anyway, I guess I finally started to forgive you when my mom and Kaylah shared how you told them, and your mom—even after you knew she hated Bomen—that you loved me."

"I did," she whispered.

"I think that speaks volumes, what you say about someone else when they're not in the room. You had no reason to say that if it wasn't true. It did nothing to help your case."

"I said it because it was true. It *is* true." Her heart raced. Her lips and tongue still didn't know how to form the words properly, but she pushed through. "I love you."

He swallowed, silent. His hands slowly clenched into fists at his sides.

"It's okay." Tears rolled down her cheeks. "You don't have to say it again until you're ready. If you ... ever..." She sniffled.

He threw his arms around her and pulled her in. No one could hug like Marcus could. "We'll get there," he whispered into her ear.

She stood there, relaxing her muscles, allowing the weight of her choices, the weight of the realm, to slowly drip from her conscience. She breathed in his cologne, calm, her heart beating to the rhythm of his.

After what had to have been several minutes, her tears had dried up. She let out a cleansing breath. "Thank you."

"Anytime. Are you ready to go back in?"

There was probably another hour left of the ball. As an official palace ball, it was going to be a long one. "Honestly, I'm pretty worn out. I might just head to my chambers."

He straightened one of her ringlets. "I wouldn't blame you. I'm sure it's been a long day. Maybe I'll rift over, drop by, sometime in the next couple of days?"

"I'd love that. Bring your throwing knives."

"I can do that."

"Or ... I could ask one of the palace archers to give us lessons."

Marcus playfully squinted at her teasing. "Maybe another time..."

She let out a breathy chuckle. "Then it's a... Well, not a date."

"Okay. Anyway, I won't hold you hostage for that second dance. I'll take a rain check."

"Actually," she stood taller, "I'd like to take you up on it now. It would be a good way to end the night."

He held out his arm, and she hooked hers through it.

"Maybe let's dance a little less conspicuously this time..." she suggested.

He winked. "I can manage that."

As they passed her security detail, who had no doubt witnessed the entirety of their conversation, Leah breathed deeply, holding her head high. She could do this. She and Marcus could do this.

They sauntered to the dance floor, nodding politely to others along the way. With impeccable timing, the orchestra struck up the next tune. Marcus held Leah's hand, guiding her to the floor.

And they danced. He wasn't a prince. She wasn't a princess. But they glided across the floor of the palace, light on their feet, peacefully gazing into one another's eyes.

In her heart, in so many ways, she was still searching for a sense of self, a sense of home. In many ways, in his arms, she was already there.

The scrutiny of the onlookers melted away in the background, hidden by the harp and the violin playing nearby. The anxiety of the evening was swallowed up altogether, replaced by hope. Hope in friendship. Hope in love. And, with the support of those who mattered most, hope in family.

To Love a Monster:

A Villain's Love Story

Prince Soren had been attending upper-class youth gatherings for the last year. No matter your station, the invite was only extended on your fourteenth birthday. It was a nice diversion, providing more entertainment and variety than he usually got at the palace and touring around with his parents.

On a beautiful summer's eve, he sat playing cards at just such a gathering with a couple of his friends and a few beautiful girls. The boys were sharp, the girls charming in dresses fitted to accentuate their features as they matured.

Live music played somewhere down the hall, colliding with the chatter of teens from various rooms in the manor.

"That's me again," a friend to Soren's right announced, laying down another winning hand. The young man beamed with arrogance.

Soren huffed. He'd been close to winning. Maybe not *that* close, but if he'd had another turn or two, he could have turned it to his advantage. "Another round."

His friend shrugged. "If you'd like. But you'll have to wait a minute." He headed toward the restroom while the dealer shuffled.

When the hands were dealt, Soren grinned. The players were busy looking at their hands, though the observers who had gathered around watched mostly Soren.

He was used to that. Being the eldest child of the queen and king had its perks, even if he wasn't the widely adored heir his little sister was.

Still holding his hand, Soren poked out a vine and peeked at what his absent neighbor had been dealt. *Not bad.* He set his own cards down and picked up the others.

"Soren!" another friend chastised.

Soren laughed. "Teaching the bastard a lesson. I think it's perfectly fair." He plucked out his friend's best cards and swapped them for his worst, just in time for him to return to the room.

Everyone remained hushed about the exchange as play resumed. Like the others, a cute young girl sitting across from Soren had her eyes focused on him, but hers were narrowed, dancing between the two young men. When Soren took his first turn, the girl rolled her eyes, setting down her hand.

"I think I'm done playing for now," she announced, standing up.

Soren stroked his cards as she walked away. Her jet-black hair was perfectly styled to frame her face, and she wore a powder-blue dress. He leaned over to the friend he'd cheated from. "Who was that girl?"

"That one? Beata Remsgard. I think this is her second invite."

Soren stole another glance as she mingled with some girls at the end of the room. "Remsgard?"

"Yeah. Those are her older sisters over there. Their father is over the reject communities."

"Ah, gotcha." It now clicked for Soren. She was as beautiful and as slim as any of the other girls. Not as many curves, but if she was only fourteen, she had time to catch up. But that look she'd given him—rolling her eyes. It bothered him.

Shaking off his distraction, Soren won the round. He even won the next round without cheating. As the dealer shuffled again, Beata exited the room. Soren stood. "I've had enough for now." He followed her out into the hallway. It was dimly lit with only a handful of people chatting yards away.

"Beata, right?"

She turned, curtsying. "Yes, Your Highness."

He approached her, clasping his hands in front of him. "You left the game abruptly."

She shrugged, giving him a courtesy smile.

"You don't approve of the way I played?"

"Does His Highness want the truth?"

"Yes."

She cocked her head. "I didn't find it particularly amusing."

He grinned. "Why? He won plenty. I was just having some fun."

Beata scanned his face with confidence. "I'd expect more from a member of the royal family."

He glared. *How dare she judge me? She's barely important enough to be invited to these parties!* "You don't think the royal family should be able to take what they want? That's a bold political stance to be sharing."

A pair of giggling girls down the hallway distracted her for a moment before she turned her focus back to Soren. "On the contrary. The royal family should know what's best for our kingdom and act to obtain it. Dissenters would call it theft. But it still requires work and ambition to take what you want."

He smiled. "So, you agree with the palace agenda, but you think something as small as a little ... sleight of hand ... in a game of cards is too wicked?"

"It's petty. Beneath you."

He furrowed his brow. "You certainly share harsh criticism openly."

She pursed her lips, not shrinking from his authority or disapproval. "His Highness said he wanted me to speak the truth. I can change to agreeing with you if you'd like."

He drew a deep breath, shaking his head. "No. I like you. You've got spunk."

She smirked.

"What about a king? Does he get more leverage in your eyes than a prince?"

She busted out laughing before raising a hand to muffle it.

Soren clenched his jaw.

"I'm so sorry." She bit her lip. "I just... You'll never be king, unless you're planning on marrying your younger sister." She raised her eyebrows. "I know it's happened in human history, but that would be a *shocking* choice for the Ivy royal family."

"No." He scowled. "I don't plan on marrying my sister." He turned to walk away.

"My apologies, Your Highness." Her voice was softer. "I meant no offense."

He faced her. "I'm not used to being mocked." His ears were warm. He didn't know what to make of her. The confidence was refreshing, the condescension—not so much.

She gave a gentle nod, frowning. "Please forgive me. You're handsome, well-educated, and well-liked. I'm not used to speaking with anyone in the royal family."

His shoulders relaxed. "I guess it doesn't really matter. Sounds like you'd enjoy being with one of those other guys out there, anyway. Why would I waste my time caring about your opinions?"

She blushed. "I didn't realize we were talking about being *with* anyone... I just thought this was a regular conversation."

He cleared his throat, looking her over. "Are you dating anyone?"

She was slow to answer. "No."

"Good." He bridged the gap and slid his hands up to the nape of her neck. They locked eyes, and he pushed her back against the wall, leaning in for a kiss. Not a complete stranger to stealing a kiss from a pretty face when he wanted, he started with a couple of small, short caresses to see how she responded. She didn't resist, so he asserted himself more. He was surprised when she reciprocated.

A couple of boys rounded the corner, laughing. "Soren, you'll never believe—"

"Oh. Never mind." They retraced their steps toward the main gathering.

Soren leaned back, scanning Beata's face. She gazed into his eyes, her cheeks red.

"I like you," he said. He leaned forward, pressing himself against her and whispering into her ear. "You said the royal family should take what they want. What if I take what I want from you?" There had to be an empty room nearby. He kissed her on the neck. When she didn't respond, he stepped back to look at her.

She averted her gaze, swallowing. "I, uh... I think *some* things are best savored when you know someone a little more."

He smiled. "You've never been with anyone, have you?"

She met his eyes shyly. "I find that an impertinent question, Your Highness."

"Call me Soren."

"Soren." She fidgeted with her hands. "I could hardly ask you that kind of question in reciprocation."

He smirked. "You haven't been."

Beata opened her mouth, but nothing came out for a moment. "No."

He drew closer again, calculating. "Good. Keep it that way."

She scrunched her eyebrows. "You may have some say, someday, in how the *stunts* handle their lives and bodies. But you don't get to tell me what to do with mine."

He found her defiance—in contrast to her acceptance of his previous advances—both frustrating and perplexing. "Maybe I'm just giving you a heads-up about my intentions and desires. That's all."

She read his face with narrowed eyes and a smile. "I will amount to more than a mere slut or mistress to a prince."

His hands glided along the silky fabric of her dress, resting on her lower back. "I don't think I could ever do that to a girl like you." His eyes softened. "Sharing honestly, would you want to date me? I'd like to call on you."

She didn't take long to think it over, reaching out and playing with a button on his shirt. "Yes."

He stole another quick kiss. "Then I will. Soon." He glanced down at her chest. "Wear something more revealing."

She gave a coy grin. "I'll see what I can do."

The rest of the evening, they caught each other's eyes across the room. It drove Soren crazy. She wasn't like the other girls he'd met at these parties. She was confident, but shy. Accepting, yet critical. Passionate, but hesitant. He wanted her. More than any girl he'd wanted before.

On his way home to the palace, Prince Soren replayed their interaction. Beata had known it wasn't appropriate to ask if he'd been with anyone, and he was grateful for that. He hadn't. He might have a reputation with his peers for being a flirt and taking a girl for a little feel-up and make-out, but he hadn't taken one to bed—yet. The prospect of his first experience being with this cute, defiant girl was enticing. But it was also horrifying.

He was a prince. He needed to appear worthy of admiration, not like an awkward, bumbling idiot.

After arriving at his chambers, he loosened his collar. Pacing his room, Soren looked at his bed and made a decision.

He opened his outer door; his personal servant was standing ready, on duty.

"Do we have any servant girls my age?" Soren asked.

The man furrowed his brow. "Yes. I believe so."

Soren nodded in thought. "Bring me one."

The man's eyes widened. "Um... Your Highness? *Here?*"

Soren crossed his arms, meeting the man's challenge. "Obviously. The prettiest one. My age, or maybe a year or two younger."

The man glanced down. "Your Highness, your parents would not approve."

"I don't give a shit! And they better not hear of it." He looked the man over; he was relatively new to this position. "Who do you think they would believe? Do you know what happened to your predecessor?"

The man gulped. "I... I'm not completely sure."

Soren sneered. He'd grown tired of the last one and his insistence on following all the queen and king's rules. It was simple enough to plant 'stolen' palace items in the servant's quarters and have him sent off to prison. "Pray you never find out the truth about what *really* happened to him."

The man looked terrified. "Your Highness... What would I even say? The kitchen staff is going to ask me why I'm calling a girl away. What if she doesn't come willingly?"

Soren's anger peaked. "I don't give a damn about the details. That's your job. Have a nurse dose her so she doesn't throw a fit. I don't really care!"

The man's breathing became rapid, his eyes darting at the floor before him. "Yes, Your Highness." He left down the corridor, and Soren mentally prepared himself for his first time.₍y₎

Beata was back home, waiting on a servant from her sister's room to help ready her for bed. Her mind was lost in thought, focused on the dashing prince. She'd heard he was passionate. That he had a temper. That he had gorgeous brown locks and bright green eyes that melted girls to his whim. He was all that and more. *And that kiss...*

Her older sister entered the room. "Callie Bremshaw said you were found in the hallway with the prince?" Her tone and expression were disapproving.

Beata grinned as the servant removed her necklace. "I won't deny it."

Her sister cocked her head. "Not a great idea, Beata. You're young."

Beata rolled her eyes. "And he's just a year older. It's not a big deal."

"Yes, but you're going to those parties to meet a *variety* of people. Not to be tainted as his plaything from an early age! He will just toss you to the side when he gets bored."

Beata gritted her teeth. "It wasn't like that. It won't be like that. We were quite frank with each other. He wants to date me."

Her sister sighed. "Just ... be careful. Normal girls don't have to be so careful with normal guys. He's the prince, for goodness' sakes. And Mom and Dad aren't in a great position for *any* of us kids to get a reputation."

Beata's annoyance grew. "I'll be careful." She fought a smile, thinking of Soren fondly. "People misunderstand him."

Her sister stood with hands on hips. "Swapping slobber in a dimly lit hallway during a party means you understand him better than the rest of the realm?"

Beata chuckled. "Yes." She didn't care what her sister thought. She was enamored with him already. Those eyes, that kiss. His absolute confidence.(z)

Her sister's voice softened. "I love you. I just think you're a bit young to play with fire."

Beata picked up her hairbrush, a warm smile forming on her lips. They hadn't even gone on their first date. And she didn't share the same qualms as her sister. "I know what I'm doing."(aa)

SOREN'S LEGACY

BOOK 2

Prologue

Leah stood outside the Ivy prison, trying to keep herself together. It was supposed to have been a normal visit with her mom. A run-of-the-mill regular visit.

And now, she was sweating and trying to breathe as she pieced together what her mom had just said, what she'd let slip, and the implications it held for Leah.

Leah wasn't going to cry. She didn't like crying. She was simply overthinking things...

But even her mother had realized the truth had hurt her, and that was before Leah had really let it sink in, before she'd cut their visit short, before she'd left the building to stand here trying not to spiral.

She hugged herself, leaning against the stone building.

I'm fine. It's fine. It's not a big deal.

She could bury those feelings, that secret, bury them so hard she could pretend she'd never felt them, had never heard it.

How many other feelings had she buried in the past?

Her mother had asked her not to share it with anyone else, anyway.

Jamming her eyelids closed, Leah thought of other things. Marcus... Sunshine... Lightning bugs... She breathed slowly in and out. It wasn't that big of a deal, really.

"Are you alright, miss?" her escort, Wren, asked from around the corner where she'd asked him to stay.

"I'm fine."

Drawing a deep breath, she forced a smile on her face.

I'll be fine. It meant nothing.

Secrets couldn't hurt anyone if no one knew them.

Chapter 1

Leah had royally screwed things up. Two years ago, that is. But she'd come a long way since then. Lots of learning, and no new assassination attempts on the Ivy queen or anyone else.

She now wore more 'appropriate' clothing for someone of her station. And her station? The ward of Queen Catrina and King Stephan.

She'd learned how to don a polite smile through almost any situation (including the lesson she was currently zoning out in), how to pretend to be interested in politicians' conversations, and how to give the rote responses people expected from her on any given occasion.

That was the thing—she'd screwed up by trying to kill Queen Kaylah, and despite her attempts to better herself, it seemed the realm would never let Leah forget that mistake. Or her parentage.

'Soren's heir,' someone had snidely called her once. Her dad had been a prince. He would have become an earl, had he not been executed for stealing the throne and naming himself king. Had he not had his title stripped from him at the time of his execution. It had all happened while Leah's mom had been pregnant with her. Many people assumed Leah had taken after her parents, and that her sad attempt at killing Kaylah had meant she'd been trying to take the throne.

"Miss Elonto?"

Leah looked up, her heart skipping a beat. She'd definitely zoned out again, but her gentle perma-smile was still there.

The instructor must have noticed she'd checked out. "What did you think of the performance, Miss Elonto?"

She cleared her throat, her palms sweaty. "It was beautiful." It truly had been. Leah only attended the local academy part time, while the rest of her education was carried out by private tutors, usually at the palace. Today at the academy, a troupe of cultural dancers had come to perform. The performance, complete with Ivy vines and acrobatics, had been elegant, but nothing she hadn't seen at the palace before.

"It was, wasn't it?" Skye said, giving Leah a reassuring smile.

Skye was there to save Leah again. But a true friend? Probably not. Leah now had a few 'friends' here in the Ivy Kingdom, in the Green Lands realm. They were really more of acquaintances, and Leah was pretty sure they were there for her only as a personal favor to her instructors or the queen.

Obligatory pals were not the kind of friends anyone really wanted.

After a while longer discussing the performance, the topic returned to women's studies in the Ivy Kingdom, and the state of current affairs. Women hadn't necessarily been *unequally* subjugated before Queen Kaylah's rule, but their powers had been suppressed, ignored, or undiscovered compared to what they now were.

Having grown up in hiding in the human world, Leah hadn't learned much about who she was or what she was capable of until she met her boyfriend and other green folk like them. Part of why Leah hadn't learned more about herself had been her mother's fault, as the usurper's wife living in exile. Another part of it had been her mother's lack of knowledge and expertise about female Ivy powers.

Leah found this topic particularly empowering. Ivy girls were now taught much more thoroughly than they used to be about all their powers. Rifting, coagulation, fertilizing, numbing—to name a few. And of course vine maneuvering.

Women's education was a heated topic in some Ivy circles. As recently as two decades ago, the schoolboys had been required to take extra classes while the girls sat them out. Now it was the other way around. Since the Ivy Kingdom no longer trained young boys to be assassins in the human world, their course loads had been slimmed down. Respectively, the discovery of extra female Ivy powers by Queen Kaylah now meant the girls had more classes to take. Some saw it as a burden they shouldn't have to deal with. Others felt it was their right to be taught in every aspect of their powers.

Leah was nineteen now, trying to figure out what she was going to do with the rest of her life. Advocating for girls being taught the full extent of their powers was something she could get behind.

Sure, she'd floundered when trying to fit in in the human world, and her grand introduction to her home realm had been far from ideal, but she wasn't ungrateful for what she was now being offered.

Queen Catrina made sure Leah's every need was seen to. She allowed her a certain level of autonomy, though not as much as Leah would like. As the queen and king's ward, Leah was afforded the best education, the most elegant opportunities, and was reassured they would help her step out on her own someday.

Once class ended, Leah said her goodbyes to her instructor and her 'friends.' They had long since learned she wasn't a hugger.

Leah's personal escort—her security detail—stuck by her side once she exited the classroom. They walked silently down the second-floor hallways of the brick academy. Other students nodded at her and her escort as they passed, not all of them making eye contact.

She was mostly numb to that kind of thing now. She'd usually been the kind to pass under the radar in the human world, at least when she wasn't getting in trouble. Now, she couldn't hide, no matter how much she wanted to. The occasional scathing remark reached her ear, muttered purposefully loud enough to bother her. But the majority of criticism about Leah reached her by accident—the gossip of classmates from outside her toilet stall, or the comment of a dignitary around the corner in the palace.

Though, most signs of disapproval for Leah's very existence were much more subtle than words. It was in the averted gaze in the hallway, the pointing and cowering child in the marketplace, the strangers who would cross the lane when they saw her and her escort coming, the Seeders that would look her dead in the eye and flash green eyes at her, or the poorly attended Boman events she'd dared to make an appearance at.

Her boyfriend's mom, Rachel, had once called Leah's dad a monster. He had been. Not in the comical ghoulish way, but a genuine piece of living garbage. And Leah's mom, Beata, had turned a blind eye to the atrocities he'd committed, and had even helped him commit crimes. She was still in prison, serving her life sentence.

Sometimes Leah felt like she might as well wear a black sash, the words *Monsters' Daughter* embroidered with bright red thread.

But everyone already knew who she was.

Leah politely waved at a few classmates as she and her escort left the building. Guys were civil, but none of them even tried to talk to her. It was also public knowledge that she and Marcus had been back together for some time.

Just the thought of him made her smile. As did the thought of him visiting her at the palace for the weekend. And the thought of the plans they'd hatched.

"Are you needing anything from the market or elsewhere before returning home, miss?" her escort asked.

"Yes. I did want to swing by the market."

As they strolled down cobblestone streets, Leah ignored the people around her, the noise, the beautiful weather.

As much as she'd become a recluse and hated being around people because of the constant scrutiny, she enjoyed the freedom of being away from the palace. No officials or servants, or little princes or princesses underfoot. No one correcting her posture or language.

Once they arrived at the small nearby market, Leah quickly zeroed in on what she wanted. Marcus was in charge of bringing something for his visit that she couldn't get away with buying, not with her constant escort. She was only responsible for pampering herself this time.

Needing to not be too obvious about her desired purchases, she took some time browsing under the awnings of each vendor. She sniffed a few perfumes, wanting something new for the special weekend. Today was almost exactly two years since Marcus had taken her back after the whole assassination fiasco. They were celebrating their anniversary.

Another shopper stepped close to Leah, reaching for a bottle of perfume. Leah's escort cut her off.

"Please allow for some space, ma'am."

The woman looked at Leah, then rolled her eyes. "Last I checked, this is a free kingdom, and she *isn't* actually royalty." She stalked away.

"Sorry," Leah weakly called after her. She didn't bother with more than that, since the woman continued to walk away.

Leah couldn't win. There had never been a right answer for what should happen to her. She didn't like that she still had an escort every time she left the palace, especially since many people felt she didn't deserve the attention, or that the kingdom's resources shouldn't be used to pay for her security detail. But the fact of the matter was ... some people still wanted her dead. She'd come a long way in the last two years, but the bullseye on her back may never go away.

It had been a gutting day when she'd had that conversation with the queen and king. She'd felt confident in her ability to protect herself against an attack, but they'd confessed they'd received multiple death threats against Leah. Some people thought she ought to have been executed as an example for trying to kill Kaylah. Many thought she embodied and embraced the twisted beliefs and prejudices of her parents. Given that fact, Leah didn't feel safe venturing out on her own.

She picked a rose-scented perfume and reached for the money in her silk satchel. After plucking out the coins needed, she hefted them in her hand, reluctant. None of this money was hers. She couldn't exactly get a job at a burger joint to earn her keep right now.

Servants, guards, food, clothes—all paid for by the Crown.

Leah glanced at her escort. Even though they were probably necessary, they drew so much attention to her. And perhaps it *was* over the top.

You should put the perfume back. You don't deserve it. You already have some at home.

And she really didn't need to buy anything at the market herself. She could have had a servant add it to their shopping list. To avoid a much longer trip back to the palace, she ought to only purchase the bare minimum, due to rifting limitations.

Moments away from putting the money back in her satchel and returning the bottle, Leah decided against it. This was a special celebration. She wanted to pick the perfume out herself, and it wasn't like it was that large.

She wouldn't steal it, either. She hadn't ever stolen anything in the Green Lands, not that the itch didn't come now and then. It took a massive amount of resolve in times like this to not scratch that itch, but she was determined to make a new life for herself, and to not undo all the hard work she'd put into her image.

Handing over the coins, she thanked the seller, then slipped the bottle into her satchel.

A few minutes later, Leah scoured the shelves at a clothing vendor's booth. Her escort gave her a little space as she surveyed the unmentionables. She quickly found something thin and cute, and paid for it, again tucking it into her satchel.

"Alright, I'm ready to go home."

Leah walked through the cave rift—the one closest to the palace, right on the edge of the Mother Vine protective border.

She hadn't returned to the human world in the last two years, though they now trusted she wouldn't run away, and Catrina and Stephan had issued her a passport and fake human ID in case she did want to go at some point. She was an adult now. But she didn't have anything to go back to in the human world.

Each footstep toward the palace was refreshing, exciting. She had a bounce in her step as she mused on the new purchases in her satchel, and her plans for that night.

As they neared the side entrance she usually used, a handsome figure leaned against the stone doorway. Brown curly locks framed a smiling face. His arms were crossed against his chest.

Leah ran to him, squealing.

"Hey, beautiful," Marcus said, opening his arms.

She squeezed him tight, breathing in his cologne. Marcus was her home, her person. The day to her night. She never smiled as widely or as genuinely as she did when she was with him. And she almost always had to wait until the weekends to see him.

He released her and kissed her on the cheek. "Let's head inside."

They didn't particularly care for the palace guards to watch their reunions, and her escort had already stepped inside. The moment Leah and Marcus entered the massive stone building and the door shut, he pulled her close, not allowing an inch between them, laying a kiss on her. She dug her hands into his hair, pressing against him.

Marcus was happiness. He was hope. He was everything to Leah.

He'd meant so much to her back in the human world, but he was so much more to her now. His kindness and forgiving nature were unparalleled.

After a minute, he leaned back, catching his breath and resting his hands on her hips. "That dress is stunning."

She grinned. She'd specifically chosen this one to see him in. It was light and flowy, with a soft pink floral print. "You say that about all my dresses."

He grinned in return. "Then it must be the girl in the dress who's stunning."

She gave him another smooch. "I love you."

"Love you too."

As much as she wanted to kiss his lips for days, and do a few other things, there was a guard or servant lurking around the corner. There always was, on Catrina's orders, to supervise the two of them.

Leah rolled her shoulder to keep her satchel's cord from slipping. "I picked up something special to celebrate our anniversary."

He arched an eyebrow. "Really? What is that?"

She leaned in, planting a kiss on his neck. "I guess you'll find out, if our timing is right."

He slid his hands onto her lower back. "I will be doing *everything* in my power to make sure that timing is right."

There had been plotting between the two. And if they'd worked it all out right, there would *finally* be passion.

Chapter 2

Two Weeks Later

Leah sat in an armchair in her chambers, staring at the wall, more than a little sick to her stomach. Her heart raced. Marcus was coming for his weekly visit to the palace.

She was excited to see him, and dreading it at the same time. Things had been good between them. Great, in fact. Two years ago, they'd started off slow, taking almost three whole months to kiss after he forgave her for using him. Marcus still lived with his parents, and was studying under his father, Guillen, and other leaders, wanting to make his own way, working in law and public policy.

Leah had done a lot of pondering over the last little while. Sure, some people would never approve of her, but she wanted to make a name for herself, as Marcus had once challenged her to do. She wanted to be an expert with her powers, and teach other girls and women to do the same. At least she had *thought* that was what she wanted.

But things were about to change.

Leah was used to change. Not that she liked it, or was good at it, but that had been how she'd had to live her life on the run. The most difficult change she'd ever made was moving to the Green Lands after discovering her parents' true identities. She still visited her mom in prison once a month. She'd only visited her dad in the royal graveyard once—that had been all she'd ever wanted or needed after discovering the truth of the man.

This particular change might not be quite that big of a revelation and shift in her way of life, but it was right up there. Leah hadn't told anyone yet, but she was pregnant. Ivy women were able to tell very early, and Leah couldn't deny the signs.

A knock sounded on her door, and Leah forced herself to stand and open it.

"He's here, miss," Robyn, her favorite servant, announced.

Leah forced a smile. "Thank you." She followed Robyn out, calming her breathing. She had to tell Marcus tonight. He deserved to know. They needed to figure things out.

Robyn led her to the smaller sitting room, where Marcus waited with a giant smile. He jumped up and pulled Leah in close.

"I missed you!" he said.

"You too." She bit her lip.

He placed his hands on her hips and laid a reunion kiss on her like he always did. Dating in the Green Lands was hard if you didn't live close. You couldn't simply text or call; it was archaic.

"Sorry I'm late." He tucked a strand of hair behind her ear.

"You're fine. Just in time for dinner."

"Mmm. Anything good on the menu tonight?" He sat back down on the sofa and guided her onto his lap.

Leah straightened her dress. At first, she'd felt silly wearing dresses so much, just because people associated that with a 'proper' lady living at the palace, but she'd warmed up to them.

I'll have to sort my closet to wear bigger sizes. Ivy pregnancies only lasted eight months, and she was two weeks along.

She tried to focus on the moment at hand. "Um, the menu... Chef Kristoff's best stew, I believe."

"Delicious. Almost as delicious as you are." He grinned, then snuck another kiss.

Her heart couldn't handle his flirtations, and luckily, she didn't have to respond.

Another servant entered. "Dinner is served."

Leah and Marcus held hands as they strolled to the dining hall. Meals at the palace were always a mixed bag. The queen and king had three little kids, with a fourth on the way. You never knew when family members would swing by, or when they'd be hosting government officials or dignitaries. Luckily, tonight would be pretty quiet. Other than the northern Boman ambassador there for the night, it would only be the royal family, Leah, and Marcus.

She had remembered right that the stew was being served. Leah stirred it in her bowl, picking out the potatoes first. Conversation was lively amongst everyone but Leah, though she tried to contribute. She paid particular attention to the ambassador. He lived in one of the Boman colonies, by choice. A blond in his thirties, he wore a wedding ring. She perked up when he mentioned having kids. That was what this child would be—a Boman, born without powers. The gene that caused the condition popped up randomly and was rare in the general populace, but Bomanism was always passed down to the children of a Boman.

Leah glanced at Marcus; he conversed easily, talking about his recent studies. Her chest only hurt more at how excited he was about a new internship opportunity.

She had always been bad for him. Even though she'd spent the last two years trying to reinvent herself, and had finally seemed to find her way, she was going to hurt him. People who loved his family hated Leah. People who loved Leah's parents hated Marcus and his family. Not that it was anyone's freaking business what they did or who they loved, and not that they had social media or tabloids in the Green Lands, but green folk knew how to gossip.

The rumor mill was always pumping out something about Leah, and about their relationship. Sadly, most of the rumors about Leah were actually true. Even *she* sometimes followed the logic and questioned why Marcus was still with her.

Leah picked up her roll, nibbling tiny pieces as well as she could manage. There was a lull in conversation, so she spoke up. "Ambassador Grayas, what's it like raising Bomen in the colonies?"

The man addressed her with a smile. "I suppose it depends on who you ask. Some say we're doing an injustice by 'separating' them from their peers with powers. But you'd have to be blind to say everything is equal in the main territories, even after all this time." He turned to the queen and king, bowing his head. "No offense, Your Majesties."

Catrina and Stephan nodded. They may be a bit strict for Leah's liking, but they were always polite and proper.

Catrina dabbed her mouth with a napkin. "That's why we're always pleased to get feedback from you. It's easier to say than do, when it comes to laws and education for such a small minority."

Look at me—helping with the numbers game. Adding to the Boman population, and we're only nineteen. Leah swallowed another bite of roll before taking a swig of water.

"And how are things for non-Bomen living out there?" She'd considered a dozen options already for her unexpected new future, but life in Boman lands was sadly not something she could seriously entertain.

Ambassador Grayas smiled again. "It may be wishful thinking on my part, but I'd like to believe non-Bomen enjoy living there, too. Takes some getting used to, away from the kingdom, but we each have our reasons."

She appreciated his kindness and smiles. She didn't get those from many adult Bomen. Leah's grandparents on her mother's side had been in charge of the 'stunt' communities, the old quasi slave communities. One of the few blessings of having her mom lie to her her entire childhood, keeping her true identity as an Ivy from her, was that her mom's bigotry hadn't rubbed off on her. She hadn't developed an opinion on Bomen until she'd met Marcus and Jake.

But life in Boman lands? Another opportunity Marcus, and now their child, could never have—life with others of their kind—if they stayed with Leah. She would *never* be accepted by the general Boman populace, even if she loved one and gave birth to one.

Most of the rest of dinner, Leah pushed the stew around in her bowl. She couldn't live in Seeder lands, either. She'd enjoyed meeting Saff when Leah had visited the Seeder nation the prior summer, but other eyes hadn't been too friendly once they realized whose child Leah was.

Leah was seriously reconsidering life in the human world now. A fresh start sounded appealing, until she considered the logistics of leaving her new home. She had no money, no one to lean on.

"Are you alright, Leah?" Catrina asked across the dining table.

Leah looked up. "Yeah, of course."

"Not hungry?"

Leah set her spoon down and sat back in her seat. "Yeah, sorry. I might have snuck a late snack from the kitchen." That was a lie, but between nerves and maternal sickness, she could only stomach so much. *Seeders have it so easy.* They didn't have menstrual cycles, didn't get morning/maternal sickness. Granted, what they considered 'birth' wasn't exactly what she had grown up knowing that act to be.

"Aha. Kristoff will be disappointed." Catrina playfully wagged a finger at her.

"Sorry."

After the waitstaff cleared the dinner dishes, they served a raspberry mousse. Leah turned it down, instead sipping water.

Once dessert was cleared, Leah and Marcus were able to slip away and let the 'adults' talk more. They strolled onto the palace grounds to their favorite spot. Tall hedges surrounded a vibrant flower garden and a viewing bench.

The couple sat down, and Leah took a deep breath of the invigorating air. Marcus pulled her in close. She smiled at the warmth of his body, and at the purple and green lightning bugs dancing in a tall tree in the distance.

"You're quiet tonight," he said.

"Mmm. Guess so. Got lots on my mind."

"Like what?"

Leah swallowed hard. This wasn't the right moment. Not yet. "What else? Studies."

"Yeah? What's your focus this week?"

"Mostly coagulation." It was all bookwork and lectures.

"Cool. What about it?"

She shrugged. "Not my favorite, but I see its use. I preferred the discussions we had on the ethics and methods of teaching various powers at young ages." Truthfully, though, she didn't want to talk about her week anymore. How could she even entertain her dream of mastering her powers and teaching them, when her own child would be deprived of them? It didn't seem right anymore. "What about your week? Sounds much more exciting."

Marcus kissed her cheek. "I'm stoked to get this opportunity with Governor Scanlon!"

She wore a soft smile. "You've worked hard for it. I'm proud of you."

He held her tighter.

"That's pretty far north. For how long?"

"Still not sure yet. Two to four months minimum. And yeah, it's in the far north, but that doesn't mean I won't make my weekly visits." He nuzzled her neck. "I never want to miss my time with you."

She frowned even as he trailed kisses down her neck.

"Not in the mood?"

Leah laid her head on his chest. "Just tired. I like how peaceful it is right here, right now."

He gently rubbed her arm. "I can be okay with that."

After several minutes of cuddling, he spoke up again. "Whatcha thinkin' about?"

"Hmmm." She figured she'd answer truthfully. "The future. And my visit next week with my mom." She and her mom had come to an agreement—her mom would try to hide her disappointment that Leah loved a Boman, and Leah would try to look past the fact that her mom was a murderer and bigot. It felt like a bit of an uneven trade, but it somehow worked.

Leah *needed* her mom in her life. She already felt like an orphan with her dad gone, her mom in prison for life. But ... eventually, her mom would find out that Marcus had knocked her up, and she'd be even more disappointed. There was no winning for Leah.

"I see. Those visits can be hard." After a minute he added, "Wanna know what I'm thinking?"

"What?"

"How happy I am to be here right now. And how much I love you."

Her lips twitched upwards.

He stroked her thigh. "And how amazing it was to sneak into your chambers a couple weeks ago."

She slid a hand to her belly, the weight of the decision ahead pressing on her. "Yeah. I think a lot about that night, too."

Leah couldn't get herself to tell Marcus the first night of his visit. Not when he'd been in such a great mood. But she wouldn't be able to keep it to herself for much longer.

Instead, she'd stayed up for hours in her chambers, examining her entire situation. She was pregnant; this she knew for certain. She'd been taught enough to read the signs, and Ivy women's bodies kinda yelled the fact at them. Since finding out a few days ago, Leah had carefully researched the birth control tonic Marcus had bought for her. It probably would have worked, had they been a little more careful about the instructions.

She couldn't blame Marcus—it had been his first time, and he'd been nervous about buying the right thing in the first place, and doing so while keeping it hidden, without drawing any attention to himself. She didn't blame herself all that much either, as this was her first time with someone who could actually get her pregnant. They were equally to blame for not being more careful or adding extra protection.

Eventually, she stressed herself out way too much, and finally passed out in bed well past midnight.

They met again for breakfast in the dining hall. Marcus excitedly chatted with the Boman ambassador. Leah dared to try to eat some breakfast. She spread some whipped coconut honey on her toast and savored the first bite. Subtle, sweet, and mellow—just right. After a few minutes of letting it settle in her stomach, she risked trying something else. She reached for a boiled quail egg—a rare delicacy in the Green Lands. She cracked and peeled it. After splitting the little thing in half, Leah reached for the salt. The smell of the yolk wafted to her nose, and her stomach lurched. Swallowing, she choked down the toast trying to make its way back up. When she realized it was futile, she dropped the egg on her plate.

"Excuse me," she squeaked out before holding her breath and standing. Trying to appear as calm and ladylike as possible, she clasped her hands before her and strode to the door. Fighting her nausea with everything she had, she made a mad dash down the hallway to the nearest lavatory, barely arriving at the toilet in time. She retched over and over again.

With the contents of her stomach expelled, she sat on the cool tile floor, leaning against the wall. She couldn't do this alone. She didn't even know if she could do this at all.

After ages on the floor, miserable but aware that her abrupt departure and prolonged absence would draw attention, she forced herself up, flushed the toilet, washed her hands, and splashed cool water on her face. She took a few slow, steady breaths and exited the lavatory.

"Hey."

She gasped, clutching her chest.

Marcus chuckled. "Sorry. Didn't mean to scare you."

She glanced to her left. "How long have you been there?" Had he heard too much?

He shrugged. "A couple minutes? Wanted to check on you after you went missing like that."

She calmed her nerves. "I'm fine. Just … a little under the weather."

"Anything I can do to help?" Frowning, he reached out and held her hand.

"No, but thanks. I think I'm going to lie down for a bit. Took forever to fall asleep last night." It was partially true. Her nausea was no doubt worse because she'd slept so little and so poorly.

"Okay. I'll, uh, be hanging out with the kids, then?" He was a great cousin to the little prince and princesses.

"Sounds good."

Chapter 3

Leah returned to her chambers and lay down. She found rest surprisingly quickly, and woke to a knock at her door.

"Yeah, um…" She brushed her hair out of her face, sitting up in bed, then raising her voice. "Yeah, you can come in."

The door creaked open, and Robyn peeked her head in, her long red curls dangling over her shoulder. "Marcus is inquiring about you."

Leah rubbed her face with her hands. "I'm fine." Her stomach ached a bit from throwing up earlier.

"Is it alright if he comes in?" Robyn asked.

"Sure." Leah pulled back the covers and stood while Robyn called to Marcus in the corridor.

Marcus entered and gave her a hug. He'd only ever been in here a handful of times before. They sat on a settee while Robyn busied herself with making the bed. It wasn't Robyn's job to do, and Leah was perfectly capable of making her own bed (though not nearly as neatly as the housekeeping staff did), but Robyn knew how to tactfully do her duty as a part-time chaperone.

Marcus wasn't allowed in Leah's chambers unchaperoned, and the reverse was true for Leah in Marcus's chambers when he came for visits. With Marcus in her chambers now, Robyn would be there to babysit the entire time.

"What's wrong?" Marcus asked.

Leah paused. 'My body is creating your child, and I'm in the middle of freaking out about it and the rest of my life' didn't sound like the right thing to say at the moment, especially with a servant nearby, even if it was Robyn.

"Like I said, just tired."

He eyed her. "When you didn't show up for lunch... Well, Aunt Catrina had a tray made up for you. Do you want to eat in here?"

It's past lunchtime already? "I'm fine, really. I'll grab something to eat later."

The words had no sooner rolled off her tongue than her stomach betrayed her with the loudest growl ever, and Marcus raised a skeptical eyebrow.

"Or maybe I'm more hungry than I thought." She glanced at Robyn, who was fluffing a pillow. "How about I get changed into something more comfortable and meet you in the small study?"

"Okay. I'll be waiting for you." He kissed her forehead and left.

Robyn exited the room after him, taking her usual place outside Leah's door while she changed.

Leah put on a pair of shorts and a comfy shirt, suitable attire for lounging around when it was just herself, Marcus, and the servants, with the possibility of running across the actual royal family. When she walked into the small study, Marcus sat at a table with her lunch tray. She crossed the room to join him, first sipping some water.

"Thanks for waking me. I love a good lunch date." She smiled.

"Of course." He pointed at the pastry on the tray. "That's really good."

She picked it up, tearing off a small chunk. "How was your time with the kids?"

He narrowed his eyes, bobbing his head. "I'd say pretty good. I became a duke today."

Leah grinned. "Really? And how did that happen? I know my nap was long, but an entire ceremony and everything to make it official?"

He leaned back in his chair, crossing his legs. "Oh yeah. You'll be sad you missed it. The whole kingdom showed up and everything."

She choked back a laugh. Dukes and duchesses were only given their titles directly from the queen, as a special status symbol for services to the kingdom. "And what did you do to earn it?"

"I'm the best in all the realm at building blanket forts. Prince Leon made it official."

Leah chortled. "Prince Leon? He has no right to issue that title, no matter how good you are at blanket forts."

Marcus looked downright indignant. "How dare you!" He put a hand to his chest. "I am *amazing* at it. And no, a four-year-old nonheir to the throne does not hold that authority, but I believe him when he says he'll convince Aunt Catrina to make it official."

She hummed. "But you said I missed the entire ceremony while I napped?"

He winked, then his gaze traveled to her hands. "You gonna eat?"

She hadn't yet taken a bite. After the quail egg that morning, she was nervous about eating anything at all, but starting with a pastry might be safe. She tried the portion she'd pulled off; it was slightly sweet with a hint of cinnamon. "You're right. That is good."

He smiled as she nibbled off another corner. "Are we still on for the boat ride tonight?"

With all her stressing, she'd almost forgotten about it. He'd arranged for them to have a special romantic boat ride on the palace lake. The thought of wobbling or rowing made her queasy all over again, but she tried to force a smile. "Yeah."

He looked like he didn't quite buy it. "Okay..."

She averted her gaze, taking another sip of her water. "The weather's nice today, though, right?" That was a pretty weak attempt at small talk. This was the Green Lands, a realm in perpetual spring. It was almost always a nice day.

"Yeah. It's beautiful. Like you." His voice was soft, almost distant or concerned, his smile only half there. "You do know that, right? That I think you're gorgeous? Inside and out. Clothed or ... not clothed." He blushed a little. "And no matter what."

He'd never once made her feel less than gorgeous. Not once. And he'd definitely made his sentiments clear the night they'd finally shared a bed.

"I think you're rather handsome yourself."

This time he gave her a more confident smile. He shifted on his chair, sitting straighter. "And you—are you happy with the way you look?"

The question sounded much more baited this time. *That's ... an odd thing to ask...* She'd always felt fairly comfortable in her own skin, even with weight fluctuations or most hairstyles. She still liked her green eyes and black hair, though not quite as much as she had before she'd found out who her parents were. "Yes...?"

He pursed his lips, not responding.

Now she *did* feel a little uncomfortable in her skin. Would he not see her the same way when she was big and pregnant? She furrowed her brow. "Why are you asking that?"

He bit his lip, then looked at her tray again. "You ... didn't eat much last weekend when I came to visit. Or now..."

She breathed a sigh of relief. He thought she was on a diet? Why would she be? Because he'd seen her naked? "I'm not trying to lose weight. I don't have any ...

eating problems, either." Maybe she should tell him here and now, but again it didn't feel right.

"Just like my nap... I've been stressed, okay?"

He nodded. "Okay."

She made a concerted effort to polish off most of her tray. There were some lovely herb-roasted chickpeas, a baked apple, and a colorful salad with poppyseed dressing. She finished half of a tropical chia seed pudding before she had to stop.

More than once, a servant entered the room to check on them and her status. Leah drained her glass of water as another servant entered and whisked away her tray.

Leah and Marcus shifted to a settee in the study and cuddled, chatting about their weeks some more.

As she shared her opinion on a topic she'd covered in her studies, he just stared at her lovingly, tickling the palms of her hands. "I think that's great." He glanced at a pendulum clock in the corner of the room. "Oh, are we still on for the boat ride? I was thinking of making a last-minute change to the picnic menu, and I should let the kitchen know."

She tried to hide a frown. He was so excited to go out on the lake. But then again, he was excited for the rest of his life and career. All of a sudden, the richness of that chia seed pudding wasn't settling right in her stomach. All she could imagine was upchucking repeatedly over the edge of the boat and then standing, bowing, and announcing that she'd ruined their date night, his reputation, and his future. At least they wouldn't be teenage parents... They'd both be twenty by the time she delivered.

"I, uh... I'm still kinda wiped out. Could I take a rain check on that? And we could do something a little more low-key tonight?"

He smiled, though it didn't reach his eyes. "Sure."

Leah felt cruddy canceling their date plans, but she felt cruddy in every way possible already. Marcus was patient as always, and they chatted and cuddled, and even went for a short stroll on the grounds. She kept waiting for a 'right moment' to pop up, but it may never. He was visiting on a three-day weekend this time, but that didn't mean she could handle another entire day of anxiety.

And she couldn't keep the secret for long anyway. Green folk were blessed with great health. Something like a prolonged stomach bug was rare, and if Marcus had noticed she'd been acting off, it was only a matter of time before others would.

After dinner. No more putting it off.

Dinner was nice, and fairly quiet. One of the twins—the princesses—was fussy, but it was a casual evening anyway, with just the royal family and Leah and Marcus.

"I thought you two were going to the lake tonight," King Stephan commented.

Leah's stomach churned, this time with nerves.

"Um..." Marcus shrugged. "Leah's tired. Maybe we'll do it tomorrow."

Catrina frowned. "Sorry to hear that. Make sure to head to bed early so you're well rested."

With her mouth full of food, Leah gave her a polite smile and nodded. It was a bit of a trek to the lake, and she doubted Marcus would be up to it even after a good night's rest, what with the bombshell she'd be dropping on him that night.

"What time are you leaving for Capital City, darling?" Catrina asked Stephan.

He clicked his tongue. "Before daylight. There's a lot to cover at that assembly."

As dinner came to an end, Leah's gut twisted tighter and tighter. She had to turn down dessert. Marcus threw a quick glance her way. If he still took that as a sign she was on some kind of crazy diet, she'd soon be dispelling that notion completely.

"Do you want to play billiards, and go to bed early?" Marcus asked Leah as servants cleared the table.

"How about another walk in the gardens?"

He smiled. "I'm down."

They rarely stole kisses in the palace itself. Usually, they snuck out to the gardens for more alone time. Of course, a servant or guard was always nearby to act as chaperone, but being outdoors meant fewer eyes in general, and less chance of an accidental audience.

Leah's hands became clammy as the couple strolled to their favorite bench. They walked in silence, their fingers intertwined.

She loved him. Irrevocably. She prayed he'd feel the same way after she told him they were going to be parents so young.

Once they got to their bench, he pulled her onto his lap. She carefully unwrapped his arms from around her and moved to the side.

He gave her a questioning glance. "Are you really okay?"

Her throat bobbed, her heart thumping against her ribs. "Not really."

Frowning, he took her hands. "You can tell me anything."

"I, um..." She pursed her lips, gathering her courage. "I'm ... pregnant."

His eyes widened, his face paled, and his grip on her hands loosened.

And he said nothing. Absolutely nothing.

It may have been only thirty seconds before he responded, but it certainly felt more like thirty minutes. She'd kinda hoped that initial look of shock would melt into an adoring smile. He was great with his young cousins, after all. But there was no smile. Only shock, possibly horror. And each second of his silence chipped at something in her heart, at her hope that things in her life could still work out.

Marcus's expression wasn't one of acceptance, or of satisfaction, as though he'd sabotaged his girlfriend's birth control tonic, or had understood she'd taken it wrong. It was the undeniable look of someone who was watching their reputation and dreams being ripped from them.

Marcus was the golden child of the realm. Leah was the black eye, the stain, Soren's heir.

"You're sure..." He gazed at her stomach. "I..."

Heat rose in her cheeks. "You better not finish that sentence the way I think you're going to." She'd slept with more than a couple of guys before him, but none since she'd met him, and she would *never* cheat on him.

Marcus furrowed his brow. "What are you talking about?"

She cocked her head, taking her hands back. "Am I sure you're the father?"

He scrunched his face. "I wasn't going to say that!"

"Then what were you going to say?"

"Just ... asking that you're sure..."

She huffed. "Yes. I know. And before you ask how far along I am, I'm going to take a wild guess that it's about two weeks."

Shaking his head, he covered his mouth. "But it was only once. Well, you know... And we were careful."

She gritted her teeth, her frustration growing. "It only *takes* once, and obviously not careful enough."

He gestured at her, exasperated. "Why are you mad at *me*? I didn't do it on purpose."

The implication hurt more than he could ever realize. "Are you saying *I* did?"

He bolted upright, pacing. "I didn't say that. Why are you mad at me?"

Nothing about this exchange had gone well, and she didn't really have an answer for him. "I... I just... Sorry."

A whistle came from over the hedge, a thoughtful advance warning. Piot was often assigned as the evening chaperone to patrol the gardens when Marcus visited, and had the kindness to alert them before he'd appear from behind a hedge to catch them making out.

Both Leah and Marcus looked toward the opening of the hedge in anticipation. Piot rounded the corner, and gave them a smile and a polite nod. "Marcus. Leah."

They both politely nodded back.

"Hi," she said weakly.

After another nod, Piot left again.

Marcus sat back down next to Leah, his voice calmer and quieter. "So, what are you thinking?"

"I don't know." Her tone was nearly as panicked as she was.

His mouth hung open a moment, and his eyes once again drifted to her stomach. "Are you going to keep it?"

"I don't know," she repeated. Despite all the time she'd had to think about it, she didn't have a single answer for any other questions he might ask, either.

Silence filled the space between them. After a moment of contemplation, he spoke again. "Well, if you decide not to keep it... You know, Tobias and Cam have talked about adopting, and—"

"No!" She spat out the word before she'd even acknowledged to herself why. Marcus was suggesting she give their baby to his brother and sister-in-law?! "No. I'm not giving it up. I'm keeping it."

"Okay. Okay." His tone was soothing. The tiniest of smiles tugged at his lips. "We'll do the right thing."

Something in her knew what he'd meant by that, and it didn't sit well with her at all. What was the *right* thing? The *wrong* thing? Leah had ... changed ... since her arrival in the Green Lands. Her moral compass had adjusted a bit. Was her shoplifting habit in the human world bad? Yes. Had she always thought so? No. Was her habit of lying, sometimes just for fun, wrong? Yes. Had she always thought so? Not exactly.

But Marcus, he was a different breed. His moral compass had always pointed due north. And the 'right' thing here meant preserving the impeccable image of the royal family they were both tied to.

"And what is the 'right' thing to do, Marcus?"

His smile widened. "We'll get married."

"No."

He frowned. "Why not?"

"Really? You have no idea how flattering that is to hear, do you? Every girl *dreams* of the guy that knocked her up saying, 'Well, I guess we're just gonna have to do the right thing.'"

He was unamused. "So now I'm only the guy that got you pregnant? As if we haven't dated for over two years? As if we haven't talked plenty about marriage and having kids someday."

"Yeah, *someday*. Down the road. *Way* down the road. When you had your career sorted, and I'd figured out what the heck I was going to do."

"Well, those plans are out the window now, aren't they?"

"I'm not going to be some stupid hillbilly shotgun bride!"

His confusion was understandable, despite how thoroughly he'd been prepared for his foreign exchange year in the human world.

"I'm not being forced to marry just because I'm pregnant."

He studied her face. "You're not exactly flattered by my proposal. I'm sorry I didn't spout off the engagement ballad. But how do you think I feel when my girlfriend, who supposedly loves me, shoots me down without even a second of consideration?"

"Supposedly?" Her voice broke, and tears gathered in the corners of her eyes. "Yeah, because two weeks ago meant nothing to me, right? I'll be in the study if you decide you want to stop being a jackass." She stood and stalked off, wiping at her eyes.

Chapter 4

A half hour later, Leah still sat in the study, wiping away tears. A servant had been kind enough to fetch her a handkerchief when they'd spotted her crying.

Who knew if Marcus would even join her? He'd essentially broken up with her for an entire month when they were a new couple, when he'd found out about her shoplifting habit.

She stared out the window, aching inside, focused on the lingering punch of color on the horizon as the sun set.

"I love you," Marcus said softly from behind her.

She sniffled, continuing to stare out the window.

The door clicked. "You know that, right?"

"Yeah," she half whispered. "I know."

He joined her on the settee, leaning against the window. "I'm sorry I didn't handle that the best."

"Me too."

"That's why you haven't been eating much? You've been sick?"

She nodded.

"Can I help?"

Her heart melted, and she hugged him. "I love you."

He gave her his signature squeeze.

After a moment more in his embrace, she leaned back. "There's not really anything you can do right now."

"Let me know if that changes?"

"Will do."

He took her hands. "So... Keeping the baby?"

"Yes." She was as sure of her answer now as she'd been when she'd said it earlier. Her heart ached at the notion of someone else raising this child. Accident or not, it was hers. It was theirs.

"But..." He pursed his lips. "No marriage."

She looked down at their hands. "I'm not saying never. I just ... don't want to be pressured into it."

"But do you want to do this together?"

She gazed into his warm brown eyes. "Yes." She couldn't fathom not having him by her side as she sorted through the mess of her life in this realm, as she carried and raised their child. She couldn't fathom not having her best friend there through it all.

"Then I'm yours."

She lunged forward, giving him a kiss. He held her by the nape of the neck, and she got lost there for just the briefest of moments.

Once their lips parted, she took a cleansing breath.

He rested a hand on her knee. "Not exactly the weekend we planned, huh?"

She frowned. "Sorry about the lake."

Giving her a half-smile, he rubbed her knee. "We've got plenty of other excitement instead, don't we?"

"That's one way of putting it." She mirrored his smile.

"Please ... try to be patient with me. Kind of my first time with this sort of thing."

"Yeah. Same. Definitely my first rodeo." It didn't happen often, but she sometimes caught herself using a human idiom he wasn't familiar with. "A rodeo's—"

"I've heard my mom use that one before."

A servant knocked and entered, lighting sconces in the room and bidding them good night.

Leah and Marcus stayed up for hours discussing things. They didn't come to any solid answers on what they were going to do, but they discussed options. He'd continue with his internship, and she would continue with her education. And despite how much they both dreaded the prospect, they would have to inform Catrina and Stephan of their news and plans. The queen and king would *not* be happy.

As Leah and Marcus prepared to turn in for the night, they walked the candlelit corridors of the quiet palace, hand in hand. They reached the hallway where they had to part ways, and hugged once more.

Marcus caressed her cheek and kissed her on the forehead. "Love you."

She smiled. "You too."

Leah tossed and turned in bed, unable to calm her mind. Life would be so much easier if there were a manual, if there were signs posted telling her to 'go this way.'

She and Marcus had agreed to sleep on the discussion they'd had, and reconvene in the morning. They planned to tell Catrina and Stephan together once the king returned from an assembly late the next evening.

But Leah couldn't handle just lying there in bed again, stressing about things, and wondering if Marcus was in his chambers freaking out about the news.

Throwing on a robe, she set her mind to go see him. It would be a tricky feat, but she'd be doing essentially what Marcus had done to sneak into her chambers, getting them into this mess in the first place.

She cracked her door open and slipped into the hallway. Light on her feet, she made her move toward the storage closet. A mere two yards away, she halted when a door clicked behind her.

"Miss Elonto? What are you doing up? Did you need something?"

Leah's heart dropped. She turned. "Robyn? What are you doing here at this time of night?"

Robyn stepped into the candlelight. "Covering a shift for Lily. Did you need something?"

Leah paused. She could lie. She could say she'd been sleepwalking, or that she needed a new towel from the storage closet for some reason in the middle of the night. She *couldn't* pretend she was sneaking to the kitchen for a late snack, since she'd been walking in the wrong direction.

She liked Robyn, and felt she could be trusted. People would find out soon enough anyway. Though ... she wasn't sure Robyn knew about the palace's hidden passageways, so she treaded lightly.

"I ... need ... to go take care of something in private," Leah said.

Robyn arched an eyebrow. "I might be able to help you if you'd like to elaborate."

Leah wrung her hands. "No, I... I kinda need you to ... look the other way."

"Hmm... Looking the other way is not something I can do much of in my position."

"Please?" She was so desperate. "If you need to go take a quick bathroom break, and then ... not check in my room..."

"Miss Elonto." Robyn's tone was more serious. "Please explain what you have in mind at this hour."

Hugging herself, Leah considered her options. She could let her plans go, but she couldn't stop that yearning, that nagging feeling telling her she had to be with Marcus right now. "I need to see Marcus."

"Absolutely not."

"I'm not asking you to lie. I just need you to not ... proactively tattle on me."

"Leah," Robyn said softly, "I have to follow Her Majesty's orders when it comes to your curfew and visitations. You know that."

Leah was close to crying. Whether from hormones or desperation or exhaustion, she didn't know. "Please? I need to see him. I'll be back before your shift is over, long before they ring the breakfast bell."

Silently, Robyn shook her head.

"I need to be with him. I'm ... pregnant."

Robyn's mouth hung open for a moment. "Does Her Majesty know?"

"Not yet. We're going to tell her tomorrow. But I need to see him." Leah wiped a tear from the corner of her eye. "Please just pretend you didn't see me leave, and I'll be back before anyone would know I'm missing."

Frowning, Robyn shifted from one foot to another. "Even if I did that, how would you get past all the other guards and servants on night patrols? They're not as likely to be sympathetic."

Leah hesitated. "I ... know how to get there without getting caught."

Robyn's gaze drifted to the storage closet behind Leah.

She does know about the passageways. The palace was Leah's residence, but sometimes she still felt more like a guest than a resident herself. No one from inside the palace had ever told her about the passageways.

"You're asking for trouble, child," Robyn said, almost in a whisper.

"I'm already in trouble," Leah replied, her stomach in knots.

After a long pensive moment, Robyn finally replied. "You and I need to be perfectly clear with one another. We never had this conversation, and I never saw you sneaking out of your room. I will *never* lie to Her Majesty. For you or anyone else."

Leah's shoulders slumped.

"But I could stand to go use the toilet. I have no reason to check your room or to suspect you snuck out. I don't expect to see you until very early this morning. Much earlier than the change of shift or breakfast bells?"

Leah's tension eased, and she almost even hugged Robyn, not that hugging the staff was allowed. "Thank you!"

Robyn shook her head. "Don't thank me. But don't get me in trouble either."

"I won't!"

Robyn scanned her. "And if you ever need to talk about it, I'd be happy to answer any questions you have about pregnancy, at least based on my experiences with my two."

This time Leah did hug her. "Thank you!"

"Sure thing. Now, I'm heading down the hallway. And I'm assuming you'll be back in your bed where you belong." Robyn released her, and Leah stood in place until the hallway door clicked shut behind Robyn.

Leah quickly pulled open the supply closet door and shut herself inside. Her heart raced in the dark, but she persevered and carefully felt her way past the shelves to the back of the closet. She crouched, finding the little lever by the floorboard. When she pulled the lever, a barely perceptible *squeak* announced her success.

She'd snuck out and explored this route before, but had been much more careful to avoid detection.

Leah slid the panel to the side, slipping through the narrow entryway, then slid it back into place. She really should have brought a candle to see better, but she'd spaced it with the moonlight and candlelight in her chambers and the hallway. She'd do fine once her eyes adjusted, and with the few tiny windows along the corridors.

She knew her way around here anyway. She hadn't explored much of the maze of tunnels and offshoots, mostly just what was needed to find a path between her chambers and the ones Marcus was usually assigned when he came to visit.

After a while spent groping the cold stone walls and guiding herself at the right turns, she arrived at the door closest to Marcus's chambers. This door wasn't as close to his room as the first door was to hers, and it required a touch more precision with the timing.

Cupping her ear to the door, Leah listened for noise on the other side, though she hadn't expected any. This particular doorway was hidden behind the curtains of a small theater and concert hall. No one would be in there at this time of night. Even then, she was careful to keep noise to the minimum as she popped the door open and stepped into the room.

She was still two hallways away from Marcus's room.

They'd spent months planning their romantic rendezvous, and it had even become a game. Based on previous observations, there were usually more guards and servants patrolling the area around Leah's chambers.

Leah sighed, pausing with her hand on the doorknob. It definitely wasn't a game this time. She twisted the knob, listening intently as she opened the door just a hair. The night was still.

Shutting the door behind her, Leah hastened down the long hallway, with only the soft *pitter-patter* of her bare feet to give her away.

As she neared the corner, someone sneezed.

Shoot.

She stopped dead in her tracks, her gaze darting around the hallway. She chose the nearest door and pulled it open, ducking inside.

A bathroom... That could be good, since it could be locked, which she did immediately. Or it could be bad, if the sneezer needed to use it!

Calming her breathing, Leah waited. And waited. And panicked as footsteps thumped closer. She held her breath, her ear pressed to the door. She finally loosed that breath after the footsteps passed her.

She waited a few minutes, mentally mapping the routes she and Marcus had discussed. The timing had to be right. She had to wait long enough for that person to be out of earshot, but couldn't dawdle, because the next patrol might not be far behind.

Leah stepped back out into the hallway and turned the corner, running to the next doorway and taking less care to open it and step inside.

Luckily, no one was in this hallway either. She passed the first door and headed straight to Marcus's, trying the handle. Unluckily, it was locked. She knocked, hopefully loud enough that he would hear it, but others wouldn't.

She danced from foot to foot, wringing her hands, waiting for Marcus. She'd just done all that maneuvering to get to him, drawing Robyn into this mess, and she'd lose it if he didn't answer, if he was fast asleep, if she got caught.

The lock clicked from the other side, giving her reason to smile, and the door opened.

"Yeah?" Marcus asked.

Leah pushed her way in, closing and locking the door behind her.

"Leah," he breathed as she turned and fell into his arms.

"I needed to be with you," she said, her hands splayed across his bare back. The last time she'd snuck into his room, it had also been for comfort, though it had been at his parents' house. He'd also been wearing only boxers on that occasion.

Marcus nuzzled her neck, squeezing her tighter, not giving a verbal answer.

He was her home. He was happiness and hope. She'd reconsidered her crazy idea to sneak over to see him a handful of times as she'd navigated the palace, but the warmth of his perfect hug steadied her heart and confirmed she'd made the right choice.

Eventually, Marcus pulled back. "What's the matter?" His gaze flickered to her stomach, and his hands rested on her sides. "Is everything okay?"

She smiled, her heart melting. "I'm fine. *We're* fine. I just ... needed to be with you."

He matched her smile. "I like the idea of that."

"Can we cuddle for a couple of hours? Then I can sneak back with plenty of time before the breakfast bell."

"Yeah." He led her by the hand to his bed. The moonlight through stained glass windows cast a beautiful pattern on the floor. She took off her robe to be more comfortable, and slid under the sheets with him.

They kissed a little, and talked a bit, but mostly just held each other. She was still lost and anxious, and could only imagine how he felt after finding out.

They checked his clock every once in a while. Every time she nodded off, she woke to a kiss on her cheek or forehead, and Marcus would ask if that was a sign she ought to head back to her chambers. She didn't want to. She didn't want to ever leave his side again.

Her arms and legs wrapped around him, she fixated on the windows. They truly were breathtaking—the stained glass in his room depicted a cherry tree in full bloom. A hint of daylight started to glow behind the windowpanes. She needed to head back soon, even though she didn't want to.

A loud knock on the door startled them. Leah's gaze shot to the clock. She still had plenty of time before she needed to be back in her own chambers.

Marcus gave her a panicked look as a second louder knock came at the door.

"Stay under the blanket," he said, covering her up.

Leah held her breath, listening. The door creaked open.

"Um... Hi..." His voice held no confidence. "Hi, Aunt Catrina."

Chapter 5

Leah's heart froze at Marcus's words. She stayed under his comforter, completely still.

"*Get. Dressed,*" Catrina ordered, her voice low and harsh. "And have Leah get dressed. The three of us need to have a conversation *right now*."

"Oh crap," Leah whispered.

"Yeah, um, I mean ... she's..." Marcus grappled for a response. Leah hadn't gotten *undressed*, but Marcus was only in his boxers, and their level of clothedness probably didn't matter in the grand scheme of things when Leah ought not to be there in the first place...

"Now," Catrina repeated.

"Yes, ma'am."

The door clicked closed, and Leah pulled back the comforter. They exchanged a panicked glance as he reached for pants and a shirt.

"Why is she even visiting this early?" Leah asked, grabbing her robe.

Marcus frowned, shaking his head. "No idea."

"What are we going to say?" Leah's heart pumped faster than she could come up with answers.

"We're just going to have to tell her now..."

She hugged him, and a thousand scenarios raced through her mind. In five minutes' time, she might be kicked out, homeless. She might be forbidden from being with Marcus, forced to raise their child alone. Possibly exiled again to the human world, permanently.

He gave her a quick kiss. "It'll be fine. We were going to tell her today anyway, right?"

What world are you living in? Sitting down with Queen Catrina to break the news was a completely different thing than Leah being found in his bed, in direct defiance of the queen's orders.

Marcus took Leah's hand, and they stepped into the hallway together.

Queen Catrina was still in a silk nightgown, her long brown hair pinned up for curls. Her arms were crossed, and her expression was also cross. But instead of starting to lay into them, she remained silent, sizing them up.

"Well..." Marcus was the first to speak.

Catrina's gaze snapped to Leah. "I don't ask much of you. I have *always* given you choices. On your education, your therapy, what public appearances you make... And I've always tried to respect your choice to be together. I don't ask much. But the rules were crystal clear—the expectations have never been muddy for the two of you." She looked at Marcus. "Were the rules ever ambiguous?"

He swallowed. "No, ma'am."

Catrina focused on Leah, expectant.

Leah gritted her teeth. Yes, Catrina had allowed her a level of autonomy, but she had plenty of rules surrounding Leah and how she should act, dress, talk, *everything*.

Ivy society wasn't exceptionally prudish. Lots of people waited to have sex until they were married, but it didn't mean there wasn't also a decent chunk of the population that thought it was fine to live together unwed. Even Queen Kaylah had done that with her husband for two years before they'd wed, though their situation had been far from typical, and he hadn't been capable of accidentally getting her pregnant...

"No, Your Majesty," Leah answered, averting her gaze.

"That's right. Crystal clear." Pain and pleading were etched into her voice. "You have come *so far* with your public image. And now this." She shook her head. "Here I thought: 'Since I'm already awake, I'll go check on Leah, because she hasn't been feeling well.' And then I was rewarded with *this*."

Maybe she only knew that Leah had snuck into Marcus's room, and didn't know about the pregnancy part yet? Perhaps they should let this blow over before throwing that gem at her...

"We weren't ... actually doing anything just now," Leah said. "We were only talking."

Catrina's eyes narrowed. "Frankly, I don't care to know what you were doing together last night. But I do know that 'only talking' doesn't end with you getting pregnant."

Yep. She knew. Marcus gripped Leah's hand tighter.

Robyn had to have told Catrina. While the betrayal hurt, Leah wasn't mad at her. She'd outright told Leah she wouldn't lie to the queen.

"Where did it happen?" Catrina asked, no doubt wanting to know *how many* rules had been broken.

Leah and Marcus remained silent.

"Where—"

"Here, in the palace," Marcus quietly answered.

Catrina pursed her lips. "I want names. Every servant or guard who knew you were sneaking around, disobeying orders."

"No one knew," Leah said.

Catrina cocked her head, clearly disbelieving. "Have you developed powers no one is familiar with? You can walk these halls without notice? When I've stationed chaperones? You've mastered invisibility now?"

"No," Leah said wryly.

"Then how, pray tell, did you sneak around the palace without a servant catching you?"

Leah's lips parted, but words failed to come for a moment. "I... We... The hidden passageways."

Rolling her shoulders, Catrina again shook her head. "And how do you even know about those?"

"I told her," Marcus lied.

"Really?" Catrina drawled. "As much as I love you, Marcus, I know you were never told about them. Only residents of the palace and those employed here are informed of their existence. They pose a security risk."

"I'm a resident," Leah countered. "Why wasn't I told? What if there was a fire, and I needed to escape?"

"Then a servant would have helped you out of one of the *many* other exits or, if needed, through the passageways. So, I'm going to ask you again. How did you even discover them?"

"Well, I..." Leah took her hand back from Marcus, hugging herself.

"Like I said, Aunt Catrina—"

"My mom told me about them," Leah confessed. "She told me my dad would sometimes sneak her into the palace before his parents warmed up to her."

Catrina's lip curled. "*Not* the best examples to be following. I shouldn't have to point that out."

Leah's stomach knotted. No, that hadn't been the wisest choice. Her mom had also escaped out those tunnels when the palace had been under attack the night her dad was captured.

"Did Robyn know you used the tunnels?" Catrina asked.

"It doesn't matter," Leah said.

"It does. I need to know who on my staff I'm able to rely on. You may not have grown up in this realm, but you've had more than enough lessons to understand what security at this palace means. Your parents might not have been able to murder your grandparents had the staff been more loyal.

"And when it comes to the security of the position I hold, and the safety of my family, my children, the people I love," Catrina's voice grew louder, "then I will *not* hesitate to dismiss anyone who would put them at risk!"

Leah recoiled a bit at that, her heart numb. Leah wasn't counted as a resident, or as a family member. Marcus was Catrina's nephew, but Leah? She was just Catrina's evil cousin's daughter, her ward, the object of Catrina's pity, her public relations project.

At this point, Leah knew in her heart she was homeless. But Robyn didn't deserve more trouble for knowing Leah had used the passageways. "Robyn didn't know. Don't fire her."

"And did *any* of the servants know you were using them? Robyn's already been dismissed for lying to me."

Leah's jaw dropped. "What?! That's not fair! She didn't lie to you. She told you where I was this morning, right?"

"Yes, but a lie of omission is still a lie, and she knew where you'd snuck off to without doing a thing about it, without proactively informing me."

"That's... No! You can't do that." Robyn was nice, and competent, and had just been showing Leah some compassion in a time when she was freaked out.

Catrina rested her hands on her hips. "I can't? I make the rules here."

Leah clenched her jaw. She was used to a sweet and caring Catrina, and a sometimes-exhausted version of her in private with the young kids and too little sleep. She'd also witnessed the more regal Catrina at formal events and with important guests. Leah hadn't yet seen this side—the *true* side of Catrina that had doubted Leah from the start, hidden under a mask of kindness.

"I will not ask again. Who else—" Catrina started.

"No one knew!" Leah shouted.

Catrina eyed her, then straightened. "I hope that's true. Back to the topic of your pregnancy. Are you keeping the child?"

Marcus slid a hand onto Leah's back. "Yes."

"Alright. Then we'll find time in my schedule today to discuss wedding details."

Marcus kept quiet.

"We're not planning a wedding right now," Leah said.

Looking mildly surprised, Catrina tilted her head. "And why not?"

Leah swallowed. "All you care about is public image, and that's already screwed now, isn't it? If you rush a wedding, people will suspect. If people with half a brain can do math, they'll know I'm already two weeks along. So why should I be forced into it before I'm ready?"

"Better to mitigate damage now than—"

A knock at the end of the corridor cut her off. The door popped open. "My apologies, Your Majesty."

"I asked for privacy, Tain," Catrina said.

"I know, my apologies. A high-priority memo arrived from that human ambassador."

Catrina blew out a puff of air. "Thank you. I'll be right out."

She faced the couple. "We'll continue this discussion later. Both of you properly dress, then see my aide to find out when we can schedule that."

"I'm not going to change my mind," Leah said.

Catrina only stared back at her.

"Give us some time to sort it all out, Aunt Catrina. We just found out."

"We don't always have the luxury of time when it comes to damage control, Marcus."

Leah needed to know where she stood in this mess, how far Catrina was willing to go if she'd fired her servant over such a small white lie. "Are you going to kick me out if I don't marry him?"

"Would that motivate you?"

"No." And it wouldn't. Leah was far too stubborn for that.

"We're going to take our time…" Marcus said. "But Leah and I are going to share a room from now on."

They'd discussed asking for that, but now was hardly the right time to assert that, and apparently Catrina and Leah were of the same mind.

Catrina wasn't accustomed to either of them breaking her rules, or standing up to her. Her exasperation wasn't veiled in the slightest. "You don't get to dictate what happens in my home, Marcus."

Leah was tired of cowering, of apologizing, of lying, of feeling this way—all of it. It had been a mistake. Her pregnancy wouldn't win her points in the public eye, but she still deserved a choice in the matter of her marital status. And Catrina ought not to be talking down to Marcus. Robyn shouldn't have lost her job.

Heat rose in Leah's cheeks and ears. "You don't have to be a bitch about it!"

A barely audible gasp came from Marcus. Leah flinched out of habit, but she hadn't needed to. Catrina could be strict, but she wasn't the type to smack someone she was angry with, the way Cheryl had with Leah when she was younger.

But if looks could kill, Leah would be in a body bag.

"Watch how you address your queen. Both of you, get properly dressed."

Leah choked down the lump in her throat. "Yes, Your Majesty."

"Yes, Your Majesty," Marcus echoed.

A hint of hurt flickered in Catrina's expression. Leah had never once heard him address his aunt so formally in private.

Without another word, Catrina turned and strode down the corridor, opening the door. "Please escort Miss Eleana to her chambers discreetly."

"Yes, Your Majesty."

As the guard headed toward the couple, Marcus pulled Leah into a hug. "We'll be okay," he whispered.

She wished she could believe that.

"Please come with me, miss."

Leah pressed her forehead to Marcus's. "I love you."

He cracked a tiny smile. "I love you too."

"Miss..."

She let Marcus go, and followed the guard down the hallway.

<hr>

Leah perched on the edge of her bed, hands in her lap. The morning could be going better. Why did this have to be so messy?

She'd been sent back to her room like a little kid to get dressed. Then she was supposed to wait around all day until Catrina could squeeze her in for a meeting to demand again that she marry Marcus?

Sounds delightful... But how much choice did she really have in the matter?

Leah went to her walk-in closet, deciding what to wear.

"Where's my most revealing dress?" she asked herself. A 'proper' lady trying to improve her reputation should look sharp and not show too much skin. She'd disagreed with Catrina about her attire from day one.

As she surveyed the closet, an ache took hold of Leah's heart. Too many of these dresses were 'appropriate.' There was nothing wrong with them, per se, but they weren't Leah. When had she allowed herself to become that girl? Wearing what Catrina would like to the balls, just to avoid a disagreement. Simply going along with it to save time and energy.

Turning her back on the dresses, Leah returned to her bed. She tucked her knees up under her chin, and allowed herself to cry. Who even was she anymore?

Her past was a patchwork of mistakes and pain. Her new future—murky and uphill. Who she was in the present—a lie coated in manners and frills.

After wiping away her tears, she slowly approached the closet again, leaning in the doorway. She usually dressed based on the occasions of the day. Marcus's romantic boat ride was out of the question now. The only things on the agenda as of right now were waiting around and lectures.

Leah's wardrobe was stunning. She'd acquired so many pieces in her two years here. From the flowing cobalt blue ball gown, to the forest green drop-waist dress with intricate Ivy-style embroidery.

But none of it was truly hers.

Hadn't Leah told Marcus two years ago that she'd never be the girl they wanted her to be? That she'd advocate for herself about what she wanted to wear, wanted to do, wanted to become?

Becoming a teenage bride wasn't on her list. Being the palace puppet wasn't either.

Leah didn't want to wear any of these clothes; they'd been purchased and commissioned with Catrina's money, with the taxes of the kingdom. But Leah couldn't simply protest by staying in her pajamas against direct orders, or by streaking through the palace.

The smallest of smiles crossed her lips as she remembered her old friends. Crouching, Leah opened a drawer deep in the closet. Her old human-world clothes greeted her—the shirt and jeans she'd originally brought with her when she'd rifted into the Green Lands. She pulled them from the drawer, hugging them.

She hadn't worn these clothes in ages, and who knew how long they'd fit before she outgrew them with her pregnancy.

One leg at a time, Leah put her jeans on, then tugged her t-shirt over her head. Each inch of fabric against her skin was an old friend reminding her of a time in her life when she was free from so much obligation and care.

"Are you ready, miss?" a servant called through the door.

Leah loosed a breath. *No.* "Just a moment."

She stood in front of the gilded mirror, smoothing the creases in her shirt. Her hand glided to her stomach, and she almost cried again. She loved Marcus. An accidental pregnancy wouldn't change that, but she wasn't ready to just hop to the next step right now.

And something deep within her was wrong, something she couldn't explain, didn't understand, couldn't yet grasp.

A part of her faltered as her bright green eyes stared back at her. She'd run away from home before.

And she could do it again.

Leah glanced around her chambers. The room was beautiful, ornate, decorated with the few personalized touches she'd been allowed. How could something this bright be such a stifling prison?

Run. Run. Run, the voices in her head told her. *Get out.*

She was used to burning her bridges. She was used to having a reputation. She could weather those storms again.

How desperately she wanted to sneak into the passageways, to find her way out of the palace, to disappear forever. Just a girl. Just a girl with a child. Not Soren and Beata's daughter. Not Matron Kaylah's niece. Not Marcus's girlfriend.

Marcus. He was the only reason she paused. That, and the fact that she now would likely have someone keeping an eye on her every moment she wasn't in her chambers or the restroom.

But she needed to leave. Maybe for a week, as a palate cleanser, giving herself more time to process her situation.

Leah quickly set to work, scouring her drawers and shelves. What if she did leave? What if she *and* Marcus left? Just for a little while... Leah would only take her belongings. But what actually belonged to her? If Catrina had her searched, would a birthday gift from the queen and king somehow incriminate her as a thief? Because they'd decide it was theirs? She longed to pocket her throwing knives from Marcus, but marching angrily around the palace with them didn't seem like the wisest thing to do. Catrina would probably think she was taking after her parents and planning a coup. What about other gifts from Marcus?

Leah shook her head. She itched to get out of here, to keep things simple. She yearned for freedom.

She grabbed only one thing, tucking it into her sock and covering it with her jeans—her unused passport with a fake human-world ID tucked inside.

The servant knocked on her door.

"I'm coming," Leah replied. She took one last look at her room. At *the* room. It wasn't hers anymore.

It never really had been.

Chapter 6

At the corner where their corridors met, Marcus stood waiting for Leah. She forced a smile. His eyes studied her, her outfit included, and his confusion at her choice of apparel was apparent.

"Hi," he said, taking her hand. "You okay?"

She bit her lip, glancing at the servants around them. "Of course. We need to meet with Her Majesty's aide, right?"

"Yeah. Let's go."

A servant led them through the hallways. All was silent as they walked. It felt like a death march. Marcus tightly gripped her hand the entire way, once giving her a questioning glance. She only shook her head. They needed privacy for this conversation.

After being led to Catrina's outer office, the couple was met by her aide on duty. "Her Majesty's in meetings most of the day, as expected, but we've carved out some time to hold a private discussion between the three of you right before lunch."

Leah groaned. She didn't want to have this stupid discussion at all, but to have to wait around for hours?

"Okay," Marcus replied, always the more level-headed of the two. "Thanks."

As the couple left the office, they agreed to grab an early breakfast from the kitchen. With Stephan away and Catrina in meetings, there wouldn't be a proper meal in the dining hall anyway.

Leah and Marcus took their breakfast trays to the small study, always escorted, and ate their food in relative silence.

She didn't eat much, her stomach in knots, and a little queasy. After a servant cleared their trays, the couple went for a long and slow stroll in the gardens. Marcus was still uncharacteristically quiet, but so was Leah.

"Are you nervous?" she asked.

He waited a moment to respond. "I guess that depends on what you're asking about..."

"About your aunt..."

He shook his head. "Aunt Catrina only wants what's best for us."

She hid her frustration. So now them getting married wasn't just the 'right' thing to do, it was the 'best' thing to do. "She wants what's best for *you*, and what's best for the kingdom, but me? Not so much."

Marcus frowned. "Come on, don't be like that. We'll get it sorted."

Sorted? Like her life was a messy room that could be folded and stacked and organized and tidied up? She'd tried that! She *did* appreciate more stability in her life, and enjoyed many things about the Ivy Kingdom, but hated fitting into a mold forced on her by her notoriety and, frankly, by Marcus's family's notoriety.

Leah's life had become a scoreboard.

Say the wrong thing at a public gathering: negative one to five points, depending on how bad it was and how much the rumors spread.

Forget to curtsy to the queen and king at a ball: negative three points, because it probably meant she didn't respect them and was planning to assassinate them.

Be found in any sort of compromising situation with her long-term boyfriend: negative three points, since she shouldn't be tarnishing his impeccable reputation.

The 'scoreboard' wasn't really discussed, but rules had been set, expectations reiterated, and criticism occasionally given.

But Leah didn't say anything. She didn't want to argue with Marcus right now. She needed him.

He continued to be lost in thought, anyway.

Approaching a massive hedge at the edge of the garden, she yearned to keep walking, to find herself at the rifting cave at the edge of the palace grounds, to simply disappear.

Leah wrapped her arms around her midsection. "I want to go," she whispered.

"Where?" he asked.

"Away. I don't want to deal with this right now." Even as the words left her lips, she knew how childish that sounded. Actions had risks and consequences.

"She just wants to talk." Marcus rubbed her arm. "She wants to help."

It took everything Leah had to not roll her eyes. When things were calm, he was the realm's best boyfriend—attentive, sweet, passionate, funny, dorky. When it came to his family and their place in society, he sometimes wore rose-colored glasses, or failed to see exactly how hard it was for Leah.

"Sure," she muttered, turning back to the palace. Only when they were halfway back did he take her hand, and she softened a degree.

Catrina sat in her office, a kind but perhaps not fully genuine smile on her lips. "Hopefully you've both had some time to calm down and discuss things properly." Her gaze traveled over Leah in her human-world clothes.

Leah bit her tongue, the heat already rising in her cheeks.

Marcus said nothing.

"We're not going to make any huge decisions in one day," Leah answered.

"Surely you two have talked about marriage before..." Catrina arched a single eyebrow, a little more pointedly at Marcus.

"Please don't," he practically whispered, gently shaking his head.

Catrina sat back in her chair, blowing out a breath.

"We're not going to get married just to make you happy or to avoid a scandal," Leah said.

Catrina pursed her lips.

"We're nineteen. We're adults. We can do what we want."

Nodding, Catrina crossed her legs. "Then please act like one."

Watch your posture. Remember the governor's name. Don't forget to curtsy. Avoid looking like you're making frivolous purchases. Keep criticism to yourself.

Leah stood. "You have enough appointments today. We don't want to burden you."

"Sit down, Leah." Catrina pointed to the chair.

"No," Leah spat out with finality. Her passport was still tucked into her sock, and she was ready for its unused status to change. "I'm going." She threw a pleading look at Marcus to join her.

He frowned, only mouthing the word, "Please."

She wasn't going to fight him, too. Leah stormed across the room, pulling the door open.

"Eleana!" Catrina yelled, and the guards outside the room closed in on her.

Leah whipped around. "Let me go. You don't want me here, so I'm going."

Catrina pointed again to the chair. Marcus ran a hand through his hair, slumping in his own seat.

"One way or another, I am going," Leah said, her voice almost shaking. "I'm done with you, and I'm done with this place."

She glanced at the guards over her shoulder; they were poised with wrists at the ready to tie her up with vines if need be.

Catrina threw her hands in the air. "Fine. Go have another temper tantrum. Marcus and I could stand to have an adult conversation."

Marcus buried his face in his hands, but remained seated.

Leah's heart begged for Marcus to join her, to show a united front, but she needed to get out of here, and she wasn't going to wait for him. The moment the guards stepped aside, Leah made a beeline for the exit. After several hallways and a couple of sets of stairs, she slammed the door behind her and breathed in the fresh air. Only a little winded from the stairs, she marched forward.

"Temper tantrum," she muttered.

She got an odd glance from a servant or two tending the grounds as she kept mumbling to herself and striding through the gardens.

After several minutes, she was past the gardens and into the forest, ducking under tree branches.

"Leah!" Marcus's voice twisted her heart, but she only slowed a little.

"Leah! Wait up!"

She didn't, but he eventually caught up to her, winded, grabbing her hand.

"Hey, wait a second."

She took her hand back and continued walking. "Like I said, I'm going."

"And I'm going with you." He strode beside her, putting an arm around her. "Where are we going?"

She wanted to cry again. "Where do you think? The rifting cave."

"Okay."

They were still a couple dozen yards away when a horn rang through the air, and they both halted.

Fear raced through Leah. She'd only heard that horn once before, during a security drill. Surely no one was attacking the palace right now.

And then her knees got shaky. Catrina thought *she* was the threat? She was just scared and angry, and wanting to leave.

"What did she say after I left?" Leah asked.

He looked flustered. "It doesn't really matter. I ... wanted to come after you and told her I was leaving, too."

In no time flat, soldiers ran through the woods, closing in on them. Even though electronics didn't work in the Green Lands, green folk had their ways of communicating. Guards in palace towers and lookouts high in the trees knew how to efficiently convey messages with codes and mirrors.

As the soldiers approached Leah and Marcus, the couple held up their hands, though Marcus didn't have his as high. Flashbacks tore through Leah's mind. Of gasps in a dining room. Of guards shoving her down a mansion hallway. Of being strapped to a chair for hours as she was bombarded with information about her parents. Of how much she'd thrown up when she'd come to accept the truth.

She didn't want to go back. If Marcus weren't next to her, if she weren't pregnant, if she didn't know better, she would have fought these soldiers. Tooth and nail. And she would have lost.

"Come with us please," one soldier said.

Leah gritted her teeth. Marcus took her hand, squeezing it. "It's really not that big of a deal to hear her out."

It wasn't to him. Neither of their aunts had ever discussed executing *him*.

"Fine." As they returned to the palace with several escorts, numbness overtook Leah. At least the archers positioned high above them didn't have their arrows aimed at her, so that was a good sign.

"I am trying to be patient," Catrina said, standing tall in her office again. "And I am not the enemy." Her soft blue eyes competed against her firm tone.

"Neither am I." Leah stood as well, refusing to take a seat. "But that didn't stop you from siccing your soldiers on me, did it?"

"Eleana!" Catrina scolded. "It doesn't have to be this way. We've treated you like family since the moment you moved in with us. Family dinners, outings, holidays..."

"But you're not my family. And I want to leave."

Catrina shook her head. "If you're going to leave this way, then—"

"Then what? You'll cut me off? I don't need your money." That was a lie. "I don't need your servants, or your palace." She shoved her hands into her pockets. "I don't need any of it."

Turning to Marcus, Catrina gestured at Leah. "Marcus?"

His expression was the epitome of discomfort. Only in that moment did it really dawn on Leah how hard this might be for him. He was being asked to choose between following his pregnant girlfriend and his own aunt, his queen.

"This doesn't have anything to do with him," Leah said, hoping to take some pressure off him. "Either throw me in the dungeon like a tyrant, or let me go. Last I checked, I'm a free citizen in this kingdom, and I haven't actually done anything wrong."

Catrina eyed her, considering. "If you want to go, then go. But you better understand the implications. You better remember the promises you've made about security measures at this palace."

Leah huffed. "Like I have anyone to tell them to."

"Passageways included."

"Done." She looked at Marcus. "I'm heading out. Again."

Marcus took her hand.

"You'll leave from the front gate," Catrina added. "You're no longer permitted to use the palace's cave."

An emotional door had officially been slammed in Leah's face. She and Marcus were to do the walk of shame, taking the much longer way out on foot.

Leah held back her tears, squared her shoulders, and choked down the lump in her throat. "Fine."

Their escort was mortifying. They hadn't stopped at their chambers for anything. And when the palace gates creaked closed behind them, Leah almost crumpled on the spot.

But she didn't. She gathered her thoughts and took a deep breath. She was *actually* homeless now.

It would be a long walk to reach a major highway.

Marcus had his hand on her back. "Do you want to take a rickshaw?"

There were always a few lining the central path between the palace and highway.

"No. I don't." She needed to work off some steam. And at least pretend to be as strong as she was stubborn.

"Alright," he said softly.

About a mile down the path, they neared the highway. Their walk had been done in silence, punctuated by the crunch of their footsteps on gravel and the occasional songbird flying above. Honey bees buzzed nearby.

Leah was thirsty, and *desperately* wanted a nap. And frankly, she didn't know where they were headed.

"Where ... are we going?" She was the homeless one, not him. He still had a home with his parents, *and* a temporary home already lined up for him for his internship up north.

He kissed her temple. "I have an idea. But..." He hesitated. "We should stop by my parents' place first."

She cringed, wilting. "Do we have to?"

Marcus blew out a long breath, tucking her hair behind her ears. "The family talks. And I'd rather give them the news myself before Aunt Catrina sends word."

Frowning, Leah nodded. He deserved as much, no matter how little she wanted to see anyone in either of their families right now. Rachel and Guillen had forbidden them from sleeping together long before they'd even gotten back together as a couple. But unlike the motivations behind Catrina's orders to wait until marriage, Marcus's parents had set that expectation out of love and concern for him. Leah had understood that. They genuinely had been astoundingly forgiving of her, accepting her into their home and family. That generosity, however, wasn't likely to extend to her anymore once they found out Leah was about to tarnish their perfect little boy's reputation.

Leah's thoughts turned to her own mother, and she couldn't hold back tears this time. She cried silently, allowing memories of a prison visit months prior to flood her mind. There was so much pain there. She still hadn't shared details of that visit with Marcus. Like a lot of her trauma, she'd buried it and tried to forget it.

She sniffled, and Marcus rubbed her back. "We'll be fine. I have a plan, I swear."

Sniffling again, she nodded. Glancing at him, she stopped thinking about herself. Why did she have to love him? If she were less selfish, she would have let him go long ago.

"I'm sorry," she whispered.

"For what?"

He was *so* close to his family. His parents, brother, aunt and uncle—the whole lot of them.

"For driving a wedge between you and your aunt."

He pressed his lips together, looking straight forward.

They neared another rickshaw, and he asked again if she was interested in taking it. It was several miles now to the nearest rifting cave, and she was crashing from her adrenaline high. She accepted, and he pulled coins from his wallet for the driver.

After they slid in and the driver began pedaling, Marcus squeezed her hand. "I will always choose you." He smiled softly, then kissed her cheek. Quiet enough for the driver not to overhear, Marcus added, "And I'll always choose our baby."

Chapter 7

After the rickshaw came to a stop at the nearest rifting cave, Leah and Marcus stood in line to go through. The cave was somewhat busy, and gazes caught on the couple now and then. That was expected, completely normal. Perhaps not at that particular cave, though, since they'd never been forbidden from using the palace's private cave. What onlookers saw—his arm supportively around her, faint smiles—was far from properly representing the chaos of the day. Eventually, their turn came, and Leah rifted first. With the help of a Seeder employee, Marcus rifted next.

Leah was tired. It would be another half-hour walk from the cave to Marcus's parents' house, and they could have rented bikes, or paid for a rickshaw to get them there faster, but she didn't want to get there faster.

She didn't want to disappoint more people today. Didn't want to see the looks on his parents' faces.

So, they plodded on. Marcus kept his arm around her, but there wasn't much conversation to be had.

"What are your plans?" she finally asked. "Where are we going to stay? What are we going to do?" She wasn't fond of the idea of him wasting his money on an inn for her, and while she was always welcome to stay in the family guest house on Rachel and Guillen's property, she imagined that open invitation was about to come to an abrupt close.

Marcus smiled. "For starters, we can stay at Tobias and Cam's cottage."

Leah arched an eyebrow. "Really?" They lived in the human world, but visited on a somewhat regular basis, and always stayed in their Ivy Kingdom cottage on visits.

"Yep. They told me I could crash over there if I ever needed some space from Mom and Dad."

"I just ... don't want to impose."

He rubbed her arm. "They're not expected to come visit for several weeks. We'll be fine."

Drawing a deep breath, she relaxed a little. She was a cloud in the wind right now—floating, directionless, not tethered or grounded. They at least had a starting point.

But they had to talk to his parents first.

Leah's legs filled with lead as they stepped onto the grounds. Marcus's hand on her back wasn't exactly *shoving* her forward ... but it was definitely doing its part to keep her upright and on her current trajectory up the lane.

"It'll be fine," Marcus whispered into her ear. "Try to be calm about it."

The lack of perfect calmness in his voice did his statement no favors. Telling his aunt he'd gotten Leah pregnant was one thing, even if his aunt was the queen. But breaking the news to his parents...

Rachel greeted them with a smile and a hug. "I love surprise visits!"

"It's good to see you too." Leah wore the best smile she could muster.

They sat in the living room, and Marcus grabbed some crackers from the kitchen to snack on, giving Leah some. He also brought her a glass of water, which she was immensely grateful for.

"So... Just dropping by because...?" Rachel asked.

Marcus cleared his throat. "Well, we, uh... When will Dad be home?"

Rachel glanced at a clock on the wall, crossing her legs. "Shouldn't be long."

"Cool..." Marcus sat back on the sofa. "I had a nice visit with Ambassador Grayas at the palace."

Leah snuggled up to him, taking sips of water. Marcus's small talk—as if life were normal—was difficult for Leah to hear, but it did the job of filling the time before Guillen would get home.

Rachel looked so young. And she *was* young. She was going to become a grandma before her fortieth birthday.

Leah's stomach churned. Maybe she should have just listened to Catrina. Should have given in. Maybe they should have eloped and lied about the date, and then everyone would be more forgiving?

People looked to the royal family expecting perfection. Wise decisions, ideal families, no missteps. Marcus and Tobias had gotten tons of attention during Kaylah's rule, as the nephews to the queen who had no children of her own. They had less focus on them now with Catrina in control, and with her bearing children, but Rachel and Guillen were still war heroes, and Leah was still a black mark.

There would *always* be high expectations.

"Anything exciting with you, Leah?" Rachel asked.

"Oh, well..." She let out a nervous chuckle. "You know, the usual..."

The front door squeaked, and Leah didn't know whether to be relieved the small talk would be over, or more nervous since they now had to fess up.

"Hey, honey," Guillen called from the foyer. Entering the room, he wore a bright smile. "Hi, you two. I expected you'd be staying the bulk of your weekend at the palace."

"Yeah, well ... plans changed," Marcus replied with a hint of unease in his voice.

Guillen sat opposite them, next to Rachel. "Well, I certainly wasn't complaining. Any fun plans?"

Leah placed a hand on Marcus's knee, squeezing it. He rested his hand on hers. "We kinda need to talk."

Rachel surveyed them, her eyes narrowing slightly. "Okay..."

"Um..." His voice was higher, all confidence stripped from it. "Well, we... Things, um, aren't going as planned, exactly..."

Guillen's eyes flickered to Leah's hand on Marcus's knee. "Go on."

"We're, uh... Well, Leah's ... um... She's...." Marcus swallowed. "Pregnant," he whispered.

Rachel's eyes grew wide, immediately looking at Leah.

"That is *not* what we were expecting to hear," Guillen said calmly.

Rachel pinched the bridge of her nose. "Where, when, how, why?"

Marcus glanced at Leah. "At the palace."

Honestly, if they were going to sneak around, they should have done it on one of Leah's visits here, because it would have made things ten times easier, and likely wouldn't have ticked Catrina off so much. But Leah couldn't have imagined doing so. She'd betrayed their family once, when they'd first welcomed her into this home. Sneaking around Rachel and Guillen's house would have felt like much more of a betrayal.

"And she's a little over two weeks along."

While Guillen did a better job of veiling his reaction, Rachel was pretty obvious in her disapproval. "How and why did this happen?"

"How?" Marcus asked in a higher octave, squirming in his seat.

"I know how babies are made, Marcus." Rachel crossed her arms. "But this is unbelievable."

The rest of the conversation went much more calmly than it had at the palace. Rachel and Guillen shared their disappointment, and reiterated the rules, and expectations the family had had for the couple. Marcus and Leah explained that it was an accident, that they were adults, and that they were keeping the baby.

Rachel focused on Leah's hand. "You're not engaged?"

"No." Marcus's response was swift, with perhaps a hint of … disappointment?

Of course he was disappointed. He was doing a decent job of supporting Leah, but he was just trying not to get crushed between a rock and a hard place with his family's reputation and Leah's proposal denial.

Rachel's brow furrowed. "Why not?" The question had been aimed at Leah.

Leah looked away. "Because we're not."

"Why?" There was something in Rachel's tone this time that Leah couldn't fully discern. Her expression was a bit confusing as well. Why didn't Leah love Marcus enough to accept his proposal right away? Why wasn't Leah immediately falling into line and marching to the beat of the royal family's drum?

They eyed each other for a minute. "Because I'm not ready," Leah finally answered with as much conviction as she could, without sounding confrontational.

Guillen sighed, rubbing his face. "Then what's the plan?"

Leah stood, unable to bear more discussion about plans they didn't have. Marcus followed suit.

"We wanted to be the ones to tell you before Her Majesty did," Leah said. She started to walk out of the room.

"We'll keep you updated," Marcus said, trailing after her.

His parents didn't come after them, didn't demand more answers.

The moment the young couple stepped out the front door, Leah fell into Marcus's arms, crying. Every moment of her life was a disappointment to others. Every ounce of her existence unwanted. The entire realm would have been happier if she would have never been born.

Marcus held her tight, rubbing her back. "Come on. Let's go to the cottage and rest for a bit."

The cottage was a tiny one-bedroom setup, and they'd been there to visit before, but it felt intrusive to sort through Tobias and Camry's things while they were away.

Leah sat on the sofa in the main room while Marcus surveyed the pantry and checked out the cellar. Worn out, practically in a trance, Leah stared at a bookshelf.

After a little while, Marcus joined her, kissing her cheek. "There's enough to piece together a few meals with whatever is growing wild in the garden, but I'll want to swing by the market."

She numbly nodded.

He pulled her into an embrace, wrapping his arms around her from behind. "Look at that pretty painting. I wonder what amazing couple gifted that to Tobias and Cam..."

Leah scoffed. "You picked it out with your dad."

"But it was intended as a gift from you and me."

She frowned. "You mean the day before I ruined their wedding by trying to kill Kaylah?"

Marcus remained silent for a moment. "We've all moved on from that. You should too."

Something deep in her soul ached. But had they? Who was 'we all'? Not the entire realm. Not Queen Catrina, since she hadn't even trusted Leah with knowledge of the palace's hidden passageways. Not even Tobias. He'd never actually said the words 'I forgive you.' At family gatherings he was polite, albeit a smidge cold, but nowhere near as friendly as he'd been when they'd first met. Marcus had been right when he'd told Leah that Tobias knew how to hold grudges. Camry, his wife, was much more generous. Granted, she was human, and hadn't grown up with the royal family dynamic and expectations the brothers had.

"Are you sure they'll be okay with us staying here?" Leah asked.

"Yeah. Of course."

Leah had nowhere else to go. She hadn't grabbed any money, any extra clothes, any ... anything, other than the passport still tucked away in her sock.

"Alright," she said, resigned to the idea, given her lack of options at the moment.

"I love you," Marcus whispered into her ear.

"I know."

"I looove you," he said in a singsong voice.

"I looove you too."

He nuzzled her neck. "I love you." His voice was comically deep this time, and she finally smiled.

"Mhmm?"

His arms tightened around her waist. "I love you both."

She melted right there on the spot, snuggling with more ease into his arms. "Thank you."

He kissed her neck.

Lying in his arms, she half expected a servant or soldier to come crashing into the cottage as a chaperone. Or to drag them back to the palace to pick out wedding linens. But they didn't. No footsteps clicked in stone hallways. No dignitaries visited who Leah needed to remember the names of.

Just silence. Just being held by her best friend. Before she knew it, she'd nodded off.

Leah woke disoriented, taking a minute to find her bearings. She'd never slept in the cottage, so she panicked a bit, but then the warmth of Marcus's body behind her brought a smile to her face. He was her home. Anywhere with Marcus could be home.

"Are you awake?" she whispered. No response, only soft breaths.

She carefully pulled his arms away from her so she could slip off the sofa. Marcus's hands suddenly pulled her back down. "Mmm, but you're warm."

She chuckled. "Yes, but I'm also hungry."

He trailed more kisses down her neck. "Fine. Be that way."

She stood, taking a moment to play with a couple of his curly locks before walking to the kitchen.

After returning with more water and a bowl of dried apricots to share, she faced Marcus, sitting cross-legged. "Where do we go from here?"

With a contemplative look, Marcus focused on the apricot he squished between his fingers. "I don't know. You tell me."

Leah swallowed hard. Just because they were pregnant and cut off from the palace didn't mean their lives had come to a screeching halt, did it? They could still keep moving forward... Minus the fact that Leah seriously doubted Catrina would have her tutors come to the little cottage, she also didn't have money for further tuition at the academy. She didn't even know how much it was or what the payment schedule was. It was more affordable and flexible than colleges in the United States back in the human world, but students still paid something to attend classes...

But Marcus had options. He had a stipend—an allowance from his family's investments. He still had his internship, which started the following week, and presumably work with his dad until then.

"You should keep working," she said. He deserved to pursue his passions and career goals. No one really knew about the pregnancy yet, and it wasn't like anyone in their families would leak that information to make things worse for Marcus.

Marcus nodded. "And you?"

"I'll..." She wasn't up to the scrutiny of the public right now.

He gave her an understanding look.

"I'm going to take some time to rest until the maternal sickness passes, and..." She glanced out the window toward the small backyard. "I'll work in the garden to help save on groceries."

He gave her a weak smile. "Sure."

After a little more snacking, they decided they needed some real food. Leah was anxious about leaving the house. The idea of being out in public without an escort, or being around people at all, was too much to stomach. Marcus volunteered to go alone.

In the hour or so that passed during his absence, Leah more fully explored the cottage. She ought to have asked him to buy more clothes for her, but she didn't know how much money he had on hand, or if he'd know how to buy her size without her trying the clothes on. Handcrafted clothing here varied a lot more than mass-produced goods back in the human world.

Leah shrugged it off, running her fingers over the embroidered waistline of a cute shirt she remembered Camry wearing ages ago. Camry had once offered to let Leah borrow her clothes, so that would have to do for now. While she was in the closet, she finally took her passport out and tucked it away for safekeeping.

The bookshelf in the main room was fairly full, which was a normal sight in the place of a wealthy family like Marcus's, but apparently not all that common in regular green-folk homes. Printing and binding were still old-school without electricity, and the paper degraded far less quickly in this realm than the human world. That meant the library systems here were generous and extensive. So Leah had been told, at least; she hadn't had much opportunity to see or learn all of that for herself.

She dared to step into the backyard and stroll around a bit. The garden was unkempt, which wasn't surprising since Tobias and Camry weren't there often. Rachel and Guillen usually had a gardener come well in advance to tidy things up if the couple was planning an extended visit.

Taking off her shoes, Leah roamed through the cool grassy yard. Despite being in a wealthy part of town, it was low-key on this property, a refreshing change of pace.

Now if only time could freeze, and this cottage was a few miles away from civilization...

Standing under a healthy chestnut tree, she got an idea. Holding her hands up, she shot vines out of her wrists, wrapping them around a sturdy branch. Disconnecting the vines at her wrists, she then extended more and quickly wove it together, making a less-than-ideal but better-than-nothing swing. She tested its hold, then carefully sat, smiling.

She softly swung, staring at the Outer Rim mountains in the far distance and the setting sun. Streaks of violet and fuchsia painted the sky, and she thought of the palace. What had they eaten for dinner? What had King Stephan thought of this whole debacle?

As it grew later, Leah started to worry. Marcus should've been back already. She considered slipping her shoes back on and trekking to the market alone, but a pair of hands suddenly gripping her sides stopped her from getting off the swing.

She startled and looked over her shoulder. Marcus laid a kiss on her.

"I was getting worried. What took you so long?"

He smiled. "Just putting up the food and preparing us something fresh."

She frowned. "You should have gotten me. I'm more than willing to help." She'd never cooked in the palace, understandably, but she often joined Rachel in the kitchen when visiting their place, and she'd helped her mom cook all the time in the human world.

"That's okay. I figured you could use a breather after today." He nodded at the cottage. "Want to see what I made?"

"Yeah." She got up, and they walked inside. He'd lit candles already, and the two of them ate the salads he'd prepared while discussing the market and the next day. He still had his third day off work, so they had nothing on the agenda.

As the dark of night enveloped the evening, Leah drank a mint tea, which helped with her nausea. She was still beat, though, mostly from the emotional roller coaster.

After the stress of the day, it was a bit awkward climbing into bed together this time, but they easily found their place, snuggling up and quickly dozing off.

Chapter 8

Leah woke early, though not as early as she normally would.

No servants knocked on her door. No breakfast bell rang through the halls. As much as a pampered life was superior in some ways, it couldn't hold a candle to waking up next to Marcus.

She watched his chest rise and fall. This wasn't their first time sharing a bed, but it was the first time they'd actually spent the whole night together.

Her happiness wavered. Had she placed all her happiness on him? Did she lean on him too much? His reputation, now his money? His kindness? Was she just using him again?

What had he told her two years ago when they'd broken up? 'I'm not your crutch.'

Closing her eyes, she pushed out those memories. She'd deserved his anger. And she'd done her best to make her own way, right? She'd become studious, without needing him to keep her on track like he had in high school.

Though ... now she might become the equivalent of a college dropout.

She breathed deeply, restoring her smile and focusing on his face. Leaning over, she gently pressed her lips against his. It took him a moment, but he soon kissed back, sliding his hands along her back to pull her in. He moaned, deepening the kiss.

After a minute or two of kissing, he gazed into her eyes, smiling wide. "First time being kissed awake... That's something I could get used to."

She agreed.

His hand trailed to her hip. "There's something else we haven't had a chance to do in the morning."

It wasn't like she needed to worry about birth control tonic anymore. "I vote we give it a try."

They lay under the covers, sharing a smile. "I love you," he said.

"I love you too." They were good at this. She'd slept with enough guys in high school to know the difference, and what Marcus lacked in experience, he made up for with passion and sweetness.

He tickled her exposed shoulder, his mouth agape for a moment. "Please marry me."

Something in her tightened, and she looked away. Each time someone brought up marriage now, it was like a vise in her chest gripped a smidge tighter. And with each addition of pressure, an anger rose in her, a part of her that fought harder to push back.

Maybe she was emotionally claustrophobic. Was that a thing?

It was probably just the stress of trying to prove herself in the Green Lands, and attempting to follow all the rules laid out for her. If people would stop bringing it up, she wouldn't push back. Right?

Part of her feared that wasn't the case. Perhaps she'd met her limit long ago. After an entire childhood of being lied to, of having zero say in where they would live, or when they would move. Of living moving box to moving box, town to town. Of not being allowed to have social media accounts like every single kid her age did. Of losing her friends and being forced to cut ties every time they relocated.

"No," she said softly, getting out of bed and grabbing a towel. He should understand that he needed to be patient with her. He should understand *her* by now.

Hadn't she been clear—crystal clear—years ago when they'd danced together for the first time at a ball, that she would never be the girl Ivy royal society wanted? She'd be herself. She'd dress the way she wanted, and act the way she wanted.

But she'd given in on so many things. And maybe he'd come to love *that* Leah too much.

She made a beeline for the solar-heated shower.

He got out of bed, following her to the bathroom, stopping her from shutting the door. "Come on." He frowned. "You act like we've never talked about this."

Sighing, she leaned in the doorway. Was this what he wanted? To get married so they could have sex all the time? To get married to appease the kingdom and his family? To keep his name less tarnished?

Or was he just that nice of a guy? The stay-with-the-girl-you-knocked-up-no-matter-what kind of guy? All obligation?

"We never did talk about *this*, Marcus. This version of things. Of me getting pregnant years before I was planning to start a family, and then having everyone in the realm pressure me into getting married."

"I'm not asking because you're pregnant. I'm asking because I love you."

In the back of her mind, a voice rose from her childhood, that of a woman in prison. *You did this on purpose. You were afraid he would leave. You just don't want to admit it to yourself.*

She swallowed as another voice took its turn. *You were always a slut. This was bound to happen. You only exist to burden others.*

"Maybe I'll consider it when people stop pressuring me into it." She forced the door closed before she began to cry. She spent half her shower doing exactly that—quietly sobbing into her knees.

***

Leah stepped out with a towel around her. Marcus still waited in the hallway, his head on his knees in a similar fashion to how she'd sat in the shower.

He looked up with a cautious expression. "I'm sorry ... if you feel pressured, okay?"

She averted her gaze. "Thank you."

Standing, he gave her a kiss on the cheek and took a turn in the shower while she dressed.

They made breakfast together—an apple salad similar to a Waldorf salad, but with a different dressing. They juiced some kittlefruit and oranges to accompany it. Only the repeated *thud* of the knife on a wooden cutting board really sliced through the thick silence between them.

"I don't want to fight," he whispered.

"Me either."

She took the bowl from his hands, setting it down, and pulled him into a long hug.

It was much needed, as was their refreshing meal. Afterward, they enjoyed some downtime playing a card game.

Leah laid down a card. "Would you mind going back to the market today? At the very least, I do need some new underwear of my own."

He lifted an eyebrow. "Yeah, guess you're not wearing Cam's, huh?"

She grimaced. "No. I'll wash the pair I wore yesterday, but," she shifted in her seat, "jeans and commando—not so fun."

Marcus's grin was mischievous. "If we're going to share a place, and you're going to go without wearing those, then I don't see why you need to wear anything at all."

He was getting way too comfortable with this lifestyle already. He rarely made her blush, but he'd succeeded. "Stop it." She pursed her lips. "Does that mean you're not wearing anything under those pants, either?"

He squinted playfully. "Wanna find out?"

She giggled, throwing a card at him.

Placing her card on the correct pile, he cleared his throat. "No, I had a couple pairs of spare clothes over here already, in case I ever wanted to crash here when we had guests over."

Lucky for him. He had a stash of clothes at the palace for his visits too.

"I don't mind going to the market. Though it might be as odd picking you up underwear as it was the…"

The birth control tonic.

"Well, anyway…" He looked at his hand, rearranging his cards. "I'll pick you up some. Since I only have a couple of pairs here, I'll swing by my place to get some of my own clothes."

She internally groaned. Couldn't they just avoid family? Boycott the rest of the world and live in a reality where it was only the two of them and no pressure? No conflict?

But it *would* be a waste of money for him to buy new clothes when his parents' place was only a mile away.

"I'll try to just slip in and out if I can, okay?"

She nodded.

Marcus returned a few hours later, hands full of tote bags holding clothes. Luckily, neither of his parents had been home, so he'd been able to grab some of his own things without any conflict.

Leah rifled through the things he'd gotten her. She couldn't help but smirk. He was like a kid in a candy store, having bought her a wide array of colors. "Interesting choices," she commented. "Was there a discount for less fabric?"

He busted out laughing. "That's what you get for letting me pick."

She kept smiling, putting them away in a drawer. They honestly weren't all that different from what she'd often worn in the human world, and she'd felt too awkward to buy that style as the ward of the queen and king. "I'll let it slide this once." She winked.

Marcus continued hanging up his clothes, putting a few pieces up on the shelf of the closet. "And if you want more clothes of your own instead of borrowing Cam's, let me know."

She perched on the edge of the bed. "I'm fine." She'd never liked taking charity. Granted, borrowing Camry's clothes was *also* accepting charity, but it wasn't wasteful...

"You *are* fine," he said playfully.

It was moments like these that gave her a glimpse of who they used to be amidst the chaos of the last couple of days and weeks. It was almost even better in a way, because they were legitimately sharing a room, and so far, she didn't hate it in the slightest. As an only child, she'd been worried about having to share.

"What in the?" Marcus reached above his head in the closet, pulling out Leah's passport. "How did Tobias and Cam get back to the human world if they forgot—"

Leah swallowed, frozen as he flipped it open to read *her* name.

He looked at her, confused and obviously hurt. "When you were heading to the cave by the palace, you were going to the human world? I thought you were just going to rift to... Well, I guess I didn't know where..."

She gingerly took the book from his hands, frowning. "I wasn't going to... Not necessarily... Honestly, I wasn't thinking straight. I didn't know where I was going, either."

He weakly nodded, but it was clear he didn't believe her.

"I swear. I wasn't going to leave you." She wasn't going to. Except she kind of had... But it wasn't like she'd planned on *actually* leaving him, on breaking things off.

But maybe he thought she was lying again. Because that certainly had never happened in their relationship before...

She set the passport on the bed and stood, taking his face in her hands. "I wasn't going to leave you."

He searched her eyes. "Okay." His voice didn't hold much more conviction than it had before.

She stole a peck on the lips, and he gave her a half-smile. So she kissed him again and again, hoping to lighten the mood.

"Alright. I get it." He wore a more convincing smile this time. "Do you want me to put that back up there?"

"Um, don't worry about it. I'm kinda starving already." She held him by the waist. "Would you mind fixing a snack for us?"

He stole one more glance at the passport. "Sure."

Once he left the room, Leah stared at the passport, her heart pounding. The way he'd looked at it made her worried he'd take it so she *couldn't* leave.

Picking it up, she ran her thumb over the gold embossing—a blossom surrounded by an ivy leaf resting on a handprint. An old impulse came to visit— one she'd long since tackled and overcome. Stealing, and then hiding the plunder in her bedroom.

It was ridiculous, really. It wasn't stealing. This passport was *hers*. But the need for secrecy, for hiding, for keeping herself safe, for relying on herself, came so naturally in the moment.

As more chopping and stirring echoed from the kitchen, Leah scoured the room for a good hiding spot. She ended up tucking it away in Camry's underwear drawer, assuming Marcus wouldn't have the guts to search through his sister-in-law's private things.

She then closed the closet door, and since it had taken her a while to decide on a hiding spot, she busied herself with making the bed.

No sooner had she replaced the pillows than Marcus came back into the room, stirring a large bowl. He glanced at the closed closet, no doubt wondering why it had taken her so long to join him.

She smiled. "I guess I've gotten too used to a tidy bed at the palace."

"Yeah." He nodded for her to join him. "Come with."

The rest of the day was spent peacefully. There was a slight bit of anxiety and tension between them, but they were just settling into new circumstances. It was reasonable to assume it would take some adjusting.

She was surprised when they headed to bed that he didn't want to do more than cuddle, but she wasn't terribly in the mood, either. It had been a weird day, to say the least.

She didn't sleep the best, her mind running through all the problems with no solutions in sight. But she did eventually nod off.

Only to be awoken bright and early by a knock on the front door. She stilled, making sure it was actually a knock and not something from her dreams.

Another knock.

"Marcus." She shook him awake. "Someone's at the door."

He blinked. "What?"

"Someone's at the door."

Rubbing his face, he groaned. "Yeah. Let me get dressed. I'm not opening doors in boxers anymore."

He stood, grabbing a pair of pants.

"Marcus?" a male voice called from a distance.

Leah froze. "Is that your dad?"

Chapter 9

Marcus's face went pale as he tugged on his pants. "Yeah, sounds like him."

Why couldn't his family leave them alone to sort things out? Give them a little privacy?

"How did he even know to find us here?"

It was probably pretty obvious. If they weren't staying at the palace or his family's estate, then the cottage would be the most likely answer.

Marcus pulled out a shirt, an apologetic look on his face. "I ... left my parents a note when I went to grab my clothes. Just in case they were worried..."

She let out a frustrated sigh, and he frowned.

"Marcus?" Guillen called again.

Marcus ran from the bedroom, and the front door squeaked open. "Dad... Hey..."

"Are you still coming to work with me?"

Leah glanced at the clock in the corner of the bedroom, blowing out a breath. They'd agreed he would go back to work as usual, and his three-day weekend was up, so they shouldn't have been surprised.

"Yeah, of course. Let me brush my teeth," Marcus said.

After a few footsteps padded down the hallway, water splashed from the direction of the bathroom, and Leah worried he might not even say goodbye. But he reappeared in the bedroom for a moment, giving her a kiss. "I'll be back right after work, alright?"

She sat up in bed. "Yeah. Have a good day."

Half expecting Guillen to mention that he knew Leah was hiding away in the bedroom, Leah was surprised when the front door clicked closed without a single mention of her. Though ... just because they hadn't talked about her while they were within hearing range didn't mean they wouldn't be discussing Leah on their trip to and from work.

She groaned, sliding down in bed, throwing the covers over her head, and falling back asleep.

It was quiet when she woke, but that extra sleep was exceptionally refreshing. Leah threw on some of Camry's pajamas. After a trip to the bathroom, she settled on cooking a decent breakfast. The pancakes she made on the griddle were fine, but her mouth watered at the thought of bacon. Oh, how she missed bacon after more than two years without it!

She blankly stabbed at the last pancake on her plate, dragging it through the dregs of crushed raspberries. Bacon—she and her mom had cooked up bacon for a nice last meal together before she'd betrayed her mom, before she'd run away with Marcus.

Before she'd tried to kill Kaylah, and had gotten her mom caught after nearly two decades in hiding.

Leah couldn't hold back tears. It was probably just hormones. Ivy pregnancies and births were very similar to that of humans. Never had Leah been more jealous of Seeders than when she found out Seeder girls didn't even have to endure periods. And here she was—knocked up, nauseous, and moody.

But it wasn't really fair to blame it all on hormones. One of Leah's 'talents' was shoving down her trauma, just to let it build and bubble over. But that wouldn't happen this time.

Leah was fine. She'd come to terms with the truth about her parents and the atrocities they'd taken part in during the old war. She'd … ignored the truth bomb her mom had dropped on her a few months ago about Leah's conception.

A hollowness threatened to take hold, but Leah wouldn't allow that.

Standing from the little breakfast nook, she refilled her water glass. She'd said she would tend to the garden, but didn't have it in her right now. Instead, she turned to the main room and perused the books on the shelf. They ought to keep her mind off everything.

The books were about seventy/thirty fiction to nonfiction. Tobias didn't seem so stuffy that he'd enjoy reading nonfiction on his visits to his home realm, so these had probably been collected by or gifted to Camry—informational tidbits to help the human fit in.

Leah related to Camry so much on that, having grown up *thinking* she was human. Then again, Leah had spent the last two years with the highest caliber of tutors and educators.

Nonfiction sounded boring, not the escape she wanted. But, she reasoned, if she took some time to read it, that would supplement her current education. She wasn't dropping out. She was ... doing independent study.

Leah pulled a book off the shelf; the spine was dandelion yellow. *Seeders: Past, Present, & Future*. It had likely been gifted by someone from Rachel's side of the family.

She cozied up on the sofa, pulling a light afghan over her lap. Then she got lost in words and pictures for hours. She took a few bathroom breaks, and a late lunch, but for the most part simply soaked up all the culture and history there.

A knock from behind startled her as she turned a page. She was of half a mind to ignore it and pretend she wasn't home, but if someone was dropping by a rarely used cottage, they probably already knew Leah was there.

Setting her book and blanket down, Leah approached the door. She regretted going to answer it once the face of her visitor came into view. Leah wilted. Guillen coming to collect Marcus for work was one thing, but why would Rachel drop by?

It was too late to duck and hide away, as Rachel had seen her too. Leah put on a pleasant smile and opened the door. "Hi."

Rachel donned a bright smile of her own, holding a huge basket of produce. "Hi, Leah." Her gaze rested on the clothes Leah wore.

Great. Not only was she sinking Marcus's reputation and future, and had become a school dropout, but Leah was braless, wearing someone else's pajamas in someone else's home. She was a leech. Rachel had to be imagining she'd spent half the day kicking her feet up and eating bonbons.

"I was studying... About Seeders, actually." Leah jabbed a thumb over her shoulder. "And Camry said I could borrow her clothes before, and Tobias offered to let us stay here." *Not really us, per se, but Marcus...*

"Looks comfy, and I'm sure she wouldn't mind," Rachel said. "Mind if I come in and help you put away the food? It's from our garden. We really should do a better job of tending to the one here for surprise visits."

Yes, I mind. Leah wished for peace and quiet, and a judgment-free sanctuary. But Rachel was the last person she could ever say no to. "Sure, be my guest."

Rachel came inside, basket in hand, and headed straight for the kitchen. She started unloading fruits and vegetables, a pair of mangos here, a bunch of carrots there.

Leah stood and watched. "I can do that. Marcus can bring the basket back later tonight…"

Waving a dismissive hand, Rachel kept unpacking. "Nonsense. I don't mind."

Maybe Rachel was bored. She didn't work full-time anymore, and hadn't for a while. Most of her work was charity work, and her schedule was sporadic. Though, perhaps this was an olive branch? Or it was a way of being nosy and making Leah feel guilty.

Once the basket was emptied, Rachel picked up Leah's dirty breakfast and lunch plates, putting them in the sink, and then proceeded to mortify Leah by lifting her hand to the water pump.

"Please don't," Leah practically begged. "I know how to do my own dishes. I'd rather you not."

"I don't mind. I just want to help."

"Please. I'm not a spoiled palace brat."

Rachel chuckled. "I'm guessing the only dishes you've helped with in this realm were at our place, because the palace staff would be utterly insulted if you tried to do your own dishes."

Leah frowned, and Rachel matched with a frown of her own. "I didn't mean it as an insult. I've spent a good amount of time in that palace. I'm just saying I know how it works there."

She left the dishes alone, facing Leah. "Can we sit and chat for a little while?"

That certainly didn't bode well for the 'get her out so I can enjoy peace and quiet' strategy, but Leah again couldn't say no. "Sure."

They moved to the sofa, and Rachel smiled when she spotted the book Leah had been reading. Leah tucked her knees up under her chin, holding her legs.

Rachel loosed a breath. "How are you doing?"

"I'm fine. Maternal sickness, but it could be worse."

Rachel nodded. "Is that what's keeping you from your studies today?"

Leah averted her gaze. "I needed to take a day off."

"Understandable." Rachel plucked a speck of lint from her shirt. "Catrina's worried about you."

Leah met her gaze, her hairs standing on end. "You guys have … talked to her?"

"She sent a note to make sure you were okay."

That had to be a fat lie. Catrina had sent a note to ensure Leah wasn't out there giving away palace secrets, or instigating a rebellion of discontented citizens, pitchforks in hand and headed straight for the secret passageways.

"Do you love my son?" Rachel asked softly.

That was unfair, and a low blow. Now Leah suddenly didn't love Marcus, just because she wasn't ready to marry him? Every relationship Leah had been in before him was short and shallow, and mostly physical. Marcus was everything to her. He was the day to her night. "Of course I do."

Rachel chewed on her lip. "Then why don't you want to marry him?"

The vise tightened, and Leah clenched her jaw. She tried to speak calmly. "Because I'm not ready right now."

Looking into her lap, fidgeting with her hands, Rachel remained silent for a little while. "I know better than anyone how complicated it can be to date and marry into the Ivy royal family. It's very stressful. And ... you knew what was expected of you when the two of you started dating again."

Leah's stomach knotted. Maybe she should have waited to tell everyone she was pregnant until she started to show—then she would have a forty-three-step plan sorted out about how she could smooth everything over without inconveniencing everyone.

"I'm sorry I'm not what you want for your son," Leah said. Flashbacks from years ago came to her. *I'm sorry I'll never be who you want me to be.* Her mom had then reassured her that she'd always love Leah, no matter what. Why was it easier for a convicted murderer to love Leah than all these upright citizens and war heroes? And then another voice reminded her of one of her darkest days. *You came into my home. You broke my son's heart. You jeopardized my husband's respectability.*

"Don't say that," Rachel insisted. "I love you like a daughter. I wish you were ready to be one."

Sometimes it was hard to know which voices to listen to. The scathing ones always felt more genuine, because the kind ones were more likely to make her look like a fool. It was particularly hard to know which to believe when the voices originated from the same source.

"And I just want my grandchild to be welcomed into this world with a supportive family," Rachel added.

"So, what does that mean for them if we don't push this under the rug and have a shotgun wedding?"

Rachel shrugged. "We'll still love them, and you. It would just be less complicated if you and Marcus took the next step sooner than later."

If this was Rachel's sole intention for her visit—to wear Leah down—then this conversation was over. "I understood the expectations when Marcus and I got back together. But he understood that I came with complications. We're adults now. Let us be."

Rachel's expression conveyed that she'd gotten the message. "I only wanted to help." She stood. "You know where to find us if you need anything."

She grabbed the empty basket from the kitchen and headed for the door. "Have a good rest of your day." Her voice was still kind, but the tension was thick.

Leah remained seated. "You too."

The door closed behind Rachel, and Leah rested her forehead on her knees. "I hate this," she muttered.

After a few minutes of gathering her thoughts, Leah got up and dressed, then set to work tidying and dusting every inch of the cottage. If they were going to get surprise visitors multiple times a day, she might as well make it look like she wasn't a useless blob and complete disappointment.

Luckily, no other visitors dropped by. Leah was just getting dinner started when Marcus returned. She gave him a genuine smile, wrapping her arms around his neck and weaving her fingers through his hair.

"Mmm." His smile was bright as he leaned in, kissing her. "I love this." He slid his arms around her waist. "Sharing our mornings and nights together. Not having to wait until the weekends." He snuck another kiss. "If I'd known how good this would feel, I'd have suggested we move in together at least a year ago."

She rolled her eyes, despite agreeing with him. "Yeah, because that would have been allowed by the committee of public scrutiny and familial obligations."

He wrinkled his nose.

"Help me with dinner?" she asked.

"Sure." He washed his hands, and they worked side by side.

"So... How was work?" she cautiously asked.

He trimmed a floret of broccoli from the stem. "Good. The usual."

"And conversation with your dad?"

He hesitated, trimming off another floret. "Good. The usual."

She passed him a skeptical glance out of the corner of her eye.

Marcus shrugged. "It was fine. I told him we were going to stay here a while and figure things out."

Leah continued plucking grapes from the stems. "How long is 'a while'? We have less than a week until you go off to start your internship up north…" There wasn't a rifting cave all that close to where he would be working, and his employer would be paying room and board. They'd planned for him to continue visiting her on the weekends when she was still living at the palace.

"We'll see. A day at a time, right?"

She nodded. "Your mom dropped by today."

"That tracks. I was curious why we have so much more fresh food. How did that go?"

"Oh, ya know. About as expected."

"What's that supposed to mean?"

She stepped behind him, using the water pump to rinse the grapes. "Trying to help. And trying to guilt us into rushing things."

"I'm sure she wasn't trying to guilt you into anything."

Why? Why did this have to happen? His family had been so supportive before she'd gotten pregnant. And now, she just wanted him to pick *her*. Not mediate. Not justify their actions.

Leah remained silent, not wanting a fight or to sour the mood.

"Have you thought more about what you're going to do with your time?" he asked. "About your studies?"

"Yep. Independent studies. I spent a good portion of today reading."

"I mean real studies."

She cocked her head, defensive. "You can be well educated without a degree or formal education, without some stupid stamp of approval." She tried to keep her tone even. "What's so special about a teacher lecturing as opposed to reading what one wrote in a book?"

He held up his hands. "Okay. So you're not keen to go back to tutors and the academy."

She frowned. It wasn't like she'd hated them.

Marcus turned, checking the heat of the coal stove. "I'm just saying, if you wanted to continue what you were doing before, I'm sure Aunt Catrina would be reasonable."

"No." If Leah never saw Catrina again, it would be too soon.

"You wouldn't even have to talk to her. You could write a letter."

"No."

He sighed, putting a pan on the stove and drizzling some olive oil into it. "Fine."

Another moment of silence passed, and she set to peeling an orange for their fruit salad.

"Do you want an escort here at the cottage?" he asked.

"What? You want to pay for a security detail? No one but the family knows I'm here so far, right?"

"Yes. Well, no. My dad asked me to ask you. The palace would still help keep you covered."

Queen Catrina's brother, Sir Guillen. Rachel had already mentioned a note. It was *so* nice to be the topic of everyone's conversations...

"I don't need an escort."

"So, you're not going back to the academy, and if I'm heading up north, you'll stay here?"

It hurt that he didn't even entertain the option of taking her with him. But he still wanted to get married; was still on his family's side of the argument about 'mitigating the damage' and 'preventing the fallout.' If there was one thing she downright *loathed* about dating Marcus, it was that the royal family was held to such a high standard compared to any other group of people.

But she considered his question. She didn't have anywhere else to go, anything else she was comfortable doing right now. "That's the plan for now. I'll get the garden going so I don't have to go to the market, and I'll study from here."

He dropped the broccoli into the sizzling pan. "Alright."

Chapter 10

The rest of the week was nice. Better than nice. Leah kept herself busy during the days, mostly with reading. No matter how boring the book was, she made herself finish it. Textbooks and history books were unsurprisingly dry. But finishing them, marking them off, gave her a purpose. No one could say she was being lazy.

And the mornings and nights were stellar. They may not be on a honeymoon, but she and Marcus sure acted like it. When they shared those quiet moments of pillow talk each night, and the smile-filled mornings alone, not a single part of Leah doubted if she loved Marcus, or if he loved her.

As they neared the weekend, however, she was a bundle of nerves. They ate breakfast at the table one morning. "You, uh, haven't started packing..." she said, spearing a piece of asparagus in her hash.

"I can't carry much through a rift..." He raised an eyebrow, taking a sip of orange juice.

"I thought you were catching a train."

He grinned. "I figured I'd spend an extra day with you, and I'll just buy new stuff up there."

She frowned. Sure, he had money, but she didn't like being a financial burden.

"Ouch," he said playfully. "I thought you'd enjoy spending more time with me, but here you are trying to get rid of me."

She rolled her eyes. "I'll tie you up, and not let you go at all."

He chuckled. "You can tie me up with your vines any day."

Her cheeks warmed. "I'm happy to have you here, but I feel bad that you're going to have to make unnecessary purchases."

"Don't worry about it. I'll have my stipend *and* a steady paycheck."

Nodding, she tried to allow herself to not take on that guilt.

"I'm going to swing by my parents' place tonight after work, though, so you can have more money here for anything you need during the week."

You're using him. He's just a tool. This baby is only a tool.

Leah closed her eyes, forcing the lies out of her head. "I don't need your money."

Marcus's mouth hung open for a moment, and she imagined his protest. She'd told him that back in high school, that she didn't want him to pay for dates when she and her mom had run into hard times financially. Or maybe he was thinking that if she'd finally agree to marry him, it would be *their* money, and not *his*.

"I just," she shrugged, "don't have any need for money if I'm not going to the market, right? No escort. I'll be fine."

He pushed around the food on his plate. "You're going to tend to the garden, then?"

Yeah, she'd said she was going to. When he was home, she spent all of her time with him. During daylight, she'd been spending it napping away her maternal sickness or reading. "Yes. I'm going to clean up the garden."

"Then I'll make sure the pantry's well-stocked before I go." He rocked his head back and forth. "But I'm still going to leave you with money, for emergencies."

She grudgingly accepted.

The day before Marcus started his internship, he was pure nervous energy. He kept checking that Leah had everything she needed, and tidied up his things, helping her fold up the freshly line-dried laundry. While he saved a lot of time by not taking the train, he'd still have to walk or ride to the local rifting cave, and then once he got to the other side, he'd need to buy new things, and make his way to the rural town he'd be living in.

The time was passing too quickly, and he was stressed. Her heart was going away for the week, and she wanted to leave them both with a reminder of how much they'd enjoyed their time together, and what they had to look forward to the next weekend.

She pulled him into the bedroom, kissing him hard. Backing herself onto the bed, she tangled her fingers in his hair, and extended vines to tug his shirt up.

He pulled away. "You're killing me. I don't have time."

She frowned. "Yes you do. It's not like there's a train schedule you need to abide by."

He raised an eyebrow. "My parents."

She internally groaned. His parents were *not* what she wanted to hear about while in bed and trying to get hot and bothered. "What about them?"

"They're seeing me off at the cave. I don't want to be late."

She leaned back on the bed, propping herself up on her elbows and retracting her vines. "When did you plan that?"

"I told you." He furrowed his brow.

"No. You didn't."

"I'm sure I did."

She huffed. No, he hadn't. "They'll survive if you're late."

He straightened his shirt. "And they'll probably guess what we were doing to make me late."

Leah pointed to her stomach. "Your child in there. They know. We've been staying here together. I think they know."

Tucking his hands into his pockets, he frowned. "C'mon. This internship is a big deal for me. My parents were already planning to see me off at the train station before I changed my plans to stay longer with you."

Why did she have to compete for his attention? Why couldn't he be an orphan like her, with no family to come between them?

"Fine," she said weakly.

He rubbed her knees. "I want you to be proud of me, happy for me."

"I am. You love what you do. You're a hard worker. You'll do great things."

"You can come to the cave to see me off, too..."

And leave with his parents after he walked through? *No thank you.* "That's okay. I'll stay here."

He pursed his lips. "If that's what you want."

She simply smiled. Marcus held out his hands, and she accepted. He pulled her to standing again, hugging her tight.

Then he gave her a solid kiss. Once their lips parted, he crouched down, lifting her shirt. He pressed his lips to her stomach. "You be nice to her," he lectured Leah's stomach.

Tears instantly pooled in her eyes, her heart melting.

When he stood tall again, his smile was warm and bright. "What?"

"I don't want you to go," she whispered. *Ever.*

He tucked her hair behind her ears. "It's only a week. We've been apart way more than we've been together." He stole another kiss. "And I will make it up to you, spending *every* free second together next weekend." He leaned forward, nibbling her ear. "Maybe I'll even bring back new half-priced clothing for you."

Okay, *that* brought a genuine smile to her face. "Go on. Don't be late."

He winked, and she walked him to the door. They exchanged 'I love yous,' and then he walked away.

He was her home, happiness, and hope. It was hard to see all of that walk away. He looked back once and waved before turning the corner. She forced a smile and waved back. And then he was gone.

And she was alone. Utterly alone.

Other than crickets singing in the early evening, it was quiet. To distract herself, Leah picked up another book, this time from the fiction options. *Valeska and the Wandering Soldier.*(bb) It was a bit of a slow-paced read, but she started to get into it. After she'd devoured a dozen chapters, her candle was burning low. It was time to call it a night. What she wouldn't do to get a text from him like when they'd dated in high school. 'Got here safe. Sweet dreams.'

She lay awake in bed half the night. After she finally fell asleep, a loud *thump* woke her. Her heart racing, Leah stayed in bed, silent and still. Another *thump*, and a slow *screech*.

Was someone trying to break in? Scare her? Now she kind of wished she'd taken Marcus up on the offer to have an escort. Sneaking out of bed with vines at the ready, Leah tiptoed to the front door and peeked out the window. Then rolled her eyes.

A storm, knocking a tree branch against the window.

She ruffled her hair, yawned, and went back to bed.

Owing to her rough night, Leah slept in much later than usual. It was closer to lunchtime when she dragged herself out of bed, but it wasn't like she had a set schedule anymore. She tried not to frown at that.

She was fine. How many people dreamed of this kind of life? No responsibilities.

As her stomach protested the lack of food, she slid a hand to it. No responsibilities *yet*.

Leah peeled a banana, deciding what else to eat, and was halfway through it when she glanced into the backyard.

Most of the garden resided in planter boxes. Rachel leaned over one, a pile of weeds beside her.

Rachel dug into the soil with a trowel, dropped a seed in, and covered it up. With a watering can, she moistened the soil, then she placed her hands over the seed. Her hands glowed with Seeder energy, and soon enough, a sprout emerged. Seeder powers were pretty amazing. The first time Leah had seen Marcus's mom actually *fly*, she was floored.

Rachel repeated the process with another seed. While it was nice to get help in sorting out the garden, it also rubbed Leah the wrong way. It was like the dirty dishes the other day. She could do it herself, and she didn't need Rachel stepping in to take care of it. It just made her feel guilty and inadequate. Had Marcus asked his mom to come over because he'd resented that Leah hadn't been working on the garden?

Leah huffed, taking another bite of her banana and setting it down. She got dressed for the day, refusing to let Rachel see her in 'lounging clothes,' and joined her in the backyard.

"Hey, there," she said on her approach.

Rachel looked up with a bright smile. "Hi, stranger. Didn't want to disturb you."

"Thanks." Leah fidgeted with her hands. "I appreciate the help, but I really can take care of this myself. It was at the top of my to-do list today."

"I don't mind. I don't have any plans until this evening." She continued working.

Leah flexed her hands. *Fine. We'll do it your way.* She bent and picked up the pile of weeds, taking them to the composting area. Then she set to work on weeding the box next to Rachel.

"Did you want to fertilize these so they'll grow faster?" Rachel asked.

Looking up, Leah hesitated. "Well, I... I could try, but I can't guarantee I wouldn't kill them."

Rachel chuckled. "You won't kill them. That's a basic Ivy power. You mastered that forever ago."

That was true. But Ivy women's powers were mostly chemical, and so were Leah's hormones. She'd learned after coming to the Green Lands that Ivy women's powers could be a bit unpredictable when they were pregnant. "Yes, but I haven't tried it on a plant since I got pregnant."

"Right..." Rachel replied in an awkward tone, as though she should have thought of that herself. "But we can test it. If it dies, it dies, and then we replant."

Yeah, that was *exactly* what Leah needed—for Rachel to nurture life, and Leah to destroy it in front of her. For Leah to cause these new sprouts to wilt and wither.

For her to poison instead of fertilize, and taint the soil. "I'd rather read up on how to do it first, thanks."

There were books out there on how to master your chemical arts during pregnancy. Queen Catrina no doubt had one on her nightstand right now. Then again, Mrs. Perfect probably had that mastered with her first pregnancy, and wouldn't need tips for her third.

"Okay." Rachel covered another seed with soil.

Leah shook her head, yanking on a stubborn invasive vine. Rachel had to be imagining Leah a coward for not being willing to try, to not perform in front of her. And Leah almost gave in, but her pride kept her back, and she envisioned Rachel taking Leah's destruction of new life as evidence of what a horrible girlfriend she was, what a horrible wife and mother she would be. She was already destroying the life of Rachel's baby boy.

Leah's side of the family only knew how to destroy. Marcus's knew how to build.

But Leah kept pulling up weeds in silence. Why was Rachel doing this? She'd always been kind and welcoming and forgiving, not overbearing.

"Do you want me to pick up a book on Ivy powers during pregnancy?" Rachel offered.

No. You're already doing too much. "I'm fine. I planned to stop by the library to get one."

"I'd love to accompany you, especially since you don't have your escort. You know—girl time."

Leah steadied her breathing, plunging a trowel into the soil to dig up a deep root. "I'll let you know."

More silence passed, and Leah eventually took her weeds to the compost pile. Rachel had moved over and started working in the newly cleared bed.

"What are you planting?" Leah asked. She'd be the one eating most of the produce while Marcus was away during the weeks, becoming a big shot. It was a little presumptuous that Rachel hadn't even asked Leah what she wanted planted.

"A little of this and that. The first box has a couple types of squashes. I'm planning for tomatoes in this box." She smiled. "And some moon melons, because I know how much you and Marcus like them."

Okay, fine. So you remember what foods I like.

"And lots of radishes if we have enough space, since Tobias and Camry love them."

Right. This is their house, not mine. Why was every action, every word, like a Seeder dart to Leah's heart? Why did the simple fact she'd gotten pregnant now make her emotions paper-thin?

People loved Marcus. They tolerated Leah.

With her mind turning to her mom, Leah sniffled. Even the few who truly loved her didn't always want her, weren't really proud of her.

"You alright?" Rachel asked.

"Yeah. Just hungry, should have had more to eat."

"Go grab something. I can handle this myself."

Leah accepted. She did need to eat and pee, but she was mostly ready to be alone again.

After fixing a lettuce wrap, Leah watched Rachel from the window. Rachel was laser-focused on the work at hand. Leah was lost in thought in her own world as well.

Why was no one trying to convince Leah to give up the baby? Rachel surely hadn't wanted to become a grandmother so young. And she wanted her son to become an important person like her husband. It had to be incredibly painful for Rachel to even be around Leah after the torture Leah's dad had inflicted on her.

But Marcus had forgiven Leah, and cared for her. And that was it, right? Marcus was simply respecting Leah's wishes to keep the baby, and everyone was respecting Marcus's choice. It wasn't about liking Leah or caring about her opinions. It was about Marcus.

After polishing off her last bite, Leah decided she was done with gardening for the day, and with having uninvited company. She walked outside, tucking her hands into her pockets. Rachel gave her yet another smile. "Just about finished with this section."

"I, uh, I'm pretty tired, actually." Leah rocked on the balls of her feet. "I was going to take a nap. You know, tired from the baby and all that."

Rachel set down the watering can. "Right. Don't worry about it." She grinned. "I've got my Seeder energy fueling me. I can take care of this."

Leah pursed her lips. "I'd feel guilty if I wasn't helping."

Only then did it seem to click with Rachel. She gave an understanding nod. "It wouldn't hurt to give myself a little extra time to get cleaned up and ready for my function tonight."

Swinging her arms with nervous energy, Leah nodded in return. "Thanks for coming over, though. I've got lots of food in the house to last me a while."

"Sounds good." Rachel gathered the gardening tools. "You know where to find me or Guillen if you need anything. Healing ... someone to shop with ... or to pick up books for you ... or anything, alright?"

I'm an adult. I can take care of myself. "Thanks. I'll let you know."

After heading inside, Leah read instead of napping. It was nice to get lost in a fictional world where no one knew her name. Where she didn't exist. Where *other people* were the main characters, and it was *their* problems that had to be overcome.

As Leah crawled into bed, she tried to shut off her brain. She hadn't been very 'gracious' with Rachel, or so Catrina would have said.

Leah was ungrateful. But was she? She acknowledged how lucky she was to have been taken in at the palace. How fortunate she was to be alive in the first place.

She rolled over in bed. How many people could relate to that? How many knew what it felt like to have your right to live deliberated over by dignitaries, by your own family members? Knew what it meant to betray those you loved, and be betrayed by them?

Leah was a tool. No, her mom hadn't trained her to be an assassin, to attack Kaylah as Kaylah had originally thought, but Leah was still a tool. She created chaos in peace. And had once created peace in chaos, but no one knew about that truth, not even Marcus, because that triumph was drowned in pain. In pain and a promise.

She was lucky to be allowed to live. Honestly, she'd be lucky to be allowed to keep her own child. Soren's heir, Soren's legacy.

Scoffing, Leah pondered that one. Maybe she should consent to marrying Marcus. At this point, it would be easier to make everyone else happier. And that was probably what they were waiting on... If Leah and Marcus didn't work out, who would everyone side with? Would Leah even get to keep the baby?

But if I marry him now, isn't that just proving the point that I'm using him, manipulating him? That—like her dad, like her parents—she treated people like tools?

Even after she finally fell asleep, Leah's nightmare of a life haunted her. Her mind gave her a front-row seat to the day she'd learned the truth about her parents. The day she'd lost her mind and almost become a murderer.

Leah, Queen Kaylah, and Leah's mom, Beata, sat together in the manor after the botched wedding luncheon. Leah's eyes were puffy from crying, her throat sore from screaming. The truth was sinking in. And she was sinking too.

Despite everything she'd learned about her mom, Leah couldn't turn her back on her. "I love you too," she said, then faced Kaylah. "What's going to happen to us?"

Kaylah glanced between the two. "It hasn't been decided yet."

Leah had nothing left. No parents. No family. No friends. No Marcus. No trust. No self. Her heart and hope were gone. "If you kill her, you should kill me too."

"No!" Beata screamed.

Kaylah furrowed her brow. "Why would you say that?"

Leah exhaled. "Because I never would have been born if you'd caught my mom when you did my dad. Why should it be any different now?"

Kaylah spun. "Is that what you told her?! No wonder she tried to kill me!"

Beata returned her anger. "You would have put me right next to Soren. Don't deny it!"

Kaylah balled her fists. "I would like to think I'd have given you the benefit of the doubt, to confirm whether you were pregnant first!"

"So, what? I'd give birth. You'd take her straight away and make her an orphan then? That's better, right?"

Kaylah narrowed her eyes. "Did you get knocked up hoping for a pardon?"

"No!"

Leah trembled, the last ounce of her identity crumbling before her. "Can I please go?" she begged.

Over two years later, that scene still tore through her mind, awake or sleeping. But now, Leah had more information. Her mom *hadn't* gotten pregnant hoping for a pardon. Her parents hadn't planned to get pregnant either. Nor was Leah an accident.

The truth of Leah's conception, if the realm knew it, would bring thunderous applause. And in so doing, would shatter her more than she already was.

Somewhere between rest and restlessness, her mom's words whispered to her: *You and me, we're the same.*

Chapter 11

The rest of the week was fine. Leah read nonfiction books during the mornings, and fiction during the evenings. For an hour or two around lunch each day, she did more work in the garden. She was surprised Rachel didn't stop by to help more since she'd seemed so insistent, but then she dared to poke her head out the front door, and found a letter Rachel had left her at some point.

Let us know if you need anything. Love, Rachel & Guillen

Leah didn't need anything. Sure, the fresh food was dwindling, and the garden was growing slowly because she hadn't dared to try fertilizing it with her vines, and she still hadn't picked up the book from the library about Ivy powers during pregnancy. But she was fine. She didn't need anything from anyone.

As the weekend approached, Leah's smile came back. She looked forward to spending every available moment with Marcus.

It was already dark by the time he returned to the cottage, but his face was heavenly and happy. They took a few minutes to talk about their weeks, mostly about his adventure with his internship, and then made their way to the bedroom. She fell asleep wearing only the new bracelet he'd brought her back, and she'd be okay if that was all she wore for the entire weekend.

The next morning, she mentioned how scruffy his face was, so he took time to shave. He was finishing up while she brushed her teeth in the bathroom.

"You know..." he said playfully. "I figured out why you don't want to marry me."

The vise tightened.

He wiggled his razor. "No *marry* me because you're not used to waking up next to the *hairy* me."

She looked away. Bad puns and rhymes were kinda their thing, but it was insensitive to keep bringing marriage up.

"Hey." His voice was soft. "It's just a joke."

"I don't like that kind of joke."

He took her hand, rubbing it with his thumb. "Sorry."

"Yeah. I'm gonna get dressed and check on the garden."

"I'll meet you out there."

Leah doubted anything in the garden actually needed attention; she'd mostly wanted to take a moment to enjoy her makeshift swing. She walked herself forward and backward, seated on the swing, her feet never leaving the ground.

Marcus joined her, holding her from behind and kissing her neck. "Mmm. Do you need any luck today?" He grazed her neck with his lips again.

"Don't you dare give me a raspberry."

"Ouch! Here I am, trying to help…"

She rolled her eyes and smirked at the same time. "Always trying to help."

"I could give you a good-luck raspberry on your belly."

That made her wrinkle her nose.

"For the baby." He stuck out his tongue.

She chuckled softly. "He or she can wait to enjoy that once they properly meet you."

He beamed. He was going to be a good dad. She hated fighting with him, and luckily, their fights were usually short.

Usually.

Marcus gently pulled her back on the swing. "So, what are our plans this weekend?"

"Plans?"

"Yeah. I've got to go to the market for a few things, right?"

"Well, yeah."

"Do you want to get out of the house and come with?"

She winced. "Would you hate it if I didn't?"

"That's fine. You grow a mini-us, and I can easily drop by the market solo."

She'd venture out there again. She would. Just … not right now.

"Any other plans?" he asked.

"No…"

He stopped swinging her, and stood in front of her. "How do you feel about dropping by my parents' place? Maybe for dinner?"

She frowned, her hands dropping from the swing's vines into her lap. "You said it would just be you and me this weekend. You promised."

"I… Well, you know… It's only a couple of hours. C'mon."

"You *promised*," she said, deflated.

"I know." He rubbed the bracelet on her wrist. "But they're excited to hear all about my internship, too."

Trying to keep calm, she took a breath. "Did you already tell them we'd come by?"

"No. But I told them I'd ask you."

She huffed, stood, and stomped back inside the cottage. *Men are stupid.*

"What was that about?" he asked, entering behind her.

"You told them you'd ask me?"

"Yeah. I didn't want to make the decision without you." He was clueless.

"And if we don't go, then they'll know it's all my fault."

He pressed his lips together.

"Yeah," she said.

"Sorry."

She rubbed her face, then tugged on her hair. "I've had enough time with your mom this week."

Don't you love my son? Why won't you marry him? I know better than you. Let me do the chores you're too lazy to do.

Marcus narrowed his eyes. "What's that supposed to mean?"

"She's dropped by twice, uninvited."

"She was only trying to help, and support us."

"Support you, Marcus. You."

He folded his arms. "My mom *loves* you. She's trying to make the best of this, okay? It would be good for you to spend more time together."

"Why? She and I were fine before we moved into this place."

"Because she knows what it's like to marry into the royal family. She understands what the pressure is like. She understands a lot of what you're going through and just wants to help."

Leah clenched her fists. Marriage, again. Pressure? Rachel was a saint who didn't tarnish the royal line. Understood Leah? Guillen couldn't even get Rachel pregnant. She had no idea what this felt like!

Someone with a perfect little tight-knit happy family like Marcus would never understand what it was like to be an orphan, to come from such a broken family.

He'd wanted the thrill of dating Leah. Of sneaking around at the palace. He liked the bad girl in the bedroom. But he didn't really want Leah for a wife, not the way she was. He wanted a girl like his mom.

"I am *not* your mother," she snapped.

His tone matched hers. "I didn't say you were. Why do you have to get so worked up about this? You know, this is your fault."

Heat rose in her cheeks.

He continued. "You didn't like Aunt Catrina's rules. Fine. But you didn't have to be so … *crazy*. You didn't have to call her a bitch."

"*My* fault?" Her voice shook. "*You* got the wrong birth control tonic for me. You were supposed to buy the clove one, *not* the tea tree one."

His eyes grew wide as he realized his mistake. The clove was effective for short-term. The tea tree was for long-term and should have been taken regularly for a while to work. "Then why didn't you tell me before we did anything?"

"Because I didn't look up the difference until I recognized my symptoms days later!"

His face was apologetic, but then he dredged deeper. "It was a mistake. But that doesn't mean you can walk all over people trying to help you."

She rolled her eyes.

"You don't like being compared to my mom?" he said. "Would you rather I compare you to *yours*?"

That was dangerous ground.

"What's that supposed to mean?"

"Just … never mind." He swiped a hand through the air, heading to the bedroom.

No. Never mind? You didn't get to insult someone, comparing them to a somewhat neglectful, somewhat homicidal person, and then simply say 'never mind.'

She followed him. "What about my mom? Where does she even play into this?"

"I don't want to argue."

"Too late."

He eyed her for far too long. "Fine. Let's get it out. Let's say what needs to be said."

She planted her hands on her hips. "Go for it. I'm dying to know."

"I don't say anything about your visits to your mother, but I hope you understand that she will *never* get to meet our child."

Leah hadn't considered it all that much. And while she agreed in concept, she didn't like being told what she could or could not do. So instead of doing the wise thing, she doubled down, she dug her heels in.

"You don't get to tell me what I can or can't do, Marcus."

He was just as upset as she was. "I do on this."

"Yeah?" Maybe she really did need a palate cleanser, and not just from his family, but from him, too. "If you say so. I'll stay away from my mom. Far away. I'm glad I thought to bring my passport."

Shock flooded his features. "The human world? No!"

"I could go. I could disappear. You wouldn't have to worry about me ruining your reputation or career, or getting between you and your mom. My mom and I survived just fine over there for years without anyone finding us."

"Yeah, that worked out great, didn't it?!"

She clenched her fists. "No one's stopping me." Catrina hadn't stopped her from leaving the palace, and she probably would be content with Leah disappearing altogether.

He looked her dead in the eyes, his voice calm but firm. "I could stop you. And you know it."

A lead weight slammed down in her gut. That was the exact kind of threat she'd heard him utter once before. Only once. *I think we both know this could get* much *worse for you.* She hadn't understood Marcus's threat to Tanner back in high school, but she did now.

That was the kind of flex the nephew to the queen could make. *He* wouldn't stop Leah from leaving. She was stronger than him with her powers. He could *have* her stopped.

And he was right. Not a single part of her doubted in that moment that Catrina would choose him, that everyone would.

Leah grasped at straws. "You don't even have proof the baby's yours. Maybe it's not. Maybe you don't deserve to have a say in anything I or my baby do."

He reached for ammunition, and found it. "Wouldn't surprise me. You did sleep around before me, right?"

Exactly one person knew how much that insult would hurt. She'd only confided in *one* person the details of her sex life. And that one person also knew that not all of her sexual encounters had been fully consensual.

She choked on her words, unable to reply. He was that one person.

"But I think we both know that's mine." He glanced at her stomach. "We both know it will come out a Boman like its father. And that there's not a *single* Boman in the entire realm, on the entire planet, other than me, that would ever screw you."

And that was it. With white-hot rage, her hand flew through the air, her palm connecting with his face with the loudest *slap* she'd ever heard.

Marcus stumbled back onto the bed, clutching his cheek, his mouth agape.

She held back a whimper, realizing what she'd just done. "Get out."

His nostrils flared as he stared at her. "Done." He got up, and she sidestepped out of the way. Grabbing his wallet from a basket near the door, he turned to her. "I'll be up north if you come to your senses."

As her heart broke completely, she gritted out her goodbye. "Don't hold your breath."

He slammed the door behind him as he exited. She watched out the window, hugging herself, her heart racing, her breathing rapid.

Only when he was far down the lane did she allow herself to fall apart.

She crumpled to the floor, sobbing and hyperventilating.

Her hand stung.

He shouldn't have said half of the things he'd said. But she'd just made things immeasurably worse for herself. His aunt was the queen. Slap a commoner—that's assault. Slap a member of the royal family?

And even if Catrina let Leah off the hook, the court of public opinion never would. She'd hit a Boman. After trying for two years to prove she wasn't an unstable bigoted assassin like her parents, she'd smacked her boyfriend.

And it hadn't been a regular slap. Her Ivy energy had boosted that. She'd used her powers against him. She'd used powers against someone born without them.

Leah would never recover from this.

Breathing and crying too hard, she threw up on the wood floor.

Much later, Leah had cleaned up her mess. She was too jittery to do anything other than go into the backyard and power-weed, yanking out everything in sight from the garden beds still needing to be overhauled. As she took the last of the weeds to the compost pile, her eyes fixed on the bracelet she wore, the one Marcus had just brought her.

She'd done the wrong thing. But so had he. He had no right to use her past mistakes against her. With tears in her eyes, she undid the clasp and let it fall into the compost heap.

After returning to the cottage, she made peppermint tea to soothe her stomach, and a light meal. And then she stared at the wall, replaying their entire day together. How had they made love that morning, and by noon, thrown away everything?

Leah flexed and unflexed her hand time and time again. She'd hit him. She'd *hit* him. After growing up with an abusive 'aunt,' Leah had promised herself she would *never* be that person. Anger didn't justify physical violence. But she didn't cry again. She was too hollow and hopeless to find tears. She just stared at her hands as the sun set.

Darkness fell. Marcus didn't return, and no one came for Leah. She needed to sleep this all off like the nightmare it was. Using a striker, she lit a beeswax candle, then took it to the bedroom.

It was comfy, and she desperately needed that rest, but the magnet had been flipped, and her safe haven now pushed her away instead of drawing her in. The thought of lying alone in the bed they'd shared was too much. She grabbed a pillow and quilt, tucking them under her arm, and picked up the candle, returning to the living room and crashing on the sofa.

Chapter 12

Leah woke late again. What was there to do or look forward to? Absolutely nothing. She stared at the bookshelf and couldn't imagine picking up a single one of those books.

Eventually, after multiple loud protests from her stomach, she found the will to roll off the sofa and get food.

As she surveyed the mostly empty counter, something through the window caught her eye—movement from the backyard.

And then her jaw dropped. Rachel was back, finishing up more seeds in the freshly cleared area of the garden. Leah's breathing became shallow. There was exactly a zero percent chance she was going to join her out there. Not after her fight with Marcus yesterday. She took a step back, hoping to slip past the windows and hide. And then Rachel glanced in her direction.

Crap. Leah swallowed and continued her retreat.

Marcus wasn't due back north yet. He might have been mad enough to storm off to the closest rifting cave and spend the rest of his free weekend there, but he might just as easily be staying at his parents' place.

Leah sat cross-legged on the bedroom floor, resting her face in her palms, waiting for Rachel to go away. How much time passed, Leah was unsure, but longer than a few minutes later, and sooner than she'd imagined (approximately when hell would freeze over), a knock sounded on the back door. Rachel's audacity...

What was Leah going to do? Huddle on the bedroom floor forever? Rachel and Guillen had bought this cottage for Tobias and Camry; they had a spare key. She and Leah had made eye contact—she knew Leah was inside.

Praying to whatever deities may exist out there, Leah hoisted herself up and approached the back door.

She shyly opened it. "Hi."

Rachel was all business, no smiles. "Everything's planted." She reached down, lifting a giant basket of fruits and vegetables far too easily. Leah's Ivy energy made her perhaps twice as strong as Marcus if she focused, but Rachel's Seeder energy was easily double that of Leah's.

"Here," Rachel said. "This should last you a while."

"Thanks..." A little perplexed, Leah accepted it.

But Rachel didn't keep her waiting. "I don't know why you getting pregnant makes me the bad guy here, Leah. I don't."

Leah set the basket behind her. *Okay, so maybe she just thinks I'm frustrated because I didn't go to dinner or the cave? Or she picked up on it when she helped in the garden last?*

Leah sighed. "I don't expect you to understand. It's complicated. You can't ... get pregnant." How could Rachel understand? Seeders didn't go through that whole thing like Ivies or humans did. And Ivies—even Ivy Bomen—couldn't reproduce with Seeders, so she and Guillen could fool around together every day of their lives without any sort of birth control or protection, without the fear of an accidental pregnancy. Leah *had* hoped Catrina would be more understanding, given she herself was pregnant right now, but she'd been born an heir to the throne, and hadn't married or started popping out kids until she was in her thirties.

Rachel nodded. "You know, Leah..." She pursed her lips, considering. "You're not the only one that's gone through hard things, or has had tough decisions to make. It's bold of you to assume I can't relate to you in any way. Or that I've never wished to experience the miracle of life in that way." There was a hint of sadness in her voice that Leah hadn't heard before.

Humbled, Leah softly apologized.

Tucking her hands in her pockets, Rachel opened her mouth again. "Has my son ever hurt you?"

Leah's heart skipped a beat. "No... Not physically."

Visibly agitated, Rachel eyed her. "So, when you hurt my son, it wasn't in self-defense?"

Leah froze, absolutely paralyzed. He had told his mom. Fear raced through Leah as she recalled with perfect clarity the most terrifying part of the day when she'd tried to assassinate Kaylah. It hadn't been Kaylah who had really frightened Leah, or even the guards who had yanked Leah away. It had been Marcus's mom.

Rachel's eyes had glowed an unnatural Seeder-green that day. *I liked you, Leah. And so did Marcus. But I've had to kill for my family. I won't let anyone hurt them.*

Her would-be future mother-in-law had essentially threatened Leah's life that day. And Leah had earned it. Had she again?

"I didn't mean to," Leah breathed.

Rachel was a war hero, as was Guillen. Leah felt two inches tall right now, easily squished under an angry boot—no Seeder blades or throwing knives necessary.

Rachel's expression was tense, but all she did was shake her head and walk away toward the side gate, which led to the front yard.

Only then did Leah let out a shaky breath, shutting and locking the door. She hefted the huge basket of produce and lugged it to the kitchen.

Still calming down, she braced herself against the counter. *Why did he have to do that?* How immature was Marcus to run to his parents and tattle on Leah? Their whole argument had started because he'd made her the bad guy with his parents over a stupid dinner visit. But now? Now he'd dragged them *fully* into their relationship.

Unable to force herself to unpack the groceries yet, she turned to the living room, ready to flop back on the sofa.

And then something caught her eye from the front door window.

"Seriously?!" It wasn't Rachel. Rachel had worn a lavender shirt; this figure wore a dark green shirt, simply standing there, not knocking.

Leah stalked to the front door, pulling it open. "Excuse me, can I help—"

The figure turned, a familiar middle-aged blond smiling back at Leah.

She didn't return the smile. "Wren? What are you doing here?" He'd been one of her regularly assigned escorts. She was nervous to hear the answer.

He nodded. "Miss Eleana. Just doing my job." He pulled an envelope from his jacket pocket, handing it to her.

She anxiously eyed the wax seal on it—Queen Catrina's.

Carefully pulling the seal off, Leah unfolded it and read the letter. It was short. She was unimpressed. "Do you know what this says?"

Wren gave a shy look indicating he did, which made sense.

"Tell her my answer is no."

"Miss Eleana..."

"No. And my name is Leah. We're not at the palace. You can call me Leah."

"Leah," he replied softly. "It would be in your best interest—"

"Her letter said it was a *request* to come to the palace to speak with her. A request can be denied. It's not a command, demand, order, or edict. I can say no, and I do." She handed him back the letter. "I have nothing to say to her. You're lucky you still have a job after working with me. Other servants aren't so lucky. That's your queen for you."

All duty, Wren nodded, tucking the letter back into his pocket. "Then I'll continue my appointment here."

"This is only a one-bedroom cottage. I don't have anywhere for you to sleep..."

"Your escorts are being put up at the nearest inn."

Great. More expense on my behalf that people can balk at.

"I'm not inviting you in, and I intend to go nowhere, so I hope you enjoy standing outside, rain or shine."

He gave her a patient smile. Or maybe it was condescending? "I do my duty as needed, miss."

Duty. Always about duty. "It's Leah. Have a good day."

She closed the door and dove back under the quilt on the sofa. And there she planned to stay the rest of the day. Maybe the rest of her life. Under guard, a pariah, she'd remain there until she and her unborn child died of old age and sheer spite.

The next few days were quiet. Leah *wanted* peace and quiet. Though perhaps not *quite* so much... Especially when it left her to her guilt and anger and thoughts.

So, she threw herself back into the books. She binged most of the fiction books first, throwing in the occasional nonfiction book, skimming over the parts that mentioned her parents. She was tired of hearing about them.

Her entire week consisted of reading, snacking, gardening, and trying to forget how much she missed Marcus. And hated him. And hated herself.

It gutted her each time she walked by the empty bedroom. Her heart ached each time she found herself with her hand on her stomach, or wanted to talk about something happening in a book she was reading, just to realize she had no one to talk to.

Her escorts were positioned at the front door around the clock. She gave them a chair to at least be able to relax. It wasn't their fault Catrina had ordered them to keep her locked up.

As the weekend approached, Leah decided to take care of something she'd been neglecting—writing a letter. She visited her mom in prison monthly, and her visit was already past due. Her mom understood Leah's life was busy, or at least that it had been, so it wasn't like they met on the same day every month, but still. Leah didn't want to worry her.

Sitting at the breakfast nook, Leah hovered a pen over paper. She needed to explain why she wasn't coming to visit. She really did need to just leave the cottage, but some overly cautious part of her feared that if she left, she might never come back. She was a squatter right now, and maybe the escorts were the family's way of drawing her out so they could evict her.

And she didn't have it in her to break the pregnancy news to her mom yet, especially not in a letter. Her mom had stressed that she would always love Leah. Would she now? As Leah rested a hand on her slowly growing stomach, her lips formed a faint smile. It was an odd connection she couldn't explain. Then her smile faded. Could her mom ever love a Boman grandchild, given Beata and her family's part in history as oppressors of Bomen?

This was definitely a conversation to have in private and in person. With the way things were going, how long would it be until Leah was comfortable going out to visit her mom again?

Hey Mom,

Sorry I haven't been able to visit. Things are going great at the academy and with studies.

She scratched out each word, recalling the runaway note she'd once left for her mom in the human world.

My schedule's been so crazy. I'll be touring a bit, and Marcus's family surprised me with some fun getaway plans, and I'll probably spend some time visiting him on his internship, so I just wanted you to know what I was up to if I'm not able to visit you for a little while. If I can't come by, I'll definitely drop you a letter. I hope you're doing alright.

Love you,

Eleana

It was bad to lie. While Leah had always technically known that, she hadn't always strictly followed the rule to not lie. Was it wrong to lie now?

She folded the letter, addressed it, and opened the front door.

"Miss." Wren nodded in greeting.

"Wren." She held the letter tight in her hand. It now dawned on her that she hadn't even taken five steps out the front door since arriving at the cottage. Sure, she'd explored the entirety of the large backyard, but she'd been holed up pretty tight here.

"Going somewhere?" he asked.

As she was still in pajamas, surely he knew the answer to that. But her legs didn't move. The backyard was mostly private, with brick walls and bushes. The front yard was so exposed.

"Would you like me to take that to the postbox?" he asked.

She gave him an appreciative frown. "Thanks."

The postbox was only a few yards down the walk, but she was grateful for the gesture.

"I needed to stretch my legs anyway." He strolled to the edge of the property, deposited the letter, and turned back with a smile. "You're making my job too hard."

She returned the smile. "You like to read, right, Wren?" He'd snuck a book out of his pocket now and then while standing guard.

"That I do."

"Have you ever read *Valeska and the Wandering Soldier*?"

"Of course."

"Is it part of a series?" she asked. "That was kind of an abrupt ending."

His eyes widened. "There are nine books in that series.(cc) You've only read the first?"

She'd read several novels from the collection at the cottage by now, but there hadn't been a sequel to this book, and the ending had stuck with her. "Yeah. We only have the one here."

"Well, you definitely ought to check out the others." He paused, surveying her. "If you'd like to dress, I'd happily escort you to the library."

She frowned again. "That's ... okay. Thanks for the offer." Resting her hand on the door handle, she prepared to go back inside.

"It's a pity." His voice was playful as he sat on the chair. "If I were you, I'd *die* to know what happens to the mutant Seeder troop we never hear from again in book one."

"Right?! Like, what even was the—" She stopped as a smirk slid onto his face. She cocked her head. "What happens to them?"

Wren shook his head, pulling his current read out of a pocket. "I don't give spoilers, Miss Eleana. I'm strictly against them."

They both knew what he was doing. It had usually been all business with her escorts during her time at the palace, but if she had to pick favorites, he'd be in her top two.

Still, she was nowhere courageous enough to venture from the cottage yet. "Maybe down the road. Thanks, though."

"Let me know when you're ready."

She wished him a good day and headed inside. It was only a silly book. She didn't *need* to know more. And she hadn't finished all the other books in the cottage yet anyway.

Settling on the sofa, Leah picked up her current read. She struggled to get back into it, her mind on the cliffhanger of *Valeska and the Wandering Soldier*, and on her letter to her mom, and the fact that she hadn't heard from Marcus all week.

Maybe... Maybe he'd realize how hurtful he'd been, how much of an idiot he'd been. Maybe he'd just needed the week to cool off, and he'd come back and apologize.

She flexed the hand she'd used to slap him, tears forming in her eyes. And then she'd apologize too, once he came back.

If he came back.

They'd 'taken a break' in the human world for an entire month when he'd found out she had a shoplifting habit. By the time he would come around after she hit him, she would probably be celebrating their child's fifth birthday.

Leah sniffled, took a sip of water, and forced herself to reread the last page she'd read without taking anything in.

Marcus didn't visit that first weekend. Leah cried herself to sleep each night.

She didn't need him. She didn't need anyone. Her life had been a revolving door of boyfriends, family, and acquaintances. Marcus was no exception. He'd stayed longer than most people in her life, but that simply meant it would take longer to get over him.

Leah didn't need Marcus. She could be a single mom like hers had been, and a better one. At least that was what she told herself every time she was on the brink of tears again.

Naps, garden, books—they became her daily life. She was fine. Just fine. Her maternal sickness was even finally easing up.

A few days down the road, a knock at the door startled her as she prepared a snack. She peeked around the corner, spotting none other than Wren at the front door, waving an envelope.

Leah wiped her hands on her jeans and ran to the front door. She took the envelope from him and immediately recognized the prison's stationery. She smiled, happy to get a quick response from her mom. "Thanks."

"You're welcome."

She paused, suddenly self-conscious. *What kind of person smiles about getting a letter from a war criminal?* She folded it and tucked it into her pocket. "So, what book are you reading today?"

Wren perched on his chair. "*Saltzer's Triangle.*"

"Never heard of it." She had admittedly not been a bookworm before this fiasco, with human literature or green-folk.

"If you liked *Valeska and the Wandering Soldier*, you might enjoy it."

She shrugged. "Cool. I just finished *The Hippo Ride.*"

Wren arched an eyebrow, clearly intrigued. All animal life in the Green Lands was small. Nothing that large and beastly resided here, but most green folk had a fascination for, or at least curiosity about, the human world.

"You know what a hippo is, right?" she asked.

"I do."

Leah sat on the step near him. "So, it's..." She almost called it urban fantasy, but that was her human-world childhood kicking in. Wren was born and raised Ivy. Since the book was written by an Ivy author, but the setting was the human world, she guessed it would be considered high fantasy for them? "Well, it's all in the human world."

"Did you like it?"

Leah briefly described the plot, which she'd rather enjoyed, but struggled to get past some of the glaring worldbuilding errors. It was obvious the author hadn't done any research. Hippos weren't bright purple, nor could they fly, though since it was fantasy, she could forgive those. But the descriptions of the setting—New York City—were horrendous. The characters walked through cornfields, and sharks swam in rivers that snaked through the metropolis.

She and Wren chatted for some time about whether the author had intended it to be read comedically or if those were in fact errors. She genuinely didn't think they were intentional.

"Well..." Wren pursed his lips. "I'll have to check it out and see if I agree with you on that."

Leah pointed to the door behind her. "Do you want to borrow this copy?"

He was hesitant.

She was sure Tobias and Camry would understand, as long as he didn't take it off their property. It wasn't like they were around often enough to enjoy it, as this was their second home and they were usually over at Rachel and Guillen's place when visiting the realm anyway.

But she understood his reluctance. He was already being paid by the queen to sit around and read fiction right now instead of using his extensive training to ensure Leah wasn't being murdered. Accepting a book was probably pushing things a bit too far.

In that moment, though, she realized how at ease she'd been, just sitting down to talk books with someone. She realized how lonely she truly was, how much she missed interactions after being surrounded by servants at the palace.

"Well, if you do decide to find a copy at the library, let me know, and we could ... talk ... about what you think... If you want."

His expression was kind and thoughtful. He had to know, right? Even if he was in the dark about what Leah was going through, he'd been there for eight hours a day, and she'd yet to leave the property, hadn't had a single visitor. The escorts always exchanged information at the change of shift, so the others would know she hadn't left, either.

Leah stood, ready to go inside.

"You know, Miss Eleana, I think I'll take you up on it."

She instantly smiled.

"I'll probably finish my current book midshift today, and I didn't bring a new one. I'd love to borrow that book. Unless..." He cleared his throat. "Unless you'd prefer to go to the library. Then we could both get a new book to read."

She gave him a look to say she knew exactly what he was trying to do, and he chuckled. Hopping inside, she grabbed the book and handed it to him. "But if I catch you dog-earing that, Tobias and Camry might kill me."

"Dog-ear?"

Then *she* chuckled. "Dogs—human pets... Sometimes their ears flop over like that." She demonstrated with her hands on her head. "Don't bend the pages."

He gasped. "I would never!" He gave her a bright, toothy smile. "I'll take good care of this."

"I hope you like it."

"Do most dogs do that? With the ears? I haven't spent much time over there on vacations."

"Um... A decent number, I guess? I'm not really a dog expert."

"Did you ever have a dog companion when you lived in the human world?"

She tried not to frown. "No. We moved around too much, and it would have been too much to keep track of." Not only had she wished for a dog as a kid, but questions like that reminded her too well that everyone in the realm knew her past. She and Wren hadn't ever conversed so casually before, but whether he thought it a sob story to pity or a sensational story to savor, he was far more aware of her story than she was of his.

"That's a shame," he said politely.

"Yeah." She rubbed the pocket she'd forgotten her mom's letter was tucked in. "I guess I'll get back to what I was doing. Thanks for my letter and for the chat. Enjoy the book."

Closing the front door behind her, Leah drew a deep breath. She quickly finished making the snack she'd been preparing before the letter came, then sat down to eat and read.

Her mom's letter was nice and long, which was unsurprising, as she had all the time in the world serving her life sentence. She expressed how much she missed Leah, the good things she'd been doing for community service from the confines of the prison, how she hoped Leah could visit soon despite her busy schedule. She seemed to have bought Leah's lies about what she was up to.

At the bottom of the letter, Leah kept reading the same words over and over.

Love always.

But did her mom really? Always? And would she really? Always?

Chapter 13

Marcus didn't visit the next weekend either. Leah was fine. Just fine.

She was fine because she *didn't* struggle to sleep. At least … not *that much*. And she was fine as she devoured more books, and found herself discussing them on a regular basis with Wren.

And she was absolutely, most definitely fine when she took down the large painting that had been a wedding gift from her and Marcus, relocating it to the bedroom closet so she wouldn't have to look at it every day.

She was a little less fine when she spent a good two hours straight staring at a photo of Tobias and Camry's human-world wedding. She'd been absent, having ruined their first wedding attempt. She analyzed Marcus's smile in the photo. She'd used him. She'd manipulated him.

And … then she bawled and turned the framed picture facedown on the bedroom dresser.

She was ashamed the first time she realized she'd lost track of the days, of what day of the week it even was. They all blended together.

The garden grew slowly. Painfully slowly. But she wasn't starving yet.

One day, Leah knelt at the garden box of tomato plants, using her own vines to wrap around stakes in the corners. She contained the growing plants, leaning them against her vines for support. She and her mom had never planted anything in all their years in the human world. They'd moved too often to be able to harvest anything they would have sown, and neither of them had really been the green-thumb type anyway. Luckily, there was a booklet in the nonfiction part of the bookshelf that addressed gardening basics.

She hadn't been inside more than five minutes before a knock at the front door surprised her. It wasn't one of Wren's special knocks, either.

When she reached the door, her stomach knotted. Guillen. Why not? One by one, every member of Marcus's family and the royal family would inevitably try to convince Leah to do the 'proper' thing and marry Marcus, to put aside her own reservations. Or ... he could be there as a government official about her battering a Boman...

Nervous, she opened the door. "Hi, Guill— Um ... Sir Guillen."

Guillen pressed his lips into a thin line. "Huh... We've never been that formal before, you and I..." His voice held its usual calm, but his eyes searched her.

"Well, I..." She just stood there. He had to know about her slapping his son. He had to have been fed up that she was squatting at his other son's property, her life and career prospects wasting away one day at a time.

"I'm not usually one to invite myself in, but could we talk?" he asked.

She gulped. "Sure, come in." As she perched on the edge of the sofa, he eased down on a chair opposite her. His gaze took in her bedding—still a mess on the sofa—and her shame was complete.

"Is, uh..." he started.

"It's more comfortable than the bed, that's all." That was a blatant lie. Night after night on the sofa was taking a toll on her back, but she still couldn't fathom spending another night in that bedroom without Marcus.

Guillen rubbed his knee, his expression somewhat skeptical. "We'll have to see about replacing that mattress, if it's not comfortable."

"No, it's... I rotate between them."

He silently nodded. "How are you doing, Leah?"

"I'm fine."

"Is that an American human fine? Or a real fine?"

She furrowed her brow.

"A polite lie? Or a genuine answer?"

She averted her gaze, fidgeting with her hands. "How can I help you?"

Guillen's voice was ever so soft. "You're his world. You know that, right?"

That wasn't fair. And that wasn't true. Marcus would be here with her if that were true.

"You've seen him?" she asked, still not looking Guillen in the eye.

"Yes."

She couldn't bring herself to ask how Marcus was doing. If he was fine, she'd die on the spot. If he was miserable, she'd feel he deserved it, but somehow also feel more miserable herself.

Guillen blew out a long breath. "My sister wants what's best for you."

Leah's jaw tightened. *Right. Defending his little sister, the queen.*

"*And* she wants what's best for the kingdom..."

Crossing her arms, Leah remained silent.

"She's not perfect," he said. "She... Well, she was more sheltered than I was about some things growing up. And she's trying her best. I wish you'd go speak with her."

Over my dead body.

"Right... I'm not her messenger. That isn't why I came today."

Leah finally met his gaze, curious, worried.

Guillen ruffled his hair. "Here's the thing, Leah. I might be the only person in the family who will say this, but I feel it's important."

She hated when people talked that way—'the family,' as opposed to 'Marcus's family' and 'Leah's family.' It reminded her that, no matter how distant it was, they were already related. Marcus was her second cousin through adoption. Guillen was her first cousin once removed. Had she understood what any of that meant when she'd moved to the Green Lands? Heck no. Had she researched it thoroughly and made sure marrying second cousins through adoption was legal and not completely freaky after they'd discovered they were? Absolutely.

Guillen continued. "If you don't love my son, I don't want you to marry him."

She didn't know whether to be relieved or insulted. It hadn't been a matter of not loving Marcus, right? This whole disaster had come about because...

"I know what it's like to be raised in a home where..." Guillen spoke slowly, deliberately. "Where my parents were not equals."

A knife to the chest. No, Leah was not Marcus's equal. Not in breeding or education. Not in action or reputation. She never had been, and she never would be. *You're only using him,* a voice not completely her own whispered.

"My parents didn't share mutual respect," Guillen said. "There was an imbalance of power, and just..." He pursed his lips, taking a long while to speak again. "I may be partial here, but I don't want my son in an unhappy marriage."

She willed herself not to cry.

"And frankly, if the two of you aren't meant to be together, then you and that child deserve better, too."

His soft blue eyes were piercing, thoughtful. It took everything she had to breathe normally, to not fall apart on the spot.

Interlacing his fingers, Guillen asked, "Do you want that baby?"

"Yes," she croaked.

This whole exchange was painful. His kind tone, his gentle mannerisms. "Then. ... congratulations."

He hadn't said it with an ounce of sarcasm or malice, but it sent her into full-on tears. No one had congratulated her yet. She hadn't even thought of it that way for herself.

Scooting to the edge of his seat, Guillen wore an expression of concern and compassion. "Do you want a hug?"(dd)

Even as tears cascaded down her cheeks, she shook her head.

"Can I help?"

She didn't like people to see her cry. "No."

"Okay..."

After a minute of her trying to regain her composure, he stood and strode to the bathroom, returning with a handkerchief.

Leah calmed herself. "Thanks."

"Of course." He stayed standing. "You know where he's staying up north, right? I could get you the address..."

She sniffled. "He knows where I'm staying too."

Guillen's smile was an ironic one. "Perhaps you two are matched. You certainly both know how to be ... a fair bit stubborn."

She blew her nose.

"Anyway," he said, resting his hand on the door handle, "it's a common trait with us Elontas, Elannas, and Elontos... I'll get out of your hair. Please let Rachel and me know if you need anything."

She nodded to be polite.

"We love you, Leah."

She choked back more tears, unable to reciprocate. Desperately wanting a hug, but far too proud to ask.

"Have a good rest of your day." He opened the door, uttered a goodbye to Wren, and closed the door behind him.

Leah stood and peeked out the door's window as Guillen strolled down the lane. She unintentionally caught Wren's gaze for the briefest moment. He examined her, a pitying frown on his lips. Ashamed, she ignored him and returned to the sofa.

She had permission to not marry Marcus if she didn't want to.

Why hadn't the weight lifted?

It doesn't matter, a brutal, icy voice whispered in her mind. *You will never deserve Marcus, and you don't deserve his child. You should have never even been born.*

The next morning, Wren's signature knock roused Leah from the sofa. She greeted him, still ashamed he'd seen her on the verge of losing it the day before.

"Miss Eleana." He gave her a single polite nod, as always. And then he handed her a book.

Holding it in both hands, she read the title. "*Valeska and the Lost Troop?*" She met his gaze. "Is this...?"

He gave her an encouraging smile. "The second book in the series?"

She could have hugged him, not that she would. Before Catrina had fully realized Leah was not a hugger (at least not with anyone other than Marcus and her mom), she'd established the rule that Leah should not hug any of the servants or staff. It wasn't proper. And when she had—that night when she'd been relieved to have Robyn's help—she'd cost Robyn her job. Maybe her poison wasn't limited to her vines; maybe her hugs and very essence were poison to people, imparting misfortune.

"Thank you," she breathed, clutching the book to her chest.

"It's from the library, though, so no dog ... earing it." He winked.

"You went to the library for me?"

He swatted a dismissive hand through the air. "Of course not. I was already going there to pick up a new read."

She glanced sideways at a book right inside the cottage, resting on the entryway table. "Did you decide not to finish this one?" He'd bookmarked it halfway through, returning it to her at the end of his shift the day before. It was another book she'd loaned him from Tobias and Camry's collection.

"Well..." Wren cleared his throat. "I sometimes read more than one at a time..."

She handed him the book, and as she met his kind hazel eyes, nothing more needed to be said, other than "Thank you."

"Happy to, miss." He gave her another polite nod, and she stepped inside, ready to finally devour the next book in this intriguing series.

The beginning was a tad slow, and her mind wandered. Was it sad that she had almost even come to consider Wren a friend? Thinking on it, she hadn't really made friends with any of her peers in the Green Lands, not in all this time.

Sure, she'd learned to socialize at balls, and she had her 'friends' at the academy. And Marcus's friends had tolerated her. But she'd become so much closer to the palace staff, honestly. Most of them were older than her, but she could relate to them in a different way. They weren't royalty; they were normal citizens. And that was how she'd always been raised—by a single mom and a hateful 'aunt,' the three of them scraping by.

Leah drew a deep breath, setting the book down after reading the same paragraph a dozen times.

Where were those 'friends' from the academy now? Did any of them even care that she'd stopped attending classes? Probably not. If they did, and they'd inquired as to Leah's location, was Catrina intentionally keeping that information private? Withholding outside contact from Leah until she capitulated to Catrina's demands? Or hiding the truth about Leah's pregnancy because she was so ashamed of it?

Lifting her shirt to expose her belly, Leah stared at it, gently caressing it. She could feel the life within her, even if she wasn't really showing yet. There was perhaps a *little* pooch there.

Just like with Leah's own birth, no one would want this baby to be born. Why did she? Why did she want to inflict herself and her reputation upon this child, just like Leah had always suffered because of her parents' choices?

Life was beautiful. Having already envisioned what the baby would look like, Leah knew this little girl or boy couldn't be anything but adorable. Maybe, in some way, she wanted to keep the baby because she was lonely.

That's not a good reason to have a child.

She swallowed. Perhaps she wanted it because she did still love Marcus, despite everything that had happened, and it was a piece of him.

You sound like your mother.

She bit the insides of her cheeks, still gently massaging her stomach.

He's already left you. You burn bridges. You push people away.

Her throat tightened.

You're selfish. That baby would be better off without you. Everyone would be.

She sniffled, wiping away a tear and promptly pulling her shirt back down.

"Shut up," she whispered, picking up the book again and finding her page. Pushing away the world and the worries, she dug back into *Valeska and the Lost Troop*, promising herself today would be a good day.

Despite Leah rationing it out, her food supply was getting dangerously low. The garden was taking ages to mature. She ought to suck it up and go to the market. Wren was more than willing to escort her.

Yet, the thought of being around so many people was crippling.

Maybe Wren would go to the market for her, like he had the library?

I can't ask him to do that. That wasn't his job. He wasn't a shopping servant; he was an escort, a guard, a protector.

But ... he *had* gone to the library for her...

Leah finished book two by the next day, and thoroughly enjoyed it. She returned the book to Wren, and they chatted a bit about the writing and plot.

"Would you like the next one?" he asked.

"Yes!"

"Would you like me to take you to pick it up?" he asked cautiously.

She bit her lip. She was an adult, and she should act like one. But...

Ending her long hesitant pause, he said, "If not, that's alright. I was already planning to go to the library after my shift."

She gave him a sad, thankful smile. Then it shrank, her nerves taking hold. "If ... if you're willing to exchange this book for me, would you be willing to pick me up another one?"

"I can do that. You want books three and four at the same time?"

Her heart racing, she picked at her nails. "Well, um, no. Actually, yes, that would be nice. But ... something else, too. A nonfiction book."

"I don't see why not."

She studied his face. He already had a faint five-o'clock shadow. His crisp uniform reminded her exactly how much of their 'friendship' was a job for him.

"Do you know ... why I'm here?" she asked. It still hadn't really been discussed between the two.

He squared his shoulders. "It's not really my place, miss."

He had to know something, though, right? "What were you told when she sent you to this cottage? About why I'm not living at the palace anymore?"

Wren's mouth opened slightly, and stayed open for a bit. "I don't know much, Miss Eleana. Obviously, Her Majesty and you are not seeing eye to eye..."

Obviously. Once a week, Catrina sent the same 'request' to come visit with her at the palace. And each time, Leah had declined.

Leah bolstered her courage. The garden *would* grow faster if she knew how to manage her powers during pregnancy, if she could safely and efficiently fertilize it. "I need a book ... about ..." She wrapped her arms around herself. "About Ivy powers during pregnancy."

Wren's eyes flickered to her arms covering her stomach, just for a moment. "Oh." His tone conveyed genuine surprise. "Well, I'm sure I could find something... And be discreet about it."

She took a full breath, relief washing over her. "Thank you."

He narrowed his eyes slightly. "I'm trusting Her Majesty knows this?"

Leah nodded.

He looked at her, his mind obviously working. Would he ask if Marcus was the father? If Marcus knew? If it had anything to do with why Marcus had abandoned her? "I'll see what I can find, then," was all he said.

"Thanks again."

Chapter 14

Wren brought Leah four books from the library—two more of *Valeska's Adventures*, and two about Ivy powers during pregnancy.

She set to work in the garden after skimming the sections on fertilizing abilities.

She ought not to have skimmed. The first plant grew limp and yellow. So, she returned to the cottage and thoroughly studied the texts.

Ivy powers were primarily chemical, mostly having to do with one's train of thought. There was a good deal of meditation required to manage female Ivy powers well during pregnancy.

Between devouring more of *Valeska's Adventures* over the next few days, and practicing meditation exercises, Leah was doing alright.

She finally gave it another go in the garden, extending vine tendrils from her wrists into the soil. She closed her eyes, breathing deeply, envisioning Ivy energy mingling with her Ivy chemicals. She channeled them down from her mind, to her arm, to her vines. Slowly, making sure she wasn't giving too much, she released the mixture into the soil through the small leaves lining her vines.

The change wasn't immediate, but she sat back on the grass to watch. It wasn't a grass yard, really, not in the way she was used to in the human world, in the US. It was a blend of grasses, clovers, and tiny wildflowers. It was cool to the touch, soft under her weight.

The excitement of watching a garden grow was akin to that of watching paint dry. But the sun was bright, the breeze light, the wild buzzing bees happy.

In the end, after a half hour, perhaps a full hour, she could've sworn the fertilizer was working, that the tomato plant she'd tried with looked greener, the vine slightly thicker.

She smiled, content. By the time dusk had come, she'd fertilized the whole garden. She couldn't stay here forever, but the garden would be left after she figured out her life, as a thank you to Tobias and Camry.

After exchanging more books with Wren the next morning, Leah strolled into the garden, her stomach growling, her mouth watering at the prospect of a faster growing garden.

It wasn't an exact science, and there wouldn't be a massive change in the plant growth overnight, especially not with Leah's limited experience.

But she smiled at the bright green garden that greeted her. Plucking a low-hanging plum from a tree, she admired her work. The spinach was broad and leafy, ready to harvest. All the other plants were looking healthy as well, though she'd hoped for more blossoms to peek out.

Reminding herself to be patient, she finished her plum. Raising her hands above her head, Leah shot out vines from her wrists, wrapping them around a sturdy branch. Flooding her arms, shoulders, and back with energy, she pulled herself up and perched on the branch, cautiously balancing herself against the trunk. With hands and vines, she harvested several plums, filling her pockets and easing some down to the ground. After getting back down, she harvested some spinach as well, and returned inside. Plums and spinach weren't exactly a delectable breakfast, but they would do until the other produce came in.

Books and watching the garden consumed more of her days. The garden had transformed into a veritable forest of lush leaves and thick stems and vines.

But ... Leah grew worried. Healthy leaves were great for spinach and lettuce, not as good for squash and tomatoes. There were no buds.

Her heart sank as she recalled more from her studies about fertilizing. This was her fault. She'd thought initially that she had mastered this power, and maybe she had, and it was just the pregnancy causing the problem. But she'd forgotten to consider the differences between the various plants' needs. Too much nitrogen in the mix, and you got all leaves, no fruit.

"Seriously?" she uttered, frowning. She tightened her ponytail, considering her options.

Leah hadn't become a master gardener overnight, and hadn't even used those skills a single time at the palace. She hadn't needed to. Now, she could refertilize, adding more chemicals to try to balance it out, but she might screw up again and make things worse.

Her mouth watered at the fruits and vegetables she could start eating again if she could just get it right. And if she didn't... Stepping forward, she rubbed a leaf of a tomato plant. There was nothing quite like the herbaceous aroma of tomato leaf.(ee) Ivies weren't susceptible to many poisons. Eating leaves from the nightshade family wouldn't harm Leah... She tore off a small leaf and tasted it.

Chewing it around in her mouth, she grimaced. It didn't taste nearly as pleasant as it smelled, and the texture was less than appealing. Still, she forced herself to swallow it.

Sighing, Leah resolved to try to fix the chemicals. She only experimented on a fourth of the garden this time, aiming to not make the same mistake of ruining all the crops.

Shaking her head, she harvested more plums and spinach. At least she hadn't tried fertilizing the trees or bushes.

Energy drained from the exertion of fertilizing, she went inside to eat and nap.

The garden was ... depressing. The correction Leah had given some of the crops seemed to be helping—they were now budding. So, she carefully applied her fertilizer to the rest of them, ensuring her concoction of Ivy energy and chemicals was well-balanced. But how long would it take for these to produce something she could actually eat?

The spinach had all been plucked, but she planted more. For now, she was scrounging what little fruit was still on the trees, and pimple berries from a bush, and picking through the limited dry storage left in the cottage.

She wasn't consuming nearly enough calories, especially not for someone with child. But she'd be okay. She'd be fine. Leah was always fine.

Leah's stomach complained early one morning. Low on energy, she rolled out of her little blanket on the sofa and ambled to the tiny kitchen.

Visions of rich banquets at the palace danced in her memories. She could almost even smell some of the exquisite food she'd become accustomed to.

Pulling herself back to her sad reality, Leah surveyed her meager spread. A healthy handful of buckwheat groats, a small container of coarse cornmeal, half a bottle of oil, seasonings, a precious bag of dried fruit.

She glanced through the kitchen window to the backyard. She'd be fine. This was the Green Lands. This realm was like a paradise. New berries matured each day, fresh sprouts emerged regularly, and things would work out.

Envisioning the worst, she pictured herself kneeling on the grass, harvesting clover—it was technically edible. That much she remembered from her courses.

Leah fought the truth tugging at her. She was doing this to herself. She was imprisoning and debasing and starving herself. No one was doing this to her.

She could trudge the mile to Rachel and Guillen's home to grovel for their forgiveness, to ask for food, to ask Rachel to come back and use her powers to boost the plants' growth.

She could take Wren up on his constant offer to leave the cottage and go to the market. Marcus had stormed out without taking the extra coins he'd brought.

She wouldn't be doing any of those things. Leah was done asking for help. Done taking people's charity and money and simply accepting that she had no other choice.

Everyone was probably aware of her status right now anyway. Perhaps that was part of the 'family plan,' to starve Leah out until she gave in to Catrina's demands.

Leah guzzled extra water and counted out a scant handful of the dried fruit. She sat at the table, nibbling and sipping. Water was good for her anyway, especially since she was pregnant.

Soon enough, Wren's signature knock sounded on the front door.

When she opened it, he gave her a half-smile, as well as the next Valeska book, and a letter from her mom.

"Thanks," she said.

He wasn't his usual self. Not bright or cheerful. He looked like he was prepared to deliver bad news.

"Is anything wrong?" she asked.

Wren bunched his eyebrows. "What do you say to us finally venturing away from here today? Checking out the library and market?"

She flipped the pages of the book in her hands. His trips to the library weren't part of his job, but had been out of the kindness of his heart. The reminder made her feel more guilty.

"I ... can just reread the books I have here," she said.

"And the market?"

That water wouldn't keep her full for long. Somehow, kneeling on all fours and eating clover from the dirt like a cow seemed less intimidating than being in public right now.

"I'm fine."

Standing tall, Wren crossed his arms. "The cold storage in a place like this can't be all that large. I'd imagine the pantry's not all that expansive, either."

She swallowed. "They're surprisingly large for a cottage this size." That was a complete lie.

He nodded, eyeing her. "And you know we patrol the entire property regularly, right? That includes the backyard?"

Her anxiety doubled. *Please don't. Just let it go.* "I know."

"I couldn't help but notice the garden's perhaps not meeting demand," he said.

"It's doing better, thanks to the books you borrowed for me." She turned to head inside.

Resting a hand on the doorframe, Wren stopped her. "We should get you food until the garden produces more."

"No." She stood there, unwilling to budge on the topic. *You've always been a burden, a mistake.*

"If you don't have proper food, I will have to inform Her Majesty." His tone was matter-of-fact.

She spun on him, her heart aching at the betrayal. "Don't you dare. I don't want help. I don't need help. I'll be fine."

"My assignment is to keep you safe," he said, sparing a quick glance at her stomach. "To keep you both safe. And if you're not getting enough to—"

"I'm fine!" she snapped, her eyes burning. "I can take care of myself. I can take care of myself and my child, and it's none of your concern. And Catrina can keep her nose out of my business."

He loosed a soft sigh. "She cares about you."

"No. She doesn't. She cares about appearances. I'm sure she's happy to be rid of me. Everyone is." Marcus, his parents, her 'friends' at the academy. "Queen Catrina doesn't care about me." Her voice shook as tears pricked at her eyes. "Nobody does."

"Miss Eleana—" he started with gentle chastisement.

Leah shoved the book he'd just given her back into his hand, pushing past him, and slammed the door closed, locking it tight.

She lay back down on the sofa, trying to find a comfortable position, slowly breaking into a fit of tears. And her mind fixated on that hidden passport.

What game was she playing? Marcus hadn't so much as sent a single letter after leaving.

She yearned to give that passport a maiden voyage to the human world. To escape this all. Marcus may never come back to her.

But a sinking anxiety stopped her from considering it too seriously. Catrina had probably reinstated the order that Leah was prohibited from leaving the realm, like she'd been for ages after her attempt on Kaylah's life.

Plus, going to the human world likely meant permanently cutting ties with this realm. Right now, she didn't have a lot to lose in that move. Except for contact with her mom as she rotted away in prison all alone.

Leah unfolded the new letter from her mom, soaking it up, cherishing each word. There wasn't anything particularly exciting about it.

As with the last letter, Leah kept reading those two words at the end. *Love always.*

Always? Really? Some things in life worked that way. Gravity *always* worked. The sun *always* rose in the morning. And Leah *always* ... found a way to screw things up.

But love and relationships? There was no always with them. People left—by choice, consequence, or death. People lied. Her mother certainly had.

About so many things. More than anyone else in the realm even knew. But Leah now knew.

The next morning, Leah stepped out the back door, praying every branch, stem, and vine in the garden had miraculously become laden with fruit overnight.

She didn't make it far. Right outside the door sat a giant basket brimming with fresh produce and dried grains. Resting on the top, dead center, was the book Leah had shoved into Wren's hands the day before.

Frowning, she picked it up. A small letter stuck out the top. She unfolded it, her hurt forming a puddle in her chest as she read it. Two words: *I care.*

Numb, trying to sort through her emotions, she summoned Ivy energy to give her enough strength to pick up the giant basket and bring it inside.

After taking her time to munch on some strawberries and mull things over, she gathered her courage and opened the front door.

Wren didn't react, sitting and reading a book.

"Thank you," she said.

"You're welcome." He didn't look up.

It was uncomfortable. He had to think she was throwing a tantrum like a child, that she was unstable like her father had been.

"And I'm sorry," she added.

He looked at her, closing the book in his lap. "No apologies necessary."

"How much did it cost?" She could pay with the money Marcus had left behind.

"It was a gift. Consider it a present for you and your little one."

"Yeah. Thanks." She fidgeted with her hands. It was time to swallow her pride. Or at least a small portion of it. Time to force herself out of her cocoon of safety. "How about we…" It pained her to utter the promise. "We can go to the market on Sunday, if the garden isn't producing enough by then." It wouldn't, not that quickly. But his gift was more than enough to last until then.

He smiled. "I'll be ready."

"And thanks again for the book." It was number eight of nine in the series.

"Of course," he said. "I'll warn you that it's a slower pace than some of the others, but vital. Stick with it, and it'll make sense."

She returned his smile, more at ease over book talk. "Sounds good."

Chapter 15

A soft knock startled Leah awake. Squinting in the daylight, she searched for the clock on the wall. It was already almost noon.

Yawning and stretching, she forced herself to fully wake. She'd gotten so caught up in book eight of *Valeska's Adventures* the night before that she'd burned through one of the precious few candles still left in the cottage. She had no idea how late it had been when she'd finally finished the book, eventually shut off her mind, and nodded off.

Rubbing her face, she approached the front door. Another soft knock disturbed the silence. It was Wren's day off, and the other escorts didn't use playful special knocks like he did, but they weren't usually this quiet.

Pulling the curtain to the side, she peered through the window in the door. Panic flooded Leah as she stared straight at Camry, who gave her a smile. Leah's heart and lungs forgot their jobs.

Her jaw dropped as she sucked in a breath. Within the span of about three seconds, a mile-long list of horrors raced through her mind. She was wearing Camry's pajamas. She hadn't showered in a couple of days, and the bedding sprawled out on the sofa definitely needed a wash, too.

The painting in the bedroom closet. The empty wall now gaped in the absence of the wedding gift she'd taken down. Their wedding photo lay facedown in the bedroom. Leah's underwear was in one of their drawers, and... *Kill me now.* Her passport was still tucked away in Camry's underwear drawer.

That didn't even touch on the messy bathroom and the unfortunate garden experiment.

Mankind truly did not understand the full meaning of the word *mortified.*

And what was Leah to do? This was Camry's home! Leah couldn't simply pretend they weren't staring at each other right now. Couldn't ask her to wait while she scrubbed down the cottage and ran away with her tail tucked between her legs.

She forced herself to open the door. "Camry," she breathed.

Camry lunged for her, sweeping her up in a hug. "Hey, Leah."

Leah wilted. "Hey." She quickly pulled away, backing toward the sofa. "I'm so, so, so sorry. I didn't even realize what day it was, and..." She tugged the blanket from between the sofa cushion and back, folding it. "I should have... I'm just going to straighten up, and I'll get out of here."

"You don't need to leave," Camry said softly, tucking her chestnut hair behind her ear.

"No. I do," Leah insisted. Granted, she needed at least half a day to properly wash herself, the laundry, *and* the house. "I'll hurry." She glanced at the door. "Where's Tobias?"

"He's at Rachel and Guillen's."

Which probably meant they'd heard it all. That she was pregnant. That she'd smacked Marcus.

"Oh," Leah replied. "Well, I'll straighten up, and then you guys can have your place back."

"Leah," Camry said a little forcefully. "We're not kicking you out."

"No, I..." Her breathing was rapid as she shook her head, stacking the blanket on her pillow. How could she have lost track of time so badly that she'd completely forgotten they were coming to visit? And not only for a weekend? It was November, and they were gathering to celebrate Thanksgiving. "This is your home. I'm sorry."

Camry cocked her head. "Are you going back to the palace?"

Even if Leah groveled, begging to return after storming out the way she had, there wasn't a chance Catrina would allow her to move back after Leah hurt Marcus.

"No."

"Then, where will you go?" Camry asked cautiously.

Leah turned to her, quieting. She had *nowhere* to go. She should have been sorting that out while here, not just hoping that Marcus would come back to fix things for her, not spending all her time lost in books to escape. "I'll figure it out."

Camry took a seat in the armchair. "We already settled in at Rachel and Guillen's guesthouse. We knew you were staying here. And that's fine."

Biting the insides of her cheeks, Leah sat on the sofa. "You know?"

"That you're pregnant?"

As she met Camry's eyes and nodded, she recalled with perfect clarity the conversation she'd had with Marcus when she'd told him she was pregnant. He had wanted to give up their baby.

Well, if you decide not to keep it… You know, Tobias and Cam have talked about adopting…

He'd jumped right to offering up their child to his brother and sister-in-law. Was Camry there to accept his offer? Had he made a unilateral decision that Catrina would surely uphold, since Leah had proven herself an abusive, unsuitable mother?

"I, uh, yeah," Leah said. "Pregnant. I'm keeping it."

Camry nodded, unfazed. "That's what I heard. How are you feeling?"

Okay, so maybe I jumped to conclusions about Marcus just turning over our baby without proper warning or a discussion…

"Better. My maternal, er, morning sickness is all gone." She did the math. She was nine weeks along. Nine! She'd spent nearly seven weeks holed up in this cottage.

"I'm glad you're feeling better."

She was still beyond embarrassed to be disheveled and squatting in their cottage, even if it was her only option at this point. "I really am sorry."

"Don't be. I brought you a gift from back home, by the way." Camry smiled brightly, pulling a tube of lipstick from her jeans pocket.

Leah couldn't hold back a small smile herself as she accepted it. They'd originally shared a bonding moment over lipstick. "The human bringing the good stuff. Thank you."

Camry shrugged. "Not exactly a baby shower gift, but we've got time for that."

Turning it in her hand, Leah studied the sleek tube, admiring the shade Camry had picked out. It was a pretty pink with a slight brown undertone. "Thank you."

"We're having a big family get-together at Rachel and Guillen's place. Do you want to join us? No rush if you want to get dressed."

Camry and Eric—Kaylah's husband—were American humans. Rachel had been raised by a human mother as well. Most Ivies didn't celebrate human holidays, but this group did, and Leah had enjoyed that part of her old home. It was still too early to gather for Thanksgiving, so this was probably just to celebrate Tobias and Camry's arrival, but Leah couldn't face either of Marcus's parents right now. And things would only be going downhill with Tobias at this point. Leah wouldn't be attending, but that didn't stop her from asking what she needed to know. "Is Marcus over there?"

Camry pursed her lips. "Not yet, but I think he's planning to come."

"No, I..." She couldn't come up with an excuse. She what? Had plans? Needed to wash her hair? At least that one was true. "I'd rather not. But thank you."

Drawing a deep breath, Camry scooted to the edge of her chair. "Do you want to hang out, just you and me?"

"Maybe another time."

"Alright. No pressure. If you change your mind, you're welcome to come over. And we'll be here for the better part of a month, so there's plenty of time. You're obviously still invited for Thanksgiving."

Leah nodded. "Yeah. Thanks."

"Well, I'll," Camry gestured over her shoulder toward the door, "head out. I just wanted to see you and say hi, and invite you over."

"Thanks again."

Camry stood, seeing herself out.

Leah sat there, numb. She stared at the tube of lipstick, musing on its familiarity. It wasn't like natural Green Lands makeup. 'A gift from back home,' Camry had said. From Camry's home, the human world. Not Leah's home. It *had* been her childhood home, but she'd been unable to call it that after she tried to kill Kaylah. She'd forfeited her right to choose which realm, which world she would live in.

Leah had nothing waiting there for her anymore. Nothing and no one.

But she didn't here either. And over there, she could at least start a new life where she wasn't the daughter of Soren and Beata, wasn't tainted by their legacy.

A familiar eerie cold settled into Leah's chest as she started to cry. She was ready to leave. She was ready to run. If Marcus had wanted to fix things between them, he could have by now.

She yearned to disappear. But how? She had an escort posted at the door around the clock. It wouldn't be that hard to sneak over one of the brick walls in the backyard and drop into a neighbor's yard to get away. She'd snuck out of her own house more than once growing up, and she'd snuck a guy into her bedroom with her mom in the other room.

But then ... what about the rifting?

She wasn't nervous about whether she could rift safely. Unlike Ivy poison and chemical arts, rifting only required Ivy energy, and that she had in spades, unhampered by her pregnancy.

Sniffling, Leah pondered her options. Sneak out and trek a few miles to the nearest rifting cave? And then what? Hand her passport to the cave employees and waltz through? Every living, breathing creature in the realm knew who Leah was, and Catrina had to have already made her passport null and void.

Most people were fight or flight. Leah was both.

She had only one option. It was illegal. She'd done illegal before, and she could do it again.

Leah set to work tidying up the cottage. She wouldn't take time to shower or wash things, but she could make it a little more presentable.

The bathroom wasn't *that* bad, all things considered. She placed her folded bedding on the end of the bed, sparing a momentary gut-wrenching frown, imagining him lying there beside her, holding her.

She retrieved the painting from the closet and hung it on the living room wall, hoping Camry hadn't noticed. She flipped their wedding picture upright, grabbed her passport from Camry's underwear drawer, and even tucked her own clean underwear in her jeans pockets after she dressed in her own clothes. The underwear was skimpy enough to all fit, and it wasn't like she could buy more anytime soon— Leah didn't have a single human penny to her name.

Last time, when she'd run away *to* the Green Lands, she'd crafted an elaborate plan. One that had imprisoned her and her mom.

Mom. Leah released a shaky breath. Maybe it was better this way. Yes, her mom was lonely in prison, but her mom's sisters and nieces and nephews sometimes visited...

Leah was leaving. This time, as she ran away *from* the Green Lands, she had no plan, but she at least knew how to get around, and could find a women's shelter...

After chucking her bamboo toothbrush, Leah peeked out the front- and back-door windows. Her escort stood guard, ever watchful, at the front door. Leah sketched out an apology on a piece of paper—a simple *I'm sorry for everything—* and left it next to her most recent read from the library.

She paused, her hand glued to the library book. She spared another glance at the front door. Her gut twisted as she considered Lycha, her current escort. Leah hadn't gotten to know her nearly as well as Wren, and she was glad Wren wasn't there right now, but it wasn't right for Lycha, either. She'd probably be canned like Robyn had been for helping Leah at the palace. No matter what, Leah was always sowing destruction, burning people in her wake.

And in that moment, she thought of her dad, Soren, of all people. Even *he* had been destroyed by Leah's existence, though he'd died never understanding that.

Slipping into the backyard, Leah picked a ripe pimple berry—white, mild, and creamy. She'd miss the unique plant life of the realm.

Her heart thumping wildly, she glanced between the handful of trees. She'd never actually rifted through a tree. It was illegal from the human world, as it required the sacrifice of the tree. Other than in the case of emergency, it wasn't even allowed in the Green Lands unless it was on your own property.

They could add this to the list of her offenses. She could handle knowing she'd be penned into the history books as a disappointment like her parents. That was the legacy she'd inherited.

Ivies, at least in the old days before rifting caves had become commonplace, generally preferred to rift through pine trees. Apparently, the energy worked differently depending on the tree, and the process imparted a flavor to the rifter. Pine trees allowed rifting with more ease, and tasted faintly of vanilla.(ff)

Tobias and Camry had no pines on their property. Leah didn't care how much energy it required or how nasty a rift might taste, as long as she could get away.

Leah stepped up to the plum tree, drawing a breath. She was really going to do this. She was making a true fugitive of herself. She was breaking the tree-rifting ban and taking her child without Marcus's permission.

Crying a little harder, she glided her hand across the rough bark of the tree. If she actually went through with this, it was a one-way ticket, unless she wanted to join her mom in prison and have her child taken from her.

Even if she wanted to tree rift home in the future, she'd be unable to return with her child after they were born. They'd require a Seeder employee at a cave to open a rift for them, and a specialty Boman jade for her child.

She wasn't giving up this child, nor was she going to come back in shackles.

"You can do this," she whispered.

As she extended her vine, touching it to the trunk, memories tugged at her. Kara, the Ivy girl who had taught her to rift in high school—they'd never talked again after Leah left the human world. Marcus—how calming it had been when he'd wrapped his arms around her when she'd been frustrated when practicing.

A muffled squeak escaped Leah's lips, and she forced down the lump in her throat.

Do it. Leave. Be a coward.

Leah pressed her vine harder against the bark, summoning her energy, focusing on the lower central channel for her energy as she'd been taught.

They don't need you here anymore. They don't want you. For good or bad, your part in this realm is done.

Tears cascaded down her cheeks as she directed her Ivy energy to her extended vine. It pulsated, lingering at the tip of her vine, waiting for her to make the final choice, to commit.

I'm not giving up. I'm giving up Soren's legacy, Beata's legacy. And this child will get the fresh start I never did.

And then she did it. Leah pushed her Ivy energy past her vine and into the tree. It instantly connected, and a coppery tang filled her mouth. Her energy mingled with that of the tree, and she slowly dragged her vine down, opening a rift, a seam between the realms.

Only a few inches into forming the rift, Leah struggled. Not physically.

The bark already hinted at peeling back, at being singed. She was stealing the life of this tree, the same one that had sustained her during her time here.

As she paused, all the self-doubt, the self-hatred, the secrets and lies and torment bombarded her. It was hell in her mind.

The same kind of hell she'd faced, the darkened haze she'd gone through, when she'd made the immeasurably rash decision to try to take her own aunt's life.

Leah reeled her vine back in, panting. And then she sank onto her knees, rested her forehead against the tree trunk, and sobbed.

And sobbed.

Why was she so broken, so wrong, so destructive?

She knew the answer to that. She'd been made that way from the beginning. It was in her very nature.

Wrapping her arms around her stomach, she stayed there. Her tears watering the ground wouldn't undo the damage she'd done to the tree, but it was the only penance she could offer. And she had nowhere to go, nothing to do, other than to let it all out.

It could have been minutes, but it felt more like hours that she knelt there, until she was interrupted.

Chapter 16

She recognized the voice. "Leah?"

Leah quieted and stilled, praying Kaylah would go away, that like a child closing their eyes and thinking they're invisible, Leah could be ignored.

"Leah?" This time Kaylah's voice was filled with urgent concern, not searching curiosity. "Are you okay?"

"Leave me alone," Leah pleaded.

"That's the last thing I'm going to do." She rested a warm hand on Leah's back. "Are you hurt?"

"Leave me alone," Leah repeated weakly.

"It looks like I've already done that for too long," Kaylah said. "Come on." A second hand grasped Leah's arm. "Let's go inside."

There was no point in fighting it. Matron Kaylah would have an escort as well who could back her up.

It took extra energy for Leah to force herself up, but Kaylah's hands were strong and supportive.

A strange man, probably Kaylah's escort, her personal bodyguard, watched on as they entered the house. Kaylah sat her down on the sofa, and eased herself onto the armchair. "Are you hurt?" Kaylah asked, her face painted with concern.

Leah averted her gaze, staring at her hands. "I'm fine."

"That's ... not exactly true, is it?"

Picking at her nails, Leah shrugged. "I'll be fine."

Warmth and caring infusing her words, Kaylah said, "Let me take you home."

All of Leah's tears had been cried. She looked up, puffy-eyed, and stated the simple but devastating truth. "I don't have a home. I never have." She couldn't recall a single postal code from her years in the human world. Not a single address where she'd lived. She and her mom and abusive 'aunt' Cheryl had moved too often, and changed phone numbers too often, to keep any of that straight.

"You're coming home with me," Kaylah said, exuding compassion. "You'll *always* have a home with me and Eric."

Leah sat there, half considering, half wishing she was in a void somewhere, not having to exist or think or feel at the moment.

"Come on." Kaylah stood, surveying the small living room. "What do we need to pack?"

"Nothing here is mine."

"That makes things easier." She stepped toward the kitchen. "Have you eaten?"

Leah's humiliation from Camry's visit had been so complete that she hadn't even thought of grabbing a bite before taking off. "No."

"Well, now, that won't do. I'm a bit peckish, too, so let me pick out a little something for the both of us." Kaylah's tone had become more cheerful. A false kind of cheerful, but she wore the mask well. Leah didn't protest.

Carrying a bagful of food from the kitchen, Kaylah rejoined Leah, her eyes resting on the folded letter Leah had scribbled out.

Leah didn't even have it in her to protest as Kaylah unfolded it and read it. She didn't say anything, but instead folded it back up and tucked it in a pocket of her dress.

"Great. We've got snacks. Anything else?"

Leah pointed to the book. "That's the library's."

"We'll see that it's returned."

Frowning, Leah added, "Please don't fire my escort."

Kaylah raised her eyebrows. "No one gets fired today unless you say so."

A measure of relief lightened Leah's load.

Squaring her shoulders, Kaylah stretched out a hand. "Let's go."(gg)

The escort on duty seemed a bit confused as they left, as Leah asked her to tell Wren thank you. Kaylah told one of her two bodyguards to inform Eric that she was taking Leah home.

She and Leah slid into the rickshaw together. "We'll be traveling to my estate, the less public roads, please," Kaylah instructed.

The driver began pedaling, and they were on their way.

"We're not going to the local cave to rift?" Leah asked. Kaylah lived far into the country. It might take days, between rickshaw driver breaks and transfers.

Kaylah hung the bag of food on a hook in front of them. After a moment of silence, she angled her body to face Leah. "Here's the thing, kiddo: most green folk your age only know what an Ivy tree rift looks like from stories and textbook diagrams, but when I was your age, I was making them every other day."

She'd noticed the damage Leah had done to the tree. They were taking hours and days to return to Kaylah's place because she didn't trust Leah to take a cave rift, nor should she. She was still a flight risk.

"Will I be in trouble for ... the damage?" She'd understood the repercussions of opening an illegal tree rift, but wasn't sure if there was some sort of lesser punishment for having only formed a partial rift.

Scooching closer to Leah, Kaylah faced forward, sliding an arm around her shoulders. "I saw nothing."

"But the damage... Will it ... die?"

"It'll be fine. It'll scar, but it'll bounce back." She squeezed Leah. "It will bounce back, and so will you."

"I hate my life," Leah confessed.

The rickshaw jostled as they hit a bump, and the driver apologized.

"Sometimes we all do," Kaylah said, giving Leah another light reassuring squeeze.

Worn out and grateful, Leah rested her head on Kaylah's shoulder and closed her eyes.

A half hour later, Leah woke to another bump in the road. She straightened and listened as Kaylah discussed travel plans with one of her bodyguards. The rickshaw was flanked on either side with a bodyguard on a bike, which had to look absolutely ridiculous for most humans to behold, but that was the life of the Green Lands, where electricity didn't properly work, even after years of joint Ivy/Seeder/human experimentation. Matron Kaylah, a retired queen, still had bodyguards with her nearly everywhere she went.

Done talking with her guard, Kaylah gave her attention to Leah. "You should eat something."

Leah pulled an apple from the bag and took a bite.

"Did the nap help?"

"A little."

Kaylah took an apple out for herself. "Good."

"Why were you even there?"

Holding out a finger, Kaylah finished her bite. "I happened to be in the area."

"In the area for a family gathering while Tobias and Camry are in-realm?"

"Hmm… As the rather barbaric human saying goes: two birds, one stone." Kaylah held her apple in her lap. "I wanted to come see you when Catrina sent word about your pregnancy, but it also sounded like you wanted everyone to get out of your hair while you sorted things…"

Leah nodded, chewing in silence. Kaylah wasn't much of a retired queen by the way she packed her schedule with causes and events. She'd probably just arrived at Rachel and Guillen's place using a cave, and was missing a weekend with her favorite people, her husband included.

"If I promise to take a rift to the cave closest to your estate, you could return and still enjoy time with the family," Leah said.

"Hmm… One step at a time. I'm okay with what we've got planned right now. Girl time—just you and me."

Right… "You don't have to lie to me, and I don't have to ruin your weekend."

"You couldn't if you tried." Kaylah crunched down into her apple once more. "Plus, road trips are good for the soul."

The rest of the day, they traveled in relative silence. Leah was grateful to not have Kaylah pry or prod. At each major city, or sooner as needed, the rickshaw driver took a break, and the women would stretch their legs. Leah's bladder was happy for the breaks as well.

They sat down for a warm meal at dinnertime on the outskirts of a town along the way. Despite it being a simple meal, it was divine after what she'd been scraping by on at the cottage. They chatted, though it was all fairly surface level—about the food, the scenery.

As the sun began to set, they pulled into another town and drove straight to an inn. The innkeeper had already been alerted to Kaylah's stay, and fawned over her on their arrival.

Kaylah requested they fetch some nightclothes and a fresh change for the next day for both herself and Leah.

The room was a two-bed suite, likely as nice as they got at inns along the path out in the middle of nowhere.

An employee of the inn rushed to light the lamps of the room, offering to draw a warm bath. Kaylah accepted.

Leah eased herself onto one of the beds and ate another light snack from the bag Kaylah had packed.

After fresh clothes had been secured from a local shop, Kaylah recommended Leah bathe, and she'd take a turn in the morning.

Whether the offer came from Kaylah having had to endure hours next to Leah's unshowered self, or to allow Leah to soak away the stress of a day as the hot mess du jour, Leah didn't want to know.

"You'll be okay in there?" Kaylah shyly asked before Leah closed the bathroom door.

Leah's heart hurt. She'd like to think Kaylah was concerned she'd slip on the wet floor, but it was probably more about Leah being reckless, and Kaylah being concerned all over again that Leah had been suicidal. They'd visited that particular concern enough shortly after Leah had tried to murder her.

"I'll be fine," Leah reassured her. "I'll leave it unlocked in case I slip."

Kaylah gave her a smile. "Thank you."

By the time Leah emerged, Kaylah had dressed in nightclothes, braiding her hair to the side. Her long hair was as black as Leah's or Beata's.

Leah combed out her wet hair. "It feels good to be clean."

Smiling again, Kaylah finished her braid. She pointed to a pitcher of water. "Stay hydrated."

After pouring herself a glass, Leah sat cross-legged on her bed, facing Kaylah.

"How's the baby?" Kaylah asked.

"She's good." The thought of the child growing within her tugged her lips upwards.

Kaylah arched an eyebrow. "She? A little predictive mother's intuition?"

Leah shrugged. "I guess I've just started to imagine it's a 'she' instead of an 'it' or 'they.' I'd be happy either way, though."

"You know..." Kaylah took a sip of her own water. "As you recall, I was super excited to find out I was an aunt..."

Nodding, Leah pursed her lips. "As *I* recall, it took a little bit. Or did you secretly like me trying to murder you?"

Kaylah donned a feisty grin. "Tosh! What aunt doesn't have a niece trying to snuff her out?"

Leah chuckled, and Kaylah winked. Dark humor had been their path to stop walking on eggshells around each other, though they never talked like this with anyone else in the room unless it was Eric. People would be too appalled at how unapologetic Leah sounded after trying to assassinate everyone's favorite queen.

"Go on, tell me how much you loved finding out about me," Leah prompted.

"As I was saying..." Kaylah flourished a hand in the air. "I thought it was fantastic to be an aunt. But I hope you don't get offended that I'm a smidge more excited about that little gremlin." She pointed at Leah's stomach.

"Really?" It sounded like there was a catch.

"Really. I mean, I'm arguably a great aunt, but now, I'll be a *great* great-aunt." She paused. "Not like a great-great-aunt, like super old, but you know what I mean. I'm great, and I'll be a great-aunt."

"Very humble, too."

Kaylah beamed.

"But please tell me you are not going to refer to my child as a gremlin."

"All children are gremlins," Kaylah stated matter-of-factly. And the funny thing was, Leah had heard Kaylah use those terms interchangeably just like that, ever since she'd met her. In private only, of course.

Kaylah continued, "I mean, diapers and screaming?" She shuddered. "I changed Marcus's once after he was adopted. Uh-uh. *Never* again."

It hurt to hear his name. Leah set her water glass down. "Are you telling me a retired queen won't deign to change her great-niece or nephew's diaper now and then?"

Wrinkling her nose, Kaylah didn't respond. Leah chuckled again.

"Fine. But if you're going to be a *great* great-aunt, then you probably shouldn't call her a gremlin like all the other kids out there. She's special."

Kaylah held a hand to her heart, playful. "I don't make the rules. No exceptions. No matter how much I will love it, that thing is a stink bomb in the making."

Leah sighed dramatically. "Then it's not my fault if I accidentally let it slip that the kingdom's hero refers to her subjects' little ones as gremlins."

"You wouldn't dare! Plus, which of us would they believe?"

Unable to mask it this time, Leah frowned. That remark hit too close to home after Marcus's threat to pull rank on her about leaving for the human world.

Kaylah's demeanor instantly changed, but she didn't ask.

"I'm pretty tired." Leah pulled back her covers.

"Yeah, same." Kaylah didn't budge from her spot. "What did you mean by your note at the cottage? That you were sorry for everything?"

Fighting fresh tears, Leah only shook her head.

Kaylah didn't press the matter. "This is a fun girl's trip, not an inquisition."

After Leah crawled into bed, Kaylah snuffed the lamps.

"Good night, Leah."

"Good night."

"Love you, kiddo."

Leah still hesitated with that one. "Thanks."

Chapter 17

Leah's eyelids fluttered open. She was exhausted and sore. It took her a moment to remember where she was. Kaylah was already up, sitting against the headboard of her bed, staring across the room, studying the wall.

Shifting to sit up, Leah caught Kaylah's attention.

Kaylah smiled warmly. "Good morning, sunshine."

Popping her neck, Leah returned the greeting. This bed was so soft and comfortable compared to the cottage sofa; the bare walls and new layout a refreshing change.

"I ordered us breakfast in the room," Kaylah said.

"Thanks."

Kaylah turned on the bed, facing Leah. "We should talk about a few things before we head out today, while we have some privacy away from the guards and driver."

Leah tensed. "Yeah?"

Searching her eyes, Kaylah cocked her head. "Nothing bad."

Swallowing, Leah nodded.

"I think we should have a little more direction about what we're doing here. Did you, or ... do you have any plans? For the future right now?"

Did she have plans and goals and aspirations? Or had she thrown her life away and given up?

"I'll figure it out," Leah said.

"I'm not trying to rush you. I just want to make sure we're on the same page. I want to make sure you have everything you need, and that I'm not cramping your style."

Something akin to a half-hearted bitter laugh made its way up Leah's throat. "I have no style to cramp." A little more humbly, remorsefully, she added, "I don't exactly have plans right now." She stared down at her hands, pushing back her cuticles with her fingernails.

"That's fine," Kaylah replied, all kindness and reassurance. "I do want to set some rules about living on the estate."

A weight pressed into Leah's chest. Was this going to be like living at the palace all over again? Being told how to talk, sit, stand, and breathe? Who she could hug, or share any affection with?

"Nothing big," Kaylah continued. "You'll be staying in the house proper."

"I really don't mind staying in the guest cabin." Out of the way, away from people.

"No. In the house proper."

They met eyes, Leah gnawing on her lower lip. She wasn't being forced out into public, but Kaylah wasn't about to let her remain a hermit.

"You can have the entire second floor of the east wing if you'd like."

"Sure."

Kaylah gave her a single nod. "When Eric and I are home, I'd like you to eat at least one meal with us a day. You're welcome to join us for all of them if you'd like, but I'd like at least one."

Not in any position to protest or bargain, Leah only nodded her agreement.

"And you and I will enjoy a weekly picnic together, just the two of us."

Leah arched an eyebrow at this one.

Smoothing the bedding around her, Kaylah said, "We've got a lot of missed bonding opportunities to make up for."

Yeah, Leah's entire childhood. And they'd spent plenty of time in each other's company over the last two-plus years, but most of that had been at official, public, or family gatherings. Not all that much one-on-one time.

"Okay."

Kaylah squinted at her. "I'm going to try to not be offended that your agreement to my terms sounds like you'd rather have all your teeth pulled."

Leah gave her a cheesy smile.

A knock at the door announced their breakfast had arrived. The inn's staff carried in a mouthwatering buffet of hot porridge and hash, fresh berries and cut melons, and a bright medley of sauteed vegetables. It was much more food than the two of them needed, and no doubt a more generous and refined spread than any of the other customers were being offered. But that was the perk of traveling with royalty, of being around Matron Kaylah.

None of the staff even passed Leah any contemptuous glances, though a couple of their gazes caught on her a little longer than she would have liked.

After they had done all of their bowing and curtsying, had deposited the dishes on a long table in the corner of the room and poured glasses of juice for the two women, they left them to scoop up.

Sitting at a small table by a large window, Leah and Kaylah dug in.

"So, anyway..." Kaylah said, spearing a chunk of honeydew with her fork. "Let me know what you need, and we'll make sure it's taken care of."

"I'll need some clothes."

"Of course, we'll take care of clothes and toiletries and all that."

Leah ate a spoonful of porridge. "I can do some extra chores to pay for them."

Kaylah looked no less than offended. "I'm bringing you home to live with me, not hiring you as a servant."

Leah didn't have it in her to ask if the funds she'd received as Catrina's ward were still assigned to her, or if Kaylah was taking on her expenses from her own pocket. And she was too weak to object, to let her pride be upset for leeching off Kaylah and Eric.

So, Leah just ate another spoonful of porridge. As she did so, she pondered her current situation further. How long she'd be at Kaylah's place, she didn't know. But something in her was more at ease at the idea of staying there a while, compared to any of the alternatives. Just until she could sort things out and make her own way.

Leah took a swig of white grape juice. "Will Catrina know I'm staying at your place?" She might already.

"Yes." Kaylah met Leah's look of frustration with a calm reply. "We only keep tabs on you for your safety. She'll know you're with family and won't have to worry about you."

Leah choked down a scoff. Catrina wasn't so much concerned about Leah as she was concerned about what Leah might do. That was a moot point right now, but Leah wanted to make sure Catrina knew they were completely done. "Could... Would you ask for my things to be delivered to your place?" She didn't have much of her own, but at minimum, her knife-throwing set was completely hers.

Kaylah finished chewing her bite. "Yes, I'll send for all that."

"Thanks."

They kept eating. Leah asked what would become of her escorts, wanting to make sure no one lost their job because she'd left the care of the palace. Kaylah assured her they'd be kept on as staff at the palace, that Catrina always had extra people staffed. Leah hoped that was true, still regretting costing Robyn her job.

After they'd both had their fill, they set out for another long day on the road. The scenery was tranquil, soothing. Leah had been at Kaylah and Eric's estate a handful of times over the last two-plus years, but never by rickshaw. It wasn't far from the end of a train line or a rifting cave, and she'd always taken either of them before.

Her view was full of pastel pink flowers on rolling hills, pineapple trees near ponds, and chatterbirds swooping in the sky. She allowed herself to admire the Green Lands, the Ivy Kingdom and its beauty. She was usually so busy with tutors and the academy, official functions, time with Marcus and his family, that she forgot what it could feel like to simply *be*.

The break from chaos wasn't healing, exactly, but it was quiet. The kind of quiet where she found herself almost even smiling as she imagined her child in her arms someday. The kind of quiet where she found her thoughts drifting to the child's father, and everything else that sucked. It was usually around those times—when her heart sank, her mind stuttered under the stress—that Kaylah conveniently wanted to muse about something from her childhood, or take a break to stretch their legs and let the rickshaw driver rest.

Leah knew what Kaylah was doing. And she let her.

They traveled all day, staying at another inn they reached at dusk.

The next day, they rode past dusk, lanterns on the rickshaw lighting their way. There was no need for an inn when they were so close to Kaylah's estate.

Dim candlelight danced in a few windows as they approached, lit by servants waiting for their arrival. Kaylah had sent word to them and Eric, who she'd left at Rachel and Guillen's house.

Shortly after the pair stepped into the main entryway, Eric rounded the corner, squeezing Kaylah tight, then turned to Leah with a soft smile.

He tucked his hands in his pockets, his arms straight and rigid. "I know you're not much of a hugger, but would you like one?"

She wrung her hands. "No thank you."

"That's perfectly fine. I'm glad you ladies made such good time, and got here in one piece."

Kaylah's escorts entered behind them, handing the few items Leah and Kaylah had collected along the way to her staff, and wishing everyone a good night.

One servant lingered at the door to the hallway.

"Acacia will take you to your room and help you get settled," Eric said.

"Thanks."

Kaylah had made it clear this was no imposition, but having Eric waiting up for them reminded Leah how much of an interruption her breakdown was causing. They were both giving up time with family—their closest friends—to coddle Leah. "I don't mind if you two go back to Rachel and Guillen's to visit while Tobias and Camry are in-realm."

The couple traded a glance. "They'll be around for a while. We'll see. We're excited to spend time with *you*," Kaylah insisted.

Eric slid an arm around Kaylah's waist. "We didn't move out to the middle of nowhere to be around large groups of people all the time. We really don't mind."

"Okay. Thanks again, for everything." She swallowed. "Have a good night." She followed Acacia down the hallway and up a flight of stairs.

Leah had only stayed the night at the estate once, and it had been in a smaller guest room on the opposite end of the house from where Marcus had slept that night. Acacia guided her to a much larger room this time, with an en suite bathroom and a door to an adjoining room. Leah explained she didn't need a huge room, but Acacia stated she was giving her the one she'd been instructed to. You couldn't really argue much with staff just doing their job.

The woman bid her good night as well, and Leah sat on the large soft bed, taking in the room in the light of a lamp. The room was smaller than what she'd been given in the palace, but still three times the size of any of the bedrooms she'd had in the human world.

Sore and tired from hours and days in a rickshaw, she barely scraped up her energy to use the bathroom and brush her teeth before she passed out on the bed.

Leah woke to a knock on the door. Daylight peeked past the edge of curtains covering the windows. Groggy, Leah rubbed her eyes and cleared her throat. "Yeah, just a second."

After rolling out of bed, she was greeted by another servant. "Sorry to wake you, miss. Matron Kaylah asked me to see that you're well, and to set your things up in your room, if that's alright?"

"Of course. And I'm fine." Her things? New things Kaylah had bought for her, or stuff from the palace?

The servant gave her a bright smile. "Lovely. Breakfast can be made for you down in the breakfast room whenever you're ready." She reached down for a large bag. "And I'm sure I'll have this all unpacked for you by the time you've eaten."

Leah considered telling her she could unpack her own things, but she'd learned at the palace to allow the servants to do their jobs. Plus, she was starving. "Sounds good."

Entering the room, the servant added, "Since the closet here is smaller than what you're used to at the palace, we already placed your finer things in the attached room next door."

That threw Leah off. "Wait, what?"

The servant gestured to the door connecting this room to the next. "Over there. The ball gowns and whatnot."

Leah furrowed her brow, heading next door. She was utterly shocked to find an armoire plumb full of her fancier dresses, as well as a couple of loaded-down makeshift racks set up alongside the wall. Some items had been placed on a shelf, perfumes and her throwing knives included.

Perching on the edge of the bed in there, Leah shook her head. *I can't believe it.*

She'd expected Queen Catrina to send her things at Kaylah's request, but not *everything* that had been in her chambers. Leah took a few moments to size it up before the servant appeared at the door. "We can rearrange it if you'd like. We'll be moving another armoire in here, but Her Highness didn't want the noise of it banging around down the hallway waking you."

Leah numbly nodded, looking at the dresses on the rack. The organization of the items didn't matter all that much to her; it was the fact Catrina had sent *all* of them that still had her uneasy.

Memories flooded Leah with each dress she studied. Embroidered, beaded, and lacy—they were all beautiful, all likely one of a kind. She'd worn them to balls and official functions where she'd needed to make a good impression. There were plenty of everyday dresses as well.

Some of the dresses held better memories than others. She just sat there and stared. Why had Catrina sent them? Leah hadn't paid for them, and in a lot of ways, they weren't even a wardrobe—they were a uniform.

Was Catrina being kind by sending them? Perhaps. Or was she sending a message to Leah? That she was done with Leah. Done with trying to help her. Done with trying to reach out to her. Done with Leah's ungrateful, selfish, stupid self. Done with the girl who was going to sink her nephew's reputation because she couldn't keep her legs closed as ordered.

Leah's gaze fixed on a deep plum dress with a sweetheart neckline. She ached. She'd worn that one to her first ball. Marcus had saved her from her misery that night.

"Leah?" Kaylah's voice was soft from the doorway, and Leah's attention snapped to her.

"Hey."

"Everything okay?" Kaylah asked cautiously.

"Of course." Leah sniffled, wiping away a tear. "I was just…" She drew a deep breath. "Why did she send all of these? It's not like I'm planning to go to any big events right now, and I won't fit into them soon, anyway." She was forming a baby bump, and it was likely already too tight of a squeeze into some of the more formfitting ones.

"I'm sure she expected you'd want them all in one place. And you may fit into them again someday."

Leah huffed. "They're not even mine. It's not like I paid for them."

Kaylah inclined her head. "They were bought for you, tailored for you. They're yours." She paused. "But if you'd rather, I could have them stored elsewhere for now."

Leah didn't want to cause the servants any extra trouble. "It's fine."

"How about we grab something to eat?"

Standing, Leah followed her downstairs to the breakfast room. Eric was off elsewhere, but Kaylah sat to eat with her.

The multigrain toast and melon-pomegranate smoothie bowl were delightful.

"Did you sleep well?" Kaylah asked, sipping water.

"Yeah. Like a rock."

She smiled wide. "Good."

Leah took another bite of her toast. "Is this our one mandatory meal of the day?"

Kaylah pursed her lips, scooping a spoonful of her smoothie. "How about we spend two together on your first day?"

It wasn't like Leah had plans, or grounds to deny her request. "That works."

Other than shared meals, what was Leah going to do with her time? She should be sorting out her life, but just the thought of that was beyond daunting. "Do you mind if I look around in your library?" There was an entire room dedicated to books—every inch of the walls lined with full shelves, comfy armchairs and sofas taking up the center of the room.

"Be my guest." Kaylah ate another spoonful. "Looking for anything in particular? Or just perusing?"

Leah shrugged. "I guess perusing." Though ... she hadn't gotten the chance to check out the last book in the *Valeska's Adventures* series... "Are you familiar with *Valeska's Adventures*?"

Kaylah softly scraped the bottom of her bowl. "I sure am. I doubt there's an Ivy who isn't."

"Do you have it?"

Twisting her lips, Kaylah searched her mind. "I don't think so."

Leah frowned, and Kaylah raised her eyebrows in question.

"Well, I just finished book eight, and it's a nine-book series."

"Aha. I'll see what I can do about that."

Smiling, Leah reached for her glass of water. "Thank you."

"Anytime."

Chapter 18

The next few days were spent in the library, on solo strolls around the expansive grounds, and with a healthy amount of napping when Leah felt like it.

Leah reconsidered the options for her future. They all relied so heavily on one person—Marcus. Her gut twisted, and her anger grew every time she recalled the things he'd said and done. Her heart hurt at the broken promise he'd given her the day she'd permanently left the palace. *I'll always choose you. And I'll always choose our baby.*

She almost wrote him a letter, on more than one occasion. But *he* hadn't bothered to, and he was perfectly capable of doing so.

At the end of the week, Leah and Kaylah set out on the first of their agreed-upon picnics. They settled down on a large blanket near a swimming pond.

"Thanks for joining me." Kaylah smiled.

Leah hadn't had much choice in the matter, but she wasn't about to insult her hostess. "Yeah, this pond is so pretty."

"First, I have a gift for you." Kaylah pulled a linen-wrapped package from the picnic basket.

"For what?"

"Because. And I promised..."

Leah unwrapped the gift, surprised to find the final book in the *Valeska's Adventures* series in pristine condition. Leah studied it. It looked brand new, not like a public library copy. Then she opened the front cover. Clear as day, an inscription had been penned on the title page. *To Leah—Enjoy the adventure.* And it was signed by the author.

Her jaw dropped as she ran her fingers over the writing. "This is for me?"

"I didn't realize you were such a bookworm."

"I'm not. Well, I wasn't..." Not until she'd walled herself off in that cottage. "Thank you." She'd never had something special like this.

"The author doesn't usually do signed books, but being me has some perks."

Leah shook her head, fixated on the book. "Thank you."

After a minute, Leah set the book down, helping Kaylah unpack their lunch. "I really like it here," Leah confessed. "More than at the palace."

Kaylah blew out a puff of air. "You didn't grow up with that lifestyle. I'm sure it was a hard transition. I wish..." She hesitated. "Do you think you would have preferred to move in with me and Eric if you'd been given the choice when you first moved over here?"

"I ... think that would have been hard at the time."

Silence hung thick in the air. She'd hated Kaylah, and she'd hated herself for what she'd tried to do.

"You know," Kaylah continued, "when we discussed what would be best for you, Catrina and Stephan were quick to offer their home."

Leah bit the insides of her cheeks. The day they'd sat in a room and discussed whether Leah and her mom would live or die for their crimes...

Kaylah gingerly opened a glass jar of peaches. She explained how Catrina truly did want the best for Leah, and how she still wished Leah would go speak with her at the palace. Leah tried not to be annoyed. "You have to make a lot of tough calls as a queen," Kaylah said.

Leah shook her head, staring at the spoon in her hand.

"Leah, I understand you're frustrated with her, with the rules." Kaylah's voice was kind but not hesitant. "But you've learned about our history. Every day of my reign, and Catrina's, we've had to be mindful about dotting our *I's*, and crossing our *T's*. It's one thing to rule a kingdom and keep up an air of professionalism. It's a whole nother issue to recover from decades, even centuries of brutality."

If Leah were more levelheaded, she would acknowledge the truth of that statement. She would also admit that even a queen was allowed a bad day. Catrina hadn't been herself that morning, just like Leah hadn't been herself when she'd slapped Marcus. Maybe the kids had kept Catrina up half the night, or her own maternal sickness had. Maybe she'd been stressed to her limits by her unending daily obligations. Maybe she had been shocked at Leah's defiance because she'd never fully understood how messy Leah's life had been before coming to the Green Lands—she'd hidden that part of herself well before that morning.

But Leah had never been all that levelheaded, and it wouldn't destroy the kingdom for someone to back her up when she desperately needed it.

Pursing her lips, Leah met Kaylah's gaze. "Is this what our picnics are going to be? Telling me why I'm wrong about everything?"

Kaylah sighed. "No. That's all I'll say about things with Catrina."

"Good. And you know, people hate me for what my parents did, but that's not my fault. I mean, obviously … the whole attempted murder thing was kinda my fault." Her cheeks warmed, but she was still stuck on the way Catrina had handled the palace's secret passageways. "Catrina even treated me different. I wasn't planning a coup. I was just trying to… It's not fair."

Kaylah frowned. "It's not. And honestly, I don't even consider your parents the worst Ivy rulers."

Leah cocked her head in disbelief. Her own dad had tortured Kaylah for days.

"I'm serious. Yes, they did horrible things, but most of what people detest were their *plans* to do things. What they *hoped* to do with Bomen, Seeders, and Ivy society as a whole. But if you ask me, I'd say Queen Lavinia was the worst we've had."

The name was familiar, one Leah had read since coming to the realm.

Kaylah spelled out her meaning. "A huge manipulation of her people, and a legitimate attempt at genocide against the Seeders."

Leah couldn't help but think of Rachel at the mention of her people. Seeder lands had been poisoned, and that poison had been lethal to every single unbloomed Seeder girl—vulnerable as teenagers or younger without their powers yet.

"Yeah, that really is worse than what my parents did."

"Plus, I look at it this way: your mother and father tried to steal my throne, but that's not any worse than your father's and my great-grandmother killing an entire downline of heirs to switch the Mother Vines' allegiance for her takeover."

"True." Leah turned the spoon in her hand. "We should bring those up more in public education, then people will hate me less."

Kaylah frowned again. "People mostly focus on your parents and what they did because it's such recent history."

Leah shifted on the blanket, crossing her legs. "So, in a hundred years' time, people will be more forgiving and might even like me?" That did a whole lot of good for Leah right now...

"Mmm." Kaylah skirted answering that one with a single understanding look. "Things will get better." She glanced at the food. "But this won't if it warms up, so let's dig in."

They sat in silence for a few minutes, munching on pastries, peaches, and broccoli slaw.

"Do you want me to arrange a counselor for you to see?" Kaylah offered.

Leah shook her head. She'd seen one for a while after the whole botched assassination debacle, but Leah had eventually come to dislike the sessions. Perhaps she'd adopted her mom's distrust of therapists, but Leah had started to fear her information hadn't been completely private with the counselor, that some of it might be given to the queen to ensure Leah was safe and proper.

She'd completely stopped counseling after a particularly painful visit with her mom at the prison. Leah had needed to bury that memory, the feelings that had torn her in half that day.

"Should I keep this baby?" Leah asked. "Or should I..."

Kaylah surveyed her, finishing a bite. "I thought you wanted to."

Leah swallowed a lump in her throat. "I do." But as much as she'd grown attached to the baby, and as much as she loved her mom, she couldn't lie to herself. More than once, *especially* in the last few months, Leah had wished her mom had never conceived her. Had found it in her to drop Leah off somewhere to be adopted as a baby.

"If you want to keep it, then you should."

"I might be a horrible mom," Leah confessed, heartbroken. "And she wouldn't have to live a crazy life like me if I gave her away, and she never knew she was my child."

"It's hard having notoriety. Marcus and Tobias know what that's like, growing up, and they're happy."

That comparison was nowhere near fitting. Their parents had been a controversial pair at the end of the war, and to some extent still were, but they were hailed as heroes. Even those who still clung to outdated beliefs were generally happy the war had ended, because it meant not sending their sons and fathers, husbands and brothers off to die in war.

"And I don't see why you'd be a horrible mother," Kaylah added.

The royal family was talking about Leah, this much she knew. But she wasn't sure to what extent. "How much do you know about why Marcus left me at the cottage?"

Kaylah cleared her throat. "I just know ... that you're pregnant, and had a falling out with Catrina, and then Marcus ... and his family. And that you haven't seen him in a couple of months?"

Tears pricked at the corners of Leah's eyes. "He... He said ... some awful things. And I... I hit him."

"Oh." Kaylah didn't show judgment or shock.

"I hit him *hard*." Leah wiped away a tear. That single action had taught her that she was capable of becoming something she'd sworn to never become—an abuser, like Cheryl. It had taught Leah that her simmering anger could go too far. What if she got frustrated some day and took it out on her own child? It was a terrifying thought.

"I didn't really mean to, but I'm pretty sure I used my Ivy energy when I hit him, when I slapped him."

"I see..." Crimes committed against Bomen carried heavier sentences, and regular green folk with powers had to be considerate of those born without them. "Have you two ever fought like that before?"

"No."

"Then ... if you're basing how good of a mother you'll be off of *one* incident..."

Leah twisted her lips, unwilling to accept the leniency.

Kaylah wouldn't have it. "Every single parent out there, no matter how kind and competent, has done something wrong. They've screamed at their crying child after they both got a sleepless night, or they've forgotten something important, left something hot or sharp within reach. No one's perfect. And whether as a parent or as someone in a serious relationship, it's their responsibility to ensure it never happens again."

"It won't."

Kaylah nodded, not responding for a while. "I'm sorry he said ... whatever he said, if it was bad enough for that to happen."

Surprised with herself, Leah felt immense relief at that. It bugged her sometimes when Marcus called Kaylah 'Aunt Kaylah.' Because she was actually *Leah's* aunt, not his. Kaylah was only his honorary aunt. But blood wasn't always thicker, and Marcus had grown up around Kaylah as the golden child, and Leah had only been in her life a couple of years, after trying to kill her.

But she felt safe in Kaylah's presence right now, as though she might be the only person who wouldn't pick sides.

"You know, he's ... immature," Leah vented, setting down her plate and spoon. "He doesn't always get how hard this is for me. And the way he... He wants me to marry him, but he won't even put me before his mom. Isn't that what adults are supposed to do? I'm carrying his child, but he cares more about what his parents think, or what Catrina thinks." She huffed, then added a couple more examples of instances that frustrated her.

Kaylah heard her out, not interrupting. She set down her plate and spoon as well. "You *are* both still young. But ... you're right. Some of that was pretty crappy." She drew a deep breath. "One thing you have to remember is that he grew up in a healthy, happy home. He's gone through some unique and hard experiences, but not nearly the way you have. And..." She shrugged slightly. "When children go through a lot at a young age like you did, they're forced to grow up faster."

Leah had told Kaylah about Cheryl's abuse, and Kaylah was well aware of the fact that Leah and her mom had moved a ton in the human world, but Leah hadn't told her even half of everything, hadn't told her anything about the sexual assaults she'd endured.

"I'm not excusing him," Kaylah said. "I'm only saying ... we all mature at different rates, and he can catch up."

Leah hoped that was true. In her heart of hearts, she still yearned for him to be next to her in that huge bed, to share meals and smiles with her, to share dreams and a future with her.

"Have you written him?" Kaylah asked softly.

Shaking her head, Leah frowned. "He hasn't written me either."

"Well, when you're ready, we could spare the paper." Kaylah smiled. "Because you two are one of my favorite couples." It was public knowledge Kaylah was a bit of a romantic, a bit of a matchmaker.

"I'll try to remember that."

"I also have some spare notebooks if you're interested. I know Rachel has found journaling helpful ... if you don't want to do counseling again."

Leah fought to not roll her eyes at yet another comparison to Rachel.

"I know... Not your favorite person right now, but I figured I'd throw it out there. You've both been through a lot. And I really do think she'll be a great support for you two and the baby. It sounds like you just need to set some boundaries."

"Yeah, we'll see."

Soon enough, a breeze blew in, the sky threatening to mist, so they packed up and returned to the house.

Leah ended up making her way to the sitting room and grabbing some stationery. After returning to her room, she penned two letters. One to her mom, to let her know she was safe and doing well, still unable to visit her. The other to Marcus, apologizing for hitting him, asking him to visit her at Kaylah's.

Only one of those letters made it to servants' hands to send in the post. The other was deposited in Leah's bedside drawer while she mulled over the matter.

Chapter 19

If her pride wasn't dead set against it, Leah might be able to entertain the idea of staying at Kaylah and Eric's estate forever. Kaylah continued to insist that Leah had the invitation to do so, and that everyone needed to accept help at times in their lives. Humble pie was a tough meal to swallow, and Leah wasn't sure she'd ever fully accept help without guilt or grudge.

But she did take her time in the library. She finished the *Valeska's Adventures* series, and reread them all again.

Kaylah and Eric stayed with Leah at their manor for Thanksgiving, a few of the staff members and their families joining them. The pumpkin pie was divine, even the crust.

On Leah's daily stroll about the grounds, she always carried a book with her; many from Kaylah's private library hadn't even been read by their owners. Granted, Kaylah and Eric were politicians, retired rulers, so a lot of their collection was dry reading, so Leah steered clear of those. Marcus might have enjoyed them, though, given his political aspirations and current internship.

Leah hiked the little hill in the back woods, made a vine hammock for herself in said woods, and soaked often in the swimming pond.

She stood a dead log up against a pair of healthy trees to use as a target. When her anger or frustration festered too much, her throwing knives got good use. She pelted them into the log time and time again. When feeling a little less violent, Leah practiced extending her vines around her palms, and squeezing them—Kaylah's tip of something she'd done many a time under the table during frustrating negotiations.

Three weeks after arriving, Kaylah and Leah held their weekly picnic, this time in the pavilion near the pond. Kaylah and Eric were having an old friend visit them, another mutual friend of Rachel's.

"And I mean it when I say you don't have to stay holed up in your room," Kaylah said. "It won't be awkward."

"Okay." Even as the word left her lips, Leah fully intended to do just that—hide away in her room.

Kaylah's Seeder friend was expected to arrive the next day for a few-day visit. Leah had met her only once before.

As soon as Leah woke, she dressed and searched the manor for Kaylah, having forgotten to ask her an important question about their agenda while the guest would be there. Eventually, Leah poked her head into the sitting room, where Kaylah already conversed with the woman—a strawberry blonde.

"Oh, sorry," Leah said. She hadn't meant to intrude, and she hadn't expected the visitor to arrive so early in the morning.

"Come on in!" Kaylah said, gesturing for her to enter.

"Well, I... I didn't mean to barge in."

"Come on. I insist."

Leah nervously entered, sucking in her gut. At three months pregnant, she was definitely starting to show. She sat down on a settee opposite the two, putting on a smile. "Good morning. And good to see you, Mrs. Murialsdotter."

"You can call me Saff." She smiled. "I didn't think you'd remember me."

In truth, Leah hadn't remembered her last name, but Kaylah had reminded her of it the day before. "I still don't know a ton of Seeders by name, but I remember you."

"I hope that's not a bad thing." Saff and Kaylah shared a playful glance.

"It's not." Leah straightened her shirt, afraid to expose her bump.

"You know, the two of you should have a chat while you're here, Saff," Kaylah said.

"Honestly, I'm going to be pretty busy," Leah lied. "I didn't mean to get in the way."

"I don't mind." Saff crossed her legs.

"Saff doesn't bite," Kaylah added. "Though..." She narrowed her eyes at Saff. "The first time we met, she *did* want to kill me."

Before she realized what she was saying, Leah grinned. "So, we *do* have something in common."

Saff's eyes grew wide, and her jaw slacked. Leah was about to explain how she and Kaylah joked about the assassination attempt that way, but she halted once Kaylah started to cackle, full-on cackle.

Leah's cheeks were warm, but Saff's face relaxed.

And Kaylah kept howling with laughter.

Leah shrugged at Saff. "That's just kinda how we roll."

Saff gave her a gentle smile as Kaylah finally took a breath.

"Gosh, I love you, kiddo," Kaylah said.

And in that moment, Leah was safe. How many people could forgive someone who had tried to take their life? And then rescue them and take them in?

"Love you too," Leah shyly confessed.

Kaylah's smile faded, replaced by a look of deep appreciation, as though she'd just been gifted the Christmas present she'd always wanted. As though she'd craved to hear that from her only niece for quite some time.

Leah still wasn't used to throwing the L-word around, and now Kaylah was the third person she'd ever used it on. And perhaps this wasn't the best time to get mushy, with a guest in the room. "Anyway, I really was going to get back to my book." She'd already forgotten her question. "But, uh, Saff, I'd be happy to chat if you'd like later."

"Sounds good."

Seeders were an odd bunch. If they chose to have children, they had twenty-four. No more, no less, and all at once. Was that why Kaylah had wanted them to chat? Because Saff had so many kids, and Leah was about to become a mom? That would require Leah to divulge that secret, assuming Saff didn't already know.

After lunch, Saff suggested they walk the grounds. Leah was always happy to do that.

"I love visiting Kaylah's estate." Saff walked with her hands behind her back. "Seeder lands are beautiful, but it just hits differently over here."

"Yeah, it's nice here."

After a moment of silence, Saff spoke again. "Was there something in particular you wanted to talk about?"

"I kinda thought you knew why Kaylah suggested we talk..."

"Nope." Saff chuckled. "I'm sure there's some puzzle to put together between you and me. Kaylah always has her reasons."

It was probably about the pregnancy thing. But really, Saff couldn't relate that much. Seeders carried their seedlings—their children—in their bodies for a week max. Not the eight months Ivies did. And the numbers game was definitely off-kilter.

But Saff had more value than just as a mother. Leah leaned into that. "Maybe it's that I spend so much time in the kingdom, and could stand to learn more about Seeders."

Saff flourished her hands. "At your service."

Leah gave her a half-smile. "Well, maybe this is selfish, because I'm a little curious about … what Seeders currently think of me."

For good or bad, most of that feedback had always been either blatantly shoved in Leah's face (through obscene gestures, scowls and flashes of glowing eyes, or otherwise), or fed to her by the palace.

"Well…" Saff bobbed her head. "Like Ivies or humans, Seeders don't all agree on everything."

That was a politician's answer if Leah had ever heard one. "So, they still hate me for my parents, and trying to take out Kaylah."

"Well, I…" Saff paused. "It's not like you're the topic of discussion every day. Most of the time, we all just go about our business. I'm sure things appear worse than they are to you because, well, it's your everyday reality."

Yeah, one I can't escape. "But when I *am* the topic of discussion?"

Saff breathed deeply. "Some say you're brave. Others…"

That sentence needed no conclusion, and it wasn't like Leah and Saff were close enough to be so frank.

"Are you thinking about doing some more travel in Seeder lands? Or doing some studies over there? I could help set you up."

Leah scoffed. "No one wants me over there. I wouldn't want to push my luck."

"Well, *I* like you."

That kind of validation from someone even older than her mom was like nails on a chalkboard. "Thanks. Now you just need to get the memo to the rest of your nation, and people can chill out."

Saff chuckled softly again. "Honestly, I can understand how some people struggle to accept you. They either have rumors to go on, or official royal tours with carefully crafted speeches. Maybe you *should* spend some time over there, and let people see the real you." She smirked. "Anyone that can joke about murdering Kaylah and get her to howl like that is redeemable in my eyes, and approachable. And Rachel likes you..."

Until her son knocked me up and I slapped him.

Leah folded her arms across her stomach. "Yeah. Get people to see the real me."

They walked for a while longer, and Leah couldn't help herself. "Is it... What's it like having twenty-four kids? Not the physical act, but raising them. Keeping them straight and caring for them all. Do you ever go crazy?" Her kids were about to all become teenagers.

With a sideways glance and the hint of another smirk on her lips, Saff said, "One kid or twenty-four, you go crazy. But I get why Ivies and humans find that kind of life so outlandish. What you have to remember is our lifestyle, our culture. Everything for Seeders is about family and community. Aunts, uncles, and grandparents are constantly around to help. It's a team effort."

Leah nodded.

"Are you and Marcus considering having kids down the road? Assuming things keep going the direction they've been going?"

Leah's heart dropped into her stomach. The direction they'd been going? "We've talked about it."

"I'd say you two have a nice support group, then, don't you?"

Did they? Marcus did. "Yeah."

Children and family support... Leah's mom still didn't know she was pregnant with Marcus's child, with a Boman. Just the night before, Leah had received another letter from her mom. That last line still haunted her. It was the one thing Leah had always needed to hear from her mom, and now always struggled to believe. *Love always.*

Leah was far too polite to ask Saff, but how many times in her stress or frustration had she ever wished she hadn't had a clutch of kids? How many times, if any, had she regretted that decision?

As much as Leah wanted to ask more about kids, she wasn't ready to divulge her little secret to a woman she barely knew. Overall, it was a pleasant walk, and gave her a couple of things to think over.

Saff's visit was only for a few days. By the time she left to return home, Leah had been at Kaylah's for a month.

Leah and Kaylah held their weekly picnic. It was nice chatting over meals with Eric, too, but Leah was growing fond of this special time with just her and her aunt. Though, she'd had some rough nightmares the night before, and was a bit on edge emotionally for this one.

"You really didn't have to hide away in your room so much." Kaylah gave her a playful look of scolding before taking a bite of strawberry.

"I know."

"You okay?"

Leah stirred her chia seed pudding. "I'm fine."

Kaylah leaned on an elbow. "Did you ever ... send a letter to Marcus?"

Frowning, Leah shook her head. "He hasn't sent one to me either." Not that she hadn't thought about her letter to him, or reread it a dozen times. She was thirteen weeks along. In three weeks, she'd hit her halfway point in this pregnancy. She'd decided that if he hadn't sent her a letter by the halfway mark, she would have to be the one to suck it up, to swallow her pride, and reach out. She couldn't keep going on like this, not knowing what her future held, not knowing how to move forward. Not knowing if moving forward meant doing so without him.

"He loves you," Kaylah reassured her.

Leah choked down the pain in that statement, battling the demons from her dreams. "No he doesn't. People tolerate or pity me; they don't love me."

"Not true," Kaylah said adamantly. "Eric and I love you, and the family loves you..." She sat up. "And I've known Marcus long enough to know that he loves you, and that you two are just ... stubborn, and this will blow over."

That deep anguish of defeat whispered to Leah that it was all a lie.

"Your mother loves you," Kaylah added.

Leah sniffled, shaking her head. "Not really."

Kaylah seemed confused, rightfully. "I knew the moment I saw her at the wedding venue that she *loved* you. She was ready to die for you, Leah."

And even as she *knew* that was true, Leah shook her head. Because it hadn't *always* been the truth.

With the haunt of a whisper, her mom's words had tortured her in her sleep last night. *You and me, we're the same.*

"What's wrong?" Kaylah asked.

Leah's throat bobbed. "Did my mom ever tell you about my conception?"

Kaylah looked surprised at the turn of conversation. "We never really discussed it much."

Leah had her confirmation. No one knew her mom's secret, other than Leah.

"She did ... *imply* ... that perhaps her pregnancy was an accident," Kaylah said.

Leah nodded. She'd kinda guessed that too.

"That doesn't mean she doesn't love you, Leah. Your pregnancy wasn't planned either, but that doesn't mean you don't love your child, or that you won't be a great mother."

The comparison was gutting, visceral, and in no time flat, Leah's eyes blurred with tears. "That's not how it happened."

Kaylah searched her face. "That's not how what happened?"

Leah swallowed hard. "My parents didn't plan me. But I wasn't an accident. *My mom* planned me." She looked down, picking at her nails. "He made it clear when they were dating that he wouldn't be faithful, and she agreed to that. She told herself she could be okay with it, as long as he made her number one. But after a while, she got jealous. She grew tired of him taking lovers." Leah dug a finger into her knee. "And she did what no woman should ever do. She stopped taking her birth control tonic, and lied. She made him get her pregnant, and lied about it being an accident to try to keep him closer."

When Leah looked up, Kaylah grimaced.

Soren had been a monster, a piece of trash that had only ever used people as tools. Perhaps he and Beata had truly been meant for each other, because Leah had been Beata's tool.

"And you know, it worked. Too well. My dad did *one* decent thing in his life; he got protective of his wife and unborn child. But then it backfired. My mom wasn't a strategist. He took care of that part of the war. But he started to act more ... erratic, less predictable. He stretched the army and assassin networks too thin. He put his focus in the wrong places." Her heart ached at the confession. "They lost the war because of me. He died giving her more time to get away because of *me*."

Kaylah wore a deep frown. "I know it's hard, and I... I know it's a barely there silver lining, but that saved my life. I have no doubt he would have killed me eventually. And it saved *a lot* of other lives."

"I know," Leah croaked. If the realm knew that Leah had helped cause Soren and Beata's downfall, they'd sing a different tune. She had no doubt they'd suddenly be a lot more forgiving to her, and even to her mom. But sharing that truth with the realm would mean accepting the piercing duality of it. Accepting the other half, or trying not to, had been destroying Leah since the day her mom had let this fact slip.

"Don't get me wrong," Leah continued. "I know they were wrong and horrible and misguided, and it's good they lost the war. But my mom is the only person that *ever* loved me growing up. She was the *only* person even remotely there for me."

Sharply engraved in the back of her mind, Leah still recalled her conversation the night she'd found her mom's journal in the human world, had discovered her parents had been rulers of some mysterious realm.

Leah had asked: "If you knew then, what you know now, that this would happen, would you have done things differently?"

Her mom had replied wistfully: "Absolutely."

"Worse than being an accident, is being a regret," Leah told Kaylah.

Kaylah looked instantly perturbed. "Your mother said that?! That she regrets having you?"

"No, she didn't." And she hadn't. She'd only spilled her secret by accident on a random prison visit, and still professed on every visit and in every letter since, that she still loved Leah, and *always* would. "But you didn't see the way she was when I was a kid. Emotionally checking out, writing in a journal, mourning my dad day and night. She wouldn't even tell me his name!" It hadn't only been sorrow that had stunted her mom all those years; it had also been guilt. "Wouldn't you, at least a little bit, regret or resent your own child if they were the reason Eric died?"

"I'm not a mother, so I can't say for sure, but I certainly hope not."

But Leah had already answered that for herself months ago. As much as part of her was getting excited for the new life growing inside her, she had regrets. No resentment, but there *were* regrets. "You know, my mom used to say we were so much alike. We look a lot alike, we like the same movies, we both ... started having sex around the same age. And I know it's not the same as what happened with my dad, but this baby, associated with me, and not conceived according to the high royal expectations, is going to take Marcus down a notch."

Kaylah looked her dead in the eyes. "You both made a choice to have sex. It's just as much his responsibility as yours, no matter who has the better or worse reputation."

"Yeah?" Leah wiped away her tears with the back of her hands. "You can't imagine what people are going to say? That Soren's daughter got knocked up on purpose because Marcus got tired of her? Realized he could do better? That I did this to trap him?"

"You're not like your mother. If you say it was an honest mistake, I believe you."

"And everyone else?" Leah challenged. "When they all know I manipulated him before? Lied to him to get close to you? When I proved I was crazy?"

"Leah." Kaylah's voice was soft, pleading, understanding. "It'll be okay."

"Right. Because a formal notice from the palace soothes all unease, rights all wrongs." She shook her head. Kaylah had commented about the strict palace rules and it being harder for Leah because she hadn't been raised royal. It was true. Kaylah was made of tougher stuff. She could handle the constant scrutiny. Leah had thought she could, had thought she was strong, but that had always been a facade, a lie.

"I'm here for you, okay?" Kaylah reassured her.

The floodgates of guilt and pain and grief had already opened for Leah, and she was far from done. She hadn't expected her pregnancy to trigger so much in her, but it had. It had shaken her to her core.

As those gates remained open, her heart raw, Leah struggled to breathe, tears continuing to cascade. "Everything is my fault. I have no one to blame but me. I built my own prison. And *every* time I think back to my life in the human world—the life I left behind—I realize I'm the one to blame.

"Because when my mom was too depressed, sad about losing my dad and not being able to see her family, not able to enjoy the ambient energy of the realm—it was my fault. And every time Cheryl hit me, grabbed me, pulled my hair, made me feel worthless—it was because my mom was too wrapped up in being sad because my very existence got my dad killed, so she didn't want to see it, didn't want to believe it."

"That's on her," Kaylah retorted.

"Every time we had to move because I acted out or because my mom was afraid of us getting discovered, every time I had to leave friends behind, every time I *hated* it—my fault.

"Every time I made stupid decisions—shoplifting, lying, sneaking out to parties—my fault."

"She was a neglectful parent," Kaylah replied.

Leah sniffled, catching a breath. "Every time I was an idiot with a guy, letting things go too far, getting hurt, earning a reputation as a slut, just because I wanted friendship and love and attention... That was my fault too. If I had never been conceived, my dad wouldn't have acted rash in the war, my mom wouldn't have lost him, wouldn't have grieved, and my life wouldn't be a living hell."

Now even Kaylah was crying. "He might have lost the war anyway. Don't internalize all that blame."

Despite her need to shove it all down, to pretend she'd never learned the truth of what her mom had done to deceive her dad, Leah had analyzed it. Knowing and feeling were two different things. Her heart and mind were oil and water.

Leah pointed to her head. "I know that here." She pointed to her heart. "But this tells me I'm lying to myself."

An unborn child held no fault because of their parents' decisions. A little girl was blameless for the neglect of her mom.

But Leah couldn't win. Couldn't accept that she had any role in ending the war, in one of the best things to happen for peace in the realm in *centuries*, without also accepting that she was scum.

Kaylah scooped Leah into a tight hug. "I'll never be anything but grateful for you."

Leah sobbed. Even as tears spilled down her cheeks onto Kaylah's back, as snot fell ungraciously onto the retired queen's shirt, as huffs and whimpers escaped Leah's lips, she sobbed.

Chapter 20

After a mortifyingly long amount of time, Leah's crying had quieted. She leaned back, and Kaylah released her. Leah tried not to be embarrassed. "Sorry."

"Don't be. How can I help you?"

Leah loosed a breath. "I have no idea."

"Does ... Marcus know?"

"No. I haven't told anyone about that. And I'm not ready for anyone to know." Her mom had pleaded with her not to share the truth of her conception with anyone.

Despite Kaylah's nod, she looked as though she didn't fully agree with that call.

"And please don't do anything with my mom, or say anything to her either." As far as Leah knew, Kaylah never visited her mom in prison, but Kaylah *did* still have some sway politically.

Kaylah didn't respond, but her expression hinted she wanted to tear Beata a new one.

"I know I should hate her, but she's the only person that's always been there for me. Even if it was ... not always what I needed." Leah sniffled once more. "She didn't tell me that to be mean. She let it slip on accident. She doesn't even realize I feel this way."

"She should, Leah. *She* deserves to feel the weight of her decisions, not you. She should be protecting you, not the other way around."

Leah frowned, glancing down at the picnic blanket. Her mom was so lonely in prison. And no one knew her mom the way Leah did. Her mom could do better, could become a better person. "Please."

Kaylah sighed. "Fine."

They continued to eat their picnic in relative silence. Leah reached for a cloth napkin at one point to wipe her hands on, but she'd used them all for tissues.

"You know, kiddo..." Kaylah scooped a spoonful of pudding. "Going back to the whole you-becoming-a-mother thing? I think you'll be a great one. You're more mature than your mother was, and you know what mistakes to avoid."

"Thanks." It hurt to be both compared *and* contrasted to her mom.

"I kinda thought you and Marcus were..." Kaylah rocked her head back and forth. "You know, talking about tying the knot."

Leah picked at a pastry. "Well, yeah, we've talked about it. But I was in school, and he was going off on his internship and focusing on his career, and..." She shrugged. "I guess it's a good thing I was never really a princess, because I suck at dating or even being remotely related to royalty."

Kaylah gave her a small grin. "I *was* a real princess, and I *still* sucked at it."

Leah chuckled.

When she retired to her room that night, Leah lay there, her arms spread wide across the massive bed. What did she want? To be in Marcus's arms. To have him warming her, kissing her, telling her it would all be okay.

But he wasn't there. She considered her letter in the bedside drawer. Perhaps she ought to not wait until this arbitrary four-month mark in her pregnancy to send it to him.

Though ... she did want to hold off a bit. She needed to process everything she'd just thrown at Kaylah, process what she wanted, and if the contents of the letter would change.

As much as she hated the idea of journaling like her mom and Rachel had, it made sense to write out her thoughts.

The next morning, Leah took Kaylah's suggestion to start one.

She didn't even know how to journal.

Do people just write 'Dear Diary' and treat the book like it's a person they're telling their story to? Or maybe that's only diaries... What's the difference between a diary and a journal?

Had she been in the human world, she'd have whipped out her phone and looked up all those questions on the internet. As she was in a realm without electricity, she had to do what came to her. It made sense to start from square one.

So ... before I was born...

The weather was tepid, the breeze light, as she sat under the pavilion and wrote. She had to admit it was cathartic. And she also had to admit that she needed a handkerchief, or two, or a dozen, if she was going to take this up.

But she spent hours pouring her soul into that thing. It was her witness. It was her warden. It was her shame and hope and sorrow.

Only when she shivered did she realize she was squinting, the light of the day fading. And she was famished.

Tucking the notebook under her arm, she headed inside. Having eaten breakfast on her own, as well as a meager snack she'd taken out with her, she made a beeline for the dining room. She halted at Eric's voice. "You're sure she'll be okay?"

"Yeah," Kaylah replied. "Sometimes we just need time and space to heal."

Leah clutched her journal, rounding the corner. "Sorry I'm late." She was *abominably* late. Kaylah and Eric's plates had been cleared, and they had dessert sitting untouched in front of them.

"I didn't mean to break my promise." She'd missed a full day of meals, not spending any with them.

Kaylah smiled, gesturing at the food dishes still on the table, and at Leah's empty dinner plate. "A little birdie told us you were busy jotting in that notebook of yours. We figured you'd join us when the light was all gone, or that pregnant body of yours forced you to seek nourishment."

Leah matched her smile, sitting down and setting the journal on the chair beside her. "Thanks."

As Leah scooped mashed potatoes onto her plate, Kaylah leaned her head on Eric's shoulder. They sat extra close during private meals, a far cry from the formal affairs they often attended. "In case you heard us on your way in, I was telling Eric why you were out there. Not any specifics, just that we had a good chat yesterday."

Eric raised his hands in a gesture of 'it's not my business if you don't want it to be my business.'(hh)

Leah liked Eric, and he'd never acted as though he judged Leah, but she was grateful Kaylah hadn't shared anything. Leah was still ashamed to be a mess. "Thanks." Though she *was* surprised. They didn't seem like the kind of couple that kept secrets from one another, or perhaps Leah didn't know them as well as she thought. They were diplomats, after all. Eric had technically been Kaylah's consort, and Kaylah had probably kept plenty of information from him during their reign. But as Leah started eating those perfectly creamy mashed potatoes, she doubted that.

She did love Kaylah. That she had saved her that day in the backyard of the cottage, that she was being impartial and helpful, and kind. That she was willing to keep Leah's secrets. And in that moment, Leah realized…

"Have you ever had servants follow me into the woods?"

"You're sturdy," Kaylah said. "We figured you'd make it back in one piece. They've only ever checked on you by tracking you down to make sure you were okay if you were gone for too long and missed a meal."

Leah nodded, scooping another spoonful, her mind in those woods. Kaylah had let her wander those woods to her heart's content, full-well knowing Leah had made an attempt at tree rifting to the human world to escape. Any number of those trees could have been Leah's ticket out of here, but she hadn't thought to do it.

She felt safe at Kaylah's. She felt free without the cage.

Just earlier that day, she could've sworn she'd felt the baby move for the first time. It had been heartwarming, and painful. Her journal entry echoed that of her own mother's, one penned long ago.

I felt the baby for the first time today. How is it the best things can bring the most pain? I'll do anything to keep it safe. But it reminds me so much of him.

Leah knew what she needed. And she needed to change that letter to Marcus.

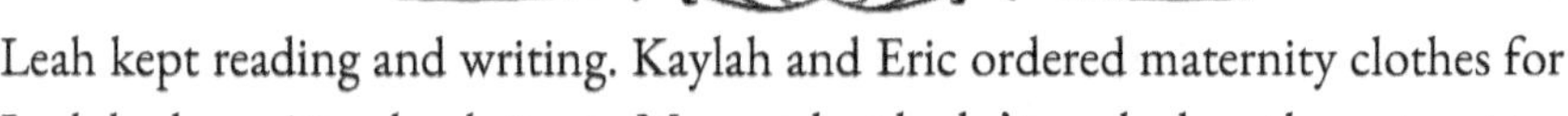

Leah kept reading and writing. Kaylah and Eric ordered maternity clothes for her. Leah had rewritten her letter to Marcus, but hadn't worked up the guts yet to send it, or to discuss her plans with Kaylah.

She could take a little more time, no rash decisions like her dad. Instead of rushing into things, she added another project to her to-do list. One that brought a smile to her face. With more movement in her growing belly, she was sure she could feel the baby now, and she wanted to do something special for her.

She started to write her stories. Stories about a brave little Ivy girl taking on a variety of adventures and challenges. She wrote little boy stories, too, in case she was wrong about the gender. She couldn't draw worth beans, though, so hopefully her future child could appreciate stick figures that looked like someone drew them with their eyes closed.(ii)

The pavilion had become one of her favorite spots to journal. The midday sun was warm on her back as she scratched out her feelings about having to move cross-country during Christmas one year. In the present, Christmas was just a few days away.

A male voice cleared his throat from just outside the pavilion.

"I packed a lunch," Leah said. "I'm fine, thanks."

"I'm glad to hear that," a hesitant and familiar voice replied.

Leah's heart ceased to beat as she looked up, taking in those warm brown eyes, that curly brown hair. "Marcus," she breathed.

Chapter 21

Frozen in place, Leah gaped. "Marcus?" she repeated.

His hands were in his pockets, his arms rigid. "In the flesh."

"What are you doing here?"

"We should ... talk."

And like that, her heart dropped to her gut. Any conversation that started like that between a couple didn't bode well. "Then say what you need to say." *Just rip off the bandage.*

He furrowed his brow. "Well, I figured *we* would talk. Not just me. Mind if I sit?"

Leah rubbed her face. "Go ahead." She closed her journal, setting it beside her as Marcus took the bench opposite her under the pavilion.

"You look great," he said, all hesitance. His eyes flashed to her stomach, and he frowned. Was that regret for getting her pregnant? Fear of her reaction about whatever he'd concluded alone? Or guilt for leaving her alone without a shred of news for eleven of the fifteen weeks she'd been pregnant?

"I think we should lay it all out there," he said. "And be honest."

"Sounds like a good start."

"And if I'm honest..." He bobbed his head. "I'm only here because Kaylah sent me a letter."

So, maybe Kaylah wasn't so great at secrets and not meddling. "What did she say?"

Marcus twisted his lips. "It was pretty succinct. That I should stop being a jackass and come visit my pregnant girlfriend."

Okay, fine. She liked Kaylah again. "About time."

"You could have visited me too." He tilted his head. "Or written a letter."

This was going to be a long chat, and a difficult one. "A lot could have been done differently. Like not dragging your parents into this mess."

He narrowed his eyes. "What do you mean?"

"You and me, we can work through problems, but once you drag family members into it, they pick sides, and they won't be on my side. You didn't need to tell them that I..." She paused, feeling every bit wrong. People who were hurt had a right to speak up, and denying him that would have been wrong, but it still wasn't right that he'd turned his parents even more on Leah. "I am *so* sorry I hurt you, and I will *never* do that again. To you, or anyone else." She rested a hand on her stomach. "I swear." She wouldn't be like the fake aunt she'd suffered under growing up.

Marcus acknowledged her words with hurt in his eyes. "I didn't tell them about that. I haven't told anyone."

"I thought we agreed to be honest. Your mom knew I hurt you. No one else was in the room to know that."

He drew a deep breath. "I told her to not say anything. I asked her to leave it alone, and give you some space."

"So, you did tell them."

"Leah, you slapped me *hard*."

Her soul shrank to the size of a mushroom. "I know. And I'm sorry."

"I didn't have to walk far down the lane before I realized I was bruising. And the last thing I needed was for everyone to notice a famous Boman with a formerly homicidal girlfriend developing a giant bruise on his face. There aren't exactly Seeder healers around every corner, so I walked to my parents' place."

Leah frowned.

"I wouldn't tell her how I got it. But she put it together when I asked her to make sure you had more food because I wouldn't be back for a while. I told her not to say anything."

Leah was at a loss for words.

"I didn't drag them into this, not intentionally."

"You shouldn't have said what you did before it happened, before you left." It didn't excuse her actions, but he had been beyond cruel.

This time he frowned, his throat bobbing. "I know. I'm sorry. I... I was trying so hard, but you were making me choose, and then you were going to leave me."

"I wasn't. And I told you that."

"Then why did you have your passport with you? Why did you hide it again after I found it?"

He *had* searched. "I wasn't going to leave you. It was just an option, one I prepared for when I was panicking."

Looking her dead in the eye, he kept a measured but unhappy tone. "You threatened to take our child and disappear in the human world like your mom did."

So many objections assaulted her. What about the fact that he'd threatened to cage her? Or literally any topic that touched on her painful feelings with her mom at the moment...

She chose the moment where this had all really started to go downhill. "Just admit you don't want this baby, Marcus."

His expression was incredulous. "Why would you think that?"

"You clearly didn't have a mirror when you had pure terror on your face as I told you I was pregnant. And you didn't want it."

"I never said I didn't want it."

"Maybe you didn't say it that way, but you made it abundantly clear."

He spoke through clenched teeth, his nostrils flaring. "I never said it, because I never *once* thought it."

She threw her hands up. "The first chance you got, you suggested we give her to your brother and sister-in-law to adopt."

"Really?!" Marcus's jaw dropped. "I'm sorry I didn't say the right words, or give you the right facial expression. You had time to process before telling me you were pregnant. You got my raw reaction. And you weren't sure you wanted to keep the baby." He gestured at her. "And if you didn't plan to keep it, you'd what? Put it up for adoption? Why the hell would that bother an adopted Boman to imagine their Boman child put up for adoption? Wondering if their birth parents hated them for the sheer fact they were born without powers?"

She should have thought of that. He didn't speak often or resentfully about his being adopted, but he'd shared how it had hurt finding out the way he'd been dropped off at an orphanage as an infant, in the way unwanted Bomen used to be.

"And honestly," he continued, "I panicked. I didn't think I could be a single dad, but I grasped on to the best option I could think of at the moment. Tobias and Cam have talked about adoption. And if they adopted it..." He paused, looking down at his hands. "Then maybe I could still be in its life."

Tears coated her eyes. "You should have said that."

He shrugged. "With your next breath, you decided you wanted to keep it, so I didn't think it mattered."

Leah scooped herself another helping of humble pie. "I should have been more understanding about all the Boman stuff."

Her mom's words replayed in her mind. *You and me, we're the same.* And that hurt—another comparison. While Soren had been the war strategist, Beata had played her role as his queen. They hadn't ruled long at all, but after their downfall, plans had been found for what they'd wanted to do with Bomen after they'd eradicated the Seeder threat. It was disgusting, and it had been planned and penned by Leah's mom, Beata—the daughter of the leaders of the former quasi slave communities.

Leah loved Marcus. She'd grown up around humans, who didn't have powers. It had never meant anything to her that he didn't have them. But she'd been culturally deaf, utterly insensitive. She needed to do better about considering his needs, too, and that of their future child. And not just because the realm would skewer her if she made a misstep as the parent of a Boman.

"I'm really sorry."

He looked at his hands again. "Thanks."

What more was there to say? "I know you don't like choosing between me and your family, but you broke promises."

"I know. I'm sorry. I thought my mom could help."

Leah fidgeted with her hands. "Did you ... have your aunt send the escorts? To make sure I couldn't leave?" They'd appeared the day after he'd left, after he'd threatened to make sure she didn't leave the realm.

He hesitated. "Not exactly. When you stormed away from the palace and I hung back, I asked Aunt Catrina to give you some space. You were acting kinda crazy, and nervous. I told her we'd be fine without your escorts while we stayed at the cottage. And then when I left the cottage, my mom wanted to make sure you were safe, so she asked Catrina to station them there for you. They were already assigned to protect you."

"They were only there on regular duty? I could have rifted to the human world with my passport?"

"I don't know," he admitted. "I haven't talked to Aunt Catrina since we left together."

She took a cleansing breath, the nightmare of misunderstanding between them laid bare. "It's already terrifying to know what kind of repercussions having your child will bring down on me, and I should have considered that more seriously before we got back together, but I'd like to think we can still sort this out."

"Leah…" He ruffled his hair. "No offense, but people bring up our relationship to me, too. It's not like I've never had someone express what a bad idea dating you is. After all we've been through. After our family's history. But I have *always* looked past that."

That stung. And he had no right to dismiss her so casually. "There's a *big* difference in our situations, though. Because *you* have always retained the ability to walk away from me and my reputation. I've never had that option in this realm, and I never will. If you broke up with me and left me for good, people would pat you on the back. I would continue to be Soren and Beata's murderous child. Any semblance of a decent reputation comes from dating you, and from 'official memos' from the palace PR team. Or from pretending to be something I'm not. I stay with you because I love you, but I'm not ignorant of the fact that I rely so heavily on you. And I hate relying on anyone." For money, for reputation, for anything. In a cage.

He sighed. "You're right. It would suck having your parents."

It did, but it was time she came clean about her parents too. "It bugs me when you talk about my mom. Especially when you compare us."

And then she let it out. Having had some time to process, and already having confessed it all to Kaylah, she explained her heartache, fears, and hurt about how her mom had betrayed her dad, and how Leah had shouldered that blame.

He mostly sat through it with head shakes and a sympathetic frown.

"I know your mom is better than mine, but I'd rather not be compared to either." She sniffled.

"I get it." He fidgeted with his hands. "Can I hug you?"

"Yes." She choked down fresh tears as they stood, meeting in the middle.

Kaylah's hugs were healing. Marcus's hugs were something otherworldly.

"I am *so* sorry," he whispered into her ear. "I'm never leaving you again. *Never.* I'll do better."

Marcus was home. He was happiness. He was the day to her night.

"I'm sorry too." She savored the warmth of his arms around her.

"This kinda feels weird," he said after a while, a smile in his voice. "Hugging you with a bump between us."

She wore a smile that she imagined matched his. "It's only going to get weirder."

"I love you," he said.

"I love you too." She leaned back, and they locked eyes. His lips begged to be kissed, so she did just that. He didn't hesitate in returning the kiss, a hand holding her hips, the other weaving into her black hair.

For that moment, it was only the two of them in that realm. The two of them, the scent of daffodils in the distance, and their hearts beating wildly in unison.

And even as they pulled apart, she wanted more. She *needed* more. "What do you say to us..."

You're nothing but a slut, Cheryl's voice taunted, a memory from her past.

There were worse things Leah could be. She could be like Cheryl. Leah promptly told the bitter old hag in her head—the one who was actually rotting away in a prison cell—where she could go, and what she could do with herself.

"What do you say to us finishing this conversation in my bedroom?" She'd wilt on the spot if he refused her. She *needed* that kind of connection with him, that happiness and hope she'd had when they'd first arrived at the cottage.

He gave her a shy smile. "Really?"

"Really."

Blinking, he looked down. "That won't hurt you or the baby?"

She rolled her eyes. "I'm pregnant. Not dying."

"Then let's see how it goes."

Chapter 22

Things went well back in Leah's room. *Very* well. That side of things had never been a problem in their relationship—the passion, the physical side. But this time was different. There was more sweetness, gentleness, intention. She loved Marcus with everything she had.

They lay cuddling under the sheets, staring into each other's eyes. "We're not half bad at this, are we?" he said.

She bit her lip. "No, we're not." She ran a caressing hand across his shoulder. "But sex doesn't fix everything... If anything, for the two of us, it kinda makes things..." She didn't want to say worse, not about their child. "More complicated."

Marcus pursed his lips. "Yeah."

"So... Assuming we both do better at being considerate, and communicating, and controlling our tempers... Where do we go from here?"

"I took the week off, told them I needed to take care of some family business." He stroked her hip with his thumb, a pensive look on his face. "I know the family wouldn't like it, but would you want to join me up north? Move in with me? See how things go?"

Her heart was full of gratitude at the invitation, but it wasn't enough. "There will be rumors."

"I know."

It felt like they'd be digging a bigger hole, digging deeper at making their families unhappy, at causing more drama. "Is it going to be that much different than hiding away here or at the cottage? I guess with the exception of spending our nights together..."

He drew a deep breath. "Option B: we go to the human world, assuming you still want to."

"Really?" Her stomach flipped. "For how long? Just this week?"

His gaze was soft, his expression sincere. "For as long as you want. As long as it takes."

"But what about your internship?"

Something flashed across his face. Guilt? Frustration? "Like you said—I've always been able to walk away unscathed. And I think I get it now. With hardly any advance notice, I told them I was taking a week off for personal reasons. And you know what they said? 'Take all the time you need. We'll hold your position for you.'"

"That's really nice of them."

He wrinkled his nose. "Too nice. Do you know how many people applied for that position? *A lot.* And I doubt they would have extended that offer to anyone who wasn't Guillen's son, and Catrina's nephew."

He'd talked about that with Leah before—wanting to stand on his own two feet. But he hadn't seemed to fully understand his privilege until now.

"That's kind of how politics go, right? It's about who you know?" she said.

Letting out a soft sigh, he shook his head. "I guess I still need to figure out how I want to fit into the politics game, because it's not just about wanting to do good, as much as I want it to be. Neither of us can escape our parents' legacies. The difference is ... mine will always give me a leg up, and yours will always be ready to tear you down."

She gave him a tender kiss on the lips. "You'd really be okay with spending time in the human world? How much time does 'as long as you want' entail?"

"I told you before Tobias's wedding that I'd be willing to live in the human world, for the right person. And if that's what it takes to make you happy, then we can stay there. Because *you're* the right person."

That gesture meant more to her than the world, especially considering what he was willing to give up.

He continued. "And even if this is a trial run, to see if you and I can really make this work..." He slid a hand to her belly. "Even if you and I don't get..."

Married?

"Well, if we can't sort out our problems, and we have to ... go our separate ways..." His voice was strained, pained. "Then we'll know we gave it a fair shot. And we'll figure out how to still get along, right?"

"Yeah." Her heart was heavy at discussing the fact they may not be able to resolve their differences in the long run. They *were* both stubborn, and so different.

"No matter what, we're always going to be family," he said.

That little part of her that got the ick at technicalities squirmed. Their relationship was legal in all fifty US states, and no one in the Green Lands thought much of them being second cousins, through adoption or not, but still... "Please don't bring up the shared family members thing when we're in bed like this."

He furrowed his brow. "I wasn't. I meant that no matter what, even if we go our separate ways, I will *always* be this child's father, and you'll always be its mother. We'll always be a family in that way, always there for him. Or her."

And in that moment, something clicked for Leah. Something deep, visceral, primal. She couldn't change the facts of her parentage, of her past. Wishing things had been different wouldn't do any good. Fearing the unknown future hadn't benefited her either. But she craved family, one of her own. One she could create and mold and nurture to be what she wished she'd grown up with. It was already staring her in the face, and growing within her.

"I'll marry you."

Marcus's eyes grew wide. "Really?" His stare was cautious. "You mean it?"

"Yes. I... I still don't want to be pressured to do it *tomorrow*, or in front of thousands or anything, but ... yes."

"Whatever you want!" And then he laid a kiss on her that would make anyone blush.

Eventually, he released her and untangled himself. "I have something for you." Sliding out of bed, he grabbed something from his clothes on the dresser. "Close your eyes."

She did as directed. A heartbeat later, the bed dipped again beside her, and his warm hands took hers. He parted her fingers, and slipped a ring on. "You can open them."

In shock, she stared at the ring. It was an Ivy design—white gold with thin details, one of a kind. "You came prepared with a ring?" With how many times she'd turned him down, and with how badly they'd become separated, that had been a lucky shot in the dark.

"Not exactly," he said softly. He hesitated, hurt or embarrassed. "I've had that with me for at least four months."

She did the math. Her pregnancy was a week shy of four months along. "You bought this before we got pregnant?"

He averted his gaze. "Yeah. I, uh, well, I was going to ask on the special boat ride."

Boat ride? "Oh," she said in a barely audible whisper. He'd planned a special boat ride and dinner, one they'd had to cancel because of her maternal sickness. The one they'd canceled on the same day she broke the news to him.

"Actually, um…" He swallowed. "I first was going to ask you the night I snuck into your chambers, but then it didn't feel right. Like it was a reward or something. 'Congratulations… We finally slept together… Enjoy this new ring!' And then there's the whole what-story-do-we-tell-our-future-kids thing. I didn't want it to be weird that we were *naked* when I proposed."

She smirked. "You mean like right now, when we're naked again, and you just slipped a ring on my finger?"

"Riiiight… I vote we omit the bedroom facts from this proposal and reunion story. This all happened at the pavilion."

She admired her ring once more. "I agree." It wasn't a harmful lie.

His voice softened again. "And about what we tell him, the baby, someday… About how this all went down? I don't want him to ever feel unwanted."

She gazed into his warm brown eyes. No, as an adopted child, Marcus would naturally *not* want his child to experience that same pain of rejection. As a deceptively conceived child, she *wished* she'd only been an accident. "I agree. People will do the math, and stories will come out—they always do. But as far as this child will ever know, it was unplanned, but *not* unwanted. Never unwanted."

He kissed her on the head, and they slipped more deeply under the covers, cuddling. She stared at her ring. It felt weird, but right.

And then something nagged at her. There was *something* about the looks Catrina and his parents had given them when they'd announced the pregnancy. A sharpness to the looks and questions they'd aimed at Leah about the young couple *not* being engaged. "Did anyone know you were planning to propose?"

"Yeah," he confessed. "My parents, and Aunt Catrina and Uncle Stephan. Uncle Stephan helped me coordinate the staff for the boat."

She let out a frustrated sigh. "Is that why they looked at me confused, even *offended* when they asked why we weren't engaged? Because they knew it was already going to happen?"

"Um… Maybe?"

She covered her face with her hands. "And you don't see why that made me the bad guy? Why everyone questioned if I really loved you?"

"Um…"

Turning to face him, she couldn't hide her frustration. "Why didn't you say something? Why didn't you pull out the ring and show me that you weren't proposing just because I was pregnant?!"

He frowned, wearing a look of devastation. "I screwed up. But I... The way you shot me down? That *destroyed* me. You were *adamant* about the fact that you didn't want to marry me. And with each mention of marriage, the thought disgusted you more and more. So, I stopped bringing it up. I asked family to stop asking, to stop bugging you."

That vise that had twisted tighter with each mention, each hint...

She hadn't appreciated the pressure. "Don't most couples *talk* about engagement before it happens? How often is it actually a surprise?"

"We talked about it. I missed you like crazy, Leah. I wanted to see you more often than on the weekends. And I figured when we started to talk about 'when' we got married instead of 'if' we got married, that you might be okay with pushing up our timeline." He quickly added, "On marriage. Not ... kids... So that sorta happened in the wrong order."

To that, she couldn't help but chuckle.

But she did have to sigh again. "I need you to man up, Marcus. This baby is yours, and we both need you. You can't make me out to be the bad guy here. I'm already the bad guy in everyone's eyes. And you can't just disappear for weeks or months at a time because you got your feelings hurt." She tried to be calm, remembering what Kaylah had said about Marcus's easier childhood meaning he hadn't been forced to grow up as fast as Leah had. Yes, she'd been as stubborn as he had been, but she'd tortured herself over it. He hadn't seemed to realize the consequences of his mistakes.

"I'll do better," he promised.

After a little more time in bed, they decided to get up. It wasn't even dinnertime, and the staff had to have informed Kaylah and Eric that Marcus was on the property...

As Leah slipped into pants, Marcus commented on her new wardrobe.

"Yeah, Kaylah helped me get some stuff that's bigger." Leah liked this deep purple shirt and the way it flared out a bit. "Sad to say, but the dress I wore to our first ball is *definitely* not going to fit me right now."

He grinned, buttoning his pants. "No offense, but I'd rather see you wearing *nothing* over any of those dresses."

"You don't blush as much as you used to."

His grin only widened.

"But you're still a nerd."

"You love it."

She eased herself down on a chair to put her sandals on. "I do." Admiring him as he combed his hair with his hands at the mirror, she couldn't resist a smirk at the irony—he hadn't been her type until she'd had no other choice than to date him. She'd never been attracted to guys like him before.

All sorted, he approached her, then knelt in front of her. "Can I see the belly?"

She lifted her shirt a bit. He gently slid his hands onto her bump, and beamed. He leaned in and kissed it ever so softly; it sent shivers up her spine, set the butterflies in her stomach loose again.

"Hey, little guy," he said. "Sorry I was gone." He lifted his gaze to Leah. "That won't happen again."

She rested her hands on his. "You think it's a boy?"

Marcus shrugged. "Maybe because I'm used to having a brother."

"I told Kaylah I thought it was a girl."

"Hmm... I guess we'll see. How does it feel? Everything's okay?"

"Yeah." She squeezed his hands. "I felt her move recently."

A subtle frown played on his lips as he nodded. "I'm sorry I missed it. I'll be around for all the other firsts."

They discussed a couple more things about their future, but some of it needed to be done with Kaylah.

Emerging from Leah's bedroom, they made their way to the dining room. A couple of servants busied themselves already with arranging the place settings for dinner. But ... there were only two settings.

"Is Kaylah or Eric gone for the night?" It wasn't like they'd babysat Leah the entire time she'd been there; they still came and went on occasion...

"No," one of the men answered. "They're taking dinner on their balcony tonight."

Kaylah. She'd sent for Marcus, and now they were leaving them to eat alone. She really was a matchmaker.

Leah didn't hate the idea of time alone with Marcus, but she was also excited for the next steps. "Do you mind if they join us?" she whispered.

"That's fine," Marcus replied.

"Could you let them know we'd like them to join us? Assuming they want to?"

"Yes, ma'am. We'll pass that along. Dinner will be served in about an hour."

While there was definitely temptation to spend that next hour back in Leah's room, Leah and Marcus decided they'd worked up enough of an appetite for now, in case Kaylah and Eric came looking for them before dinner.

Instead, they snuggled in the library, with her sitting on his lap, him nuzzling her neck.

"I want to hear all about your internship."

Marcus explained how he'd spent the better part of the last three months—learning public policies, formal manners, how laws were handled between the elected officials and the queen and king. Politics weren't really Leah's cup of tea, but she listened intently.

"And ... you?" he asked, drawing a spiral on her thigh.

"Oh, ya know... The equivalent of a college dropout still... I don't know." Her shoulders slumped. "It feels wrong to focus so much on powers when our baby won't have any."

"Hmm..."

She smiled. "But I've been reading a lot. And I've even written a few books."

He raised his eyebrows high. "What?"

"Well, it's not like they're novels, but more like little stories for us to read to her." She rested a hand on her bump.

Marcus trailed kisses down her neck. "That's brilliant. Can I see them?"

Leah cringed at the thought of anyone reading or seeing them in their current state. "Uh... Maybe down the road. They could be better. And the drawings are, well, *interesting*."

After a while, they were summoned for dinner by one of the servants. The servant informed them that Kaylah and Eric would be taking dinner with them.

And now, Leah and Marcus were about to discover if they could actually make their plans work.

Chapter 23

Kaylah and Eric stood from the table and exchanged hugs with Marcus after he and Leah entered the dining room. "Thanks for inviting us to dinner," Kaylah said.

Leah squinted as they all took their seats. "Mmhmm... We had an agreement. I can't believe you were going to back out of a shared meal together."

Kaylah grinned wickedly as she unfolded her napkin, placing it on her lap. She was the master orchestrator, and Leah could never be mad at her again.

"Congratulations, you two," Eric said, taking a sip of his wine.

"On...?"

"Your engagement. That's what your ring means, right?"

Leah blushed. She hadn't realized they would have noticed so quickly. But then again, they were diplomats. They knew how to read people and pick up on small details. "Thanks."

Marcus sent a smile her way. "Thanks."

They began serving themselves from the generous spread on the table—rice pilaf, roasted yams, a black bean spread with flatbread, and more.

"Bacon," Leah whispered. *Bacon. Ham. Steak. Chicken. Meat!* The human world had more meat, and that reminder made Leah's mouth water.

"Busy mentally planning the wedding?" Kaylah kidded. "Or are we needing to change Christmas plans?"

Leah had zoned out. "I was just thinking about, well, yeah, some of our plans for the future." She treaded lightly, nervously. "Marcus and I are hoping to leave and spend some time in the human world."

In unison, Kaylah and Eric's gazes dropped to their plates, Kaylah's lips pressed into a thin line. And Leah's heart stuttered. "Am I not allowed to leave?"

Kaylah drew a deep breath, her silverware clinking as she set it down. "Catrina … put orders in place when you left the palace, when the two of you left and refused to go talk to her."

"I can't leave either?" Marcus asked.

"The orders only pertain to Leah," Eric said, giving her an apologetic glance.

"It was just a security measure," Kaylah said. "And I'm sure if you two want to pay her a visit, she'd lift it."

Leah groaned internally. This wasn't the start they wanted, not if their reunion and future plans involved sitting down with the queen to be lectured, scolded, and possibly punished or forced into something they weren't ready for yet.

"Can't you do anything about it?" Leah asked. "You know, as Matron?"

Kaylah sat up straighter. "I'm not the queen anymore. My authority doesn't override her orders."

"But you still have pull," Marcus countered. "Diplomatic visas and whatnot?"

It might not be fair to drag Kaylah into their mess, but Leah still held out hope. "We figured you two would understand, with how you kept your relationship a secret when Eric first moved to the Green Lands. You two didn't want people to have their noses in your business."

Eric winced. "Those were different times and circumstances."

Kaylah studied the couple. "We can try."

"Thank you!" Leah said, all smiles.

"When are we planning on this?" Kaylah asked.

"Maybe a couple of days?" Leah said. That way Kaylah and Eric could enjoy time with family during Christmas. They'd allow Kaylah to tell the family a partial truth—that the young couple had made up and were choosing to spend their time alone getting reacquainted. They'd just omit the human-world part of the equation. "As much under the radar as possible, but we have some things to take care of."

Then Kaylah asked which property the couple would be staying at in the human world, as the royal family had a handful they kept up. Leah and Marcus wanted freedom, a clean break from their families. They weren't planning on staying at any of them. And they weren't planning on using either of their allowances, their stipend money.

Kaylah swirled her wineglass. "But neither of you have ever paid bills."

"I'm getting a job first thing," Marcus said.

"As am I. Until the baby comes, at least," Leah added. Her mom hadn't allowed her to help when they were in a pinch back in the human world.

"It's ... pricey to step out on your own. Especially in the human world. They have nasty inflation, and neither of you have marketable skills or job experience you can lean on, not to put too fine a point on it."

Kaylah's skepticism was logical, but Leah and Marcus were determined. "We'll make it work," Leah said.

"Until we leave, I was planning on staying here," Marcus said.

"We assumed as much," Eric replied. "You both always have an open invitation in our home."

"And we were planning on having me stay in Leah's room," Marcus added, his tone landing between the fear he'd exuded about breaking the pregnancy news to his parents, and the boldness with which he'd outright told Catrina they'd planned to room together at the palace.

"Obviously," Kaylah said.

"And if my parents or Aunt Catrina ask?" Marcus asked. Technically, Leah and Marcus were still breaking their rules.

Kaylah gave him a smirk. "If there's one thing I've learned while wearing a tiara and a crown, it's how to lie without lying."

"Okay..." Marcus still had a nervous edge to his voice, and Leah tried not to be annoyed by it.

Kaylah, however, *didn't* try to mask her feelings. "You are adults. You're going to have a child together. You are engaged. It's not my place to babysit you and make sure you look just right for the PR portraits." She pointed her dinner knife at Marcus from across the table. "And I care more about what my niece wants right now than what your aunt wants. And so should you."

Well, this is awkward. The room went silent. That was a little harsh on Marcus, but it meant the world to Leah to have someone in her corner, to have someone sticking up for her.

"I want Leah happy," Marcus muttered.

Kaylah looked between them and added, perhaps to keep things in perspective, to keep things fair, "And you better not hurt my nephew."

Leah ached inside. Was that about her slapping Marcus? Whether or not it was, she wouldn't hurt him again, and intended to not hurt his heart again either. "Yes, ma'am."

With a single nod, Kaylah continued her meal, as did the others. Leah and Marcus only exchanged a small glance about the awkwardness of being put in their places.

The rest of the meal was much less tense. Dessert was served—a selection of pastries and fruit puddings.

"Did anyone ever tell you the story about ornery little Marcus and that tree house in his parents' backyard?" Kaylah asked Leah, selecting a pastry.

The tree house they'd made out in? "Um... No."

"You see, Marcus can be stubborn, as we all know." Kaylah tore off a piece of her pastry. "So, the tree house..."

"She doesn't need to know about that," Marcus said, squirming in his seat.

"No, I think I do."

Kaylah grinned. "Oh, she does."

Marcus groaned, and Eric snickered knowingly.

"When he was little, whenever he'd get in a fight with Tobias or his parents, whenever he'd get in trouble, he'd climb that tree and refuse to come down."

Leah smiled, picturing him as a little boy defiantly climbing up and sticking it out.

"All there is to the story," Marcus declared.

"Not even close." Kaylah's tone was honey-thick. "One day, Little Marcus was particularly angry about something, climbed up to that tree house, and hunkered down. For hours. But he'd enjoyed plenty of juice and water earlier that day."

Marcus was most definitely blushing. "The end."

"But he wasn't coming down from that tree. He pronounced he never would. And when he couldn't hold his little bladder any longer..."

He covered his face, slumping into his chair. "Kill me now."

Kaylah flourished a hand in the air. "He watered the lawn from up in the tree house. As any dignified member of the royal family would be expected to."

Leah choked on a laugh.

"And he still refused to come down, even after skipping dinner. After multiple attempts to talk him down, Guillen went to the shed and brought out an axe."

Leah's eyes grew wide.

"He wouldn't have hurt Marcus, but a single solid blow to that tree trunk had Marcus surrendering in no time flat."

"I was *little*," Marcus defended.

"And I thought he'd learned his lesson about running away from problems."

"I did. I have," he said humbly at the subtle reproach.

Returning to her jovial tone, Kaylah smiled at Leah again. "The best part? The new gardener was out touring the grounds that day as Marcus performed his 'waterfall.' Saw the whole thing."

"I didn't know!" Marcus laughed.

Leah joined in with a laugh. "I hear plenty of stories about Marcus as a kid, but you and I need to talk more. I have a feeling everyone's gatekeeping all the juicy stuff."

"That's it," Marcus said. "Change of plans. We're headed to the human world first thing in the morning." He and Leah shared a grin.

The rest of the evening was filled with easy conversation as they enjoyed their small family reunion. Once the two couples said good night, Marcus and Leah continued to discuss their plans and rekindle their flame in the privacy of her room. *Their* room.

Chapter 24

Leah woke the next morning to a soft kiss on her bare shoulder.

"Good morning, gorgeous," Marcus whispered, his voice groggy.

She moaned. This wasn't a dream, but it sure felt like it. "Good morning."

He kissed her shoulder again. "Are we still on for our plans today?"

Drawing a deep breath and stretching, she finally opened her eyes. A soft glow from behind the curtains lit the room. She turned to face Marcus. "Yes. We have to hope Kaylah can get an exception for us. I don't want to derail everything." Leah didn't want to talk contingency plans.

He slid a hand to her hip. "Okay. And you're sure you don't want to just write your mom a letter?"

Leah's heart was heavy. She wasn't really ready to see her mom, and didn't want to lie to her. But Beata had to be lonely and worried that Leah hadn't come to visit in months. And the couple didn't know how long they were going to stay in the human world.

"I need to see her. I just have to."

"Okay."

"And I promise, no funny business with rifting," Leah added. The prison was quite a ways away, but Kaylah and Eric trusted that Leah wasn't a flight risk at the moment, and a cave rift would be the quickest way to get there. Eric and a couple of their bodyguards would be escorting her.

Marcus gazed into her eyes. "I trust you. I look forward to seeing you again tonight."

Dressed in a shirt that did a decent job of concealing her growing belly, Leah set out on the daunting trip to visit her mom. The shirt hid her stomach well enough, and didn't scream 'I'm a maternity shirt hiding something.'

Preparing to walk into the public gaze, Leah had slipped her engagement ring into her pocket, and was ready to exhaust every ounce of her Ivy energy, if needed, to engage her core, to suck in her gut as far as possible, to appear completely normal.

Eric did a good job soothing her nerves on the ride to the cave, shooting the breeze about the weather, about recent scientific discussions the United Green Folk Alliance had been working through with some humans.

Leah tried not to be insulted when the employees didn't let her create her own rift at the cave. Since the destination a person rifted to was determined by what the rifter envisioned, what they mentally dialed in when rifting, the cave employees had no way of ensuring Leah wasn't leaving the realm, wasn't disobeying Catrina's ban on her going to the human world.

So, Leah and Eric went through the same Seeder-created rift, exiting at a familiar cave nearest the prison her mom was being held in. Luckily, Cheryl was locked up to rot elsewhere.

Leah's heart beating wildly, her hands clammy, she straightened her shirt, made sure she was still standing tall and sucking in her gut, and strode alongside Eric to the prison. He gave her frequent calm, reassuring smiles.

More there for support and security than anything, Eric stayed in the waiting area. Leah always visited her mom alone. The guards guided her into the visiting room, with one stationed in the corner. They didn't usually require that, but perhaps that had been another of Catrina's requirements. It *was* Beata who had told Leah about the palace's secret passageways, after all.

Leah paced the small room—like most buildings in the Ivy Kingdom, it was built of stone. The walls, floor, and ceiling were all grey, depressing. A water spigot and glasses were situated on a ledge in the corner. Sweating, nervous, Leah filled a glass for herself and sipped.

"Sweetheart!" Beata said from behind, all excitement and warmth.

Setting her glass down, Leah turned and gave her mom a hug. *Suck it in. She can't notice.*

It didn't exactly feel *good* to hug her mom, but bittersweet. "Hey, Mom. Sorry I was away for so long."

Her mom squeezed tighter. "You have a life to live. That's okay. I'm just glad you're alright."

After a minute, they finally broke apart and sat at a small wooden table. Leah wasn't too fond of having the guard still in the room, having eyes on her, but she didn't have much choice in the matter.

Beata took Leah's hands in her own, a mirror image of Leah, only older and with dark brown eyes. And she did look older, like she'd aged more than she ought to have since Leah's last visit, but that might have just been Leah's guilt tricking her senses.

"You *are* okay, right?" Beata asked.

"Of course. I'd tell you."

Beata's hesitant expression implied she knew Leah better than that, that they were both inept at baring their souls.

"I'm good," Leah calmly stressed. "How are you?"

She always tried to listen to her mom, tried to show interest. The modern Ivy prison system was strict on making sure prisoners were treated fairly, that fights didn't break out, that there wasn't abuse. Leah didn't worry about that so much anymore. Her mom was allowed to work on projects within the prison for community service during her life sentence, as a small way she could make amends for her crimes, as a way to keep busy and have meaning in her life. But it was dull, day after day, life on repeat.

Her mom summed up the past few months, and Leah did her best to listen, despite her nerves, despite the strain on her energy to keep her facade and keep her stomach tight.

"I want to hear more about your adventures, though!" Beata said.

Leah slowly exhaled. "I'll have to tell you more next time. I hate to say it, but I have somewhere I have to be later today."

Beata frowned.

It killed Leah to do this, to lie straight to her mom's face. It was just like she'd done when running away to this realm, and now she was doing it to run back to the human world. Running away with Marcus.

"Either way, I'm always glad to see you." Beata gave her a smile.

"Me too." Leah gathered her courage, and leaned in a bit. Hopefully not so much that the guard caught on that it was a conspiratorial stance. "I know I haven't been able to visit for a while, and I'm ... going to be gone for a while again..." She cringed.

Beata looked confused. "More traveling? You'll send word?"

Leah swallowed the lump in her throat. "Well, um... I changed my plans, and I got accepted into a university in the human world." She quickly whispered, "Please don't say anything." She indicated with her eyes that she meant the guard, that she didn't want anyone to know.

"Oh." Beata searched her expression. "I know you've had it rough because of your father and me, and the 'incident,' but you... Why over there?"

"I miss it. You know... Electricity, meat, cars, human holidays. I thought I'd give it a try."

Beata nodded. "It's what you grew up with. But you'll still write? Come back when you can on school breaks?"

Leah's stomach knotted. She and Marcus were separating from the family for now—a full cutoff. "I ... might not."

Profound sorrow filled Beata's eyes, torturing Leah. Leah pitied her *so* much. "I'm sorry. I don't know. I'm not sure when I'll be back or send word. It may be sooner than not. I just wanted to give you a heads-up."

Beata rallied a weak smile. "Okay."

Taking a shallow breath, desperately fighting to both breathe and relax while simultaneously clenching her muscles, Leah prepared for the second part of what she needed to say. "I've told you Marcus and I have talked about marriage, right?"

They didn't discuss Marcus much on their visits, mostly to avoid contention.

Looking down at her hands, Beata cleared her throat. "Yes, you've mentioned it."

"I don't have any official announcements, but I need you to ... get on board. Because I love him, and he's going to continue to be in my life." Leah *knew* her mom could do better, could become a better person, could grow and overcome her prejudices. And Beata hating Marcus for being a Boman was one thing, but the thought of her hating their child? Leah couldn't handle that. It almost destroyed her knowing her own mom might have regretted or resented *her* growing up.

Beata didn't reply.

"You say you want me to be happy," Leah said.

"I do. But can he protect you? Are you equals? Does someone without powers even understand you?"

Leah's jaw tensed. "He makes me happy. He understands me and is equal to me in different ways. Were you and Dad equals?"

"That was different." And it had been. While many still didn't believe it, didn't *want* to believe it, Leah was convinced Soren had been a rare form of Ivy, born with extra powers like King Stephan was.

"Not really," Leah replied. She sighed, unhappy with the way the conversation was going. She wasn't there to convince her mom, just to hopefully point her in the right direction, giving her a nudge to reconsider her prejudices, so she'd be prepared for the big news down the road. Because the road was short, and permanent decisions hung in the balance. "I'm asking you to try to see things from a different perspective, okay? That's all I'm asking. Because someday when I come to visit, I'm going to have a ring on my finger, and when that day happens, I don't want to have to choose between you and Marcus." *And it's going to be a heck of a lot sooner than you think.*

"And I might have his kids someday. We know they'll look like me." Leah looked so much like her mother because of the family genes in their line, because of the ancient clan they'd descended from. "But they would be like Marcus." She searched her mom's dark brown eyes. "Will you hate my children? Will I have to tell my children their grandmother hates them?"

Beata averted her gaze, her mouth open for a moment. "I couldn't hate any part of you, Eleana. I will *always* love you."

"That's not true if you hate Marcus."

"Then maybe you should reconsider your choice. I'm sure there are tons of nice Ivy guys out there who aren't *stunts*."

Leah bristled. Stunt was an old term—stunted—and not a kind one. "Bomen, Mom. They're called Bomen."

Her mother looked her dead in the eyes. "Why are you so determined to make your life harder? Loving one of them, with our family history? You will *never* be accepted into their little circle."

It hurt that it was true. Bomen were a tight-knit group. And Leah wouldn't just be another standard Ivy with powers going to playgroups with other moms who had Boman children. They wouldn't be soccer moms hanging out. Not with Leah's family history. But she'd loved Marcus too much to consider the easy path. Nothing in her life had been easy.

Sitting taller, Leah gathered herself. "I came here to let you know that I'm okay. That I'll be gone for a while. And to give you the courtesy of knowing that I would still like you in my life down the road. But if you ask me to choose..." Tears threatened to emerge. "If you ask me to choose, you may not like my choice. Please don't make me choose."

Beata studied her, not responding. She had to know that something was in the works, that a proposal was imminent if Leah was broaching the topic. She even glanced at Leah's hands, checking for a ring.

Leah guzzled the rest of her glass of water. "Like I said, I've got somewhere to be." She stood, and her mom followed suit.

"I love you," her mom said softly, awkwardly opening her arms.

Leah gave her another hug. "I love you too."

She couldn't stay long, couldn't handle the stress, and she refused to cry, refused to turn into a ball of mush in that visitors' room. She released her mom. "Sorry I couldn't stay longer, but I really have to go." She added a little more uncomfortably, "Happy holidays."

"You too, sweetheart."

As Leah reached for the door, Beata spoke again. "Your last letters came from Kaylah's estate..."

That was a can of worms Leah wasn't about to open. "Long story. I'll tell you all about it when I come next time. Love you."

And then she left, clicking the door closed behind her. As a guard guided her back to the waiting room, Leah fought tears with every step. That hadn't gone well, and would probably make her mom worry even more. She hadn't even told her what she'd planned to study at this fictitious university. Hadn't explained herself. The brevity of the conversation hadn't been reassuring to her mom at all. But at least there was something, and hopefully some kind of a seed planted about changing her thoughts on Bomen?

When Leah entered the waiting room, Eric stood to greet her. His two bodyguards and a prison attendant were in the room as well, on the other side.

Leah faced the wall, releasing her tense muscles for a minute, angled away from the others who might notice too much. She tried to catch her breath, tried to not hyperventilate. Eric slid an arm around her shoulders. "Are you okay?"

"Yeah." She gulped for air. "I'm fine. I'll be fine."

"Do you need anything, Your Highness?" one of the others asked.

"No thank you," Eric answered.

Grateful for his support, Leah took another minute to gather herself before setting out again, heading straight back to his and Kaylah's estate.

<hr>

Leah ambled along that last stretch of the path to Kaylah and Eric's home. Once they were within the gates at the end of a long dirt drive, she assured Eric she'd prefer to walk by herself, taking her time, that she was grateful for his support but no longer needed the escort.

Rubbing her belly, glad to not have to be sucking it in unnaturally anymore, she pondered on the last thing Eric had said to her at the prison before they'd left:

"Ready to go home?"

"Yeah, let's go home," she'd said. "Well, to your home."

"Your home too."

She wore a thoughtful smile. It was a transient home like any of the others she'd lived in her entire life. But she *did* like the way it felt there. It *felt* like a home. Yes, there were servants and visitors, but not the way there had been at the palace. And even with Marcus, they had enough privacy in the eastern wing to enjoy each other, but were close enough to be near family to chat or spend dinner together.

It wouldn't last forever, but it was nice.

Once she arrived at the house, a servant told her Marcus could be found out back at the pavilion. His primary task of the day had been to rift to the apartment he'd been staying in during his internship, pack up his things, and have them shipped here for safekeeping. He'd also collected his remaining pay, telling them he wasn't sure how long he'd be gone.

Strolling to the backyard, she found him at the pavilion, where he worked away at the other task of the day: writing letters.

"Stealing my favorite writing spot?" she asked on her approach.

He smiled wide, his gaze still fixed on his paper. "Great minds..."

She stepped up, slinging an arm around a pillar. "Do you want privacy?"

"You're fine." He glanced up. "Do you want to talk about your visit?"

She twisted her lips. "Hmm..."

He set the paper and pen on the bench next to him, holding out his arms. She smiled and accepted the offer, sitting on his lap.

"You okay?" he asked.

"I will be." *I hope.* "How was it, settling things up north?"

He shrugged. "It was fine. It was a little weird when they tried to pry, asking if there was anything wrong. It just felt like they wanted dirt on the family, you know?"

Leah wrinkled her nose.

"And..." He rubbed her thigh. "They reassured me they'll keep the position open for me, because I'm *such* a valuable asset." He rolled his eyes.

"You are."

He raised his eyebrows. "I'm a beginner intern."

"And you'll be brilliant in what you do someday. Even if your career has a ... gap in it." She frowned, intertwining their fingers.

"Worth it."

Giving him a hesitant smile, she studied his warm brown eyes. "Are you sure you'll be okay with working construction in the human world? That's hard work."

"It pays well, doesn't require as many fancy fake IDs, and it's pretty much the only skill I can think of that can get me a job right away when we go over there."

His father had worked in construction before the war ended, and built the house he and Rachel now lived in. Marcus had been too young to help with that, but he had enjoyed spending time with his dad learning some of the basics with renovations over the years and improvements to the tree house.

"If you say so," she replied, kissing the palms of his hands.

"Is *that* it? You're afraid I'll get callouses? You don't want rough hands on your body?" He grinned mischievously.

She leaned in, brushing her lips against his ear with a sensual whisper that would have made the songbirds in the distance blush. "I've never complained about you being rough with me, have I?"

He groaned. "We have a lot to do today, and you are not going to make it easy on me."

"I bet there's a nice cozy spot out in these woods. I've never made love out in the open." As she whispered, his breathing became labored, and she poked out a vine, slithering it up his shoulder, to his neck, and then tickled his ear.

"Ack!" He wrenched his head away, and she giggled.

He threw her a dirty look, and she got off his lap, settling on the bench beside him. "There *is* a lot to do." It was already nearing dinnertime, and she had letters of her own to see to. They were both taking the day to write to Catrina and his parents—apologies, explanations.

After fetching paper and a pen for herself, Leah rejoined him, and they worked in silence, side by side.

Kaylah was gone all day, running errands, personal and official, with her charity work.

The next morning, Marcus and Leah ate with Eric. He said Kaylah had been delayed, but would be there by lunchtime.

Leah was a bundle of nerves, pacing around. She offered to pack up her things so Kaylah and Eric could have their guestrooms back, but Eric insisted it wasn't a bother, and it was something that could be dealt with when she and Marcus returned and had decided what they were going to do.

Kaylah returned right in time for lunch, and they all sat down together. "Some of your favorites." She smiled, gesturing to the dishes One was loaded with mashed potatoes, another with sliced moon melon.

As they ate, they discussed their plans for the evening. Leah was ready to get it over with. When the time came, they handed their letters to Kaylah, who promised she'd deliver them once the couple was out of the realm. Leah dressed in clothes that would help conceal her stomach, though she still planned to suck it in while in public. She and Marcus tucked away his internship earnings and anything else they could use that would fit in their pockets.

And they were set to go. Eric and Kaylah stood ready in the entryway; Eric planned to stay at the estate to help the group keep a lower profile.

"Before we go, Eric and I have something for the two of you," Kaylah said. She held out an envelope sealed with her official insignia.

Chapter 25

Leah eyed the envelope Kaylah offered. "What's that?"

"Open it, and you'll find out."

Leah took it from her, popping the green wax seal and opening the envelope. Out slid a single item: a shiny brand-new human-world debit card. The sticker was still on it. "No. We told you. No family money. We're doing this on our own." She held it out to Kaylah.

Kaylah did not take it back. Eric only shook his head, wrapping an arm around Kaylah's waist. Kaylah turned to Marcus. "How much do you have from your internship?"

"Three hundred bronze marks."

"The conversion rate is lousy, and that won't get you far."

"That's why I'm applying for jobs first thing tomorrow morning," Marcus replied.

"It takes time to find jobs, to find apartments, to get *approved* for an apartment. Especially around those human holidays."

Leah sighed. "And I'm going to—"

This time Kaylah turned on her. "It's your inheritance."

Leah scoffed. "I don't have an inheritance."

"Well, that's what I'm calling it. When you first came here, when we brought your mother and that other horrible woman in, they had cars; they had possessions. When we packed up their things, we sold a lot of it. It had no use over there. You deserve every penny of that."

Leah furrowed her brow. She hadn't thought of those logistics. "But that money would have gone to the queen's coffers to take care of me, right? That money has to be long gone for my upkeep."

Kaylah shrugged. "Your mother's car was a really nice model."

Hmm... Leah held up the card. "How much?"

"Enough to get you by for a while."

"*How much?*"

"I have pretty lucrative investments in the human world. Great interest rates. So, there's a ... small bonus."

Leah held it out to her. "No. We don't want your charity."

"It's not charity. Christmas is in two days. It's part of your gifts."

Leah continued to hold it out to her.

Her expression firm, Kaylah remained still. "We *all* need a hand sometimes. Financial stress doesn't help in relationships." She gently cocked her head to the side. "You don't have to spend it. Keep it for emergencies."

Leah's pride fought tooth and nail, despite the perfect logic. "Fine," she grumbled, sliding it into her pocket. "But don't be offended when we return it someday completely full."

Kaylah only gave her a soft smile. "We won't be."

"I don't like you right now." Leah pouted. "But I still love you."

"Come here, kiddo." Kaylah reached for her, and the group exchanged hugs.

"All set, then," Marcus said, squaring his shoulders.

"One last thing." Kaylah pulled a ring off her finger. "I want you to take this with you. *Do not lose it.*"

"Are you serious?" Marcus asked in full disbelief.

Leah took a step back, nearly terrified of the offer. "That's *definitely* too far. Your royal ring?!" Only official Elontas—those in the proper Ivy royal family line of heirs—were assigned insignias, and they each had *one* ring. One official ring they wouldn't let someone pry from them.

"I can do with this as I please. You may need it."

Staring at it, Leah stood frozen. "We don't know how long we're going away for. *You* might need that. And people would think I stole it from you!" Even if this realm didn't know about her previous shoplifting habits, they'd think it.

Kaylah let out a composed breath. "Eric still has his. I trust you. And while this may not do you any good in the human world other than earn you a few bucks at a pawnshop, this will do nearly anything for you in a pinch in this realm. If you two have an emergency, all you need to do is rift over, or show the ring at a cave. It will stop a train. It will send people to track me down from anywhere. They will take care of you and do as you say, *then* verify that it wasn't stolen later." Her expression and tone were stone-cold sober. "Take it."

"Aunt Kaylah," Marcus interjected. "It's not like I'm banned from leaving the realm. If something happens, I can ask for help."

She was losing her patience. "I love you, but it is not the same. And you're about to defy your queen's explicit orders, nephew or not, by taking your fiancée out of the realm. And if you break your neck working construction, I have a feeling Leah would appreciate having a safe way to approach a rifting cave to call for a Seeder healer to make a special visit for you."

With that devastating vision dancing in her mind, Leah palmed the ring, sliding it into her pocket. "Okay. I'll make sure not to lose it."

The walk and ride to the rifting cave were beyond tense. Leah focused on sucking in her gut, breathing calmly, putting one foot in front of the other, and not crushing Marcus's hand.

Not wanting to involve more people than necessary, they lied to the customs official, stating Marcus and Leah were traveling domestically.

When they got to the rift coordinator, the panic fully set in. With Catrina's ban, Leah still wasn't allowed to create her own rift. And since Marcus was a Boman, he wasn't capable of making his own, either. They needed a Seeder to open a rift for them.

"We will be going to Selen, these two first," Kaylah calmly instructed the Seeder employee.

The employee gaped. "Um, Your Highness, we're not allowed to… What I mean is, the girl's not allowed to … leave the realm. Domestic only."

A bitterness lingered on Leah's tongue. The unused passport felt like a useless brick in her pocket right now.

"I understand the current orders," Kaylah said. "This is an exception."

The employee cringed. "Matron, all due respect, but the orders come from Her Majesty, and I can't lose my job."

"I'll make sure you won't."

When the employee wouldn't budge, Kaylah took them to the side to chat in private.

Marcus kissed Leah's shoulder, holding her arm tight. "It'll be fine. Everyone in this realm owes her."

"Yeah," Leah whispered. "Kinda wish she hadn't handed the crown over to your aunt already."

A couple of minutes later, Kaylah and the tense cave employee returned. "I appreciate your cooperation," Kaylah said.

Pursing their lips, the employee nodded curtly. "Selen?"

"Yes please."

The Seeder stepped into the center of the cave space and swiped a hand through the air. A shimmering rift opened, and Leah approached.

"What's holding up the line?" a voice called from behind.

Crap.

Kaylah looked Leah dead in the eyes. "Love you, kiddo. We'll be right behind you. *Go.*"

Leah panicked. Kaylah helped her with a gentle shove.

"Who is that? Hold up now, I need to see—"

The voice cut off the moment Leah entered the rift. Her field of vision swiftly transitioned from the back of a cave to a yellow glow, then into an inner cave. The lack of ambient Green Lands energy was an instant and staggering contrast.

Before Leah could process everything, the arrivals coordinator beckoned her to move forward. "Wait... What are *you* doing here?"

Correction. Leah hadn't been panicking before. *Now* she was panicking. "I, uh..." They'd hoped the human-world employees wouldn't care, or hadn't been informed of the ban. And if she had been any Regular Joe, she'd have waltzed right by with the employee assuming she'd shown her passport and it wasn't a big deal that she was there right now.

But Leah wasn't a Regular Joe. She was notorious.

Leah threw her thumb over her shoulder. "Kaylah's right behind me."

The employee looked insulted. "*Matron* Kaylah?"

Ugh. Why hadn't Leah at least used Kaylah's title? She sounded ungrateful. People didn't understand how close she'd grown to Kaylah, and that she was grateful she'd spared her life after the botched assassination attempt.

"Yes, Matron Kaylah."

The employee stared at the rift, disbelief plastered on their face.

Come on, guys. Marcus should have already come through, and then Kaylah through her own rift. *Come on.*

The rift closed.

"Right," the employee drawled.

"I swear. She's right behind me."

"How about you follow me, and we'll find out?"

Leah planted her feet. She wasn't going to be separated from Marcus. She wasn't going anywhere. "She'll be right through."

"Security!" the employee called out.

"Security? There's no need for security!"

"Please calmly follow them."

Leah clenched her fists, her mind racing. They didn't need a scene. They were trying to avoid a scene! Why weren't Marcus and Kaylah coming through?

"Send someone over to confirm. Kayl— Matron Kaylah will confirm it's okay for me to be here, that the order was ... rescinded..." She used to be a much better liar.

The employee gave her an incredulous expression. Inter-realm rifts weren't something you sauntered back and forth through willy-nilly. Seeder or Ivy, you could only physically make a round trip between the realms once a day. Most of the cave employees probably lived in the Green Lands, and would be cutting their shift short by going back. Shift coordination was fine-tuned, and Leah was the wrench in the works they weren't willing to deal with.

A uniformed security officer approached. "Please come with me, Miss Elonto."

Leah shook her head. *Kaylah will be through in two seconds.* How many dozens of rifting caves were there in the entire Green Lands realm and human world combined? And *all* the employees knew Leah was banned? She didn't need the rumor mill churning about the ban, and then that she'd been taken into custody for directly disobeying her queen's orders.

The officer—a male Ivy—extended vines, wrapping them around her upper arm. "You can follow me, or we can do this the hard way."

Gutting memories flashed through her mind. Being shoved down a hallway at the wedding venue by Kaylah's bodyguards. Being strapped to a chair for hours.

Sweating, Leah could sense the Ivy energy burning and surging in her, her own vines prodding at her wrists. "*Get your vines off me,*" she muttered through clenched teeth, her voice low and threatening.

"I explained your options, Miss Elonto."

Should she pull out Kaylah's ring? *It will stop a train.* It would *force* them to rift over to check her story.

It didn't feel like the right moment to play that trump card. That ring was supposed to be for an emergency. This wasn't an emergency. She didn't need that ring right now, because Kaylah was just on the other side of a rift, arriving any moment. Right? "I'll come with you if you take your vines off me."

The officer considered. "Do you have any weapons on you?"

Leah's lip curled. *Seriously? Who did I come to assassinate? A no-name employee? Some random human?* "No."

Cautiously, the officer released her. "Hands where I can see them, and keep your vines to yourself."

"Done."

She followed the officer. He kept a close eye on her as he guided her to a small room and closed the door behind them.

"Matron Kaylah will be over to vouch for me."

"The orders come from the queen."

"Then there's a delay in the update on those orders. I was granted an exception."

He scoffed. "That's likely." He eyed her, pointing to a large wooden table in the room. "Empty your pockets."

Her passport? The debit card? Kaylah's ring that they'd assume she'd stolen? Her extra pair of *underwear* she'd tucked in there? "No."

"We're well within our rights, especially given your history."

"I was acquitted of all charges. I've been living in the palace. Official notices went around the *entire* realm explaining my innocence! Don't give me this 'given my history' shit! I don't have any weapons on me. I have no reason to."

He stared right at her, and with that scathing look, it was clear she really didn't have a place back there. People tolerated her because the government said to, but they didn't understand her, didn't respect her. "I can have a female come in and do a strip search."

Her face heated with rage. "Over my *dead body*. My *aunt* is just on the other side of a rift. And if anyone touches me... I'd hate to find out what she'd be willing to do for her only niece."

"The one who tried to murder her?" he said flatly.

Kaylah's forgiveness had never been anyone else's to give but hers. Nor had Marcus's or anyone else's. Green folk worshipped Kaylah, and loved Marcus. But they were so blind at times, even when Kaylah and Catrina had tried to clean up Leah's mess with their PR teams.

Luckily, the security officer did seem to weigh the relationship, and the faint possibility that Leah might not be making this all up. He didn't pull out the restraining straps normally used for Ivy vines.

Instead, he jutted his chin to the end of the table. "Over there. Sit down. Hands on the table. No sudden moves. We'll see how this pans out."

For the next several minutes, he interviewed Leah. He asked about her purpose there, and details about this 'change in orders' that didn't actually exist. After a few lies, she stopped answering his questions. She finally released her death grip on her Ivy energy clutching in her gut once she realized the table covered her stomach, and settled in, drawing patterns on the table. "Matron Kaylah will explain," she said over and over and over.

He eventually got tired of that phrase and left, locking her in the room.

A breath whooshed out of Leah, and she laid her forehead on the table. No one had luck like she did. What kind of cruel irony was it that she'd plotted and snuck into the Green Lands in the first place, and now she'd plotted and snuck out of that realm? Neither time had gone off without a hitch.

Leah was thirsty and ready for a good night's rest. There was a time difference when rifting, so it was still earlier in the day here, but she was beyond ready to call it a day and be done with this.

Eventually, her lungs didn't appreciate her bending so far forward, so she sat back in her chair, watching as time ticked by on an electric clock. She mused on that, on her old friend—electricity. How much had changed since she'd left the human world? Was there a new president in the United States? Had any major hurricanes or earthquakes happened? What was the weather like outside this cave?

One minute crawled by after another on that clock.

More than a half hour later, the door *finally* opened again.

Chapter 26

More calm than Leah had expected him to be, Marcus stood at the door. "Are you okay?"

"Yeah." She stood and rushed into his arms. "What took so long?"

He sighed, threading his hand into her hair. "I'll tell you all about it later. Let's head out of here. Do you still have everything you came with?"

"Yes."

"Good. Let's go. Our ride is on its way."

"So, we can stay? Is Kaylah not going to say goodbye?"

He pursed his lips, shaking his head. "She's... Yeah, we can stay, but we should get going."

Leah wasn't about to argue with that. She took his hand and followed his lead. The cave was near silent; all employees they passed had their eyes on the couple.

They wove the reverse route Leah had taken two-plus years ago to get there, eventually ending up in the fake nature preserve's display room. They had a little while to look it over this time since they were waiting on a rideshare to take them away instead of going to a car in the parking garage. A giant tan moth with a broken wing hung lopsided off a single pin in the other wing. A coyote looked like it had been taxidermied by someone while blindfolded. They really did go to great lengths to deter humans by making this place dumpy.

A single cashier stood in the gift shop.

"What happened?" Leah whispered to Marcus.

He rolled his eyes. "A cave supervisor with balls the size of the Grand Sea? He came to see what was causing the holdup, and once he saw me, and you... He tried to uphold Aunt Catrina's orders, and wouldn't budge."

Could Leah have found a way to be content as a shotgun bride? Maybe she should have just sucked it up months ago... But that wouldn't have resolved everything. Not even close.

"That is *seriously* ballsy, with Kaylah there and everything."

"Right?"

"But where is she now? What happened? What took so long?"

Marcus ruffled his hair. "We were trying to minimize the damage, to keep it under wraps. In the end, she pretty much put both caves under lockdown, staff sworn to secrecy until she could bring proof from Aunt Catrina that her orders regarding you were rescinded."

Leah angled her head. "But they're allowing us to leave."

He rubbed the back of his neck, pulling a cell phone from his pocket. "Under the condition we carry this with us. For 'emergencies and updates.'"

She wilted. Her mom had tracked her via cell all her life. "You mean so they can track wherever we go?"

Huffing, he tucked it back into his pocket. "I swore I'd take it. It was either that or they'd send you back home until it was all sorted out."

Yuck. "I guess I'll take the phone."

He nodded. "So right now, I'm pretty sure *your* aunt is on her way to storm the palace to have a few choice words with *my* aunt. And I'm putting my money on *yours* winning this one, or at least hoping... She was *scorched*."

Catrina hadn't even fought in the old war. Kaylah had taken multiple lives. "I'm putting my money on Kaylah, too. Plus, Catrina wouldn't even be the queen yet if Kaylah hadn't given the position to her."

"Shh," he whispered.

"Right, sorry." The employee was still in the room, and that kind of talk wasn't ideal from the usurpers' daughter.

Marcus kissed Leah's forehead, and soon after, his phone dinged, notifying them that their ride was there.

They slipped into the back seat of a pristine blue car and headed out. They'd decided ahead of time to go to a somewhat familiar area, but not too close to where Tobias lived, or Marcus's grandparents. They'd be about an hour away.

Marcus rested a hand on her leg, and she leaned her head on his shoulder, dazed.

"Is that place any good?" the driver asked as he pulled away. "Such a weird out-of-the-way place for people to come and go without their own cars. And at the weirdest times of day. And around the holidays..." Caves were open around the clock.

"No. It sucks," Marcus said.

"Dang. Then they must pay for some good advertising, huh? To con people into checking it out?"

"Guess so."

After a couple more questions from the driver and disinterested answers from Marcus, the driver got the hint.

Leah closed her eyes and let herself simply be. Her life was a disaster. From conception to the foreseeable future. Part of her said the only way out of that would be to take that phone in Marcus's pocket and chuck it out the window, and tell the driver to drive any which way until sunset.

But that would be too rash. Rash decisions rarely paid off for Leah.

After a while in silence, the driver turned some music on.

"Are you okay?" Marcus whispered into her ear.

She swallowed. Being grabbed like that by the security officer... And threatened to be strip-searched? *Not really.* "I will be." She rested a hand on her relaxed baby bump. "I will be."

An hour later, they rolled up to a hotel in the city they'd chosen, thanking their driver.

"You have that debit card Kaylah gave you?" Marcus asked as they stood outside the hotel.

"Yeah... But didn't you exchange your Ivy money at the cave?"

He frowned. "I wanted to get you out of there."

And with that, she pulled it out, and peeled off the sticker. "Our independence lasted long, didn't it?" She gave him an ironic smile, and he chuckled.

They paid with the card, presenting fake IDs, and headed to their room. Starving by now, Leah gulped down water while Marcus ordered room service. If they were having to utilize Kaylah's generosity already, they were going to enjoy a good meal. It kinda felt like a last meal, given that the phone dangled over their heads like an axe, so they ordered extra dessert.

Leah turned the debit card in her hand. "I swear Kaylah can see the future."

Marcus plopped on the bed next to her. "I think if she could, she'd have split us up and had a whisper rifter sworn to secrecy help you get out."

She cringed. "If we'd decided to go that way, I could have just tree rifted myself."

No, they'd wanted to do this smoothly, and as legally as possible. Kaylah could smooth-talk, though apparently not everyone once she'd passed on the crown and entered retirement. Bomen could only rift through caves anyway, and Leah hadn't wanted to be separated.

"How do you feel energy-wise?" Marcus asked.

Leah rubbed her face. "It's weird. I'm sure I'll get used to it." She hadn't known the Green Lands energy growing up. But the difference between realms was palpable. It had been invigorating as it flooded her upon her arrival when she originally went over there. Now, as she stepped back into the human world, she already understood why most green folk only came to *visit* over here. She'd wondered if that difference, that lack, had contributed to her mom's depression over the years, to Cheryl's bitterness toward Leah. Leah feared that for herself now. If her biology, her cravings to return to the realm and that unique energy, would trump her craving to be free.

Then again, if Catrina dispatched guards to drag the couple back, Leah wouldn't have to find out for herself.

"On a scale of one to ten, how much would you hate me if that phone smashed itself during the night?"

Marcus lifted an eyebrow.

"Fine. I'm just throwing it out there. If they're going to keep thinking I'm a villain, might as well see how badly we can blow things up."

He placed a soft kiss on her lips. "Kaylah will come through for us."

She snuggled up to him as they waited for their food. All she could think about was how she never wanted to go back, would *never* forgive Catrina, and how excited she was to eat meat-lover's pizza after two and a half years without it.

In the middle of the night, Leah's bladder happily reminded her she was pregnant. She reached for the striker on the nightstand to light a candle, only to remember she was in the human world. With a smile on her face, she clicked the button on the lamp next to her, then tiptoed to the restroom.

When she finished up in there, she decided to sneak one of the leftover breadsticks. As she was midchew, something caught her attention from across the hotel room. A tiny blinking red light—the cell phone.

Her gut twisted with dread. Was it a message from Catrina to make sure they were dressed because a dozen guards were on their way to drag them back?

Please leave us alone.

Leah sat on a chair next to the small table where they'd emptied their pockets into a pile. Drawing a deep breath, she grabbed the phone and turned the screen on. Two texts from an unknown number.

<Free as a kite, kiddos! Keep this phone and number for emergencies. Merry Christmas. Love you!>

<P.S. I'm not saying you have to, but if you wanted to name your gremlin after me, I wouldn't be mad. ;) >

Leah's heart swelled. They were free. Kaylah had come through for them. She hadn't signed her name, but it had to have been Kaylah. No one else would have called their unborn child a gremlin, and she wouldn't have sent a servant through a rift to type that. That was a private joke.

The timestamp showed it had been sent a couple of hours ago. Kaylah wasn't likely lingering in the human world for a response, but she might rift over now and then to get in cell phone range. Leah typed up her own message.

<And Happy New Year. Love you too!>

After sending it, Leah gingerly set the phone on the table. The room was silent other than Marcus's soft breathing behind her, the occasional hum of a car on the street, and the clunk from the ice machine down the hallway.

Leah sat there a moment, surveying their tiny cache of belongings, and considering the many tasks ahead of them in the next few days. She plucked out two of the things that made all the difference in the world right now: a debit card and a gold ring.

In that moment, Leah came to a realization that was both heartwarming and heart wrenching. Kaylah had done more for Leah in the two and a half years she'd known her than her mom had her entire life.

Even as she thought it, guilt rose within her. Her mom wasn't *all* bad. She *was* bad. She had let her husband do unspeakable things in war and in his personal life. And she'd manipulated him by getting pregnant with Leah. And she still clung to old prejudices.

But Beata had also kept Leah safe... *Somewhat* safe. Clothed and fed. And she'd done her best to keep Leah out of trouble with regards to shoplifting and school and boys. Yet, she had been grossly neglectful. She was horrible at communicating, at keeping harmful secrets. She had refused to see the things her aide was doing to Leah, refused to listen to Leah, calling her a drama queen about Cheryl's insults and abuse over the years. She'd taught Leah to run away from problems instead of trying to calmly face them.

Kaylah always gave Leah the benefit of the doubt. Space and freedom and a listening ear. Encouragement and even calling her out when needed, in a way that helped Leah.

Leah wiped away a tear, hugging herself. "Thank you," she whispered.

After another minute, she turned off the lamp and crawled into bed with Marcus, laying her head on his bare chest.

He stirred a little, and she adjusted her engagement ring, happy to wear it now that they were away from green folk. She kissed his chest. "We're free."

Marcus was over the moon the next day after he read the texts. After ordering more room service for breakfast, they had to prioritize their to-do list.

The Ivy money Marcus had brought would do no good in the human world. Green folk had allies amongst the humans—some minor politicians and scientists, some family members and friends—but for the most part, they were still very disconnected worlds. The only place to exchange that money was at rifting caves, and they didn't want to step foot in one until they were sure they were ready to return, just in case. They'd stop by an ATM to check how much Kaylah had loaded into that account.

They needed to look into apartments, apply for jobs, get new toiletries and clothes and personal phones, and figure out transportation. They took time to enjoy each other, but this wasn't a vacation. This was a trial run to ensure they could make things work between them.

They spent the next few days getting things lined up, taking a little extra time to celebrate Christmas. They didn't exchange gifts, but they took a stroll in the snow. It rarely snowed in these parts, and it was exciting to witness it after its absence in the Green Lands.

The ATM revealed that Kaylah had indeed been absurdly generous, and while they still intended to try to do as much of this as they could on their own, it was comforting to have a safety net. They purchased the necessities, and started applying for jobs and apartments. It was tricky, having no references, no listable work experience.

Ivy royalty had connections in the human world, and they could get you any sort of fake background you wanted. The old assassin networks had been dissolved long ago, but their connections were still helpful for green folk who wanted to explore the human world.

Marcus still had his fake persona intact from when he'd come over as a foreign exchange student. For Leah, they'd taken one of her most recent photos and made her a fake driver's license that they'd presented to her with her passport. Her mom had never let her get a license when she was a high schooler here.

But if a company did a background check, the couple didn't have much set up to help out. Marcus's job would be the easier one to come by. Hard labor paid well, trained on the job, and sometimes hired undocumented workers.

Soon enough, Marcus snagged a job, and they found an apartment. Without work or rental history, they paid a huge sum for a deposit on a dumpy third-story apartment in a busy neighborhood near a bus line. They quickly realized how naïve they'd been about finances.

Before moving into their apartment, they figured out how to disable the tracker on the phone they'd been given. Not wanting to worry Kaylah, they sent a text to her, letting her know they'd done that and were fine. A week later a text came in with a single heart emoji.

The couple didn't waste money on decorations, so the apartment walls remained bare, dozens of poorly plugged nail holes dotting them.

Furnishing their new place was an adventure. Most of the stuff was secondhand. Leah's Ivy energy, even when dimmed in the human world, became immensely helpful when they carried it all up the stairs to their place. She had to be extra careful to not use her vines in public—it had become second nature in the Green Lands, and they were useful for gripping things. Leah almost had a heart attack when she nearly dropped a couch they were carrying up the stairs. A pair of neighbors came running up to help, shocked a young pregnant girl was hefting a couch up to the third floor with her fiancé. She wasn't wearing shirts designed to hide her fast-growing belly anymore, and wasn't sucking in her gut. She chose to believe she was only getting bigger so fast because of the baby, and not because of the bacon and other things she'd missed and was now consuming on a regular basis...

Finding Leah a job was a harder task. She was trying for entry-level positions, but wasn't getting many callbacks or return emails. They considered breaking their no-contact rule with family to ask his brother or grandparents to be references, but they chose not to, at least not yet.

So as Marcus worked full-time, Leah spent her days applying for jobs, reading books she got from the local library, and journaling. In the evenings, they enjoyed cooking together, relaxing, and chatting.

Marcus came home from work, day after day, exhausted but happy. He admitted it was awkward to learn to use power tools, but he never complained about having to work a hard job, not once. Not when he'd fall asleep while sitting on the couch. Not when he came home with a gash on his arm that Leah could only help bandage and kiss better, when his Seeder mom could have instantly healed it with a mere touch of a finger.

Separated from the stress and scrutiny of their home realm, they were doing well.

Chapter 27

Eventually, Leah landed a part-time job, working at a dollar store as a cashier. It didn't help all that much with the finances, but she at least had some satisfaction that she was contributing.

With her spare time, she gave something else a try. She'd enjoyed *Valeska's Adventures* so much, and found herself reading more often than not, so she decided to give writing a go. Not just the kids' stories back in the Green Lands that she hoped to finish for their child someday, but stories for an older audience. Maybe if she'd gotten into books in middle and high school, she'd have avoided a lot of the drama and trauma. Plus, *Valeska's Adventures* was pretty light on the romance, and Leah had a feeling she could do better.

With a notebook and pen, she started to write.

Things were genuinely going smoothly between Leah and Marcus. They were best friends. They took time on the weekends to go for walks. He endured her talking about books, and she always listened to his stories about what happened to coworkers she hadn't met on his worksite.

Were things perfect? No. They were still very different people from shockingly different backgrounds. They were young, and trying to figure out how to make things work. They both forgot to pay a utility bill, and had to pay an extra charge. The minutiae of sorting out things like who was going to pay the bills and how to remember to do it on time were daunting.

And they both still had their tempers. Leah remembered the tips Kaylah had given her about dealing with frustrations.

One evening after Marcus came home and showered, he sat on the floor while Leah massaged his shoulders. She used her Ivy energy to put some extra pressure into his knots. He squirmed a little as she did so, but was grateful.

"You're sure you don't want to go alone?" he asked.

Leah sighed. To try to make things work, to find a better way to meet in the middle and deal with stress, they'd looked into counseling. There was a local program available that helped with low-income sessions. A limited number of sessions were covered, so they'd agreed to take them as a couple.

She leaned forward on the couch, wrapping her arms around his neck, and rested her chin on his head. "Yeah, I'd rather go with you."

It was tempting to see a counselor for herself, because no one here would have preconceptions about who Leah was. They would have no background on her, would have no need to report to the queen or anyone else. But ... Leah's heartache was deep and complex, and she'd have to walk on eggshells to discuss it with a human. 'So, when my dad was king... Oh, um, I mean... a CEO of a company you've never heard of...' 'After I tried to assassinate my aunt, the queen... No, I mean... Um...'

She'd either slip on that kind of information and earn a grippy-socks vacation because they thought she'd lost it, or she'd have to lie so much that she doubted any sort of soul-baring would be effective.

No, she'd sort through her stuff—someday, somehow. And in a way, she already was. Just voicing it with Kaylah and Marcus had been immensely helpful. Just jotting it in a journal helped her release her anger and think things through.

Marcus kissed her hand. "Okay. I'll make it work with my schedule."

The first session was mostly a meet and greet to discuss what they wanted out of counseling. The second session was surprisingly productive. Though, Leah was mortified to find herself crying in front of a stranger about how she felt regarding always losing people. She was honest about her mom being sent to prison for life, about her dad dying before she was born, about having to move all the time growing up. She was perhaps a *little* hazy on the details.

She and Marcus had agreed ahead of time to go out for ice cream after sessions to decompress, and it was a fun reminder of their original dates as high schoolers.

"I'm really sorry," Marcus said quietly, pushing his ice cream toppings around as they sat in the shop.

"It's okay. It was my fault, too," she reassured him. It was true. When they'd 'taken a break' in high school for an entire month, during Christmas Break, it had been because Marcus had wanted it. It had been torture for Leah, but she'd earned it by shoplifting. And him being gone for nearly half of her pregnancy? She could have reached out to him as easily as he could have to her.

"Still." He frowned. "I think her advice will help."

Leah nodded. They'd talked about how to pick their battles in their session that night, and also different fighting styles. It was weird to be told it was okay to fight, but that they needed to set boundaries. They needed to agree together on what was too far in an argument. Bringing up past mistakes and hurtful trauma was a no-go.

And Marcus was an avoider in arguments. In his heart, he was still that little boy who didn't want to deal with contention, and ran off to a tree house. But if he needed space and time to work through a problem, to properly handle it, then Leah agreed to give it to him, but there had to be rules. He could halt an argument and go for a walk, but he'd have to promise to not be gone for more than a couple of hours. They both needed boundaries.

Not once was a rationale given that they needed to handle things a certain way because of how it would affect Leah's public image, or Marcus's reputation, or the royal family's.

It was impartial. It was helpful. It was encouraging.

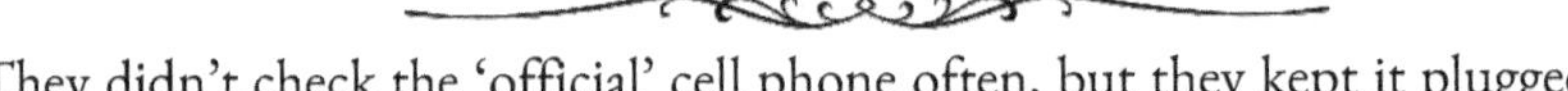

They didn't check the 'official' cell phone often, but they kept it plugged in on a side table.

Around Leah's five-month mark in her pregnancy, Marcus started to act antsy, staring at the phone.

What was going through his mind? Did she even want to know? Could she handle the truth?

At some point, she couldn't ignore it. One Sunday afternoon, Leah lay with her feet propped up on the armrest of the couch, her hands resting on her rapidly growing bump, her head in Marcus's lap as he gave her a relaxing scalp massage.

"Why do you keep looking at the phone?" she asked.

He pressed his lips together, hesitant. "I've been thinking a lot about Aunt Catrina, is all."

Leah's stomach tightened. "What about her?"

"That she's due any day. I've just been thinking it would be cool to know what she ends up having."

The vast majority of green folk still didn't come to the human world for health care, for obvious reasons. They didn't know the gender of Queen Catrina's baby, or if there would be multiples. Twins and triplets weren't uncommon for standard Ivies.

Leah closed her eyes, processing. She wanted nothing to do with Catrina, with official palace news, with any of it. They'd agreed upon a full cutoff. But ... Catrina was his aunt, and they had always been close. And it would be a major cause for celebration in the Ivy Kingdom, so perhaps they should be aware of that sort of thing?

Drawing a cleansing breath, Leah opened her eyes. "I'd be okay with us texting Kaylah for an update once she's given birth..."

He instantly beamed. "Thanks!"

They texted the number they had for Kaylah, and a few days later got a reply. Catrina had given birth to another set of twin girls.

"Poor Leon," Marcus said. "Outnumbered four-to-one."

"Right? And *four* daughters, *four* downline heirs of her own. One more, and she's single-handedly taken care of the Elonta line!"

Ivy royalty had complex rules about names and titles, mostly based on the way the Mother Vines assigned their allegiance. The first five female Ivies after the queen in the Elonta bloodline held the power.

Leah's mom had never truly held the power of the Mother Vines, had never *truly* been a queen. She wasn't an Elonta. Leah was grateful to not be an Elonta or Elanna either. While these births were celebrated, it would no doubt stir up unwanted feelings and resentment in some of those further down the bloodline who were now taken a notch down because new heirs above them had not only claimed an exclusive title, but access to a power that only six people at a time could hold to any discernable degree.

Leah was fine being an entire realm away from those considerations. The enormous celebrations welcoming the new little princesses, and the subtle passive-aggressive greetings from Elontas or Elannas down the bloodline. But it brought her peace to see how much joy a little news from family back home brought Marcus.

Not much later, Leah's peace turned to guilt. How could she not feel guilty? Marcus's family was so close. He would never be living over here if it weren't to be with Leah. He'd said he would be willing to move to the human world permanently if that was what it took to make Leah happy, to make things work between them.

But part of her knew, no matter how much she wanted to deny it, that this was a *temporary* situation. Even if they did set up a permanent home here, would they never visit the Green Lands again? She couldn't do that to Marcus. Rachel wasn't capable—as a fully-rooted Seeder matriarch—of entering the human world anymore. They couldn't expect family to come to them. Marcus could go there. And what? Take the baby with him? Leave Leah behind because she couldn't stomach facing the public again? She'd always be the bad guy.

But every single time she imagined going anywhere near a rifting cave, she panicked.

Marcus had picked up some extra hours one Sunday, and Leah hadn't been put on the schedule that day at the dollar store. She lounged at home, cross-legged on their bed, writing in her journal.

If people only knew her—the real her. If they understood what she'd been through, how she'd misunderstood everything when she'd tried to kill Kaylah...

Leah had gone on tours with Catrina, had been formally presented and acquitted of any crimes. But people still judged.

Tapping her pen on the notebook, Leah recalled something that Saff of all people had said. Leah had asked Kaylah and Rachel's Seeder friend about current Seeder feelings regarding Leah.

As she'd suspected, Seeders had never grown that fond of her.

I can understand how some people struggle to accept you, Saff had said. *They either have rumors to go off of, or official royal tours with carefully crafted speeches.*

Yeah... Those 'carefully crafted' speeches had been dry and official and everything Leah wasn't. No matter how the palace's PR team packaged Leah, it had never felt authentic, and people probably saw that. Catrina had asked her more than once if she'd wanted to say anything for herself, but public speaking was *not* her thing. Even if she'd worked up the guts to try, she'd be a sweaty mess, likely stumbling over another preapproved message.

Leah lamented her position, until something clicked.

Marcus returned home a few hours later, coated in sawdust. Leah didn't wait for him to shower. She grabbed him and pulled him in for a kiss. He didn't hesitate to reciprocate. Holding her waist, he eventually pulled back. "If you want a little something more, I can take a quick shower..."

"No. Well, maybe a little later, but I couldn't wait. I think I know what I want to do..."

"Okay..."

"I want to write another book."

He set down his lunch bag and took a spot on the floor. "Another one for the baby, or like that older one you won't let me see?"

She wrinkled her nose. "You'll think it's crap."

Marcus rolled his eyes. "I'm sure it's not half as bad as you think."

"And if my writing *is* crap, you're going to lie and tell me it's good so I don't feel bad."

He clasped his hands, resting them in his lap. "I can be impartial. And my grammar is better than yours. I can proofread..."

It was true. He'd had a better education and had been a better student. "Maybe... But I'm not talking about fiction. I want to write a nonfiction book. An..." She cringed. "Autobiography of sorts? Or memoir? Something that tells my story. Something that gives me the opportunity to change the narrative. More personal?"

He furrowed his brow; she might die on the spot if he thought it was a stupid idea. 'Autobiography' sounded so dry. She wasn't even twenty yet. Presidents and other famous people had books like that published about them, not the villain's daughter, right?

"If you want to, you could give it a go?" Marcus said.

Not exactly a pat on the back.

"But how much are you willing to include?" he asked.

She sat on the couch, blowing out a puff of air. "I don't know yet. I'm still figuring that out." How much of her life did she want to share? How much did she *need to* for people to give her a chance? Would she divulge that she'd shoplifted? That she'd suffered sexual assault? And if she did, to what end? To what extent?

Leah picked at her nails. "I think the only way people will really give me a chance is if they learn more about me, directly from me. Not rumors. Not dry, carefully crafted speeches, you know?"

He nodded, still pensive. "But if you did that, you know it would have to be approved by Aunt Catrina. Royal family involvement and all..."

She frowned. "I know. But I'm willing to try."

Folding his arms, he shrugged. "It's your story. I support you however you want to go about it."

"And the fact that you're part of my story?" She glanced at her round protruding stomach. "A pretty big part of it?"

"I don't expect you to lie," he said softly. "But I *would* like to be able to read it. Have some say, perhaps?"

"Of course!"

"Then it's settled. If it makes you happy, and you think it can make things better for you and that little guy." He pointed at Leah's stomach. "Then I'm on board."

She smiled. "Good. How about you clean up, and I'll see about dinner." She stood, pulling down her shirt. "And then we'll decide what kind of *dessert* we want."

A few days later, Leah allowed Marcus to read her progress on the romantic adventure story she'd been working on. It made her cringe to share her work, so she sat on the bed outlining her life story while Marcus read her other book in the living room.

Leah had a lot of work to do. Her journal was helpful, but it wasn't perfectly organized chronologically or by topic, so she still needed to decide how she wanted to approach this.

The blinds were drawn closed, and the overhead light illuminated the room. She dug around the comforter with her bare toes.

"Are you kidding me?" Marcus said from the living room.

"What?"

"No." His voice was firm as he appeared at the bedroom doorway, holding her notebook. "No. Absolutely not."

She hid a grin. "What? You told me you liked my writing."

His eyes were wide. "Yeah. I do. You're actually really good. But this? *No.*"

She feigned innocence. "It's a rough draft. It'll get better."

"A sex scene?"

Releasing that grin, she kept a tone of confusion. "I thought that was some of my best writing yet."

Marcus glanced at the page. "I'll give you that. It's ... not bad... But not exactly appropriate for the age range your books are supposed to be written for!"

Leah shrugged.

As he cocked his head to the side, it was more than evident he was willing to die on this hill. "People will assume you wrote this about *us.*"

She waved a dismissive hand. "Psh. That's the fiction one."

"If you ever publish this, *in either world*, green folk will find it and still make assumptions."

Drawing a deep breath, Leah stretched out her legs. Her tone was sweet and seductive. "Marcus... I didn't write that scene for any of these books. I wrote that for *you.*"

He slowly straightened, considering. "You promise? It's not for the books?"

"Yes."

"Okay..." He relaxed, holding the notebook in front of him again. "It is actually really..." He swallowed. "I don't think we've tried a couple of the things in here..."

With an absolute smirk, she replied, "No. We haven't."

He cleared his throat. "You know, I was thinking of going to the store. We're kinda low on bread. And I could ... pick up some extra things..."

He understood the assignment.

"Only if you want to." She winked.

He looked like he could pounce right then and there. "I'll order a rideshare. Way faster than taking the bus at this time of night."

She acted casually disinterested. "Up to you. We *are* low on bread."

They shared a grin, and he left the doorway.

"Marcus?"

"What?"

"Can you pick me up some pickles, too?"

"Sure."

His keys clinked from the other room, and he reappeared in the bedroom doorway, a finger extended. "When you say pickles... Is that a ... euphemism?"

She laughed. "Dill. The kind I've been eating a lot of."

He chuckled. "Okay. Pickles."

An hour later, he brought back two full grocery bags. Amongst the collection, he had remembered the pickles, but not the bread. That was fine. They had not, in fact, been low on bread.

Chapter 28

As Leah neared the seven-month mark of her pregnancy, she and Marcus decided they could make do with her quitting her part-time job. It would be tight on finances, but he was bringing in a steady paycheck, and they still had Kaylah's money for emergencies.

Since Ivy pregnancies only lasted eight months, Leah was large. *Really* large. And tired of the comments and questions of strangers.

And she loved working on her books.

And ... she was getting more nervous about the next steps.

From what she'd gathered, Ivy births were similar to human births, with some essential differences. Her mom had escaped the palace with aides who had helped her deliver Leah. Leah had Marcus, but the thought of delivering a child in secret like that was terrifying.

She was about to acknowledge they'd have to go back to the Green Lands for the birth. She was nowhere ready emotionally to go back there, but she didn't have much choice in the matter, not when it came to her safety and that of their child.

"How do you want to go about this?" Marcus asked, massaging her feet as they sat on the couch.

She frowned and groaned. Sneak back and see if they could retain some semblance of privacy somehow?

One of the phones dinged, and they both perked up. It wasn't one of their personal phones. They'd turned the sound up on the one they'd been given at the cave, so they wouldn't miss any pertinent updates.

Marcus grabbed it from its spot on the side table, clicking the screen on as he sat back down. He silently read, surprise on his face. "Well, that's an option." He handed the phone to Leah.

<Hope you kiddos are doing well. Would you like an Ivy nurse to come check you out and prepare for that gremlin?>

Leah smiled. "What do you think?"

Marcus held his hands up. "It's up to you."

Even if they'd still go back, advanced preparations would put Leah much more at ease. She still didn't trust her chemical powers, not after she'd botched the garden at the cottage. She'd felt bad when she couldn't even inject Marcus with numbing when he'd gotten an injury at work, because they weren't willing to experiment on him, not on a Boman.

She wished she'd have studied more from the library book Wren had checked out for her, other than just reading about fertilizing powers during pregnancy.

And in regard to her delivery, Leah didn't want pain. Ivies with powers metabolized things like alcohol and human painkillers a lot faster. Minimal pain during birth was natural for Ivy women, assuming they knew how to balance their energy and their chemical arts. But Leah was in the dark.

"Definitely." She typed out a response and sent it off.

A few minutes later, the phone dinged again with an address, date, and time for an appointment.

<Renting out a private exam room. You'll be in good hands. Love you two!>

Leah's heart warmed. Kaylah was in-realm, though likely more than an hour away at the cave. The address for the nurse's appointment was in the city nearest the cave.

She would've hugged Kaylah if they'd been closer.

Less than a week later, Leah and Marcus arrived at the clinic Kaylah had specified. Marcus's boss wasn't all that fond of him taking the afternoon off, but they hadn't been given options, and he wasn't about to miss this.

Leah was sweaty and nervous as they entered and checked in. The receptionist swiftly led them to a private room where a brunette stood and surveyed the equipment, looking sharp in a white button-up shirt and dark grey pencil skirt.

"Hi," Leah said as they popped into the room.

The woman turned.

"Olivia!" Marcus practically lunged for the woman, hugging her.

Olivia smiled. "Hey, Marcus. It's been too long."

Leah closed the door behind them, a little awkward about not knowing the woman.

"Leah, this is Olivia. The best nurse in the kingdom."

Leah shook her hand. "Nice to meet you. How do you guys know each other?" Olivia had to be about Guillen's age.

Olivia kept smiling. "I was the palace head nurse for a time, under Queen, well, Matron Kaylah."

"Oh."

"Take a seat." Olivia gestured to an exam table, and Leah settled onto the edge.

"Aunt Kaylah didn't say it would be you!" Marcus said, standing next to Leah.

Olivia busied herself again with the equipment in the room, inspecting. "Her Majesty and Her Highness were probably working out details, and we had to see if I could clear my schedule."

Leah was a bit iffy on the details of this woman. Never once had Leah been to a doctor, at least according to her recollection, in the human world. Her mom had been too paranoid about them doing an exam that would reveal her green-folk nature. Green folk with powers were also blessed with quick healing and good health.

So the idea of a stranger fiddling around with her body was ... new, and uncomfortable.

It was also weird that this nurse and Marcus were close enough to hug.

"Did you leave the palace because the throne changed to Queen Catrina? Or to pursue pediatrics?"

"Neither," Olivia said, clicking on a machine. "But you don't have to worry. I've assisted with several births."

That wasn't reassuring. It wasn't even her specialty...

"She's the best there is," Marcus whispered, and Olivia blushed.

"Do you have kids of your own?" Leah asked.

Olivia faced her, an air of professionalism about her. "I never found the time to start a family of my own. But I assure you, I'll take good care of you." She paused, leaning back against the counter. "I head the Sanath Institute."

Leah's eyes grew wide. "Oh!" That was huge. "Oh." The Sanath Institute had the most progressive and prestigious nursing program in the entire Green Lands. She'd studied it when trying to peg down a career path. "That's amazing. I considered seeing if I could study there, but I realized how far behind everyone else I'd be since I didn't grow up knowing how to use my powers."

"I'm sure we could still get you an interview with the entrance board for consideration."

Leah rested her hands on her huge stomach, trying not to frown. It still didn't feel right to focus her career on powers when her child would be born without them. And she wasn't fond of the idea that she'd only be extended that special exception because of her connections to the royal family.

And, even though it wasn't doing anything for her financially at the moment, Leah was growing more attached to the idea of becoming a writer, a real author with books published.

"Thanks, I'll think about it." She gave Olivia a half-smile.

"Right." Olivia stood tall, gesturing to the machine she'd turned on. "I've trained on human equipment, and this is top of the line. Want an ultrasound? Just to take a peek?"

Leah instantly beamed. "Yes!" The human world had its perks.

As instructed, Leah lay back, and Marcus held her hand.

Olivia prepped a wand with gel, explaining a little about the equipment. The image might be a bit fuzzy due to Leah's Ivy energy, so it would help if Leah could force it away from her stomach where it naturally pooled to support and protect the baby. She channeled it to her extremities. It felt weird, as did the cool gel on the wand. But soon enough, little whooshes filtered through a speaker, and Leah had to fight not to cry. That was her baby. Her and Marcus's actual baby. A little heartbeat.

Marcus kissed her hand and squeezed it tighter.

"Mhmm," Olivia said, facing the screen. "Good job parting your energy. I've got a pretty clear view. And look at that Boman energy." Her voice was sweet, her bedside manner friendly.

"You can tell?" Leah asked. "The difference between an Ivy baby with powers and without?"

Olivia nodded, moving the wand. "Fainter glow. And if you're *really* looking for it, you *might* be able to check for vine nodules, but that's harder."

Leah was over the moon. It made it all so real.

"Did you two want to know their genders today?"

"We were talking about that, and—" *Wait, what?* 'Their' could have been interpreted as gender-neutral, but... "Did you just say genders, with an *S* at the end?"

Olivia smiled brightly. "Yes. Twins."

Leah's jaw dropped.

"Really?" Marcus asked, his voice as confused as Leah's.

"I thought all Bomen are single births..."

"Me too," Marcus echoed.

The *last* thing Leah needed was for more attention because she was having some sort of freaky pregnancy no one had ever heard of. Strike that—the *actual* last thing she needed was for people to assume she'd cheated on Marcus and these children were standard Ivies with powers...

"Can you count again?" Leah asked, a hint of panic in her voice.

Olivia hummed confidently, swiveling the screen. Clear as day—two babies. "See that fuzziness on the screen? That glow?" She pointed to their tiny heads and necks. "Boman glow. This is the third set of Bomen twins I've heard of, actually."

Leah breathed a smidge easier. At least she wasn't going in the history books as a first on this one. But then the reality of having twins smacked her. One was going to be enough to manage, an arm and a vine full. "Two?"

"Isn't that exciting?!" Marcus's tone echoed his sentiments.

Leah, however, was still stunned. She turned her head, enunciating clearly. "You don't get to be excited about that. You don't have to push them out of your body!"

His unadulterated joy was unwavering. "Twice the cute!"

"When you think about it, it's not that much extra work, because—" Olivia stopped and cleared her throat at Leah's reproachful glare, returning her attention to the screen.

"Come on. We've got this," Marcus added a little more calmly.

Leah looked at him. And then it hit her... She allowed his glee to rub off on her, to calm and reassure her. What she would've done to have him be this excited when she'd first broken the pregnancy news to him... She returned his smile.

"They're going to look just like you," he said. "Perfect." He kissed her forehead.

"I'm fairly confident in the genders, if you did want to know them," Olivia said.

They'd agreed to be surprised, but Leah was already surprised by the twins detail, and now she wanted as much information as possible for preparations. *No wonder I'm so huge. At least it's not all the bacon and tacos...*

She looked at Marcus. "I kinda want to know now."

"Sure, why not?"

Olivia pointed out the anatomy. "This one's a girl."

Leah threw Marcus a subtle 'I was right' look.

"And a boy."

Marcus snickered, nudging Leah. So, they both had guessed right.

After another minute of pointing out anatomy and answering questions about what the equipment showed, Olivia turned it off and sat on a stool in the corner of the room. "Do you know what your plans are? Have you been preparing with energy and chemical arts exercises?"

Leah bit her lip. "I didn't study... And I don't have a book about all of that... And Kaylah didn't exactly say what our options are..."

"Well... It's up to you." Olivia folded her arms. "I highly recommend starting the exercises right away, because that makes an Ivy birth massively easier. And *you're* going to be the only one who can regulate your pain. Another Ivy's numbing won't work on you when you're pregnant. It's tricky, but you have to self-regulate."

That sounded both oddly empowering, and frustratingly daunting. "Are you going to be able to teach me?"

"That's part of why I'm here. Were you planning to give birth over here?"

Leah blinked. "If it's an option, then absolutely."

"It is. If you've got the time, let's discuss it."

They spent the next hour forming a plan. Olivia would be rifting over to the human world on the weekends, and stationing another nurse she trusted over here during weekdays. The other nurse would meet with Leah to coach her on exercises in preparation.

The scanning equipment was ideal here, but the couple confessed they didn't live all that close. With Olivia sworn to secrecy, they told her what city they'd settled in, and she said she'd scout out another birthing location. Given Leah was a mother with powers, her pregnancy was very low risk, even with twins.

"And then the last week, both of us will plan to be here full time until these little ones arrive."

Leah was *so* relieved and much more confident in the path ahead of her. Marcus was excited and supportive.

But they also had to decide who would be clued in on their news, assuming they even had a choice in the matter. Catrina and Stephan would be notified, as well as Kaylah and Eric, and Rachel and Guillen. It didn't feel right to keep them all in the dark, and they'd keep the secret.

Leah and Marcus left the appointment after exchanging contact details with Olivia. She'd have the other nurse reach out soon about helping Leah prepare.

Needing groceries anyway, Leah and Marcus swung by the store on the way back to their apartment. Once home, they sat on the couch, enjoying a quart of rocky road ice cream straight from the carton.

"Here's to *two* of them." Leah held up her spoon, wide-eyed. Marcus grinned and clinked his spoon against hers.

This was perfect, absolutely perfect. They hadn't been ready to return to the Green Lands, and they'd be able to have the kids here. But a nagging feeling slowly brought Leah's spirits down.

Rachel. Leah remembered Rachel's reproach, how she'd shared that she had once yearned to experience the gift of life. Now she was becoming a first-time grandmother, and her future daughter-in-law was at fault for cutting her out of the equation.

Rachel wasn't the entitled type. With extra time and perspective, Leah now genuinely regretted how things had gone down between them at the cottage. Had Rachel been a bit overbearing? Yeah. And she'd reacted to the news in a way that had ruffled Leah's feathers. But she'd been trying to help, and some of those problems were of Marcus's causing. Rachel was sweet and kind and forgiving. And unable to come to the human world. Even if Leah chose to make an exception to their no-contact rule with their families, Rachel couldn't be there for the birth.

Leah stared at her spoon, frowning. "Do you think your mom will ever forgive me for doing this over here?"

He matched her frown, his eyes conveying he understood. "She'll be sad. But she wants you to be happy, too."

And then Leah remembered everything her parents had put Rachel's family through, and how extraordinary it was that she had forgiven Leah, that she even tolerated Leah.

Neither a human-world birth laden with guilt nor a Green Lands birth filled with anxiety was ideal.

Marcus reached over, taking Leah's hand, and kissed her engagement ring. "This is about *our* family. You and me and our *mini-me*s."

She nodded, forcing a smile. She'd be able to come to terms with it. And then she gazed down at her ring. They hadn't held any real conversations about marriage since Marcus's proposal months ago. He was probably too scared of her running away again or thinking twice about it. But this had also been a bit of a trial run to see if they could make things work. She was confident now that they could.

"What do you want to do about the wedding?" she asked.

Chapter 29

Marcus eyed Leah, finishing another spoonful of ice cream. "What about the wedding?"

"What do you want it to look like? Venue? Timeframe? People?"

He scrunched his eyebrows in thought. "I dunno. What do you want?"

"Nope. I asked you."

Sighing, he set down his spoon. "I always imagined, you know, the whole big wedding thing. My aunt *is* the queen, after all. But I know that's not what you want."

She mulled it over. It wasn't what she wanted at all. She'd faintly learned to *imagine* getting to a place where she was capable of enduring a giant ceremony with all eyes on her, back before she'd gotten pregnant, but now...

That didn't mean this was going to be one-sided. He deserved to get something he wanted, and maybe that was a sacrifice Leah could make. Or maybe even if it was something small in the Green Lands, his mom could be there, to make up for missing the birth?

"You know me: crowds and I don't get along. And I would have *literally* no one on my side of the wedding that wasn't already on your side, because I'm *absolutely* not inviting anyone from my mom's side of the family. But I can ... do what you want..."

"That doesn't exactly sound like an ideal bridal situation."

Her heart was heavy. Couldn't she just have this special day without guilt? A bride getting what she wanted? "I know, but we agreed to compromise, to meet in the middle."

His eyes were warm, his voice soft. "All I've ever wanted was *you*."

She had to blush at that. Since they weren't eating the ice cream anymore, she put the lid back on and took it to the freezer. "You know, that's not completely true. You haven't *always* wanted me."

"Lies."

"Hmm." She nestled into his arms on the couch. "Exhibit A: dating that human girl after I asked you out."

"What? Exhibit A: I thought a super pretty and bold girl asked me to shoot archery, and I made an idiot of myself by calling it a date and finding out she did *not* consider it a date."

Leah let out a breathy chuckle. "But after I asked you on a real date, you went on *two* dates with some human girl! I was throwing myself at you!"

"Hey, now. I'd already asked her on the first, and I didn't want to be rude."

"And the second? That was *torture* waiting for you to decide."

"She asked, and I felt bad saying no."

"You admit you were spineless?"

His lips brushed against her ear as he whispered playfully. "You don't get to be mad, because you didn't even like me yet."

She pouted. "I liked you as a friend. And I *definitely* liked the way your butt looked in jeans..."

He nibbled her ear, exploring her body ever so gently with his hands. She was putty in his arms.

"So, what do *you* want?" he asked.

"Right now?"

He knew exactly what he was making her want.

Kissing the back of her head, he slid his hands to her giant stomach. "How about we figure that out in a few minutes? For now, what do you want with the wedding?"

Right. Yes. That...

"Honestly, I'm willing to compromise, but my ideal right now is just ... us. Make it official. I kind of even would like to do it before the babies come. Is that weird? Would you hate having me this big for our wedding?"

"I'd be okay with all of that. I was the one who wanted to move up our timeline, remember?"

She narrowed her eyes, resting her head on his chest. "You'd really be okay with an elopement?"

"We're already halfway there."

There were two bridal shops in the area, and Leah went to them both. It was depressing. Unsurprisingly, they didn't have entire sections dedicated to dresses designed for superpregnant mothers. And the plus-size options were abysmal.(jj)

And she was shopping alone. Marcus offered to join her, but she wanted to keep *something* a surprise for the wedding. If she hadn't nearly died of mortification from her visit at the cottage, Leah might have considered breaking the no-family ban to shop with Camry.

This was one of those events she imagined she would have loved to do with her mom... At least ... the mom she'd known before coming to the Green Lands.

At the first shop, a spiteful voice told her it was a joke for a slut like Leah to even consider a white dress. She almost listened to it. But she wanted white, so she reminded that voice to take a hike. She prayed that someday down the road, it would be faint enough for her to not keep hearing those kinds of comments.

At the second shop, her own guilt told her she didn't *need* a special dress to elope, and it wasn't her money to spend. This was going to go on Kaylah's card.

She tried to push past that one, because Kaylah would want her to be happy. But ... it was a hefty fee they were quoting to take a frumpy plus-size option and rush fit it to her.

Leah stared at herself in a mirror, adorned in a ghastly lace-covered dress that was tight on her stomach and baggy everywhere else. She did *not* feel like a bride.

They still wanted to make a sale. "I think it's great you're doing it now; that way you and your babies can share their dad's last name, right?"

Leah laughed way more than she ought to. Ivy society was matriarchal. With some exceptions in the Elonta and Elanna royal line, the woman's surname was taken by her husband and children. But none of that actually mattered for Leah and Marcus. They already had the same last name—Elonto. Exactly five people in both worlds—human or Green Lands—shared that last name, one designated for royalty-adjacent misfits like them...

After the failed assassination attempt, Leah was offered a choice as to what she would be called. She wasn't fond of keeping her human-world alias—Edwards. It had all been a lie, and she'd wanted to leave it behind as she started a new life. She'd wanted nothing to do with her mom's family because of the way they'd treated Bomen, so she also turned down their surname—Remsgard. As her dad had been a prince, Leah was given the Elonto option.

Leah's shoulders slumped. Why was she in a dress shop letting someone try to talk her into this gosh-awful getup that she was going to pay way too much money on and feel guilty about, just to hate it?

"I'm going to have to think about it, but thanks."

With all the charm and sweetness of condescension coated in a bucket of sugar, the saleswoman addressed her. "No offense, honey, but your wedding is soon, and that baby bump isn't getting smaller."

Yep, that sealed the deal. "Then I'll pass, thanks."

Leah returned home and did some online searching. She found a website that offered beautiful bridesmaids dresses, including maternity options, and you could change the color to white. Happy to pay for rush shipping, she whipped out the card and let out a huge breath of relief.

Human–green-folk relations had become more complex in the last two decades as Seeder and Ivy societies made drastic changes, and their interactions with humans took on new purposes.

Admittedly, a lot of what green folk did in the human world was technically illegal. They all used fake identities to travel, obtain bank accounts, and study. But as long as it was done in the right spirit, keeping the Green Lands secret and safe, then those in the know overlooked it.

The marriage license would be a fake, but despite that, all human-world marriages were recognized as legal back in the Green Lands.

Leah's wedding dress arrived. It was a simple flowy design, and it made her smile. It fit just right around her stomach and chest, so she was grateful she'd ordered a size up.

They found a local pastor to perform the ceremony, but they needed a witness. It was awkward to confess they didn't have anyone. The pastor offered to have his wife attend. Leah and Marcus said they'd think about it.

Lying in bed, they snuggled up to each other, chatting about their day and making final decisions.

"How was your meeting with the nurse today?" Marcus asked.

"Pretty good." She threaded her fingers through his curly hair. "I definitely wish I'd started learning earlier."

If left untrained, she'd have to endure the birth much like unmedicated humans did, which was a terrifying thought. With her trained, it should go much smoother—quicker and minimally painful, fast to heal. But the training was complex. It was similar to how she'd heard Seeder flight was achieved, in that she'd have to shift her energy to the right places in her body to help the process along. It would help prevent injury and aid healing, all the while she'd try to keep her calm and focus on her chemical arts to balance things out.

Marcus smiled. "You'll do great."

She adjusted herself on the bed. "And what are your thoughts on the wedding witness?"

He softly grunted. "It's weird having someone witness who we don't actually know."

"I've been thinking about it, and there's another option that doesn't involve family... And they're *kind of* mutual."

"Yeah?"

Leah bit her lip. "What about seeing if Jake can make it?"

Marcus instantly lit up. "Really?"

She smiled as well. "Really. Why don't you message him and see if he wants to come? As long as he can keep a secret. And ... you can enjoy a bachelor's night with him."

Marcus kissed her, then grabbed his phone from the bedside table. He typed up a message. After sending it, he gave Leah another smooch and cuddled back up. "But if we do a bachelor's night, what will *you* do?"

Jake and his girlfriend, who Leah had met in high school, were still together, but long distance, as she'd started to attend a university a few states away.

Leah breathed deeply, something that came with more effort these days. "I'll be happy here. I've been neglecting my journal with all the wedding and baby preparations."

Marcus wouldn't get drunk or have strippers; neither he nor Jake were like that. They'd probably play video games all night. "Are you sure?"

"My gift. Go have fun."

He eyed her skeptically. "We'll see what Jake says."

Jake responded soon enough and cleared his schedule. It didn't take much convincing for Marcus to agree to a bachelor's night since they hadn't seen each other in nearly a year.

And Leah really was fine hanging out at the apartment. Marcus came home shortly after midnight. He took a half day at work that Friday, and cleaned up, donning a sharp black suit. Leah wore a cute pink maternity dress she'd found, and Marcus carried her wedding dress in a garment bag.

It was a calm day in late April, and Leah's birthday.(kk) She'd always grown up celebrating her birthday in late November. That had been one of many lies told to her by her mother. The lie had been somewhat understandable, given Beata's paranoia about being found while in hiding. More than one of her aides had gone missing, and she'd always been afraid they had ratted on her, disclosing that she'd given birth in the human world.

Leah might have continued to celebrate on the November date if it had been *any* other day. Beata had been paranoid, but also too sentimental and guilt-ridden about her husband. She'd always celebrated Leah's birthday on *Soren's* birthday. The moment Leah had learned that, she'd chosen to celebrate on her true birthday.

It was a fitting day to be a bride. She celebrated another year of her life, and would soon bring new life into the world. This wedding would give her and Marcus a new start.

They met the pastor at the church, and Leah excused herself to get changed. Marcus lingered outside the door, and soon enough his voice became louder, joined by Jake's. Leah had only seen Jake once since she'd moved to the Green Lands. This would be fun for her too.

As the guys shot the breeze, Leah struggled to zip up the dress; it got caught on the fabric. Her vines could reach the zipper, but couldn't grasp it well enough to tug it free. She carefully cracked the door. "Marcus, I need your help," she muttered.

"Yeah, sure." He stepped up to the door. "But you said I couldn't see you yet."

She huffed. "Then close your eyes. It's not that hard to feel a zipper."

The door creaked as it widened, and his hands slipped inside the changing room. And then those hands roamed everywhere but the zipper. "I can't seem to find it."

"Stop it," she scolded.

"Ope, there it is. I'm usually much better blindfolded, aren't I?"

She blushed. "Stop it! We're in a *church*," she whispered.

"You never attended church a single time in this world," he whispered back, freeing the stuck zipper.

"So what? I know how to act in one…"

He softly chuckled, zipping it and kissing her on the neck.

"Thank you. I'll be out in a minute."

She straightened her dress and touched up her kissproof lipstick. Did she feel like a bride? Kinda? None of this was going the way she'd imagined growing up. But a smile still came to her lips, her anticipation building.

Leah took a deep breath and stepped out of the changing room for her big reveal, into the hallway where the guys chatted again.

She smiled brightly at Jake. "Hey!"

He did not smile. His jaw dropped, and his eyes widened, staring right at her baby bump. "*Wow*, Leah, you're... Wow!"

Rolling her eyes, she stood taller. "Pointing out how huge a massive pregnant bride is *isn't* the most polite thing to do."

Jake looked confused. "No. I just ... didn't know you were!"

Placing her hands on her hips, she turned to Marcus. He stood there smirking. "You didn't tell him?!"

Marcus let out a goofy laugh. "I thought it would be more fun if it was a surprise!"

She lightly smacked his arm. "Not funny."

He kept laughing.

Jake recovered enough to pick up his jaw. "I mean, you look *great*, Leah."

"Mhmmm..."

"And it's *twins*," Marcus said.

Jake looked as confused as they had been about that announcement, and Marcus clarified that they weren't the first Bomen twins out there.

"Cool," Jake said. "I was wondering why you guys weren't having a big wedding back in the kingdom... So, this is why?"

Leah bit her lip. *No talk of back home. No guilt or spiraling.* "Nope. We just wanted it to be small, and to collude with our friend again. Like old times." She winked.

He gave her an ironic grin.

"We shouldn't keep the pastor waiting," Marcus said, offering his hand.

Leah took it, and they headed toward the room the pastor had designated for the ceremony.

"You do look breathtaking," Marcus whispered in her ear.

The ceremony was short. No pomp and circumstance. Just three friends and a stranger with authority to seal the deal. Leah held a bouquet, and they exchanged simple vows. She didn't cry, but she was at peace, a calmness settling into her soul. Marcus's smile was a mile wide.

They took a few pictures on their phones at the church and on the surrounding grounds. Everything was in bloom, and even if the spring here didn't hold quite the idyllic beauty it did in the Green Lands, this particular one couldn't be beat.

After Leah changed back into her more casual dress, the trio of friends went out for steak.

They gabbed and laughed. It wouldn't be everyone's idea of a successful wedding day, but it worked for them.

After occupying their table for far too long, the group said their goodbyes and parted ways.

Marcus had rented a car for the weekend, and he drove Leah to a resort forty-five minutes away.

It wasn't until they checked in and settled in that Leah fully relaxed, fully processed everything. A simple brand-new ring she'd bought for Marcus now gleamed on his finger as he carried in their things.

They were *married*. Man and wife. Woman and husband. Soon-to-be parents. Best friends.

Leah rested on the sofa, glancing out the sliding glass door to a balcony.

"I only have one regret about our wedding," Marcus said.

She frowned.

"We didn't get to dance. But we can do that now..." He pulled out his phone, selected some music, and extended his hands.

Smiling, she took them and hoisted herself up. She wrapped her arms around his neck and let him lead.

"Music," Marcus said. "I think I miss music most about the human world when I'm back home. Because you don't need a band over here to listen to it. And you don't have to hear me screeching out songs like a tree full of chatterbirds during mating season."

Leah chuckled as they swayed. "You're not *that* bad."

He beamed, sneaking a kiss. "How does it feel to be married?"

She drew lazy circles on his neck with her thumbs. How did it feel? They'd already been living together. Had already started a family together. People said it was only a piece of paper all the time. Leah used to think that way. But something special clicked into place for her in that moment, as he held her in his arms, her belly poking against his. He'd promised in his vows that he would always be by her side, and she believed it. They'd come so far, grown so much.

Her life had been an incomplete puzzle, all askew, a mess. She'd been fighting to line up the pieces, to match up the colors and patterns, and most of the time floundering.

There were still a lot of pieces left to sort, so much unknown about the future. But this day, this little step, was like snapping the last piece of the border into place. It gave her a secure framework. It gave her hope and happiness. And Marcus had always been that for her. Marcus was her home.

Her heart full, tears gathered in her eyes. "It feels great."

Chapter 30

The newlyweds enjoyed the weekend alone on their little getaway. It was hard to not acknowledge how blissfully silent it was at the resort. The absence of traffic, or neighbors with their movies and video games up too high, was stark.

They sipped smoothies their last morning there, sharing a wicker bench on the balcony, discussing preparations for the babies' arrival.

One baby was expensive. Two babies... Someday they'd find a way to pay Kaylah back.

Marcus's eyebrows knit as he sat pensive. "Did I ever apologize for getting you the wrong birth control tonic?"

She searched her memories. "I don't remember." They'd been in a pretty heated conversation when she'd told him.

"I am sorry. I mean, not that I'm sorry that we're having them, because I want them, but you know..."

She smiled softly. "I know." One of the babies kicked, and she moved his hand to feel it. He always ate that up.

"I promise I'll be more careful," he said. They hadn't brought any tonic with them, and as the tonics required ingredients only available in the Green Lands, they couldn't brew up their own even if they knew how to. Hormonal birth control wouldn't help either, as Ivy chemistry didn't align closely enough with that of humans. They'd have to use other methods of contraception while in the human world.

Like the dimmed energy over here, and the constant noise of electronics, ease and comfort of contraception was one more mental tally mark in Leah's mind as she processed where they were going with their lives. And the fact that she had to keep her vines hidden when in public sometimes brought back hurtful memories of her childhood and being forced to repress that side of herself.

Marcus broke her from her reverie. "We should peg down baby names. Or do you think we should wait until we see them?"

She slurped up the last of her smoothie, setting the glass down beside the bench. "I think one less unknown makes me less crazy. What are your thoughts?"

He shrugged.

Leah adjusted her seat. "I know Kaylah was joking in her text, and Ivies don't normally do middle names, but what would you think about giving them middle names? And having the girl's be Kaylah?"

Marcus smiled. "I'm okay with that." He rested a hand on her leg. "Any other suggestions?"

She chuckled. "I'm all out of names from decent people in *my* family, unless you want to include Eric." As soon as she said it, guilt weighed her down for so easily dismissing her mom. But Beata would never be a complimentary name for a child in the Green Lands. It was like a modern human naming their child Stalin or Putin.

"Mmm…" Marcus rocked his head back and forth. "No offense to Uncle Eric, but how would you feel about the boy's middle name being Guillen?"

Marcus respected his father *so* much. Guillen was kind. He had kind of implied that Leah wasn't equal to his son when he'd visited at the cottage, but she'd come to understand where he was coming from. His parents' marriage had been disastrous. He had also given Leah permission to not marry Marcus, and that was a bit awkward now that they'd tied the knot. But he'd given her permission no one else had. And he'd been the first to actually congratulate her on her pregnancy.

Leah rested her hand on Marcus's. "I think that's a great idea."

And then to decide on the first names… They considered other Ivy and human traditions. In the end, they agreed upon Aspen for the girl, Ash for the boy. It made Leah twice as excited to finally meet them.

Marcus carefully lifted Leah's shirt, exposing her stomach. He leaned down, pressing his lips to her skin, and then blew a massive raspberry.

Leah gasped, clenched, and pushed him off. "I swear you made them both just kick my bladder!"

He laughed. "Sorry."

She offered him a dirty look.

"I *am* sorry." His tone was all but apologetic as he lifted a hand to his heart. "But I've been neglecting giving you good luck. I think we're gonna have to do it three times a day until we meet them, to make sure everything goes smoothly."

She threw him a death glare. "You can give them luck once we meet them. I will continue to exercise my powers *without* your special brand of good luck, thank you very much."

He only smirked in response, and it took everything she had to not cave and kiss that smirk right off his face.

Seeder reproduction worked like clockwork; it was extremely predictable. Ivy pregnancies weren't on that level, but they were still far less risky and more predictable than those of humans.

Almost to the day, Leah went into labor around her eight-month mark. Olivia and her accompanying nurse were ready for her at a private birthing center.

She hadn't mastered the techniques the nurses had tried to teach her. The birth was painful and stressful, and involved a little swearing, a lot of sweat, and plenty of tears. Marcus gripped her hand tightly through it all, much calmer than she'd expected him to be.

Aspen and Ash were beautiful, their little cries music to Leah's ears. There weren't words to express their perfection and how much it meant to finally meet them.

As the nurses cleaned them up, Leah rested, taking slow breaths. Her Ivy energy and chemical powers surged within her as they tried to find a proper equilibrium again. Her stomach cramped as it set to work healing already. "If we ever do that again, I'm practicing those exercises from *day one*," she said.

"You'll want to have more kids?" Marcus asked sweetly, brushing aside a wisp of hair plastered to her forehead with sweat.

She stared at him. "Not the best time to make that decision."

He chuckled, kissing her cheek. "You were great, Mom."

And then she started to cry again. *Mom.* She was a mom.

They set little Aspen and Ash on Leah's chest, and her heart overflowed. They were *perfect.* They both had a full head of hair, and as expected, it was black like Leah's. They also had her and her mom's nose. Eye color could change a little with time as they grew, but for now, their eyes were light brown, and she hoped they'd stay that way. Leah's love for her own green eyes had been tainted by learning about the man she'd gotten them from.

Nursing the twins was intimidating, especially with two of them, but they sorted it out. She was grateful for that. They could have survived off formula, but it was expensive, and she planned to stay home. Plus, they didn't have any kittlefruit in the human world, the type of nourishment green folk used when babies over there couldn't nurse.

By nightfall, the couple returned to their apartment with two little swaddled ones in car seats. Leah rested, cuddling with the twins in bed while Marcus ordered them dinner. This had been such a massive hurdle in her life. From her puzzle box, it felt like a lot more than just two pieces clicking into place. It was more like an entire row.

She beamed as Ash made an adorable soft baby grunt in his sleep. With Marcus, this was her world. She'd never wanted to rule the kingdom, even if people misinterpreted the assassination attempt that way. She'd never been big on traveling, not when her mom had forced her to move so much growing up. She was a homebody. She wanted a place to call home, and people who wouldn't leave her, who she wouldn't have to leave. For once, she had that.

It took time to get their routine down as a family of four. Marcus couldn't take much time off if he wanted to keep his job, not as a newer employee with questionable work history, references, and legal paperwork.

Both Leah and Marcus gave their all, taking turns with shopping, cooking, and changing diapers. When she wasn't too exhausted and could make the time, Leah continued to work on her stories. The adventure in her fictional novels was enough for her. The truths in her memoir were hard to face, but also freeing, especially when she considered how it might change people's perspective of her.

On one of his days off, Marcus prepared dinner while the twins napped. Leah sat on the couch, scratching away at the plot of her adventure romance work in progress. Marcus kept encouraging her to continue. She definitely needed more opinions than his, but she enjoyed imagining herself as an author. She'd be crushed if other people read it and decided it was rubbish. But even then, she was willing to learn, to improve—as a writer and as a person.

In some ways, she'd corrupted Marcus, changing him from the shy, obedient, nerdy kid to a runaway, and one who was not shy in the bedroom. But he'd tamed her, too. She wasn't chasing the thrill with the next guy or party or shoplifting haul. She was a bookworm and a mother.

Marcus handed Leah a plate of taco salad, and she set her work aside. "I like what you did with the last chapter," he said, easing down next to her.

"Thanks." She smiled. "I've been doing some thinking... If we're serious about this being my thing, I want to publish the adventure romance books here, in the human world."

He raised an eyebrow. "That's ... not going to go well. We should stick to Green Lands publishing, where it's, you know, legal..."

She sighed. The secrecy from humans was understandable. Imagine the uproar if the masses of humans discovered there was an alternate realm filled with botanical beings on their own planet? "I know... But it's fiction. People will think it's fake, like fairies and dragons and all that."

He eyed her, and she huffed. "Blah, blah, blah. Joint laws with Seeders, Ivies, and Bomen. I get it. But I could change the details. Instead of green folk in the Green Lands, they'll be ... butterfly people in the ... Blue Lands?"

Marcus laughed. "Butterfly people? Blue Lands?"

She pointed her fork at him. "Don't judge me. I'm sure most humans would think *we're* ridiculous."

Shrugging, Marcus dug into his salad.

"There's a wider audience in the human world, ya know? Instead of a few million potential readers, it's a few billion."

He crunched down on a piece of romaine. "If you do butterfly people, you could publish in both worlds."

She wrinkled her nose. That was true, but she also kind of didn't want people in the Green Lands to read those books. It felt weird to mingle her memoir and identity with something fun and playful. "We'll see." Maybe she'd use a pen name to separate them.(11)

"What about those stories back at Kaylah's?" he asked. "The ones you wrote for Aspen and Ash?"

That brought another smile to her face. "I still want to get them made up. But I'd want them professionally illustrated." She cringed. "I don't want to give our kids nightmares."

"You should ask Saff."

Leah furrowed her brow. "Your mom and Kaylah's Seeder friend? I'm sure she's got enough on her plate."

He shrugged in reply.

Leah recalled a painting at Kaylah's estate. "Kaylah probably doesn't even know who painted it, and I don't know if they can do people, but there's a painting in her library I love. The colors are really soft. It's of daisies in a vase.(mm) I think I'd like the style if it were in watercolor."

Marcus choked on his salad and laughed. "Saff painted that."

Leah pursed her lips. "Fine. Point made."

<hr>

Day after day, week after week, time passed, and they found their groove. Before Leah stopped meeting with Olivia for checkups, Olivia delivered congratulations from Marcus's family back in the Green Lands. No official announcements had been made. Olivia provided Leah and Marcus with two Boman jade tokens for Aspen and Ash so they could rift. And ... to their discomfort, they discovered people were looking for the couple, here in the human world.

Had Marcus never gotten back together with Leah, he probably would have faded more into obscurity once there was a proper prince in the Ivy Kingdom to dote over, and now four princesses. But ... Leah was gossip-worthy. They were a pair people kept tabs on. She'd been in hiding too long; they'd both been missing for far too long to go unnoticed. People had even stuck their noses in Marcus's family's business on this side of things, showing up at his grandparents' house, and that of Tobias and Camry.

As Leah healed physically and emotionally, she fought against the tug to go home, at least to the home Marcus had grown up in. *This* world had been her home. With the comforts of modern electronics, planes that could take you anywhere you needed, *light bulbs*.

But every day, she felt that subtle tug, that her time here was running out. She wasn't a Seeder; cut off from the energy of her ancestral realm, she wouldn't die like they did. But she *did* feel that lacking in her Ivy energy, every day.

Marcus, Aspen, and Ash wouldn't feel it nearly as much since they were Bomen with only wisps of Ivy energy. Aspen and Ash probably wouldn't even know the difference, since they'd never experienced the Green Lands. But could Leah really take them away from family, from their heritage? Just because she didn't like the attention over there?

No one had ever hunted for Leah when she was a child. They'd tried to hunt down her mom, but had eventually given up. They hadn't known about Leah until she'd revealed herself.

Now, she'd never be left alone. How long would it take for people to track them down? Would she and Marcus move to Argentina to run away? The thought of forcing her children into a life of hiding was nauseating.

So, she continued to write her memoir. Hopefully, someday it would make a difference.

And as she did so, Leah started to forgive herself. As she and Marcus grew into their parenthood and proceeded to focus on being better communicators, she started to see others' perspectives better, and began to forgive some of them too.

But she worried... Where would her relationship with her mom come out at the end of it all?

Chapter 31

Aspen and Ash were nearly five months old. Leah's manuscripts were getting close to completion. Marcus kept working construction, and he seemed to really enjoy it.

In the haze of a dream, Leah sat tall in a fancy dress purchased and fitted for her by the palace. She crossed her ankles as a proper lady ought to, wearing a perma-smile for the crowd. This meeting was taking place in Capital City, a gathering of mostly Bomen.

Leah tried not to sweat, tried not to show fear or panic. She was well-mannered, repentant—everything she should be to win over the people.

Queen Catrina, King Stephan, and other politicians and public servants took turns addressing the crowd. They shared plans for the future of Bomen, and more than one gestured to Leah, commenting how she'd come to realize the error of her ways. She was a shining example of how far people could come in accepting those born without powers. Leah tensed to not squirm, to keep that smile on her face as eyes rested on her.

Luckily, it hadn't been all about her, but it was an opportunity to show her off, to clear her name, to help her settle in.

As the rally came to a close, Leah and the others on the platform stood. She tried not to fidget, keeping that smile that told everyone she wasn't crazy or hateful.

To her surprise, a redheaded woman approached the platform, right in front of where Leah stood. She must have been an Ivy Boman, assuming the child she held in her arms was hers. The adorable little child had deep red splotches on its face and neck—the mark of a *Biman*. Less than a handful of Bimen existed in the Green Lands, the offspring of Ivy Boman mothers and Seeder Boman fathers.(nn)

Leah marveled at the child, at the miracle of unity it represented. She wished Marcus could have attended with her that day, her smile becoming more genuine.

And then the woman's gaze turned harsh, and she gave Leah a vulgar gesture. She stared Leah dead in the eye as Leah's heart faltered, as her smile faded. No, the woman hadn't wanted to talk. Hadn't wanted to give Leah a chance. She'd wanted to show her child and remind Leah that had her parents won the war, had things turned out according to their plans, this child would have been born into slavery, or more likely—wouldn't have existed at all.

Leah wanted to vomit. The child began to wail. Leah tried to open her mouth to say something, to reassure the woman she wasn't like her parents, didn't think that way, that she *loved* a Boman. But her mouth wouldn't budge.

The child continued to wail, louder and louder, as the woman simply turned and walked away.

Come back! I can explain everything!

Why is the crying getting louder?

Leah woke with a start, her heart racing. *What the... No, that's...* The crying was from one of hers. Either Aspen or Ash was crying.

She blew out a breath to collect herself, closing her eyes. The mind sucked when it played tricks like that. That rally *had* happened in real life. That interaction with the mother had happened.

It didn't matter. Hopefully, Leah's book would make a difference someday?

The bed was cold next to her, a dim light glowing through the open bedroom door. Marcus must have gotten up with one or both of the twins at some point.

Leah pulled back the covers and stumbled to the doorway. Marcus sat on the couch in his boxers, softly shushing Aspen. "No waking Mommy," he whispered. "Mommy needs sleep." His voice was groggy but gentle.

He lifted Aspen, sniffing her diaper. "Oh, man! What is Mom feeding you?!"

Leah watched while leaning against the doorframe.

"No more tacos for Mom, that's what I say, Stinky One," he cooed in the most adorable baby talk. Setting her next to him, Marcus grabbed a diaper and wipes, then proceeded to clean her up.

Leah held a hand to her heart, smiling wide as he took care of a now-calm Aspen. He continued to talk to her, animated and sweet.

Marcus was always like this with the twins. He'd been a great cousin to the prince and princesses. He was a great father.

And then Aspen giggled at his silliness. Her first giggle.

Leah turned to mush, her heart full, her smile gone. A thousand emotions flooded her, pouring out in the form of tears. Marcus was the type of dad she'd imagined she would have had as a little girl. The kind of dad she *wouldn't* have actually had if he'd lived—not with a monster like Soren.

With Marcus, she never once feared her children wouldn't be safe with him. Never once feared she'd have to choose between her kids and her husband.

That dream, that memory of the Boman mother... Even if it was the case that Bomen never came to accept Leah, they accepted Marcus. There was confusion about why Marcus would still be with Leah after what she'd done, but he was an insider they respected. And even if it hurt Leah to never be included in their circle, despite being a mother to Bomen, Marcus was a Boman and could help their kids where she lacked, where she was unwelcome or uncomfortable.

He deserved the world. He deserved to be happy.

Leah sniffled, wiping away tears. Marcus's gaze shot up to her. He only now realized he had an audience. "What's wrong?" Concern painted his face. "Are you okay?"

She nodded, sniffling again. "I'm fine."

"Do you want to talk?"

As she walked in, Aspen stirred once more.

Leah picked her up, supporting her with vines. "Might as well get a two-in-one diaper change and feeding." She sat back on the couch. "We all know you like Mom's *taco-flavored milk*." She gave Marcus a look.

He snickered. "You heard that, huh? I'm just saying, it might be the hot sauce..."

Leah rolled her eyes.

"Did you hear her giggle?" Marcus asked, wearing a broad smile.

Aspen latched on. "Yeah," Leah whispered. "It was cute."

He sweetly ran a finger up and down Leah's arm. "So, what's wrong? Why were you crying?"

They'd been happy tears. Mostly... "I..." She wanted to say it, but it was almost impossible to push out, and once she did, she couldn't take it back. She couldn't dangle that carrot in front of him and then take it back, not when he'd been so patient. "I think it's time to go home."

He studied her a moment, cautious. "Really?"

There was indeed hope in his voice. He'd been patient as she'd healed, as they'd worked to figure out what they'd needed as individuals, as a couple, as a family. But he had always wanted to be home, even if he'd never said so.

"Really." She explained her reasoning. She could continue working on her manuscripts anywhere. His family deserved to see him and meet the twins. And they couldn't hide forever.

"If you're sure, then I'm on board."

"I'm sure."

As she nursed and rocked Aspen back to sleep, they discussed their timeline and how they'd go about everything.

Long after Aspen drifted off, they continued to chat. Something nagged at Leah, her heart hurting as they discussed returning home.

And normally, she'd have buried that feeling, would have suppressed it until it probably came out in some unhealthy form of resentment. But they'd promised to be open and honest as a couple. And even though she knew it wasn't exactly right, she couldn't deny her feelings.

"When we get back ... I know that..."

He'd explicitly declared during their big argument—before he'd left her—that she couldn't do what she wanted to right now.

"I know my mom can be a better person. And I know it's wrong, but I... Part of me wants her to be able to see the kids." Her mom hadn't been there to dress shop with her. To plan things. To help in the delivery room. Her mom had missed the most important moments of her life. And even though Leah recognized her mom's faults and shortcomings and sins, a part of her ached to have her in her life—the one constant she'd always known. And if her mom accepted her kids, maybe she'd finally recognize how twisted her prejudices were.

Marcus pressed his lips thin, looking down. He had to be angry, disappointed. "Let's talk about that."

⁂

The next day, after taking time to sleep on their decisions, they used their extra phone to text Kaylah. They didn't really know the state of things or how they'd be received when they arrived at the cave. This was going to be a *huge* move, and there were preparations to make.

A few days later, a text arrived from Kaylah.

<So excited to see you!!! Safe to head over. Give me forty-eight hours heads-up whenever you're ready, and I'll be there.>

She also provided a different number to text, that of a cell that would stay with a cave employee in the human world. They'd be dispatched to send for her.

Leah battled her nerves, but pushed forward. What they'd do with their belongings was the easiest decision to make. You couldn't rift with much other than what was stuffed in your pockets. Most big things they'd acquired were secondhand anyway, so they started to redonate them along with other items. It chipped a little at Leah's heart that they'd have to give up most of the clothes and toys they'd bought the kids. But they would never lack in the Green Lands. She picked out her favorite ones and donated the others to a women's and children's shelter.

They gave their apartment notice and cleared the place out. Marcus quit his job and collected his last paycheck. They took a rideshare to the city Marcus's family lived in, and rented a hotel room.

After their whirlwind of preparations, they texted the number Kaylah had given them, and quickly received a reply that they'd send for her.

Needing to keep their most important belongings compact, Leah had spent time at the library typing up her manuscripts and printing them in small print with narrow margins. They went to a drugstore and printed tons of photos of them, their wedding, and the kids.

Now, it was a matter of waiting the forty-eight hours, and visiting people in town. They met up with Jake for breakfast at a pancake place. It was his first time meeting the twins. Aspen made a mess by grabbing a syrup-covered pancake from Marcus's plate, and Ash cried for the last ten minutes. Parenthood had its perks. Since Jake would likely marry a human and be unable to have children with her, the twins' antics probably didn't serve as birth control, but still...

Despite the chaos with the kids, that was the visit she'd been looking forward to the most. The next was nerve-racking, and Leah considered having Marcus go without her, but she needed to get to a place where she could stand tall and endure scrutiny. Because scrutiny *would* come.

They each carried a car seat as they approached Tobias and Camry's house. Marcus squeezed Leah's free hand.

As Marcus rang the doorbell, Leah took a breath to bolster herself. *I can do this.*

Camry opened the door, all smiles. "Come in!" After the family of four entered, Camry lunged for hugs from Marcus and Leah, and Tobias emerged from the kitchen, hands in his pockets.

Leah prepared herself for embarrassment and resentment. They didn't know what the family had told Tobias and Camry about everything. All Leah knew was that she'd nearly died of mortification when Camry had come to visit her at the cottage, and that she already hadn't been one of Tobias's favorite people.

Marcus and Tobias exchanged a quick hug, and Tobias curtly nodded at Leah. "Leah."

That was basically what she'd gotten from him the past three years, so she could manage.

They sat and gabbed for a while, introducing the twins. They shared pictures and stories. It was a little weird talking about their wedding. Leah doubted she'd share pictures of her casual superpregnant wedding with many, but it was extra awkward since she'd ruined *their* wedding. But Camry asked, and they shared. They ordered food in, caught up on family gossip, human-world stuff, and just settled in.

It was uncomfortable, but bearable.

After another night in the hotel, they visited Marcus's grandparents. Leah firmly believed theirs would be one of the most uncomfortable relationships she had in her life. She'd apologized to them after the assassination attempt, and they'd forgiven her, but it was weird. Not tense like it was with Tobias, but ... more uncomfortable than not. There was shared guilt there from the old war, and Leah's assassination attempt after having spent so much time in their home had only made it worse. Unlike with Kaylah, there was no dark humor about the debacle. Just a silent understanding that they'd all rather forget what had happened, would rather never speak of past mistakes in this group. And Leah could be content with that.

Samantha and Brad were happy to meet the twins as well. Who wouldn't be? They were freaking adorable. Leah couldn't help but smirk when Marcus's grandma commented on how grownup he looked. He really had matured a lot in the last year.

The next day was *the* day, the big day. They were both excited to see Kaylah, but nervous about stepping back into the public eye. They'd be recognized on sight.

Aspen lay asleep while Marcus paced the hotel room, burping Ash. "It'll be great," he coached. "We'll be fine." There might have even been a bit of an edge to *his* voice.

Leah stared at the pile of things on the bed in front of her. They had their pictures, her printed manuscripts, the jade tokens, and several other things. Pacifiers for the kids and a change of diapers, of course. The thing that claimed Leah's attention was Kaylah's ring. She turned it in her hand, examining it. They'd never had to use it. They weren't in the clear quite yet, but still... They'd never had to resort to using it in an emergency, and for that she was grateful. Kaylah had to be ready to be reunited with it.

And then there was the debit card. It was still in good shape. They'd used it far more than they'd wanted to, but not more than they'd needed to when things had gotten tight.

"Things will work out," she said.

Chapter 32

Leah's guts were a twisted mess of panic and anxiety as their rideshare rolled up to the 'nature preserve.' Somewhere in her traitorous mind where her Ivy energy resided, there was a yearning to return, like her body understood she was about to be flooded with Green Lands energy again, like a junkie with their favorite drug.

As it was early November, the nature around the fake preserve was lovely, at least to Leah. Fall had always been her favorite season(oo), with the way trees sprinkled the world with varying shades and hues of red, yellow, gold, and brown, accented by sturdy evergreens. Leah halted before entering the building, to enjoy this last moment here. Eternal spring was nice, but mild seasons were hard to beat.

They couldn't take the car seats with them through a rift, and they didn't have cars over there, but they brought them inside, prepared to donate them to the cave for the next set of incoming parents to use on their arrival.

The solo employee at the decrepit nature preserve display did a double take, then gaped.

Yes, we're that couple. Yes, we've been missing for months, and people have been looking for us. Yes, these two children that look remarkably like me are indeed ours. Marcus and Leah gave them polite smiles as they passed. If the Green Lands had electricity, the employee would have likely already snapped a picture and scattered it on social media.

After winding through the hallways and back rooms to get to the cave opening, they finally arrived, having passed a few people, most of whom also eyed them.

Kaylah's text had been brief. They didn't really know what to do, but they assumed they should mention they were supposed to meet with her when approaching the customs employee. There would probably be a long list of paperwork to fill out for the twins since they didn't have Ivy Kingdom passports yet.

But they didn't have to get that far. Halfway across the room, a guard approached, nodding. "Mr. Elonto. Miss Elonto. Please follow me."

She wasn't about to correct him about it being Mrs. They'd almost pocketed their rings, but they were holding infants, so...

They'd specifically planned an early-morning arrival to hopefully avoid the employees who had been working the evening they'd arrived all those months ago.

Even then, as they neared that waiting room, the one where Leah had been detained, she felt sick. Emotionally, she was digging in her feet, clawing her way back. Marcus put a reassuring hand on her back, guiding her slowly forward.

It had been so traumatic, so violating when the previous guard had wrapped his vine around her, then threatened to have her strip-searched. But the place was small, and they probably didn't have a lot of meeting rooms like this here.

Leah's anxiety melted away once the guard opened the door and ushered them in. Kaylah *and* Eric greeted them, jumping up from the table they'd been waiting at.

Kaylah squealed, leaping to give Leah and Aspen a hug first. Eric more calmly strolled to Marcus and Ash, hugging them.

They spent a few minutes meeting the twins, gushing over their excitement to have Leah and Marcus home again. Eric assured them everything was ready for them at their estate, and that made Leah breathe easier, because they hadn't coordinated anything yet.

"Oh yeah, here," Leah said, digging Kaylah's royal ring from her pocket. "I don't want to have to keep track of it anymore."

Kaylah slipped it on her finger, smiling. "I knew it would be safe with you."

"Thank you."

Kaylah then showed Aspen some more attention, and she cooed. "For the record, I don't do diapers. I was traumatized enough the one time I changed Marcus's."

"Hey!"

Leah snickered. "Stinky, huh? Rachel and Guillen didn't pour hot sauce in his kittlefruit juice as a baby, did they?"

Marcus guffawed.

The inside joke lost on Kaylah, she looked a little alarmed. "I certainly hope not."

Kaylah explained they wouldn't need passports for the twins this trip, but they each already had one prepared for them back at the estate. They'd do a quick customs check and then rift back to the Green Lands. Kaylah hesitated in the last part of her delivery, albeit only slightly. "Just to prepare you, we won't be arriving at the cave by our estate. We'll be arriving at the palace's cave."

A tiny squeak of terror rose in Leah's throat. "Can't we settle in first?"

Kaylah locked eyes with her. "It's time."

The rifting process went smoothly. Leah and Marcus each carried an infant through a Seeder rift. To make sure Aspen and Ash had the necessary engravings touching their skin, Leah and Marcus held the jade stones in their little hands with them. No fuss, no muss. They were happy, relatively unfazed.

A familiar warmth of energy rushed into Leah as she filled her lungs on the other side of the rift. Even if the people here weren't fond of Leah, at least Mother Nature had nothing against her.

The guards at the reception cave made Leah uneasy, but she'd known they'd have to pay the piper eventually.

"Matron, Your Highness," a guard addressed Kaylah and Eric. "Please follow me."

This isn't a death march. It's going to be fine. Perfectly fine. She repeated that to herself with each crunch of twigs, leaves, and gravel underfoot as they marched through the woods and palace grounds.

Stepping inside the palace felt both nostalgic and foreign at the same time. Marcus tightly held her free hand as they walked.

After one long and one short set of staircases, they were taken to a waiting room. A couple of Catrina's nursemaids reached for the twins. "We can see to their needs."

It took everything Leah had to give up Aspen. Marcus's expression made it clear he wasn't excited to give up Ash, either.

"They'll be fine," Kaylah assured them. "Eric and I will stay here with them the entire time."

Leah allowed the nursemaid to take Aspen, then fidgeted with her hands. She wanted Kaylah to be there in Catrina's meeting with her, too. But Leah and Marcus were adults. They needed to rip off the bandage.

"Their Majesties are waiting," the guard said.

Leah and Marcus followed. She slipped her clammy hand back into his. She hadn't even noticed she'd extended a vine tendril and wrapped it around Marcus's wrist, binding them together, until he glanced down at their joined hands. He met her gaze. "We'll be okay. They just want to talk."

It was to be a private meeting. A *formal* private meeting. Upon entering the queen's office, Leah and Marcus curtsied and bowed, something they hadn't done in so long.

Queen Catrina and King Stephan sat together on an elegant settee. Catrina gestured to another opposite them. "Please take a seat."

The young couple followed directions, sitting thigh to thigh, arm to arm.

"We're glad you're home safe," Catrina said, all business. "And congratulations on your wedding and children."

"Thanks, Aunt Ca— er, Your ... Majesty?" Marcus said.

Catrina sighed, softening a touch. "We're in private, and we're still your aunt and uncle."

Leah couldn't fathom ever addressing them as such, even as Marcus's wife, though the comment hadn't been aimed at her.

As Catrina eyed them both, Stephan spoke up. "We *are* glad you're back. And we look forward to meeting the twins..."

Leah smiled slightly at that.

"I didn't realize you were so unhappy here, Leah," Catrina said, letting the statement hang in the air.

"It wasn't that I was unhappy, or ungrateful, because I *am* grateful..." She dug a fingernail into her jeans. "I just didn't feel it was fair the way you expected me to follow stricter rules than any of your other subjects."

She and Marcus had done plenty of preparation for this discussion. Leah wasn't about to grovel, or apologize more than she needed to. But she was going to keep her temper in check, and use more 'I' statements. She was going to prove she'd grown since leaving.

"Most subjects don't live under our roof or have access to palace secrets," Catrina said. "And most of them don't date our nephew. You knew what you were getting into when you signed up for that."

Leah gritted her teeth, keeping silent, because she didn't have anything kind to say.

"I'm disappointed," Catrina continued. "In both of you."

Don't say anything. Don't say anything. Don't say anything.

"Respectfully, Your Majesty, I never asked to join your household, or to use your money. And I hoped that you allowing me to live and you taking me in meant you trusted me. But you never did. Not when you reacted that way about the passageways. I was *never* staging a coup, or trying to undermine you. I'm nothing like my parents." Her nostrils flared as she tried to keep her cool. "And I lost all respect for you—"

Marcus squeezed her hand in warning.

"You lost my respect when you fired Robyn. Maybe you don't know what it's like to be afraid of a pregnancy, but you didn't have to fire a servant when all she did was look the other way when I was panicking."

Leah could provide a laundry list of reasons as to why she'd acted the way she had, most of which were in her manuscript, but that wasn't the plan today. Today was about burying hatchets with the least pain possible.

Catrina waited a moment to respond. "No, I don't know what that feels like. I was raised with high expectations, so I know they're achievable. As for the passageways and security protocols... You're a mother now. I would hope you would do everything in your power to keep those children of yours safe."

In truth, Leah's understanding *had* changed, but it didn't all become rosy. They were still miles apart in their upbringing and temperaments, and always would be.

"As for Robyn, you were right."

What? Leah was dumbfounded. Was that the closest people got to an apology from a queen?

"I still stand by what I said."

Or not...

"For my children, for this palace, and for this kingdom's security, I *do* need staff who are unfailingly loyal, who do not disobey orders on a whim when a scared girl makes a plea."

She made it sound like Leah was a five-year-old.

"That said, I do believe in second chances, just like I gave you a second chance. I rehired Robyn the week after the two of you threw a tantrum and left."

Leah's eyes grew wide. "Really?"

Catrina's face was hard. "The two of you would have known that, had you deigned to accept my requests to visit."

No one expected a queen to chase down teenagers refusing to meet with her... Leah slumped a little on the settee. "Thank you, Your Majesty, for giving Robyn her job back."

"Are there any other objections you have about your queen and king?" Catrina asked. "Anything else we should know about?"

Stephan hadn't even been there the day Leah and Marcus had left; he hadn't been part of the drama. And did Leah have more to say? Absolutely. Was it wise and necessary? Absolutely not.

And that was the compromise she and Marcus had come to. Leah couldn't care less at this point if her relationship with the queen and king ever fully recovered. But Marcus still loved them. She didn't need to have their relationship in a place where they hugged. Leah didn't even like hugs from most people, and she wasn't the type to run after people until they liked her. She could be okay with civility, even if it was cold civility like she had with Tobias.

If they could sit at the same banquet table and exchange necessary small talk while Marcus still got to enjoy his family, then Leah could choke down her pride.

"That's all, Your Majesty," Leah answered.

Catrina switched her focus to Marcus.

"No, ma'am. I'm good."

They'd written letters of apology before leaving for the human world, so he'd already explained that the birth control tonic had been his mix-up, and that he hadn't told Leah how long he'd been holding on to her engagement ring.

Stephan rubbed the back of his neck. "And what are your plans moving forward?"

Leah let Marcus take it from there. He explained that they weren't sure yet. That he'd inquire about the possibility of returning to his internship, even though he'd been away for so many months. They planned to move in with Kaylah and Eric again until they could find a place of their own. Leah hoped to stay home with the twins. That part was a little more complicated, but he waited to address the book.

"And will you be needing to keep an allowance, Leah?" Catrina asked.

"No thank you, Your Majesty." She wouldn't be their ward anymore. She and Marcus agreed they *were* going to dip into Marcus's stipend again. That was his family's money allotted to him, and wealthy parents could do as they pleased with their investments. It would be helpful and necessary. But taking a payout from the queen's coffers didn't feel right anymore.

"Even after leaving the palace, you'll have access to escorts for security. We can add another allotment to ensure the children are safe."

That was kind of a tricky topic between Leah and Marcus. They didn't fully agree on this one. But Leah did want to publish in both worlds, and he might be busy with work, and they didn't always want to burden family with the twins if they needed help.

"I know it's not my place to ask, but... Well, I... Sometimes I feel like having escorts makes me *more* of a target. So, maybe if I go out on my own, I don't always need them, and maybe we could have a helper for the house instead?" She winced. "Obviously, the twins' safety is the priority, but..."

"I think we could manage to add an extra helper to your allotment without compromising your escorts," Stephan said. "Parenthood is hard, especially for new couples."

Leah tried not to cringe. It was true, but how many people were as lucky as them to have servants help them through those hard times? "Thank you."

"She's not currently trained as a nursemaid, but would you like to have Robyn assigned to your household?" Catrina asked.

Leah's jaw dropped. Was Catrina offering Robyn as a peace offering? Or as a way to get rid of a servant she still wasn't completely trusting of? Leah didn't care. "Yes, we'll take her. I don't care if she's trained."

Catrina cracked her first smile of the meeting. "Consider it done, whenever you're ready for her to start."

"Thanks," Marcus said.

Nervously rubbing the knee of her jeans, Leah knew she ought not to push her luck, but she couldn't help herself. "If we're picking which staff gets assigned, can I make another request? Can Wren be reassigned to my escort duty?"

Catrina cocked her head, curious. "Wren?"

"Yeah, he did a really good job when I was at the cottage." She'd love to see her old book buddy on a regular basis.

"What did he do a good job of?" Catrina furrowed her brow. "We didn't receive any reports about security threats during your time there."

Leah swallowed hard. There hadn't been. And she might have just opened her mouth and gotten him in trouble. Wren had undoubtedly crossed the line professionally, but Leah and her children likely wouldn't be here if it weren't for him. "When I say he did a good job, I mean overall, even before the cottage. He just ... you know... I felt safe around him."

Marcus lovingly ran a thumb over the back of her hand. She'd confessed it all to him. He knew how much this man had done for her.

"We'd hope you feel safe with *any* of the staff, Leah," Stephan said. "But I'm sure we can arrange for this one to be reassigned as well."

Leah smiled, relieved.

Catrina's focus shifted to their hands. "Now about the wedding, the twins, and the announcements... This obviously got messy. Nothing that happened here was ideal. But I suppose, despite the fact we've been combating rumors regarding your disappearance, your returning married and having delivered is in your favor."

It was a politician's job to weigh things like this, but it still rubbed Leah the wrong way to have her marriage and children discussed so clinically.

"I think the best course of action would be to do something a little like what your parents did with you and Tobias, Marcus."

That was actually what Marcus and Leah had been hoping for. It wouldn't be as grand, but it honestly wasn't all that different. It had been extremely controversial at the time of Rachel and Guillen's wedding for them to be married, and for them to adopt their boys. They'd done it all in private, only announcing it publicly when the time was right. When done properly, it gave the kingdom an opportunity to celebrate, from a subtle position of power at the palace. They'd told the kingdom 'we're an item,' with the comment section closed. It didn't mean everyone had liked it, but the deed had been done, and they weren't offering apologies for being who they were or for loving whom they would. Leah adored Rachel and Guillen's love story.

"We're on board," Marcus said.

"Very well. We'll discuss details. It would be good to do it soon, to get ahead of the rumor mill about your return. Perhaps with a ball at the palace?"

Leah smiled once more, happy about getting to dance with Marcus again in a formal dress. She might even fit in her old gowns—Ivies tended to bounce back pretty quickly from pregnancy.

Stephan drew a deep breath. "We do still believe it would be best to keep details a little fuzzy, or ... perhaps altered, about the timeline. We can word the announcement so people will hopefully not pay attention to the order things happened in, but will only recognize that you wished for privacy, so you awayed to enjoy a private ceremony, and started your family."

It pained Leah to entertain that, just for the fact that it was all to help the royal family's image. But it *would* help Leah and Marcus's image to look tidy. There would be less judgment. And anything that deterred scrutiny toward them would benefit Aspen and Ash. "Sure," she forced herself to say.

Catrina smoothed her skirt. "Lovely. Then we're settled?"

Leah bit her lip. "Well, one more thing..."

Chapter 33

Catrina and Stephan were all ears.

"There's something I need your permission for," Leah said.

"She's amazing at it," Marcus said.

She gave his hand a little squeeze. She had this one. "I've been writing a book…" She wasn't going to address any of the fictional books right now. "A memoir. I want to publish it. And since there will obviously be mentions of the royal family, I know I need your permission."

"I don't know how comfortable we'd be with that," Catrina stated. Despite her queenly nature, her voice was gentle.

Leah caught herself biting her nails. She needed this and the hope it would provide. "It's mostly about me. About my parents and their secrets and what it was like for me growing up. And … why I was confused enough to try to hurt Kaylah. And maybe people would understand that I just want to be a good citizen, normal." She swallowed. "Please just consider it. I already have most of the first draft written. I want to do this for me, and Marcus, and the twins. They deserve this."

Stephan crossed his legs. "I'm assuming Marcus would be in this book?"

"Yes," Marcus answered. "And I support anything she writes in there. Good or bad. I've … made my mistakes, and she doesn't deserve to take the blame for them."

Nodding, Stephan turned his focus back to Leah. "And the palace family and staff?"

"Yes. I'll be fair, but honest. And I'll obviously make sure there aren't any unnecessary details or things that would compromise security." She hesitated. "I'm grateful you've tried with the rallies and announcements and stuff, but people still hate me. *You* get the rare death threat about me, but *I* get the stares and glares and comments on a daily basis. Maybe you're used to that, but I'm not. And I don't want my kids to have to live through that if there's anything I can do about it."

Catrina spoke again. "A book like that has the potential to make you a lot of money."

It wasn't like Leah hadn't thought of that. She was notorious, and people loved gossip. Even if they didn't go into it wanting to side with her, she had to take the chance she could win some people over. "I'm sure it will. And I'm not ashamed of that. If it means financial security for Marcus and me and the twins, then that's a bonus."

Leah cleared her throat. "And I don't want it published by the palace or backed in any way by you guys. I respect your opinions, and I'll follow your guidelines as I have to, but I don't want people thinking it's propaganda or lip service."

"If we said yes…" Catrina angled her head. "You should obtain written permission from those you share stories about."

"Not a problem." She *was* a little worried about that, including Rachel and Guillen and their parents, but she hoped they would understand the value, especially with Marcus on her side. "Do I … have to get permission from my mom?" She was obviously going to be front and center in Leah's memoir, like she had been in Leah's life.

Catrina pursed her lips. "As your mother and as a citizen, Beata has had her rights stripped from her for her crimes. You don't *ever* need permission from her for *anything*. Do you understand?" Her tone conveyed her distaste for Beata. Queen Catrina hadn't been victimized the same way Kaylah had, so she didn't loathe Soren and Beata as much, at least not openly. Maybe Leah read into it too much, but Catrina's tone almost sounded protective of Leah. "Write your story, Leah. All we ask is that you give us a chance to review it before letting outside eyes look it over."

Relief and hope washed over Leah. "Yes, Your Majesty."

After agreeing their main concerns had been addressed, the four of them adjourned to the waiting room, and Catrina and Stephan's kids joined the group. Marcus enjoyed introducing everyone to Aspen and Ash, and they got to meet the two new little princesses. It was heartwarming to watch as Marcus interacted with his young cousins.

"How was it?" Eric asked, now standing next to Leah as she lingered in the corner of the room.

She smiled. "It was fine."

"Hmm... 'Fine' as in 'not really fine' or 'fine' as in 'actually fine'?"

Leah grinned. "I like you, Eric."

He ran a hand through his blond hair. "Most people do." He squinted playfully. "I look innocent."

She let out a breathy chuckle.

"I'd say Aspen and Ash already have a couple of built-in playmates," he said.

Her eyes on the group, Leah nodded in agreement. "I guess you're right." Family trees were confusing, so Leah had to think about it a moment. Technically, Catrina's kids weren't cousins to Aspen and Ash. Aspen and Ash were to the princesses and prince what Leah was to Catrina—a cousin's child. Catrina's kids were grouped pretty close in age, and the youngest set of twins was just months older than Leah and Marcus's. Leah smiled more genuinely. She didn't want her kids to grow up pariahs like her, and even though she had a lot of hope with her memoir, she feared that down the road, her children would still grow up outcasts. But even if they were shunned by most, they had instant friends right here. She was grateful they'd managed to piece together civility with Catrina and Stephan, even if it was mostly for the sake of Marcus and the twins.

Leah studied Catrina as she crouched and listened to Prince Leon telling her something. Leah doubted she'd ever really see eye to eye with her. They were just too different. But she couldn't forget what Kaylah had said, that when they'd deliberated on the day of the assassination attempt, Catrina had been the first to open her arms to Leah, to invite her into her home. She couldn't overlook that kindness.

Leah had her rough edges, her painfully sharp moments. The stress she faced was small compared to what a ruler like Catrina endured on a daily basis. Leah had hated the pressure placed on her to be perfect. Had she expected Catrina to never make a mistake?

From the corner of her eye, Leah spotted Kaylah as she perched on a settee near the larger group. Kaylah gave her a reassuring smile, and then a wink.

***

Kaylah and Eric accompanied Leah, Marcus, and the twins as they entered the palace's rifting cave.

"Have one more stop in you before heading home?" Kaylah asked.

Leah grimaced.

"If not, I'm sure Rachel and Guillen would understand."

Marcus bounced Aspen, keeping his mouth closed.

"Sure. Let's go." It wasn't Leah's first choice, but she needed to push through that discomfort. Catrina's had been the visit she'd been fearing the most today anyway.

They gave the Seeder on duty the coordinates for the cave closest to Rachel and Guillen's home, and she opened a rift for Marcus and Aspen to go through first.

After their entire party had arrived and Marcus had tucked the twins' jade tokens into his pockets, they rented a pair of rickshaws to get to the house faster. Ash fell asleep on the ride, and Aspen looked pretty tired, too.

Leah was nervous. But also oddly excited as they got closer. It was hard to grasp her feelings. She didn't know how her and Marcus's apology letters to his parents had landed. And Leah didn't know if they'd forgiven her for slapping Marcus. She hoped they had, or that they could.

The more she'd reflected on her interactions with her now in-laws, the more Leah had made sense of how things had fallen apart during her time in the cottage. She had no beef with Guillen, and he didn't seem the type to hold grudges. And Rachel—Rachel was a protective mother, and a good mother. Leah had come to see why Marcus had pushed the two together after the pregnancy news came out. Leah could learn a lot from Rachel.

Society hadn't been prepared for a couple like Rachel and Guillen when they'd married, or even when they'd adopted Tobias and Marcus.

Despite that, they'd raised their boys in a loving home, and even with outside pressure on their blended family soon after the war ended, Tobias and Marcus had turned out relatively well. Leah's upbringing, on the other hand, hadn't done her many favors. She'd been a lying, thieving almost-murderer.

Marcus again rested a supportive hand on her back as they reached the front door. "I love you," he mouthed.

"You too," she returned.

Guillen opened the door with a smile, welcoming the group in. Leah and Marcus indicated with fingers to lips that the twins had both nodded off, so everyone was quiet.

Rachel stood from an armchair, shyly hugging herself.

Kaylah and Eric first exchanged hugs with Rachel and Guillen.

"Congratulations," Guillen said. "On your marriage." He nodded at the twins. "And on those two. Pretty exciting to have a rare set of Boman twins."

Marcus teemed with pride, giving his dad a side hug. "This is Aspen. Want to hold her?"

"Oh goodness," Guillen said softly as he carefully took Aspen from Marcus's arms.

"Congratulations, Leah," Rachel said, just above a whisper. She was acting as timidly as Leah was at the moment.

"Thank you. I'm sorry it was all ... away. That family wasn't there."

Rachel had taken lives in the old war. She was as intimidating as anyone when she wanted to be. Leah had witnessed that heated rage only once, after the assassination attempt. But on a daily basis, Rachel was simply kind. She was tenderhearted, soft. No matter what Rachel would say, Leah would always know she had been hurt by missing their wedding and the births.

"It's okay, Leah." Rachel gave her a gentle smile. "You're your own family now, and I have to remember that. I didn't mean to step on your toes. I'm sorry."

Leah shook her head. "It's not your fault. And I'm *really* sorry I lost my temper with Marcus. That will *never* happen again." It was inevitable she'd lose her temper, but they both understood what she was getting at.

Rachel glanced at a smiling Marcus as he and Guillen chatted quietly over Aspen. She faced Leah and nodded.

"He's a great dad," Leah said. "He had great examples growing up."

"Thanks." Rachel blushed. She glanced down at Ash as he slept in Leah's arms. "Black hair like you."

"But they have brown eyes, like Marcus."

Technically, Leah had descended from a clan with mostly dominant traits. Without similarly dominant whisper rifter genes to compete with, like how Leah's dad had likely contributed to Leah's green eyes, Aspen and Ash's brown eyes had probably been inherited from Beata, not Marcus. Still, Leah was glad to have them look like their father in that way.

Rocking on her feet, still hugging herself, Rachel looked antsy.

"Do you want to hold him?"

"Yes!" Rachel swooped in, snatching Ash up and clutching him to her chest. "Oh my gosh," she whispered, positively lost in the moment. "Babies!"

Leah's heart warmed. A long time ago, Leah had asked Rachel how she was capable of allowing Leah into her life, given how much Leah's parents had traumatized her. Rachel had been frank with her, had told Leah that it *was* hard. But she'd wanted Marcus to be happy. More shyly, she'd confessed that it helped for her to think of her best friend, Kaylah, as Leah's mother, instead of the truth that Kaylah's brother Soren had been her father. It hadn't made as much sense to

Leah back then. But she appreciated Kaylah's part in this more now, in helping them bridge a massive gap.

Rachel kissed Ash's head. "Leah, I will *never* forgive you for making me a grandmother so young. But I will *always* forgive you, because they're so *adorable*."

After a few minutes, Kaylah and Eric excused themselves, letting Leah and Marcus know they were safe to take the nearest cave back to the estate whenever they were ready. Escorts would be left behind for them.

Eventually, Leah and Marcus sat on a sofa together, while Guillen and Rachel eased down onto armchairs next to each other, still holding the twins.

"Do you want to see pictures?" Leah offered. The palace staff had given them a bag they could unstuff their pockets into, so they'd be more comfortable, and their items safer.

"Of course!" Rachel answered.

As they talked about the wedding and birth and everything in between and after, Leah realized how much she'd miss having a cell phone with her for quick communication and for constant picture-taking. Rachel and Guillen had visited the human world often for family trips before she'd fully matured as a Seeder and become incapable of rifting over. Leah hoped she and Marcus would take the twins on plenty of adventures back there as well, and would definitely take the opportunity to snap pictures to bring back.

"So, do you plan to stay in-realm, then?" Rachel asked timidly.

Tobias had settled down in the human world for Camry, his human wife, leaving his little brother as the one to be there for his parents. Rachel would be devastated to have them both gone, even if they visited often. With how warm their relationship had been before the pregnancy drama, and how that was already rekindling, Leah wasn't afraid to spend time with her in-laws. They'd find healthy boundaries. "Yes. I might do some work in the human world on projects I'm working on, so I might travel often at some point, but we're planning on making things work here."

Rachel beamed. "That's great to hear. And projects in the human world?" She raised an eyebrow.

Leah wasn't ready to divulge anything about the books today, except perhaps... "It's a work in progress. But do you have your friend Saff's address in Seeder territory? I want to ask her about something."

Marcus quietly snickered, wearing a know-it-all grin about the painting in Kaylah's library. Leah gave him a dirty look.

By the end of their hours-long visit, they'd eaten a late lunch, Rachel had given Leah Saff's address so she could send her a letter inquiring about possibly painting for the twins' books, and the twins had woken, both needing diaper changes.

It was going to be hard to get used to cloth diapers, but at least they were covered already at the palace and at Grandma and Grandpa's place.

They stood at the doorway saying their last goodbyes before heading back to Kaylah and Eric's estate.

"And I mean it," Rachel said. "We don't want to step on toes, but we're happy to watch the kids if you need sitters, if you need breaks for date nights or anything."

Leah gave her a warm smile. She didn't trust many people enough to allow them to hold or watch her kids, but she had no doubt they'd be safe with Rachel and Guillen. And a date night with just her and Marcus sounded *amazing*. They hadn't had one since the twins were born because they hadn't had anyone in the human world they felt comfortable visiting and leaving them with. "I'm sure we'll take you up on that."

Chapter 34

It was still light outside by the time they reached the estate. The servants greeted Leah, Marcus, and the twins, fetching Kaylah and Eric.

"Good visit?" Kaylah asked.

"Yeah?" Marcus answered, half-question.

"Yes," Leah confirmed.

Kaylah smiled brightly. "Great. Let's show you some improvements around the house! We gremlin-proofed a bit."

"Are you *seriously* going to call them gremlins?" Marcus asked.

Kaylah clasped her hands in front of her, her posture, expression, and tone all exuding the authority of the queen she'd once been. "Yes, Marcus. As I've explained to your wife, *all* children are gremlins. I just happen to like some more than others. And I like these two." She grinned, holding up a finger. "But if you tell anyone outside of my household that I use that term, I will absolutely deny it. And I'll remind you there are no recording devices in this realm."

Eric shrugged. "Sorry, I just put up with her."

Kaylah's jaw dropped. "Ouch."

He chuckled. "C'mon, guys, let's go see the playroom."

While Leah and Marcus had been away in the human world, Kaylah and Eric had converted one of the smaller spaces downstairs into a kid-friendly room.

"No sharp corners or easily breakable things," Eric said. Wooden toys filled the room, as well as sewn plushies, bright colors, blankets, and a basket system for diapers.

"Wow," Leah whispered, dumbfounded. This was huge, given Kaylah and Eric had never wanted kids of their own. "Thank you. I'm sure they'll love it." She glanced at Marcus.

He raised his eyebrows. "Thank you. We're not sure how long we'll need to stay with you guys until we get a place of our own sorted."

Kaylah and Eric exchanged a look. "Take as long as you need," Eric said. "And it's really no bother. Even after you move out, we wouldn't hate it if you wanted to visit often, come for dinner now and then."

Leah smiled, but still felt a little guilty. "We'll try to keep them quiet. But ... they *are* kids. Kids are messy and loud. We'll do our best."

Kaylah sighed. "We are well aware of how children work, Leah. We're happy to have you here. And you're *not* a burden."

Her cheeks warmed. "Okay."

"How about you two go check out the changes upstairs? Up in the adjoining room. We'll take care of these guys for a bit."

Excited, Leah and Marcus handed Aspen and Ash over and headed upstairs to their room. It looked identical to how they'd left it. Opening the adjoining guest-room door, however, gave them a big shock. More armoires lined the walls, probably holding Leah's gowns like they'd discussed before. But the big bed had been removed, replaced with two new cribs. Leah almost cried as Marcus held her from behind. It was going to be nice having more privacy with the kids in the other room, but also having the ability to open the door to hear if they cried during the night.

"What do you think, beautiful? Isn't it nice to be home?"

A calm smile graced her lips. The energy of the realm, having made amends with his family... This still wasn't her home, even if they had an extended invitation, but it was the closest to one she'd ever really had. "Yeah. It's nice to be home."

After a couple of hours catching up again downstairs, they ate dinner with Kaylah and Eric. A blanket had been laid in the dining room for Aspen and Ash to play and wiggle on.

"We're hoping you two have tomorrow free?" Kaylah said, slicing into a stuffed portabella mushroom.

"I was planning on rifting up north to ask about my internship. I doubt they actually held it for this long, but it would be good to check."

"Hmm... And after that?"

Marcus shrugged, glancing at Leah.

"That was the main priority. We should get clothes for the twins at the market."

"Oh," Kaylah said. "One of the dressers in the adjoining room upstairs is full of baby clothes. But if they're not to your taste, we could go to the market. I'd love to join you, if you want."

"We didn't even look in the dressers. I'm sure they're fine. Thanks again."

"Great. So, when Marcus returns, you're both free?"

"I suppose so," Marcus said. "What's up?"

Kaylah grinned. "A surprise. I think it's too late in the evening to plan on taking care of it today."

More surprises? "I'm sure we can make space in our schedule."

After finally getting the kids to bed, they quietly closed the door between the rooms. Only hints of colored light still danced on the horizon. Marcus lit the lamps in the room.

"Definitely one thing I'll miss," Leah said. "Electricity."

"Yeah... But it sounds like they're still hopeful about the static nettle research program."

"It's so peaceful, though," Leah said, perching on her side of the bed. "Listen." Not a single car drove in the vicinity. The train station was too far away to be heard. No loud TVs. "It's nice. I hope if they figure out how to get electricity working someday, that it doesn't change things too much over here."

"Agreed."

Leah sorted through the bag of things they'd brought from the human world. For now, she tucked most of it away in her bedside table drawer. Her gaze caught on a folded piece of paper in the drawer. "Huh..."

She pulled it out and unfolded it. "Oh."

"What's that?"

She swallowed. "It's ... a distant memory." Part of her wanted to toss it, hide it away. It was something she would have done before leaving for the human world. But she'd changed. She'd grown. "Here. It was written for you."

Marcus came around the bed, standing in front of her. His face tensed into a frown as he read the letter she'd never sent him. It took him a while to read it; she'd been thorough.

Slowly, he folded it back up. "Wow," he whispered. "You really were going to leave me."

She frowned as well, taking the letter from his hands and setting it on the bedside table. "I would have come back, but I needed to get away to heal and sort things out." The letter had said as much. She'd come to realize during her time here that the *only* thing that would help was time away from this realm, whether with him or alone.

Leah took his hands in hers. "We're here now. That's what matters. That's very outdated."

He slid to his knees, kissing the palms of her hands, still frowning, hurt. "We lost time and memories that could have been shared. I'm glad I came back when I did."

"Well, you're stuck with me now. We'll have plenty more time and memories. And I'm glad you came back when you did, too, so I never had to send that letter."

He nodded pensively. She had figured he'd take it as a sign they'd done the right thing by leaving, and doing it together. She hadn't realized he'd take it this hard, hadn't meant to dredge up old hurt.

"I love you," she said.

A small smile quirked his lips. "I love you too."

"And you know..." She raised his hands to the bottom of her shirt. "The kids are sleeping. And I don't care what all those people out there say about you. I think you're pretty amazing."

He grinned, taking the bait. "Don't care what all those people out there say about *me*, huh? What exactly are they saying?"

She shrugged. "Oh, ya know. I've ignored them for so long, I've forgotten what they even say."

Sliding the first of several buttons on her shirt undone, he gazed into her eyes. "Do they say I'm handsome?"

"Nah. I'm sure that's not it." She couldn't resist digging her fingers into his curly locks.

He traveled to the next button. "Do they say I have the best wife?"

Leah chuckled. "They *definitely* don't say that."

"How about..." He unbuttoned two more. "Do they say I have two amazing kids who look just like their mother?"

"Psh. They wouldn't even know that yet."

He unbuttoned one more, leaving the last, top button done. "Well, I've never cared much what they think about me. So, I guess it doesn't matter." He snuck a kiss, stood, and turned to walk away.

She shot out her vines, wrapping them around his waist. "Don't you dare."

He laughed as she reeled him back onto the bed.

"You think you're so funny." She faced him.

Raising a hand to his chest, he smiled wide. "I'm the funny one in this relationship."

"Perhaps funny, but not smart. Because we both know something was a little less than ideal in the human world, when my energy and chemical powers were lower or off-balance. And if you were smart, you wouldn't have left this last button done up."

Without a word, he continued to smile, ever so slowly undoing it and gliding his hands down her bare sides. Her spine shivered.

In less than a minute, they were lips and hands, fast heartbeats and quick breaths. Only as he started sliding her pants off did she remember something crucial, and panicked.

"Wait!" That was the last thing her heart and body wanted to do, but she and Marcus hadn't stopped by a market. "We don't have birth control tonic. And I'm *not* ready to be pregnant again already."

He panted out a couple of breaths. "That's fine. We can do other things. Or…" He kissed the nape of her neck. "Or we can use the last of the protection we had in the human world. Which I just so happen to have tucked in my pocket."

"You are the best man I know." She crashed her lips back into his.

Only the crickets and the clouds knew how late it was as they faced each other under the sheets.

"There *are* perks to you being at full energy." He planted a kiss on her forehead.

She giggled. "Drop by the market for that tonic, and you'll remember how good it can *really* be."

"Everything with you is good," he replied sweetly.

She wore a contented smile. "Speaking of tasks tomorrow… What are you going to do if they don't give you your internship back?"

Marcus drew a breath. "I'm actually rethinking going tomorrow. Maybe I should wait until the palace announcement about us. Keep under the radar."

"Aren't you afraid of pushing your luck by waiting longer?"

He hesitated. "Would you be disappointed if I didn't go back to my internship?"

She frowned. "I'd feel guilty I lost it for you because we were gone so long."

"No," he replied softly. "I mean if I *chose* not to."

"But I thought you loved it."

"I did. I do. I think I do… I just… I didn't hate working with my hands on construction, though I can only imagine the disappointment my parents would have in that. I'd prefer to do something that makes a difference, but politics can suck at times. And then you and the kids… I don't want to be gone on long trips away from you. I want to support you in your writing and help with the kids. I guess I'm saying I don't know what I want to do anymore..."

Leah bit her lip, considering. For now, they had a roof over their heads, and he would start taking his family stipend payments again. "Your parents would be proud of you no matter what, and I would be too. But if you need time to explore your options, we can work around that. If you want to stay home more and watch the kids while I work on my books, I can get them published faster..."

"You're sure?"

She slid a hand to his heart. "Take your time. It's *your* turn to explore what you want to do."

After breakfast, Marcus traveled to the nearest market to purchase a few necessities, including two sets of wraps for baby-wearing. Kaylah and Eric said their surprise would take a bit of hiking, and that they'd set out on foot from their home.

For nearly an hour, the group chatted as they climbed around boulders and over downed logs, deep into the woods. Their grounds were expansive, and Leah had explored them, but not this far out, not in this direction.

It was heavenly to be able to use her vines freely again to help steady her over some of the more precarious spots. The trees suddenly thinned, opening to a wide clearing—and in the center lay a stone foundation.

"What's this?" Leah asked.

Kaylah kept quiet, giddy with anticipation as Eric retrieved a rolled-up paper from a storage box.

"Here." He handed it to Leah and Marcus.

They gave each other a glance and unrolled it together. "Blueprints for a building?"

"A home," Kaylah said. "*Your* home."

Leah was stunned speechless.

"We can't accept this," Marcus said.

"Yes, you can," Eric replied. "We've already partitioned the property. We'll have a main path cleared to meet our driveway so rides and walks will be much faster."

"No." Leah shook her head in disbelief. "This is too much."

"Like hell it is," Kaylah replied. "Eric and I worked our asses off for years getting this kingdom to a place of tolerance and peace. And you guys deserve it as much as anyone else."

"Yeah, but—" Leah started.

"No buts." Kaylah put her hands on her hips. "I never got to spoil my niece growing up. I never gave her Christmas presents or birthday presents, or baby shower gifts or a wedding gift. You can't tell us how to spend our money." She gestured to Marcus. "Rachel and Guillen got Tobias and Camry a cottage they barely ever visit for *their* wedding. If you don't like the location out here and you'd prefer to move somewhere in town, then consider this a vacation home away from the chaos and noise." She crossed her arms, not backing down. "Plus, you don't want to offend Rachel and Guillen, because they're planning on furnishing it for your wedding and baby gifts."

Marcus and Leah shared another glance.

"Can we, uh, talk about this a second, in private?" Marcus asked.

"We'll be right here."

He and Leah stepped a few yards away.

Leah struggled with guilt, but also yearned so badly for this. Not just a home. *Her* home. One of her own, like she'd never had. No moving. And quiet, peaceful, but still with decent access to a town, train, and rifting cave. "I want to say yes."

Marcus smiled. "Then let's say yes."

Leah wrinkled her nose. "Are you sure?"

"It's going to take a while for this place to be ready, but I could help build it. I'd love that." He changed hands supporting Ash against his chest. "And it might be fun for something my dad and I can do together when he has time off."

She considered, rubbing Aspen's back. "Even with bikes or rickshaws, it's not a five-minute trip to the market. There better be a big cellar, and a big garden." Her chemical powers were back to normal, so she wouldn't botch the garden anytime soon. "I bet your mom would love helping me get it started."

He smiled wider. "So...?"

Leah rocked her head side to side. "You know, we never *did* have sex out in the woods, and with the privacy out here—"

Marcus covered Ash's ears. "We'll take it!" he yelled to Kaylah and Eric in the distance.

Kaylah let out a celebratory whoop, and Leah laughed.

"I love you." She kissed Marcus.

"I love you too."

They returned to Kaylah and Eric, exchanging hugs, careful not to squish the kids strapped to Leah and Marcus. Leah stayed in Kaylah's arms just a touch longer. "Love you, Aunt Kaylah."

Chapter 35

She'd thought it before, and she'd likely think it again, but *today* would be the new hardest day of Leah's life.

Aspen and Ash were back at Kaylah and Eric's place, watched by Robyn. She had kids of her own, so Leah didn't see a need for tons of formal training on how to take care of them.

Leah and Marcus walked hand in hand to the prison Beata served her life sentence in. Leah was already sweating and nauseous. She was seriously doubting whether she'd keep down her breakfast.

Marcus squeezed her hand. He hadn't seen Leah's mom since he and Leah had run away together to his brother's wedding in this realm over three years ago. He'd been on decent terms with Beata in the human world, but once he'd discovered who she really was, he'd never wanted to see her again.

Leah had never pushed it. She'd kept those parts of her life separated, compartmentalized. She couldn't blame Marcus, or any Boman, given her mom's history in the war, and her plans to further victimize Bomen.

Leah squeezed his hand back. He was all sorts of tense, but his presence there today was part support, part compromise. And she didn't think she could do it without him.

The guards welcomed them into the massive stone building. "Mrs. and Mr. Elonto." One nodded. "Congratulations."

"Thank you," Leah said. The palace announcement about their private wedding and Boman twins had just gone out, and word traveled fast, at least when it was the juicy kind.

The couple stayed in a waiting room while the guards fetched Beata for the meeting. Marcus paced the room while Leah sat, bouncing her knee and biting her fingernails.

A guard opened the door. "She's ready in room one."

Leah filled her lungs to capacity. *I can do this...*

Hands gripping each other, Leah and Marcus entered room one together. Beata smiled wide at Leah, but quickly dropped her expression at the sight of Marcus. She looked nervous. But she recovered, opening her arms to Leah.

Only then did Leah let go of Marcus's hand as she hugged her mom.

"I've been so worried," Beata breathed, holding Leah tight. "You said you'd be gone, but I didn't think it would be *this* long!" She stepped back, tucking Leah's hair behind her ears. "You're okay?"

Leah gave her a forced smile. "I'm great. Let's sit down."

Marcus had already sat at the round table in the small room. There would be no hugs between him and Beata, and everyone in the room was well aware of that.

"Marcus," Beata acknowledged as she took a seat, her wrists bound so her Ivy vines could cause no harm.

"Beata," he replied a little sharply.

Beata turned her focus back to Leah, not bothering to inquire why Marcus had joined her on this visit. "How was the human world? You didn't even tell me what university you got into, or what you're studying."

Leah blew out a breath. "That wasn't ... completely true. I *was* in the human world for most of the time, but not in school. I needed a break from the realm."

"That bad?" Beata frowned.

"I mean, not everything was bad... It's a long story. But I'm in a good place, Mom." She held up her hand, showing her ring. "Marcus and I got married."

Beata took a moment to react. She couldn't be that surprised, not when Leah had outright told her to prepare for this eventuality when they'd last seen each other nearly a year ago. But Beata didn't deign to offer her congratulations. She turned to Marcus, giving him a little nod. "You *were* good for her in high school. She stopped stealing for you."

Marcus's jaw tensed. "Yes, I *was* good for her. I *am* good for her, and I will *continue* to be good for her." His tone dangerously rode the line of civility.

Leah rested a hand on his thigh under the table, giving it a gentle squeeze. Leah had been forced to sacrifice her pride to keep things civil with Catrina and Stephan upon their return. This time it was Marcus's turn to keep the peace. He deserved to tell Beata off however he wished, but that wasn't what they'd agreed upon for this particular visit.

"What was the wedding like?" Beata asked. "I assumed you would let me know before it happened..."

Leah stared at her wedding ring. She was a tiny bit mortified by her wedding pictures, with her ginormously pregnant, wearing a cheap dress in some random church in the human world. "It was beautiful and private. We did it in the human world while we were away. I'm sorry I didn't give you a heads-up. I ... didn't think to bring pictures on this visit."

"Well, I'd love to see next time. Are you back to living in-realm now? You'll visit more regularly?"

Choking down the lump in her throat, Leah took a moment to respond. She didn't have that answer yet. Depending on how this visit went, she might make time for visits with her mom, or she may never see her again for the rest of her life. And that terrified her. "We'll have to see. I'm really busy right now. I have a job."

Beata smiled. "That's great! What are you doing?"

"And we're building a house."

"That's nice. What part of the kingdom? I assume you're staying in the kingdom?"

Leah's courage wavered, her hand shaky as she pulled a photo from her pocket, resting it in her lap. "Yeah. Staying in the kingdom. And honestly, a lot of time will be taken up with family. With ... our kids."

Beata was rightfully confused. "Your what?"

Slipping the picture of Aspen and Ash onto the table, Leah tried to breathe regularly. "Marcus and I had twins."

Her mouth wide open, Beata slid her hand across the table, taking the photo. "You can't be serious." She stared at the picture of the two of them. "But they look like you." Her gaze shifted up in a subtle glare at Marcus, with a hint of 'you knocked up my daughter?!' in the mix. "That's why you were gone for so long?" She returned her focus to Leah.

"Yes."

Beata shook her head, studying the picture again. "I can't believe..." And the wheels churned, then it clicked. "Well, they're obviously not Marcus's. Sweetheart, I know the ins and outs of stunts, and they don't carry in multiples."

A low, rumbling exhale came from Marcus, a warning, or a sign that he and his balled fists were barely keeping back his absolute hatred for Beata.

Leah's heart broke. Not at Marcus's anger, but at her mother's continual use of the term 'stunt.' That was like 'weed' or 'leech'—terms that hadn't been commonplace since the old war, not with anyone civilized or tolerant.

"I'd like the picture, please," Marcus said, plenty of edge to his voice. He extended a hand. "The picture of *my* children."

Beata handed it to him.

"Mom, they *are* Bomen. They *are* Marcus's. There are actually a couple of other sets of Ivy Boman twins on record since I was born."

Beata furrowed her brow. "Oh..." It still didn't seem like she believed it, but that was the least of Leah's worries. "I guess they're old enough to have been confirmed as ... what you say they are..."

"They're *Bomen*, Mom. Not stunts. Please stop calling them that. My children are *not* stunts. Neither is Marcus, or anyone else born without powers."

"Sorry," Beata muttered. "I'll try to do better." She studied Leah. "They're healthy? You're healthy? Were you okay?"

Leah nodded. "We're all fine. They're angels."

Beata smiled softly. "If they're yours, then I'm sure they're perfect. I'd love to meet them on your next visit."

Marcus's nostrils flared, and Leah's heart dropped into her gut.

"That's not going to happen," Leah said with as much confidence as she could muster. "I won't be bringing them."

Beata frowned. "I wouldn't *say*— I wouldn't *do*— I just want to meet them. I'd love them, because they're a piece of *you*."

Before they'd left the human world, Leah and Marcus had had a real heart-to-heart. She'd desperately wanted her mom to meet her kids, and Marcus had been adamantly opposed to it. Instead of fighting it out, they'd addressed it calmly, with an open mind.

The thing was, it didn't matter how much Beata repented of her actions and prejudices—she had committed crimes, she had planned heinous things. Bomen would never forget that.

And it didn't matter that Leah had never cared one way or the other that Marcus was a Boman, born without powers. But just because she wasn't a bigot didn't mean she'd understood his struggle. She had plenty of prejudices stacked against her personally, but she'd never been part of *that* marginalized group, and she wasn't necessarily the best advocate. She had to default to Marcus for that, trusting he knew best when it came to that aspect.

Leah wrung her hands in her lap. "No, Mom. You won't get to see them until they're old enough to understand who you are and what you've done. And then they can decide for themselves if they ever want you to be part of their lives."

Beata's eyes filled with tears. "I can be better. I promise. I can be better."

Leah still hoped with all her heart that her mom *could* be better, do better. But she and Marcus had agreed upon this ahead of time, and their decision was as immovable as the Outer Rim surrounding this realm.

They would not budge.

Yes, Beata still had to change, and she had, to some degree, already. She was civil with Marcus, making a tiny bit of effort in this meeting, but she still was cold toward him, and she still called him a stunt. But even *if* she had changed her tune without prompting, if she had turned a complete one-eighty and was now a saint, they wouldn't have budged on this.

Because children were not tools. Aspen and Ash were innocent and perfect, not born for the purpose of changing the minds of bigots. It wasn't Leah's responsibility to change her mother's mind, and it certainly wasn't her children's. Beata's story was tragic and pitiable, and her parentage had done her no favors morally. But the fact remained that she was a grown adult, and it was no one's job to fix her but her own.

Leah's children would *never* be tools. Not the way she'd been when her mother had conceived her as a manipulation against Leah's dad. She was breaking that cycle. She may *look* like a carbon copy of her mother, and they may have a lot in common, but Leah was *not* the same as Beata.

Aspen and Ash were not there to manipulate or educate, and even as tears moistened Leah's own eyes at witnessing her mother's devastation, that fire burned within her.

Leah could only imagine the hurt and horror and distrust it would earn her if her children eventually learned that she'd taken them to see their grandmother—a war criminal—when they were too young to consent.

To the entire realm, Beata was a villain. To Leah, the lines still blurred on a personal level. No one else had been protected by her the way Leah had been, even if she'd been somewhat negligent. No one else had loved Leah when she was younger. Beata would always be her mother, but she was selfish and toxic.

Leah's lip quivered. "No, Mom. That decision's final."

Beata continued to cry, her frown deepening. "Could I at least keep the picture? I'd love one with the three of... Well, with your family..."

Leah shook her head. She didn't imagine that would be much better for her kids. Leah's children were descendants of slaves, and she couldn't give her children's photo to someone who still believed slavery wasn't all that bad. Even if Beata considered this particular set of slave descendants somehow *alright* just because they were half-breeds of her daughter's.

Beata pursed her lips, staring at the table between them.

The silence was deafening, and it was time.

Leah rested her hand on Marcus's thigh again. "I need to talk to her alone, okay?"

He rubbed her hand. "Sure. I'll be right outside."

Chapter 36

The door clicked closed behind Marcus. Beata wiped at her tears. "What's going on, sweetheart? Is he making you—"

Leah gritted her teeth. "Marcus isn't making me anything." He hadn't been there to strong-arm Leah. She'd agreed to everything she'd said, and she'd asked him to let her say it herself, but to be there for support if he could stomach it.

"But Eleana, twin stun— Twin Bomen? And not ... letting me see my own grandchildren?"

"It's all true. And the decision is mine as much as it is Marcus's."

"I promise I'm trying here. And I'll do better."

"Good. Because I hope someday I can be proud of that change, and that they can see it in their hearts to forgive you."

Beata scrunched her eyes closed, shaking her head.

Leah looked at her, angry, hurting, and sad. This next part wasn't going to be any easier, but it was a different issue, more personal, and it hadn't felt right to have Marcus here for this one.

"About the job I mentioned." She rested her hands on the table. "It's more like, uh, a work in progress. I love books now."

Beata opened her eyes, gently smiling. "I'm happy you found a good hobby."

"I'm hoping to make it more than a hobby. I'm actually a writer now. I wrote some stories for the twins, and I'm hoping to have them illustrated and published." *Illustrated by a Seeder, who you also hate.*

A genuine look of pride graced Beata's face as she wiped away the rest of her tears. "That's great."

The adventure romance was being put on the back burner for now. The twins weren't getting any younger, and Leah was ready to get her personal story out into the world. Plus, Kaylah had mentioned reaching out to the author of the *Valeska's Adventures* series about seeing if they'd be willing to personally mentor Leah, and Leah was over the moon about that opportunity.

"I have another book that's almost finished that I need to tell you about." Leah sat straighter. "I'm not doing this lightly, but things haven't been easy. People hate me."

"And that's not fair."

"No, Mom. It's not. And the queens have tried to help, but I need to do this for me, okay?"

"Do what?"

Leah rubbed at a scratch in the wooden table. "I'll be publishing my story. My life story. I can't change the past. I can't change the way people look at me or think of me. But I *do* have the opportunity to change the narrative put out into the world about me, sharing my truth and allowing people a deeper look into who I am."

Beata was thoughtful. "I know it's been hard. If you think it would help..." Her eyes worked, her mind worked, and her fear became apparent. "What all are you going to tell them?"

"Everything that matters. I need people to know why I tried to kill Kaylah, why I lost hope that day. I need them to understand that I'm not like you." Saying the words tortured Leah, but she remained strong. "Because I'm not."

Beata's eyes filled with tears again. "I'm sorry I wasn't a better mother. It wasn't on purpose."

And ... that made Leah start to cry, too. "But the fact is, you weren't better. And I've forgiven you for the past. Because you had crappy parents growing up, and times were different. But you let Cheryl hurt me. You lied to me about my dad and about *so* much."

"I'm sorry," Beata whispered, staring down at her hands. "Please don't do this. Please don't make people hate me more."

How selfish.

"You're serving a life sentence in prison. I'm sorry you'll be embarrassed, but I honestly don't know that people will care much about what's said about *you* in my book. But hopefully they'll better understand *me*. Because to them, Mom, you're a murderer, a hateful bigot, and a pawn. You *knew* my dad had Kaylah in the dungeons on your own wedding night, that he was torturing her, the rightful queen. You knew, and you did nothing." Leah sniffled, taking in a sharp breath. *And for me, Kaylah's done everything.* She almost uttered it, but it felt like too much. This wasn't about spite or revenge, and it wasn't for comparison or to make Beata feel worse.

"I'm telling you as a courtesy," Leah said. Her guts twisted. "I'm going to tell them what you did to my dad. That you got pregnant on purpose to trick him, and what it did to him."

Regret and ghosts of Beata's past flashed across her face. "I never meant to tell you that. It doesn't mean I didn't love you. I still love you, Eleana. I will *always* love you. No one else needs to know that about your conception. You said you wouldn't tell anyone."

Leah buried her face in her hands. "I know. But it's important to me. And I'm sorry if you've carried guilt over that all these years, that it might have been your fault you lost the war and my dad died, but most people nowadays are *happy* the war ended and are *happy* he died."

Beata sobbed. "I'm sorry! I didn't mean to! I didn't mean for any of this to happen!"

The door clicked open behind Leah. "We're fine," she answered. She didn't need Marcus or a guard checking in on them.

It softly closed.

As Beata gathered herself, Leah waited patiently, sopping up her own tears with a handkerchief she'd brought. "I'm not saying or doing this to be cruel or to punish you, but I'm going to do it. I'm telling the truth." She rubbed at that same scratch in the table. "Frankly, the guards might even like you more. I think people will like you more. Because of what happened, even if you didn't intend it."

Beata gave her a look of almost contempt, her eyes cold. "They will cheer me on because I got my own husband *killed*. You want me to be proud of that? Would you be proud of that if it were Marcus?"

That touched an unexpected nerve, and yet... "You want me to be happy? You say you love me, that you will *always* love me. If you do, and you do want me happy, then you'll understand that it's hell for me on a daily basis out there. I'm tired of being hated and misunderstood when it wasn't my fault. I want a better life, and I want a better life for my children. I'm not exploiting you. I'm allowing people to know the truth with hopes of a better future."

"I do want you to have a better life," Beata whispered.

"Then don't be mad at me for doing this." Leah pointed to herself. "Because I've had to live this, and I will continue to live this. And I plan to pass down a better legacy to my children than what I received."

Beata let out a shaky breath in resignation. "Then do what you have to."

Leah hadn't needed her permission, but her heart was lighter knowing she had it. "Thank you. I'll be honest and fair. I'll tell them the good too."

Something like an attempted smile twitched at Beata's lips.

Picking at her nails, Leah processed her thoughts. Tons more could be said, but how much of it was necessary? She'd said what she'd come to say. "Like I mentioned, I'm going to be busy. I'm a wife and a mother. We're building a home and starting a garden, and I'm writing books. I..." Guilt weighed her down, because it wasn't wholly the truth. "I'm going to be busy, and I don't know when I'll be able to see you next."

Leah was going to be swamped. A happy kind of swamped. But she needed time to process this visit, this day. And after she left this room, she wasn't sure when she'd next see her mom, or if her mom would want to see her after she'd had a chance to mull it over.

"Will you write me?" Beata asked.

"I don't want to make a promise I'm not sure I can keep."

"Can I still write you?" She was grasping at straws, and Leah couldn't blame her. Life in prison would be lonely.

"Yes. I'll be at Kaylah's. But I don't know how quickly I'll respond." And she wasn't sure when or if she'd be able to get herself to read any letters.

Leah stood, but she couldn't hug her. Not after all that. "I've got to go."

"I... I love you."

Swallowing, Leah acknowledged the truth. More than ever, she disliked her mom, and resented her, and was unforgiving. And in the most unreal way, the little girl who resided in her heart would always yearn for her mother. "I love you too." She turned and walked out the door.

"Eleana!" Beata pleaded.

She wanted her hug goodbye, not the vision of her daughter turning her back on her, but Leah was done giving. She was done baring her soul to her mother, and done ripping her mother's heart and hopes away from her.

In the hall, Marcus took Leah into his arms. And then sobs came from the other side of the door. Leah completely shattered in Marcus's grip.

A guard approached. "Are you alright, Mrs. Elonto? Were you harmed?"

"I'm fine," she croaked. "The visit's over."

He opened the door behind Leah. "Visit's over, Mrs. Remsgard. It's time to go back."

Even with the door closed behind him, Beata's screaming and crying was loud and clear. "No! Make her come back. I want to see my daughter! I want to talk to her. It can't end like this."

Leah whimpered, destroyed, burying her face in Marcus's neck. Should she go hug her mother? Should she give her more of her time? Leah had to choose herself in that moment, and doing so meant she needed to walk away for now.

The guard issued more orders, but Beata was nothing short of distraught. "I don't believe it!"

"Come on, let's get you out of here," Marcus whispered, pulling Leah away from the noise.

Soon, Leah filled an empty waiting room with sniffles and whimpers and tears. At this point, it might have been less painful to stab her mom in the heart.

"I'm proud of you," Marcus soothed. "I love you. It's going to be alright."

Cutting people out was hard. Choosing between people was hard. Setting healthy boundaries could be devastating.

After eons of calming her breathing, drying her tears, and gulping down water, Leah was numb and ready to see adorable faces that loved her unconditionally, and supportive family who were there for her no matter what.

They walked from the prison in silence for some time, Leah staring down at the picture of Aspen and Ash to remind her why she'd just done this.

"I really am proud of you, Leah," Marcus whispered, his arm around her waist.

Why did it have to hurt so much?

"You know, I got to thinking about how we talk about legacies," he continued. "Escaping our parents' legacies—yours *and* mine... But really, I feel like people mostly talk about legacies when they talk about people who have passed, and it's about good things they've contributed to the world."

So, my dad ... and that would be nothing.

"And if Soren has a legacy, even if he never realized it or how it came about, that one good thing is you." Marcus leaned in, kissing her gently on the cheek. "And I wouldn't give you up for anything. Not for the realm, not for the world."(pp)

Epilogue

Leah rested in her Adirondack chair, watching the kids play with Grandma Rachel and Grandpa Guillen in the backyard. Marcus was in the front yard with Tobias, Camry, and the human girl they'd adopted through the foster care system.

Catrina approached Leah from behind, resting a hand on her shoulder. "We're taking off. Thanks so much for having us."

Leah smiled. "Thanks for coming!" She and Marcus were happy to host a large family picnic on their property, and glad to have Catrina and Stephan and their kids come all the way out there.

Things were monumentally better, in so many ways. Leah's relationship with Catrina and Stephan, for one. When she'd finished her life story and submitted it to them for approval, it had opened the door for more honest communication. She'd included the truth about them. How she'd been grateful for them welcoming her into their home. How they'd been kind and extremely helpful as she'd tried to find her bearings in her ancestral realm and powers. But she'd also shared, with as much tact as she could, how hard it had been for her to follow strict rules, how hard the royal family had to fight to avoid any image of impropriety because of their sincerity to steer clear of past mistakes in the Elonta ruling family. They appreciated her candor and gratitude. There had been more sincere apologies from both sides once Leah had laid everything bare, and they were in a less heated, more casual meeting.

Catrina had even taken the opportunity to meet with Leah in private after that, and had shared more about her own life story. Leah had been sworn to secrecy about the matter since it was private information, but she and Catrina shared more than Leah could have imagined. Catrina and Guillen had endured rough childhoods, which Leah had already been told, but many dark secrets had been buried that the public wasn't privy to. If the Elonta family knew how to do something well, it was making and keeping secrets.

Leah and Catrina would still never be best friends, and that was fine. Catrina was born and raised to be a queen, an heir to the throne, a holder of the power of the Mother Vines. Leah's upbringing was far from that. But they always tried to meet in the middle now.

Stephan and Catrina gathered their children and said their final goodbyes. The backyard fell nearly silent without so many kids there.

"Mind if I join you?" Wren asked minutes later. "Their Majesties and Highnesses are off now."

Leah gestured to another chair. "Be my guest."

It had taken Wren a while to fully accept the casual atmosphere with which Leah and Marcus ran their household, but he didn't hesitate to join them now for a good chat when work allowed.

"Thanks for all of your hard work," Leah said.

He took a sip of watermelon juice. "Family visits are *always* fun days."

"Leah?" Robyn called from behind. "Oh, there you are." She straightened her dress once in view. "Is it still alright if I head out early? You don't need anything more for the little ones?"

"We'll be great, thanks. And don't forget to take the gift by the door." Robyn's oldest was celebrating another birthday this weekend.

"He'll love it. Thank you. I'll see you Monday."

After Robyn left, Leah and Wren chatted about security details for the rest of the weekend.

The house was completed, and the surrounding woods were always an escape from the crazy of life. Leah couldn't have picked a better location for their home if she'd tried. The property that Kaylah and Eric had partitioned off for Leah and Marcus was so beautiful, but also well protected from wandering eyes.

Kaylah and Eric had an outer gate on their lane that was always guarded, so for someone to sneak by would be an astounding feat already, and then they'd have to somehow get past the larger estate and the on-site security to continue on to Leah and Marcus's house. It was virtually impossible for lowly busybodies to invade their privacy.

Though, the busybodies and haters had lessened in their numbers eventually. The royal family's introduction of the married couple and their children had definitely helped. And Leah's book had made a significant difference. In their finances and in the way Leah was treated.

People nodded more, averted their gazes less. She'd actually had people approach her to sign her book, which had made her nervous because she hadn't practiced for that. People sometimes approached to thank her for sharing her story and for being a good example.

That didn't mean everyone loved her. No one was loved by everyone. No matter how kind a person was or how many mistakes they corrected, they would always be a villain in someone's story.

Leah wondered how much of a villain she was in her own mother's story. They still exchanged the occasional letter, but she hadn't found it in her to ever visit her mom in prison after setting the much-needed boundaries regarding Aspen and Ash. Maybe she was a coward, but any time she'd considered it, she imagined telling the twins that she was leaving them for a few hours to visit a woman who would have oppressed people like them. If it was between her twins and her mother, she would always choose her twins. If it was between Marcus and her mother, she would always choose Marcus.

The handsome devil himself stepped onto the patio, plopping on a seat next to Leah. "They're off. Tobias and Cam decided to take off too, but they'll be over first thing in the morning for breakfast."

Leah held out her hand, and he took it, resting it on his knee.

There wasn't a piece of her heart that didn't belong to him. He was a better husband than she ever could have hoped for. Shortly after her life story had been published, she'd sent a copy to her mom in prison. The letter she'd received in response had not been kind. Beata had essentially rescinded her permission to share anything about herself that she didn't want people to know, and she had accused Leah of using her. All because Leah hadn't visited her. Marcus had supported and consoled Leah. After Leah had responded with a strong letter of censure, setting limits and not apologizing, her mother had eventually written with an apology of her own. It may have been a desperate attempt to not lose Leah completely, but it kept things civil.

"The two of you are still planning on a human-world visit Monday?" Marcus asked.

"Yes, sir." Wren nodded.

"Yep," Leah said, kicking her feet up on a footstool. She still brought in decent income from sales of her life story, though that wouldn't last forever. There was a limited audience in the Green Lands, especially with the library systems being so popular. That book had never been about making money anyway. It had helped her heal, had helped her explain herself.

Marcus and Leah visited the human world a lot to get away and for outings with the twins. Leah also rifted over often to work with her agent on her romantic adventure stories, and Wren usually accompanied her for those trips. She was now publishing under a pen name in both the human world and the Green Lands realm. The stories were essentially the same, with obvious changes for those in the human world to follow laws green folk had about not disclosing their existence to humans. With Marcus's stipend from family investments, and Leah's income from publishing, they weren't stressed. And he'd had a chance to discover what his passion really was.

"Sounds good," Marcus replied, putting his feet up next to Leah's. "I'll have plenty of homework back here." He smiled as Aspen giggled at Guillen while they continued to play. Marcus had indeed been offered his internship again. He'd turned it down. Instead of going into public service full-time, he did volunteer work on the side like Rachel, Kaylah, and Eric did.

As much as he respected his dad and his profession, Marcus had gained the courage to pursue something he'd come to love. Not only had he worked tirelessly to help build this home, he'd made the twins a mini palace. Whereas Guillen had built his boys a nice sturdy tree house, Marcus had built the twins a miniature palace to play in, big enough for the adults to join them inside.

And right now, Ash was on the second floor, popping his little head up in a window and then ducking and running to the next one over. Leah couldn't believe how fast the twins were growing. They were like weeds, just not the ... awkward derogatory nickname kind...

The playhouse they enjoyed right now was just a little thing for fun compared to what Marcus aspired to create. He was studying architecture and structural engineering while Leah worked on her books. He wanted to leave his mark on the world in a more physical way than his father. Unintentionally, his chosen path in architecture also helped their little family fade into private obscurity more than politics would have. It was a win-win.

Leah, Marcus, and Wren chatted a while longer. Like any other day in the Green Lands, it was warm, the breeze gentle, and songbirds whistled in distant treetops.

Wren eventually called it a night. Kaylah and Eric finally showed up, apologizing for arriving so late from a trip to the human world.

"I don't miss the crazy weather back there," Eric said. "Especially when it delays our flights to come home." They always made time to go on getaways together, and to visit his family.

They enjoyed some dessert, the twins with sticky fingers and trying to steal drinks from everyone's glasses. As it got dark, the older couples bid everyone good night, and Leah and Marcus prepared the twins for bed.

They loved being read stories by Mom and Dad from Mom's books at bedtime. That was the one thing Leah had decided to keep for herself. She and Saff had finished the children's books, and they'd had several professionally printed, but they hadn't put them out into the world. They were a passion project for Leah's kids, and for a few kids of close family and friends of either Leah or Saff. They were too close to Leah's heart to share with the world.

Once the twins were tucked in, Leah and Marcus returned outside, cuddling on a porch swing and staring at the dying embers of a fire pit.

"Today was fun," Marcus said, planting a kiss on Leah's cheek.

She couldn't hide a smile. It had been utter chaos. How could it not be, with that many people, that many kids? But she loved being able to host the gathering, being treated like an adult.

"It was," she said wistfully.

As they slowly swung, the realm became calm again. Crickets serenaded the couple, a frog in the distance accompanying them. As full darkness fell, bioluminescent moss on trees in the distance glowed softly.

Leah massaged Marcus's scalp, soaking in the moment. But she had news she couldn't wait any longer to share. "What would you say..." She drew a deep breath. "If I told you I was pregnant?"

"Really?" The level of excitement in his voice was beyond compare. The moonlight lit his face enough to show that excitement.

She beamed. "Really." This one they had planned for. He'd been ready for another one for some time, but she'd needed to mentally prepare herself. Her studies on maternal sickness were helping keep it at bay.

"Not joking?" he asked.

Laying a hand on his chest, she leaned in for a kiss. "I wouldn't joke about that."

He pressed his lips against hers and didn't hold back. They hadn't lost their spark, and she prayed they never would.

Eventually, they pulled themselves apart before the kiss turned into something that led to the bedroom. "What do you want to do about announcing it?" he asked. "About telling the family?"

She caressed his cheek. "I'm letting you decide this time."

"You're sure?"

Her heart beat wildly after that kiss, but her soul was at peace. He was a great father, a great husband. Along with Kaylah, he had helped her understand who she was, what powers she held. Had given her a home and family—what she'd never had growing up, what she'd always wanted and needed.

"Yes." She placed another kiss on his lips. His lips followed hers this time as she leaned back.

"I'm okay with whatever you decide. You mean everything to me." She still recalled what he'd told her when she'd needed it most. "I wouldn't give you up for anything. Not for the realm, not for the world."

Annotations

The Heir of Exile

Symbol	Page #	Annotation
a	3	I had fun continuing this series, considering how green folk use their powers on a daily basis. We get to see a few creative uses in this duology that help us glimpse into their lives.
b	5	From descriptions of some buildings to several names, Ivy culture is often touched by Polish influence. I lived in Poland for a short time, and had fun incorporating a piece of my heart into one of the cultures in this fictional world.
c	5	As an author, I impart a piece of myself into each character I write. In a lot of ways, I'm not like Leah at all, but we definitely have some shared trauma. Her anxiety of moving is absolutely something I've experienced. From preschool to university, I attended thirteen different schools. And that doesn't speak to all the moves I've had in my adult life. It's hard to make friends, and I often made the wrong ones at a new school. The lack of stability is tough and lonely, a struggle many don't understand when they haven't experienced it.
d	8	I had fun with this misunderstanding. The play on words was a happy accident after I'd already come up with the term for green folk without powers. My editor and I had to consider how to spell it, too. At what point do you spell it correctly vs incorrectly based on the close third person point of view and their misunderstanding? Readers who've read the central trilogy may remember the proper spelling from the final epilogue, but if not, they'd possibly be as unsure about the spelling as the main character until it's explained.
e	9	I love this kind of subtle miscommunication. Statistically, Seeders probably have the same ratios of eye colors as humans, but if you're including their shift to green eyes with their powers, well over half the adult population also has green eyes.
f	14	I used to have my own bow, and my family would go to local shooting ranges to learn and practice (and in the case of my dad—to compete). It was during high school, and my bow was bright lime green, and as a double-jointed gal, I knew all too well the pain of letting your form slip and not using an armguard. From the ambiance of the shooting range in this scene to the overly helpful older gentleman, it all felt like I was back in a certain shop in Oregon state as a teen.
g	24	In this book, we explore several types of bias, and Tanner tips his hat early about his generational bias. Granted, Leah doesn't understand what's going on, but you and I know he's the Green Land's Draco Malfoy.
h	51	Beata is one of, if not the most complex characters I've written. It's hard to tell when she's truly innocent and guilty. When she's spinning the truth, is it because she's delusional? Or is she trying to protect herself? Or someone else?
i	57	When you remember Seeders are inspired in part by dandelions, that symbolism has some real zing!
j	61	This book is unlike any I've written before, an exploration of bias, motivations, and the downhill spiral of an average person. As contemporary fantasy characters, my main characters are meant to represent the standard American teenager. In epic fantasy, nobody bats an eye at an assassination plot, but the average American teenager? It was also a delicate dance of motivations, each character having their reason for saying or not saying what they do at any given time, often unaware of how they contribute to Leah's journey.
k	72	My little murderous and clueless Leah... She may be hotheaded and confused, but her logic is sound.

Symbol	Page #	Annotation
l	82	There are a lot of moral boundaries explored in this book, and I may not see them the same as my characters or readers. Is Marcus being too strict? Is Leah's mom being too permissive?
m	87	Gotta love that combination of confirmation bias and Marcus's ignorance.
n	93	If you read the central trilogy, you partially understand how bad this was for Jake's family, but we'll get to see in the Spy's Duology just how serious a situation they were in.
o	135	This series is intended for a young adult audience, so I've had to evaluate over time how mature the content gets. Even when the characters are adults, I keep intimacy behind closed doors, but I think it's healthy to discuss things like safe sex. There's no harm in acknowledging teens are curious and have drives. That said, I've thoroughly considered the biology of green folk, and how their powers affect their cultures, their reproduction processes, and their sexual habits. I don't explicitly go into many details, though I plan to dole out more information with future books. For now, I'll let you make your own conclusions based on things you know, like Seeder roots, how their energy reacts to emotion, and the fact Ivies can control chemicals and have extra appendages.
p	135	Samantha's trauma is certainly mentioned in the central trilogy, but many questions are left unasked. After years of being married to a horrible person who manipulated her, this is nice validation to know he was never fully able to enjoy intimacy with her.
q	147	One more instance of confirmation bias as she builds up a case in her mind to fuel her pain and anger!
r	182	That unanswered question at the end of the trilogy—was Soren actually a whisper? As the author, I don't even always know the answers. Many things in my mind fall on a scale, and that scale tends to tip one way or another over time. When I first had him assert he was a whisper, it was 50/50 as to whether or not he was honest about that. I wanted him to be a charlatan, simply a manipulative smooth talker, but in the end, I don't think he would have stood nearly as much of a chance as he did were he not a whisper. Additionally, some Ivies (like Guillen and Catrina) hold a strong family resemblance, while we know Seeders canonically do not. Seeders are truly more of a monolith in their own wild way, but Ivies are a wealth of variety with the powers, much of which hasn't been explored. Some of that will be further unraveled in future books, and the Elonta royal family still has more secrets to uncover ;)
s	192	In many ways, Leah in *The Heir of Exile* and Mel in *Seeder Shadow Wars* are mirror opposites, or perhaps other sides of the same coin. Mel had never dated, but Leah has slept with multiple guys. Mel had a healthy and happy family, but Leah has had a rough go of it. In *Seeder Shadow Wars*, Mel understands that no one ever owes anyone a date (or any sort of romantic or sexual attention). In *The Heir of Exile*, Leah has an unhealthy and confusing understanding of sex and relationships. She's always been with the wrong sort, and doesn't understand her own worth. So when she thinks she might *owe* it to Marcus to sleep with him, it breaks my heart, but it's very true to character for her.
t	193	Yes, this was painted by Saff!
u	219	We don't get much understanding about Marcus's motivations, since we don't get his point of view, but this is a good insight into his mindset. The realm loves Marcus—he's famous. He absolutely could have tried to use that to make him look cooler in Leah's eyes, but he'd been used by a girl before for popularity, and that had burned him. He was elated to be anonymous, and put a gag order on Jake and Tanner to keep his identity from Leah until he was ready to share it himself.

Symbol	Page #	Annotation
v	223	Beata is a villain, though not nearly as much as Soren was. She has goodness in her and she's strong, but she has her missteps. Her assertions and mindset are not always consistent with other canon because she's not only biased, but she also remembers things the way she wants to. Beata, Leah's mother, isn't that same girl as the younger version of herself in the prologue. Nor is either adult version of her the same as the teenager we meet in *To Love a Monster*. And we'll have even more exploration of her character in Soren's Legacy. When was she manipulated and pitiable, and when was she the manipulator and worthy of our anger?
w	231	Did Beata truly choose Leah? Would she have, had Soren not died? And what did she do on Leah's behalf that she's so ashamed of? We never actually find out. If you want to continue to speculate, then you can skip this next part or wait to read the below at the end of the book or duology, but in my head canon, it likely would have looked like this: Beata got them money by sleeping with and extorting her boss. She's so fiercely loyal to Soren, even after all these years, that it kills her to break her promise to him about never being with another man. But in the end, she did choose Leah by letting go of that promise so she could provide for her daughter. Would Beata have protected Leah if Soren had never died? Like with Cheryl, it would have been too little, too late. Soren was much more cruel and perverse than we get to see, and Leah wouldn't have been safe with him as her father. In the end, I think Beata *would* have stood up to Soren about the way he hurt their daughter, and I don't think it would have ended well for Beata. Leah has a special place in my heart, because so many people don't have the kind of parents Mel did.
x	258	I love seeding my stories with callbacks and hints for future plots. This is such a simple, benign confession, but we'll eventually learn how genuinely massive this event was that Kaylah's referring to.

To Love a Monster

Symbol	Page #	Annotation
y	270	Here, we get another hint about Soren's depravity. Some people may prefer I write all I know about Soren and the things he's done, but the majority of it will remain off page. I don't personally like writing dark stories, but I can confidently say *no one* should swoon over this kind of villain.
z	271	Even from a young age, Beata is willfully ignorant. She focuses on and believes in what she wants to.
aa	271	Beata had so much potential to make Soren a better person, but we see a hint of her own ambition in this last line. She didn't understand how evil he was, but they really did trap each other in different ways.

Soren's Legacy

Symbol	Page #	Annotation
bb	348	I hope to someday write the books mentioned within this book!
cc	366	A little easter egg about how many novels I currently have planned for this *Seeder Wars* series.
dd	374	The relationship she has with Guillen in this scene reminds me of my Uncle Lance 💜
ee	381	Genuinely though... The aroma of tomato vine and leaf is superior! If you haven't grown your own tomatoes, you haven't known true joy.

Symbol	Page #	Annotation
ff	391	While much of the magic system is well thought out, I sometimes throw in random factoids for fun. The ease of travel and flavors associated with different types of trees hasn't been mentioned or important before this. But having grown up around many pines, I noticed I always default to having Ivies rift through them. Instead of it being a 'they picked a pine because that's what the author's used to,' I decided to make it far more fun.
gg	394	I have to admit I haven't been as close to my nieces and nephews as I'd like. I didn't live nearby when they were little, but Kaylah is to Leah what I'd love to be to my own nieces and nephews if they need me.
hh	427	I once had a teenage boy look at this series skeptically and say, "It's one of those 'girl power' books, isn't it?" Well... Yes... There are two matriarchal societies featured, the women have stronger powers, and I try to make my female main characters strong in spirit. But I like to celebrate equality, and positive contributions as well. Eric, Guillen, and Wren have my heart completely in this book.
ii	428	I've already started drafting some children's books featuring green folk. Start 'em young!
jj	489	From experience as a plus-size bride, this commentary is on point. As a side note, if you're looking for a body-neutral plus-size romance to read, check out my novelette *The Hatanii Bride*.
kk	492	Author confession: I botched Leah's birthday in *The Heir of Exile*, so this detail is a bit of a backpedal. I'm not afraid to admit my mistakes as a writer. When plotting a single book, and even a trilogy, it can be easy enough to keep things straight. But crossed and expanded timelines are trickier, and it wasn't until after I published *The Heir of Exile* that I realized I hadn't more correctly considered what time of year Beata had gotten pregnant. Luckily, Beata's lies and sentimentality for Soren makes this addition very believable, and that much more painful for Leah.
ll	500	Avoiding spoilers, I will simply say that we will hear more about Leah's writing exploits again in a future book 😊
mm	501	A fun callback to *Seeder Shadow Wars* and that vase of daisies!
nn	503	What's that? Something in the magic system is changing? Definitely not foreshadowing for a future book...
oo	510	Self-insert? I'd definitely *never* include my own trauma about moving a lot. Or my love of tomato leaf smell. Or my favorite season which is clearly superior...
pp	542	To be clear, I bawl every time I read Leah's story. Our girl has it rough, and she's known so little love in her life, but I still stand by her decision here. Aside from Leah's need to prioritize her own children, Beata was a very neglectful mother. Many issues have to be read between the lines because Leah herself doesn't acknowledge the problems or she doesn't realize how severe they are. One example is medical neglect, and another is dismissing instances of sexual assault. We're told that Leah has never once been to a doctor because her mom was afraid of discovery. That means no matter how sick or injured Leah had ever been as a child, no matter how traumatized she was by the sexual assaults she hints at having endured, her mother always dismissed them and simply packed up the house and left. Beata does love her in the capacity she's capable of, and she does right by her on occasion, but I would never praise her parenting after her neglect, persistent racism and ableism, and allowing Cheryl to abuse Leah.

Don't forget to leave a review!

On Amazon, Goodreads, StoryGraph and/or anywhere else this book can be found.

Don't forget to sign up for J. Houser's newsletter for publishing updates, promotions, and bonus content!

JHouserWrites.com

Also, connect with the author here:

On YouTube, TikTok, Facebook, and Instagram under:

JHouserWrites

About the Author

J. Houser has spent most of her life in the Pacific Northwest of the United States. Her writing philosophy aligns with 'write what you want to read' and 'let the characters be who they are.' While her life is not nearly as exciting as that of her characters (and luckily less heartbreaking), she enjoys the journey, the thought process, the romance and relationships.

Also by J. Houser

Decorative Lined Notebooks

558

Reading Journals

Writing Planners & Notebooks

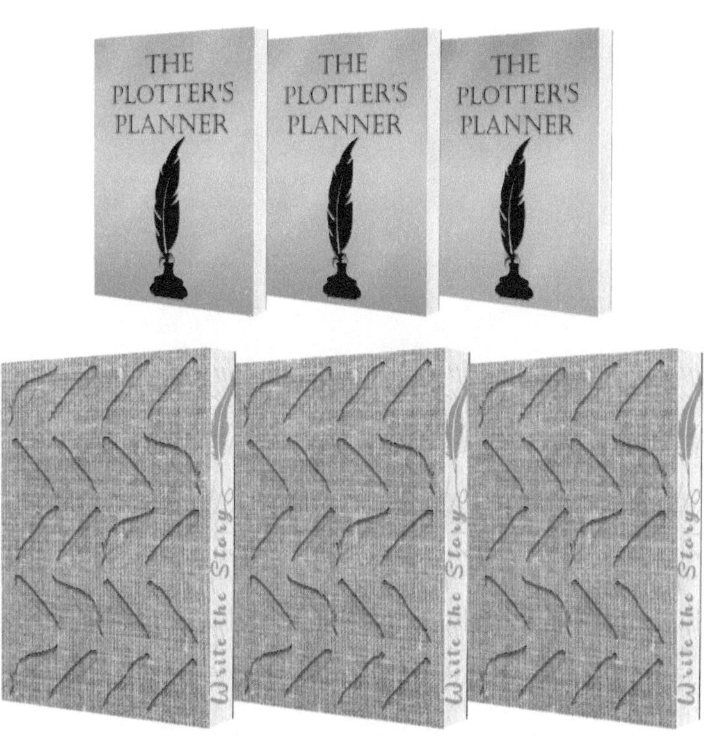

www.ingramcontent.com/pod-product-compliance
Lightning Source LLC
Chambersburg PA
CBHW021725190726
48289CB00008B/2695